# Grace Livingston Hill

## A GIRL TO COME HOME TO
## THE BEST MAN
## LADYBIRD

# Grace Livingston Hill

## A GIRL TO COME HOME TO

**LIVING BOOKS**®
Tyndale House Publishers, Inc.
Wheaton, Illinois

This Tyndale House book
by Grace Livingston Hill
contains the complete text
of the original hardcover edition.
NOT ONE WORD
HAS BEEN OMITTED.

3-in-1 ISBN 1-56865-290-9
Printed in the United States of America

THE stars were all out in full force the night that Rodney and Jeremy Graeme came home from the war. Even the faraway ones were peeping eagerly through the distance, trying to impress the world with their existence, showing that they felt it an occasion when their presence should be recognized. And even the near stars had burst out like flowers in the deep blue of the darkness, till they fairly startled the onlooker, rubbing his eyes in wonder if stars had always been so large. It was early evening, scarcely six o'clock, but it seemed so very dark, and the stars so many and so bright.

"It almost seems," said Jeremy, "as if all the stars we have ever seen since we were born, have come out to greet us when we come home. They've all come together. The stars that twinkled when we said our prayers at night when we were little kids, and seemed to smile at us and welcome us into a world that was going to be full of twinkling lights and music and fun. The stars that bent above the creek where we were skating, and seemed to enjoy it as much as we did. The stars that smiled more gently when we drifted down in the old canoe, and sang silly love songs, or lay back and grew dreamy with unnamed ambitions."

"Yes," said Rodney, with a grin down at his brother, "the

5

stars that blessed us with a bit of withdrawing when we walked home from church, or a party at night with our best girls. Right, Jerry? There must have been girls, somewhere in your life, after I left. There'd have been stars for them, too, of course. That's a swell thought that all those star fellows have sort of ganged-up on us for tonight. Nice to think about."

"It seems an awfully long time ago, though, all those other things happening," said Jeremy thoughtfully. "Like looking back on one's self as an infant. After all we've been through. I wonder how we're going to fit into this world we've come back to."

"Yes, I wonder!" said Rodney. "I sure am glad to get back, but I've sort of got a feeling every little while that somehow we oughtn't to have come away till we'd finished the job, and had 'em licked thoroughly, so they can't start anything again."

"Yes, that does haunt you in the back of your mind, but anyway we didn't 'come' away. We were *sent,* and *had* to come. They thought we were more important over here."

"Of course," said the older brother. "And I'm satisfied, understand. Only somehow there's a feeling I ought to take hold and do some more over there yet. But I guess that'll wear off when I really get into this job over here they think is so important."

"Yes, of course," said the younger brother. "But there's this to remember, we aren't like some of the other fellows. I heard one fellow on the ship complaining the folks over home didn't understand. They hadn't an idea what we've been through. They've been just going on gaily having a good time between their good acts of doing a little war work. But our family isn't like that. Our dad and mother understand. Dad's never forgotten his own experience in the other war. You can tell from their letters."

"Yes, of course," smiled the older brother. "Our family has always been an understanding family. But you're right about this world we're getting back to, I suspect. For a while it will be like going out to play marbles or hide and seek. The trouble is one can't go out to meet death without growing up. We've grown up, and marbles don't fit us any more."

"Sure!" said Jeremy thoughtfully. "We'll just have to get adjusted to a new world, won't we, and somehow I don't see how we're going to fit any more. I don't really have much heart for it all myself, except of course getting back to dad and mom and Kathie. But the others will seem like children. Of course you don't feel that way because you have Jessica. You'll get married I suppose, if it really turns out that we get that job they talked about overseas. You planning for a wedding soon, Rod?"

There was a definite silence after that question and suddenly the younger brother looked up with a question in his eyes:

"I didn't speak out of turn, did I, Rod?" He looked at his brother anxiously. "You and Jessica aren't on the outs, are you?"

Rodney drew a deep breath and settled back.

"Yes, we're on the outs, Bud. Our marriage is all washed up."

"But *Rod!* I thought it was all settled. I thought you bought her a ring."

"Yes, I bought her a ring," said the older brother with a forlorn little sound like a sigh. Then a pause.

"She sent it back to me a year ago today. I guess by now she's married to the other guy. I don't know, and I don't want to know anything more about it. She just wasn't worth worrying about, I suppose."

There was a deep silence with only the thunderous rumbling of the train. The younger brother sat and stared straight ahead of him, his startled thoughts taking in, in quick succession, the sharp changes this would make in his idolized brother's life, the things he knew in a flash must have been being lived down by Rodney all these silent months when they had not been hearing from each other. And then his comprehension dashed back to the beginning again.

"But the ring!" he faltered, thinking back to the bright token that had meant to him the sign of everlasting fidelity, the lovely peerless jewel that they had all been so proud their Rodney had been able to purchase with his own well-earned money, and place upon the lovely finger of the beautiful girl who was his promised bride.

"What will you do with the ring?"

Jeremy was scarcely aware he was asking another question. He had been merely thinking aloud. Rodney turned toward him with a look almost of anguish, like one who knew this ghastly thing had to be told, and he wanted to get it over with as soon as possible.

"I sold it!" he said gruffly. The brothers' eyes met and raked each other's consciousness for full understanding. And in that look Jeremy came to know how it had been, and how it had to be with Rodney. Rodney was four years older, but somehow in that look Jeremy grew up and caught up the separating years, and understood. It did not need words to explain, for Jeremy understood now. Saw how it would have been with *him* if he were in a like situation.

But after a moment Rodney explained.

"At first I wanted to throw it into the sea. But then somehow that didn't seem right. It wasn't the ring's fault, even though it was of no further use to me. Even supposing I should ever find another girl I could trust, which I'm sure I never will, I wouldn't want to give her a ring that had been dishonored, would I? No, it would never be of any further use to me, or to anybody unless they were strangers to its history. Yet what to do with it I didn't know. I couldn't carry it on my person and have it sent back to my mother sometime after I had been killed, to tell a strange story she wouldn't understand, could I?"

"Then mom doesn't know?" asked Jeremy.

"Not unless Jessica has told her, and I doubt if she has. She wouldn't have the nerve! Though maybe there was some publicity. I don't know. I haven't tried to find out. There hasn't been a word of gossip about it in any of my letters. My friends wouldn't want to mention it, and any others didn't bother to write, so I've had to work this thing out by myself. After all it was my problem, and I worked at it part time between missions when I wasn't out killing Japs and Germans. It helped to make me madder at the enemy, and less careful for myself. What was the use when the things I had counted on were gone? And what was the ring that I had worked so hard to buy but a costly trinket that nobody wanted? So I found a diamond merchant who gave me a good price for the stone, more than I paid for it, and I was glad to get rid of it. That's the story, Jerry. It had to be told and there it is. At first I thought I couldn't come home, where Jessica and I had been so much together, but then it came to me that there was no point in punishing mom and the rest just because Jessica had played me false. So I'm here, and I only hope I shan't be subjected to too much mention of the whole affair. Jessica I'm sure will be out of the picture, thank Heaven! She spoke of being married in another part of the country. Certainly I never want to lay eyes on her again of course, and perhaps in due time, with the help of a few more wars, I may forget the humiliation I have suffered. But I don't want pity, kid. I'm sure you'd understand that."

"Of course not," said Jeremy, giving a sorrowful comprehending look. "But Rod, I don't just see how she *could*. She always seemed to be so crazy about you."

"Well, let's not go into that. I've been through several battles since that thought used to get me," said Rodney.

"The little vandal!" said Jeremy. "What did she do? Just send the ring back without any letter or explanation?"

"Oh, no, she sent a nice little letter all right, filled with flowery words and flattery, to the effect that she was returning the ring, though she did adore it, because she thought I might want to use it again, and that I had always been so kind and understanding that she was sure I would see that it was a great deal better for her to frankly tell me that she had discovered she didn't care for me as much as she had supposed; and as she was about to marry an older, more mature man, who was far better off financially than I could ever hope to be, she wished that I wouldn't feel too bad about her defection. She closed by saying that she hoped that this wouldn't be the end, that she and I would always be friends as long as the world lasted. That we had had too much fun together to put an end to it altogether. Words to that effect, said in a flowery style, quoting phrases that had been supposedly dear to us both in the past, showing me plainly that they had never really meant a thing to her but smooth phrases."

"The little rotten rat!" ejaculated Jeremy. "I'd like to wring her pretty little false neck for her!"

"Yes, I felt that way for some time, but then I reflected that I didn't want to even give her that much satisfaction. She isn't worth so much consideration."

"Perhaps not," said Jeremy, "but all the same I'd like to class her with our enemies and let her take her chances with them."

The older brother gave an appreciative look.

"Thanks, pard!" he said with a wry grin. "Well, enough said. It's good to know you'll stand by if an occasion arises."

"Yes, brother, I'll stand by," said Jeremy solemnly, and then after a moment:

"And what about mom and the rest?"

"Oh, they'll have to be told I suppose, but at least not the first minute. The time may come soon, but probably not tonight."

There was silence for several minutes, and then Jeremy spoke slowly, speculatively:

"Ten to one mom knows," he said. "You know she always had a way of sort of thinking out things and knowing beforehand what had happened to us before we even got home."

"Yes, that's true. Dad always said it was her seventh sense. That she sort of smelled 'em out ahead of time. Still, I don't see how she could this. However, it's all right with me if she has. I guess I can take it. Gosh, I hate to tell her. I hate to be pitied."

Another long silence, then Jeremy:

"Yes, I know. But I guess you can trust mother."

"Yes, of course," said the older brother, lifting his chin with a brave gesture. "Yes, mother's all right. Mother's wonderful! And it ought to be enough for any fellow to be getting home to her without worrying about some little two-timing brat of a gold-digger."

Jeremy flashed a quick look at his brother.

"Was that what she did? Was it money?"

"Yes, I figured that was what did it. A guy I met in the navy mentioned his name once and said he was just rolling in wealth. Had something to do with the black market he thought, though when I came to question closer he wouldn't tell any more. He said he guessed he oughtn't to have mentioned it. Seems the fellow is an uncle of a buddy of his on his ship, and he was afraid it might get back to him that he had been talking. Well, what difference did it make? She'd thrown me over. Why should I care what for?"

"But Rod, we're not exactly poverty-stricken. And as for you, Jessica knew your Uncle Seymour left you a nice sum. You had a good start in life for a young man."

"My shekels wouldn't hold a candle to what a black market man could make now," grinned Rodney.

"No, I suppose not," said his brother with an answering grin. Then there followed a long silence, the brothers thinking over what had been said. Rodney had perhaps been more confidential with Jeremy than ever before in his life, and the younger brother had a lot to think over.

Rodney had dropped his head back on the seat and closed his eyes, as if the confidence was over for the time being, and Jeremy stared out the window unseeingly. They were not far from home now, another half hour, but it was too dark to notice the changes that might have come in the landscape. Jeremy was interested, after his long absence from his own land, in even an old barn, or a dilapidated station they passed. Anything looked good over here, for this was home.

But there were adjustments to be made in the light of what Rodney had just told him. He had come home expecting a wedding in the offing, and now that was all off, and there was a gloomy settled look of disappointment on the face of the brother who had always been so bright and cheery, so utterly sure of himself, and what he was going to do. Was this thing going to change Rod? How hard that he not only had the memory of war, and his terrible experiences at sea, but he had to have this great disappointment too, this feeling of almost shame—for that is what it had sounded like as Rod told it—that his girl had gone back on him. The girl whose name had been linked with his ever since they had been in high school together. What a rotten deal to give him! Good old Rod! And he had always been so proud of Jessica! Proud of her unusual beauty, proud of her wonderful gold hair, her blue eyes, her long lashes, her grace and charm!

Jeremy searched his own heart and found that for a long time he himself had never cared so much for Jessica. Perhaps it was because she had always treated him like a younger brother, sort of like a little kid, always sending him on messages, asking favors of him, just a sweep of her long lashes and expecting him to do her will, go her errands, give up anything he had that she chose to want, like tickets to ball games. Well, he thought he had conquered those things, because he had been expecting ever since he went overseas that she would sometime soon be his sister-in-law, and he wanted no childish jealousy or hurt feelings to break the beautiful harmony that had always been between his brother and himself. The family must be a unit. And so he had disciplined his feelings until he was all ready to welcome his new-to-be-sister with a brotherly kiss.

But now that was out! And mom didn't know anything

about it yet? Or did she? Could a thing like that fail to reach their mother?

If she didn't know, how would she take it? Had she been fond of Jessica? He tried to think back. He could dimly remember a sigh now and then, a shadow on her placid brow. When was that? Could that have been when Rod first began to go with Jessica? But mom had later seemed to be quite fond of Jessica, hadn't she? Jeremy couldn't quite remember. He had been more engrossed in himself at that time. About then was when he got that crush on Beryl Sanderson, the banker's daughter. Of course that was ridiculous. He, the son of a quiet farmer, living outside the village, on a staid old farm that had been in the family for over a hundred years, without any of the frills and fancies that the modern homes had. And she the daughter of a most influential banker, who lived in a great gray stone mansion, went to private schools, then away to a great college, dressed with expensive simplicity, and never even looked his way. Beryl Sanderson! Even now the memory of her stirred his thoughts, although he hadn't been pondering on her at all, he was sure, since he went away to war. Well, that was that, and he wasn't mooning around about any of his childhood fancies. He had a big job to do for his country and there wasn't time for anything else then.

Suddenly Rodney broke the silence.

"How about you, kid? Did you pick up some pretty girl across seas, or was there a girl you left behind you? Come, out with it, and let us know where we both stand now we're getting home."

Jeremy grinned.

"No girl!" he said.

"No kidding?" said the older brother, turning his keen eyes a bit anxiously toward the younger man, with a pleasant recognition of the goodly countenance he wore, his fine physique, his strong dependable face. There was nothing of which to be ashamed in that brother.

"No kidding," said Jeremy soberly. "Not after the line of talk mom gave me before I went away. She didn't exactly hold you up as a horrible example of one who had got himself engaged before time, but she did warn me that it was a great deal better to wait for big decisions like that till one was matured enough to be sure."

"H'm! Yes, well maybe mom felt a little uncertain about what I'd done, though she never batted an eye about it. Of course I went away so soon after Jessica and I thrashed things out, and mom was always fair. She never jumped to conclusions, nor antagonized one of us. Probably she didn't want to have me go away with any unpleasantness between us. She took her worries if she had any about us, to God. She was that way. She had a wonderful trust that God could and would work *any*thing out that she couldn't manage. Mom was wonderful that way. It somehow bore me up a couple of times when I had a near call, just to remember that mom was probably on her knees putting a wall of her prayers around me, maybe right at that time."

"Yes, she's been a wonderful mom," said Jeremy thoughtfully. "That's why I don't want anything to upset her now. I gotta go slow and let her know I haven't got away from her teaching. But say, aren't we coming into our station? Isn't that the old Clark place? Yes, it is. Now it won't be long before we're home. Boy, but I'm hungering for a sight of the old house, and mom and dad, and Kathie, and even old Hetty. Won't it be good to eat some of her cooking again? I'm hungry enough to eat a bear."

"Here too," said Rodney, looking eagerly out of the window. "But a bear wouldn't be in it compared with Hetty's fried chicken. Nobody ever fried chicken to beat old Hetty. Maybe we ought to have let 'em know we were coming. It takes time to go out and kill a chicken and cook it."

"Have you forgotten, brother, that they have an ice plant in the cellar? Ten to one mom's had chickens galore, frozen and ready to fry, just in case. You know mom never got caught asleep. She's probably been getting ready for this supper for the last two months. She won't be caught napping."

"No," said the older brother with solemn shining light in his eyes. "Well, here's our station. Shall we go? It's time to get our luggage in hand."

"Here, I'll reach that bag, Rod. You oughtn't to be straining that shoulder of yours, remember. You don't want to go back to the hospital again you know."

And so, laughing, kidding, eager, they arose and gathering their effects trooped out to the platform.

Casting a quick glance about they made a dash toward the upper end of the station, and using the tactics known to them of old in their school days they escaped meeting the crowd that usually assembled around an arriving train. They cut across a vacant lot, and so were not detained, but strode on down the country road toward their home. That was where they desired above all things to be as rapidly as possible. That was what they had come across the ocean for. Mother and home were like Heaven in their thoughts, and at present there was no one they knew of by whom they were willing to be delayed one extra minute.

They were unaware, as they hurried along with great strides, of the eyes of some who had sighted them as they dashed around the end of the station, and pointed them out, questioned who they were. For though the uniforms of servicemen were numerous, in that town as well as in others, they shone out with their gold braid and brass buttons and attracted attention, as they passed under the station lights.

"Well, if I didn't know that man was overseas, in a hospital, I'd say that was Rodney Graeme," said one girl stretching her neck to peer down the platform behind her. "He walks just as Rod did."

"Oh, for Pete's sake," said another. "You're dreaming! Rodney Graeme has been overseas over four years. Besides, there are two of them, Jess. Which one did you think looked like Rod?"

"The one on the right," said the first girl. "I tell you he walks just like Rod."

"I guess that's wishful thinking," said Emma Galt, an older girl with a sour mouth, a sharp tongue, and a hateful glance.

"That other one might be Rod's younger brother, Jerry," said Garetha Sloan.

"Nonsense! Jerry wasn't as tall as Rod, he was only a kid in high school when Rod went away."

"You seem greatly interested for a married woman, Jess," sneered Emma Galt.

"Really!" said Jessica. "Is your idea of a married woman one who forgets all her old friends?"

But out upon the highway the two brothers made great progress, striding along.

"Well, we beat 'em to it all right," said Jeremy.

"Okay! That's all right with me," said his brother. "I'll take my old comrades later. Just now I want to get home and see mom. I didn't notice who they were, did you?"

"No, I didn't wait to identify anybody but old Ben, the station master. He looked hale and hearty. There were a bunch of girls, or women, headed toward the drugstore, but I didn't stop to see if I knew them. I certainly am glad we escaped. I don't want to be gushed over."

"Well, maybe we've escaped notice. You can't always tell. We'll see later," said Rodney. "But there's the end gable of the house around the bend, and the old elm still standing. I was afraid some storm might have destroyed it. Somehow I forget that they haven't had falling bombs over here. It looks wonderful to see the old places all intact. And a light on our front porch. Good to see houses and trees after so much sea. And isn't that our cow, old Taffy, in the pasture by the barn?"

"It sure is," said Jeremy excitedly, "and my horse, Prince! Oh boy! We're home at last!"

They did the last few laps almost on a run, and went storming up the front steps to meet the mother who according to her late afternoon custom had been shadowing the window, looking toward the road they would have to come if they ever came back. Not that she was exactly expecting them, but it seemed she was not content to let the twilight settle down for the night, without always taking a last glimpse up the road as if they might be coming yet before she was content to sleep.

In an instant she was in their big strong arms, almost smothered with their kisses, big fellows as they were.

"Mom! Oh, mom!" they said, and then embraced her again, both of them together, till she had to hold them off and study them to tell which was which.

"My babies! My babies grown into great men, *both* of you! And both of you come back to me *at once!* Am I dreaming, or is this real?"

She passed her frail trembling hand over eyes that had grown weary watching out the window all these months for her lads.

"This is real, mom!" said Jeremy, and then hugged her again. "And where's dad? Don't tell me he's gone to the village! We can't wait to see him."

"No, he's hereabouts," said the mother's voice, full of sweet motherly joy. "He just got back from bringing Kathleen from her day at the hospital, nursing. He went out to milk the cow. Kathie, oh, Kathie! Father! where are you? *The boys* have come!"

There was a rush down the stairs, and the pretty Kathleen sister was among them, and the kindly father, beaming upon them all. It was a wonderful time. And good old Hetty came in for her share of greeting too.

And then the boys hung their coats and caps up on the hall rack, in all the glory of gold braid and decorations, dumped their baggage on the hall table and chair, and went to the big living room where the father had already started a blaze in the ever-ready fireplace that was always prepared for the match to bring good cheer.

Then as they sat there talking, just looking at one another— even old Hetty having a part of the moment—smiling, beaming joy to one another, somehow all the terrible impressions, so indelibly graven in the consciousness of those fighters who had returned, were somehow softened, gentled, comforted by the sight and sound of beloved faces, precious voices, till for the time the past terrible years were erased. It seemed almost like a look into a future where Heaven would wipe out the sorrows of earth.

Then, softly, old Hetty slipped out into the kitchen. She knew what to do, even if Mrs. Graeme had not given that warning look. So many times, dark days, when there had come no expected letters, and news was scarce, and bad when it did come, these two good women had brightened the darkness by making plans of what they would do, when, and if, the boys did come suddenly, unexpectedly.

Hetty hurried to the freezing plant and got out her chickens. All the children home now, all the family together at last. And Hetty was as happy over the fact as any of the family, for they were her family, the only family she had left any more.

And presently there was the sweet aroma of frying chicken, a whiff of baking biscuit at the brief opening of the oven door, the fragrant tang of applesauce cooking. Oh, it was going to be a good supper, if it *was* hastily gotten together. There would be also mashed potatoes and rich brown gravy, Hetty's gravy, they knew of old. And there were boiling onions, turnips adding to the perfume. Celery and pickles. They could think it all out in anticipation, and Mother Graeme could smile and know that all was going on as she had planned. Little lima beans. Her nose was sensitive to each new smell. There would be coffee by and by, and there was a tempting lemon meringue pie, the kind the boys loved, in the cold pantry. The boys would not be missing anything of the old home they loved.

They had asked about the horse and the cow and the dogs, the latter even now lying adoringly at the feet of their returned masters, wriggling in joy over their coming.

They had heard a little of the welfare of near neighbors, a

few happenings in the village, the passing of an invalid, the sudden death of a fine old citizen, but by common consent there had been no mention as yet of the group of young people who had been used to almost infest the house at times, when the boys were at home before the war. Of course many of the men and a few of the girls were in the service, somewhere, and there was a shadow of sadness in that thought. A sadness that no one was quite willing to bring upon their sweet converse, in this great time of joy. Jeremy, sitting quietly, watching his mother's sweet happy face, suddenly realized that she had not ventured to tell them about any of their old friends and comrades, and wondered again if she knew what had befallen Rodney. He wished in his heart that the matter might not have to be mentioned, at least not that night. There would be time enough for the shadow of a blighting disappointment to one of their number, later, but not tonight. Not to dim the first home-coming. They were there, just themselves. It was almost as they used to be before they grew up, when they were a family, simple and whole. Oh, that it might be that way for at least one more night before any revelations were made that might darken the picture!

He gave a quick look toward Rodney, sitting so quietly there watching his mother. Was Rod wondering about the same things? Of course he was. Somehow he and Rod always seemed to have much the same reactions to matters of moment. And this surely must have been a matter of moment to Rod.

Good old Rod! These first few days might be going to be tough for him. He must be on hand to help out if any occasion for help should present itself. People were so dumb. There were always nosey ones who asked foolish prying questions, and would need to be turned off with a laugh, or silence. A brother could perhaps do a lot.

It was just then it happened.

The blessing had been asked. That seemed this time such a special joy to be thanking God for bringing them all together again. Father had served them all to heaping plates of the tempting food, Rod had just put the first mouthful in his mouth. Jeremy watched him do it. And then the doorbell rang, followed by the sound of the turning doorknob, the opening of the big front door, the entrance of several feet, the click of girls' heels on the hall floor, just as it used to be in the past years so many times. For all their young friends always felt so much at home in their home. But oh, why couldn't they have waited just this one night and let the home folks have their first inning? Just this first night!

A clatter and chatter of young voices, as Kathleen sprang up and hurried into the hall.

"Oh, there you are, Kathleen," said a loud clear voice that Jeremy knew instantly was Jessica's, "Oh, you're eating dinner, aren't you. Never mind, we'll come right out and sit with you the way we've always done. No, don't turn on the light in the living room, we'll come right out. Of course we've had our dinners before we came, but we simply can't waste a minute, and no, we won't hold you up. I know you must be hungry—"

Jeremy's quick glance went to Rodney's face, turned suddenly angry and frowning. Yes, he had recognized the voice. His reaction was unmistakable.

In one motion as it were, Rodney swept his knife and fork and napkin and plate from the table as he sprang stealthily to his feet, and bolted for the pantry door, carrying with him all evidences of his erstwhile presence at the table. Only his mute napkin ring remained to show there had been another sitting there at the right hand of Mother Graeme. Then quickly, quite unobtrusively, the mother's hand went out and covered that napkin ring, drawing it close to the other side of the coffee pot, entirely out of sight from the door into the hall by which the bevy of guests seemed about to enter. It was then that Jeremy came to himself and realized that this was his opportunity. He swung to his feet and grasped the chair that stood by his side where his brother had been sitting, giving it a quick twist, and placing it innocently off at one side, where any unsuspecting person might sit without noticing that it had but a moment before been a part of the family circle of diners.

Jeremy came forward courteously and met the guests as they entered, ahead of the disturbed Kathleen, who had done her best to turn them aside and failed. But no one would ever have suspected that Jeremy was playing a graceful part, or that he was at all anxious about the present situation. Rodney was definitely out of the picture, that was all that mattered. The pantry door was closed, and there was not even a shadow of the passing of a blue coat with brass buttons, gold braid, and ribbon decorations.

Jeremy glanced at his mother, but she was coolly welcoming the guests, seating them around the room, not saying a word about Rodney's absence. Perhaps she hadn't even noticed yet that he was gone. But you never could tell. Mother was a marvelous actress.

## 2

OUT on the road going slowly by, two old men were jogging along, as much as an ancient Ford could be said to jog, even in war times, and as they passed the car standing in front of the Graeme house, they even slowed down their war-jog and stared at it as they were passing.

"Ain't that the car Marcella Ashby bought off that Ty Wardlow jest afore he left fer overseas? Seems like there ain't another one jest that make an' color in these parts. And I seen her driving by a while ago with Emma Galt an' Garethy Sloan, an' another gal. It looked very much like that highflier that married that old gray-headed ripsnorter of a so-called stockbroker from the West, her that useta be Jessica Downs. Poor old Widow Downs done her best by that gal, but she was a chip of the old block I guess, and couldn't get by with that temper'ment she inherited from that flighty ma of hers, an' her good-for-nothing' pa, Wiley Downs. He was jes' naturally a cussed young 'un from a three-year-old, up, when they all thought he was so sweet and cute. Well, he was cute all right. I never did see no sweetness about him though, did you Tully?"

"Not so's you'd notice it," answered Tully glumly. "I

know he was anythin' but sweet when I knowed him in school, and I guess his teachers all felt the same way. And that Jessica, she had every one of his traits, including that washed-out yella' hair that she flung around sa proudly, 'zif she was the only one had any. Oh, she was sorta pretty, I'll own, but she had sly eyes, and I allus wondered how it was that Rod Graeme ever took up with her. I sort of figured that his pop an' mom was a'most glad ta let him go to war jesta get him away from that little gold-digger.

"Well, she does seem like a gold-digger, doesn't she? How she shelved Rod Graeme and took up with an old man just because he was said to be rollin' in wealth."

"Oh, she's a gold-digger all right, Tully," said Jeff Springer, turning out for the car they had just been discussing. "They do say that old guy, Carver De Groot, is rich as they make 'em. Ur leastways that's the talk. Though I'm wonderin' what she came back here fer, if that was her in that car with the other gals. I heard tell it was some likely that the Graeme boys might be comin' home soon on a furlough."

"Yep," said Tully. "They hev. I seen 'em jest a little while ago. They got in on the late train and shied off across the medder 'zif they was tryin' to escape notice. Beats all how shy some o' them heroes are."

"Well, mebbe the gals seen 'em," said Jeff, "an' they've come here to find out ef it's so."

There weren't many in the town that could beat Jeff and Tully figuring out what had happened and what people were going to do about it.

"Wal, I don't see what she'd wantta come back here fer," said Tully thoughtfully. "She's married all righty, fer I heard that Marcella Ashby went out to the weddin', an' it ain't so long ago, neither."

"Yep. But then, there's such a thing as *di*-vorces, ya know."

"Shucks!" said Tully, "no gal brought up in this here town would think about gettin' a *di*-vorce. Why, it ain't considered *respectable* here."

"Wal, you needn't tell me that gal Jessica would ever stop anythin' she *wanted* ta do fer respectability's sake. It ain't in her."

"Mebbe not," said Tully speculatively, "but it would any of those Graemes. You know that, Jeff."

"Yas, I s'pose so," reflected Jeff, "that is, of course, mom and pop Graeme would feel that way. But that ain't sayin' the boys would feel that way *now*. They've been ta war, ya know, an' they do say that war changes men a whole lot. You can't jus' say fer sure them Graeme boys feels that way now, ya know."

"It may be so," said Tully unbelievingly, "but I don't believe it. I've knowed them Graeme boys since little-up, an' I never seed a look or an act that would lead me ta believe they would think a *di*-vorce would be right. Not them with their bringin' up. Not them with a father an' a mother like they got."

"Well, tha's so too," said Jeff thoughtfully. "There's a great deal in what's before you. Your forebears mean a whole lot, even in these days. Well, mebbe you're right! But ef tha's so I can't figger out what that ripsnorter of a gal has gone there fer."

"Look here now," said Tully protestingly, "I didn't say nothin' about that highflier gal bein' against *di*-vorce did I? *She'd* prob'ly be *fer* it, I s'pose, but that ain't sayin' what she could do about it, bein' as one of the parties was a *Graeme.*"

"Wal, I hope yer right. I sure do, Tully! It sure would be a contest worth watchin', and I'm somehow bettin' on the Graemes my own self, if you ast me. I sure hope I'm right."

They drove on down the highway and their voices were lost in the distance.

But inside the Graeme house the contest had already begun.

It was such a pity that Jeff and Tully couldn't have been present to see the start.

It was Jessica who opened the first round, with a quick glance around the table, taking in the place where Rodney should have been and wasn't, and not even a napkin ring in sight to mark where he had been.

Her eyes came back quickly to Mother Graeme's face with a quick suspicious glance. She had always felt that there was not full harmony between herself and Mother Graeme even in the days when she was the acknowledged fiancée of Rodney, and supposed to be under the advantage of a blessing and the full acquiescence of his parents. She had none of her own, living, to worry about. Just the one quick glance, searching to see if the mother had somehow managed to spirit away the desirable son in that brief space of time. Then her face melted into a sweet tender look, for she was very versatile, and well knew what kind of a look she should put on to deceive these elect people.

"Oh, dear Mother Graeme!" she said tenderly, meltingly, "it's so good to get back to you. I have come to believe that there is no mother in the whole wide world as good and dear as you are."

Mother Graeme looked at her with an inscrutable, unbelieving smile, that showed this false girl's words had not gone even skin deep into her heart. But even her son Jeremy couldn't be sure just what his mother felt about it when he saw.

"There are a great many mothers in the world, Jessie. You haven't been away long enough to have seen them all, child." And then Mrs. Graeme turned away and greeted the other girls graciously.

"Mom is a perfect lady even though she's never been much out of Riverton in her life," decided Jeremy as he watched the quiet poise of his lady-mother. And then he noted that her brief acceptance of the gushing compliment had been enough to put the showy admiration out of running, and Jessica turned quickly to her next interest, which was really what she had come for. It began with another quick survey of the table, dwelling brittlely on each vacancy where another might have sat, and then she addressed a remark to the whole table:

"But where is *Rodney?*" she asked, letting her eyes touch each face tentatively, and coming back decisively to Jeremy. "I was told that he had come home also. Surely he hasn't left already?"

Jeremy caught the question midway before anyone else could answer, the way he used to snatch the football out of the very teeth of the enemy when interference hadn't been suspected from his direction.

"Rod had to go out," he said, quite casually, as if it were a thing to be expected, and not at all as if he were apologizing for his absence. And he noted that their mother did not look astonished at his words, and not even Kathleen seemed surprised. Strange. Even his father, after a quick sharp look at Jeremy, went right ahead with his eating, and kept his genial family atmosphere intact. He had a great family, Jeremy reflected. And oh, but they must surely know that something was wrong. Didn't they know that Jessica had married somebody else? Or hadn't she married him yet? Maybe she didn't get married. Maybe she had got over that and had come out after Rod again. Well, if she had he personally would devote himself to seeing that she did not get him. After what she had done to Rod, she was less worthy than he had thought her long ago, not fit for such a prince as his brother. He would keep out of this as far as he could, but if it came to a showdown he would go out for Rod in a big way and save him, even from himself, if she should prove canny enough to lead him so far afield as that.

So Jeremy devoted himself to the other girls, asking them questions about their families and what they had been doing for the war during the years of his own absence overseas.

But presently, as Rodney did not appear, and time went on while Jessica watched the younger brother, she became quite intrigued with him, and broke into his conversation with vivacity:

"Do you know, Jerry, you've quite developed," she said
patronizingly. "You're really a man now, aren't you?" and she
lifted her eyes with that long appeal from under golden lashes
that he used to watch her give to his older brother, and wonder at so long ago. It fairly sickened him now, the memory
of it.

He grinned his slow indifferent grin.

"Well, I guess that's what was intended I should be, wasn't
it?" he said. And then he turned to his sister and said:

"By the way, Kath, we met an old crush of yours in New
York as we came through, Richard Macloud. He asked after
you and wanted to be remembered. He's going back in a few
days now, and is slated for some big job, the powers-that-be
aren't saying what just yet."

Jessica gave full attention to Jeremy during this brief conversation, and took a hand at once.

"Do you know, Jerry, you look very much like Rod. I
hadn't noticed before, but of course now you're older the resemblance is very marked. You're even taller than he is, aren't
you?"

"Oh no, he's an inch and a half taller," the younger brother
answered with a gleam of amusement. But he did not further
pursue the subject. Instead he turned to his mother and began
to ask questions about her old neighbors, women his mother's age who used to give him cookies when he was a child.
He told one or two amusing stories of things that happened
long ago.

Jessica was watching him, and deciding that when his
brother was not present there would at least be Jerry, and he
really seemed to be worth while. In fact anybody in a uniform
was interesting to Jessica.

Meanwhile he kept wondering what Rod was doing, or
going to do, and was Hetty giving him more chicken out in

the kitchen, and would she give him coffee? Rod hadn't had his coffee yet, and he knew he was hungry and anxious for a cup of real home coffee. And what would Rod do if these tormenting callers continued to stay far into the night? Could he possibly steal up to bed without being heard and lock his door and go to sleep? Or was it thinkable that he himself could help out somehow by making an excuse to get Rod's coat and hat out of the front hall and throw it down the back-stairs? There were complications any way he saw it. And it certainly wouldn't be a good thing for these callers to go out the front door again and pass those two identical overcoats and caps hanging there together. They would know in an in-stant that Rod hadn't gone out of the house, that he had mere-ly been hiding somewhere. Well, perhaps that was what Rod wanted, to let Jessica know definitely that he did not wish to see her.

However, as he talked, he continued to work away at the problem in his mind and wonder if this was possibly where his own helpfulness and initiative should work in.

So presently he brought the conversation around to talk of people he had met overseas, and spoke of one he was sure was known to them all.

"Just wait!" he said springing up, "I think I have a snapshot of him upstairs. I'll get it. It was taken just after he came back from his most dramatic mission and won a lot of honor."

He went hurrying out, snatching the two overcoats and caps from the hall rack as he passed them and bore them up-stairs, striding to his room, and dropping them on a conve-nient bed out of sight. Then he plunged his hand even in the dark into the collection of hand luggage, located his own bag which he knew carried some photographs, and hurried back down stairs, producing the picture, with a few others but tak-ing care he did not show them any in which his brother fig-ured. Let that highflier girl forget Rod if she could. Rod definitely wanted none of her; or if Rod only *thought* he didn't, and there was a doubt, there was no doubt in Jeremy's mind about whether *he* wanted that girl for a sister-in-law.

Now Jessica was accustomed to getting all the attention there was from every man within her charmed circle, and she didn't like it that Jeremy divided his attentions so thoroughly, so she set herself to achieve interest in this new man who had only been a kid before he went away, and had turned man overnight as it were. But Jerry wasn't interested. Perhaps if he let her know he wasn't she would get tired and go home.

At last Jessica looked straight at Jeremy.

"When is Rod coming back?" she asked directly, and her eyes demanded the truth.

Jeremy laughed lightly.

"That's hard to say," he answered. "Men don't usually confide little matters like that."

Without really repeating her own words Jessica turned to the quiet mother, and managed to shift both her glance and her question to her, as if she were the one she had meant to interrogate in the first place.

Mrs. Graeme met the shifted glance with an odd quietness and answered promptly, calmly.

"He didn't say when he would be back."

Jessica seemed a bit perplexed at the answer, and the calm demeanor. She shifted her sparkling nervous fingers, so their load of glittering diamonds would shine directly into the lady's eyes, and asked impertinently:

"Where did he go, Mrs. Graeme?" in the tone of one who has an undeniable right to ask.

"He didn't tell me," said the mother quietly.

There followed a deadly moment of silence in which it was evident that the visitor was a trifle disconcerted. Then Mrs. Graeme lifted a sweet smile and asked quite casually:

"Is your husband in Riverton with you, Jessie?"

Jessica's cheeks flamed into crimson above the lovely make-up, and her eyes went down to her glittering fingers nervously. "Why, no, Mrs. Graeme," she answered indifferently. "He's too busy. His business engrosses all his time. He seldom goes anywhere away from home."

"Oh," said Mother Graeme, "then I suppose you're not remaining here long."

"Well, I don't know just what I shall do," flashed Jessica angrily, "I'm quite free to stay as long as I please if it suits me. Depends upon how interesting you folks can make it for me. But I certainly do want to see Rod."

"Yes?" said the calm mother voice. Then after another instant's silence: "What a pity Mr. De Groot couldn't have come with you, just for once. Your old friends would certainly like to meet him."

"What a mother!" commented Jeremy in his heart. "She certainly is tops. Then of course she has known about the break between Rod and Jessica, perhaps for a long time, and never breathed a word of it to Rod! Even called her husband by his name! Rod needn't have worried lest there would be a scene. Mother never would permit a scene. She isn't a day older than when we were little kids and she always kept her hand on everything! Bless her! And dad follows right along with her!"

He cast a quick look toward his father, and saw him eating quietly along, enjoying the festive dinner, not seeming to question what had become of Rod! Not being upset nor allowing any tenseness in the pleasant home atmosphere since these old-time friends suddenly dropped in upon them so unexpectedly. Just taking it as if it were an everyday happening.

"Jeremy," said his mother pleasantly, "take this coffeepot out to Hetty, and ask her to make a little more coffee. These friends will have a cup of coffee with us surely, even if they have had their dinner."

Jeremy arose promptly, smilingly, took the coffeepot and vanished kitchenward.

Then arose Jessica scowling.

"I think we should be going," she said sharply. "I want to find Rod."

"Oh," said Marcella Ashby, whose car they had come in, "but how will you find him? You don't know where he's gone."

"Oh," said Jessica scornfully, "we'll just scout around until we find him. I imagine he'll not be hard to find. Will he, Mr. Graeme?"

Father Graeme looked up with an inscrutable smile.

"I wouldn't know, Jessie," he said. "Rodney has always been a bit unpredictable, and there's no telling now, since he's been off to war on his own."

Jessica turned angrily and marched toward the hall door looking back to say, as Jeremy came in with the coffeepot:

"No coffee for me, thank you. I'm going out to find Rod."

But suddenly Marcella spoke up.

"Speak for yourself, Jess, I'm staying for coffee. I haven't had any of the Graeme coffee in ages, and there's nobody else in Riverton can make coffee like old Hetty."

Jessica paused angrily.

"Oh, well, then give me your keys to the car. I haven't any time to waste. I can pick you up later when I'm ready to go back to your house." It was spoken quite haughtily, as if Marcella might be a sort of a hired servant.

"No, you don't get my car keys," said Marcella, reaching out to accept the cup of coffee Mother Graeme made haste to pour for her. "I'm not running any risks like that. You always do make a car act all haywire. And besides I know the hours you keep. I'm not going to wait around here and make everybody stay up entertaining me, nor walk home without the car."

"Oh, very well," said Jessica disagreeably. "Next time I'll *hire* a car of my own, or get a gentleman to accompany me."

So Jessica stood pettishly in the doorway, staring down the hall, wondering what had become of the coats and caps she had sighted on the hatrack when she came in. And there she stubbornly stood while the rest of the party lingered drinking their coffee in a leisurely manner, reluctant to leave the pleasant old home, and the charming family circle that had once been so dear to them all.

OUT in the pantry Rodney, boiling with rage, slammed his plate down on the pantry shelf and scowled. What right did those girls have to come here the first night he was at home and barge into the dining room? Yes, they were old friends, most of them, but they ought to have better sense. And *that* girl! What was her idea in coming? He and she had nothing in common any more and he didn't want to see her ever again. Rotten little double-crosser! And then presume to think she could smile and smooth it all over and be just as good friends as ever. Not on yer life he wouldn't.

He didn't know what the family would think of his having run away, when perhaps mom didn't know anything about it all, and wouldn't understand. Though he could usually depend on his family to stand back of him whatever he did. And of course those others. He didn't know what they would think about him and he didn't much care. Had any of them seen him go? He thought not, for the hall wasn't exactly in line with where he had been sitting. But he was most troubled about mom. Of course she might have heard some gossip, and might have got on to the fact that there was a break between him and Jessica. Still he hadn't meant to have it come to her knowledge in such a way as this. But since it had come, it had, and he would have to take it and get it over with, no matter what. Of course if Jessica had carried out her threat and got married mom would certainly have heard some gossip, but he was definitely not going to be friends with Jessica, nor even acquaintances if he could help it. He thought of the hours of peril and danger through which he had lived, and of how he had all this time also battled with the thought of her disloyalty to him, disloyalty to the tender vows of everlasting love she had uttered before he went away, and how many times he had writhed in their memory as he went forth to fight the enemy! He had thought over all the precious times of their youthful association, her professed overwhelming love for him which she had so utterly repudiated afterward, all those treasured looks and touches of her hands and lips! Now he had torn them from his consciousness, flung them away to some foreign breeze in a strange land, renounced them forever, erased them from his memory. And now that he had come back to a pleasant homeland did she think that he could smooth them all over and be *friends?* Could she think that for a smile from her he would take her back into his friendship? No, a thousand times *no!* He was done with her forever. If she forced him ever to have to see her again, or speak to her, he would certainly make her understand clearly that he had no faith in her whatever. Not even if she should repent and say she was sorry, and want him back, would he ever love her again. For strange to say, the separation, and the peril and her own disloyalty had utterly killed all the love he used to think he had for her. And suddenly, sitting there in the pantry, he saw that it never had been real love, but only imagination. He had taken her lovely image, beautiful features, a flawless complexion, gorgeous hair that seemed so like the crowning of a young saint, and upon those outward forms he had built up a character for her which was not really hers.

And now, was it possible that he could ever be *glad* that all this had happened, and that her action would in a way set him free from what, if it had gone on as he had planned, would have been a galling life of torture for him? Disillusionment had come early and in a hard way at a hard time. But how much better that it had come now instead of after they were married and he was doomed to a life that would have been worse than imprisonment or death. Come back to her and be good friends? Well, she could guess again. He was done with her forever. He didn't ever want to see her again, and wouldn't if he could help it. But if he had to see her again under circumstances where he couldn't help it, he would give her to understand once and for all that he was finished.

Just then Hetty tapped softly at the pantry door.

"Mr. Roddy," she whispered softly, using his old pet name by which she used to call him when he was a child, "I'se got some moh good chicken for you, an' some mashed taters real hot, an' some o' them yeller turnips you useta love so much, an' nobody won't know you'se here. They all think you'se gone away."

Cautiously Rod shoved away the chair he had braced under the latch of the door and held out his empty plate, grinning sheepishly.

Silently the old servant filled his plate with choice pieces, and much hot gravy, added a cup of coffee, and an extra understanding grin, and Rod attacked his second helping with much gusto. Somehow he would have to make his peace afterward with his mother, but after all mom always understood, and maybe she never had cared much for Jessica, anyway. He tried to think back, and began to see a glimmer of half-disapproval in the past. Well, anyway it was good to be at home, and his hunger was getting appeased. Good old Hetty, who had always understood, too! Now, whenever those stupid visitors departed he could come out of hiding and be none the worse for wear.

As he finished off the last breast of chicken Hetty had brought him and started in on the applesauce and hot biscuits he grinned across the kitchen at Hetty, as she hovered just outside the dining room door with her ear trained near to a hearing crack, and an interested eagerness on her kind old face.

He lifted his hand with a summoning gesture, and Hetty stole noiselessly across the smooth kitchen floor, with a questioning look on her faithful old face.

"Who's in there Hetty?" he asked. "Anybody I know?"

"Dey sure is!" said Hetty in her low soft voice. "Dere's Miss Emma Galt, an' Marcel' Ashby, I reckum dey come in her cyar, and dere's dat rattle-pated Miss Jessie wif her fingers all dolled up in di'mon's, 'Rings on her fingers an' bells on her toes,' like de old hymn useta say. An' she's usin' her tongue for bells for she's done mos' all dat talkin' like she always done when she useta come ta see you. An' she come ta see you dis time too, leastways dat what she says, an' now seem like she's goin' away ta hunt you up. It's my 'pinion you all bettah get ta bed 'fore she gits back, ur you'll git cotched fer sho.'"

Noiselessly shaking her sides with laughter, old Hetty rolled softly away and took up her stand at the crack of the door again, until finally she came back to report that they were all getting ready to go, and pretty soon he could go back and finish his dessert with the family.

But Rodney was taking no chances. He waited patiently for Hetty's signal. He even opened the pantry window a crack to wait until he heard the car driving away.

The cold air came in refreshingly against Rodney's hot forehead, and the quiet out-of-doors seemed to make him understand that he must be patient. He ought to know by this time that those girls never left when they got to the door, but just stayed and talked and talked. Well, this draft was getting chilly. He reached out and drew the window shut, and straightway his mind jumped back to the present situation, and what he was going to do next. Well, if those unwanted guests ever took themselves away definitely, he must go out at once to the dining room and make his peace with his family. It was going to be a bit embarrassing of course, but after all he had been through in the war why should he mind a bit of embarrassment? It certainly would be great to get his family all alone again.

Eventually the group in the dining room gathered themselves in the hall to leave, and Kathleen went to the door with them. The rest of the family remained seated in silence until Kathleen came back and sat down. They waited even then a second or two till the sound of the retreating car driving away came to their ears, and then the father looked up with a comical twinkle in his eyes.

"Now," he enquired mildly, "is it perfectly safe to ask what this is all about? And does anybody know what suddenly became of Rodney?"

They all burst into laughter, and the sweet homey sound of it reached to the kitchen, even as Mother Graeme reached out and tinkled the little silver bell for Hetty to take the plates and bring the dessert.

"Do you know what this is all about, son?" asked the father, appealing to Jeremy innocently.

"Why certainly, dad," answered Jeremy jovially. "It simply means that someone was about to come in that Rod didn't want to see, and he scrammed. That was perfectly natural, don't you think?"

"Well, yes—how do you say it?—'Could be'? But there was more than *one* somebody here. *Which* one?"

Jeremy grinned at his father.

"Do you have to ask that? Wasn't it obvious?"

The father sat thoughtfully for an instant, and then he said slowly, nodding his head half amusedly.

"Yes? I suppose you are referring to the glittering one. If that's so I wouldn't judge Rod *would* want to see her. A girl that would turn down a single real good stone, for a display like that! I'm not surprised! I somehow thought that Rod would find out what that girl was before it was too late! Well, we've got nothing to worry about in her loss. And now, where's Rod?"

"He's right here in my kitchen," said Hetty, appearing on time with her tray in her hands and beginning to gather up the plates. "Dat boy ain't ferget whar ta go when he's hungry, no mattah who barges inta de dinin' room."

"Oh, so he's up with the program is he, and doesn't have to be waited for while he catches up on the first course," said the smiling father.

"No sah, he ain't behind. Fact is he's had somethin' like three good-sized helpin's of the fust co'se."

Mother Graeme's smile and Mother Graeme's eyes thanked faithful old Hetty.

"I knew he'd be all right in your hands, Hetty," she murmured quietly, as Hetty took her plate away.

"Yes, ma'am, I knowed you'd be sure o' that," answered Hetty happily.

It was just then that Rodney came grinning out of his hiding with a quick apprehensive glance toward his mother's beloved eyes, a wink and a grin toward Jeremy, answered by a salute from the brother in true military style.

"Pretty slick, old man," said Jeremy in an undertone as Rodney sat down.

Rod grinned like the sun shining from behind a thunderhead. Then with a courteous smile toward the family he added in his pleasantest voice:

"Sorry folks, I couldn't take time to say excuse me!"

And that understanding family only smiled comfortably. That was the great thing about that family, whether they understood or not, they always took startling things with a smile, quite as if they expected them.

But Jeremy was sure by this time that his mother understood. Just how much she understood, or how it had come about that she knew anything about it, didn't matter. Mom was all right, and she would never bungle things by throwing a monkey wrench into the works.

So the happy silence settled comfortably down upon this reunited family, and they were just getting ready to savor the joy of it all, when there came another interruption.

But this time it was not the sound of the doorbell, but the rattle of a latchkey in the lock, and they all looked up astonished. Evidently Kathleen had locked the door after the other guests left, but who had a latchkey? Their eyes went around the circle, a question in each face, and Rodney sprang to his feet as if for another flight. This was an evening of surprises. Who was using that latchkey?

There were only three outside the immediate family who had a latchkey to that front door. One was Hetty of course for the rare occasions when she took her day off and went out to spend it with some of her old friends. The second was Mrs. Graeme's brother now overseas on confidential business for the government, and not likely to return for some months. The third key was in the hands of the widow of a distant cousin of Mr. Graeme who had spent some weeks with the family, professedly on business connected with her late husband's will. She had recently departed for another city, and had neglected to return her latchkey. Her departure had been a great relief for the family, and they had not anticipated her soon return, so when they heard someone walk into the door after Kathleen had locked it they could not understand it.

But Cousin Louella Chatterton was stealthy. She came rubber shod, for she loved surprise-effects, and it also gave her the advantage of hearing words not intended for her ears. So she stood silently observing them, and not a thing missed her sharp eyes.

Suddenly Rodney subsided and dropped easily back to his chair again, slickly as if he had not intended otherwise.

"Yes, Rodney, it's no use for you to attempt to slide away," said Cousin Louella, "I was too quick for you. You can't get by with a thing like that with me. I know what I'm about."

Rodney grinned.

"Could be," he said mischievously. "I haven't seen you in a good many years, but you certainly sound to be in good form."

"Take care, now, Rodney!" said the lady stiffening up as if Rodney were a child of three. "You needn't try any of your impertinence on me. I know what you have just done, and I have come in for the distinct purpose of telling you just what I think of you. Of all the rude things for a young man still in the service to do, I think what you have just done was about the rudest. And you presuming to wear all those ribbons of honor on your breast and then running away when ladies, some of your oldest friends, came in to welcome you! I'm surprised. I really think this ought to be reported to your chief officer, and you disciplined for it. What are we coming to when the men we have sacrificed for, and given bonds for, and sent munitions to, come home and perform like that? And the worst of it was that one of those girls was the girl who used to be your former fiancée, or maybe is yet for all I know. Though I have heard rumors that she is about to marry some one else. Did you know that, Margaret? Had you heard there was any break between your son and that lovely girl with the wonderful gold hair that he used to be so crazy about?"

Rodney went white, his black brows drawn in a terrible frown, but nobody but Jeremy saw him, and he looked quickly away toward his mother. How would she take this announcement?

But Margaret Graeme was a thoroughbred, and she lifted calm eyes to the unwelcome relative, and answered in a low quiet voice without a quaver in it:

"Why certainly, Louella, that engagement was broken long ago, soon after Rodney went away to war."

"It *was?* But Margaret, you *must* be mistaken about that. You know I was here for a long time and no one ever said *a word* about it to *me*."

"Why should they, Louella? It wasn't a matter that any but the two concerned had any right to talk over. Won't you sit down, Louella and have a piece of Hetty's lemon pie, and a cup of coffee with us? Jerry, bring that chair over here by me for her."

"Well, yes, I don't mind if I do have a cup of coffee," she said in a parenthesis, "but Margaret, *who* broke it, Rodney or the girl?"

Then before the gentle-voiced mother could reply, Rodney spoke up haughtily.

"That's not a matter for outsiders to discuss, Cousin Louella," he said, and Jeremy, listening, caught the look that Rodney must have worn when he went out after the enemy, and felt like cheering for him.

It was then that the wise quiet father put in his voice.

"Cousin Louella, did you ever succeed in getting in touch with that lawyer out west who had had to do with that property that you were so worried about when you were there last?"

The cousin turned annoyedly and answered sharply, "No, I didn't, not yet. We'll talk of that later. You know, Donald, I hate to be interrupted when I'm talking about something else, and I'm not through with this matter yet. I want to know the truth about this before I speak of other things. Rodney, suppose you tell me the whole story, and then I shall know what to answer when I'm asked."

Then Rodney sat up straight and faced the curious cousin sternly in most decided tones:

"I've nothing to say Cousin Louella, and I should think if anybody asked you impudent questions like that the only answer would be to say it was none of their business."

"Oh, but Rodney! That would not do at all. If the engagement is broken why did that girl come here to see you tonight? Does she want to make it up?"

"I really don't know," said Rodney in a cold voice. "She couldn't have known that I was here, unless some lousy sneak who had seen me get off the train told her. Even mom didn't know I was coming."

"Oh, *I* told her," said the cousin serenely. "I met her as I was coming away from the post office where I had stopped for a package. They sent me a notice that it had come for me postage due, and *I* told her."

"Oh, *you* told her," said Father Graeme. "And how did *you* know, Louella?" His face was grave and his voice very stern.

"Why the taxi cab driver told me. He had sighted the boys as they went across lots from the station and he was eager to tell me. And later, coming out of the post office I met Jessica, and she said she wondered if Rodney had come home yet, and I said, yes, he had."

"Oh," said the master of the house. "Well, now, Louella, if you've got that off your chest I think you and I will go into the other room and talk over that matter of business."

Mr. Graeme took his last bite of pie, and the last swallow of coffee, and arose with finality. But the persistent guest sat still, her full coffee cup in her hand and shook her head with firm determination:

"No indeed, Donald, I intend to finish this lovely pie and coffee before I talk business, but I certainly have to get a little more data about this broken engagement."

Then she took her first bite of her pie, and the children by common consent arose from the table and followed their father from the room, wearing amused and angry looks, if one can combine those two adjectives.

And there were only Margaret Graeme and Louella left at the table, while Louella took another bite of the pie, and cast an eager enquiry toward her hostess.

"Now, Margaret, they've gone, and you'll tell me all about it, won't you? I feel terribly hurt to have been left out of this important happening of the family. When did you first find it out, and weren't you *terribly* disappointed and grieved?"

"No, I'm sorry you feel that way, Louella," answered Rodney's mother, "I don't feel that it was so important a happening. It was just a youthful high school attachment you know, and things of that sort are better ignored, don't you think?

No, I wasn't disappointed. I knew if it wasn't the wisest best arrangement all around it would work itself out, and we were all quite satisfied that it did. But I do feel that it is a thing of the past, and not to be brought into our conversation again. And now Louella, what plans have you made? Are you to be in this region long, or do you have to go right back? And where is your luggage? I ought to have asked you if you didn't want to go upstairs and freshen up. Did you come right here from the train?"

"No," said Cousin Louella coldly, "I went to the inn first and left my things, then took a taxi over here. You see I had no idea of course if you would be home, or gone perhaps to Florida."

Louella finished her coffee hurriedly and rose. "Thanks for the coffee. It just touched the spot. And now if you don't mind, I'll run on. I've a room at the inn, and there are people I want to see, who may be waiting for me so I better go at once. As for the business, it can wait, or I may find a lawyer who can help me. No, don't call a taxi, *I'll* phone the inn to send their cab for me, and don't disturb yourself for me. I'll be seeing you again before I leave, that is if I get time. Good night!" and Louella walked angrily to the telephone in the hall and sent for her cab. It was not long before she was gone, and the family were rejoicing in her departure. Then Mother Graeme gathered her children around her and beamed on them, and Father Graeme poked the fire into brilliancy again, drew down the shades as for a black-out, turned out the lights in the hall, locked and chained the front door, and in every way made sure that no more callers would seek welcome that night in the Graeme home.

"Maybe it's selfish," he said as he came smiling back to the library again, "but I declare if we can't have one evening with our children to ourselves after all these long months of anxiety and waiting, I'll do something desperate!"

And the children lifted proud happy eyes.

"Thanks, dad. That's what we wanted!" said Jeremy.

"Here too!" said Rodney.

"And mom, if anybody else tries to get into the family sanctum, let's make them have an examination on what topics of conversation they are going to select to talk about before we pass them in," said Kathie.

"That's all right by me," said the smiling lips of the mother in her best imitation of the present-day slang. And then they all burst into a joyful round of laughter, and the mother had to wipe some happy tears away before she could hold hands with her two boys, seated on the floor one on each side of her.

And then began the happy converse which they had been anticipating all the way across the sea.

4

IF the Graemes had been able to look in on their last caller in her comfortable apartment at the inn, and seen the luxurious appointments, the elaborate little evening repast that was being set out for her expected guest, they would no longer have been under the impression that she was hard up financially. She had spared nothing to give the right touch of festivity to her setting, including candles on the little table, set in readiness.

She hurriedly changed into a charming negligee, gave just the right touch to her coiffure with a charming artificial rose that drooped becomingly to one side. Then she took up her position in a comfortable chair with one of the latest bestsellers, the kind of book that was the rage in the fashionable world. A glance at the clock and she settled herself for at least five minutes of pleasant relaxation.

But in less than five minutes her telephone rang.

"Is that you, Louella?" asked the dashing voice that answered her acknowledgment of the ring. "This is Jessica! You are back? Okay. We're on the way. Be there in five minutes."

And it was less than five minutes when Jessica marched in, followed by her three friends, and sat down to sip tea and eat cakes and bits of sandwiches and confections. But Jessica did not waste much time.

"Well, what did you find out?" she asked with eyes that grueled the eyes of her hostess. "Did you find out where he is? Was he there?"

"Why certainly," said Louella. "I told you he would be there."

"He was there? You *saw* him?"

"Why certainly."

"Where was he?"

"Sitting at the dinner table, enjoying his meal with the rest of the family," said Louella with satisfaction. She adored playing such an important part and being able to prove her prognostications. "Did *you* go out and look for him?"

"I certainly did," said the vexed Jessica. "I went simply everywhere that he used to go, to all his old haunts, or telephoned where it was too far, and none of the people had even heard he was coming home. But do you mean he was there *all the time?*"

"I shouldn't be at all surprised. He had that home atmosphere about him, in spite of his uniform. I doubt if he had been any further away than the garage, or even just the pantry. Of course I don't know, but I just have a hunch," said Louella.

"But didn't he act as if he knew that I had been there?"

"My dear, he didn't act at all. He just sat there and glowered. In fact when I entered silently with my key and watched them all an instant before they saw me, I think he had heard me and was on the point of leaving the room quite suddenly, and then when he saw it was only I, he sat down in his chair and began to eat again. But he certainly was in a poisonous mood. He was as rude as he could be to me, declined to answer any of my questions, and positively shut me up. Said if anybody asked me any questions about you and himself I might tell them it was none of their business."

"Oh, *really?*" asked Jessica with a defeated look on her

handsome face. "Well, I suppose I might as well give up and go back west and work things out some other way."

"Not at all, my dear," soothed Louella. "I should say from what I used to know of Rodney in his youth that the outlook is very hopeful."

*"Hopeful?"* said the younger woman, astonished. "Why you have just given me to understand that he is very angry with me, and doesn't want to see me. I don't see anything hopeful about that."

"Then you can't know Rodney very well. Don't you understand that the very fact that he is angry at you and doesn't want to see you, shows that he is still deeply in love with you, and you will have no trouble at all in getting back his admiration when once you get really face to face with him and have a good talk? I'd be willing to wager that you with your beautiful face and your gracious graceful ways, can easily win him back to love you more than he ever did before."

It was then that Emma Galt plunged into the conversation.

"But Jess is married, Mrs. Chatterton. You forget that. And Rod was brought up with very strong moral ideas about the sanctity of marriage."

"Fiddlesticks for any moral ideas nowadays," said Louella grandly, as if she were empowered to speak with authority on the new moral standards of the present day.

"But you don't realize at all, Mrs. Chatterton, how intensely those Graemes feel on moral questions. Those boys have very strong ideals, and real conscientious scruples about things. They were brought up that way, and it has taken deep root in them," said Marcella.

Louella smiled.

"Piffle for their conscientious scruples! You seem to have forgotten that those boys have been to war. You will probably find that out when you come in closer contact with them. I don't fancy many conscientious scruples can outlive a few months in the company of a lot of wild young soldiers or sailors off on their own. And remember *Rodney* has been away from his hampering, narrow-minded parents for at least three years!"

Then up spoke Marcella Ashby again.

"I think that is perfectly terrible, Mrs. Chatterton, for you to call those dear people narrow-minded. All the years while we were growing up, they have been the dearest people to us all. Their house was always open to give us all good times, and they never showed a bit of narrow-mindedness. They were ready to laugh and joke with us all, and spend money freely to give us enjoyment."

"Oh yes, children's stuff, picnics and little silly games, and nice things to eat of course, but did they ever have dances for us, or cards, or take us to the theater, or even let us play kissing games?" spoke up Jessica. "No, indeedy. Everything was very discreet and prim, and of course we are no longer children and times have changed. You couldn't expect people like the dear old Graemes to be up to date. They are old people, and can't understand the present-day needs of young folks. But I think myself that it is quite possible that the boys may have changed. They've been out in the world, and seen what everybody is doing. I don't believe for a minute that Rodney would be shocked at all if I told him I'd made a big mistake in marrying a man so much older than myself, and that I was going to Reno to get a divorce as soon as I've finished up a few matters of business here in town. Isn't that what your idea was, Mrs. Chatterton?"

"Well, yes, I think myself you'll find those boys, at least Rodney, is much more of a worldling than his folks give him credit for, and I feel sure Jessica, if you give your mind to it, that you can win him back."

And then they went into a huddle to plan a campaign against Rodney Graeme.

And even as they plotted, with the devil whispering advice secretly to them, and only Marcella Ashby of their number protesting at their plans, the Graeme family were kneeling in a quiet circle about the fire in the library, while Father Graeme thanked God for the return of his children, and petitioned that they might be guided aright in the days that were ahead, that none of them should be led astray from the way in which the Lord would have them go, and that His will might be done through them all, to the end that they might become changed into the image of His Son, Jesus Christ, and be fit messengers for the gospel of salvation.

And he prayed also for the rulers of their beloved land that they too might be led by the Holy Spirit to make right laws and decisions, and to govern the beloved country ever as God would have it governed, and that all spirit of unrighteousness might be put down, and any mistakes inadvertently made might be overruled, and the land saved from mere human guidance or acts ordered by warped judgment.

And he prayed for his boys, who had been so graciously spared from death or torture or imprisonment, that they might understand that God had thus spared them so that they might be the better fitted to do His will in the life that was still before them, that they might live to serve their Master even more fully than they had served their country.

As they rose from their knees, and brushed away tender tears that had come to all eyes, the plotters were just starting out on their second attempt to start their campaign.

"Now," said Father Graeme as they stood a moment thoughtfully before the fire, "I think these boys should get to their rest at once, especially this wounded shoulder needs to have complete rest. Besides, if thoughtless friends are contemplating any further raids on the household tonight, it seems to me that would be a good way to head them off. Just let us get to bed as quietly, and quickly, and as much in the dark as possible, and when and if they come again, let them find it all dark. I suggest if they ring the bell and continue to ring, that you let them wait until I can get my bathrobe on and go down and meet them. I think perhaps I can show them that any further visits tonight will not be acceptable to anyone."

He grinned around on them pleasantly, and they all responded gratefully.

"All right, dad!" said Rodney happily. "This has been our family's own night, and we don't want it spoiled in any way. You don't know what it's meant to me to hear you pray for us all again, and to know that we are back together again, after so many terrible possibilities."

"Here too," said Jeremy huskily. "You got me all broken up with that prayer, but perhaps tomorrow I'll be able to tell you all about it. What a memory I had of your prayers when I was out on a mission meeting bombs and knowing the next one might carry me up to God, and I wanted to go from my knees to meet Him, so my heart knelt as I flew along, and perhaps that was how I came through. I felt God there!"

The testimony of the two boys stirred them all deeply, and they lingered in spite of themselves, and then suddenly they heard a car coming.

"That wouldn't be our friends, would it?" asked the father anxiously. "Perhaps you better all scatter as swiftly as possible. Here, mother, you take this tiny flashlight. I don't want you to fall. I guess the rest of you can manage in the dark, can't you? I'll wait a minute and make the fire safe for the night."

Swift embraces, tender kisses, and they scattered silently, and when Marcella's car arrived before the door the house was dark as a pocket, and silent too, everyone lying quietly under blankets, and almost asleep already.

"Why the very idea!" said Jessica sharply as she clambered out of the car. "They *can't* have gone to bed this early, and they wouldn't have been likely to go out anywhere this first night."

"You seem to have forgotten that Rod was wounded and has been in the hospital for sometime," said Marcella.

"*Nonsense!*" said Jessica. "Anyhow I'm going to ring the bell good and loud. I guess they won't sleep long after that."

5

THREE girls were grouped together in a pleasant corner of the Red Cross room sewing as if their very life depended upon their efforts. One was running the sewing machine gaily, putting together tiny garments for the other two to take over and finish. The second girl was opening seams, and ironing them flat, and then finishing them off with delicate feather-stitching in pink and blue, binding edges of tiny white flannel jackets and wrappers with pink and blue satin ribbon. The third girl was buttonholing scallops with silk twist on tiny flannel petticoats. They were making several charming little layettes for a number of new babies who had arrived overnight without bringing their suitcases with them, and these three girls had promised to see that the needy babies were supplied before night. And because these three girls were used to having all things lovely in thier own lives, it never occurred to them to sling the little garments together carelessly. They set their stitches as carefully, and made their scallops as heavy and perfect as if they had been doing them for their own family. Others might sling such outfits together by expeditious rule, but they must make them also beautiful.

"Aren't they darling?" said Isabelle Graham. "I feel as if I were making doll clothes, and I'd like to play with the dolls myself. They say that a couple of these poor little mothers have wept their hearts out mourning for their husbands and they haven't taken time to get anything ready for their babies. The husband of one baby's mother has been reported killed, and another one is taken prisoner. A terrible world for a little child to be born into."

"Yes," said an elderly woman coming over from a group across the room to take the measurement of the hems the girls were putting into the little petticoats, "I think it's a crime! Bringing little helpless babies into a world like this. And all because their silly mothers couldn't wait till their men came back from fighting. It's ridiculous!"

Alida Hopkins shut her pretty lips tightly on the three pins she was holding in her mouth, ready to set the measurement of the little petticoat she was working on and cast a scornful look at the woman.

But the woman pursued the subject.

"Don't you think so, Alida?"

"I don't think it's any of my business," said Alida with a gay little laugh. "It certainly isn't the poor babies' fault, and they're here, and can't go around without clothes in this freezing weather, so I'm here to make clothes for them. Beryl, have you got any more of that lovely white silk twist? I've an inch more scallops to make on this petticoat, and I don't like to change color."

"Oh yes," said Beryl Sanderson, fishing in her handbag for the spool and handing it out. "I have a whole lot at home. I bought it before they stopped selling such things. I thought it might fit in somewhere."

"Well you certainly were forehanded," said the critical woman sharply. "But I wouldn't waste real silk twist on baby garments for little war foundlings. It won't be appreciated I tell you. Better save it for your own children some day."

Beryl smiled sweetly and covered the rising color in her cheeks with a dimple.

"Well, you see, Mrs. Thaxter," she said amusedly, "I haven't reached that need yet, so I guess we'd better let this little war baby have the benefit."

Mrs. Thaxter cast a pitying disapproving glance at the girl, pursed her lips and tossed her head.

"Oh, well, I guess you're as improvident as the rest," she said sharply. "I thought you had better sense."

"Improvident?" laughed Beryl. "Why should I provide for children I don't possess and may never have, and let some other little child suffer?"

"H'm!" said Mrs. Thaxter, "I guess they won't do much suffering for the lack of a few needlefuls of buttonhole twist," and she marched off to the other end of the room with her head in the air. Her departure was announced to the room by little rollicking ripples of laughter from the girls she had left.

"Shhh!" warned Beryl softly. "There's no need to make her angry, even if she is an old crab. Do you know she has worked all this week cutting out garments, worked hours over time?"

"Yes," said Bonny Stewart with a twinkle, "and ripped every last worker up the back while she did it. I was here. I heard her, and believe me it was the limit!"

"Well, I guess she's pretty sore that her Janie got married without letting her know before her soldier went away. And now he's got himself killed and Mrs. Thaxter has to keep telling Janie 'I told you so' all the time," said Isabelle with a gay trill of a laugh.

"Oh, but he didn't get himself killed, he's only a prisoner. Hadn't you heard?" said Celia Bradbury drawing her chair over to join the group, and getting out the little pink booties she was knitting. "The word came last night from the War Department. Janie called up and told my sister. She's in her Sunday School class. She's very hopeful that he will get home now."

"Being taken prisoner by the enemy is almost worse than death these days," commented Beryl sadly.

"Yes, I think this war is *horrid,*" said Bonny with tears in her voice. "I don't see why somebody doesn't put a stop to it."

"That's what they are trying to do, child," said Beryl with a smile.

"Yes, I suppose it is," answered Bonny. "But say, did you know both the Graeme brothers came home last night? I was on the train. I saw them, and they're perfectly stunning looking in their uniforms. Not all the service men get killed or taken prisoner. Say, Beryl, didn't you used to know those Graeme boys?"

"Why yes," said Beryl looking up interestedly. "I went to high school with Jeremy. He was a fine scholar and a swell person. I didn't know his brother so well; he was older than I, and out of high school, in college, but I've always heard good things about him. They've got a wonderful mother and father. My mother has often told me nice little kindly things they've done for people who were in trouble."

"Oh, yes," said Alida with a half-contemptuous smile, "they're like that. Always doing good. Terribly kind, but kind of drab and uninteresting."

"No," said Beryl suddenly, "they're not drab and uninteresting. My mother has told me a lot about them. She loves to talk with them. And certainly Jeremy was interesting. The whole school loved to hear him recite. He could make the dullest study sound interesting. He always found so much to tell that wasn't really in the books."

"You mean he made it up, out of his head?" asked Alida.

"Oh no," said Beryl, "he'd looked it up in other books, the dictionary and encyclopedia, and sometimes several other books. He always told where he'd found it, and who had written things about it. He studied up all his subjects that way."

"My word!" said Isabelle, "he must be a hound for hard labor."

"But he seemed to like it," said Beryl, "and certainly the class liked it, and the teachers were crazy over him."

"I'll bet they were. It probably saved them a lot of work preparing for the class, and they likely lauded him to the skies. I suppose he's as conceited as they make 'em."

"No," said Beryl gravely, "he didn't seem to be. In fact he always appeared to be quite humble, in spite of the fact that he was well thought of in athletics."

"Well, speaking of Jeremy Graeme," said Bonny Stewart, "he's going to speak at our church next Sunday night. I just remember it was in the church paper that my sister brought home from Sunday School, and I happened to read it. It was headed 'Local hero will speak at the evening service'!"

"H'm!" said Mrs. Thaxter appearing on the scene to make sure she had the right measurement for petticoat hems, "I guess you mean his older brother, Rodney Graeme. They wouldn't ask *that* little squirt to speak. He's only been in service a little over a year, and Rodney has been there three years. I understand Rodney did some notable things during his service."

"No," said Bonny firmly. "It was Jeremy. Definitely. I remember thinking what a queer name he had. And it said he had only been over a few months over a year, and was once reported missing, but was saved in some unusual way. Say, girls, let's all go to our church next Sunday and give him a good send off. Is he shy, Beryl? We won't embarrass him, will we, and spoil his speech? We might hide in the Sunday School room where he wouldn't see us."

Beryl smiled.

"No, he isn't shy."

"Well, girls, will you go? You will, won't you, Beryl?"

"Why, I might," said Beryl. "I'll see what plans mother has. Perhaps I'll go. But if I were you I wouldn't hide. He wouldn't mind your being there I'm sure. He isn't that kind."

"But say, girls," said Isabelle thoughtfully, "wasn't that brother Rodney the one who was engaged to some girl with bleached hair? Jessica. That was her name. And she sported around with his ring on and made a great fuss over being engaged, and then after he went away she got married to some rich old man? Wasn't that Rodney Graeme's girl?"

"I'm sure I don't know," said Beryl Sanderson. "He always impressed me as a grave quiet kind of man, the few times I ever saw him. The kind you would trust, you know."

"Oh, *that* kind. Well, a girl that was gay wouldn't stick by a fellow like that, of course," said Alida. "Say, what's this Jeremy like? Awfully religious? Because if he is I shan't go Sunday. I don't care much for religion anyway. It always makes me cry, and wish I'd never been born."

"I really don't know, Alida," said Beryl almost haughtily. "I only knew him in high school, but he seemed very cheerful then."

"Why, he'll likely just talk about the war I suppose," said Isabelle. "They all do. I adore to hear the fellows tell about their experiences, how many enemies they killed, and all that, and how they just got off by the skin of their teeth."

"Isabelle! You bloodthirsty thing! How dreadful!" exclaimed Bonny.

"Well, isn't that the way we're supposed to feel during this war? We're out to get the enemy as quick as we can and finish them up so they can't start anything again, not in our lifetime, anyway. Isn't that the idea?" said Isabelle.

"Well, anyway, girls you'll all go, won't you?" said Bonny Stewart. "I'll get some credit up in Heaven for bringing so many to church, won't I? Come and meet at my house. It's near the church and I know my way around you know. I'm supposed to be a member of that church. Meet at my house and we'll have a cup of tea and some little frosted cakes before we go over to the church. Beryl, why don't you invite Jeremy Graeme to come over along with you, and we can all get acquainted with him."

"No," said Beryl with dignity. "He wouldn't want to go to a reception before he spoke, and anyway I wouldn't do that sort of thing. I'll be at church I think, but I'm not sure I'll be over at your place, Bonny, beforehand. Mother has company and I may be needed at home until time for church to begin. I'll look you all up if I can."

Then the noon whistle sounded and there was a general movement to put away work, and go out to lunch. Beryl slipped away out of notice to think over what she had been hearing.

So, Jeremy had been doing notable things in the war and was going to speak about them. It would be interesting of course, and she was sure she would like to hear him. Yet she recognized in herself a certain shrinking from seeing him again lest the grown-up Jeremy might disappoint her. For he had been one of her childhood's admirations, and she didn't want to think that he had failed to turn out the kind of man his boyhood had promised. She did not like to think her little-girl ideas of people had been wrong. Somehow they made a happy young background for the childish self she had been.

When Beryl reached home she went to her own room and sat down to think. Her mind was going back to her days at school and to the times when she was interested in this one and that. It was very plain to her as she thought back, remembering the boy they had but just a few minutes before been talking about. Presently she got up and went to her bookcase where were several big books full of snapshots and photographs of her school days. She had scarcely looked them over since she was graduated from high school. Yet she knew exactly where to find the ones she wanted. They were grouped together in the middle of the book, flanked on either side by other members of her class. And there was one a little larger than the rest, not really a photograph, just a page cut from the class yearbook. For some time she studied the pictures, and when she put the book away she decided that definitely she wanted to go and hear Jeremy talk, and see if he had carried out the promise of his childhood. Then she put away the thought of it all and went to her appointment at the hospital where she was taking a friend's place nursing for the afternoon.

There was another woman interested in the one who was to speak in the Harper Memorial Church next Sunday night, and that was Louella Chatterton.

Louella had gone into the city to visit with an old friend, also to be near the lawyer whom she wanted to consult about some business matters, and as she was passing along the street a name on the advertising board in front of a church caught her eye. GRAEME. Why, could this be the Riverton Graemes? Louella about-faced and drew up in front of the church, studying the notice.

Lieutenant Commander Jeremy R. Graeme will speak in this church Sunday evening at 8 P.M. Come and hear the thrilling experience of this young service-man. Come and bring your friends.

Louella read the notice over several times and when she started on her way she headed for a drugstore where there would be a telephone. Seated in the booth she called up her number and asked for Mrs. De Groot, and when a voice responded she said gushingly:

"Is that you Jessica? I've got the most exciting news to tell you. Can't you take dinner with me tonight? We can talk so much better in my room at the hotel, and no interruptions, and meantime I'll be looking up details and be able to tell you more than I can give you now over the telephone."

"Oh! Louella, what *do* you mean? What is it all about? Has it anything to do with Rodney Graeme?"

"Well, yes, in a way. I've got to find out a little bit more about it, but I've got a scheme and it ought surely to give you an opportunity to meet him, and have a good talk, which ought to clear the atmosphere, don't you think?"

"Well, yes, it might. But what *is* all this? How did you hear about it, and what is it really?"

"Why it's just that he seems to be advertised to address an audience in the Harper Memorial Church, here in the city. I have seen the notice outside the church so that's how I know about it. He's a lieutenant commander, isn't he? I thought so. They've got the names mixed somewhat, but I know it must be Rodney. It says Jeremy *R.* but that means nothing. Notices often get the names or the initials wrong, and anyway, even if it should be Jeremy, Rodney will probably be with him on the platform, and perhaps we can work it so he will come and sit with us. I'm sure this is a break for us. I knew I'd find a way for you to see him in spite of his stubbornness. I'll find a way yet."

"Where are you?" asked the fretful voice of the girl.

"Why, I'm down in the city at a drugstore phoning. No, I'm *not* in the village of Riverton. I'm down in the *city.* I've been staying all night with a friend I met out west, and I'm coming home tonight. Will you be at my hotel by six-thirty? All right, I'll be seeing you then, and we'll fix something up."

KATHIE came in from a trip to the grocery, her arms full of bags, bundles and baskets.

"Have the boys come down for breakfast yet, mother?" she asked eagerly, "because I've brought some simply wonderful fruit, and I know they will enjoy it."

"No, they are not down yet. I thought they ought to sleep a little while, as long as they seem to want to, now that they are at home, and there is no one around to say 'Thou shalt, and thou shalt not.'"

"That's nice, mother. Isn't it wonderful to have them both home again and have a chance to spoil them just a little? Only, do you know, mother, they somehow don't spoil. I think that's a tribute to the way you brought them up. I do hope, perhaps, some day, somebody will think *I'm* a credit to your bringing up, too."

"You dear child! Of course they will. Kathie, you have always been a wonderful daughter," and the mother stepped over and stooped to lay a kiss on the sweet white forehead, as Kathie was bending over the table to arrange a great dish of fruit.

"Look, mother, *pink* grapefruit, Florida oranges, lovely red apples, and see these luscious yellow bananas. They have sunshine in their skins."

"Yes, aren't they beautiful? I'm so glad you found them. But there, the boys are coming down. They must have been waiting for you to get back. Tell Hetty won't you? Tell her she better get the griddle hot. We're having buckwheats you know."

"Yes, I'll tell her," said Kathie happily, and skipped out to the kitchen. Her mother could hear her eager young voice calling to Hetty: "All ready, Hetty, put the griddle on!"

Then the brothers barged into the dining room, breathing joyous good mornings, and in the same breath Jeremy cried: "Oh, *boy!* What do I smell? Buckwheat cakes! As I live. Rod, what do you know about that? We're really home at last and going to have genuine buckwheat cakes. And maple syrup from the row of maples on the meadow lots! Can you beat it?"

"No, I can't beat it, brother. I can't even in my thoughts come up to it. Sometimes on far seas I have laid in sacks and dreamed of buckwheat cakes. I've seen the butter melting on their hot brown surfaces, I've closed my eyes and tried to think how maple syrup would fall from the old silver cruet, and how it would taste as I put the first luscious mouthful in my mouth. I almost thought there was syrup on my lips, and I must be careful not to drop any on my uniform and get myself all sticky."

"Oh, Jerry, what a boy you are," said his smiling mother. "Sometimes I was terribly afraid that you would be so grown up when you came home that I wouldn't feel you were my little boy who left me and sailed away to foreign lands, but you're just the same, Jerry. There! Sit down and begin. Do you want fruit first, and cereal?"

"Not on yer life, mom. I want a buckwheat cake the first off the bat, and no kiddin'."

And so amid laughter and joking the morning began, with Rodney not far behind in his appreciation of the buckwheat cakes.

Though it was three days since that first night that the brothers had arrived, yet it seemed to them all as if they had just come. The long months and years of their separation were still sharply in their minds, and they had to savor every moment of their presence together again. Oh how they had feared and dreaded that home might be sorrowful, might be filled with disappointment, worry for fear of disablement or incurable illness, or a burden of sorrow and inability for their dear ones, and that very morning as the loving mother had knelt to pray for the opening of the day, she had thanked the Lord fervently that He had brought her dear ones home safely, not lamed nor blinded nor stricken with some fatal illness. And so she had gone down to meet the day with her heart filled with wonder and her face shining with joy and the glory of the Lord. And those boys saw the glory and rejoiced in it.

The brothers were just beginning to feel really at home again, ready to kid each other and feel thoroughly as if they had not been away at all. Their mother was beginning to hold her breath every time the telephone rang lest it might be some new orders from Washington, and the boys might have to go away again. Although they had told her that they had been given to understand that their next assignment would likely be in the United States, but her mother heart kept turning wistfully to her Lord, just to help her trust. For all her petitions had to go through the permission of her Lord.

So it was a very happy family at that breakfast table the third morning of their stay at home, and they were beginning to plan what they would do, and where they would go, and who of the old friends they must be sure to see first. Though at any mention of leaving home even for a few hours they all groaned.

"Mom, if I was to be going to live a thousand years, I'd like to make sure I could come home here every night to sleep.

Just you try to sleep once in a sack overnight, or on a ship that is being bombed, and you'd know what I mean. I have great sympathy for the man who wrote *Home Sweet Home,* 'Be it ever so humble, there's no place like home.' And this is anything but a humble home."

"Dear boy!" said Mrs. Graeme tenderly with sudden tears of joy in her eyes.

"Please make that plural, mom," urged Rodney. "I could echo every word of that sentiment."

"Dear *boys!*" said the mother, suddenly smiling brightly through more tears.

And it was just then that Kathleen sprang from her chair and stepped over to the window, then backed away.

"Good night, mother, don't cry! Look who's coming in the gate. Mop up your eyes and pretend you're laughing."

"What! Who?" said Rodney springing to his feet and stretching his tall height to look out the window from the vantage of his place at the table.

"It isn't that girl again, is it?" he ejaculated.

"No, no, Rod," laughed his sister. "Not quite so bad as that. It's only Cousin Louella!"

"Good night, it is indeed," said Jeremy. "And I was going to eat another plateful of pancakes, but this has to do me till tomorrow morning. I can't stand another session with Cousin Lou." He grabbed the last two cakes on the plate, emptied a couple of spoonfuls of sugar on one, folded them neatly together and scuttled up the back stairs, calling back in a sepulchral whisper:

"Mom, if anybody asks for me, tell 'em I didn't say where I was going, just errands."

Rodney stopped long enough to get the last swallow of coffee before he departed, and he could just hear Cousin Louella's key in the front latch as he closed the back door, pulling on an old sweater and making his way to the garage where Kathie kept the old car.

"It's all right, Rod," said his sister hurrying after him, "I put the chain on the front door last night and the latchkey won't do any good. She'll have to ring and wait till somebody comes to open the door."

Rodney grinned.

"Thanks awfully, Kath. You're a good angel," he said. "You might hang a handkerchief out your window when she leaves. I won't come back till she's gone." With another grin and a wave of his hand he vanished into the garage.

Kathleen hurried back into the house to save her mother from going to the door.

"You aren't going to ask her to stay to lunch, are you, mother? Because the boys won't come back if you do. I promised to hang out a flag for Rod when she's gone."

"No," smiled the mother, "not today. I have to go down to the village on an errand. I can perhaps ask her to go along."

"But Rod's got the car."

"Oh, well, that's all right. I'll go later. You leave her to me. If I give her some work to do she won't stay long. I'll let her put those hems in my new aprons. You bring them down to me and I'll sit right here and sew on them. You can be dusting the hall and library and be near enough to hear any signals I send out. She will maybe like to take a walk with you."

"Not she," grinned Kathleen. "She always says she has sprained her foot, when I ask her to take a walk. But you might try her on going down behind the barn to see the little new colt. I have to take some feed down to the colt's mother."

Mother Graeme grinned mischieviously, showing how much she resembled her two boys.

"Okay," she said calmly, "I'll try her, but you just watch her face when I do."

So Kathleen walked to the front door, which was now open about four inches, and being banged impatiently, indignantly back and forth against the chain.

Kathleen with firm hand closed the door, released the chain, and then opened it, so quickly that the indignant semi-relative was flung almost bodily into the hall.

"Why, the very idea!" said Cousin Louella indignantly. "Whoever put that thing on, I should like to know?"

"Oh, didn't you know we used the chain now?" asked Kathleen coolly. "I guess nobody thought to take it off this morning. Won't you come in Cousin Louella? Mother's in the dining room sewing. Just go right in there. I think Hetty is going to sweep in the living room so it will be pleasanter sitting in the dining room."

"Oh, *really?*" said the cousin with a lofty insulted air. "Well, of course if your mother is there. But it was really the boys I wanted to see. More especially Rodney. Where is he?"

"Why, I'm not sure. He went out to the garage, and I think I saw the car go out. You know you can't keep track of the boys when they once get in their home town, after their long separation."

"Rodney wouldn't by any chance have gone to see his old friend Jessica, would he?" asked the cousin pryingly, with an insinuating smile, as if she had a secret that Kathleen probably understood.

"Why no," said Kathleen calmly. "I don't think he went there. I don't think he has much to do with her any more. You knew she is married, didn't you?"

"Oh, yes, I knew she was married, poor dear. But I feel so sorry for her, and for Rodney too. Such a pity, a nice suitable match like that broken up. What a foolish boy he was to let that happen. Of course what he ought to have done was to have married her before he went away. Then this couldn't have happened. But I suppose your mother blocked that. She always was opposed to having her children grow up."

"I beg your pardon, Cousin Louella, I don't quite understand you. Mother had nothing whatever to do with the breaking of that engagement. And I don't think we ought to talk about it, do you? Rodney would be furious, and I shouldn't think Jessica would care for such comments. At least *I* wouldn't. She's a married woman you know."

"Yes, poor dear, I'm aware of that. I feel so very sorry for her. But there are ways of getting out of a situation like that of course."

"Is that the way you look at it, Cousin Louella? I don't think so. But here comes mother. See what pretty aprons she is making. Here, sit down in this little rocker in the bay window. I think the view of the yard all snow is pretty out there, don't you? And Hetty is making hot doughnuts. Shall I get you one, or do you think it is too soon after breakfast?"

"Yes, I certainly would like some doughnuts. But I'd want a cup of coffee with them. Wasn't there some left from breakfast, Hetty could heat up for me?"

"I'll see," said Kathleen, and vanished grimly into the kitchen. "The *idea!*" she muttered to Hetty. "Doughnuts and coffee, when she probably ate a huge breakfast at the hotel. Well, perhaps she won't attempt to stay to lunch if I feed her now."

So Kathleen got ready three hot doughnuts and a cup of coffee and brought them on a tray to the guest-cousin, and then vanished to her dusting lest more would be demanded.

Meantime Hetty was filling two large platters with doughnuts already fried, and hiding them on the top shelf of the pantry, where no snooping relative could find them.

So the guest settled back in her rocker with her coffee and doughnuts to enjoy herself, and see how much information she could pry out of Mother Graeme.

"Well, so it seems Rodney is becoming a public speaker," she said as she took a large sugary bite of doughnut, and began to rock slowly, balancing her coffee cup neatly on the arm of her chair, with a careful hand guarding it.

Mother Graeme smiled.

"Oh no, not Rodney," she said pleasantly. "He was pretty badly wounded you know, and until his shoulder gets better he has been distinctly ordered not to do anything for a while. They wanted him to broadcast from Washington, but the doctors said no, not now, so they are putting that off till spring, or even later if his condition is not good yet."

"But what possible harm could a wounded shoulder get from his just getting up and telling of his experiences? I think that's ridiculous!"

"Well, the Navy doesn't think so," said Mother Graeme smiling quietly.

"Well, I guess you'll find that a spirited fellow like Rodney won't be tied down that way by any Navy, now that he's home. Besides, I guess you don't know he's going to speak next Sunday night at the Harper Memorial Church in the city. I saw the announcement myself today when I was in town. In front of the church. I certainly thought it was strange that you hadn't told me, but that seems to be the way I am treated by my family in everything. However, he's going to speak, even if you don't know it. These boys think now they have been off to fight that they have a right to run their own lives without consulting their parents. I presume that was it. He wouldn't want to decline an honor like that, in that big important church. There'll be a big audience there and you ought to be ashamed to try and stop it."

"No, Louella, you are mistaken," said Margaret Graeme with an upward quiet look. "It is *Jeremy* who is to speak at Harper Memorial."

"*Jeremy!*" almost screamed the cousin. "You don't mean that they would ask the *younger* brother to speak and leave out the older more experienced man, who has been in the service so much longer? Why, Jeremy is nothing but a kid, just a child. He couldn't speak."

The mother went quietly, patiently, on with her sewing and let her guest rage on explaining why this could not be, but when Louella stopped talking to begin on her second doughnut she spoke quietly.

"Why, you see, Louella, Jeremy has already done quite a little speaking on the radio, and other places, and of course

Rodney has also, for they have been through some great battles. But this Harper Memorial engagement came through a buddy of Jeremy's who is a member of that church, and he wrote home to his friends about Jeremy, so he had the engagement to speak there before he sailed for home."

"You don't *mean* it!" said the astonished cousin. "Well, that'll be quite a feather in Jerry's cap, won't it? And aren't you afraid it will create jealousy between the brothers, having Jerry speak instead of Rodney?"

"No, Louella. I don't see why it should. They don't regard it in that light at all. It's merely another duty in the winning of the war. Besides, the boys each have had experiences that may help someone. And now, Louella, I wonder if you wouldn't like to go down behind the barn with Kathie and see the new colt. It is very cunning and attractive, and Kathie is taking a pan of mash down for the mother. There is a nice path all the way down and you won't get your feet wet."

Cousin Louella took her last swallow of coffee, and arose.

"No thanks, I don't care for animals, and colts don't in the least appeal to me. But I think I'll be going now. There are several people I want to see and I have an appointment with a lawyer in the city this afternoon. Well, I'll be seeing you, as the young folks say. I suppose, Margaret, even if it's only Jerry that's going to speak, you'll all be going in to hear him, of course."

"Why, we haven't talked that over yet, Louella. There's a possibility it may be on the radio and then everybody will be able to hear it."

"Really? Well, Jerry must be quite set up having such a fuss made over him. I suppose of course Rodney will at least go in with him, won't he?"

"I really wouldn't know what Rodney's plans are. But you needn't worry about Jerry. He doesn't get set up with things like that. He just wants to do the right thing."

"Oh, yes, Margaret, you always did think your children

were models of every kind. Well, I'm sure I hope you won't be disappointed in them."

"No? Well, thank you Louella. But I feel rather happy that both my children are saved. That's the only thing to be proud of."

"Yes, of course," said Louella. "Most parents are proud when their children get honor to themselves doing hard things and being courageous and all that, and then get safe home without any very bad scratches. Yes, they are *saved* from this horrible war. I don't suppose they'll have to go back again will they? So you can really count them saved. Saved and *all* through with it."

Mother Graeme looked at Louella perplexed.

"Oh Louella, you *know* I mean saved from something far worse than any war. I mean saved from sin—from eternal punishment. Saved for Heaven."

"Oh! *That!*" said the cousin sanctimoniously. "Well, I guess you never can tell about that until you get there. Of course some do say that if you died in the war, you did what the Lord did. You died for others, and therefore you are saved. But your boys didn't *die,* so they wouldn't be saved on that score. I wouldn't count on that too much if I were you though. You might find out when you get over there that you were mistaken. It sounds rather far-fetched to me, and boastful."

"No, Louella, I won't find out, I'm not mistaken and it's not boastful, because it's nothing the boys have done themselves, only their trusting in what Christ has done on the cross. The Lord has promised, and my boys have accepted the promise, and believe in Him as their Saviour. The Bible says, 'He that believeth *hath* everlasting life,' so I *know* my boys are saved. But Louella, you go and hear Jeremy, and you will understand."

"Oh, *really!* Well, I *may* go, I'm not sure. If I can get my friend to go with me I might go. It will be odd to hear him speaking in a big church. Little Jerry! Do you think he'll be embarrassed? Talking about himself and what he's done?"

Jerry's mother smiled.

"No, Louella, Jeremy won't be talking about himself, and his achievements. He'll be talking about his Lord and what He has done for Jerry."

"Oh!" said the cousin uncomprehendingly. "Well, I'm not sure I know what you mean, but maybe I'll go and see if I can understand. Well, good-bye," and Louella Chatterton went out of the house, and wondered at herself, how very little she had been able to find out about Rodney.

Then came Kathleen with her duster in her hands, smiling at her mother.

"That was great, mommie dear," she said, coming over and kissing her mother on the top of her head. "You certainly did give her something to think about, although I don't believe that poor soul understood at all what you meant."

"Yes, dear, I'm afraid you're right," sighed the mother. "I was just thinking of the Bible verse that describes her. 'If our Gospel be hid, it is hid to them that are lost.'"

"Oh, mother!" said Kathleen solemnly. "Do you really think she is lost?"

"I'm not her judge," said the mother sweetly, "but she certainly is not saved yet, and doesn't know what it means. But it isn't too late yet for her to believe."

"But I don't think she even wants to believe, mother."

"A great many don't," sighed the mother. "I guess we ought to pray more for her, and criticize less."

"Well it isn't a bit easy to pray for anybody that has such a vitriolic tongue as our cousin," laughed Kathleen. "But say, I must run upstairs and put out my signal for Rod to come back."

Then there came a voice from the top of the front stairs—Jeremy calling to know the signs of the times.

"Mom, has that old harridan gone yet?"

The mother smiled.

"Why Jerry, I thought you went with Rod. Yes, the coast is

clear, son, but what kind of a cataclysm would you have precipitated if she hadn't gone yet, and you had called those words down in time for her to hear? You know that would not have been an easy thing to live down."

"Oh," said the grinning young man, "but perhaps I wouldn't want to live it down."

"Oh, but you must, dear. For I was just about to ask you to help us to pray for that unpleasant cousin. You can't exactly feel that way toward her if you are going to pray for her."

"H'm!" said Jeremy thoughtfully, "I hadn't exactly thought of her as a candidate for prayer."

"Well, perhaps that's the reason she is that way. Nobody has been praying for her."

"Why this sudden anxiety, mom?" asked Jeremy. "I never heard you mention her as a subject for prayer. What started you on this line?"

"Well, I don't just know, dear. We got to talking. She asked about your engagement to speak. She had seen a notice of it in front of the church. Only she thought it was Rodney, not you, who is going to speak. But I think she is coming to hear you. Perhaps you'll be given a mesage that will reach her heart."

"Say, mom, you know how to go to the heart of things, don't you? But I'm afraid it would take more faith than I've got to get up a message to reach that woman."

"Oh, you wouldn't have to get one up, Jerry. If you did it would be powerless. That's the trouble with so much of the preaching, these days. Remember the Holy Spirit will do that for you. Just be sure you have your heart open to be led, and don't clutter up your mind with all your childhood's dislikes and prejudices. Just ask the Lord to show you what He wants for you. And then don't worry about it. You are well taught in the Bible and the Holy Spirit can speak through you if you are fully yielded to Him. That's all. Now what are you going to do, Jerry? Any plans?"

"Not 'specially, not today. I'm expecting a phone call tomorrow night, but till then I'm free to do anything I please, that is anything *you* please, mom!"

Mom Graeme's eyes grew misty.

"Dear boy!" she said. "To think I have you home again. To think I have you *both* home! If I only could be sure it was to stay."

"Well, mom, it might be you know. That is it might not be far away. There's something in the wind, but we'll let you know as soon as we find out."

A sweet tender look came into her eyes, a kind of a light as if some great hope were shining in her heart.

They were still for a minute and then the mother spoke again.

"Jerry," she said, "tell me something. Rodney isn't quite happy, is he?"

"Well, I'm not sure. No, I don't know as he is, not exactly the way he used to be."

"Do you think it's that girl? That Jessie?"

"I'm not sure, mom," said Jerry looking troubled. "I don't want to force his hand."

"Of course not," said the mother. "But I wanted to find out what your reaction is to the whole thing. Do you think Rod is mourning for that girl?"

"No, mom, I don't think so. I was afraid that might be the matter with him when we first talked it over, but after that gal appeared on the scene I saw he wasn't grieving after her. And didn't you take notice how gay he was when he came back from the pantry and settled down to eat his pie? No, mom, I don't think he's grieving. I don't think he has been anything but *mad* for a long time. I think he has sorted her out with the enemy. I don't know whether he counts her a Jap or a German, or just a plain spy, but he labels her 'enemy' good and large, and I don't believe he's in any further danger from her. Except, of course, she can annoy him. But he's had experience enough fighting the enemy, not to be caught napping now. After all, mom, he's your son, and he has eyes to see a whole lot."

"Yes," said mom thoughtfully, "I could always trust Rod. Of course—" she hesitated thoughtfully an instant, "of course I was troubled when he first began to go with Jessie. She didn't seem up to him, but I realized he was a young boy, and then a good deal of their intimacy probably came from the girl. Some girls seem to be born that way, or else, well she didn't have much upbringing, I'm afraid."

"That's it, mom. Now you've reached the point. I don't think you ever knew what her mother was, or you would have done something about it sooner. However, I guess there's no harm done. And a fellow has to grow up sometime and learn how to judge the world. Besides, you'll have to remember this, mom. Rod has been to war. He wouldn't pick out the same girl now that he would before he went through the service. Of course if she'd been half decent and hadn't gone back on him herself, he'd have been true to her, because he wouldn't think it was right to do otherwise. And that's partly it now, he couldn't believe at first that Jessica had done this to him. He knew he was true to her. And when he finally reached the stage where he accepted the truth it made him angry. It took the heart out of him so much that he flung himself into this war business, not caring what became of him. It was partly what made him such a wonderful fighter. Mom, I guess God has everything worked out for all His children. He sees they need some hard going, and when He can trust them to take it right He gives it to them. Isn't that right, mom?"

Mother Graeme looked at her boy, who such a little while ago was just her little boy, her mere baby, as she heard him utter these words of wisdom, and wondered.

Then her face blazed with that rare smile that she sometimes wore, that suggested nothing else but glory in her face.

And then after a moment of deep thought, as if she were receiving a revelation, she said:

"Oh, my dear son, God has been wonderfully teaching you, too. You are speaking thoughts I never knew you could understand. My boy. My *two* boys! How proud I am of them, proudest of all that you have been taught of God. Thank you for telling me that!"

And then Hetty came in with her brooms and sweeper and cleaning cloths and announced that she was going to clean the living room if that was agreeable to the family, and the conference between mother and son broke up.

# 7

IT was the next afternoon that Jeremy met his old admiration, Beryl Sanderson.

He had wondered about her, and almost decided that before he had to go away from that region he would perhaps call on her, just a brief call of greeting as an old schoolmate. But he wasn't at all sure that he would. Before he ever decided to do anything like that he would have to find out all about her. Maybe she was married, or engaged. Maybe she had moved away. Certainly he did not wish to bring either himself or her into the limelight by making too pointed enquiries about her. No, he would go slowly. He had nothing to lose by going slow, and perhaps nothing to gain, nevertheless he kept thinking he would like to meet her again and see if she was as interesting as he had thought several years ago. But he wasn't bothering himself about it yet. It would all come in good time, if it came, and perhaps would only upset him, and make him discontented, if he should discover that she was definitely not for him. One night as he knelt beside his bed before retiring, the thought of this girl had come to him, and he had definitely laid the matter before his Lord.

"Lord," he prayed, "this is a matter I can't very well do

anything about. I don't want to make any mistakes. So I'm laying this in your hands. If you want us to meet, please make it plain. If not, please help me to put her out of my thoughts. I leave it with you."

It was a habit he was forming, to leave important matters, or even trifling ones, to his Lord. And each time he did it somehow the matter seemed to be settled for him without his worrying about it.

That was two days ago that he had made that prayer, and he had scarcely thought of her since.

Today Rodney had asked Jeremy to drive with him to see the family of a buddy of his who had died in combat overseas. He was a stranger to them of course, but he had been close to their son, and he could tell more than anybody he knew, of the last days, even the last few minutes of his friend's life, and he felt he ought to go as soon as possible. So he had asked Jeremy to drive him, and after the call was made they would go to the hospital where Kathie was working today and bring her home.

So Jeremy had agreed, not realizing that Rodney's call would lead him into the region where the Sandersons lived. When he did draw up at the curb and let Rodney out, he saw that the Sanderson house was not more than a block and a half ahead. Still it did not matter. It was not in the least likely that he would see Beryl, and if he did why worry? That was something entirely in his Lord's hands now.

So he sat quietly behind the wheel and waited, gazing idly about at the pleasant surroundings, thinking how glad he was that the girl of his fancy lived in such a lovely spot. She was the kind of girl that it seemed to him fitting that all should be quite perfect about her.

It occurred to him to make the contrast between this sort of life and the places where he and Rodney had been in their war service. It was good that fine sweet girls and women had places like this street, and these attractive houses where they could be cared for and safe. So good that these nice people were not subject to some of the terrible things that had happened to beautiful homes abroad. There had been no bombing in his own blessed country, thank the Lord. Not as yet, anyway.

It was just at that point he looked up and saw her coming straight toward him, just walking briskly down the sidewalk, not at first noticing him at all. But then suddenly she stopped and looked straight at him, a little rosy glow in her cheeks, a sparkle of welcome in her lovely eyes.

"Jeremy! Jeremy Graeme! It is really you, isn't it? I am so very glad to see you."

She put out both her hands with a real welcoming gesture, and Jeremy sprang out of the car and took both her hands in his, and there they stood looking down, and up at each other and reading great joy and deep interest in each other's eyes.

Somehow they didn't have many words at first to express their joy in finding one another, but something in the touch of their hands spoke, something in the glance of their eyes, and presently the words came.

"What are you doing over here, Jeremy?" she asked, her cheeks brightly rosy now. "I don't think I ever saw you over here before."

"No," faltered Jeremy. "I often wanted to come. I always liked it over this way. But I never seemed to have time, and then I went across."

"Yes, I know," said the girl. "I've been reading about some of the things you did over there, some of the decorations you've had. But what are you doing here today? Don't tell me you have friends over this way that I don't know about."

"No, I have no friends over here, unless I can count you one," said Jeremy smiling.

"You may," said Beryl. "Go on."

"Well, you see my brother wanted to call and see the mother of one of his friends who died over there. He asked me to drive him over. He has a wounded shoulder and mustn't drive yet. He's in there now." He nodded toward the big brick mansion before which they were standing.

"Oh," said Beryl, "you mean Carl Browning? How wonderful! Poor dear Mrs. Browning. She knows so little about Carl's death. It will be great for her to talk with a young man who knew him well. I've heard about your brother. He was quite distinguished, too. But I understood he was badly wounded."

"Yes, he was, but he's recovering rapidly, especially since we got home, and he's had mother to take care of him."

"Yes. I imagine that would make a difference for all wounded men. And is he in there? I'd like so much to meet him. I wonder if you couldn't both come into my house for a few minutes after he comes out."

"Why, we'd love to, I know, but we're supposed to go to the hospital after my sister Kathie who is doing some nursing today, and it's almost time. Perhaps another time, if we may."

"Oh, of course! And I shall want to meet your sister too. It isn't far to the hospital from here. Couldn't you bring her down here and all come in for a little while, just till we get to know one another?"

"Well, we might work something. Why couldn't you get into the car with us and drive over after Kathie, and then you come over to our house to dinner with us? I think that would be swell. Mother would be delighted to meet you. I used to tell her a lot about you when we were children in high school. Will you come?"

"Oh, wonderful! Why of course I'll come!" and then those two suddenly discovered that they were still holding hands, with bright cheeks flaming, bright eyes glancing, like a whole battalion of homecomings. And it was so, suddenly standing apart consciously that Rodney saw them first as he came out of the house of mourning.

"There's Rod, now," said Jeremy, thrilling at the thought that Beryl Sanderson had just been holding hands publicly with him and she didn't seem to mind at all.

Then Rodney stood beside them enquiringly.

"Rod, this is Beryl Sanderson. You know, I've told you about her, and she's going with us over to the hospital to get Kathie, and then she's coming home with us to dinner."

"Swell!" said Rodney, looking with fine appreciation at the sweet face of the girl his brother admired. "Why that's great! I've wanted to get acquainted with you, and I'm sure dad and mother will be terribly pleased. Say, getting home is something real, isn't it Jerry."

Soon they were all in the car speeding away to the hospital after Kathie, who presently looked at the new girl with shy interest. Oh, Kathie had seen her before, had known who she was in school days of course, although Kathie was younger than Beryl, but she added her invitation to the new girl to stay to dinner with the Graeme family.

"You know mother always likes to have lots of company. She always did, and we're just delighted to have you. I've known all about you and often admired you in the past."

"Why, you dear," said Beryl. "You don't mean to tell me you are the little girl that used to come to school and go home with your brother? I often watched you and thought you were lovely."

"Well, this seems to be sort of a mutual admiration society, Jerry. What do you think of that? All of us friends in a hurry."

From there they went on making a brisk acquaintance and all of them liking one another.

The road lay through the town of Riverdale on the way to the Graeme farm, and who should be walking down the street as they drove through town, entirely engrossed with their guest, but Jessica De Groot, and Alida Hopkins, slowly window-shopping by the way, and turning to look sharply at each car that passed them.

"Why, who was that with the Graemes, Jess? That girl? Haven't I seen her before?"

"That, my dear naive little Alida is Beryl Sanderson, the exclusive daughter of the great banker, Sanderson."

"Well, but didn't you know her in school once? Wasn't she in our high school for a time before her father bought that big stone mansion on Linden Shade Drive?"

"She certainly was, my lamb."

"But she didn't speak to us, Jessica."

"No, she certainly did not. She's too much of a snob. She never did have anything to do with me you know, and of course just now she was entirely too much taken up with those two navy men to know that anybody else existed. She's too snooty for words, Alida. I'm glad she didn't see us. I would have frozen her with one of her own cold looks if she had tried to speak to *me*. Of course I used to be a poor girl when she knew me, but now I'm even above her class financially I suspect so what does it matter?"

"Well, I wonder if that's what Rodney has on his mind now?"

"Oh no, lambkin," said Jessica, "guess again. *She* belongs to little brother Jeremy. I used to watch them in school. He was just nuts about her."

"But they never went together at all in high school."

"Oh no, mamma wouldn't have approved you know. She's a very carefully brought up girl."

"But who was the other girl in the car?"

"Why that was Kathleen Graeme, the boys' sister. She certainly has grown up fast, trying to get in the swim I fancy."

The girls passed on to other topics, now and again recurring to the Graeme family, in one way or another, and finally ended up at the hotel where Cousin Chatterton was temporarily abiding, because there was almost always some interesting information to be got out of Cousin Louella, after any brief absence. If she didn't really have further information she could always invent some, which was almost as interesting.

And this time it was interesting, if not exactly accurate.

"Yes, girls, I really have some news for you. I went over to see dear Margaret Graeme this afternoon, and uncovered a bit of information sort of unawares. That is I walked in on it when there was a private conversation between two members of the family going on. They didn't know I had come in. ·I found out that the Graeme boys are likely to stay in this country permanently, or at least for a time. There is some notable position being suggested for them. I didn't discover just exactly what it is, but I think—now you mustn't say anything about this of course outside, for it is a family affair, and of course I always try to be loyal to my family. But you, Jessica, were at one time almost family, so I know you won't say anything, but I think—mind you I don't *know* for sure, I only sort of *think* whatever this job is, it may have something to do with Naval Intelligence. I'm not sure that I know exactly what that is, so I may be incorrect in my judgment, but I just thought it had to do with spotting spies in this country, or else teaching young navy men just before they go over what will be expected of them in going among the enemy. But anyhow it sounded interesting, and if I work judiciously I can find out a great deal that you might like to know. Of course I know I can trust you girls that you won't betray me. I would never be forgiven by the Graemes if they dreamed I was reporting things I'd overheard. But you know those Graemes are so terribly shy, and retiring, afraid of publicity that is, that often I'm quite ashamed of them. Everybody knows that I am related to them, and of course I'm expected to be kept informed of their moves, and it's so embarrassing to have to say, 'I'm sorry, I haven't heard yet what the decision is,' or something like that. So I'm simply forced to obtain my information by backhanded means. And I don't like it at all. I'd much rather be treated like one of the inner circle, and be told frankly everything, and not made to appear as one who is not honored with the confidence of those near and dear to me."

"Of course," said Alida in a pitying tone.

"But I imagine you with your cleverness," put in Jessica, "can really obtain a wider scope of information than even if you were wholly in their confidence. Sometimes these underhanded ways are more productive than a closer relationship.

Oh, you are clever, Louella, and no mistake. Do you know what I would do if I were you? I'd get a connection with some rather outspoken daring magazine, or newspaper, and then write some spicy little articles anonymously that would set people wondering, and get them all agog. You could really sway governments that way, and if you made the right contacts you could make oodles of money. Believe me, I know. I haven't been asleep all the time since I got married, and my husband is as smart as a whip. Perhaps I'll put you on to two or three matters, if you stick by me long enough, Louella. And believe me, my clever friend, life isn't just made up of catching the right man and making him fall in love with you. It's nine tenths of knowing what to do with him when you've got him, and how much you can make out of him."

"Now, Jessica, that sounds very wordly indeed. I never would have suspected you of having been at one time almost a member of this dear silly Graeme family. And now my dear, since you don't seem satisfied to be utterly done with those innocent dears, I have a little scheme for you, and it has to do with your attendance at that church service in Harper Memorial Church next Sunday night. I would suggest that you plan to be there, and to perhaps sit in the top gallery. Get Alida to go with you, and keep a watchful eye out for Rodney. I'm almost positive he's going to that meeting, and will probably sit in the gallery himself. He seems to want to keep in the background at present. And if you and Alida should be sitting near by it will be easy to slip over and sit beside him, and get to talking. I can put you on to two or three matters that Naval Intelligencers ought to be able to answer without a suggestion that there was anything out of order in your asking questions, or their answering them, especially if it was done under the guise of a very loving old friend, merely wanting to get near Rod's work, because of old times. And my dear, I'll write two or three questions for you, which if you could write up the answers you get, I could get you good pay for the articles. You would be just the one to write them, for you are clever enough to disguise your intentions, both in asking the questions, and in writing them up, anonymously of course, afterward. Think it over my dear, and I'll see what I can do. And now, really, I must go. I have an appointment at the hairdresser's."

"Well, that sounds most interesting. I certainly could use a little extra money," said Jessica, "even though I am married, and if I couldn't win the personal attention I'd like from my old lover, at least I could find a way to punish him for his indifference."

And so the interview ended, and the girls went out to talk it over. Not that Alida was a very wise adviser, but she certainly could gush and encourage anything that sounded like a lark, or an interesting intrigue.

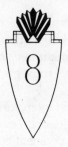

8

"DAD," said Kathie quietly the next morning when her father came downstairs a bit early to attend to something in the barn, "wouldn't there be some way to get that key away from Cousin Louella? I was worried to death all last evening while that lovely Sanderson girl was here, lest Cousin Louella would barge in on us again, and butt in on all the conversation. Dad, she is simply impossible!"

"Yes, I know," said Father Graeme, "I have been thinking about that. I'll get the key. There's no reason why she should have a perpetual right to open our door without notice. I'll see to that today. But don't say anything to anybody about it yet. I don't want your mother worried."

"Yes, I understand, dad. Thank you so much. You don't know what a trial she has been. I'll be kind to her when we meet, but it's awful to have her turning up in the most embarrassing times. You know how she comes right into the room when we are having family prayers, and sits there scorning us. She takes no pains to hide her dislike of it. She told me the other day that she couldn't understand why we hadn't protested against such old-fashioned ideas. She said nice people nowadays didn't flaunt their religion in the faces of outsiders."

"Poor soul!" he said with a sad little smile on his kindly face. "Poor soul! She certainly needs praying for, and the day may come when she'll be glad to have some religion to flaunt, even if it is old-fashioned. Don't worry, Kathie, I'll see to it."

Father Graeme came in very soon, ate his breakfast and then took the car and went down to the village.

"The boys won't be down for a while," he said as he went out. "Let them sleep as long as they want to. They've had to do a lot of getting up early over there in the war. I'll be back by the time they want to use the car."

Kathie flashed a twinkle of a smile at her father. She knew what he was going out for, although she couldn't imagine how he was going to work it. Sometimes there were things that only dad could accomplish. Things that were difficult, yet dad could always manage to get them done without definitely offending anyone.

As he drove down the street into the glory of the morning he began to think over the night before, and it gave him great comfort that a girl like Beryl Sanderson had come to their home and seemed to be so glad to be there, and to like his boys and his girl so much. He thought it all over, recalled the lovely smile she wore, the sweet unspoiled look of her, the gay happy way in which she entered into the conversation, the reverent way she bowed her head during the blessing at the table, with not a trace of sneer on her lovely face afterward. She had stayed for the evening and entered into the family life as if she had been one of them, as if she had real sympathy for the things they liked and did and said. And mother liked her too. He always knew when mother liked a girl. Yes, she was the right kind. How was it that her boys hadn't found Beryl before? He recalled also that he had met her father, a few years ago, and liked his attitude on certain questions in the Presbytery. He was a right-minded man. On the whole Beryl Sanderson had made a good impression on Father Graeme, and he hoped in his soul they would see more of her. She was like a breath of fresh air in a stifling atmosphere, after that other girl with the bleached hair that Rod used to affect. He prayed in his heart that they would not have to see more of her. Well, of course they said she was married now, but that didn't seem to mean a thing in these days when there were almost as many divorces as marriages. He hoped with all his heart that his two sons had not come to feel lightly about marriage.

Thinking these thoughts he soon arrived at his destination, a place to which he did not often go, the hotel where Louella Chatterton was staying for the present.

He parked his car and went to the desk, asked if Mrs. Chatterton was in, and being told that she was, sent up his name. He was informed that she would presently come down, as she was planning a trip to the city that morning, so he sat himself down to wait, well knowing that he must have patience, for he had had experience in waiting for Louella before and knew that she would not hasten.

When she arrived he made haste to come toward the elevator to meet her.

"Good morning, Louella. I hope I didn't interrupt you seriously, but I shall not keep you long. I came to ask you for my house key which I loaned you over a year ago you remember. And now the time has come when I need it, so I thought I would stop by and get it."

Now Louella had made her mind up that he had come to invite her to dinner perhaps, and she had come down all smiles. The dinners at the Graemes' were always good, and cost her nothing. So the little matter of a latchkey did not interest her. The interest went out of her eyes.

"A key?" she said meditatively. "Oh, yes, a key. I believe you did give me a key. I thought of course you meant me to keep it. Let me see, what did I do with that key? I think I may have brought it east with me. I'm not sure. I'll have to look through my things and see—" Louella gave an obvious glance toward the clock as if she had no time now to look it up.

"Oh yes, you brought it with you," said Father Graeme. "You used it to open our door the night the boys came home, and walked right into the dining room, don't you remember?"

"Did I? But no, I think you are mistaken. I think the door was not locked."

"Yes, the door was locked, Louella. We always lock it at night, and we heard the key in the lock before you came in. I'm sorry to ask you to go back upstairs and get it now if you are in a hurry to go out, but I really need that key this morning."

"Oh!" said Louella with annoyance in her voice. "What's the hurry? Wouldn't it do if I brought it over this evening?"

"Sorry, no, Louella, I need it this morning. Would you like to have me go up to your room and try to find it for you? I really want it now, if you please."

"Oh, no, of course not," snapped Louella. "But wait! Maybe I have it in my purse."

She opened her man-size trunk of bright red she was carrying under her well-tailored arm and rummaged through it, and there right in the compartment with her change was the key, just where her cousin was sure she would find it.

"Well, of course, here it is, if you must have it, but I shall feel rather lost without it. Giving this up makes me feel that I have no family any more." She managed a break in her voice. "But—how long will you need it? Perhaps I can call tomorrow and get it again. Will you be through with it by that time?"

"I'm afraid not, Louella. My family is all home now, and we need our keys. But I am sure you will always be able to get into the house if you ring the bell or even knock. Thank you, Louella, and now I won't keep you any longer. You have a nice day for your city trip. Have a good time. Good-by," and Father Graeme lifted his hat, and bowed himself out. Louella looked after him angrily and began at once to plan how she could get that key back. Perhaps she could bribe Hetty to give her her key. The very idea! Give a servant a key and take it away from a blood relation, at least a relation by marriage! There is no denying that Louella was very much upset about that key, and decided to get it back at the first possible moment. As she climbed into the bus that would take her to her lawyer's in the city, her mind was occupied with the problem of how to get that key back, and also incidentally to get a little more information concerning the doings of the Graeme boys.

The best way to do that would be to go there this afternoon and get Margaret by herself. She could always get things out of Margaret Graeme if she worked it in the right way. She was sure she could get that key. Margaret was soft-hearted and if she showed that she was really hurt by not having that key she was sure she could get it.

So she hurried through her business with her lawyer and took the return bus that would go by the Graeme house. That would not waste so much time.

So, Margaret Graeme, fresh from a nap, and her heart at rest because her two boys were at home, took her sewing and went downstairs to sit by the library fire and wait for her family to drift back from their various wanderings and interests. She was no sooner comfortably seated than the doorbell rang twice, sharply, aggrievedly, and Margaret sat placidly as she heard Hetty go in a leisurely lope to open the door.

"Well, you decided to come at last, did you?" came Louella's sharp faultfinding voice. "Where were you? Up in the third floor? Because I should think you'd arrange to be downstairs in the afternoon when calls are likely to come, or else get somebody to look after the door when you decide to go up to the attic and take an afternoon nap."

Then Hetty's indignant tones boomed out.

"No ma'am, I wasn't takin' no nap. I nevah takes no nap. An' I wasn't up in the third stoh'y neither. I was right in the kitchen, just liftin' out some chicken thet was 'bout to burn, an' I come as quick 'z I could."

"Oh, yes, I suppose you'd have an alibi. You never did learn how to be respectful."

"No ma'am, I don't have no Al Lebi. I don't eben know him. Ain't been no man at all around here."

"Well, never mind. Don't talk forever about one thing. Just answer the door sooner the next time. Now, where are the family?"

Hetty in her haughtiest manner shut the front door definitely, and then turned toward the caller.

"Mistah Graeme, he has went to a special meetin' of the Presbytery. De young gemm'l'men tuk him down to de chu'tch, an' dey'll went after him when he's done de meetin' an' meanwhiles dey'll go roun' an' about an' call on dere frien's; Miss Kathie, she's off to her horspital wurk; an' M'is Graeme, she's settin' in de li'bry. You can went in ef yeh like." And Hetty sailed nonchalantly into the kitchen.

With a sniff of disapproval Louella marched into the quiet atmosphere of the library.

Margaret Graeme looked up with a pleasant smile. Not quite so pleasant perhaps as that smile would have been if the person arriving had been one of her boys or her girl. But she had heard most of the dialogue between Hetty and Louella, and was prepared with quite a pleasant welcome, a little bit troubled, perhaps, and worried lest Louella might stay longer than would be pleasant, that she might insist upon staying until the boys got back, and that would be altogether unfortunate. She didn't want her sons to have anything to mar the sweetness of home. Especially if it should so turn out that they had to go back again to the horrors of war. She must be cautious. She must be quiet to be guided. "Oh God, help me!"

Perhaps it was a petty trial to bring to the great God for help, and yet Margaret Graeme had learned through long years that there is no trial so petty that may not work out to unpleasantness and even sin if allowed to sway the spirit. Mrs.

Graeme had learned through long years how to keep that spirit of hers placid, unruffled by little things. She was always looking to her Guide for strength.

It is a pity that Louella could not have learned from the same Teacher, for she would have been a much more welcome guest if she had.

"Well!" she snapped from the doorway, "here you sit as quietly and contentedly as if all the world was moving in oiled grooves according to your plan. Guests may come and ring at your doorbell and pound on your knocker and that lazy so-called servant of yours opens the door when she gets good and ready. Really, Margaret, if I were in your place I would dismiss that Hetty before the day is over. I'm sure I could get you a servant that would be far superior to her at her best, and for less money I'll warrant you. The trouble with Hetty is that she doesn't know her place. You spoiled her, and she thinks she can do anything she pleases."

"Good afternoon, Louella," said Margaret Graeme, "won't you sit down by the fire? I know it isn't a very cold day, but yet there is still a little sting of winter in the air. And throw aside your coat, won't you? Then you won't be chilly when you go out again. Did you walk over?"

"*Walk? Me?* Mercy no. I never walk if I can ride. I came on the bus of course. I came after my key. It worries me not to have it on hand when I want to come over here."

"Your key?" asked Margaret. "What key, Louella?"

"Why, my key to this house. Don't you remember you gave it to me when I was living here, and I've kept it ever since. And this morning Donald came over and asked me for it. Where is he? He said he had need of it. He didn't say what for, and I told him I would come over and get it. Is he here?"

"No, Louella, he isn't here. He went to a meeting. I don't know when he will be back. He may stay for the evening session."

"Well, then won't you go upstairs and look in all his pockets and get that key for me? I haven't much time just now and

I can't be easy without that key. It has been in my inner consciousness so long it seems a part of me, and gives me a feeling of belonging to a family."

"Oh, I'm sorry, Louella. But you see we need that key. There aren't keys enough to go around, and when we have a guest for a day or so, it is rather embarrassing not to have a key to give them. Donald has been going to ask you for it ever since you were here the other night, and he has just put it off."

"Well, that's ridiculous!" said Louella. "You can always get Hetty's key. She doesn't need a key anyway. Or you can get another made from one of yours. I insist, Margaret, that you get that key for me, and hurry up. I have other calls to make."

"I'm sorry, Louella," said the sweet Graeme mother firmly, "but I just wouldn't know where to look for that key. And anyway if Donald asked you for it, he likely had a reason. Besides, Louella, you don't need a key now that you are not staying here. Forget it, Louella, and let's have a nice talk. Are there any pleasant people staying at the inn now?"

"No!" snapped Louella. "None that I care for. I tried playing bridge with some of them last night but do you know Margaret, they cheated! Yes, they actually did. And then they charged me with not being honest. But of course they were strangers to me, and if I were going to stay here long I certainly should change my hotel. And that's another reason why I want that key back. Won't you please go upstairs and try to find that key for me?"

"Why, no, Louella, I wouldn't like to do that when Donald went after it. There must have been some reason why he wanted it. But really, Louella, there isn't any reason why you need a key. Especially if you are expecting to go home soon. It wouldn't be of any use to you. By the way, Louella, you hadn't seen Rodney since he was a very little boy until the other night. He was away in service when you were here before. Didn't you think he looked well? And did you notice how much he looks like his father?"

"No, I hadn't seen him in a long time, but I'm sure I

couldn't tell who he looks like. He was so horribly cross and rude to me that night I couldn't bear to look at him. I can't see how he could possibly look anything like his father, for Donald never looks cross at anybody. He is always placid and polite."

"Well, I'm sorry, Louella," said Rodney's mother. "You just didn't understand. It happened that someone had been in just before you arrived, and it had upset him very much, and when you asked him those questions it simply made things worse. You didn't understand of course, and wouldn't have hurt him for all the world if you had known. You were always kindhearted when you understood."

"Well, what is it? Why don't you explain? You can't expect me to be kindhearted if I don't understand."

"No? Well, what is it you want explained?"

"Well, I would like to understand, first, just why this ideal engagement was broken?"

"I'm sorry, Louella, but I don't believe I would have a right to explain those matters. You see they are not mine to explain. Isn't it enough to say that the engagement is broken, and that Rod is entirely satisfied about it, but he doesn't like to have that girl flung in his face continually, nor to be asked questions. After all it is his affair, and nobody else has a right to know all the details. I don't know them myself, and I've never asked about it. Boys don't like to have their intimate affairs talked over, and I've never asked him a thing. I felt that he had a right to his own privacies, and I would rather have him *give* me any confidences he wants to give, than to have him feel that I have been trying to dig them out of him."

Louella shut her thin lips tight, and pursed them while she shook her head, disapprovingly.

"Now Margaret Graeme, you know perfectly well that you had no right to take that attitude. You should have insisted on making Rod tell you *every*thing. After all, that is the way to encourage deception. And you have just deliberately encouraged Rodney in deceiving you. I certainly am glad I came in that night and brought the matter out in the open, even if Rodney didn't like it. And furthermore I'll do all I can whenever I see him, in trying to make him see that the way he has treated and is treating that lovely girl is all wrong, utterly unmanly, just the part of a scoundrel!"

Mother Graeme gathered up her knitting and tucked it into her knitting bag, and then looked at her visitor more indignantly than Louella had ever seen that placid cousin-in-law look.

"Louella," she said, and her voice was firm and angry, "what in the world do you mean? What an outrageous thing for you to say! You certainly will have to explain those remarks, or we cannot talk together any more. I will not have my son maligned."

"Oh, yes, your poor little son!" taunted Louella. "Yes, of course you would defend the poor child. After all, if he has been able to fight in a grown-up war, I should think he could do his own defending."

"Now look here, Louella, I'm not trying to defend my son, because there is nothing to defend. I am trying to find out what you meant by saying that he has, and is, treating his former fiancée outrageously? What right had you to say that? Who has been talking to you? Where did you get any reason to speak like that?"

"Why, I got my information from the lady herself. She told me herself that when she came into the dining room the other night Rodney took his dishes and dinner and marched out of the room without speaking to her, and that he did not return while she was there. She said you told her that he wasn't there. At least Jerry did, and that she couldn't find out anything about him from any of you. And she said she knew he must be there for his coat and cap had been hanging in the hall when she came through. Besides he was there at the table eating pie when I came in."

"I see," said Mother Graeme. "So you have turned detective. Just why are you doing that, Louella? Is it merely out of

curiosity? I didn't know that you were especially curious."
Mother Graeme was growing quieter, more self-controlled.

Louella bridled indignantly.

"Really!" she said indignantly. "Since when did you take up
this offensive way of talking? I certainly wouldn't know you,
Margaret! But then I have heard that even a dog who is very
gentle will snarl and bite when her offspring is attacked."

Margaret Graeme arose quietly, laid down her knitting bag
on the little table by her chair.

"That will be about all, Louella. Excuse me. I'll get us a cup
of tea. Perhaps you will be less excited after that."

"Excited! *I* excited! I should say it was you who is excited."

But Mother Graeme had gone out and closed the door definitely. She had not heard what the annoying guest had said.

When Mrs. Graeme returned she was carrying a tray. Two
steaming cups of tea, lemon and cream and sugar, a plate of
cookies and another of tiny sandwiches. Mother Graeme had
a theory which she often put into practice, "When in trouble
always feed the troublemaker." She was working her theory
now. She put the tray down on the little table, removed her
knitting bag, and drew up a chair for the cousin.

"Now," she said cheerily, "let's have a good time and stop
arguing."

"But I wasn't arguing," said Louella belligerently. "I was
just *telling* you."

"Lemon or cream? I can't ever remember which you take,
Louella?"

"Lemon!" snapped Louella. "I can't imagine how anybody
can take cream. That's why so many people have to reduce,
they take too much cream. And lemon is so much smarter."

"Here are napkins, Louella."

Louella accepted a napkin and thereby lost her line of argument.

"Help yourself to sandwiches, Louella."

"Are those cookies made by your mother's recipe?" asked

the guest, her mouth filled with delectable sandwiches. But Louella never praised anything if she could help it.

"No," said Margaret Graeme. "I don't think they are made by mother's recipe. I had loaned my recipe book. I think this was a recipe that Kathie got over the radio the other day. Have a cooky and sample it."

"Thanks!" said Louella, and took a generous bite. "Yes, this seems very light and tasty. I always thought your mother's recipe didn't have enough shortening in it. This seems better. Light as a feather. I wish you'd give me half a dozen of these to serve with five o'clock tea when some one comes in to call."

"Why surely," said Margaret Graeme pleasantly, wondering how long this unwelcome guest was planning to stay, and what subject she could start next that would be argument-proof. But the guest did not wait for a subject. She had one right up her sleeve, the real reason for her coming.

"By the way, what are the boys going to do now? They don't have to go back overseas again, do they?"

"They haven't received their orders yet," said the mother.

"Do you mean they don't know? But I understood they knew before they left the hospital. I heard they had a good job provided for them, and they were done fighting."

"Oh," said the mother, "just where did you hear that, Louella? It's strange they wouldn't let us know, if the matter is decided yet."

"Do you really mean that you *don't* know yet, or are you just trying to put me off again? Because, really, I don't think that's very kind of you, Margaret, to keep me in ignorance, when practically everybody else knows, and is talking about it."

"The next time they tell you that, Louella, suppose you ask them where *they* got their information. Because there really has been no word come yet for the boys. In fact they didn't expect it for a month yet. They were sent home for a good rest, and they will not be told the decision about their future work until they go down to Washington, and have a thorough physical examination, to see how they have progressed since they left the hospital on the other side."

"Oh, how perfectly silly! Those boys are in fine physical shape, don't you think, Margaret? Their mother certainly ought to be the best judge."

"I don't think I'd be the best judge, under the circumstances. You know I wouldn't understand all that they've been through, and what reactions I should look for. It's the Navy's responsibility you know, not mine. And whether I thought so or not wouldn't make any difference to them. The boys belong to the Navy, and they have to do as the Navy says."

"But I thought they were out for good. Mrs. Hopkins says her boys are home definitely to stay. And she says they were practically in the same company with your boys. She says her boys said they heard overseas that your boys were slated definitely for something else. Something over here, they said."

Margaret Graeme looked at the cousin thoughtfully.

"I'm afraid I wouldn't know," she said quietly.

"Oh, now Margaret, don't be so closemouthed. You know perfectly well you just don't want to give out information."

"I'm sorry, Louella, I've told you the truth. But if you don't choose to believe me I've nothing further to say. Won't you have another cup of tea? Another cooky?"

"No, Margaret, I've had plenty. And besides, I feel very much hurt at the way you are treating me. I know perfectly well you're not telling me all you know. I feel very much offended at your attitude."

"I am sorry Louella, that you take it this way. I have no intention of refusing to give you any facts that I have a right to give, even though I feel that your attitude of demanding to know everything about the family is unjustifiable. However, in this case I do not know what the boys are going to be ordered to do, and shall probably not know for several weeks.

And by the way, here are the cookies you asked for. Take the sandwiches too, if you like. Good-bye."

Louella accepted the neat package done up in paper napkins, and took herself out of the picture.

Margaret Graeme turned thankfully away from the door, grateful that this trying relative was gone before her family got home.

On her way back to the hotel Louella remembered that she had neglected to ask whether the whole family were going out Sunday night to hear Jeremy speak. Well, never mind. She would insist that Jessica carry out the plan of sitting in the gallery. She felt reasonably sure this plan could not but succeed.

9

BUT Rodney did not sit in the gallery, as Louella had been sure he would do, confirmed in this belief by Margaret Graeme's statement that the boys did not care to be in the public eye, and be lauded for what they had been in combat. And so Jessica sulked in a dark corner of the gallery without a gallant to comfort her lonely state.

She had not taken any of the girls with her because she felt her part in the drama she was expecting to play would be more effective if she went alone and slid unaware, as it were, into the vacant seat beside her ex-lover. But just before the meeting began, the other girls of her "gang" as she called it, came into the church, and finding no seats downstairs, went grumbling up the stairs to find her. They could not understand why she had put them off, and refused to go with them. And so when they had found her they squeezed into a seat across the aisle from where she was sitting, in behind a post where they could scarcely see the platform, and sat staring around them.

"Say, are you sure Jerry is going to speak here tonight?" whispered Emma Galt to Alida Hopkins. "He isn't down there on the platform, and there are quite a lot of people sitting up there behind the pulpit."

"Yes, Jerry is speaking all right. I saw his name on the Church Bulletin Board outside the church as we came in. Didn't you?"

"Sure!" said Isabelle. "Wait! Some more are coming. There! There he is! The last one. And see. Down there, coming in the middle aisle. That's Rodney Graeme, isn't it? And who are those girls with them? As I live, isn't one of them that Beryl Sanderson? It surely is! And who is the other one, oh boy! Gaze on that outfit. I'll bet she's some swell friend from New York. Girls, we made a big mistake. We should have come early and sat down in that front row of seats."

"You couldn't," said Alida, "there's a rope across the aisle. Those seats are reserved. Look! They're opening the aisle. They're escorting those people into those reserved seats. Why, look! Isabelle! Isn't that Rodney Graeme with them? And who *are* the girls? Beryl Sanderson and who else? I never saw her before. I *wonder* who she is."

Isabelle leaned forward and looked, whipped out her little old-fashioned opera glasses that she had lately inherited from an old aunt, and stared at the group being seated.

"Yes, that's Rodney and Beryl all right. And wait. I know who that other girl is. She *is* from New York. She's been here before to visit Beryl. Her name is Diana Winters. Well, that's some set up. Just how do you suppose Rod got in with them? For the love of Mike, won't Jess be angry? This is what she gets for following the drivel of that poor old gawk of a cousin of the Graemes. That's what I told her when she insisted on going to that poky old hotel to call on her. I think that woman's a flop, and everything she tries to do is silly."

"Oh, keep still, Isabelle. That old man is looking at us. He wants us to stop talking."

"Well, this church doesn't belong to him. I shall talk if I like and he can't stop me. There! There! See they've given those reserved seats to the Graemes. Say, I think this is a rank trick the old girl played on us, bringing us to a church to sit away up in the gallery where we can't possibly see anything or hear anything. Let's go downstairs and get a better seat."

"There aren't any seats, Isabelle," said Emma Galt, leaning over Alida to speak to her. "I stood up and looked, and I just now heard that usher that passed down the other aisle at the end tell that old man that there wasn't even standing room left down there. We better sit still. At least Jerry has a good strong voice, and I'm sure we can hear him."

"Not unless you girls can stop your talking," said the old man leaning forward and looking at them sharply.

That made Isabelle angry, and she was about to tell the old man what she thought of him, but suddenly the organ rolled into attention, and fairly thundered, and not even Isabelle could be heard over that. Then all at once everybody began to sing:

> It may be in the valley, where countless dangers hide,
> It may be in the sunshine that I in peace abide;
> But this one thing I know, if it be dark or fair,
> If Jesus is with me, I'll go anywhere.

It was an old song, and most of the people in the audience knew the words. They had sung it in the Primary class long ago, and it was still familiar in their different churches. But it was wonderful how the audience took hold of it and swung it along, setting a keynote for the meeting that was to follow.

The little crowd of indifferent ones in the gallery whose whole plan for the evening had gone far astray looked only bored. They did not care for this style of music. It seemed to them childish, belonging to an earlier age when men prated of sin and salvation and Jessica sat back with a sigh of disgust. Jessica had distinctly not come here to listen to religious songs, even if they were so well sung that they filled the air to the exclusion of other thoughts. What did they have to sing such songs for?

But with scarcely a word from the platform the throng drifted into another:

> *We have an anchor that keeps the soul*
> *Steadfast and sure while the billows roll,*
> *Fastened to the Rock which cannot move,*
> *Grounded firm and deep in the Saviour's love.*

Jessica with another audible sigh looked toward her gang across the aisle and curled her lip. She was all but ready to go out of this silly childish gathering. What did she come here for anyway, to listen to a young boy who just a few days ago was nothing but a high school student declaiming? How much more of this did she have to sit through? If it wasn't for these obnoxious people who had crowded in beside her and shoved her even against her protest all the way to the inside end of the seat, making it impossible for her to leave without climbing over them, she would leave at once.

And then came another tiresome song. How perfectly pestilential! Probably this was somehow a work-up to get the younger boys ready for going overseas. There was no telling. But how could a thing like that help anybody to be patriotic? They ought to sing *The Star-Spangled Banner* or some really patriotic song. Who in the world arranged a stupid program like this anyway? She wished they had asked her what to sing. Even though it was in a church they were entertaining a returned serviceman, weren't they? Why go so ultra religious?

> *There is a Shepherd who cares for His own,*
> *And He is mine;*
> *Nothing am I, He's a King on a throne,*
> *But He is mine.*

The melody was carried as a solo by an exquisite voice, but everybody seemed to know the song and the choral accompaniment of humming voices was rather wonderful.

There was not much time for Jessica to be thinking about leaving, for the program hurried along almost breathlessly, and somehow even the sneering gang *had* to listen.

Suddenly seven servicemen in uniform marched up to the platform and it was announced that instead of having the scripture read these seven men would recite it, as each had experienced it overseas.

Then each spoke, with heartfelt accents, what was evidently a truth each had felt.

"The angel of the Lord encampeth round about them that fear Him, and delivereth them. PSALM 34:7"

said the first, a tall Marine.

"We will rejoice in Thy salvation, in the name of our God we will set up our banners: the Lord fulfill all thy petitions. Now know I that the Lord saveth His anointed; He will hear him from His holy heaven, with the saving strength of His right hand. Some trust in chariots, and some in horses: but we will remember the name of the Lord our God. PSALM 20:5-7"

This was the word of a corporal in the army.

Then came a private on crutches, his face emaciated, his skin sallow, his eyes with haunting memories hidden by a great light. It was whispered about among the audience by some who recognized him that he had recently escaped from a prison camp after two years' confinement, and his contribution, spoken in a clear ringing voice was:

"Praise the Lord, O my soul. The Lord looseth the prisoners. PSALM 146:1, 7."

Next came two Navy men. The first a tall fellow with a clear voice and many decorations, and he spoke a ringing word like a testimony:

"He that dwelleth in the secret place of the most High shall *abide* under the shadow of the Almighty.

"I will say of the Lord, He is *my* refuge and my fortress: my God; in Him will I trust.

"Surely He shall deliver thee from the snare of the fowler, and from the noisome pestilence. Psalm 91:1-3."

Then without a pause his companion went on:

"He shall cover thee with His feathers, and under His wings shalt thou trust; His truth shall be thy shield and buckler.

"Thou shalt not be afraid for the terror by night; nor for the arrow that flieth by day. Psalm 91:4, 5."

Then followed a young army officer. In a steady voice like an official oath he was taking, he said:

"In Thee, O Lord, do I put my trust; let me never be ashamed: deliver me in Thy righteousness.

"Into Thine hand I commit my spirit: Thou has redeemed me, O Lord God of truth.

"My times are in Thy hand: deliver me from the hand of mine enemies. . . .

"Be of good courage, and He shall strengthen your heart, all ye that hope in the Lord. Psalm 31:1, 5, 15, 24."

And next came a Navy flier with a kind of ringing triumph in his voice:

"I love the Lord, because He hath heard my voice and my supplications.

"Because He hath inclined His ear unto me, therefore will I call upon Him as long as I live. PSALM 116:1, 2."

"It is better to trust in the Lord than to put confidence in man. PSALM 118:8."

The gang in the gallery listened astonished. They could not laugh, they could not sneer, for those words were too solemnly, too earnestly spoken, from men who obviously had been but lads so short a time ago. They bore marks in their faces of having been through fire and flood and death, and even worse than death. For just an instant, while those boys were speaking, even Jessica got a little glimpse of what the war must have meant to these men who but recently were to her just so many more to dance and flirt with. Now they were living souls who had been through something of which she had no conception. She was frightened. Her impulse was to turn and flee, but she had not the courage to do it.

And then there came another surprise. Another soldier in uniform stepped up beside the seven, and they all began to sing, a double male quartette.

*Be still, my soul: The Lord is on thy side;*
*Bear patiently the cross of grief or pain;*
*Leave to thy God to order and provide;*
*In every change He faithful will remain.*
*Be still, my soul: thy best, thy heavenly Friend*
*Thro' thorny ways leads a joyful end.*

*Be still, my soul: thy God doth undertake*
*To guide the future as He has the past,*
*Thy hope, thy confidence let nothing shake;*
*All, now mysterious, shall be bright at last.*
*Be still, my soul: the waves and winds still know*
*His voice Who ruled them while He dwelt below.*

The voices were beautiful, and the words were distinct. The audience was very still as the singing went on to the end. Then very simply the pastor of the church introduced Jeremy: not giving his history, nor a list of his great achievements in the war. His decorations could tell that tale to those who understood.

Jerry stepped forward quietly and began to talk:

"I asked the fellows to sing that song for me," he said, "because it was a verse of that song that came to help me when I started out on my first bombing mission. Up to then I hadn't been greatly stirred by the things I had been through. I had rather enjoyed it all while in training, and I hadn't been in any serious fighting. I knew my duty and it hadn't seemed to me anything very difficult to do as I had been trained. The element of fear hadn't been in it yet for me. Not until I was in my seat ready to go out on my first serious mission, did I realize that I was going into possible death.

"Of course when I enlisted I saw by the expressions on the faces of my family that there was dread and fear ahead for them. But I laughed at them, and went gaily on my way, enjoying every hard thing that came my way. My mother was brave and courageous. She never voiced her fears. She did not try to dissuade me. 'We are putting you in God's hands, son,' she said with that sweet patient look in her eyes. That was mother. I expected cooperation from dad and mother.

"Oh, there had been prayers for me every night and morning in the few days before I left, and I listened to them as if they had been unnecessary farewell presents to bear me on my way. My family had always prayed for me, and I would be sure they would now as I was going off to war. We always had family worship morning and evening in my home, and sometimes as a little kid it had rather bored me, but that last morning, it seemed the right and fitting thing. My father always read a passage of scripture and prayed, and sometimes, when we had more time, we sang a hymn. That morning I went away we sang that song the boys just sang.

"I remember when we reached the second verse that somehow those words seemed written for my mother, and I felt she was singing them to herself, although all our voices were joining in.

*Be still, my soul; thy God doth undertake*
*To guide the future as He has the past.*

"Those were the words that stuck in my memory, and for an instant I had a brief vision of the night my older brother went away to war and I had a passing sympathy for what she must have suffered during the months he had been away. Now she was having to take it again! But she was brave, and she would stand up and trust, with that wonderful faith of hers. A gallant little mother. And a father with a strength and a faith like a rock.

"So I went out.

"I didn't have any fear then. I think I must have supposed that when *I* got into the war, that would end everything. But it didn't take me long to find out my mistake. Nevertheless I went through the preliminaries, thrilled with the enormity of the undertaking to save the world for peace and prosperity. And it was not until I was seated in my bomber, awaiting the word for me to start out on my first solo mission that I began to realize what it all might mean. Oh, I had been out with others, I had watched some battles, I had seen some of my comrades fall, but as yet I had no fear that it could come to me. Death? Why I was young and strong. I was *trained*. I had courage to go right among the enemy and down them. Of course I didn't exactly say that to myself when I started.

"Now I couldn't understand this feeling of fear that had come over me. It was like the time when I began to play football and I saw the other side rounding up against me. Suddenly I found that I hadn't had experience in meeting just such a set-up as was coming, and I began to quake. How I despised myself. Then I was just a sissy after all. Afraid to go out and fight. Me! Jerry Graeme!

"Then strangely there seemed to come to me a strain of a song. But it was very far away, like all my old courage that I had always been so proud of. And then at that instant came the signal to start, and I *had* to go. I must not be an instant behind.

"I started. My hands did the things that they had been trained for, my brain out of habit directed my actions, but I was going out all alone with nothing but the strain of a hymn to give me heart:

>   *Be still, my soul: thy God doth undertake!*

"But it was so far away, as if it scarcely belonged to me, as if it was a song out of some other fellow's memories. But my mind grasped out for it, to make it mine. 'Thy God doth undertake.' Would God undertake for me? I had always supposed of course that God was on my side. But now I wasn't so sure. I began to go over my life, swiftly. There wasn't much time to take stock of one's self then, but I had heard that when a person faces sudden death his whole life in every little detail comes over him in a flash, and it was so with me. I thought I had been fairly good, no sin, except the original sin I had been born with and taught about. Or was that true, no sin? Well, suddenly I wasn't so sure. I had lived a clean moral life. Yes, but was that enough to help me meet God if I had to go at once into His presence?

"It was almost as if I were talking the matter over with God, presenting my claims to enter His presence.

"'I've always gone to church? Why, I *like* to go to church. Of course I'm a *member* of the church!' But still that did not seem to make things any better, or give me any comfort. Well, I wasn't a liar or a thief. I had never killed anyone, no, nor hated anyone enough to *want* to kill them. I began to count over the cardinal sins, and my estimate of self began to bulk up before me, but none of those things seemed to count, and then I remembered that my mother used to teach me that the one great sin that included all others was unbelief. But even that was not my sin—*was* it? I had grown up knowing the Bible, believing in God, that is in God with my mind. I believed what God had done, I believed that Jesus Christ had lived, and then died for me. I had accepted all that as a sort of a formula of doctrine. I believed He was the Son of God, and that He not only died, but had risen from the dead. I knew and believed that when Christ died He took my sins upon Himself as if they had been His own, He who never sinned Himself, and that He bore the sins, as well as the penalty for my sins. I could remember that when I united with the church they had asked me if I would accept what He had done and take Him for my personal Saviour, and I had assented. Quite casually it must have been, or so it seemed to me as I rode along in God's air, about to come into His actual presence, perhaps, and I didn't feel ready. I just didn't *know* the Lord. Oh, I had prayed, and read my Bible, but now it began to seem to me that it had all been almost nothing but a mere form, done because it was the thing a Christian was supposed to do. And my heart quaked within me.

"I began to see planes ahead of me. I would soon be at the scene of my first great activity, and I was so engaged with thinking that I didn't know God and might be going right into His presence that I couldn't seem to be giving my mind to the duties that were before me.

"And then, suddenly, as the critical situation approached, I felt I was not alone. A Presence was there beside me. There was glory in the air. And then I realized it was the Lord. He had come to me in my need! And I felt a sudden strength, and the fright that had made me weak before went away. I looked into His face and I was not afraid any more. 'Don't be afraid, I will go with you,' He said, and His voice was clear, in my heart. And I wondered why I had never taken such joy and strength from Him before. Then I realized that I had never really looked into His face. I had not seen Him before. I had not *known* Him. But now I knew Him *Himself,* and I could do *any*thing. That is anything He wanted me to do. I could accomplish my mission. I could crush the enemy. And if so be that it meant I was to meet my death too, it would not matter, for I would be with Him, either in life or death, with Him forever more!

"The enemy was all but upon me then, the sky was full of the sound of battle, but I was not afraid because God was with me, and He was undertaking. One swift resolve I made, and that was that if I went through this war, and ever got home, I would go to all the fellows who were going over pretty soon, and would tell them that they must get acquainted with God before they went. It made no difference how much they were trained, or how skillful they were in the use of the implements of war, if they didn't know God their preparation was not complete, for only in the strength of the Lord Jesus Christ could they be fully prepared to do the best that a serviceman could do. And that is the message that I am bringing you tonight. If there is only one fellow here tonight who is pretty soon going out to the great fight, my message is to you. Get acquainted with the Lord Jesus Christ, *now* while there is time. Get to know Him so well that there will be no fear in your heart no matter what situation you may be called upon to go into. But there is one thing about it, once you have seen Him with the eyes of your believing heart—and you cannot help but believe in Him when you have *met* Him—once you have seen Him you can never be afraid any more of anything that your enemy the devil in the form of evil men and arms can do to you."

From that thrilling moment Jeremy went on to tell of the battle into which he presently went, making it so vivid that the audience felt that they were looking into reality. They could even see the smoke and the fire, hear the bursting of the bombs. And for an hour and a half Jerry held that audience, yes, even to the gang in the gallery, listening, with tense attention, clenched hands, eyes blurring with tears at times. And yet Jeremy was only telling in simple vivid terms just what had happened, and how through it all there was that majestic Figure by his side, that glory in the air that did not come from fire of battle, the glory of the Lord in the face of Jesus Christ, protecting Jeremy as he went on in the way his duty ordered.

The story of the young man's work in the service was not being told for Jerry's glory, it was openly apparent that every word was spoken for the glory of the Lord Christ, Whose he was and Whom he served. He kept the Lord ever present as he spoke, and never once lost sight of that Central Figure.

As he sat down and dropped his face behind his hand as if in prayer, the minister came to the front. His voice was husky with tenderness as he spoke:

"I do not feel that I have fitting words to thank our brother for his wonderful message, or that any words should be added. I am going to ask our speaker's brother, Lieutenant Commander Rodney Graeme to close this meeting with prayer."

And then from that front row tall Rodney Graeme arose and lifting his face began to pray. "Our gracious God Who hast made Thyself known to us through Thy Son, let Thy Spirit work in all our hearts tonight to humble us before Thee. Show each of us our sin and guilt. May every one of us receive in the blood abundance of that life which Thou alone canst give, and may we be so yielded that Thy life may be lived through us, to the glory of our Lord Jesus Christ. Amen."

THERE was something in the timbre of Rodney's voice that stirred old memories in Jessica's mind, and suddenly she sat forward and looked down. She saw his face uplifted; she caught the strong sweet expression as he prayed.

He was standing so that the full light of the great chandelier was flung upon him, and it brought out a face that was both strong and engaging. So he used in school days to lift his head and look up at her and smile, and the strength and courage he had gained amid the terrible surroundings of war, had in no wise diminished the stunning charm of him. And he *used* to belong to her! And would yet if she hadn't of her own accord given him up for what she had *thought* to be wealth and fame and a great position. What a fool she had been! Would it be worth her while to win him back again? Divorce her elderly husband, whose charm had already vanished for her?

Then suddenly that vibrant voice caught her attention, and she began to listen to the prayer, till it seemed to her that he was praying just for her. Yet of course he didn't know she was in the audience. She never used to be eager to go to church or attend any sort of a meeting. He couldn't suppose that she would be there. Yet because the old charm of his voice stirred her she listened to every word and wondered. Why, Rodney never used to pray in meeting. She was sure of that. Oh, his family were religious of course, had family prayers, and went to all the services of their church and all that, but Rodney had never talked about such things.

So Jessica sat in startled wonder and stretched her neck to look down and make sure that it was really Rodney who was praying, although of course his voice was unmistakable.

She listened to that prayer that seemed to be directed at herself. Talking of *sin,* that horrid antiquated word, in which nobody now believed any more. The prayer was a direct charge of sin, coming straight at her shivering heart. The words stung frightened tears to her eyes. They flowed down her face like rain, and a great anger arose within her. How dared he pray like that? *Sin! She* had committed no sin in returning his ring, and marrying another man, and if he was daring to take a chance of her being present and say those things to make her ashamed he would find himself greatly mistaken. She was no sinner and he had no right to think of her as such! She would get out of this awful place before the prayer was over, before people would see she was crying.

She arose precipitately, and stepped across the other people in the pew, making her way silently and swiftly to the aisle. She climbed like a quick-moving shadow to the top of the aisle, dashed down the stairs, and out the open front door into the darkness of the street—fairly ran to the next corner, hailed a taxi, and was borne away out of sight before the notes of the organ proclaimed the service was over.

And when Louella Chatterton looked up with an interested smile Jessica was not there! She tried in vain to find her among her other friends. She had simply vanished.

Louella bustled down the aisle to the other girls who were standing there talking together, pointing out different acquaintances down on the main floor. They were mostly watching Jeremy and Rodney, and the girls of their party; wondering, speculating as to how they came to arrive together. Trying to decide whether they would go down and give old friends greeting and congratulations. "Yes, let's go," whispered Louella. "Tell him what a perfectly beautiful prayer that was!"

"Yes, wasn't it sweet?" exclaimed Bonny Stewart. "I just adore men that can pray like that."

"But where is Jessica?" asked Alida Hopkins. "Did she go down alone to speak to the boys?"

"I don't see her down there anywhere," said Isabelle, leaning over the edge of the gallery to look.

"Oh, she's probably just going down the stairs," said Garetha Sloan. "Come on, girls, let's go down. We don't want to get left out of the affair," and Garetha started up the aisle followed by the others, Louella, bringing up the rear breathlessly, said to herself what selfish things young girls were anyway. Never waiting for an old friend, even though she was the one who had brought the news of the meeting to their attention. But she puffed excitedly along after them, stretching her neck to try and find Jessica.

But Jessica was not in sight anywhere.

And now Louella could see the top of Rodney's head towering above the crowd, and she rushed the harder. Jessica of course must have gone straight to him and she wanted to be in at the meeting herself.

But, unfortunately for her plans, it happened that Jeremy who was just coming down the steps from the platform, caught sight of the pestiferous cousin, and casting a quick glance behind her saw several of Jessica's girl friends, also coming on, and took instant alarm. Quickly he reached his brother's side and said in a low penetrating whisper, "Watch out Rod, Louella and her gang are coming."

Rodney cast a hasty glance up the aisle, wondering if that meant Jessica was there also, but could not see her.

"There's a picture of your friend Carl Browning back in the Sunday School room, they tell me," went on Jeremy in a low tone. "If you need an out that might be an excuse."

"Thanks Jerry," said Rodney with a swift grateful smile, and went on shaking hands with the old friends who were still swarming up to greet the brothers.

It was several minutes however, even with all her talent for getting ahead, before Louella and her crowd managed to penetrate the outer edge of the crowd. And there they won from the brothers only a friendly handshake. Even Louella's voluble tongue failed to carry on much of a conversation over the heads of the crowd.

Just as Louella thought the crowd was thinning and they might have a chance to monopolize the heroes, suddenly Rodney leaned over and spoke to the girl from New York who had come in with him. Then without warning the Sanderson crowd followed him out the little door at the side of the platform, into the Sunday School room, closing the door behind them, and not even Jeremy was left where they had all been standing but an instant before.

"Well, upon my word!" said Cousin Louella, indignation and dismay in her voice. "What do you think of that?"

"Well, if you ask me I'd say that Sanderson crowd don't intend to let other people have a chance at them," said Isabelle, "perhaps we'd better just go to the house. I'm sure the Graemes were *here*. I sighted them once, and they've probably gone home and prepared some refreshments. We'll just go and get in on it."

"Well, if you ask *me*," said Bonny Stewart, "I'd say they've all gone to the Sandersons' house. They brought Beryl Sanderson and her friend. They would naturally have to take them home."

They looked at each other dismayed.

"Well," said Cousin Louella brightening up, "then I think we better go at once to the Graemes' house. We'll be there when they get home. They won't stay at Sandersons' long tonight, with a wounded serviceman in their company, and if we're there when they arrive they'll have to let us speak to them for at least a few minutes."

So they went back to Riverton, and drove to the Graeme farm.

The house was all dark. "The family hadn't come home yet, or perhaps father and mother Graeme had arrived first and retired," suggested Louella. "But that's all right. We can sit in the car till the others arrive."

But where was Jessica, they began to question.

"You don't suppose she's gone with them to Sandersons', do you?" asked Isabelle.

"Mercy no," said Marcella Ashby. "Not to Sandersons'. Don't you remember there was always a feud between Beryl Sanderson and Jessica? At least I don't know how Beryl felt, but Jessica always despised Beryl because she was rich and everybody admired her."

So they sat in the car under the tall old trees, and yawned, and waited, and discussed what could have become of Jessica. Finally Isabelle said:

"Well, what are we waiting for anyway? It's after midnight, and they won't want to see us when they do come. They'll be tired and want to get to bed. And if it's Jessica we're waiting for I don't see waiting any longer. She went off and left us without telling us where she was going, and now if she went with them let some of them bring her home, or let her get home the best way she can. I don't see sitting around for her any longer. We've got lives of our own to live without hanging on to the fringes of Jessica's performances. Drive on, Marcella. We'll take Louella to her hotel and then we'll go home. I'm fed up with this act, and if you don't start now I'm getting out and walking."

So they drove away, and went disappointedly to bed and to sleep, dreaming over the strange unexpected meeting on which they had been in attendance. Somehow there was nothing to gloat over in the whole time, and deep in their hearts there remained an uneasy feeling that perhaps there *was* a God and a Heaven, and sometime they too might get into a situation where they would need both, and couldn't find the way. It certainly had been strange to hear merry-hearted Jeremy Graeme talk as if he knew God personally, had met *Him* out there high in that awful sky with terrible death, menacing below, and little hope of ever getting through alive.

And what had become of Jessica? Could it be that she had gone with the rest to Sandersons'? Could it be that she would even descend to putting on a religious act to subjugate Rodney Graeme again, now after she had married a rich old man?

The clock in the old-fashioned tower of the town hall was striking a solemn one o'clock as the Graemes turned into their driveway. Their voices sounded sweetly happy, full of a quiet joy, as they got out of the car and went into the house. They had all been to the Sandersons' and got well acquainted, old folks and young folks alike.

Mother Graeme had a moment's talk with Rodney at the foot of the stairs before he went up to bed.

"Son, I cannot tell you how happy I am that you have learned to know God well enough to pray as you did. That prayer of yours was the answer to all my prayers for you while you were away fighting, and tonight has been a blessed time for me. I can truly say I am thankful that the Lord sent you to war, since it has resulted in bringing you to know Him."

Rodney took his mother's soft hands gently in his and stooping gave her a tender kiss.

"Thanks, mother dear," he said. "I've been wanting to let you know how it is with me, Heavenward, but somehow there hasn't been much time yet."

"Dear son!" she breathed. And then in a minute, "And I'm glad that you have found such nice Christian people for friends. I like the Sandersons so very much. And that girl from New York, that one they call Diana. She's so very sweet and dear. It somehow struck me that that was the kind of a girl for a young lad to come home to, after he's been off in peril and death. I wish you had known her years ago."

"Yes, she seems to be a grand girl," said Rodney simply.

And then after a minute he added, "You never did quite like Jessica, did you, moms dear?"

Mother Graeme lifted honest eyes to her son's face.

"Well, no, Roddie dear. Not for *you!*"

"And yet you never said a word against it, moms! You're a brave little woman. Why didn't you?"

"No," said mother Graeme. "I figured it wasn't for me to decide your life. It was your life and I'd done my best to give you right ideals, and if you couldn't figure out what you wanted to do with your life I didn't think I ought to interfere. So I just prayed, and trusted that the Lord would show you what He wanted you to do."

Rodney looked deep into her eyes with a great adoring tenderness.

"He *did!*" said Rodney solemnly. Then added, "Dear mom, you're wonderful!"

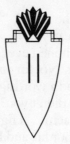

## II

DUMPED in front of her hotel by the unfeeling girls who had brought her home from meeting, Louella unlocked her door and went to her telephone, calling up Jessica.

She was answered after some delay by a very cross voice, that sounded strongly of tears in the offing.

"Oh, my dear! Is that really you?" said Louella excitedly, "I've been so worried. I nearly went wild about you. Whatever became of you? I looked everywhere and you weren't in sight. What happened to you?"

"Happened to me? Why nothing happened to me. That was the trouble. I was bored to death. I couldn't see staying there any longer and listening to that religious twaddle. They certainly have got it bad!"

"Then you didn't go with the rest to the Sandersons'?"

There was just a fraction of hesitancy before the answer.

"*Sander*sons'? Did they *all* go to the Sandersons'? Heavens, no! I wouldn't be seen drunk with those people. I despise them. *Did* they all go to Sandersons'?"

"Apparently," said Louella in a mortified tone. "That is they suddenly all disappeared together, out through the back of the church somewhere. I heard them say they were going to see a picture of one of Rodney's buddies in the war, but they went, definitely, and didn't return. Then the janitor began to put out the lights, so we came out and drove over to the Graemes', and waited till now, and yet they hadn't come home."

"So they went to Sandersons', did they? H'm, well! I suppose that means something. But if I couldn't compete with that little washed-out Diana I definitely would give up. But since I've heard that religious twaddle I don't know as I'm interested any more, anyway. I feel that this has been an utterly wasted evening. I really do. I don't know why I ever got the idea of coming back to Riverton. It is always disappointing, don't you think, to go back to little primitive country hometowns? The things and the people that used to interest you seem very tame after you've been in a city and got used to city ways."

"Well, yes, I suppose they do," said Louella. "Still, you've only been in Chicago, and that's almost a little West, don't you think?" said Louella. "While Riverton is decidedly East you know. Not too far from New York to run up a little while very often."

"Yes, New York, of course! But it's not what it used to be, I understand."

"Oh, why, my dear child! Who've you been listening to? You're all wrong you know. New York is definitely the tops of course."

"Well, if you want to pose as belonging to the East of course. But say, what did you find out this afternoon? You thought you were going to have something worth while to listen to. Did you find out what the boys are going to do as soon as they are out of service?"

"Well, I found out that they are not going out of service. That was stated as a fact."

"You don't mean they're going back overseas, Louella?"

"Well, no, not that, but they are to have some very responsible position here at home I believe, and still be in uniform."

"You don't say!" said Jessica all interest. "Well, that's quite exciting, isn't it? It might be really well worth my while to play up to Rod and get to find out a lot of dope I could write up for my editor. I'll have to look into that. You don't know what branch of the service they are to be in?"

"Well, no, they seemed very reluctant to say. Perhaps Margaret Graeme didn't know, but she's not so dumb. She probably was just keeping her mouth shut about it. You know so many of those things are being kept secret these days. It seems ridiculous."

"Why that sounds really exciting," said Jessica. "I was thinking of seeing if I could get reservations for tomorrow night, but in that case, maybe I'll stay a day or two more and see if I can find out where he is and what he is doing. It might help me in my writing. You know if I could get into something really new and thrilling I would just be on easy street."

"Well, why don't you stay a while, and I'll do my best to find out what it's all about."

"All right, Louella, maybe I will. I'll think it over. But make it snappy, won't you? I'll have to be sure there's something worth while in all this, for I mustn't waste my time."

"All right, Jessica. I'll do my best, and call you up and let you know as soon as I find out anything," said Louella.

Louella cast a quick eye at the clock, wondering if she should venture to telephone Margaret Graeme tonight, make up some plausible excuse for disturbing her; but decided against it. She would begin the first thing in the morning. That would be better and not get everybody in the family up-in-arms against her, as so often happened. It really wasn't good policy, for one could never find out facts from people who were angry and disturbed at you.

So very early in the morning Louella began.

"Is that you, Margaret? Oh, so you did get home at last, didn't you? I was really worried last night. We drove over to congratulate Jerry, and we waited until after midnight, thinking you would surely be home pretty soon, and then after I got home I got to worrying about you lest you might have had an accident on the way home from meeting and been taken to the hospital. Are you all right?"

"All right? Why certainly! Why shouldn't I be all right, Louella?" said Margaret Graeme with a touch of asperity in her tone.

"Well, you were so late getting home last night, I was really afraid something had happened to you, an accident, or something."

"Oh, no! Nothing happened. We were with friends for a while."

"Friends?" said Louella in a tone that asked a question, pointedly if ever a simple word ever did.

"Yes, Louella. We do have a few friends you know."

"Oh," said Louella and waited for an explanation, but none came.

"It was kind of you to call, Louella," said Margaret Graeme as the pause grew irksomely extended. "By the way, are you going to the Red Cross meeting this morning? If so I'll meet you there. It's almost time to start, and I have two or three things to do before I leave."

"Oh, *well,*" said Louella offendedly, "if you haven't time to talk to me of course I'll get off the line. Goodbye!" and Louella hung up sharply.

It was just about that time that Beryl Sanderson and her guest, Diana Winters, got up from a late breakfast and went slowly into the sunny sitting room, settling down with businesslike knitting bags, and took out their knitting, socks and sweaters for servicemen.

"Now," said Beryl settling herself comfortably and pulling out her work. "Let's have a real old talkfest. We haven't had a minute for one since you came. And first, let's begin with yourself. Are you really engaged to that splendid-looking officer I saw when I was at your house? I had a letter from Rose

Alters and she said that it seemed to be a settled thing, although you hadn't announced it yet. Is that so? *Are* you engaged?"

Diana's lovely face flushed a little, and a troubled frown rumpled her delicate brows. She didn't answer at once, but spent time straightening out her yarn which had tangled itself around her needles. Then she said slowly, almost hesitantly:

"Well, no, not definitely."

Beryl laughed.

"Will you tell me how you would manage to be *in*definitely engaged?"

"Well," laughed Diana amusedly, "that is a funny way to put it, isn't it? But the fact is Bates Hibberd has been hanging around a lot, insisting on an answer, insisting on being at least engaged, and I didn't seem to be ready with an answer yet. In fact he wanted to be married right away before he has to go overseas, but I just couldn't see that. I don't really know him well enough to be sure I want to spend the rest of my life with him. I told him I had to have more time to decide, and I ran away to you here to think it over. I knew if there was any place in the world where quiet and sanity reigned and one would have a chance to really think, it would be here."

"Thanks, Diana," said Beryl. "I consider that a great compliment. And does that mean that you would rather not be questioned about this matter, while you are thinking it over?"

"Oh, no," said Diana. "I shall need your help to make a sane decision."

"Say, that's a pretty big order. I don't know that I'm equal to advise on a subject like that. I know so little about the man."

"Oh, I can easily tell you. He's rich, handsome, has personal charm, well-educated, comes of a good family, one of the best. Several signers of the Declaration in his family, several noted writers, scientists, a poet, an essayist, even two millionaires and one preacher among his forebears. He's bright and smart, a man full of good ideas, and fine morals and manners, a leader in society, and popular everywhere. Before the war he had some thought of going in for politics. But I don't know what he'll do when the war is over. Well, I guess that's about the picture. What do you think I ought to do about it?"

"What's the matter with him?" asked Beryl matter-of-factly.

"Matter with him?" questioned Diana perplexedly. "Why, there is nothing the matter with him. That's it. That's why I can't decide what to do. There is *nothing* whatever the matter with him!"

"Well, then, why don't you marry him?"

"Well, I don't quite understand it, but I'm not just sure I *want* to marry him. Isn't that silly?"

Beryl looked at the other girl keenly.

"Do you mean you don't love him?"

There was a long pause before Diana answered, then she said slowly as if she were considering each word as momentous:

"*Love* him? I don't know. No, I don't suppose I really *love* him," she said. "But nice people don't really *love* one another before they are married, do they? I mean that emotional, demonstrative kind of love."

"Why, *Diana,* where did you get such an idea as that? Of course nice people love one another. If they do not why should they ever marry? And if they are not *sure,* beyond a shadow of doubt that they love each other with all their hearts, how *could* they ever bear to live intimately with one another? How perfectly terrible to be tied for life to a man you did not love and honor and respect with all your heart!"

"Oh, I could honor and respect him, of course," said Diana. "But I doubt if I could *love* anybody that wasn't really a saint, a real angel of a person, you know."

"But my dear, doesn't he seem that way to you?"

"No," said Diana thoughtfully, "he doesn't, and I'm sure I *don't* love him, not now. But I supposed I'd grow into loving him if I lived with him."

"You *never would*," said Beryl out of her deeper teaching from a mother who knew how to instruct her daughter in the intimate things of life. "Don't marry him, dear, not unless the time comes when you feel as if you would die if you could not be with him always. Do you feel that way about him?"

"Mercy no," said Diana. "Sometimes I'm really bored with him, and wish I could get away."

"Then don't marry him, Diana! That's not love. You'll never be happy with a man who bores you. Say, tell me something. Is there anybody else you love, or ever did love?"

Diana looked away thoughtfully, and then slowly shook her head.

"No, not anyone."

"Are you *sure?*"

"Yes, positive. Oh, there was an ugly little boy in school when I was in the third grade. He was always getting into trouble with the teacher and getting a whipping, and I used to feel sorry for him, and wish I could comfort him. It went on for several years till he left school and moved away somewhere, and I never saw him again. But that wasn't real love I suppose. Anyway I was only a child. And the last I ever heard of him was that he died in the war. I haven't thought of him in years, except when I heard of his death. And then there was another boy in high school. I thought I adored him till I heard he had run away with the worst little rat of a girl who lived down in the slums. Oh, Beryl! How can you ever tell about *any*body?"

Beryl looked at her pityingly.

"You *can* tell," she said positively. "That is," she added, "if you turn down the man you *aren't* sure you love, and just wait till the man God has planned for your life comes along."

"Do you think God does that? *Plan* somebody for your life?"

"Yes," said Beryl with her eyes cast down, and her cheeks a little more rosy than usual.

"Well, but suppose you don't like the man God picks out."

"Oh, but you would, I'm sure you would, Diana. God would understand and send the right one."

The visitor gazed at her perplexedly.

"Beryl, how long have you thought God cared what became of us?" she asked. "You never used to talk this way."

"Well, perhaps not. But Diana, I was very early taught that God cared about us in every little detail. Perhaps I never paid much attention to it when I was a child, but I think in the back of my mind I have always *believed* it. But anyway, Diana, I'm quite sure you ought *not* to marry that man whom you do *not* love. Don't tie your life up with someone, before God has shown you what you might have."

"Well, perhaps you're right. I don't know, Beryl, but somehow you have impressed me. But tell me, Beryl, are you in love with anyone?"

Beryl looked at her friend with a startled glance, her cheeks grown rosy.

"Why, no, Diana—not in love. There is someone I admire very much, but I'm not sure he's ever looked at me. We are just good friends, that's all, but it's very pleasant to have even a good friend that you really like, and feel at home with, even for just a few minutes' talk."

"Yes," said Diana thoughtfully. "Do you know, it's queer, but I felt that way, just a little, last night when I was talking to that nice Rodney Graeme. I had a feeling that I would like to know him better, and that I could really enjoy his company. But of course he's a perfect stranger, and is probably very much engaged to someone else."

"Oh, yes—Rodney. He's nice, isn't he? Those brothers are both nice. They couldn't belong to that family and not be, of course. But no, I don't think Rod is engaged now. It seems to me I heard he was once engaged to some girl he had known since childhood. But I thought I heard that was all off and she is married to someone else. But now, *there's* a man that a girl could trust. *He* would never bore you."

"But Beryl, I'm afraid a man like that would be too far

above me," said Diana. "A man who could pray like that! I shall never forget that prayer. It was like a creed, so brief and yet so very clear and comprehensive."

"Yes, wasn't it!" said Beryl. "My dear, if war does that to all the boys who have been over, what will the world be like when they all get home? We shall have to look to ourselves, or we won't be good enough to company with them even now and then. Do you know I was thinking that while Jeremy was talking. He has grown up so wonderfully. Although he was always a wonderful boy, even in his school days."

"How well did you know him?" asked Diana.

"Not so very well," said Beryl thoughtfully. "I thought he was wonderful in school, but we never saw each other outside of classrooms. I used to often wish I knew him better, but he was not at any social affairs, and neither was I. I don't know how it happened. Of course we lived in separate townships. My father picked out that high school over in Riverdale because it had several quite superior teachers. He had to pay to get me in there and I had to be driven over every day, which was another separating fact. But I never forgot Jeremy, and I was so delighted when I met him a few days ago, and had an opportunity to greet him."

"Well," said the other girl, "if you would ask me some of the questions I've been asking you, I think I could unequivocally answer yes, by all means let your interest center around that lad. I liked him a lot too, and what a wonderful message he had. He almost made me believe a lot of things I never was sure about before. Do you know his brother? Is he as nice? I certainly enjoyed him last night, even just sitting by him in a meeting. He made me feel as if I had known him a long time."

"No, I never knew him at all until a couple of days ago. He was off at college when Jeremy and I were in high school, and then he went right overseas. He enlisted you know, and he's been a long time away. They tell me he has done a lot of marvelous things in the war, and won a lot of honors. You saw the ribbons he was wearing."

"Yes, but you mustn't interest me too much in him," sighed Diana, "for it isn't thinkable that he isn't already taken. I simply must not complicate my life any more than it is already, with any more *impossibles,*" and Diana laughed rather bitterly. "Perhaps I don't know what love is all about. And anyway I wouldn't be up to a notable Christian man like that one." Diana sighed almost enviously.

Then they heard Mrs. Sanderson calling them to come upstairs and see some photographs of Beryl's baby-days she had promised to show them, and they sped up to answer her call.

"We'll talk again," whispered Diana, and Beryl, with a sweet smile, caught her fingers in her own and squeezed them lovingly.

A couple of days later Jeremy Graeme called up Beryl Sanderson.

"Hello there! Are you busy today, you and Diana? Because Rod and I have to take quite a drive on some business errands for dad, and we thought you girls might like to go along. It's business so it's legitimate to use the gas. My sister can't go because she has to be at the hospital all day, but Rod thought it would be great if you girls should want to go. We're putting up a lunch, coffee and sandwiches, enough for a regiment, and we thought we'd start right away if it was all right with you two. How about it? Like to go?"

"Oh, wonderful! Wait a minute till I ask Diana."

She was back in less than a minute with a gay little voice full of eagerness.

"Yes, Diana thinks it will be wonderful too. We'll be ready by the time you get here."

The two excited girls hurried up to make ready, and to explain to Beryl's mother, who seemed well pleased when she heard who they were going with.

"Take that box of candy your father brought home last night," she said smiling. "That will help out with the lunch."

And so in a few minutes they were off.

It was a glorious day. One of those perfect days in the opening of spring, and the sunshine had that yellow quality that is so alluring after a long dreary winter of cold and fog and gloom.

"It almost seems as if the war was over!" said Beryl with a relieved sigh as she settled back in the car. "Here we have real sunshine, and flowers and birds, and two of the best fighters home from the war."

"Thanks awfully!" said Jeremy with a grin. "Hear that Rod? Better salute after that." So Rodney stood up and gravely lifted his cap. "It's something fine to have won that title," he said.

That was the beginning of a wonderful day. Not even an April shower to mar its loveliness.

Occasionally Beryl cast a glance over her shoulder at the back seat of the car where Diana and Rodney were sitting, deep in talk, and she couldn't forget the last thing Diana had said to her before they left the house. "Oh, I'm just scared to death," she had breathed as they hurried downstairs.

"Scared?" said Beryl looking surprised. "Why in the world should you be scared?"

"Why, I'm scared to talk to that wonderful man. A man who can pray as he can must be a very holy man indeed, and I'm sure he thinks I'm a little heathen. I shan't know what in the world to say to him."

"Nonsense!" laughed Beryl. "He's not like that at all. Don't worry. You'll get by all right."

And there sat Diana in the back seat laughing and talking vivaciously. She seemed to be enjoying herself immensely. What's more the navy man looked very pleased himself. So Beryl cast off her anxieties and gave herself up to the enjoyment of the day, and the company of Jeremy whom she admired greatly.

It was a long delightful drive to the three towns which were their destination, and every minute of the time was filled with joy for all concerned. Even the three stops were interesting, the first at an office, where they could see Jerry through the window, spreading out papers on the desk, pointing out certain items to be noticed, waiting courteously for the signature, and then talking genially with the man they had come to see. He was evidently being asked questions concerning his war service overseas, for the stranger pointed to his decorations, and Jerry was laughingly explaining, then perhaps telling a few words of what he had been through.

The next stop was a small grocery where the proprietor came out to meet them, arguing about some matters in the papers before he glumly took Jerry in, and signed.

The third was a large old farmhouse. A very old man on the piazza with a big old-fashioned gray shawl over his knees, and a gray felt hat pulled down to shade his eyes. They could hear the converstion at this stop, a learned discussion of roads and why this protest was necessary.

Jerry got away at last with only a brief sketch of his experiences in service, and climbed back to his seat in the car with a sigh of relief.

"There, that's that!" he said. "Now we can start to have fun."

"But it's all been fun," said Beryl.

"It certainly has," said Diana with shining eyes, and Beryl settled back, content that her guest was enjoying herself.

"Now," said Jeremy, "how about lunch? I'm hungry as three bears. What about the rest of you?"

"There couldn't be a better suggestion," said Rodney. "I'm always hungry now."

"That sounds wonderful!" said the girls in chorus.

So Jeremy turned down a dirt road leading into the woods, and presently they were winding among hemlocks and pines and maples, with bird songs overhead, and chattering squirrels skittering from limb to limb on the trees.

The lunch was ample with many surprises in the shape of delightful sandwiches and little frosted cakes, and berries, olives and pickles and cheese and jellies. There just seemed to be nothing that could have been thought of that had been forgotten, including plenty of hot coffee in the thermos bottles. They ate it in a leisurely way, with many a joke and a laugh, Beryl twinkled her eyes at Diana as if to remind her of her fear that these young men would be too grave for her light-minded self.

It was after they had finished, washed the dishes in a convenient little brook, and packed away all that was left in the basket, that Rodney suggested a walk.

They locked the car, left it in a nest of trees, and started off for a stroll.

"There are some pretty spots around this woods," said Rodney as he and Diana went along. "Some of my old haunts of bygone years, if they haven't been destroyed during my absence. If you'd like to see them, this way," and he parted the branches and showed her a hidden path that a stranger would scarcely discern.

Diana stepped into the opening he made for her, and Rodney turned his head before he followed her, and called back to the others:

"So long! Be back in an hour or two!" and grinned as the answer came back, "Okay! See you subsea."

It seemed to Diana as they penetrated into the green depths of that lovely woods, that she had never seen such beautiful quiet remoteness.

Rodney made a delightful escort. He found pleasant walking for her feet, and when they came to rest while he arranged a seat from hemlock branches, and when they were seated in the beautiful stillness he finally said, looking into the greenness above him, where little glimpses of sunlit blue sky were visible:

"Isn't this great? It seems as if this must be one of the places in which God delights, doesn't it? It seems as if He were here with us. Or—don't you feel that way?"

Diana looked up fearsomely, and half shuddered:

"Oh," she said in a little frightened tone, "I don't know much about God. But you—" she paused and gave a shy look toward the young man, "you seem to know Him so intimately." Her tone was almost envious.

Rodney looked down and smiled:

"Yes, I do," he said pleasantly, as if he were owning to an earthly friendship, "but no better than you may know Him too, if you want to. I was brought up to know all *about* God when I was a child, but I didn't get to *know* God until I met Him out in the air over enemy fire."

"Oh!" said Diana. "Tell me about it please, if you don't mind."

Rodney smiled.

"No, I don't mind. I love to talk about my Lord. Since I've met Him and know Him so well, it gives me great delight to talk about my Lord."

And so he began to tell the thrilling story of how he started out in his own strength to fight the enemy, and began to realize that Death was waiting just ahead for him, and perhaps the end of things down here. And then as he drew nearer and nearer to his doom, he heard the Lord calling to him through all the thunder of shells and planes. And the words He called were the same words he could remember his father reading at family worship, those mornings away back home when he was wishing the morning prayers would be over and he might be free to go to his work or his play. They were words that God spoke: "'Fear thou not: for I am with thee: be not dismayed; for I am thy God: I will strengthen thee; yea, I will help thee; yea I will uphold thee with the right hand of my righteousness.' It reminded me," went on Rodney, "of the time when I was a little kid, and my dad sent me out in the dark to get something I had left out there, and I was afraid. I was just a little kid you know, and dad came and took my hand, and said: 'Don't be afraid, Roddie. I'll go with you. I'll help you.' It was just like that. It was as if I heard Him call me. 'Rod! I'm here. I'm come to go with you!'

"And over and over again when I grew fearful, there was my Lord beside me. Sometimes going before me, right into battle, and the fire whistling all around me, but none of it touched me. I was safe because He was there!

"It happened again and again, and always when I had to go on some fearful mission He was there with me. It was almost as if I could look up to the clouds above me, and say, 'Come, Lord, are You going with me this time? I'm not afraid if You'll stay by!' And that's how I came through. Do you wonder that I feel I know Him, that I can talk with Him as if a man were talking with his friend? He's my friend!"

There were tears on Diana's cheeks as he was telling this.

"Oh, that is wonderful!" she said. "But does one have to go through death to know Him?"

"No, oh no! Not if you will take Him without having to be shown *that* way."

"But you were taught when you were little. You sort of grew up knowing Him, didn't you?" There was almost a hunger in Diana's tone.

"Yes, I knew *about* Him. I knew His history, the story of His life and death, and that it was for me, but I never took it to my heart until Death drew near, and I had to fly for refuge. Many times at home when I was young I might have got to know Him, and didn't. I just couldn't take time. I knew it was all true, but I'd never looked into His face before. Not until He took me up there in the sky alone with Himself and menacing Death just below, and all around. Then I looked up, and I saw Him. But that is something that cannot be described. You have to see Him yourself to understand. You have to know Him."

"Oh!" said the girl disappointedly. "Then I'm afraid there is little likelihood that I could ever understand. I can't go overseas and get into combat."

Rodney looked at her quickly.

"No, you're wrong," he said. "You don't have to go overseas to see Him. I had every chance to know Him before I went into death, but I was just too much interested in my own affairs, and in the world and worldly people to look up. I just wouldn't look at Him. But you—you would like to see Him? If you long to find Him He will come to you. The only condition is that you believe. That is believe that He took your sin, and took your place and suffered your death penalty. Take Him for your personal Saviour, that is. Are you willing to do that?"

"Why yes. I could believe because I have seen the faith in your face, I have heard it in your words, and in your wonderful prayer. Is that the right kind of belief? Because I don't really know much about Him, only the set stories that churches talk about, and I never paid much attention to them before. But I'd like to know Him now."

"That's great!" said Rodney with a joyful ring in his voice. "Shall we tell Him so?"

They were sitting on a smooth bank of lovely moss, under a great tree. The young man bowed his head, and Diana, awed at what might be coming, almost frightened again, bowed hers.

"Lord Jesus," said Rodney in his quiet conversational tone, "I'm bringing this little girl to You because she wants to know You and says she will take You for her Saviour. Please show her how You love her, how she needs You, and to understand what You have done for her. May she now be born again, and will You let her see You as You are, and get to really know You, and love to serve You in her daily life.

"And now will You listen to her while she tells You what is in her heart? Thank You, my Father."

There was a long pause in the still greenness of the woods, while a thrush trilled out some high sweet notes of praise, and then Diana's little frightened voice trembled on the air:

"Dear God, I want to be saved. I want to know You, as Rodney does. Won't You please show me how? I do believe, as far as I understand."

Into the silence that followed this brief prayer came Rodney's ringing Amen, and after a moment of silence he reached over and took her hand in a strong firm clasp.

"Welcome into the family, little sister!" he said tenderly. She looked up into his eyes and her own were filled with tears of joy, and there was a smile on her lips.

They lingered for some time in the quiet retreat, talking over what the Christian life meant, what it was going to mean to her, and to him now that he had come back to his own country, and had to live with a world that hadn't been to war, and hadn't met Christ in the clouds above Death.

Then suddenly Rodney looked at his watch.

"Say, do you know, our two hours are more than up! What do you know about that? How fast time can go in a place like this, the two of us alone with God."

Diana looked up at him, her eyes full of gratitude.

"I shall never forget it," she said. "It's been the most wonderful two hours of my life."

Rodney smiled down at her.

"I'm glad," he said. "And I'm greatly glad that you know my Lord. For now, you see, we have much in common. I had begun to think there were no Christian girls except my sister in the world. I'm awfully delighted that I know you."

"And if I hadn't met you," said Diana fervently in a soft little voice, "I probably never would have been saved."

"I don't know about that," said Rodney with a smiling acknowledgment of her words, as he caught her hand and pressed it gently, "I'm glad to have had the privilege of leading you to know my Saviour, but you know the Lord isn't entirely shut up to my services for bringing souls to know Him. He has other servants who know and love Him as well as I do."

"Yes? But I'm glad He sent you."

"Yes, so am I," he said, and this time he caught her hand again and drew it within his arm, helping her over the rough ground as they slowly made their way back toward the rendezvous.

And at that they got back to the car before the other two wanderers had come yet, and climbing into it resumed their talk.

"How much longer are you going to be in this vicinity?" asked Diana suddenly. "I do so wish it would be long enough for me to ask a lot of questions that I know will come to me when I get by myself and try to read the Bible alone. You're supposed to read the Bible, aren't you, when you are a saved person?"

"It's the best way," smiled Rodney. "Prayer and Bible reading are the great helps to knowing God and living as He would like to have you live."

"Yes, well, I never could make anything out of the Bible. I tried several times to read it by myself, and it didn't mean a thing. Then someone told me it was only tradition and wasn't meant to be read literally. Is that so?"

Rodney grinned.

"That's what unbelievers tell you, and many college professors, when they even mention it at all. But there are wonderful Bible Schools of course, in almost every region. I certainly would enjoy introducing you to Bible Study if it might be my privilege. I'm not a Bible teacher, and only know my Bible as my mother taught me long ago when I wasn't paying much attention, and as the Lord has taught me to live it since I met Him in the way. I'll be pleased to tell you what I know while we are together, but there is a better teacher than I am, one Whom it is every Christian's privilege to study under, the Holy Spirit. Christ promised He would come and 'He shall lead you into all truth,' He said. Reading your Bible with the help of the Holy Spirit makes all the difference in the world. Even with no earthly teacher, men have found the way to understand. But to answer your question, I'm not sure just how long I can stay here. I may get orders to report in Washington soon, or at the hospital for examination."

"Oh, will you have to go back overseas?"

"That isn't settled definitely yet. Perhaps not, and then again, perhaps yes. I ought to know in a short time. In any case I'm glad I found you. I shall always feel glad. And I wonder if I may have the privilege of getting you a Bible? Or have you one already that is precious to you?"

"Oh, no," laughed Diana. "Not precious. I have a tiny red leather one with gold lettering on the back and very fine print, which I won in the Primary class in Sunday School when I was five years old for perfect attendance for one year. But I have never even tried to read it. Only its red cover ever appealed to me. But I shall treasure a Bible that you gave me, because you are the one who helped me get acquainted with Jesus Christ."

"Thank you," he said, "I am proud to have you feel that way. And I shall always remember this day, even if orders come to move on at once. I should never forget the sweet converse we have had today. But there! Look ahead! Isn't that my dallying brother and your friend Beryl? I guess our talk is at an end for the time. But, I'm going to be praying for you. Do you mind?"

"Oh, *will* you? That will be wonderful! And I'll pray for you too," Diana said shyly, "though I don't suppose my prayers will do you much good, I'm so new at it."

"Thank you. Yes, they will. The Lord is ready to answer even the newest of His children." The look he gave her seemed afterward as she remembered it to be almost like a caress, or maybe a better word would be "blessing" she decided as she thought it over.

13

THAT was the beginning of ten days of delightful fellowship between the four young people, with sometimes the addition of Kathie and her special army chaplain, John Brooks. They all fitted together beautifully, and had many grand rides and walks and picnics and meetings together. And then there was the day that they planned to run down to the shore for a few hours for a dip in salt water. They were to go down on the train, and they had taken special pains to keep Cousin Louella from knowing their plans, lest she might want to go along.

For Jessica was still in town, hobnobbing with Louella constantly, and very subtle in her methods. They thought they had been very clever in their plans, but when they were waiting for their train at the station, Jessica and Louella came walking down the platform together. They were obviously not planning to take the train, for they were wearing house dresses, and no hats. It was of course quite early in the morning and Jessica had come out to hunt up Louella and ask if there was any news of what the young naval officers were going to do. They had walked together down to the station to mail an important letter Jessica had just written her husband—demanding money, on the early train, and there they were waiting for the train to come in.

"Can you beat that!" said Jeremy under his breath as the two hove in sight. "Such luck! Come on around the other end of the station, over in the edge of the meadow, as if we were picking violets."

Rodney seized Diana's arm and propelled her swiftly out of sight behind a lilac bush. And the two conspirators walked on slowly down the platform, without seeing them, while the travelers scuttled down to the other end of the station, and bore up against the wall, with a kindly syringa bush sheltering them.

"Isn't this too ridiculous!" giggled Kathie. "I hate to be always on the sly."

"How could you help it with a cousin such as we possess?" grinned Jeremy. "She's got eyes like a gimlet that would go through a steel helmet, and a tongue that can talk faster telling gossip than an electric fan. I hate to say it about anyone who is somewhat related to my revered father, even if only by marriage, but it is the truth. And as for that other person, we certainly want no part with her. She's deadly."

"Yes," said Beryl sympathetically, "I always did dread it when she came around. But wasn't she once pretty intimate with your brother?"

"Oh yes, she tried to be when Rod was a mere kid, but that's all off. She's married now. Married some rich old guy and took herself out of the picture for a while, though it looks as though she was trying to get in the spotlight again, but I guess she won't make it. Rod is pretty fed up with her. She isn't exactly his kind, you know. Listen! There comes the train now. Skim across behind the shrubbery to the last car. The enemy is up front mailing a letter."

When they were safely seated in the train Jeremy returned to the subject.

"I wondered," said Beryl, "I never could feel quite com-

fortable in her company. She always managed to say something catty. Well, that's not the way to talk about a former
classmate is it? And it certainly isn't the kind of thing your
Christian principles advocate."

"No," said Jeremy with a wry grin, "it isn't. But it always
makes me furious to see that girl barge into the scene, just to
annoy my brother! Well, maybe there's some reason why he
needed this, so I guess we better take it smiling, keep our eyes
on the Lord, and let Him work it out. It's curious sometimes,
to watch how He does that, and remember that He is both
omniscient, and omnipotent. He knows all and has power to
do anything that needs doing."

"I guess you're right, Jeremy. But you didn't always feel
this way about Christian things, did you? I remember thinking you were a keen scholar, but I did not know you were
interested in religious things. Oh I knew you were upright
and all that, but nobody ever told me you went to church
much, or cared for things like that."

Jeremy answered her soberly, after a moment's pause.

"Well, I always went to church. It was the rule of our house.
And I always believed the main things about the Bible that I
was taught, but I didn't waste much time over doctrines and
things like that till I really knew the Lord. It was probably my
mother's prayers that followed me and kept me, laid me open
to meet the Lord when I got frightened and didn't know
where to turn."

"Oh," said Beryl, "I suppose any of us might feel that way
if we were suddenly confronted by death. But isn't it queer
we feel so easy about things like that when we all know everybody has to die, and it may come suddenly to any of us."

"Yes," said Jeremy, "it is. And there's another queer thing,
and that is how much we miss living an indifferent life like
that. You know I've never been so happy in my life as since I
found the Lord and was sure that I knew Him forever!"

She looked at him wistfully.

"You know, Jeremy, you're rather wonderful."

"Oh, no," said Jerry shaking a decided head. "I'm not wonderful at all. I've just got my eyes open suddenly. Do you know I found myself described wonderfully in the Bible the other day when I was reading about that fool guy Balaam, the fellow who had the wonderful privilege of being God's prophet, and didn't know any better than to use his great gift of divination for his own glory and personal aggrandisement. And then after he had missed a lot of chances to make good in God's sight, God had to send a poor old donkey and an angel to teach him. He knew what God wanted, but he wanted to serve himself. He hedged and hedged trying to get God to give in, until the Lord finally got his eyes open and then he saw. And after that he called himself the man 'whose eyes are open.' That's me, now, I hope. I'm the man whose eyes are open, opened by the Lord, and I pray that no more I shall go around equivocating, and viewing questions from this mountain peak, and that one, trying to get God to agree with me. I pray that I may always be the man 'whose eyes are open' to what God wants me to do."

"Oh, Jeremy! Is that what that story about Balaam and the ass means? I always wondered why that was put in the Bible."

Just then two seats in front of them were vacated and the young people moved together. Then they had a jolly time and almost forgot for a while that there was a war on the other side of the world, and the servicemen might have to return to it. The day was bright and the water just right. By the end of the day all felt rested and had got to know one another wonderfully well.

Back at Riverton there was gloom.

"Whatever becomes of those two navy men?" asked Jessica impatiently. "They never seem to be anywhere, and I really can't waste my time hanging around for them. I've got an order for some writing, but I simply must have a few facts, and I'm dead sure I can get better ones if I could just once get Rod started talking. I always used to be able to do that in the old days, and if I had a good chance at him all by himself I'm sure I could again. You promised to make this possible you know, Louella. And you haven't even found out yet what service those boys are likely to be called into when their leave is up. By the way, isn't it almost up?"

"Why yes, I'm sure it is," said Louella. "Their mother was sighing the other day that she might soon have to be saying good-bye to them again, for they were sure to be going away somewhere."

"Well, Louella, I've promised my husband to get some really authentic news from my old friends who have been all sorts of places and will be able to tell me lots of stories about the enemy and their plans."

Then Louella, interestedly:

"Why that sounds wonderful, Jessica. It sounds like your old self, and I'm sure you are on your way to fame. But don't get impatient dear. I'm doing my best for you. I'm almost sure I'm on the right track. I was over at the house yesterday morning and I happened to mention a phrase or two I had heard, and I was sure Margaret Graeme pricked up her ears and gave a swift look toward Kathie. I didn't say anything more about it just then, because I didn't want them to know I was getting on to any of their secrets, for then I know from past experience that they would shut right up. But I'll be mentioning it again, and then I expect to have a more enlightening report to give you."

"What were the phrases you mentioned, Louella? You haven't forgotten them already have you?"

"Why of course not. Did you ever hear of a place in the city called Bankers' Security, Jessica? I think it's a whole building somewhere. But I wasn't quite sure what it had to do with the other phrase."

"How aggravating you are, Louella! What was the other phrase? How can I make head or tail out of the things you say if you can't be a little bit more explicit in telling me?"

"Now Jessica, that's very rude of you. I don't know at all

why I take all this bother for you when you are so cross and unpleasant about it."

"Oh, well, Louella, you're very trying. But what was the other phrase?"

"Well, the other phrase was Naval Intelligence. Does that mean anything at all to you? And I'm quite sure it's something very secret, for the way they guard their looks, shows that they are really afraid I'll find out something."

"Well, yes, Naval Intelligence might be a branch that would interest me very much if I could really get at any of their vital matters. Find out if that is the branch they are really going to be in, won't you, and how soon they start? Gracious! I wonder how they got into that, if they really did. Well, get a hustle on and see what you can find out."

Therefore Louella took her way to the Graeme house the next morning. She arrived not more than ten minutes after the young people had left for the day and Margaret Graeme gave thanks silently that she had not come sooner.

"Well," said Louella, settling down in the most comfortable chair and getting out her crocheting, a delicate little nothing of pastel shades of silk, or nearsilk, designed eventually to hold sachet powder, and figure as an asset to handkerchiefs, "what's new, Margaret? Don't tell me the boys aren't up yet? They'll be getting lazy, and that won't be a help when they get back into service. And of course you are keeping their breakfast hot for them. You always did spoil your children terribly, Margaret, and I'm sure you'll be sorry for it yet. You can't get by without such things catching up with you."

"Yes?" said Margaret Graeme lifting a smile to her unpleasant cousin, "and what do you think is going to catch up with me, Louella?"

"Why, your pampering of your children. It will surely bring sorrow to you in some way. You'll see."

Margaret Graeme laughed lightly.

"And how am I pampering my children now?"

"Why, letting them lie in bed a lovely peppy morning like this, and then cooking them a separate breakfast when they choose to get up."

"Oh," said Margaret Graeme, "but my boys are not lying in bed. They were up an hour ago and had their breakfast, and milked the cows and curried the horses, and now they are off on their own business."

"Oh, *really*, Margaret? How did you manage that? Why, that's wonderful! But where have they gone? Then it's true, isn't it, what I heard last night. They are in the Naval Intelligence Service, aren't they? I was so hoping it would be that, for that would keep them at home, wouldn't it? And I know it would so break your heart to have them go back overseas again, and go on any more of those terrible 'missions' as they call them, out to bomb human beings. It seems a terrible misnomer to call them by the name of Missions. I supposed missions were for Christianizing heathen, not killing them."

Suddenly Margaret Graeme was overcome by merriment, and she burst into a bubble of laughter. But Louella who had never quite understood her cousin-in-law's laughter, turned an offended eye to look at her.

"Well, really, Margaret, is that a new way you have acquired to escape answering my question? Laughter?"

Margaret Graeme sobered down till only her sweet eyes bore the merry amusement.

"Question, Louella? Did you ask a question?"

"I certainly did. I asked you if it was true that your sons are being assigned to the Naval Intelligence Service? I was told so last night by someone who certainly *ought* to know the truth."

Louella reconciled this statement with the truth and her conscience by her emphasis on the word ought.

"Oh, is that so!" said Margaret Graeme gravely. "Well, I wouldn't know about that," she said pleasantly. "You see no one has told me anything about that. If it is so I suppose it will come to light in due time. If the boys have heard any such thing they may have kept it to themselves that I might not be disturbed. They have always been thoughtful of me that way. But I doubt if any order of any sort has come through for them yet. I am sure I should have known it if there were anything important in the offing. Of course ultimately, there will be something. We are expecting that. But we do not know what form it will take as yet. And now, Louella, tell me about your plans. You told me a week ago that you were obliged to hurry right home because an important deal was likely to come. Did it come through all right?"

"Oh," said Louella, with a confused look. "Why no—yes—that is, not yet. There was an unexpected hold up. The people who were thinking of buying my house felt that they first had to sell the one they were occupying, and I thought it best to wait here for their decision."

"Yes? Well I should think that might be very wise. A bird in the hand is worth two in the bush of course." Margaret Graeme's voice was steady and her lips did not twitch, but there were little lights twinkling in her eyes. She was used to Louella's boasting, and knew pretty well that Louella's property in the West was a mere mirage, that had faded long ago into a hopeless mortgage-foreclosure, but why let Louella suspect that she knew it? There were unpleasant points of difference without adding an unnecessary one. Margaret Graeme was used to looking upon these séances with Louella as a sort of game wherein the winner was the one who could keep the question going back and forth over the net without answering it out and out. Thus she made it interesting rather than a bore, and always kept her temper. Though Louella, not having a keen sense of humor, kept dropping stitches in hers. Then Margaret Graeme took pity on her.

"How would you like to go out on the porch, Louella? It's a glorious morning, the sun so bright, and the perfume of the flowers is beginning to scent the air. I just love these early spring mornings."

"Oh, yes, they're well enough, if it's not too chilly. I never like to get a cold in the spring. It's so apt to linger all summer and keep one's nose looking red, and one's eyes full of tears. But perhaps if you can lend me a shawl, or a sweater . . ."

"Why, of course, I have shawls and sweaters, but if you are afraid perhaps we'd better stay right here. Just move your chair over by the window and get a little more light on your work. How pretty that is, you are making. Is it to be a handkerchief?"

"No, a sachet for a dear little old lady at the hotel. She does admire my work so much."

"How sweet of you!" said Margaret. "I often wish I had leisure to do nice things like that for people, but somehow the days are not half long enough for all I have to do."

"Well, I say you do too much! You ought not to pamper your daughter. You make all her clothes, don't you? And she's always dressed like a doll. You would have plenty of time for anything you want to do if Kathie made her own clothes. When a girl gets to her age she ought to understand the art of sewing thoroughly."

"Oh, she does," said Kathie's mother with a loving smile. "She's made all her own clothes since she was in high school, and often has made some of mine. She seems to be very gifted in that way."

"Oh, really? You don't mean *all* her own clothes do you? I'm sure she never could have managed that lovely suit she was wearing last Sunday night. It fitted too perfectly to be homemade."

"Yes, she made that last spring. It does fit nicely, doesn't it? And she takes such good care of her clothes that it's always well worth her while to get good material. After all it does make a lot of difference if you have good material to work with."

"Well, I suppose it does, but after all if you encourage a young girl to spend a lot on her clothes what kind of wife will she make for some of these poor soldiers when they come home?"

"I trust that Kathie will have good sense about spending her money. But after all she is making a very fair wage in her hospital work, and I think she will know how to spend what she has worked for."

"Well, you always think your children are perfection, Margaret, don't you? But if she works so hard and makes her clothes besides how will she ever get out to know any young men? You know she might not get married at all. Then what would you say?"

"Well, I think I could bear even that, Louella, for then I should have my girl with me a little longer," smiled Kathie's mother.

"Margaret! You wouldn't want your only daughter to be an old maid, surely!"

"Why not, Louella? There are worse fates. But unfortunately for your theory, Kathie isn't likely to be unmarried. She is already engaged to a delightful young man whom we all honor and love."

"Margaret! You don't mean it? When did this happen? And why wasn't I told?"

"Well, it happened in the winter sometime. The last time he had a leave of absence before he went overseas. He is a chaplain in the Army, under some special orders. He was just back again last week for three days, and he's likely to be back again next week for three days before he goes again."

"Oh, Margaret, isn't that too delicious? Somehow I thought that would never happen to Kathie, she's so quiet and unworldly."

"Oh, do you think all men prefer noisy worldly women?"

"Well, no, I suppose not. Not if they know they are good cooks."

"Mercy!" said Margaret Graeme with an amused laugh, "what an unpleasant idea of marriage you must have!"

"Why no, I haven't really, Margaret, only naturally a man would take some account of what he was getting into when he set out to get married, and if a girl wasn't stunningly pretty, or a smart dresser, or a good cook and housekeeper, why naturally he wouldn't let himself get crazy about her. Oh, of course, Kathie is fairly good-looking, not stunningly pretty as Jessica was you know—"

"There are differences of opinion you know, about looks. I certainly never felt that Jessica was even pretty, certainly not beautiful."

"How funny, Margaret. You certainly are queer. I always thought Jessica was a raving beauty, but your ideas and mine never did jibe. However, as I was saying, I never did think Kathie had enough initiative to go out and get her a man."

"I should hope not!" said Margaret fervently. "Of all disgusting things the worst I think is a girl who lowers herself enough to let it be seen that she is out to try to *catch* a man. That isn't a girl's place, Louella, to go out after a man. If the man wants her it is his place to seek her."

"Oh, Margaret Graeme, you are so far behind the times you don't understand that no man in these days would ever go out after *any* girl unless she first courted him. Certainly not one as quiet as Kathie. I used to think it was hopeless for Kathie ever to expect to get married."

Margaret Graeme only smiled.

"Well, I'm glad my daughter isn't of the type to go out after a man. Better a thousand times that she go unmarried than that she should demean herself by setting out after a man. What kind of a marriage would that make? There would be no happiness at all where the girl had lowered herself that way."

"Oh, Margaret! You certainly are old-fashioned! But that isn't the way the world looks at that question today. The girls all understand that they must do all they can to get them a man before somebody else gets him, and I'm sure Kathie is to be congratulated on getting one that you think is so fine, but remember, after she's got him she must keep him, and she'll never do it by being such a demure little thing as you've brought her up to be. She simply can't compete with the girls of today."

"I'm afraid I wouldn't want her to do that, Louella. A happy marriage is not built along such lines, and there is nothing worse than an unhappy marriage."

"Oh, no, you're mistaken, Margaret, not in these days. There is always divorce now, and it is so common today that one is not outlawed by it. In fact divorcées are very attractive to men. They really have the advantage of young girls in many cases."

"Well, Louella, divorce is something we do not consider in our family. In fact I don't think many Christians do. We just don't believe in it you know."

"Oh! *Chris*tians!" said Louella with a shrug and a sneer. "Of course, I forgot how narrow-minded you are. By the way, Margaret who is that coming up your front walk? Isn't that a telegraph boy? He's on a bicycle. Yes, I'm sure it is. He has brass buttons on his cap. Would you like me to go to the door for you? Then you won't have to disturb your knitting."

"No, thank you, Louella," said Margaret Graeme gently. "I don't disturb so easily."

"Well, I'm sure I only offered to help you," said Louella offendedly. Quietly, without replying, Margaret Graeme laid her knitting down and went to the front door. She came back immediately with the telegram in her hand, and stepped into the kitchen to give an order to the servant, Hetty, and then came back standing the telegram up on the mantel by the clock, where Louella tried in vain to read the name it bore.

"Well," said Louella at last, impatiently, "what was it?"

"A telegram. You were right Louella, it was the telegraph boy."

"But what was the telegram? How really trying you are, Margaret. I've just been quivering to know what has happened. Was it from Washington? I'm dying to know what the boys' orders are."

"Oh! Why Louella, the telegram was not for me, so of course I do not know what it was about."

"But it was for some member of your family, wasn't it? Didn't you open it? Aren't you *going* to open it, and find out?"

"Certainly not, Louella. I don't open other people's telegrams. What do you think I am? It is a private message and I would not think of opening it."

"But—your own family, Margaret. How ridiculous! If it's for some of your children, or even your husband, surely you have a right to find out about it. It might be something quite important that ought to be attended to at once."

"No," said the mother, "it would not be my business to open it, unless I had been told to open it and find out, and send them word."

"How perfectly silly you are. I'm sure I wouldn't like to live with your conscience. Well, then, suppose *I* open it for you, and if anybody finds fault you can blame it on me."

"No!" said Margaret with finality. "The telegram is not ours and you will *not* open it."

"Well, I'm sure I never heard of anything so silly! Suppose we dampen it and pry it open and find out if it is anything important, and then seal it up again. I used to be quite expert at that sort of thing when I was a girl."

"No," said Margaret firmly, "we do not do underhanded things like that in this house. Let's forget the telegram, Louella, and suppose you show me how to make that crochet stitch you told me about the other day. Here is some pink wool. Is this the kind of needle you use or would you rather have a larger one?"

And so for the time being the subject was changed, but Louella kept turning wistful eyes toward the mantel shelf where the yellow envelope stood. Twice she tried strategy, inventing reasons for her hostess to go into the kitchen and see who was at the back door, after she had heard Hetty go upstairs, so she would have an opportunity to get nearer to the address on that envelope. She was consumed with a desire to know whose name it bore. But Margaret Graeme was canny, and could explain every noise at the back door, and did not leave her trying guest alone with that letter. At last Louella got discouraged and decided that it was high time for her to get home and telephone Jessica if she expected to catch her before she went out for the afternoon. But she felt that she had at least some progress to report. And then of course she was never at a loss for filling in from her prolific imagination, what facts did not give her. And there was that mysterious telegram on the mantel for a start.

And so at last Louella departed. Making excuse, however, to return to search the floor and her chair for a possible dropped handkerchief she was sure she had with her when she came. And during her careful search she had opportunity to see that the telegram was still on the mantel, and Margaret Graeme had been as good as her word and had not taken opportunity to open the envelope as soon as she had left. That was what she had hoped to catch her doing, and then surely she might be able to discover to whom it had been sent.

But Margaret was sitting there serenely where she had left her, still thoughtfully, almost wearily, knitting. Louella always did make her very weary. Her mind had to be so keenly on the alert to avert disasters of one sort and another, especially the leaking out of private family matters that Louella ached to discover and broadcast.

So at last Louella was gone, and Margaret might draw a free breath. She walked to the window to see her going down the hill toward her hotel—just to make sure she would not be returning within the minute.

Rodney came in a little while later and read his telegram.

"Has Chatty been here yet today mom?" he asked as he cast his eye about the room and noted Louella's favorite chair brought in from the other room, and placed to good advantage for conversation.

"Chatty" was the nickname given the unloved cousin in derision. The mother smiled.

"Why yes, how did you know?"

"Isn't that her ball of yarn under the chair, and a handkerchief with red cherries around the border? They could belong to none other than our garrulous relative." He grinned, and the mother smiled sympathetically back again.

"Well, mom, that telegram is my bid to come down to Washington next week and broadcast, but don't tell her, in case she comes back to find out what it was."

"Oh no, of course not," said the mother with a twinkle. "I've already had my troubles to keep her from opening the envelope and discovering for herself what it was."

"Brave woman. I'll pin a medal on you for that," said the boy, stooping over and planting a kiss on his mother's smiling lips.

Jeremy stood at one side grinning and watching them.

"What do you suppose she wants to know for?" he asked. "Is she just curious, or did she have some ulterior motive?"

"I'm sure it would have been ulterior, whatever the reason," said Rodney with a wry grin.

"Well, if you ask me, Rod," said Jeremy, "*I* think she was gathering fodder to feed to your old flame Jessica."

"*What?*" said Rodney, looking at his brother sharply. "What makes you say that? Have you got some dope you haven't told me about?"

"Not definitely, but I know the habit of the woman—or perhaps I should say women. What do you suppose your former fiancée is hanging around here all this time for, anyway? I understood she was only here for a day or two, didn't you?"

"I didn't understand anything about it," grouched Rodney. "I wasn't interested."

Afterward, upstairs in their room together:

"Well, if I might advise," said Jeremy loftily, "I should say it might be to your advantage to find out what's going on, brother. You know that baby isn't one who ever does anything without reason, and it's just as well to find out and take the sting out of it before she gets in any of her deadly work."

"H'm!" said Rodney thoughtfully. "Perhaps you're right. I'll look into it. But you understand Jerry, I don't want to be connected with Jessica in *any* way. I'll look into it, but it will have to be through you, or somebody else. I simply *will not* have anything more to do with that double-crossing, slippery little sneak. She is not to be trusted for an instant, and I want nothing more to do with her. Not even to stop her connivances. However, I'll take some means to let her understand that it is of no use to try anything more with me, and I feel it in my soul she's plotting something of that sort, and is trying her best to make that silly cousin of ours help her get it across."

"Well," said Jerry, "I'm glad you see that much. I certainly am. I was afraid there one time you were going to feel sorry for the poor little brat, the way you used to do sometimes when you caught her in one of her flirtations in high school, and then she turned weepy on you and you made it up with her."

"Yes, I know," said Rodney with his brows in a heavy frown. "I was a fool then, but I've found it out now. I didn't spend all those days and nights up in the sky with nobody but God and the enemy around, for nothing. I found out a lot of things about myself, even besides my sins. But Jerry, you were only a little kid in those high school days, just in the freshman class. How did you know anything about all that?"

"What do you think I was? Dumb? I reckon I saw a whole lot that you didn't even know. I saw, and I heard, and I watched, and I grew up watching. And maybe I did worry a lot about my big brother. For I didn't trust that sleek hypocrite of a girl, not one little bit. I saw and heard a lot more than you thought I would, and I'm not meaning mebbe."

Rodney studied his brother's face searchingly for a minute, and then he said, "I'll bet you did, kid, and the more fool I was that I didn't see it, too. Yes, with the kind of mother I've got I ought to have seen it myself, first off the bat. Thanks, awfully, kid, for having seen it, and stuck by me, and kept your mouth shut. But now I hope I can get by without any more contacts."

"Well, it may be so," mumbled Jeremy, half whistling as he talked, "but knowing that gal as I've watched her, I think not. I think she means to get it back on you yet, unless you're mighty cautious, lad."

"I guess you've forgotten something, haven't you buddy? I've got a Lord now, and He's keeping guard over me. 'He'll not let my soul be lost,' you know, 'He will hold me fast.'"

"That's right, brother," said Jeremy with a lovely light in his eyes. "Sure, brother, I forgot you had that now. The enemy may be strong but he can't get by that defense. I say, Rod, it's something great, isn't it, to be at home again, and to live this new life together, with a Saviour like ours. 'Able to keep, and to present us faultless!' Sometimes I just revel in that thought, 'able to keep' and 'to present us *faultless.*'" And then in the dimness of the hall as they started downstairs for lunch, the two brothers felt for each other's hands in a strong happy clasp of rejoicing.

## 14

BUT the next day there were letters, and phone calls, some of which sought to change the bright future good times the young people had planned.

The letters were for Diana. One from her mother, saying she was so glad that her daughter was having a delightful visit with her old college mate, but wasn't she almost ready to come home? Didn't she realize how many gay affairs she was missing, how many old friends were home on furloughs, who would be going back again overseas, perhaps for a longer stay? And they were being given parties. There were even a few weddings, unexpectedly soon, weddings in which of course Diana must participate. There was Rush Horrmann's and Lannie Freeman's wedding. She mustn't miss that, and Lannie had just called to say she wanted Diana for her maid of honor. And there was a simply huge affair for the Red Cross Drive. She mustn't miss that on any account. She owed that to her mother who was president, even if she were not interested on her own account.

"And then my dear," went on the mother, coming gently to the crux of the matter in her last few sentences, "do you realize at all how you are treating poor dear Bates Hibberd? Does that seem quite fair to him that you should go flying off after an old college mate, just at the time when Bates was coming home with new honors? And he has always been so devoted to you. Why he confided to me only yesterday that he had hoped to get you to name the day while he is home this trip, and was planning to coax you to get married right away. And just think my dear how much you'll be missing of pomp and ceremony if you should happen to wait so long that the war would be over and you couldn't have a real military wedding. Uniforms do make a wedding so picturesque you know, and it would be simply calamitous if you were to miss that. I could never forgive you. I was looking at Bates yesterday while he was talking with me and he did look so handsome in his new officer's uniform. It is just gorgeous. And so my dear I wish you would bid good-bye to your fascinating new friends and come home not later than Monday, but really I suggest that you come Saturday. Say to your friends there that it is *imperative*. After all you've certainly outstayed your invitation I am sure, and we all are getting quite hungry to see you again. The house seems terribly empty without you."

The other letter was from Bates Hibberd, perfect of diction, impeccable of stationery, demanding of tone, as if he had a perfect right to demand, and didn't understand why she hadn't come home of her own desire days ago.

> Dear Diana:
>
> I cannot understand your absence. After all, since we are engaged, it seems high time that it should be announced.
>
> How long do you intend to keep me waiting? I told you that I was coming home especially to talk over a very important matter with you, and I simply cannot understand why you are treating me this way.
>
> I wish you would come home AT ONCE, taking the first train after you receive this. I am making plans for a delightful surprise for you, and it is necessary that you be here before I fix the date.

There was more in this general line, in a most possessive tone, indicating that the young officer felt that she was virtually his to order around, and that his usually reasonable temper was roused beyond further endurance.

Diana sat pondering this letter for a few moments with a frown of worry on her lovely face, and then she went to her room and wrote an answer to that letter.

> Dear Bates:
>
> I am sorry that you feel that I have not treated you fairly, but it was just your very insistence that made it necessary for me to run away for a little while and do some thinking.
>
> You know, my friend, I have *never* agreed to your desire that we should be engaged. I have told you more than once that I do *not want* to marry *anyone* at present, nor to be engaged. We are *not* engaged, Bates, and it has been made very plain to me during my absence that I do not want to be engaged to you at all. You are my good friend, and that is all, and I wish you would accept that statement as final. I do not care for you as one should care for the man one is to marry, and I mean that definitely.
>
> I am sorry if I am hurting you by saying this, for you have always been my good friend from childhood, but this is truly the way I feel, and I would have no right not to make it plain to you.
>
> But I do hope you will understand, and that someday soon you will find someone else for whom you can truly care, who will make you very happy.
>
> Please forgive me for not having told you this sooner. I did not realize the situation fully before. But someday I hope you will be glad that I have written you this letter.
>
> Your true friend,
> Diana Winters

The answer to her mother's letter was not so easy to write, because she knew her mother would be terribly disappointed at her decision.

Dear Mother:

I'm sorry not to be able to come right home as you request, but Beryl has planned several lovely affairs for the next few days, in which I figure of course as her guest, and it would be quite disappointing both to her and to me if I could not be here. So I feel, after the Sandersons have gone to a good deal of trouble to show me a good time, that it would not be courteous for me to leave so abruptly. I cannot possibly see my way clear to leave before the middle or end of next week. One of the expeditions planned is a trip to Washington with a few friends, and they have secured us some rare privileges. Some returned officers from overseas are to broadcast, and it will be an interesting experience to be a part of the group.

And now mother, you speak of Bates Hibberd, but you know I have told you several times that we are *not* engaged, and he has no right to attempt to order my comings and goings. He is only an old friend and I have just written him quite definitely that I do not want to be engaged to him, and that this is *final*. I wish you would understand that I mean this mother.

I'll be home in time for your Red Cross Drive if possible. And I'll wire Lannie about her wedding. But meantime I'm having a delightful time here, and I wish you wouldn't worry about me.

Your loving
Diana

These letters were dispatched special delivery, Air Mail, and Diana drew a long breath and took courage. She felt that she had taken a very decided step in her new life, and that she was being honest with her own heart for the first time since Bates Hibberd had begun to pester her to marry him. In the light of the new life she had she was surprised to find how such questions fell into place, and were clear and plain before her. For one thing Bates Hibberd wouldn't be in sympathy with her living a Christian life, that she knew definitely. He did not go to church and hated religious things. But clearest of all came the knowledge to her that she did not love him, and that she could not enter into a close relation like marriage with one whom she did not love. Yes, he was handsome, and rich, and influential, and could give her a fine social position, but those things did not count now. She had found a Saviour, a Redeemer, a Guide, and she had found a joy that no royal social position could give her. She was content.

So Diana had one night of restful happy sleep, and then very early the next morning, the telephone rang, and her mother's angry voice called her, demanding that she come back into the world from which she had fled.

"I'm sorry, mother," she began, but the sharp voice at the other end of the wire interrupted her.

"No, there is no use for you to begin making excuses," said the angry voice of her mother. "I'm not going to have any more of this. You are my child and I know what is right and fitting for one of our family. I'm not going to have you play-ing fast and loose with a man as fine and distinguished and definitely wonderful as Bates Hibberd. It just can't be done, and I *demand* that you come home at once, starting this morn-ing! That is an order from your mother!"

There was a distinct moment of silence and then Diana, trying to keep her voice from trembling, said firmly:

"Listen, mother! Have you forgotten that I am of age, and have a right to control my own movements?"

"*Indeed!*" said the icy voice of the parent.

"I don't like to talk like that to you, mother dear, but this is something that I have to decide for myself. I am *not* going to marry a man because he is fine and distinguished and wonderful. That isn't what you married my father for, I know, for you've often told me how you cared about him, and I certainly do not care for Bates in that way. I think marriage would be awful without love!"

"Nonsense!" said the mother. "You don't know what love is! You're too young to know!"

"Then I'm too young to get married," said Diana firmly.

"That's ridiculous! If you are as young as that you'd better realize that your mother knows what's best for you, better than you do. You'll love him all right when you are married to him. Besides he's likely going away to war again very soon, and you'll have plenty of time to get used to the idea after he's left for overseas. It would really be best for you to marry him at once, and get the question settled. It isn't fair to him to keep him uncertain."

"He need not be uncertain, mother. I have written him very fully, and I'm sure he could not misunderstand. I told him I hoped he would soon find someone else to make him happy, and that we would of course always be friends."

"Yes, I know what you have written. Bates brought your letter over to me to read the first thing this morning, and I consider it was a most insulting letter for a daughter of mine to write to a good respectable young man, one who belongs to a fine old family, and has always been most kind and attentive to you. A man who had offered you his love and his name—"

"I beg your pardon, mother, I don't think he ever did. He just ordered me to be engaged to him, and told me we were going to be married, in spite of the fact that I told him I wasn't *ready* to marry *anyone* at present; and that isn't my idea of love. I said no, every time he talked about the subject, and that is the reason that I ran away from home when he came back. I wanted to think this thing all out and know exactly how I felt. And now I know, mother, and I am *not* going to marry Bates. I'm not even going to be engaged to him *tentatively*, or anything like that. And I *mean* what I say! I've grown up, mother, and I know what I *don't* want. And I'm not coming home just now. I'm sorry to disappoint you, but I've made certain engagements to do things and go places here, and I'm going to keep them. I'll run up to New York for a day or so for your drive, just to go on record, but I'm coming right back here until you've put aside all idea of this Bates Hibberd proposition, and I can come home and be myself without danger of running into an argument."

"Diana, I *insist* that you come home at once!"

"No, mother, not now."

"Diana, you don't know what you are doing to your life!"

"Yes, mother, I definitely do, and it's what I want to do."

"You'll be sorry!"

"No, I won't be sorry!"

"Diana, you never talked to your mother this way before."

"No, mother, and I wish I didn't have to do it now, but if I had done it before perhaps I wouldn't have to be doing it now. I mean if I had told you long ago how I felt about Bates, and the way he took me for granted as if I belonged to him, ordered me around and everything, I think you would have understood that I would *never* care for him."

"Diana, I can't listen to any more of this silly twaddle over the telephone. You simply must come home at once! If you think you are grown up, then act it. This isn't the way a refined well-bred woman acts toward her mother. I want you to come home now and get this straightened out at once. It breaks my heart to have any differences come between us. You must come without delay. I am sure I'm on the verge of a nervous breakdown over this, and you must come today if you want to prevent any such result."

"Well, mother, I'm sorry I can't come for an appeal like that, but it just happens that I have promised to go with Beryl this morning and she really needs me. There is quite a good deal involved in this. We're going down to the canteen to teach the servicemen to sing in a chorus for an hour on the radio that we're preparing them for, and I have to play for the singing, because we have only one copy of the music and I'm the only one who knows it."

"How silly! Let them choose another song then."

"It's too late, mother. Beryl has already gone, and I wouldn't know how to reach her. She had to go early to get the chairs arranged. And besides, it's almost time for their last rehearsal, and they come on at two o'clock, so you see I've got to rush, even now."

"Well, then, come on the three o'clock train."

"But mother, we're due at a dinner right after that. We've barely time to get dressed after we get back from the broadcast. And mother, it's just as I told you. Every minute is arranged for up to the last of next week. I really couldn't change things. It would be awfully rude, after Mr. Sanderson has spent so much time and money arranging to get us tickets and reservations for all the activities we've planned."

"But Diana, I don't know you. You never acted like this before when I asked you as a favor to me to do something."

"Mother, you were always reasonable, all my life. You never wanted me to do rude things, simply for a whim. I am quite sure anything you want to say about this matter of Bates can wait until I come. And I'm sure if I came now you would get no other answer from me than the one I have given. I am not engaged to Bates, and I never will be, no matter how desirable you may think he is. It would be I who would have to live with him afterward, and that I *never will* do."

"Oh, Diana. How you are grieving me! I am sure when you think this over you will be ashamed, and I shall be waiting to see you arrive on a later train this evening."

"No, mother, I can't do that. Good-bye now, I must go." And Diana in response to a call from downstairs, hung up the receiver, snatched her hat and gloves and hurried down the stairs, and out the door. She was almost sure she heard the phone ringing again as she went down the street, but the bus was almost to the corner and she had to run to catch it.

Diana, as she settled down in the only vacant seat, was not

very happy in her heart. Somehow it came to her that this did not seem to be a very good way to begin a Christian life, being almost rude to her beloved mother, refusing to grant her request. But what else could she have done? If there had been any real need of her at home, if her mother had really been ill, of course she would have gone at once, no matter how many engagements had to be broken. But she knew her mother's ways, and she was well aware that if she had been quite free to go it would only mean a long session of arguments, with Bates dragged into them, until she was wearied of her life. She could not yield this time and get into the toils of those two again. Too many times she had been aruged with until she scarcely knew how to answer, and this was what she had come off here for, to get away from that demand to marry Bates, or at least to let her mother give her an announcement party and be in the public eye in such a way that she could not get away from it without seeming to be dishonorable, or what would be worse in her mother's eyes, without making it appear that Bates had let her down. How her soul shrank from such dishonorable actions!

All the way in to the canteen hall where they were to practice, Diana sat with closed eyes and quietly prayed in her heart:

"Dear Lord, show me what to do. Help me somehow to keep my obligations and yet not to hurt my dear mother."

"Now," she said in her heart as she got out of the bus at her destination, "please help me to forget this and do my duty till it is over, and then show me what is right."

The rehearsal went well. Diana roused from her distractions and played with abandon, and interest, and the sailors sang well. The radio man came in as they were singing the final song, and applauded.

"That's great!" he said genially. "If you do that well this afternoon you'll bring the house down."

The rest of the day was so full that Diana had no time to think any more of her own perplexing problems. She had cast them off on her new Burden-Bearer, and she was just resting on that.

But when they got back to the Sanderson home just at dinner time, there was the telephone ringing, and Diana looked up alertly as the maid said, "Miss Winters, that phone is for you. Your mother has been trying to get you all the afternoon." Then the great burden of worry dropped down upon her young shoulders again like a heavy weight. As she went toward the telephone, her hands trembling almost too much to take down the receiver, she was praying in her heart: "Oh my Heavenly Father, please help me. Show me what to say, make me understand what I ought to do."

Then came her mother's voice, no longer sharp and implacable. Just hurried, almost apologetic.

"Diana, is that you? Have you come at last? Well, I've been trying to get you for the last two hours. I'm glad you've come, for I have to leave almost at once. Your father is preparing to go to California for a couple of weeks and he wants me to go with him, so you better delay your return till I get back. I have just been talking with Bates, and he has received unexpected orders to report back at camp as soon as he can get there. He will be back again later, and all these matters can be settled then. So now you can keep your promises to your friend, and turn over in your mind this question about your engagement, and see if you don't want to change your mind. So I hope you will be satisfied. But meantime I forgive you for your rudeness, and I hope you will be able to see things sensibly by the time I get back. I will write you on the way, and give you our address later so you can write me. Meantime, have a good time, darling, and get ready in your mind for a grand big announcement party when we get back. Now good-bye dearest. I must go. Your father is calling."

As Diana hung up the receiver and turned to go her face was alight.

"What's the matter, dear?" asked Beryl. "You look as if you had received a reprieve."

"I have," said Diana smiling. "I was afraid I was going to have to go home at once and miss all your nice times, but now the plans have changed and I can stay till we get back from Washington."

"How grand!" said Beryl. "But somehow the look on your face was more than just being glad over a good time."

"Well, it was," said Diana. "I was wondering if God always arranges troublesome things for you when you cry to Him for help?"

Beryl's face grew suddenly grave.

"Oh, I wouldn't know," she said. "I don't think I ever tried it. But I shouldn't be surprised if He *did*. You ask the boys. They'll know."

"I will," said Diana with a sweet look in her eyes. "But oh, I'm so glad God worked this out for me, for I was terribly afraid I was going to have to go home and have a very hard time, with my mother arrayed against me, and an old playmate determined to marry me right away—and I didn't *want* to."

"My dear!" said Beryl. "I'm so glad for you. I knew you didn't love that man you talked about yesterday. Well, now we can have a nice time going to Washington, can't we?"

"Yes," said Diana with a happy smile. "And I'm so glad that my mother isn't angry with me. She has always been very domineering and insisted I should go her way, but I do love her, and I hate to have her out of harmony with me."

"Of course you do, dear. I understand."

"Beryl, you are the most understanding friend I have. Except perhaps my father. He always seems to know what I mean and to feel just as I do about things. He's a wonderful daddy!"

"So is mine," said Beryl. "But my mother usually understands too."

"Yes, you have a wonderful mother!"

"Yes, I have," said Beryl, "except perhaps sometimes she's a little bit afraid of things I want to do."

"But that's because she loves you so, and wants to put a hedge around you to protect you."

"Yes," said Beryl. "And perhaps if you would study the subject carefully you might find that the things your mother wants for you are things she *thinks* would protect you."

Diana studied her friend's face seriously.

"Perhaps you're right," she admitted slowly. "She probably thinks Bates' riches and power and influence will be a wall around me to make me safe everywhere, and she doesn't at all realize what it would be to marry someone I do not love. She is so thoroughly sold on Bates herself, having always admired him from the time he was a child, that she cannot take it in that I am not. She thinks I haven't grown up yet and don't know my own mind, but that it would be all right if I found myself married to such a wonderful young man. This I suppose is because I was so undecided myself when I came away from home. I was trying to please everybody except myself, and yet not yield to my own uneasy feelings. Thank you for giving me that thought. I must treat my mother much more tenderly in the future. I can see I have not always done that, especially yesterday, on the telephone. But I am thankful that she was in such a hurry getting ready to go with father that I think for the time being she had forgotten it. I must write her a sweet letter, and help her to keep forgetting."

And then there came a call from the Graemes, proposing a tennis match for the morning, dinner in town, and a meeting in the evening at which a wonderful Bible teacher was to speak, and the conversation ended with joy on their faces. Still there was something about it that could not be forgotten, and its essence returned to Diana's newly awakened conscience again and again.

15

THE next two days were quiet ones, little excursions planned on the spur of the moment. It was taken for granted that all the group would go everywhere together. No more apologies for keeping up this constant friendly fellowship. It was as if they were a lot of children, brought up together, glad that they belonged together. Yet behind it all was the constant realization that this could not last forever. It would soon be over when the boys were sent somewhere. There would be lonely days after this delightful companionship.

They were taking every day as if it were something precious, dealt out to them hour by hour, knowing that when it was gone there might be no return of the joy they were spending so lavishly. Not that they thought it out in these phrases. They would none of them perhaps have reached the place where they would be willing to admit how much it all meant to them, but at night, when each was by himself, they would think the day over almost breathlessly, and plan that the next day should be savored even more happily.

They were doing all their planning toward their trip to Washington for the broadcast, as if it were a kind of climax of their happiness. When they returned, well, there would doubtless be something soon to separate them, at least for a time. For one thing Diana was likely to be called home by an irate and demanding mother, and she had hinted more than once that there would be problems for her to solve, problems which would not only affect her new Christian life, but might even make trouble for her at home. Rodney had thought a great deal about the few words she had dropped along these lines, and had been praying for her, not only that her anticipated trials might not be as great as she feared, but that she might be able to bear them, even if they were worse than feared.

She had noticed that a great gentleness had come upon him of late, and when they walked together his words would be low and quiet, and now and again his strong comforting hand would be laid over hers as it rested on his arm. And once, when they were walking so, quietly, on the shady side of a moonlit street, it suddenly came to her to wonder what it would be if this were Bates walking so with her, and she knew that she would shrink from such contact with his hand. Bates' immaculately cared-for hands! And yet their touch would not be welcome to her. Would not be so comforting, would be almost revolting to her. Then suddenly she knew beyond the shadow of a doubt that she did not love Bates Hibberd.

Oh, she had been saying so for several days, to her mother over the telephone, to Beryl, tentatively to herself, reassuring herself, just to be sure she hadn't made the mistake that her mother and Bates would keep telling her she had made. For she had been dreading the time when she would have to go home, very soon, and meet all this again. *How* she had been dreading it! But now, she was not afraid any more, for something new had come to take the place in her heart that had been so uncertain. What was this something new? Was it just that she had a new friend, who had taught her to love the Lord? Was that a little thing? It seemed so great, so wonderful. And it was something apart from the friendly relations of earth. Something that almost seemed like a holy relationship, one that had nothing to do with world-ideas of jealousies. A relationship that had its center in Jesus Christ, that did not base its being on good looks, although there was plenty of that if one were counting it, or on wealth, or even on possession. It was something bigger than worldly relationships.

Of course it would be a wonderful thing if a man like this one loved her and wanted to marry her. She would not have to wait and ponder over a question like that. She would feel that just to walk with a young man like Rodney through her life on earth would be the greatest blessing Heaven could bestow. But she had not a thing like that to consider. He had not asked her, and it was not a thing that was likely to come to her. She was not good enough for him. And she had not been thinking of love with reference to him. But she could see that God had sent him her way that she might know, and understand, what a man whose life was hid with Christ in God, could be; and how she must on no account link her life with a man who did not know Christ. And while this was no time for her to be considering any new idea of marriage, it certainly was a time to decide whom she should *not* marry.

And suddenly with that thought a great burden rolled away from her. She did not have to consider marriage any more. Not unless God sometime sent her a companion of His own choosing. She might be just happy now, and have a good time, learning to know God and to follow her new Guide.

But while Diana was thinking these thoughts, Jessica was on her way to a consultation with the husband she had married so hasitly, called to him by an insistent telegram, peremptorily ordering her attendance at once.

Jessica was very much annoyed about it, because Louella had particularly promised to have some more news for her this very morning, news that would have reference to the immediate movements of the Graeme brothers, and she had not had time to get Louella on the telephone before she took the train designated in her husband's orders. She had already learned by the hardest way that it did not do to disobey orders. No one else in the world but Carver De Groot had ever been able to make Jessica do anything unless she wanted to do it, and she certainly did not want to drop her present pursuit of her former lover and go traveling away off out in what she called "the Sticks" after a mere husband, from whom the glamour had long since worn off. But Carver De Groot had ways of his own, severe ways which did not waste time in coaxing. He gave the word of command and expected it to be obeyed, and one disobedience needed but the one penalty to bring about a future obedience. Jessica had learned her lesson the hard way, but she had learned. And perhaps her almost penniless condition made her the more easily adaptable.

For Carver De Groot had a deep purse, though he held the purse strings exceeding tight. Still there was great wealth behind those purse strings, and when they were loosed to an obedient one there was a generous sum, and sometimes a jewel now and again. So it behooved Jessica to go when he called, and to cast about her a cloak of unaccustomed humility.

So it was with haste and a meek spirit that she walked into the old De Groot homestead, set away back from the highway amid shrubbery well hidden from curious eyes, and maintaining a shabby outward show, to further camouflage its inner glories. This quality of staid ancient shabbiness was by no means an asset to Jessica, and she had wasted many precious tears, and angry words to try to change this feature, but found she could in nowise change a jot or tittle of the place. At last she began dimly to understand that behind it all there was some fixed and unchangeable reason, something that had to do with the war mysteriously, and because it frightened her to think of it she calmly put it out of her mind. It wasn't her problem. And when she protested that he had promised her good times—how could she have good times so far away from everything and everybody at all interesting?—she was told that she need not stay there for her good times. There would be plenty of opportunities to go out and away, and she would be hindered in nothing she wanted to do except at certain times when he would demand her attendance, and help, often in matters of great importance to his business. But she need not ask about that business. When the time came he would tell her all she needed to know to help him, and nothing more, so she would be in no danger of giving out forbidden information. He had impressed it upon her that he was working for the government (what one?) and she certainly knew there were many matters that for the time of war must be kept secret. So there would be no use of her asking questions just to satisfy her curiosity. In fact, she had considered this matter before marrying, and decided that she would be a girl most discreet, able to keep her mouth shut and do as she was told.

So she walked hastily up the steps of the old shabby house, down the luxuriously furnished hall, to the door of her husband's office, otherwise designated as the library.

She tapped lightly with the tips of her well-cared-for fingers a kind of a code which she had been carefully taught.

There were sounds of voices inside the door, which ceased with her knock, and a cold voice bade her come in.

Chin up she walked arrogantly into the room and faced the hard cold eyes of her elderly husband. The man with the cruel mouth, and the sharp, sharp eyes that always saw too much, and searched back into any past in which he cared to interest himself.

The cold eyes were searching her face now, and the cold voice said:

"Well, so you decided to come back at last!"

"I came as soon as I got your message," drawled the girl indifferently. "I understood you to order me to stay there until I heard from you."

"H'm! I didn't notice that it was a very great trial to you to go to the town your former fiancé was soon to come to."

"I understood that was the reason you sent me there," said Jessica. "You distinctly asked me to look him up at once when he arrived and get in touch with him."

"Did you do it?"

"I certainly did my best."

"Just what did you do? I haven't had any report yet."

"There wasn't anything to report," said Jessica in a calm tone. "I wasn't able yet to get in touch with him."

"Just what did you do? Why couldn't you get in touch with him? He arrived at his home, didn't he?"

"Yes, he arrived, and I went at once to the house and entered just as I used to, going right out to the dining room where they were all sitting down at the table, but by the time I got there Rod wasn't there, and nobody seemed to know where he was."

"Well? What then?"

"He didn't come back. And nobody would tell just where he was. If it had been in the old days of course I would have gone through the house hunting for him, but they didn't give me any chance to do that."

"I thought you were a clever girl."

"Yes, I thought so too."

"Why didn't you go to some of his family?"

"I did. I did everything I knew how, but apparently they are all in league with him. I chased him everywhere I heard of his being, but there was always somebody with him. I even went to an old religious meeting to try and see him, and he just walked out on me before I could get near him. I got close to a stupid old gossip of a cousin of his and she tried to work things for me, and she's getting news about his movements for me now, but so far I haven't got any definite news. If you hadn't sent such an imperative order for me to come back I should have stayed, for today was going to be a critical time. The stupid cousin seemed to think she was right on the verge of a discovery. She thinks it's going to be Naval Intelligence. Does that mean anything to you?"

"It certainly does,' said the man with a glint of fire in his stony eyes. "It's most important. I had begun to think you were a flat tire, but if you can manage to get into an office where that matter is carried on, especially if you can manage an intimate interview where you would have opportunity to ask a lot of questions, perhaps overlook some papers with important writing, get familiar with the office, arrange to meet him at his place of work. Of course it will likely be well guarded, but you would have to plan a way to get in there. You would probably know how best to get around your man, having known him for years. Then when you get that far there will be a way to get hold of some important papers we want, and you will have to keep your eyes open. I'll write a list of words and phrases you are to look for. And there is a paper we very much need for evidence that must be destroyed."

"Destroyed? How could I destroy anything?" asked Jessica with a startled look. "You promised me there would be no danger connected with what I had to do."

"No, no danger. There are ways you know. Little time bombs that can be left around near a safe, or close to a file of records, or wherever you discover they are keeping the kind of papers we need. That of course is the most important part of your mission. And the danger will be scarcely appreciable. Of course when you have arranged your blast—it is just a little thing like a pencil, scarcely noticeable—you will have to arrange to get out quickly and get downstairs out of danger, but I'm sure by that time you will be familiar enough with the place to have that all fixed up beforehand."

"But there must be danger connected with a thing like that!"

"Look here, Jessica. Did you ever see a stone like this?"

Jessica turned frightened eyes toward the velvet case the stern husband was holding out toward her. It was white velvet, and in the center shone a great blue diamond, its wonderful lights stabbing her in the face, stirring her heart with envy, and longing.

"Oh, that's wonderful!" said Jessica. "It's a blue diamond, isn't it? Yes, I saw one once in New York in an exhibit of stones, but I never saw such a lovely one. Oh, Carver, where did you get it? Is it yours?"

The sinister eyes were gloating over the look in the girl's eager face. Then he pronounced the words for which he had demanded her presence.

"It is yours, if you carry out my orders!"

"Oh, Carver! I'd do *any*thing to own that!"

"Even if there were danger connected with its possession?"

The frightened look came back and peered out through the eager light, but it was as if with an impulsive movement of her hands she brushed the fear aside and made her quick decision.

"Yes," she said. "Yes, no matter what the danger. I should worry. I want that stone at all costs."

"Very well!" said the cold voice, now full of calm satisfaction. "Just do your part and the stone will be yours! Now, you better get back to the job and don't let any opportunities pass you by. Get intimate with that old-time boy-friend, and I don't mean maybe."

There followed instructions, some in code which she had already learned, some given orally.

When Jessica started back to Riverton, she carried in her mind's eyes the gleaming stone of which she had just been given another gorgeous glimpse. She had even been allowed to hold it against her white hand, and note the rainbow tints that shot through it, her face full of gloating eagerness. To have that jewel for her own! What more could any girl desire?

All through her return journey Jessica was thinking about that jewel, though occasionally her conscience, or whatever it was she used for a conscience, told her that she really ought to be planning how she was going to recover her old hold on Rodney Graeme.

But it was the thought of the jewel and how it would look on her slender hand. That sustained her. She could go in triumph back to Riverton. She would show it to Rodney and let him see how she had gained by giving up his little white diamond. Oh, of course his wasn't really little. It was wonderfully large for a boy in college to be able to get with his own savings, and she had been proud of it then, but of course it was silly to try to stick to it when she had a chance at bigger things, and she was glad she had had the courage to send that ring back. Perhaps she had been foolish. She might have kept it, and strung him along. Then she would have had another ring in her collection. Of course there was the emerald she got from the French diplomat that winter she spent in Washington, and the star sapphire the young Russian officer had given her at the beginning of the war, and the ruby from that silly man she met at the mountains that last summer before she was married. Why hadn't she kept Rodney's diamond? Just because she hated to tell him she had let him down. She had sent that ring back to break it to him gently. Just because the Graeme family were so frightfully conscientious, and would think she was so awful to keep a diamond ring for nothing.

Wild thoughts like these kept flashing through her mind, and then an idea came to her. After all it was what she was supposed to be doing on this journey back to Riverton, thinking up some way to get back into Rodney's good graces, and wasn't that ring a key to it? That was it. A legitimate reason for getting into touch with him. She would ask to have the ring back!

How could she manage it? Well, there would be a way. And that nice little diamond would make a good guard for this lovely big blue jewel!

So visions of diamonds with big blue lights danced through her empty head as she settled down in the Pullman coach and went to sleep. What would Louella say when she told her about the blue diamond? Or should she tell her? No, probably not. Part of the agreement was that she could keep her mouth shut.

16

AS the trip to Washington drew nearer the little company of young people who met almost daily at either Graemes' or Sandersons', grew more tense and almost excited. It wasn't the young man who was to speak on the radio who was tense or excited. For Rodney had been too long in the service to count a little testimony over the radio as anything much. Rodney was excited for entirely another reason. For he knew the time of their companionship was drawing nearer and nearer to a close, and he knew that in a very few short days now his own fate was to be decided, whether he would have to go back overseas, or serve in some way in this country, as had been hinted to him more than once by subtle questions.

And it wasn't that he was so deeply concerned about where he was to be located, on his own account, except that he wanted to be near home if possible. But it had come to him more and more every day that this companionship with the lovely Diana might be almost over. For Kathie had hinted to Jeremy, who had promptly conveyed the news to Rodney, that Diana was more than half committed to a rich handsome officer in the army whom she had known since childhood, one of a noble family, and greatly favored by Diana's people. So not only Rodney but equally his brother and sister were deeply disturbed over the possibilities of the future.

Now was the time of course when Rodney had opportunity to make sure about this, to offer his own love, and hope to win the girl who had come to mean so much to him. But Rodney did not feel that he had a right to commit himself to any girl until he knew what his immediate prospects were to be. He was just as old-fashioned as that. If he only could have asked her out plainly if she were engaged it would have been so much easier for him, but there was something innately fine about him that forbade him to rush her into an affair with one whom she scarcely knew as yet, and she was too fine herself to show more than lovely comradeship in her association with him. So it was only through their great expressive eyes, by a stray smile now and then, that any preference had been actually shown by either of them. Yet the eyes and a smile now and again can often start the heart beating, and so it was that these two were occupied with thoughts of one another, pleasant dealings with the outer edges of one another's lives, hovering around great questions each would like to ask, yet dreaded to broach lest the present joy of their fellowship should be in any way spoiled by bald facts.

And the other four young people were equally engaged in watching them. Kathie and her young chaplain as much interested as Jeremy and Beryl. For little by little Beryl had spoken of Bates Hibberd, and with an occasional question now and again Jeremy was pretty well acquainted with the complications, and dreaded lest his beloved brother had another disappointment in store for him. Oh, no, not *that,* dear Lord, not for Rodney!

As the day of the Washington trip drew near Jeremy came in the night before looking troubled.

"Say, Rod, that young highstrike of a Jessica didn't stay away after all. You know I told you I saw her taking the westbound train the other day. Well, she's back. Yes, I saw her this morning, and I'm almost certain she'll try to horn in on our trip if she finds out, and we don't do something about it."

"H'm!" said Rodney with perplexed brows. "What would you suggest we do? The railroad trains are free, we can't stop her, and we can't likely get gas enough to *drive* down. Besides dad needs the car."

"No, I don't need the car today," said the smiling father walking in just in time to hear the talk. "Take it and welcome. If that brazen girl once gets the idea that you are going some-where she'll manage somehow to go too. She's like a leech when she once gets hold. As for gas, Rod's broadcasting for the Government isn't he? He'll have no trouble getting what gas he needs."

"Sorry!" said Rodney looking exceedingly troubled. "Dad, I know you do need your car. It's all my fault of course. I should have had better sense than ever to have thought she was worth anything. Somebody ought to teach little kids that a pretty face isn't everything. But there, probably my mother did, only I didn't take it. I'm the sinner. I ought to pay the penalty. I might take the midnight train and go down by myself."

"No you won't, Rod. I don't intend to use the car today anyway," said the father again.

"Okay," said Jerry. "We'll start an hour earlier than we had planned and go in the opposite direction. Get mom to send a jar of honey to Aunt Polly, over in Andersonville, and go around by Prattsville. It can't be more than two or three miles out of the way, and we can get into the highway easily from there. And then when 'Chatty' comes over to mom to find out what has become of us she can tell her we took some hon-ey to our old cook. See?"

"Good scheme, brother. That ought to relieve the situa-tion," said Rodney. "I don't know what I'd do in my little old life without you, Jerry."

"Okay! Let's get to work. I'll call up the girls and tell them to be ready an hour sooner."

The next morning was bright and clear, and the young people were ready even earlier than necessary.

"Say, this is grand!" said Diana smiling at Jerry. "When did you think of this?"

"It's just a scheme to get away without having uninvited guests," said Jerry, grinning.

"Uninvited guests?" said Diana with a puzzled frown. "Would anybody try to do that?"

Jerry gave another wry grin.

"There are that would," he said with a comical wink. "Ever meet Jessica De Groot? Ever know our cousin Louella?"

"Oh! Would *they? Both* of them?"

"They work in pairs just now. Besides they know the car is seven passenger. One too many more or less means nothing to either of them in their young lives."

"What impossible people!" said Diana. "Of course I don't know them. I think I was introduced, perhaps at that meeting we attended when you spoke, but I didn't talk with them even, and I've only seen either of them in the distance since."

"They're best seen from a distance," said Jerry grimly. "Avoid them if you can!" And with another grin Jerry swung himself into his seat behind the wheel, and they were soon on their way.

There was perhaps more joy in that little carload of six young people on their way to Washington, than in any place in that land. Oh, there were still possibilities of separations and dread in the future of course, but for that day at least they had sunshine and a blue sky, they had each other, and no jealousies, no bitterness, no animosity in that whole company. Just gladness that God had made them and brought them together, and let them have this day with each other. They had escaped from a possible enemy of discord, and were having a nice time.

But back in Riverton the two allied enemies were holding a conference and getting ready to go to work in earnest, for now Jessica had something real to do, and she knew what she wanted to find out, and had spent some of the hours in the train when she ought to have been sleeping, planning out just how Louella could best help her. She had planned also just how she would open her campaign in order to lead her elderly ally to see what was expected of her, and would not be startled into drawing back, or hesitating. For at present Louella was Jessica's only possible connection with the source of her needed information, and Louella was not only proud but flattered to be her emissary on so important an errand.

They held their conference in the morning, and after a heartening lunch, Jessica went back to her room to take a restful nap, feeling that her morning had been well spent, and Louella put herself in battle array, and betook herself to the Graeme house to begin her first engagement of the new campaign.

She arrived at the Graemes' house just as Margaret Graeme had retired to her room to get a much-needed nap while her household moved on smoothly without her. The children would not be at home to dinner that night. They would probably all stay over in Washington, to drive home by moonlight if the weather continued favorable. So this was a good time to rest. She and her husband were going to be on hand to listen to the radio of course when Rodney was speaking, and then they were going to take the bus over to a friend's house to dinner. It was almost an unheard-of thing for them to be able to get away together this way, and it made a real holiday for them both. So Margaret had gone to rest with a real feeling of luxury upon her.

Father Graeme was out about the farm, looking over his fences to see if there were any places that needed mending, and getting things ready for the evening milking so that he would not be late in starting to the dinner party.

Hetty had gone on her semi-annual visit to a cousin in the

country, so there was nobody at home to go to the door when Louella rang persistently, over and over again, and Margaret Graeme slept calmly on, not aware of its ringing, nor of the feeble angry pounding of Louella's fist on the door. Just for once, perhaps because she was unusually weary, or because she was so fully relieved of the constant pressure from the daily routine, she slept on.

Louella at last was furious. She stepped out into the driveway and looked up at the windows, where the muslin curtains were blowing pleasantly in the afternoon breeze.

"Margaret! Oh Margaret!" she called insistently. "Where on earth are you?"

After several more calls she gave up and sat down on the steps to consider what she should do next. Then she heard the ring of a scythe against a stone, and listening sharply she located the sound over behind the barn. She got up forthwith and marched around the house till she could look out over the meadow and there she saw Donald Graeme. Climbing fearsomely up the rails of the fence she called in her refined angry little voice:

"Donald! *Oh,* Donald: Donald *Graeme!"*

Most emphatically the words rang out over the meadow, chiming in with the occasional ring of the steady scythe, going on with its rhythmic swinging.

Growing more and more indignant, Louella at last climbed the fence, at great risk to her treasured stockings and, incidentally, starting a run in one of them, and after stopping to express a few anathemas at the splinters on the fence rails, she arrived on the ground, struggled to her feet, and went storming over a strip of plowed ground that lay between her and the field where Donald was mowing.

He sighted her plunging among his carefully planted furrows of corn, and finally laid down his scythe and came to her rescue.

"Why, Louella!" he said sternly. "What is the matter? Has something happened?"

"Happened!" said Louella almost in tears. "I should say there had. I can't get into your house. I've rung and rung at that old bell of yours, and I've knocked till I've got the skin all off one knuckle, and then I went out and called and *called* up to your wife's window, but not a response could I get. I should like to know where that lazy Hetty is, and why doesn't she answer the bell? I wouldn't put it past her to have looked out the window and seen who it was, and refused to answer the bell just because she saw it was me. I declare Donald, I must have my key back again. I can't get on this way. It is too inconvenient. Here I've put a run in my new expensive stockings getting over that fence to reach you. I ought to charge those stockings up to you, Donald."

Donald grinned, looking very much like his son Jeremy:

"On what ground, Louella?" he asked.

"On the ground that you took away my key."

"But it wasn't your key, Louella, it was mine. And besides, if we are going to pay for things in that way, how much do you think I'm going to charge you for tramping and wallowing all over my nicely planted corn field?"

"Corn?" said Louella, looking wildly around. "I don't see any corn."

"No," said Donald. "But it's there. I just got it planted yesterday and now you've stepped everywhere over it."

"Well, how was I to know? There's no sign of any corn. It's all smooth. I don't think you should leave corn lying around loose that way if it's so valuable. But anyway, I came over here to find out where everybody is. I'm sorry if I've spoiled your cornfield, but I guess it'll come up just the same even if it is all messed up. Now, Donald, tell me where everybody is."

"Well," he said pleasantly as he guided her carefully over to the grassy edge of the field where she could do no more harm, "I think this is Hetty's day out. I saw her go down the lane a little while ago with her best bonnet on, and I don't think she's coming back before tomorrow morning."

"The very idea! Giving her all that time. No wonder she's

so horribly spoiled. I shouldn't think you'd allow Margaret to spoil her that way."

"What was it you came over for, Louella? Why did you want to see Margaret?"

"Oh, I just wanted to ask her a few questions."

"Well, suppose you ask me," smiled Donald genially. "You see I don't want to waken Margaret up just now. She got very tired yesterday and I've made it my business to keep it quiet for her till she wakens of her own accord."

"Is Margaret sick?" asked Louella sharply. "I'm afraid you spoil her just the way she is spoiling Hetty."

"Well, that's the way I like to have it," said Donald Graeme pleasantly. "That's the reason I married her. I loved her and wanted to take care of her always, and I'm doing it, Louella, to the best of my ability. So, now, what was it you wanted to ask?"

Louella was annoyed. She hadn't exactly formulated her questions to meet Donald's clear comprehension, and sharp eyes. He wouldn't just smile and pass it off the way Margaret was apt to do, nevertheless letting out a glint of information now and then so that she could enlarge upon it for her own purposes.

"Well," she said, fabricating a story in her mind rapidly as she was wont to do when she got in a corner, "I was thinking of having a little tea at the hotel for a few of my friends, and I wanted the boys to meet them. They are crazy to know them, and I thought Margaret would tell me just when she thought it would be convenient for them."

"Well, I'm sorry about that. I wouldn't be able to tell you about the boys' engagements. They change everyday you know. But I can tell you that they are not keen for any teas or anything of that sort. I warn you they'll get out of anything of that sort if you let them know about it beforehand. I haven't seen a single returning soldier or sailor who wants to be shown around and exhibited and asked what they did over there, so if you take my advice, Louella, you'll forget it. If you happen to meet them on the street or somewhere and have any of your curious friends along with you, well snap up your chance and introduce them if you can catch them long enough to accomplish it, but otherwise I'm sure you'll miss out. And don't ask me or Margaret when and where they'll be, for we really don't know. The boys have been so long under discipline that all they want now is freedom to do as they please. So we're determined to help them get it as long as they are with us. Of course we don't know how long it will be before they are ordered off again. And of course we don't know but they may be sent off to the Pacific. After all they are trained men, and will perhaps be needed."

"Oh, you don't really think that, Donald. You are expecting the boys to stay over here, you know you do. Why somebody told me the other day that they were almost positive those boys would both be retained over here for very important positions."

"That being the case we have not yet been informed, and I think it not advisable to say any more about it. If it were so we should probably not be allowed to say anything about it, so we'll just change the subject, shall we? Suppose we go over to the springhouse, shall we? I could get you a glass of ginger ale, or some grape juice.

"The boys took a lot of bottles down and left them in the springhouse last night. It's handy to have some cold there when we're working in the field you know. And there are two or three glasses there. Come on. It's just as easy for you to get to the highway back to your hotel as to go back the way you came. I don't think you're much of a fence climber. Come on."

So Louella was definitely cajoled across the rough ground to the springhouse where she was served with delightful cold drinks, apple juice first, and then a mixture of ginger ale and grape juice which proved a pleasant change from the ordinary drinks Louella was used to. Of course she wouldn't have minded if there had been a dash of something a little stronger in it, but for an afternoon refreshment at her dull over-conscientious cousin-in-law's house, especially when no one but this tiresome cousin seemed to be obtainable, it was better than nothing. And at last baffled in spite of herself, Louella went back to her apartment, and took to the telephone, calling up the sleeping Jessica, and complaining to her of her inability to get information whatever for her.

But Jessica was all filled with her new ideas of how she was going to get back her hold on Rodney, and she had a lot of questions to ask. What had been going on during the few days she had been away? Had those Sanderson people been around any? Had that Diana gone home to New York yet?

Of course Louella was in no position to answer these questions. In fact she hadn't been around much even with the Graemes during Jessica's absence. But always what Louella did not know she could easily make up, and she managed a fitting little story which hovered near the truth while allaying the fears of Jessica.

"I'm satisfied I shall be able to answer all those questions after I have seen Margaret Graeme for a few minutes. I am expecting to have a long talk with her tomorrow, in the morning I hope. And don't you worry, for I am sure from what my cousin Donald said today that the boys have not received their orders yet, and that nothing at all is settled. Donald even spoke as if there might be a possibility that the boys were to be ordered to the Pacific, but he said it in such a satisfied tone as if he were not worried that I'm sure that is not it."

"Well, I've got to have some more definite information than that immediately," said Jessica annoyedly. "I thought you promised to have it for me by the time I got back."

"Well, I didn't exactly promise," drawled Louella. "I said I'd do my best. If you think you can do any better, why don't you go over there and try? I shouldn't think it would be so impossible for you to talk to some of the family."

"Well, if you can't do any better than you have I may do

just that. I can't simply fool around and wait much longer. I have a job to do, and the people I work for are getting impatient."

"Well, I'm doing my best," said Louella offendedly. "After all I'm simply doing this for you because I like you, you know, and if I do not please you perhaps I better go home. I'm simply staying around here because you asked me to."

"Suit yourself," said Jessica. "Don't let me hinder you. If you can't find out a thing for me, I'm sure I don't know why you should stay. Unless of course you could find out something else for me."

"Such as what?" said Louella's cold voice.

"Well, I should like to know whether that Diana girl is still hanging around Rod, or whether she's gone home to New York."

"Oh! Why didn't you say something about that before? This is the first I've heard of that. I would have had plenty of chances to find out if I had known it was important."

"Well, go to work on it then and see how far you can get with that."

"I'm not sure there will be any way to find out. Especially if she's gone back to New York."

"You might call up on the phone and ask for her," suggested Jessica.

"H'm! You might try that yourself, you know."

"Yes, but I don't think I should care to. I might run on that disagreeable Beryl. I can't abide her."

"Oh, well, I'll think it over and see if there's anything I can do about it before I go home. I really ought to hurry away. There's a possibility that somebody wants to buy my house, and I really need to sell it. I need the money."

"I see! Oh, well, see what you can do and let me know. I really have some letters to write. But, by the way, if you find out where she is you might get some further information about her. I heard the other day that she is as good as engaged to some big guy over in New York. If I knew all about that I might even get somewhere with Rod. He might not have heard it you know."

"Yes, that's quite true," said Louella thoughtfully. "It seems to me that I heard something about that too, but I'm not sure. Well, I'll see what I can do. Will you be home this evening?"

"I'm not sure," drawled Jessica. "I had thought of going out for a while, but I may not go."

"Well, if you do, suppose you drop in here on your way. I may have something more to tell you. I have more than one source of information you know."

Louella waited until she was sure Jessica would not be likely to call her back, and then she called up Isabelle Graham and asked quite casually if she knew Diana, that girl from New York who was visiting Beryl Sanderson.

Isabelle did. She was fairly gushing with news. She had a friend in New York who had just written her the latest about her. She was engaged to some rich guy in the army who was coming home soon and they were going to be married at once, and she'd been down at Riverton killing time until the wedding came off. She had her trousseau all bought, and everything ready to be married. Weren't some people lucky?

Louella finally hung up after she had extracted every bit of information she could possibly get, and sat back to digest it and turn it over, with bits of her own devising, and then she called Jessica again.

But Jessica's line was busy. To tell the truth she was actually calling up the Sanderson number, and about to ask for Diana, but there was no one at home to answer that call, so Jessica after trying for some time hung up, and so was ready for Louella's next call.

17

IT was that same evening later that one of the girls called up and asked Jessica if she heard Rodney broadcasting that afternoon, and "wasn't he great?"

Jessica paused long enough not to show her astonishment and vexation that she had missed it, by not knowing about it, and resolved to blast Louella for that, and then she said with a characteristic drawl, "Oh, well enough, but I can't say I care for that line he has now. I thought he'd get over that religious twaddle, didn't you, when he went to war? He seems to have sort of stolen his little brother's theme, doesn't he?"

"Well, no, I don't think he has," said Alida who happened to be the girl who had called her, "I thought it was so entirely different, and yet just as interesting, and just as convincing. The war seems to have affected a good many of our boys that way."

"Oh, I hope not! What a bore that would be," said Jessica. "I hate boys to turn old before their time. Just think what it would be to go dancing with a fellow that talked religion all the time."

"But the Graeme boys never did go dancing, did they?" asked Alida.

"Well, no, I suppose not. They were too much mamma's

little boys to do a wicked thing like that. But I did suppose that they would get over such silly old-fashioned notions when they got away from mamma's apron strings."

"Well, they haven't," said Alida sharply. "If anything, they are more markedly old-fashioned than ever, and do you know I *like* it. They sound like real men."

"Oh, merciful heavens, *you too?* Have they converted *you,* Alida? This is too much. And you used to be such a good sport."

"Well, I can't help it. I think they are fine. I never heard young men talk like that before. If everybody felt that way there wouldn't be so many wars and bad things in the world. There wouldn't be so many divorces, and drunkards and gangsters."

"Oh, heavens, Alida! Cut it out. Tell me something. Do you know how and when they went down to Washington? Was it just Rodney all alone? Didn't he have anybody with him?"

"Why sure he did. They drove down. My brother met them early this morning going over toward Prattsville. They had their big car and there were six of them. Jeremy and Beryl, Rod and Diana, Kathie and her young chaplain."

"Rod and Diana!" said Jessica in disgust. "Do you mean that unspeakable girl is sticking around yet? I declare she is disgusting, and she's supposed to be engaged to some big rich guy in New York, and getting ready to be married when he comes home on furlough."

"You don't mean it! Where did you hear that? I don't believe that. Diana is not that kind of a girl. She's sweet and quiet and lovely."

"Oh yeah? Who told *you* that? I heard very differently. That sweet quiet character she is putting on just now is just an act to deceive poor blind Rod. You know really he's awfully easily deceived. Anybody can make him think he's talking to an angel."

"Yes, I remember when *you* did that little act yourself, back in our happy school days. But remember that Rod is grown up now and has been to war and done great things. You'll find he's as sharp as a needle and can see through anybody. Remember he's been through an experience with you, and has learned quite a little. There was a time when he simply adored the ground you walked on, but not any more. You have thoroughly disillusioned him, and you did your work all too thoroughly. You couldn't deceive him now, and I don't mean mebbe."

"Oh yes? Well, I'll wager I *could*. Just watch me and see."

"For sweet pity's sake, Jessica, you're married! Lay off that stuff and act like a decent woman, or we'll be ashamed we ever knew you."

"Ashamed? *You?* Well, I like that! I could rake up a few things you've done in your time, if I cared to take the time to try."

"Jessica, you're quite impossible," said Alida harshly. "I'm sorry I called you up. Yet I suppose it is rather hard to watch your discarded lover take so kindly to a rich cultured girl, and find her so entirely willing."

"Yes?" said Jessica hatefully. "Well I could fix that too if I wanted to. There isn't much you can't do with a nice little sweet mamma's child like Diana if you go about it in the right way. So long, Alida. I'm going out this evening so you'll have to excuse me from further talk. Good night."

But Jessica made no further attempt to go out that evening. Instead she sat in deep thought, into the small hours of the night, making plans.

The next day Diana had gone down to the city on an errand for Mrs. Sanderson, while Beryl was addressing some of the Red Cross notes for which her mother was responsible and had promised to get into the mail that day. Diana had finished her errand and was walking briskly through the store on her way back to the house when Jessica sighted her, gave her a quick sharp look and then quickened her own steps and caught up with her.

"Aren't you Diana Winters of New York?" she asked.

Diana turned with a quick look at the other girl and smiled.

"Why, yes," she said sweetly. "Are you somebody I ought to know? I seem to have seen your face somewhere, but I just can't remember your name. I'm sorry."

Diana's manner was altogether disarming, but Jessica was in no mood to be disarmed. She had come out to fight, and she meant to do it.

"I'm Jessica De Groot," said Jessica. "I think we were introduced at that meeting where Jeremy spoke, but it was such a mob I don't wonder you can't remember my name. However, that makes no difference. I thought it was high time you and I had a little talk. There are some things I think you ought to know. Shall we go somewhere where we can talk without being interrupted? Right up these few stairs to the half gallery there is always a place to sit."

Diana, a bit perplexed, glanced down at her watch.

"Why, I think I can spare a few minutes, if it won't take long," she said, and allowed herself to be led up the stairs, and seated on a long bench overlooking the many counters below.

"Now," said Jessica, "I have seen you going around with Rod Graeme a lot, and I thought it was high time you understood that he's not for you. He really belongs to me, you see. We were engaged long before he went to war, and he just isn't for you, that's all. And I decided to tell you to lay off him. I won't stand for anybody else taking him over. He's mine, see?"

Diana sat there in amazement staring at Jessica, and for the moment saying nothing, so Jessica went on.

"Besides, I've been finding out a lot about you too. Things I suppose Rod doesn't know or he never would be going around with you. He's so nasty-religious that he would drop you like a hot cake if he knew. And if you don't let up on this

I'll good and well see that he does know. See? You see I have friends in New York, and they tell me you are engaged and going to be married right away to a swell guy who thinks you're all right, and naturally *he* doesn't know what *you* are doing in Riverton. But if you keep this thing up I'll see that he *does* know all about it. I often go to New York and I can hunt him up and tell him *everything* that goes on here, see?"

Diana looked at the girl as if she were crazy, and in her heart she was saying: "Oh, Lord, what is this? What shall I do? Help me, please."

She was smiling faintly when this tirade began, and the startling things this girl said had for the instant driven away her usual calm from her expression, leaving only that faint smile set there like something that might fade quickly.

Then, as if some unseen strength had come to her she began to speak in a steady voice:

"Are you quite through? Is that all you wanted to say? Then if you'll excuse me I think I must go, for someone is waiting for this package," and with all her old sweet self-possession, the result of years of cultured training, she arose, walked quickly across the gallery, down the steps and out through the crowded store, head up, shoulders back, and an undistrubed expression upon her face.

And Jessica sat in amazement and watched her go. Her hateful words had not even phased the girl. What kind of a girl was she anyway? And somehow Jessica almost envied Diana, to be able to take it that way. That was what it meant, probably, to be "to the manner born," while *she* was only born to the wrong side of the tracks and couldn't seem to get away from it no matter how hard she tried, nor how hateful she was to other people. She simply could not understand it. What did it mean? Wasn't it true about her being engaged? Well, why didn't she say so then? Or was there nothing much between her and Rod? Or what? Had she only put herself in worse with Rod by attacking the girl he had been going with? Well, it was done, and now what? She must follow this up somehow. She would have to go to Rod, get to him somehow even if he didn't want to see her, and tell him what kind of a double-crosser his latest girl was. With all his religion he couldn't stand a girl doing that. She would get in touch with Rod tomorrow in spite of all his scruples. In spite of the Graemes. In spite of Louella. She would beat them all, and get it back on everybody. Get it back on Rod and perhaps get him just where she wanted him, and then she would ask him to give that ring back, and have it to show to other people. She would do that little thing tomorrow morning. She certainly knew how to make plenty of trouble for a lot of people when she really set about it.

So, dressed in her most innocent morning frock of delicate wash material, fragilely trimmed with simply expensive lace, and a wide hat with a wreath of wild roses, the kind of thing Rod used to admire, and delicate white sandal slippers, she took her way slowly up the old familiar drive. She went to the side door where she always used to go, knock, and walk in without ceremony or waiting for anyone to admit her. But she did not wish to anger anyone now, so she stayed a little on ceremony, and stood with her wide hat in her hand, sweetly smiling. And Jessica knew how to smile, sweetly, *almost* innocently.

"Are you here, Mamma Graeme?" she called in a pleasant voice. "I've come to see you. I hope you're home, and not busy."

Margaret Graeme came out a little anxiously, not knowing just what to anticipate, and she looked at the smart girlish figure and was thankful in her heart that this girl was not for her boy. She had never felt her to be the right girl for either of her children, though there had never been a danger from her for Jerry, for he had openly despised her, raging to his mother now and again on Rodney's account.

"Why, no, not too busy. That is not for a while. I believe I have to go to a committee meeting at eleven. Sit down won't you?"

So Jessica spread her filmy orchid-sprigged skirt out engagingly in the rocking chair that was offered and settled herself for a good homey talk, with a nice air of pleasant anticipation.

She spoke of the lovely weather they had been having, rattled on a little about her brief trip west, with a unique fabrication of a story to explain her going. She told enlarged stories of her husband's estate, described the wonderful old house and its fine costly antique furniture. She told of a wondrous blue diamond her husband was getting for her which was to be set in a new fancy way, and at last she looked at her little trick of a watch and remarked nonchalantly:

"I hope I haven't come too early to catch the boys when they come down. I know they like to sleep late these furlough mornings. Dare I stay till they come down?"

"Come down?" said Margaret Graeme lifting amused eyebrows. "Why, bless you child, they aren't even here. They left late last night."

"Do you mean they've been sent back overseas?"

"Oh no, not that, that is not yet."

"But where have they gone? I'm always asking that question about Rod, and never getting an answer. Is this intentional?"

Margaret Graeme smiled.

"Well, it has been rather hard to place them. They've so many things to see and do, and they have felt that perhaps they had so little time in which to do it."

"Well, then, suppose you give me an answer now, Mamma Graeme. Where have they gone?"

Mrs. Graeme laughed merrily.

"Well, I'll have to give you the same answer," she said, "they didn't tell me. They simply said they were called to headquarters."

"Do you mean they've been called back to Washington?"

"It might be, of course, but I'm not sure. It depends on what headquarters it is I suppose. I really don't know much about these things. I haven't had much chance to talk over their affairs with the boys yet. It seems there are several head-quarters, I think, depending on whether you are talking in terms of military orders, or personnel or home efficiency. I'm not even sure I'm using the right terms. I'm afraid I'm rather a dummy about such matters, and it hasn't seemed too impor-tant to take time to understand. But undoubtedly we'll learn in time, and be able to give them their true standing in the eyes of the world, that is, as far as the world is going to be allowed to know. If it is, yet."

"But don't you really know pretty well where they are going? Surely you could tell me that much. Remember, Mamma Graeme how near I came to being a member of the family, and then I would have had to know."

Margaret Graeme laughed.

"I'm afraid not," she said amusedly. "We don't know yet, and may not be told everything even when the boys get their orders, for the Government has found that there are some things that *must* be kept absolutely secret, even from the near-est and dearest."

"But I think that's perfectly horrid. That's unreasonable. No families would stand for that."

"Oh, yes, they would. They have to, you know. Why there were months and months when the boys were overseas that we had no definite idea at all where they were. It was understood that we wouldn't. It was the only safe way to win the war."

"Nonsense!" said Jessica. "I think that's ridiculous! As if all those thousand of soldiers would stand for that! Why they wouldn't stay there and fight if they were treated like that."

"Oh yes they would. They understood, themselves, why such orders were given, why such precautions were neces-sary. No, we got rather used to not asking too many ques-tions. We knew that if we asked one that shouldn't be answered they would just laugh and give an evasive reply. So we just waited till the boys got ready to tell us. If they didn't we knew it was because they were forbidden."

"Well, I certainly wouldn't stand for that."

"I would rather stand for that and help the war along, than just to satisfy my own curiosity and persist in demanding to know everything. You know you want your dear ones to be true soldiers, and to submit to laws and ordinances."

Jessica was vexed and showed it. At last she got up and started toward the door.

"Well, it seems I came on a fool's errand," she said.

"Oh, I wouldn't call it that, child," said Mother Graeme. "We've had a nice talk, haven't we?"

"We didn't get anywhere, and I wanted to talk to Rodney. There is something important I want to ask him about. When do you definitely expect him back?"

"I'm afraid it will have to be the same old answer. I just don't know. It might be a day or two or more even, or a week, or a month. Depends on what changes are going to be made in their work."

Margaret Graeme was getting to be a master of evasion indeed. Of course she did not actually know definitely what was to be done with her sons in the immediate future, though she could guess perhaps and not fall far short of the truth. But she had been adjured not to tell *anything*, not even what she *knew* to be true, so she told nothing. And at last Jessica, much vexed in spirit, took herself away, went and hunted up Louella, and complained to her.

"Well, Jessica," said Louella sympathetically, "that's exactly the way Margaret Graeme always treats me. You wonder why I can't get any of the information you want. Well, now you see, I simply can't get anything out of her no matter how hard I try. I'm glad you've seen it yourself, and then you won't be so hard on me."

"Well, at least now we know they've gone somewhere, and it ought to be definitely settled soon where they are to be permanently. I wonder if we could get anything out of the postman?"

"I'm afraid not," said Louella. "I tried him a while ago,

asked for the address of somebody overseas, and do you know he wouldn't give me the address, not without an order from the person. He said he would mail my letter, but he had no right to give me the address. It seems to me that Government affairs take too much on themselves, refusing to give out the address of your best friends, or next door neighbors, perhaps."

"Well, there must be some way," said Jessica. "I'm not one to give up so easily. I'm going to find out where they are as soon as they are located definitely, and believe me I'm going to visit Rodney in his office, too, Government or no Government. They can't simply turn a lady out of an office."

"Well, I don't know about that," said Louella doubtfully. "You know the Government is very severe. Army and Navy regulations are simply unreasonable, *I* say. And I wouldn't hesitate to step over some of their old regulations myself. Nobody would certainly put *me* out of anywhere, office or whatever. But maybe *you* ought not to try. You are a young woman, you know. And perhaps your husband wouldn't like it if you did. You might get your name in the papers or something, and be misunderstood."

"Well, anyhow I'm going to talk to Rodney Graeme. I've got things to tell him that he ought to know, and I intend he shall know them. Remember I used to be very close to him, and if I know something to his advantage I think *I'm* the one to tell him, don't you?"

"Well, of course, Jessica, if you put it that way. But you must remember there are always consequences to things like that, rash actions especially when you're dealing with Government regulations. I'd be careful what I did, Jessica."

"Oh, I'm not afraid. Just wait till I find out where that office or plant or whatever it is, is located, and I'm going straight in and track Rod to his office. Then believe me, nobody, not even a mother, is going to put up any bars to keep me out. I'm going to his office and I'm going to stay there till I've told him plenty about that little white-faced Diana that he's trotting around with, and when I get done you won't see him out riding with her any more I'll guarantee. One thing that Rodney Graeme is mortally afraid of is to do anything that will make narrow-minded people talk about him. He seems to think God is just waiting around the corner, watching, to see if he goes wrong some way, or if anybody can find anything to accuse him of. I'll show him that that girl is no mate of his. A girl that would be all ready to be married and then go off and visit and run around with other men when she's got a perfectly swell guy of her own who is expecting to marry her. I know he'll draw the line at that."

"But after all, Jessica," said Louella, "isn't that something like what you did, sending Rodney's nice pretty ring back to him and marrying another man?"

"Well, I sent it back didn't I? I didn't keep it, though I wish I had. I may go and ask him for it. I wonder if he has it in the bank? See if you can find that out for me, Louella."

## 18

DIANA walked all the way home instead of taking the bus as she usually did after shopping. Somehow she wanted to be alone to think, and not be herded in a bus with a lot of other people to distract her thoughts. She felt as if she had been struck sharply, or had a shocking fall, and didn't want even to think for a few minutes, till some of the pain was past.

She was thankful that the way she had chosen had very little traffic, and few pedestrians. She walked rapidly as it seemed easier that way, but when she came to the park that was across the road and only a block below the Sanderson home, she turned sharply into it, and sought out the bench where she had often gone to read when Beryl was busy or away at the Red Cross for her mother.

There was no one there now, and the sunshine was shimmering through the lacy hemlock boughs that were planted behind it. She sat down under the shadow at the end of the bench, and drew a relieved breath, feeling as if she had reached a real refuge. For an instant she just sat and looked out over the lovely scene, and tried to realize that she was no longer under the fire of that awful girl's eyes, her look of contempt and challenge. Then the memory of it all rolled over her like a great wave of trouble, and fairly took her breath away.

She dropped her face into her lifted hands, her head bowed over, and if she hadn't been still so conscious of the great world outside which might at any moment step into the picture, she certainly would have groaned. The whole matter seemed so utterly sordid and humiliating. To think any girl would dare to talk to another as that girl had done. Real trouble she was in, and she had no one to go to. She would be ashamed to tell Beryl, or her mother, and as for her own mother, even if she were home and she might go to her at once, her mother would only be very angry, and annoyed with her. She had stayed away against her advice, and laid herself open to gossip and criticism.

Somehow the only one she wanted to go to with her trouble was Rodney Graeme, and of course she couldn't do that. She wouldn't for the world have Rodney know a thing like this. It seemed to put a great blight upon her soul, a great insult to her life which she had always hoped was sweet and clean. She felt as if she had suddenly fallen into pitch and did not know how to get rid of its stains. If only there were somebody to whom she dared talk! But the only one who came to her mind as possible was Rodney, and that was impossible. Perhaps she never could talk to him again. And there would be his sweet mother too, but of course she wouldn't have her know for anything in the world that a girl like that would dare to talk to her the way Jessica had talked.

Then suddenly there came to her, like a voice speaking quietly behind her: "Fear thou not for I am with thee. I will help thee." Where did that come from? Out of her childhood past, or out of the meeting where Jeremy had spoken, or had she heard Rodney repeat it lately? Why, surely that was the verse Rodney had used among others when he was telling her about the Lord, and it reminded her at once that she need not cast about for someone to comfort and help her. She had a new Helper, a Lord Who cared, and Who had promised to be with her everywhere. She had no need to go to earthly friends, to men and women, or even her girl friend. There was One closer to her now. Who would understand fully. Before Whom she need never feel humiliated, even though He and she both knew she was a sinner. But He had taken that sin upon Himself, for her sake.

Then she remembered how she had once before cried unto the Lord in trouble and He had helped her, smoothed her troubles all out without any effort on her part. Would He do it again?

So she prayed:

"O, my dear new Lord, I am in trouble again, and no one to help but You. I can't do anything about it myself. Won't You please take over? I don't understand why this thing has come upon me. Was it something I did wrong? But somehow I'm sure You can make it right. And if there is something I should do, please show me what it is, and give me guidance now, and strength. And now, please help me to go back to the house, and the hours that are ahead, and not act frightened. I will trust You all the way, and listen for Your guidance. Thank You. Amen."

She remained with bowed head for a moment, and it seemed to her she felt a hand upon her head, laid there in blessing, and a promise. And again came that voice from far away, back down the ages, and yet as if the words were just spoken. "Fear not. *I* will help thee."

A moment more and then Diana lifted her head, and the trouble and burden seemed to be gone. God was there, and what *she* could not, He would do for her.

She brushed her hair back from her hot face, straightened her hat, and got up, gave one glance around the quiet park, and then started briskly back to the house. It did not matter now what that girl had said, what she had threatened to do. God would take care of that for her. What a wonderful thing was this that Rodney had done for her, whether she ever saw him again or not! Whether his steps ever crossed her path again, that was in God's hands too, but at least she would always be glad that she had known him, and that he had introduced her to God. Perhaps in Heaven they could talk it over, but maybe by that time all this would be as if it had not been. Just like that trouble with her mother and Bates Hibberd. It might go away. Of course there might be more of that coming to her again when she got back to New York, but God had helped her once. He could, and would surely help her whenever the time came that she needed help.

So she went smiling into the house with a real glad light in her eyes, not any artificial smile either, but a smile of resting and trusting.

But over in her own room, not many miles away, Jessica was fretting and fuming.

For three long days she waited for her chance to get it back on this gay little indifferent New Yorker whom she hadn't been able to down with the bitterest most unpleasant words she could find. She had gone each morning early to the Graeme house, telling Mother Graeme that she simply *must* see Rodney at once, and gotten the same answer, that he had not yet returned. And she knew no more of what was to be his orders now than she had known when Jessica was there before.

"Well, then, you'll have to give me his address, Mamma Graeme. I've simply got to ask him some questions. I've got an order to write an article, and I told my editor that I had a friend just returned from service, and I would get some local coloring from him, and I've only a few more days to get this article in, so please give me his address."

"But I don't know what it is, Jessica," said Margaret Graeme, glad in her heart that she didn't know. "You see the boys know that I understand I mustn't worry if I don't hear. I've been through months and months of that you know, and so have they, and they would be sure I would wait, and know that they would write as soon as they had anything definite that they had a right to tell."

"But they are not overseas now you know."

"No, I wouldn't know that for sure. You know the war needs are peculiar and changeable. They might have been sent right off to the Pacific, without a chance to either telephone or write. They would feel that I would understand. But then again they may be returning tonight or tomorrow, or even sometime today. They'll come when they come," and she smiled quietly with a faith that was used to trusting her very life to God.

But that utter trust only made Jessica angry.

"You're the most unfeeling mother I ever saw," she snapped, "or else you're holding out on me for some reason."

"Why no," said Margaret Graeme, "I'm not holding out on you. I just haven't the information you want, that's all."

But Jessica had slammed away and gone over to Louella's hotel to blame her. She was due to report to her husband either by letter or in person in three days, and as yet she hadn't got anywhere, except to blast Diana, which though it gave her personal satisfaction, had left a great uneasiness because she couldn't interpret aright her reaction. She had never seen a girl react to an insult as Diana had done, and with apparently no after-climax of retaliation, and she was constantly fearing what form it might take when it did come. For she was sure a girl with spirit enough to have such steady poise to walk out on an insult, head up, shoulders back, must have initiative enough to bring a real sting when she finally decided to act. She knew that Diana was no mollycoddle, even if she didn't wear lipstick and paint her finger nails. So she watched and planned, and tried to bully Louella into doing something drastic. She hadn't been even able to find out whether she had driven Diana back to New York yet, or if she was still at the Sandersons.

But at last the boys came home again, arriving on the late

train Saturday night, to stay just over Sunday, they told their mother as they kissed her joyously. And from that embrace she gathered that their news was good, whatever it was. She could wait till they told her.

The news of their arrival got around the town by way of Bonny Stewart whose brother spent much of his time hanging around the station, especially at the time of the arrival of the late trains, hoping to pick up an extra dollar or two conveying late passengers to their homes to eke out his depleted bank account.

In due time the word got around to Jessica, by way of several of the other girls, and she lost no time in going to the Graeme house, but found them of course all gone to church.

"The very idea!" she said to Hetty who had informed her. "I should have supposed they would have stayed at home together, if the boys are going away again. A strange kind of a mother they have that she would let them go to church, and go herself when they may be going away again, perhaps never to come back."

"Dat's mostly de case wif every one," said Hetty wisely. "When you go out an' away you can't say ef you'll ever come back again. But dat ain't sayin' you shouldn't go right on livin' de best you can. But dat's how it is. Ef you want's ta see dem boys you'd best go ta church yourself."

Very angry at this, Jessica walked out, but decided on the way to the gate that she would go to church and hold up Rodney, *make* him walk home with her, and show the town who had him now. So she went to church.

She entered noisily and took a back seat, and the first sight she saw was the Graeme family all sitting together in their usual pew. Later her eyes wandered to the other side of the church and there sat the Sandersons, with that Diana in their midst! The effrontery of her. After all she had said to her to think she would dare come to a public place and appear with Rodney's friends. Well, she would settle that once and for all. She would get hold of Rodney before any of them, and make him promise to walk home with her. He simply couldn't say no, or get out of it in public this way.

So while the last words of the benediction were still echoing in the air, and while the soft tones of the organ began to play for the close of service, Jessica was halfway up the aisle, marching straight to the Graeme pew, and making everyone turn and stare wondering if someone had died, or something strange had happened. Jessica had not been seen with the Graemes for several years, yet there she was leaning over Father Graeme and Mother Graeme, to speak most earnestly to Rodney. Well, that was something to look at and no mistake!

"Rod," she said with her sweetest smile, recalling with her tone the days when he always sprang to do her bidding, "will you please walk home with me? I have something very important to tell you, and it won't wait. And can you come at once, so I won't take too much of your precious time?"

She was waiting, still leaning over the Graemes, effectually blocking the way for them to get out into the aisle. Margaret Graeme's heart almost skipped a beat, as she heard the request made of her boy. Just how would he handle this matter? Then the assurance came back to her eyes and she knew that God was managing this affair as well as the war, and she might relax and just trust.

But Father Graeme's face was stern, and his jaw grim. Most of his fellow Christians could tell pretty well how he felt about the matter, for well they knew that expression, and didn't care to get into any argument with him when he looked like that. Then they all looked quickly at Rodney, especially Jeremy, who was just beyond his brother, at the other end of the seat, and his eyes were both stern and anxious.

But Rodney had a calmness about him that his brother knew was not his own. Jeremy felt he had just been praying.

Rodney gave Jessica one sharp, stern, searching glance and then he let his lips relax, and he answered in a pleasant voice that all around could hear: "That would be quite impossible, Mrs. De Groot. Someone is waiting for me with a car, and I have to leave at once. Mother, Dad, will you kindly let me pass? I promised not to be late," and though Jessica put on an act of trying to detain him:—"But oh, Rod, this is most important! Then when *can* I see you? Sometime today?" he brushed by her brusquely and went marching down the aisle, smiling at everybody but getting quite away.

And though she did her best to follow him up for just one other word, trying to think which ugly truth she could convey briefly to fling at him, she only arrived at the church steps in time to see Rodney assisting Diana into the back seat of the Sanderson car, and sitting down beside her. So, that was the way it was, was it? That girl hadn't taken her warning, and now she was due to get her full punishment. Well, she, Jessica, would do her worst. She would go to the Sandersons' and ask to see him. He surely couldn't get away then. And she would tell him all she knew, and more that she had made up, about that girl Diana.

Jeremy watched her from afar, but she wasn't noticing Jeremy. The fire was in her eyes and he knew she meant to do mischief. He had watched her too many years, to protect his brother, not to know what her expressions portended.

So as soon as he reached home he went to the telephone and called up the Sandersons'.

Rodney came to the phone.

"Hello, Rod! I just wanted to tell you that you left an enemy in the church aisle when you went away, and you better be prepared for almost anything. I think you're due to meet her shortly, so get in touch with your Guide. I don't know just what form this will take, but I didn't want it to get you unaware, and it will be plenty. Get on your armor. And oh, Rod, tell Beryl I'll be over in about an hour, and if you need any help call me also. See you subsea!"

So Rodney was warned, but not definitely. And certainly Mr. Sanderson was not warned, for it was he who opened the front door for Jessica when she arrived, just as dinner was being put on the table and the family were on the way to the dining room.

Mr. Sanderson bowed courteously and showed the caller into the small reception room nearer to the front door than the living room, where the more intimate guests were always taken. Then he stepped to the dining room door and called, "Rodney, here's a caller for you." Then under his breath he whispered as Rod went by him, "Got your pen ready? It's probably an autograph!"

So Rodney came to stand in the doorway and looked into the room.

Jessica had taken pains to sit in the most sheltered corner of the room where she would not be seen, or at least recognized at once by the person entering, and so Rodney came all the way into the room and looked around, and then seeing her he said "Oh!" in a tone that was anything but flattering.

Jessica put by a delicate handkerchief wherewith she was doing a preliminary plaintive weep, and rising came toward him.

"Rodney," she said softly so that her voice would not reach to the other room—not *yet*—"I have something very important to tell you. Something that when you have heard you will be glad I told you. It is something I felt you ought to know, and for the sake of my old-time fondness for you I have put aside my natural timidity—"

"*What?* said Rodney sharply. "What did you say? Your *natural timidity?* I don't remember that. But go on. Let's get it over quick. You are holding up my host's dinner."

"That won't matter when you have heard what I have to say."

"Go ahead," said Rodney flinging up his head impatiently.

"But Rodney, there is something else I want to ask first, for my own sake. I want you to do a personal favor for me."

"Yes?" said the young officer looking her straight in the eye with a wry grin on his lips, "I thought there would be some catch. Proceed!"

Jessica drew a quivering breath and swept a swift glance of reproach at the young man, but she hurried on, knowing that he was quite capable of terminating this interview without notice, but she meant to get in her work this time.

"Well, then, Rod, I want my ring back again! I've suffered no end of trouble to think I ever gave it up, and I want it back again. Please, Rod. Be good to me. I'm so sorry I ever gave it up. Please give it back!"

"What do you want it for?" asked the young man with almost a sneer on his nice lips, because he didn't believe anything this girl was saying.

"I want it to remember you by!" she said with almost a sob, and a quiver between every word.

"Yes? Well, I wouldn't care to be remembered by you, even if I had the ring. And I haven't got it!"

"You haven't *got* it? What have you done with it? You haven't given it to that other girl *yet,* have you? Oh, *Rod!*" and Jessica's head drooped and she bowed her face in her hands. "Oh, Rod! I didn't think you'd do that!"

"I certainly did not give it to any girl," said Rodney severely. "I wouldn't dishonor any other girl by giving her a ring that had been returned to me in scorn by a girl who had no honor herself."

There was a solemn pause while Jessica took in this implication, and then she cried out in a good simulation of despair, "Then what *have* you done with it?"

"I sold it to a dealer in China two years ago. I didn't want a thing like that cluttering around my life. I hated the light of it and the thing it stood for. Thank God it is gone from my thoughts even, forever!"

"Oh, Rod! How *can* you be so cruel to me? You once used to love me!"

"The more fool I," said Rodney. "I only thought I did, but I am grateful that I was made to see what you really were before it was too late. And now, was that all you came to say? I could not get that ring back even if I wanted to, and I would not even if I could. So that is my answer to that. Now, what else?"

Then Jessica lifted her anguished head and looked him in the eyes with fire of anger in her own:

"Yes, there is something else. And this is for *your* sake. I have found out that the girl you are going with now has a false heart. It is ironic that you should select two girls who are neither of them true to you. This girl you are rushing here in Riverton is engaged to be married to a rich handsome fellow, of high birth, in New York, and she is to be married to him within a very short time. She has her trousseau bought and her wedding dress is waiting for the time when he is expected home to claim her. I thought you ought to be told that before your affair here goes on any further. I had intended leaving Riverton myself a couple of weeks ago, but delayed till I could get opportunity to tell you this before it was too late. Now, I don't expect you to be grateful at once, but I'm sure when you find out that what I have said is true, you will write and thank me."

Rodney stood looking at her with almost fury in his eyes for a moment, and then he said with dignity and severity,

"I am too angry to answer you as you ought to be answered. It would be better for you to go now. I don't care to talk with you any more. Shall I open the door for you? Good afternoon. And don't try anything like this again."

Rodney's voice had been clear and decided, and the people in the other room could scarcely help hearing, though Mr. Sanderson did his best to create a diversion by dropping the brass tongs on the tiles of the hearth, and tapping a spoon against a glass by his place. The family had not sat down, they had been sort of waiting for Rodney, but little by little they all perceived that Rodney was anything but pleased by his caller,

and they all had more or less the feeling that he might presently need them to come in and say something that would make
her leave. Mrs. Sanderson even ventured the thought to herself, that if she went in and invited the girl to stay for dinner
with them she would then take the hint and go, and she suggested this in a low tone to Beryl, but Beryl shook her head
decidedly. "No, mother, you don't know her. She would
stay and put a crimp in the whole works." So the mother
desisted, meditating whether it wouldn't be best for them to
sit down and start dinner.

But just then to their great relief Jeremy breezed in and
walked right into the dining room with his cheery greeting.
This made the conversation so general that it could but be
heard in the front reception room. The next sound they heard
was the front door closing emphatically after the unwanted
guest.

It did not take Jessica long to realize as she walked angrily
down the pleasant street toward her bus that she had over-
stepped herself in this visit. If she had only stopped after the
request for the ring, and not gone on to tell about Diana, with
all that horde where they could hear what she was saying, she
might have had some effect. But now she saw that she had
only made Rodney very angry by trying to run down Diana.
Well, at least Diana had heard her, and had known that she
had made good her threat. She had attained that much. And
she had made known the truth, or what she supposed was the
truth, to Rodney. Though it really never made much difference to Jessica whether what she told was the truth or not, so
it hit home on somebody, and hurt, preferably the people she
didn't like.

So Jessica went on back to Riverton, and hunted out
Louella to commiserate with her. Of course Louella told her
she had been very, very brave, and she was sure something
drastic would come of all this, but secretly she decided that
she would stay away from the Graemes' for a while till this

blew over, or else she would be blamed with it all by Donald, who was rather plain-spoken and didn't mind hurting when he thought it would do some good.

But Jessica, weeping herself angrily to sleep, resolved that next she would go up to New York, hunt out that officer Diana was engaged to, and put trouble to brewing there for Diana when she got home to put on her wedding dress, which she felt pretty sure Diana would do, now that Rodney knew the truth about her. He hadn't said anything, still these close-mouthed soldiers knew how to shut up, but they smoldered inside. She was sure she had seen fire for somebody in Rodney's eyes. He might blame her at first, but Diana would have to account for it all, and it wouldn't be so fine for him. She doubted if he would go to church tonight with her. Perhaps she would go herself just to find out.

Before Jessica fell asleep that night she decided it would be a good thing if she were to go up to New York the next morning and hunt out that bridegroom of Diana before Diana got home. For undoubtedly she would be leaving Riverton in the morning, after what she must have overheard today.

Then, after she had made that New York swell understand what had been going on, and put a crimp in Diana's plans, she had only one more thing left to do. She had to find out just where Rod and Jerry were located, what work they were doing, and somehow get into their offices and hunt up those papers her husband wanted. Then she would have her blue diamond and that was all she cared for in life. After she had that maybe she'd get a divorce and hunt up some nice returning officer for herself, for she was done with Rod. The way he had looked at her when he put her out of the house had settled that for her definitely.

Then she went to sleep.

19

IT had been a bit embarrassing for Rodney when he came back to the dining room, to meet the family that he had come so to respect, and love. He felt shamed and humiliated, until he suddenly realized that that was what Jessica had wanted, and that was why she had come there, just to humiliate him, in return for his avoiding her. He smiled to himself wryly.

"What's funny, Rod?" asked his brother. "You certainly didn't sound like a comic opera in there. We could hear a lot of what was said. I suppose you realize that?"

"Yes," smiled Rodney. "I knew you couldn't help it, unless you all got up and shouted, or went out in the kitchen and got spoons and pans and had a band parade. In fact I *wanted* you to hear *some* of it. Though I certainly am ashamed, Mr. Sanderson, that I should have disgraced your home where you have so kindly made me welcome."

"Not at all, boy! Don't worry about it for a minute. We all knew of course that you couldn't be enjoying the session very much yourself."

"No," owned Rodney, "I wasn't. It was just the dread of something like this happening sometime that made me almost not want to come home from war, but I knew that was foolish. It had to be got over with, and that was all. But I had hoped that fool-girl had grown up, since she got married, and learned a little sense. But it seems I was wrong. Mr. Sanderson, I'd like you and your wife to know that at one time when I was a kid in high school I thought that girl was the most beautiful creature on the face of the earth, and I fancied myself very much in love with her. I even got her a ring. And then when I'd been over in the war about a year she sent that ring back to me with attempts at proper apologies. She said she was going to marry a rich man, and she knew I would understand and forgive her. Well, I was pretty young then and the war was grim, and for a while I thought everything was gone. Death was everywhere. Nothing was genuine. But after a while I met the Lord, and then all was different. I was glad He had saved me from a girl like that.

"Forgive me Mrs. Sanderson for spreading my mistakes and troubles out before everybody, but since you had to hear some of it, I'd rather you would understand."

"Go on Rodney," said the smiling mother. "Just act as if we were your own people and tell what you want us to know."

"Thank you, Mrs. Sanderson," said Rodney with gratitude in his voice. "I appreciate that. There isn't so much more to tell, but—do you know what that girl said she came here for today? She wanted me to *give her* BACK the ring she had returned!"

"I hope you didn't do it," said Mr. Sanderson amusedly. "Though I don't suppose you've carried it around in your vest pocket all these years."

There was a twinkle in his eyes which set everybody laughing merrily, and relieved the tensity of the atmosphere somewhat.

"No, I didn't give it back," said Rodney fiercely, "I told her I had sold it to a dealer in China, and that even if I *had* it I wouldn't give it to her. But there, I'm just ashamed that you had to meet up with my poor young mistakes. I hope I'm not that bad any *more,* but still one can never tell. I guess Heaven may show up some more mighty big failures yet."

"Well, we won't worry about those now, not with the God you have, to forgive and cover them up with His own righteousness. Mother, I wonder if there are more hot mashed potatoes out in the kitchen? And more gravy, too? Jeremy and I both want some more, don't we, Jerry, my boy?"

And so the routine of the pleasant dinner table went on, and the incident of Jessica passed into the annals to be forgotten. After all it had not troubled anybody but Rodney, and they all loved Rodney and wanted to comfort him.

The talk fell into more practical lines. The young men told as much as they could, as much as regulations allowed them to tell, of their own present prospects. The place where their work would be located at first, and the importance of what they were to do. There were shining eyes about that table as they all realized that immediate far separation was not to be their lot.

"Does mom know yet?" asked Rodney anxiously, looking at his brother. "She's been rather worried I know, though she hasn't said much. I hope you told her something, Jerry. We hadn't much time last night, or this morning before church."

"Oh, I didn't tell her much, only that she needn't worry, we were not going far, not at present. That satisfied her for the time. You know mom has always been wonderfully understanding."

"Yes, I know," said Rodney. "She's about the best soldier in our family. Dad always wants to understand everything."

"Yes," said Beryl's father, "I'm like that too. I run my family pretty well, and I sometimes think I could run the Government too, better than most other people. Well, couldn't I, mamma?"

Such a pleasant understanding family they all were, and so much like the Graemes, thought Diana, wistfully wishing her own family were like them.

Then suddenly she looked up and her eyes met Rodney's eyes, and there was something in them like a blessing. Her cheeks turned rosy, and somehow unexplained matters seemed all at once set right between them. Her heart grew gladly light, and she knew she was not going home to New York in the morning. Not *yet,* not a little-yet, anyway.

After Jerry saw that look pass between them he settled down to enjoy his third helping of mashed potatoes and gravy, and spent the rest of the time looking at Beryl.

The afternoon came at last and Rodney could take a shy Diana out and have a talk with her.

"Well, Diana, are you off me for life since you found out about my foolish past?" he asked after they had found a pleasant grassy place to sit among the trees.

Diana's eyes lighted happily.

"Everybody has a silly past," she said wisely enough. "Perhaps it isn't always their own fault entirely. It is sometimes the fault of older people who ought to know better. They fairly fling people at you and insist on making something of their companionship. That was my trouble. I was sort of paired off with a boy I had known all my life, and I couldn't seem to get away from it. He just ordered me around as if I belonged to him, and he got around my mother, till I finally ran away to visit Beryl and get away from it all, so I could think out what to do."

Rodney was watching her as she talked.

"Then you hadn't got your trousseau and wedding dress all ready when you came away? And you haven't set the date for your wedding yet?" he asked, watching her meanwhile keenly.

"Mercy, no!" laughed Diana. "I hadn't any idea of getting married." Then she turned to him suddenly and looked him sharply in the eyes:

"Did *she* tell you that?" she asked.

He looked astonished.

"Yes, Jessica told me. How did you know?"

"Because she threatened to tell you unless I went home to New York at once."

"She *did?* The little rat!"

"And she threatened to go up to New York and find the young man she said she heard I was going to marry, and tell him how I had been running around with all of you down here."

There was a kind of a frightened smile on her face as she said this, and Rodney knew it was troubling her.

"Do you mind her doing that?" he asked, a tender note in his voice.

"No, only it may get to my father and mother if they come home soon, and it will trouble them. They have been awfully worried because I wouldn't come home and fix up an engagement right away."

"And you don't want that?"

"No, I certainly do *not*," said Diana definitely.

Rodney looked at her earnestly another minute and then he said firmly, "Well, then, I guess we've got to do something about this right away. I wasn't going to rush things because I felt perhaps you didn't know me very well, and I was so uncertain about my future, but the immediate future is sort of settled for the present, anyway." He reached out and took both her hands in his. "You *dear!*" he said tenderly. "I love you, my sweet!"

Then he bent down and kissed her softly, and Diana looked up with a glad light in her face like a glory light. Their lips came together again in a long sweet kiss, as he drew her closer.

"I love you too," said she softly. "I think I've loved you ever since you prayed for me in the meeting that night when Jerry spoke."

He drew her closer and looked down into her face.

"Yes, I was praying for you then," he said, wonderingly. "How did you know?"

"I just felt it in my heart," she whispered softly. "It frightened me a little and made me feel a sinner. I never had known I was a sinner before, although I joined the church when I was a child. But how did you know I needed praying for?"

He smiled.

"I guess the Holy Spirit told me. I kept wondering and wondering if you knew the Lord, and tried to say you wouldn't have been in the meeting if you didn't, yet I knew that was no proof, and so I began to pray that you should know my Lord."

"Oh, my dear! This is wonderful! I never knew God could speak to people and guide them on this earth the way He is doing now. I am so glad I have found you. I didn't think there would ever be a man I could love. That is why I ran away down here."

"Then you didn't love the man they thought you were going to marry?"

"No, I didn't love him, and I didn't want to marry him. He is nice, you know, a really good moral fellow, but I didn't love him. Not even if he had been a Christian I wouldn't want to marry him. I couldn't *love* him."

"That's good," said Rodney. "That makes it all right with me. And Jessica can go around telling all the tales she wants to tell. It won't bother me any. But now, here's something else. Your mother and father. What will they say?"

"Well, of course they won't like it very much, not at first, anyway. At least mother won't. She's very much sold on Bates Hibberd. And she doesn't know you. But she will. I'm satisfied she will. She'll like all those ribbons and decorations you're wearing on your uniform too. Those things count a lot with her. Of course you're an officer too of some kind, aren't you?"

"Oh, yes, of a sort," laughed Rodney. "But will this mean we will have to wait a long time to get married? How old are you anyway?"

"Twenty-one last April," said Diana with a glad smile. "I'm of age. I can do as I please, although of course I don't want to hurt my parents, but if they object I'll have to do what I think is right, even in spite of them. And I know my father won't object. He'll like you too, I'm sure."

"But you said this other guy was rich, didn't you? And I'm as poor as that typical church mouse. Of course I've got a job with the Government just now, but the war is almost over. There is no telling what will come afterward for me. I might have to be just a plain farmer. That's something I understand, at least."

"That's all right with me," said Diana happily, nestling closer to the strong arm that held her.

"Yes, but it might not be all right with your dad, my dear. And perhaps it's all right for him to feel that way too. Parents don't like to hand their children over to penniless strangers."

"They won't object after they know you. Anyway I love you."

"You dear!" he said bending to touch her lips with his own again. "What a girl to come home to! And to think I was bitter when I returned because my girl had gone back on me, and I hated her for it. When all the time she wasn't my real girl at all. She was the girl I *thought* would be a right one, and then found out that God had something better waiting and ready for me. What a girl to come home to! My dearest, the best in all the world! But now, see here, we've got to do something about this matter of your mother and father at once. If Jessica goes up to New York as she threatened, and gets in touch with that Bates Hibberd, he'll beat us to your parents, and that will not be so good. When do you say they are coming home?"

"Probably not till the end of the week," said Diana.

"Then we better go Saturday morning. I can get off then, I think. This isn't a thing that can wait. Do you think so?"

"Oh, yes, I'd like to get it over. I warn you it won't be easy. Mother is very much set on Bates. She'll probably call up when she gets home, and I dread that for she might insist on sending Bates down to accompany me home. That would just fit right in with her plans."

"Then don't say when you're coming. Say you'll try and arrange things here to get back soon. I believe perhaps we better just go ourselves early in the morning unannounced and then there can't be anything like that sprung on us. You see I've had experience in this long-distance calling back and forth. There generally is some mix-up, especially when there is a difference of opinion. I'll be ready to go on that early train, if you are. Are you sure you can get away?"

"Yes, I can go. Perhaps that is the best way, just take things in our own hands and announce what we are going to do, and say we've come for their blessing."

So they sat and made their lovely plans.

"Oh, it is going to be so wonderful to have somebody planning for me, somebody I can love and trust," said Diana. "It was awful to be ordered around by Bates. Oh, he was nice and pleasant you understand, but I constantly resented his possessive manner."

"I'm glad of that," said Rodney fervently. "But maybe you'll find me developing a possessive manner, too. What will happen then?"

"Oh, but I *love* you! And that makes all the difference in the world."

"Darling!" said Rodney gathering her close again, and sealing the word with a kiss.

"It's queer, but Beryl said something like that to me the first day I came, and I didn't know just exactly what she meant. You see I didn't know what love like this meant. I hadn't known you yet."

Time went very swiftly and happily out there under the sheltering trees, for those two. Occasionally they would pause in their gladness and make a plan or two about Saturday, and then slip back again to merely exulting in the presence of each other.

"And it's so wonderful that you belong to the Lord. You seemed to understand and take Him into your heart right away. That set the seal right at first on my love," said Rodney thoughtfully. "I knew you were the right one by that very sign, for I had been knowing all the way home that I couldn't ever love anyone who did not give allegiance to my Lord."

"Oh," said Diana with wonder in her eyes. "And I told Beryl that I was afraid of you after hearing that prayer. You were so religious I was just afraid to talk to you lest I couldn't measure up to your heights. And just to think, you reached down to the level where I'd been living and lifted me up where I could see the light and glory in Jesus' face. I would have loved Him long ago if I had really ever seen Him. And oh, I'm so glad it was you that helped me find Him."

And out in another green place in the woods where there were no people, and only a sweet silence punctuated now and again by piercing sweet bird notes, Jeremy and Beryl were walking arm in arm, or sometimes hand in hand, according to the roughness of the going.

They had been talking about Jessica. In fact it was almost impossible, after the scene that noon, not to talk about her. And Jerry had been telling Beryl of the early years when he was always anxious because that girl fairly possessed his brother and he couldn't do anything about it.

"For he was always such a wonderful chap!" said Jeremy soberly. "I just couldn't bear to see him get in her clutches. And then to come home and find her messing around in the way again. I just couldn't stand it."

"Yes, he is wonderful," said Beryl. "And he seems so very much like you in many ways."

Jeremy looked down at her with a quick appreciative smile.

"Thank you," he said. "You couldn't have said anything that would please me better. I always adored him."

It was then that Jerry reached down and took her hand, drawing it up within his arm, and holding his own over it. It was the first time he had done it just this way. He had been almost shy with Beryl.

They walked along silently for a little, thrilling over the touch of their hands, the look in each other's eyes. Then Jeremy, pressing the small hand he held, said with a relieved sigh:

"Well, now, I've got my brother's worries off my hands, let's talk about us. We've known each other a long time, far off. Very far, for you always seemed unattainable to me. You were so beautiful, and so perfectly dressed, and so very gracious and full of lovely manners, that I felt like a gawky country boy, all hands and feet, whenever I came into your presence. But I think I've been loving you all these years. How about it? Could you stand me for the rest of your life?"

The shade of the woods was very dense just where they were walking, and Beryl turned and put her face against his arm.

"Oh, Jerry!" she breathed softly. "I have always loved you. I sometimes was afraid you would see that shining in my eyes and written on my face."

And then Jerry folded her in his arms.

"Sweet! sweet! sweet!" sang a knowing little bird in a high tree above them, turning his bright little glance down at them, just as if he understood. And who knows, perhaps he did.

The shadows were low on the mossy way as they went slowly back to the house much later.

"Now," said Jerry in a practical voice, "tomorrow morning you and I are going to the city to buy you a ring. Not any seven-by-nine one, but a *real* ring that will match your dear self, and all that you stand for in my life."

20

JESSICA had thought she was going up to New York that Monday morning to interview the would-be bridegroom and show up her hated enemy, Diana. But there came a telegram before she was awake, ordering her to meet her husband out West on important business, and so she had to pack up and get off on another train, in another direction entirely.

She had only time to call Louella before she left, and order her to find out certain things for her definitely, before her return, which she hoped would be in the course of two or three days. And she promised to reward her well if she got all the answers to her questions ready for her return.

So Louella arose and set forth on her quest for answers. For to tell the truth she sorely needed the reward promised. She had lazed around too long running up hotel bills which she hadn't paid, and which would eventually fall to her relative to pay, as heretofore.

She went first to the Graemes' of course, for that was her main first source of information, provided she could get *any*.

But the boys were both gone. Where? "To the city I think," said Margaret Graeme. "They said they had some shopping to do."

"Shopping?" said Louella curiously. "What kind of shopping? I didn't know servicemen ever did shopping when they got home."

"Now Louella. You never can bear not to find out everything, can you?" laughed Margaret. "But won't you come in?"

"Oh, yes, just for a minute. There are some questions I want to ask you. What about the boys? Are they any better informed than they were?"

"Oh, yes," said the boys' mother. "They are not to leave the country for the present. They have a job here, that is not far away. I wasn't given the exact location yet. It seems hard for us to get time to ask questions. It's so good to know they are not going back to combat, for the present anyway."

"Well, what are they to be doing? What is their title? They surely have some designation."

"Why, you see I didn't think to ask that. They'll just be Rodney and Jeremy to me, just the same as they always were."

"Oh, Margaret, you're simply impossible," said Louella, and she finally took herself away, much to the relief of her relative.

But Jessica was by this time speeding away on an express train and trying to figure out just what she had to do in the near future, how soon she could hope to get that blue diamond.

The next day she was closeted with her husband and two other men in a bare little room in a dowdy boarding place, getting instructions.

One of the two strange men seemed to be a foreigner. He had a pompous disagreeable air, and talked with a strange accent, which she could not quite place. The other man was a sort of high-class secretary perhaps, for he wrote everything down, including the papers she was given to guide her in the work she was to do. And strangely he seemed to be somebody who was over her husband in this work she was doing

A Girl to Come Home To

which he said was for the Government. She kept asking herself *what* government, and why he was telling Carver what to
do? It was a new role to find her husband taking advice, or
rather orders from anybody. It gave her food for thought,
and a sort of a frightening background for this work she had
been ordered to do.

Carver, it developed from the talk between the men, was
expecting to leave the country for a time, possibly soon.
There seemed to be an uncertainty about it, maybe dependent
upon her own success in the mission they were about to send
her on. If he went she would ask him to take her along. She
was about fed up with this country, and it would be a relief to
travel. Afterward, if she still was out of sorts with her husband, she could probably get a divorce over in Europe as well
as in this country, and could make her plans accordingly.

They suggested that the war might be over soon, and the
possibility seemed fraught with peril for some of them. She
tried to figure that out, but couldn't quite make it. However,
if anything unpleasant developed, she would just get away
somewhere. It hadn't been hard to do so far, though she
sensed that she had not been so clever as her husband had expected she would be when he married her. She really must
exert herself and get this one across, for there was that blue
diamond. She mustn't miss out on that.

The tiresome session was ended at last, the men departed
one by one by devious unexpected ways, the foreigner going
by way of a window and a fire escape. He was hurrying to
catch a train he said, but when she looked out of the window
he was walking away toward the woods as fast as he could
go, with his hat pulled down over his face. It was all very
queer and bewildering, and when she asked a puzzled question her husband reminded her that she was to ask no questions whatever, and it was best to forget all that she had seen,
or thought she had seen. There seemed to be something
crooked somewhere, though she couldn't quite make out
what. Not that Jessica objected very seroiusly to crooked

ways of doing things, but it didn't seem quite to fit with her well-dressed, immaculate, severe husband, and she did like to understand things. However, this wasn't the way to win blue diamonds.

So, reluctantly, she gave attention to the instructions that were being given her.

"This paper is the most important. You will put it in the small white bag, and pin it inside your garments, right over the heart. Don't let anyone get possession of it. Guard it with your very life. Do you understand?"

Jessica blanched.

"But you said there was to be no danger," she faltered.

"No danger if you do your work fearlessly. No possibility of being suspected if you work calmly, fearlessly. It is safer that way."

Jessica caught her breath and kept on listening, and the stern old voice continued:

"Now here are the papers that you will need in getting into the plant."

"Plant? What plant?" she asked with wide eyes. "Have I got to go and work in a plant?"

"Nonsense! Give better attention or you will never be equal to this. I would have sent someone else, but the one I had chosen was killed in an accident, and this matter is urgent. Listen carefully."

"Killed?" said Jessica in a frightened tone. But the hard old voice went right on:

"Yesterday your friends, those two officers you know so well, entered new positions in the service, and it is necessary that you make immediate contact with them and get to work. There are important papers which will be under their care, and you can better find them than someone your friends do not know. The elder of the two men, your former fiancé, will be your special object of interest. By nine o'clock tomorrow morning you should be entering his office. The office is located on the top floor of the building, and this paper contains the address. It is just outside your city and can be reached by bus or taxi. I should suggest taxi, unless you find the bus not too crowded. We don't want too many witnesses. You will have to use your discretion in some of these moves. Don't take any chances unless it is the only way. Remember I have told you. Don't blame me if you get into any trouble. You'll be all right if you just follow instructions."

Jessica flung a bitter look at her husband, but said nothing.

"And when you get to the plant," he went on, "you will need identification papers. Here is your pass into the place, and your badge. I used an old snapshot of you to put on it. You won't have any trouble getting in, only remember you are Commander Graeme's private secretary, and if you should get there before he arrives in the morning so much the better. If possible manage it so that you are alone in his office for a few minutes, even a short time might accomplish what you want. The main thing is to get this paper, the original of the one you have in the secreted bag. You will have to study it so that you will recognize it at once, even if you see only a part of it. We *must have* that paper before it has a chance to be sent to the Government. If Mr. Graeme comes in while you are searching in the safe, as you may well have to do, you will know how to kid the gentleman along, even with endearments if necesary. Let him think you were hunting for a record you put in the safe Saturday. He won't know. He wasn't there then himself. Yes, I know definitely. I've had him watched for a week. Remember, the paper is the main thing and it *must* be had!"

When Jessica came out from that interview she was trembling from head to foot, and greatly impressed with the importance of the errand on which she was about to embark.

She had just had a ravishing glimpse of the blue stone in the white velvet box, fed to her as a cat would tantalize a mouse. If it had not been for that stone she would have taken the next train as far away from that frightening husband, and his kind, as it would be possible to get, but she simply must finish this engagement out and get that stone. Then she could stand any-thing. Just get away from Carver De Groot as fast as she could and never lay eyes on him again. She could dye her hair and change her make-up, and he might never know her, even if he hunted for her. Well, she had got to get through this somehow.

She went to sleep on the train and got a little rested, and then she began to study her papers, and get into her memory what she had to do, for she had been ordered to commit all these notes to memory, and then destory all but that one pa-per which was so important, and must be kept until the last minute.

Jessica found the way back to Riverton most tedious and tiresome. There were three changes, with long waits between trains, and nobody about the waiting places to look at or talk to, just little sheds, with a platform and a bench, and open country sizzling in a hot sun. She thought of the pleasant quiet sunny home of the Sandersons where she had been for a few minutes to fling her ugly words into Rodney's nice life, and a passing twinge of envy went through her. After all, what had she gained? She might have married Rodney if she had kept that ring, and been a part of that nice respectable crowd at the Sandersons', or at the Graeme house where she had spent so many pleasant days in her childhood. Awful bores they all were, and Rodney the worst bore of all of course, now that he had thoroughly adopted this religious phase, to which he seemed to have become heir. What a family! But better than her present lot, full of intrigue and peril and doing hazardous jobs of which she would have to take the blame if they went wrong.

She sighed heavily as she gathered up her bags from the hard bench and stood up to take the train as it crept along the rails to the shed where it was supposed to stop. Oh, she wished this whole thing was over. There was nothing pleas-ant to count on. Not even the small contact with Rodney was going to have any thrill about it, and to judge by the way he acted last Sunday there was no telling what attitude he might take toward her. She was definitely frightened, and wished she might run away and hide. She had entirely forgotten the scheme she had entertained of going to New York to find and inform that rich young officer about the defection of his supposed-to-be-bride. Later it would come to her, and she would wonder if there were any chance for her to charm him away when she got rid of her old husband, but now she was entirely engrossed with the thought of what she had to do, and she did not like the idea. There would be guns around, perhaps, and she detested guns, and firing. She never had wanted to learn to shoot.

So now while the people she had wanted to harm were having a happy time selecting rings, engagement and wedding rings, and making a memorable day of it, Jessica was beginning some of her punishment already.

JESSICA got back to her room in the Riverton Hotel very late Tuesday night, and went right to bed. It was too late to call Louella, so she did not know what had been happening during her absence, but it likely didn't matter. She would call her in the morning, and besides she was too tired to care.

However, she awoke very early the next morning, suddenly aware of the unpleasant errand she had to do for her husband, and filled with excitement over it.

She should of course call Louella the first thing now and make sure that the Graemes really had that new job. She wondered what she should do if there had been some hitch, and they were not there.

But when she called Louella she was informed that Mrs. Chatterton had checked out early yesterday morning. She had received a telegram calling her west on important business, and might or might not return later, depending on how the business came out.

This cut off Jessica from her only source of information about the Graemes, for she knew that her girl friends were all gone to the shore for the week, and anyway they would not know much about the Graemes. Jessica suddenly felt very much alone, and quite frightened.

How she hated this town! How she wished she could get away from it at once. She dressed rapidly, resolving that as soon as this horrible business for her husband was finished she would pack up and vanish utterly from Riverton, and all that could remind her of it. Just as soon as she had that blue diamond she would go away from everything. From Carver De Groot most of all. She shuddered as she thought of the look in his hard eyes when he threatened her. When he said, "Don't blame me if you get into trouble."

With that in mind she began swiftly to fold up her garments and lay them in her trunk. She didn't want to be delayed a moment in getting away when she got her work done. She was also very nervous about that approaching mysterious errand she had to do. She had not expected to be afraid, but she was. Unaccountably she was wondering what might happen to her if she should get caught. Rather frantically she was considering what she should do in case she had to get away from this vicinity quickly. She wouldn't want to leave her clothes behind her. More and more as the moments went by she grew panic-stricken. She must prepare for any happening, and there wasn't so much time. If she could just get everything into her trunk and lock it, then if worst came to worst she could send for her baggage afterward, say her husband had been taken sick and she had to go to him at once, or something like that. Just in case she got very much frightened.

She glanced at her watch. There wasn't so much more time before she should start, and perhaps she should have had something to eat before this trying expedition.

So she called up and ordered coffee, toast and orange juice, sent up to her room, and continued with her packing. At least everything should be under lock and key if anybody tried to go through her belongings. She didn't know why they would want to do that, but at least she was taking no chances now. It made her feel more safely comfortable to know that her affairs were all out of sight, and ready to meet the most inquisitive eye, even if she got into some kind of trouble through this doubtful escapade of her husband's.

She had thought out the different stages of this affair most carefully, so that no one around this part of the world would need to know where she was and what she had been doing today. She had arranged for the taxi to take her to the station for the very early train to the city. Then she was planning as soon as the taxi had gone to walk swiftly away and get a bus going in the opposite direction, so that if afterward there should be anyone questioning her movements, there would be no link left unguarded to tell any tales. After that she would get another bus, and then perhaps another taxi, whichever seemed to be most convenient, and by devious ways she would arrive at that plant in plenty of time to get in before the brothers came. Most of these movements had been planned by a sharp-seeing husband, but she had added a few of her own, instigated by fear, and some of her plans were clever indeed. That was what Carver De Groot had seen in her, that she was exceedingly clever.

So before Jessica left her room she went carefully about, examining even the waste basket to make sure there wasn't a scrap of precious notes, or papers that could possibly tell any tales about what she was doing.

Her baggage was locked, her door was locked, when she came down the stairs, for it was too early for the elevator boy to be on duty. She gave careful directions to the office man at the desk, explaining that she was going to see a member of her family who was very ill, and she was not sure how long she would be gone. If she found she was needed she might remain a few hours and return this evening. On the other hand she might stay for several days, or even for a week or two. In which case she would telephone for some of her baggage, but for the present she was retaining her room.

Then with high head she went briskly out of the door as if

for a pleasant visit, and got into the taxi, feeling perhaps, much like the fliers about to start on their first bombing mission.

Jessica had started early, following minutely the careful directions she had been given by her husband, and she arrived at the plant early, even earlier than she had hoped, and some minutes before the brothers reached there. She had made her entrance carefully, showing the badge and card and identification papers as she had been directed, and she had no trouble in getting to the office where Rodney was soon to arrive. A pretty woman seldom had difficulty in getting by, she reflected with satisfaction. She was beginning to get back her self-confidence.

The officer in charge of the rooms on that floor had given Jessica a sharp looking over, wondering a little at the style of secretary the new man had selected, but he let her in, and hovered near the door to explain, when Rodney would arrive, that he had let in his secretary just a minute ago. Was that all right? She had all her papers and badge, he said.

"Secretary?" said Rodney sharply, lifting his eyebrows, "Why—I—*haven't*—any—secretary." And then he stopped short and remembered that he was still a serviceman and there was no telling what the regulations here were to be. Perhaps they picked out his secretary for him! He didn't like that. But perhaps it was only temporary.

Then the door swung open and there was a woman, working away at the safe!

Jessica had been furnished with the safe combination, and been drilled carefully on how to open the safe swiftly. Moreover, she had just found the paper she was ordered to take, and as she heard the doorknob turn she dropped the paper inside her handbag, and turned smiling pleasantly, toward the stern face of Rodney who at once recognized her.

"Good morning!" said Jessica sweetly. But Rodney's face did not relax.

He took one step to the desk that stood near the door, and

whose accessories he had carefully studied before when he came to look things over. He slipped his hand across the top, down to the edge next his chair where two small unobtrusive bells were located, and touched them, one and then the other, twice. And instantly the door was stopped in its progress of closing and swung open again with the orderly standing there and the sound of tramping feet coming down the hall toward the door. Two burly officers came and stood saluting. "You called?" they said.

Rodney answered their salute:

"Take this person down to Major Haverly's office at once," he ordered. Gravely the officers advanced impersonally to the handsome, astonished, frightened young woman who stood before the safe with her hands full of papers.

"But—but—I'm Commander Graeme's secretary!" she said in a frightened voice.

But Rodney paid no heed to her.

"See that she is thoroughly searched!" he ordered. "She has no right to be up here."

"But her papers seemed all right," said the alarmed orderly.

"They can't be all right," said Rodney. "Take her at once, and don't let her out of your sight. I'll call Major Haverly."

He went to the telephone.

"Major Haverly," he said in a low voice when the door was closed again, after the frightened girl and her escort, "I have just sent a young woman down to you under guard. I found her in my office standing in front of the safe, taking out papers. Please see that she is thoroughly searched, and pay no attention to any of her claims. She is *not* my secretary and never has been, and you cannot always believe what she says. This is important. I haven't had opportunity to see what is missing from the safe. I will check the list at once."

"Yes, Commander Graeme. I will attend to your order. She has just arrived. Reporting later."

Jessica was stiff with fright, yet she knew she must somehow brazen this out. If she only could get that terrible paper out of her bag. No matter what became of it, it wouldn't be in her possession.

But when she tried to fumble with the clasp of her bag the sharp-eyed keepers watched her every move, and there presently arrived a woman to search her, who seemed to miss nothing. The officers were at a distance, but she knew she could make no move without their notice. Now if only that woman would only pass by that paper and not notice it!

But no! She opened the bag last, and found the paper the first thing. A gimlet-eyed woman who knew every sign of official paper, and knew what was important and what was not.

"Officer!" she called, and handed over the paper, also the handbag.

Jessica began to cry.

"But I need that bag," she said, "and I need all those papers; some of them aren't mine."

"That's right, they're not," said the officer coldly. "You took some of these out of the safe."

"No," she said. "No, I didn't. I only took out what I was told to take out. I'm a secretary, you know. I was sent to get them."

"Who sent you?" The sharp eyes of three officers were instantly upon her. They saw her flinch. They knew her guilt. The head one spoke a single word, and the others put handcuffs on her slender wrists and marched her away to a small room that was like a prison cell. More orders were given in low tones, and then she was left there with two women police, and one orderly at the door.

She cried a lot, and begged them to send for her friends. She said she had many friends both in the Army and the Navy that would help her. At last she asked them to send for her husband, and was frightened afterward when she saw a knowing look pass between the men who were guarding her. Also she remembered Carver had told her *never* to speak his name or he would be in trouble. But surely he didn't expect her to get arrested, did he? It was time he did something about this himself. He had no right to let her suffer. Even the blue diamond wasn't enough to pay her for going through a thing like this.

By night Jessica was taken to a place of safe keeping. She was fed and made comfortable, but she was definitely a prisoner, and from remarks she overheard now and then she gathered that there were a lot more suspects in this also. Oh, what was she in for?

At last she wrote a most piteous note to Rodney, telling him what trouble she was in and asking him to come to her at once, but though they took the note, they did not give it to Rodney. He was having trouble enough rounding up others of this gang, and going over a mass of important papers that had been tampered with. Of course this was something that had been going on before Jessica had arrived on the scene, but she was definitely linked up with it, and he suspected that the honorable old De Groot was at the bottom of the whole matter, which probably originated out of the country.

So that night Rodney did not get home to the delightful dinner that had been prepared. Instead he telephoned that there was trouble at the plant and he must stay till things were straightened out.

Jeremy came later for him in response to his phone call, and they felt that the real work of their new labors had begun in earnest.

Jeremy frowned when he heard that Jessica was connected with the trouble, and blamed himself.

"I knew *some*thing was going on," he said, "but I didn't suspect it was as serious as this. There'll be a trial of course?"

"Sure," said Rodney.

"She'll try to get you to help her out," said Jeremy.

"Nothing doing," said Rodney. "They wouldn't allow it, even if I would, and I don't see getting into this. If she's guilty she's guilty and they'll soon find it out. And even if she didn't know any better, she has to learn her lesson. These people that play fast and loose with their country's honor are just as bad as our enemies, and need punishment every bit as much."

"Certainly," said Jeremy. "But what do you think will happen to them? Will they be shot?"

"Some of them, perhaps, but most of them will be put in jail well guarded. Better off than some of the war prisoners of course, but they'll not be able to carry on any of their machinations. They'll be out of circulation till they learn how to be decent. Some of them will be out of circulation for life. But that's the only way to make the world safe for the coming generation. Of course we can't make the world perfect, and it won't be, till the Lord Jesus comes, but it will help to have right living possible for everybody. They won't all want it, nor take it, but those that want it ought to be able to get it, and not be under the domination of cruel fools."

So they talked it over, these two, who were sorely heavy-hearted over the world, and the way that Satan had deceived the multitudes. But they went on, living near to God, and trying not to bring their daily worries into the dear homes that were so precious to them.

A little later came the trial, for they had rounded up Jessica's husband and his gang, and were sifting the whole matter down to facts, and later the names all came out in the paper. They had all been sent away to a safe place, Jessica with the rest, and poor Louella read about it in the paper, and cried a great deal. She went off to a lonely little hotel in a far part of California, and disguised herself, fearing that she too might be rounded up with the criminals, because of her close association with Jessica.

But the dear young people about whom all this trouble had circulated and tried to harm, went strongly on in the power of their Lord, and were glad that they had found each other, and found a Lord who could sustain them.

Saturday was on its way, and Rodney was very glad that he need not worry any more about Jessica, nor have to deal with her in any way. He knew she was in the hands of right and just men, who would find out the truth if anybody could, and deal with her as she should be dealt with in order to teach her righteousness of a sort, and make her see that she could not play with sin and treachery, and not take the punishment when a law of the land was broken.

**22**

ON Saturday, up in New York, Diana and Rodney walked into the Winters' apartment just half an hour after the arrival of the father and mother.

They found Diana's mother frantically trying to telephone her daughter back in Riverton.

It must be owned that Mrs. Winters was at once impressed by Rodney's uniform, not to say stripes, and other decorations, all of which she took in thoroughly at a glance, even while she was standing by the telephone, receiver in hand, insisting that the operator ring Riverton again.

Then when she sighted Diana, who rushed to embrace her at once, she hung up the receiver and turned to face her, and the young Lieutenant Commander with such notable decorations, and such a handsome face.

It certainly was incredible, she thought, the way Diana always managed to attract the good-looking men, and high officers. This young man was almost better-looking than Bates Hibberd. Where did she find him? Not surely in that little backwoods town of Riverton! Then she smilingly held out a welcoming hand and was introduced. Diana with pride gave Rodney all his titles, even the newly acquired one, that he had only worn a day or two, and she had the great pleasure of seeing her mother look him over with eyes of approval.

Then she heard her father coming downstairs, and she called:

"Daddy, come here! I want you to meet somebody I've brought home," and there followed another introduction.

"I knew dad would like him, I knew, I knew," she whispered to her heart, as she saw the hearty grip he gave Rodney, and his smiling interested glance.

Suddenly, as they all sat down and the mother was prepared to ask a few routine questions about their journey and so on, Diana burst in with her news:

"Mother and dad, this is a very special person I've brought home with me, because I am going to marry him just as soon as we can arrange it. We love each other, and we think that's all that matters. He has a good government job, so I won't starve, and I hope you'll approve. This is Rodney's place to say all this first, I know, but I wanted you to know where I stand before he begins, so there won't be anything said that you'll be sorry for afterward, because this is the man *I'm going to marry!*"

Then Rodney came to the front.

"I didn't know she was going to do this, first, but I hope you'll excuse me for being slow. I came up here to ask your permission to marry your daughter. I've brought all my credentials with me, which you can examine at your leisure, but I sure hope you'll approve, for I love her a lot and I'm going to make it my chief business to make her happy as long as I live."

Then Father Winters fell in line gallantly.

"Well, young man, I don't know you of course, but I like your looks, and I'm willing to take you on faith until I can know you better."

"Thank you, sir," said Rodney warmly, grasping the offered hand of the man whom he had been afraid was going to be just another enemy to be conquered, as he had conquered the enemies across the water. But suddenly he knew that the eyes into which he was looking seemed definitely to be friendly eyes, and his heart grew warm and happy. Then he turned to meet the mother whom he had been led to understand would be the hard one to please.

But amazingly Mrs. Winters was smiling, looking almost shy as she held out a lovely hand.

"Well, I guess what papa has approved, I will have to approve too," she said in her most gracious manner. "But we love our girl a great deal, you know, and you'll have to measure up to requirements if you're going to please us."

"With God's help I'll try to do that, Mrs. Winters," said Rodney with a grave happy salute.

The mother gave him a quick scrutinizing look. Good Heavens! Was he *reli*gious? Or was this just put on for the occasion? But Rodney was smiling, and drawing Diana close to his side with her fingers squeezed tightly in his own, and he suddenly turned and gave her a kiss, so tender and genuine that the mother was won entirely over.

"And now," said Rodney, standing there with Diana's hand still in his, "we'd like, if you don't mind, to go right to the authorities and get a marriage license, for I have to go on duty at my new job on Monday, and I'd like to take my wife down with me just as soon as possible. Could we possibly have it the next Saturday?"

"But—but—*But!*" said Mrs. Winters, "we couldn't possibly arrange a wedding that soon. There are clothes to be bought, a whole trousseau, a wedding dress. It takes time to get clothes together to be married, my dears. Make it six months at least. Clothes take a lot of time!"

"*Clothes!*" sniffed Diana gaily. "What are clothes? I've got plenty for the time being, and even if you insist on a new one for the wedding, I can get that in an hour, I'm sure."

"But my dear! You couldn't get the invitations out in that time. A *week!* It's preposterous!"

"But why have invitations? We can call up the few people we like best, and just have it a quick war wedding. I don't want a lot of fancy truck to put away in a trunk in the attic for the rest of my life the way you did with your wedding dress. I have it, mother, I'll wear your wedding dress if you'll let me."

"Why of course," said the father. "That would be great. It will fit her, I'm sure. You were as slim as she is when you were married, my dear."

But Mother Winters drew her fine proportions up, and lifted her chin haughtily and said:

"Now, Edward, I haven't changed so much."

"Why no, of course not, my dear. You're just as charming as when I first fell in love with you."

So great joy descended upon the two young people, and even the dazed parents began to think that life was pretty nice.

It helped a lot, too, when there came a telephone message from the other would-be bridegroom, saying he was to be sent overseas at once, and wouldn't be able to come back to see Diana at present. But nobody was thinking anything about him, only Diana who wrote a nice little note of farewell and good wishes, and called that part of her life a closed incident.

They had a lot of fun and were very busy that week.

Of course Rodney had to get back to the plant early Monday morning, but as soon as the marriage license was arranged for, he had gotten in touch with his family at home and told them the good news so they could rejoice with him as soon as he returned. They were overjoyed at the news, and they all promised to come up to New York for the wedding, just for the day of course. So Mrs. Winters had plenty to do finding rooms for them all, and getting ready for a real house party, a thing she adored doing.

Diana tried on her mother's dress and found it needed very little alteration, and they simply eliminated all shopping for the time being.

It was a trial for the mother to give up all this delightful shopping, for the present, but she surrendered gracefully, with a resigned smile.

"I'll get you a lot of lovely things afterward," she said, "when we have more time to find what we want."

It was a goodly trainload of guests who came up the morning of the wedding day to see Diana and Rodney married.

Margaret Graeme wondered on the way whether Louella would ever forgive them that she should have started away only the day before the knowledge of the wedding came to the Graeme family. But Louella hadn't left an address where they could have reached her, and of course they were all just as well pleased not to have to have her.

And so it was going to be only the real families, Graemes, Sandersons, and a few very intimate friends and relatives of the Winters family. Though all their New York friends were given to understand that they might come to the church if they cared to, as it was to be quite an informal affair.

The wedding was to be in the great stone church which the Winters family had attended for generations, and Mother Winters was having her own way about the decorations, costly, refined and beautiful as any dream. Lilies and roses and palms and great lacy ferns, and masses of white azalias. But then the decorations were only a matter of an order to the best florist of New York, so everything was fitting and beautiful, and everybody satisfied.

The reception was supposed to be private, for the families and *very* intimates, but that too, was only the matter of an order to the best caterer in the city. Mrs. Winters had nothing to weary her naturally sweet temper. There were no hitches nor mistakes, nothing to show the difference between the quiet station of one family, and the smarter station of the other, with the sensible lovely Sandersons in between.

Jeremy of course was best man, and Beryl maid of honor.

The flowers were wonderful, and Diana's bouquet was as lovely as if she were marrying a millionaire. It was Rodney's one chance to show what he liked best for his dear bride. White roses, many of them, with maidenhair ferns; and smiling mistily in between, giving lightness to the whole spray, little waxen lilies of the valley. He enjoyed getting that armful of flowers for his dear girl. He had had so little opportunity as yet to show her how he loved her.

And even his new mother-in-law said it was exquisite!

The wedding was in the early evening, and they were going away soon after the ceremony so they might have one whole beautiful day to themselves before they had to go back into the world and begin to live. Rodney regretted so that they might not have a regular honeymoon, and go away somewhere together, but Diana only smiled and said that was the way most servicemen were having to do now while the war still lasted. And they were going to be together now in their own little home, a cottage at the upper end of the Graeme farm for the present, so it didn't matter.

Thank God Rodney didn't have to leave the next day and go back overseas, as so many warmen had to do, and leave their brides alone with an ocean and peril between.

Besides, Diana was in a hurry to get home and get her house ready for her parents' first visit, when the Winters would really get acquainted with her dear Graemes.

And now, let's go to the wedding, all of us.

The organ was playing sweet hymns.

"But *hymns!* Darling! *Not* hymns for a *wedding,*" protested Diana's mother. "*Just* hymns! I never *heard* of such a thing! You don't want to be outlandish. You *couldn't* really have such an innovation. It would scarcely be—well—respectable! Just hymns and no other music! I thought you were talking about that wonderful singer. Aren't you going to have him sing something? Yes, I thought so! And the wedding march, you know. It wouldn't seem right without that of course. But hymns are not at all fitting at such a time of rejoicing. Hymns are so sombre and gloomy."

But Diana was firm.

"It's *my* wedding, isn't it, mother? Well, that's the way I want it. That's the way we *both* want it. It's to be a kind of declaration of our faith!"

"What *nonsense!*" said her mother with a worried frown.

But the organ was playing sweet old hymns that meant very much to the bridal party. Softly, tenderly, the organ spoke, like a prayer breathed for the lives of those two who were to be joined in marriage. Some were lovely like the evening, some gay like the morning, and some triumphant, as when the words that belonged to their harmonies spoke of the coming of the Lord to those who understood.

Diana had compromised on having the wedding march played just as she stood at the door ready to enter, for her mother had been so aggrieved, and felt its absence so keenly, that she could not seem to be comforted to have it left out.

So the great organist somehow was made to understand about these two with shining eyes who went to explain it to him, and so he made the wedding march sound very far away at first, then drawing nearer, and nearer, till when the bride stood at the very door it melted into a triumphant note or two and went gloriously into another great sounding hymn.

Diana's mother frowned and caught her breath, turned quickly and cast an anxious glance back at the door. What was the matter? Hadn't Diana arrived yet after all? How strange! She was all ready when she left home. What could have happened? Was she taken suddenly ill? But Diana was almost never ill? She gave another anxious glance back again, and there she could see by the door a vision of white, the wonderful old veil! A lovely vision!

The audience had caught its breath and looked back, too, saw her there, while that triumphant hymn went on for an instant, filling the church with its sweet glad harmonies, and then suddenly a thrilling voice took up the strains with wondrous words. They were new to Mrs. Winters. What did this mean? Wasn't the organist going to go on with the wedding march while the bride came up the aisle? But then she had to stop her puzzled worries and listen as the great singer made the words of the song live.

And so when Diana walked softly up that richly carpeted

aisle in the beautiful old white satin wedding gown, trimmed with rare old costly lace, her lovely face alight with joy that had a touch of real glory in it, it was not to the conventional wedding march that she timed her footsteps, but to the fine old hymn as that wonderful voice sang the words:

> *When He shall come with trumpet sound,*
> *O may I then in Him be found;*
> *Dressed in His righteousness alone,*
> *Faultless to stand before the throne.*
> *On Christ the solid Rock I stand,*
> *All other ground is sinking sand,*
> *All other ground is sinking sand.*

Rodney, in his handsome uniform, with the glory-light on his own face, watched her come up the aisle to him, leaning on her father's arm, and said to himself in his heart, as she came:

"What a girl to come home to!"

## About the Author

Grace Livingston Hill is well-known as one of the most pro-lific writers of romantic fiction. Her personal life was fraught with joys and sorrows not unlike those experienced by many of her fictional heroines.

Born in Wellsville, New York, Grace nearly died during the first hours of life. But her loving parents and friends turned to God in prayer. She survived miraculously, thus her thankful father named her Grace.

Grace was always close to her father, a Presbyterian minis-ter, and her mother, a published writer. It was from them that she learned the art of storytelling. When Grace was twelve, a close aunt surprised her with a hardbound, illustrated copy of one of Grace's stories. This was the beginning of Grace's journey into being a published author.

In 1892 Grace married Fred Hill, a young minister, and they soon had two lovely young daughters. Then came 1901, a difficult year for Grace—the year when, within months of each other, both her father and husband died. Suddenly Grace had to find a new place to live (her home was owned by the church where her husband had been pastor). It was a struggle for Grace to raise her young daughters alone, but through everything she kept writing. In 1902 she produced *The Angel of His Presence, The Story of a Whim,* and *An Unwilling Guest.* In 1903 her two books *According to the Pattern* and *Because of Stephen* were published.

It wasn't long before Grace was a well-known author, but she wanted to go beyond just entertaining her readers. She soon included the message of God's salvation through Jesus Christ in each of her books. For Grace, the most important thing she did was not write books but share the message of salvation, a message she felt God wanted her to share through the abilities he had given her.

In all, Grace Livingston Hill wrote more than one hundred books, all of which have sold thousands of copies and have touched the lives of readers around the world with their message of "enduring love" and the true way to lasting happiness: a relationship with God through his Son, Jesus Christ.

In an interview shortly before her death, Grace's devotion to her Lord still shone clear. She commented that whatever she had accomplished had been God's doing. She was only his servant, one who had tried to follow his teaching in all her thoughts and writing.

# THE BEST MAN

**LIVING BOOKS®**
Tyndale House Publishers, Inc.
Wheaton, Illinois

This Tyndale House book
by Grace Livingston Hill
contains the complete text
of the original hardcover edition.
NOT ONE WORD
HAS BEEN OMITTED.

Copyright © 1989 by Tyndale House Publishers, Inc.
All rights reserved
Cover illustration copyright © 1989 by Lorraine Bush

*Living Books* is a registered trademark of Tyndale House
Publishers, Inc.

3-in-1 ISBN 1-56865-290-9

Printed in the United States of America

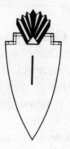

CYRIL Gordon had been seated at his desk but ten minutes and was deep in the morning's mail when there came an urgent message from his chief, summoning him to an immediate audience in the inner office.

The chief had keen blue eyes and shaggy eyebrows. He never wasted words; yet those words when spoken had more weight than those of most other men in Washington.

There was the briefest of good-morning gleams in his nod and glance, but he only said:

"Gordon, can you take the Pennsylvania train for New York that leaves the station in thirty-two minutes?"

The young man was used to abrupt questions from his chief, but he caught his breath, mentally surveying his day as it had been planned:

"Why, sir, I suppose I could—if it is necessary—" He hesitated.

"It is necessary," said the chief curtly, as if that settled the matter.

"But—half an hour!" ejaculated Gordon in dismay. "I could hardly get to my rooms and back to the station. I don't see how—Isn't there a train a little later?"

"Later train won't do. Call up your man on the 'phone. Tell him to pack your bag and meet you at the station in twenty minutes. You'll need evening clothes. Can you depend on your man to get your things quickly without fail?"

There was that in the tone of the chief that caused Gordon to make no further demur.

"Sure!" he responded with his usual businesslike tone, as he strode to the 'phone. His daze was passing off. "Evening clothes?" he questioned curiously, as if he might not have heard aright.

"Yes, evening clothes," was the curt answer, "and everything you'll need for daytime for a respectable gentleman of leisure — a tourist, you understand."

Gordon perceived that he was being given a mission of trust and importance, not unmixed with mystery perhaps. He was new in the Secret Service, and it had been his ambition to rise in his chief's good graces. He rang the telephone bell furiously and called up the number of his own apartments, giving his man orders in a breezy, decisive tone that caused a look of satisfaction to settle about the fine wrinkles of the chief's eyes.

Gordon's watch was out and he was telling his man on just what car he must leave the apartments for the station. The chief noted it was two cars ahead of what would have been necessary. His gray head gave an almost imperceptible nod of commendation, and his eyes showed that he was content with his selection of a man.

"Now, sir," said Gordon, as he hung up the receiver, "I'm ready for orders."

"Well, you are to go to New York, and take a cab for the Cosmopolis Hotel — your room there is already secured by wire. Your name is John Burnham. The name of the hotel and the number of your room are on this memorandum. You will find awaiting you an invitation to dine this evening with a Holman, who knows of you as an expert in code-reading. Our men met him on the train an hour ago and arranged that he should invite you. He didn't know whom they represented, of course. He has already tried to 'phone you at the hotel about coming to dinner to-night. He knows you are expected there before evening. Here is a letter of introduction to him from a man he knows. Our men got that also. It is genuine, of course.

"Last night a message of national importance, written in cipher, was stolen from one of our men before it had been read. This is now in the hands of Holman, who is hoping to have you decipher it for him and a few guests who will also be present at dinner. They wish to use it for their own purposes. Your commission is to get hold of the message and bring it to us as soon as possible. Another message of very different import, written upon the same kind of paper, is in this envelope, with a translation for you to use in case you have to substitute a message. You will have to use your own wits and judgment. The main thing is, *get the paper, and get back with it,* with as little delay as possible. Undoubtedly your life will be in danger should it be discovered that you have made off with it. Spare no care to protect yourself *and the message,* at all hazards. Remember, I said, *and the message,* young man! It means much to the country.

"In this envelope is money—all you will probably need. Telegraph or 'phone to this address if you are in trouble. Draw on us for more, if necessary, also through this same address. Here is the code you can use in case you find it necessary to telegraph. Your ticket is already bought. I have sent Clarkson to the station for it, and he will meet you at the train. You can give him instructions in case you find you have forgotten anything. Take your mail with you, and telegraph back orders to your stenographer. I think that is all. Oh, yes, to-night, while you are at dinner, you will be called to the 'phone by one of our men. If you are in trouble, this may give you opportunity to get away, and put us wise. You will find a motor at the door now, waiting to take you to the station. If your man doesn't get there with your things, take the train any way, and buy some more when you get to New York. Don't turn aside from your commission for anything. Don't let *anything* hinder you! Make it a matter of life and death! Good morning, and good luck!"

The chief held out a big, hairy hand that was surprisingly warm and soft considering the hardness of his face and voice, and the young man grasped it, feeling as if he were suddenly being plunged into waves of an unknown depth and he would fain hold on to this strong hand.

He went out of the office quietly enough, and the keen old eyes watched him knowingly, understanding the beating of the heart under Gordon's well-fitting business coat, the mingled elation and dread over the commission. But there had been no hesitancy, no question of acceptance, when the nature of the the commission was made known. The young man was "game." He would do. Not even an eyelash had flickered at the hint of danger. The chief felt he would be faithful even in the face of possible death.

Gordon's man came rushing into the station just after he reached there himself. Clarkson was already there with the ticket. Gordon had time to scribble a message to Julia Bentley, whose perfumed scrawl he had read on the way down. Julia had bidden him to her presence that evening. He could not tell whether he was relieved or sorry to tell her he could not come. It began to look to him a good deal as if he would ask Julia Bentley to marry him some day, when she got tired of playing all the others off against him, and he could make up his mind to surrender his freedom to any woman.

He bought a paper and settled himself comfortably in the parlor car, but his interest was not in the paper. His strange commission engaged all his thoughts. He took out the envelope containing instructions and went over the matter, looking curiously at the cipher message and its translation, which, however, told him nothing. It was the old chief's way to keep the business to himself until such time as he chose to explain. Doubtless it was safer for both message and messenger that he did not know the full import of what he was undertaking.

Gordon carefully noted down everything that his chief had told him, comparing it with the written instructions in the envelope; arranged in his mind just how he could proceed when he reached New York; tried to think out a good plan for recovering the stolen message, but could not; and so decided to trust to the inspiration of the moment. Then it occurred to him to clear his overcoat pockets of any letters or other tell-tale articles and stow them in his suit-case. He might have to leave his overcoat behind him. So it would be well to have no clues for anyone to follow.

Having arranged these matters, and prepared a few letters with notes for his stenographer, to be mailed back to her from Philadelphia, he reread Julia Bentley's note. When every angular line of her tall script was imprinted on his memory, he tore the perfumed note into tiny pieces and dropped them from the car window.

The question was, did he or did he not want to ask Julia Bentley to become his wife? He had no doubt as to what her answer would be. Julia had made it pretty plain to him that she would rather have him than any of her other admirers; though she did like to keep them all attendant upon her. Well, that was her right so long as she was unmarried. He had no fault to find with her. She was a fine girl, and everybody liked her. Also, she was of a good family, and with a modest fortune in her own right. Everybody was taking it for granted that they liked each other. It was time he was married and had a real home, he supposed, whatever that was — that seemed to have so great a charm for all his friends. To his eyes, it had as yet taken on no alluring mirage effect. He had never known a real home, more than his quiet bachelor apartments were to him now, where his man ordered everything as he was told, and the meals were sent up when wanted. He had money enough from his inheritance to make things more than comfortable, and he was deeply interested in the profession he had chosen.

Still, if he was ever going to marry, it was high time, of course. But did he want Julia? He could not quite make it seem pleasant to think of her in his rooms when he came home at night tired; she would always be wanting to go to her endless theatre parties and receptions and dances; always be demanding his attention. She was bright and handsome and well dressed, but he had never made love to her. He could not quite imagine himself doing so. How did men make love, any way? Could one call it love when it was "made" love? These questions followed one another idly through his brain as the landscape whirled past him. If he had stayed at home, he would have spent the evening with Julia, as she requested in her note, and there would probably have been a quiet half-hour after other callers had gone when he would have stayed as he had been doing of late, and tried to find out whether he really cared for her or not.

Suppose, for instance, they were married, and she sat beside him now. Would any glad thrill fill his heart as he looked at her beautiful face and realized that she was his? He tried to look over toward the next chair and imagine that the tired, fat old lady with the double chin and the youthful purple hat was Julia, but that would not work. He whirled his chair about and tried it on an empty chair. That went better; but still no thrill of joy lifted him out of his sordid self. He could not help thinking about little trying details. The way Julia looked when she was vexed. Did one mind that in the woman one loved? The way she ordered her coachman about. Would she ever speak so to her husband? She had a charming smile, but her frown was —well—unbecoming to say the least.

He tried to keep up the fallacy of her presence. He bought a magazine that he knew she liked, and read a story to her (in imagination). He could easily tell how her black eyes would snap at certain phrases she disliked. He knew just what her comment would be upon the heroine's conduct.

It was an old disputed point between them. He knew how she would criticize the hero, and somehow he felt himself in the hero's place every time she did it. The story had not been a success, and he felt a weariness as he laid the magazine aside at the call for dinner from the dining-car.

Before he had finished his luncheon he had begun to feel that though Julia might think now that she would like to marry him, the truth about it was that she would not enjoy the actual life together any better than he would. Were all marriages like that? Did people lose the glamour and just settle down to endure each other's faults and make the most of each other's pleasant side, and not have anything more? Or was he getting cynical? Had he lived alone too long, as his friends sometimes told him, and so was losing the ability really to love anybody but himself? He knit his brows, and got up whistling to go out and see why the train had stopped so long in this little country settlement.

It was just beyond Princeton, and they were not far now from New York. It would be most annoying to be delayed so near to his destination. He was anxious to get things in train for his evening of hard work. It was necessary to find out how the land lay as soon as possible.

It appeared that there was a wrecked freight ahead of them, and there would be delay. No one knew just how long; it would depend on how soon the wrecking train arrived to help.

Gordon walked nervously up and down the grass at the side of the track, looking anxiously each way for sign of the wrecking train. The thought of Julia did occur to him, but he put it impatiently away, for he knew just how poorly Julia would bear a delay on a journey even in his company. He had been with her once when the engine got off the track on a short trip down to a Virginia houseparty, and she was the most impatient creature alive, although it mattered not one whit to any of the rest of the party whether they made merry on the train or at their friend's house. And yet, if Julia were anything at all to him, would not he like the thought of her companionship now?

A great white dog hobbled up to him and fawned upon him as he turned to go back to the train, and he laid his hand kindly upon the animal's head, and noted the wistful eyes upon his face. He was a noble dog, and Gordon stood for a moment fondling him. Then he turned impatiently and tramped back to his car again. But when he reached the steps he found that the dog had followed him.

Gordon frowned, half in annoyance, half in amusement, and sitting down on a log by the wayside he took the dog's pink nozzle into his hands, caressing the white fur above it gently.

The dog whined happily, and Gordon meditated. How long would the train wait? Would he miss getting to New York in time for the dinner? Would he miss the chance to rise in the chief's good graces? The chief would expect him to get to New York some other way if the train were delayed. How long ought he to wait on possibilities?

All at once he saw the conductor and trainmen coming back hurriedly. Evidently the train was about to start. With a final kindly stroke of the white head, he called a workman nearby, handed him half a dollar to hold the dog, and sprang on board.

He had scarcely settled himself into his chair, however, before the dog came rushing up the aisle from the other end of the car, and precipitated himself muddily and noisily upon him.

With haste and perturbation Gordon hurried the dog to the door and tried to fling him off, but the poor creature pulled back and clung to the platform yelping piteously.

Just then the conductor came from the other car and looked at him curiously.

"No dogs allowed in these cars," he said gruffly.

"Well, if you know how to enforce that rule I wish you

would," said Gordon. "I'm sure I don't know what to do with him."

"Where has he been since you left Washington?" asked the grim conductor with suspicion in his eyes.

"I certainly haven't had him secreted about me, a dog of that size," remarked the young man dryly. "Besides, he isn't my dog. I never saw him before till he followed me at the station. I'm as anxious to be rid of him as he is to stay."

The conductor eyed the young man keenly, and then allowed a grim sense of humor to appear in one corner of his mouth.

"Got a chain or a rope for him?" he asked more sympathetically.

"Well, no," remarked the unhappy attaché of the dog. "Not having had an appointment with the dog I didn't provide myself with a leash for him."

"Take him into the baggage car," said the conductor briefly, and slammed his way into the next car.

There seemed nothing else to be done, but it was most annoying to be thus forced on the notice of his fellow-travellers, when his commission required that he be as inconspicuous as possible.

At Jersey City he hoped to escape and leave the dog to the tender mercies of the baggage man, but that official was craftily waiting for him and handed the animal over to his unwilling master with a satisfaction ill-proportioned to the fee he had received for caring for him.

Then began a series of misfortunes. Disappointment and suspicion stalked beside him, and behind him a voice continually whispered his chief's last injunction: "Don't let anything hinder you!"

Frantically he tried first one place and then another, but all to no effect. Nobody apparently wanted to care for a stray white dog, and his very haste aroused suspicion. Once he came near being arrested as a dog thief. He could not get rid of that dog! Yet he must not let him follow him! Would he have to have the animal sent home to Washington as the only solution of the problem? Then a queer fancy seized him that just in some such way had Miss Julia Bentley been shadowing his days for nearly three years now; and he had actually this very day been considering calmly whether he might not have to marry her just because she was so persistent in her taking possession of him. Not that she was unladylike, of course; no, indeed! She was stately and beautiful, and had never offended. But she had always quietly, persistently, taken it for granted that he would be her attendant whenever she chose; and she always chose whenever he was in the least inclined to enjoy any other woman's company.

He frowned at himself. Was there something weak about his character that a woman or a dog could so easily master him? Would any other employee in the office, once trusted with his great commission, have allowed it to be hindered by a dog?

Gordon could not afford to waste any more time. He must get rid of him at once!

The express office would not take a dog without a collar and chain unless he was crated; and the delays and exasperating hindrances seemed to be interminable. But at last, following the advice of a kindly officer, he took the dog to an institution in New York where, he was told, dogs were boarded and cared for, and where he finally disposed of him, having first paid ten dollars for the privilege. As he settled back in a taxicab with his watch in his hand, he congratulated himself that he had still ample time to reach his hotel and get into evening dress before he must present himself for his work.

Within three blocks of the hotel the cab came to such a sudden standstill that Gordon was thrown to his knees.

## 2

THEY were surrounded immediately by a crowd in which policemen were a prominent feature. The chauffeur seemed dazed in the hands of the officers.

A little, barefoot, white-faced figure huddled limply in the midst showed Gordon what had happened: also there were menacing glances toward himself and a show of lifted stones. He heard one boy say: "You bet he's in a hurry to git away. Them kind allus is. They don't care who they kills, they don't!"

A great horror seized him. The cab had run over a news-boy and perhaps killed him. Yet instantly came the remembrance of his commission: "Don't let anything hinder you. Make it a matter of life and death!" Well, it looked as if this was a matter of death that hindered him now.

They bundled the moaning boy into the taxicab and as Gordon saw no escape through the tightly packed crowd, who eyed him suspiciously, he climbed in beside the grimy little scrap of unconscious humanity, and they were off to the hospital to the tune of "Don't let anything hinder you! Don't let anything hinder you!" until Gordon felt that if it did not stop soon he would go crazy. He meditated opening the cab door and making his escape in spite of the speed they were making, but a vision of broken legs and a bed in the hospital for himself held him to his seat. One of the policemen had climbed on in front with the chauffeur, and now and again he glanced back as if he were conveying a couple of prisoners to jail. It was vexatious beyond anything! And all on account of that white dog! Could anything be more ridiculous than the whole performance?

His annoyance and irritation almost made him forget that it was his progress through the streets that had silenced this mite beside him. But just as he looked at his watch for the fifth time the boy opened his eyes and moaned, and there was in those eyes a striking resemblance to the look in the eyes of the dog of whose presence he had but just rid himself.

Gordon started. In spite of himself it seemed as if the dog were reproaching him through the eyes of the child. Then suddenly the boy spoke.

"Will yous stay by me till I'm mended?" whispered the weak little voice.

Gordon's heart leaped in horror again, and it came to him that he was being tried out this day to see if he had the right stuff in him for hard tasks. The appeal in the little street-boy's eyes reached him as no request had ever yet done, and yet he might not answer it. Duty,—life and death duty,—called him elsewhere, and he must leave the little fellow whom he had been the involuntary cause of injuring, to suffer and per-haps to die. It cut him to the quick not to respond to that ur-gent appeal.

Was it because he was weary that he was visited just then by a vision of Julia Bentley with her handsome lips curled scornfully? Julia Bentley would not have approved of his stopping to carry a boy to the hospital, any more than to care for a dog's comfort.

"Look here, kiddie," he said gently, leaning over the child, "I'd stay by you if I could, but I've already made myself later for an appointment by coming so far with you. Do you know what Duty is?"

The child nodded sorrowfully.

"Don't yous mind me," he murmured weakly. "Just yous go. I'm game all right." Then the voice trailed off into silence again, and the eyelids fluttered down upon the little, grimy, unconscious face.

Gordon went into the hospital for a brief moment to leave some money in the hands of the authorities for the benefit of the boy, and a message that he would return in a week or two if possible; then hurried away.

Back in the cab once more, he felt as if he had killed a man and left him lying by the roadside while he continued his unswerving march toward the hideous duty which was growing increasingly more portentous, and to be relieved of which he would gladly have surrendered further hope of his chief's favor. He closed his eyes and tried to think, but all the time the little white face of the child came before his vision, and the mocking eyes of Julia Bentley tantalized him, as if she were telling him that he had spoiled all his chances — and hers — by his foolish soft-heartedness. Though, what else could he have done than he had done, he asked himself fiercely.

He looked at his watch. It was at least ten minutes' ride to the hotel, the best time they could make. Thanks to his man the process of dressing for the evening would not take long, for he knew that everything would be in place and he would not be hindered. He would make short work of his toilet. But there was his suit-case. It would not do to leave it at the hotel, neither must he take it with him to the house where he was to be a guest. There was nothing for it but to go around by the way of the station where it would have to be checked. That meant a longer ride and more delay, but it must be done.

Arrived at the hotel at last, and in the act of signing the unaccustomed "John Burnham" in the hotel registry, there came a call to the telephone.

With a hand that trembled from excitement he took the

receiver. His breath went from him as though he had just run up five flights of stairs. "Yes? Hello! Oh, Mrs. Holman. Yes! Burnham. I've but just arrived. I was delayed. A wreck ahead of the train. Very kind of you to invite me, I'm sure. Yes, I'll be there in a few moments, as soon as I can get rid of the dust of travel. Thank you. Good-bye."

It all sounded very commonplace to the clerk, who was making out bills and fretting because he could not get off to take his girl to the theatre that night, but as Gordon hung up the receiver he looked around furtively as if expecting to see a dozen detectives ready to seize upon him. It was the first time he had ever undertaken a commission under an assumed name and he felt as if he were shouting his commission through the streets of New York.

The young man made short work of his toilet. Just as he was leaving the hotel a telegram was handed him. It was from his chief, and so worded that to the operator who had copied it down it read like a hasty call to Boston; but to his code-enlightened eyes it was merely a blind to cover his exit from the hotel and from New York, and set any possible hunters on a wrong scent. He marvelled at the wonderful mind of his chief, who thought out every detail of an important campaign, and forgot not one little possible point where difficulty might arise.

Gordon had a nervous feeling as he again stepped into a taxicab and gave his order. He wondered how many stray dogs, and newsboys with broken legs, would attach themselves to him on the way to dinner. Whenever the speed slowed down, or they were halted by cars and autos, his heart pounded painfully, lest something new had happened, but he arrived safely and swiftly at the station, checked his suitcase, and took another cab to the residence of Mr. Holman, without further incident.

The company were waiting for him, and after the introductions they went immediately to the dining-room. Gordon took his seat with the feeling that he had bungled everything hopelessly, and had arrived so late that there was no possible hope of his doing what he had been sent to do. For the first few minutes his thoughts were a jumble, and his eyes dazed with the brilliant lights of the room. He could not single out the faces of the people present and differentiate them one from another. His heart beat painfully against the stiff expanse of evening linen. It almost seemed as if those near him could hear it. He found himself starting and stammering when he was addressed as "Mr. Burnham." His thoughts were mingled with white dogs, newsboys, and ladies with scornful smiles.

He was seated on the right of his hostess, and gradually her gentle manners gave him quietness. He began to gain control of himself, and now he seemed to see afar the keen eye of his chief watching the testing of his new commissioner. His heart swelled to meet the demand made upon him. A strong purpose came to him to rise above all obstacles and conquer in spite of circumstances. He must forget everything else and rise to the occasion.

From that moment the dancing lights that multiplied themselves in the glittering silver and cut glass of the table began to settle into order; and slowly, one by one, the conglomeration of faces around the board resolved itself into individuals.

There was the pretty, pale hostess, whose gentle ways seemed hardly to fit with her large, boisterous, though polished husband. Unscrupulousness was written all over his ruddy features, also a certain unhidden craftiness which passed for geniality among his kind.

There were two others with faces full of cunning, both men of wealth and culture. One did not think of the word "refinement" in connection with them; still, that might be conceded also, but it was all dominated by the cunning that on this occasion, at least, was allowed to sit unmasked upon their countenances. They had outwitted an enemy, and they were openly exultant.

Of the other guests, one was very young and sleek, with eyes that had early learned to evade; one was old and weary-looking, with a hunted expression; one was thick-set, with little eyes set close in a fat, selfish face. Gordon began to understand that these three but did the bidding of the others. They listened to the conversation merely from a business standpoint and not with any personal interest. They were there because they were needed, and not because they were desired.

There was one bond which they seemed to hold in common: an alert readiness to combine for their mutual safety. This did not manifest itself in anything tangible, but the guest felt that it was there and ready to spring upon him at any instant.

All this came gradually to the young man as the meal with its pleasant formalities began. As yet nothing had been said about the reason for his being there.

"Did you tell me you were in a wreck?" suddenly asked the hostess sweetly, turning to him, and the table talk hushed instantly while the host asked: "A wreck! Was it serious?"

Gordon perceived his mistake at once. With instant caution, he replied smilingly, "Oh, nothing serious, a little breakdown on a freight ahead, which required time to patch up. It reminded me —" and then he launched boldly into one of the bright dinner stories for which he was noted among his companions at home. His heart was beating wildly, but he succeeded in turning the attention of the table to his joke, instead of to asking from where he had come and on what road. Questions about himself were dangerous he plainly saw, if he would get possession of the valued paper and get away without leaving a trail behind him. He succeeded in one thing more, which, though he did not know it, was the very thing his chief had hoped he would do when he chose him instead of a man who had wider experience: he made every man at the table feel that he was delightful, a man to be thoroughly trusted and enjoyed; who would never suspect them of having any ulterior motives in anything they were doing.

The conversation for a little time rippled with bright stories and repartee, and Gordon began to feel almost as if he were merely enjoying a social dinner at home, with Julia Bentley down the table listening and haughtily smiling her approval. For the time the incidents of the dog and the newsboy were forgotten, and the young man felt his self-respect rising. His heart was beginning to get into normal action again and he could control his thoughts. Then suddenly, the crisis arrived.

The soup and fish courses had been disposed of, and the table was being prepared for the entrée. The host leaned back genially in his chair and said, "By the way, Mr. Burnham, did you know I had an axe to grind in asking you here this evening? That sounds inhospitable, doesn't it? But I'm sure we're all grateful to the axe that has given us the opportunity of meeting you. We are delighted at having discovered you."

Gordon bowed, smiling at the compliment, and the murmurs of hearty assent around the table showed him that he had begun well. If only he could keep it up! But how, *how,* was he to get possession of that magic bit of paper and take it away with him?

"Mr. Burnham, I was delighted to learn through a friend that you are an expert in code-reading. I wonder, did the message that my friend, Mr. Burns sent you this morning give you any information that I wanted you to do me a favor?"

Gordon bowed again. "Yes: it was intimated to me that you had some message you would like deciphered, and I have also sent a letter of introduction from Mr. Burns."

Here Gordon took the letter of introduction from his pocket and handed it across the table to his host, who opened it genially, as if it were hardly necessary to read what was written within since they already knew so delightfully the man whom it introduced. The duplicate cipher writing in Gordon's pocket crackled knowingly when he settled his coat about him again, as if it would say, "My time is coming! It is almost here now."

The young man wondered how he was to get it out without being seen, in case he should want to use it, but he smiled pleasantly at his host with no sign of the perturbation he was feeling.

"You see," went on Mr. Holman, "we have an important message which we cannot read, and our expert who understands all these matters is out of town and cannot return for some time. It is necessary that we know as soon as possible the import of this writing."

While he was speaking Mr. Holman drew from his pocket a long, soft leather wallet and took therefrom a folded paper which Gordon at once recognized as the duplicate of the one he carried in his pocket. His head seemed to reel, and all the lights go dark before him as he reached a cold hand out for the paper. He saw in it his own advancement coming to his eager grasp, yet when he got it would he be able to hold it? Something of the coolness of a man facing a terrible danger came to him now. By sheer force of will he held his trembling fingers steady as he took the bit of paper and opened it carelessly, as if he had never heard of it before, saying as he did so:

"I will do my best."

There was a sudden silence as every eye was fixed upon him while he unfolded the paper. He gave one swift glance about the table before he dropped his eyes to the task. Every face held the intensity of almost terrible eagerness, and on every one but that of the gentle hostess sat cunning — craft that would stop at nothing to serve its own ends. It was a moment of almost awful import.

The next instant Gordon's glance went down to the paper in his hand, and his brain and heart were seized in the grip of fright. There was no other word to describe his feeling. The message before him was clearly written in the code of the home office, and the words stared at him plainly without the necessity of study. The import of them was the revelation of one of the most momentous questions that had to do with the Secret Service work, a question the answer to which had puzzled the entire department for weeks. That answer he now held in his hand, and he knew that if it should come to the knowledge of those outside before it had done its work through the department it would result in dire calamity to the cause of righteousness in the country, and incidentally crush the inefficient messenger who allowed it to become known. For the instant Gordon felt unequal to the task before him. How could he keep these bloodhounds at bay—for such they were, he perceived from the import of the message, bloodhounds who were getting ill-gotten gains from innocent and unsuspecting victims—some of them little children.

But the old chief had picked his man well. Only for an instant the glittering lights darkened before his eyes and the cold perspiration started. Then he rallied his forces and looked up. The welfare of a nation's honor was in his hands, and he would be true. It was a matter of life and death, and he would save it or lose his own life if need be.

He summoned his ready smile.

"I shall be glad to serve you if I can," he said. "Of course I'd like to look this over a few minutes before attempting to read it. Codes are different, you know, from one another, but there is a key to them all if one can just find it out. This looks as if it might be very simple."

The spell of breathlessness was broken. The guests relaxed and went on with their dinner.

Gordon, meanwhile, tried coolly to keep up a pretense of eating, the paper held in one hand while he seemed to be studying it. Once he turned it over and looked on the back.

There was a large crossmark in red ink at the upper end. He looked at it curiously and then instinctively at his host.

"That is my own mark," said Mr. Holman. "I put it there to distinguish it from other papers." He was smiling politely, but he might as well have said, "I put it there to identify it in case of theft;" for every one at the table, unless it might be his wife, understood that that was what he meant. Gordon felt it and was conscious of the other paper in his vest-pocket. The way was going to be difficult.

Among the articles in the envelope which the chief had given him before his departure from Washington were a pair of shell-rimmed eye-glasses, a false mustache, a goatee, and a pair of eyebrows. He had laughed at the suggestion of high-tragedy contained in the disguise, but had brought them with him for a possible emergency. The eye-glasses were tucked into the vest-pocket beside the duplicate paper. He bethought himself of them now. Could he, under cover of taking them out, manage to exchange the papers? And if he should, how about that red-ink mark across the back? Would any one notice its absence? It was well to exchange the papers as soon as possible before the writing had been studied by those at the table, for he knew that the other message, though resembling this one in general words, differed enough to attract the attention of a close observer. Dared he risk their noticing the absence of the red cross on the back?

Slowly, cautiously, under cover of the conversation, he managed to get that duplicate paper out of his pocket and under the napkin in his lap. This he did with one hand, all the time ostentatiously holding the code message in the other hand, with its back to the people at the table. This hand meanwhile also held his coat lapel out that he might the more easily search his vest-pockets for the glasses. It all looked natural. The hostess was engaged in a whispered conversation with the maid at the moment. The host and other guests were finishing the exceedingly delicious patties on their plates, and the precious code message was safely in evidence, red cross and all. They saw no reason to be suspicious about the stranger's hunt for his glasses.

"Oh, here they are!" he said, quite unconcernedly, and put on the glasses to look more closely at the paper, spreading it smoothly on the table cloth before him, and wondering how he should get it into his lap in place of the one that now lay quietly under his napkin.

The host and the guests politely refrained from talking to Gordon and told each other incidents of the day in low tones that indicated the non–importance of what they were saying; while they waited for the real business of the hour.

Then the butler removed the plates, pausing beside Gordon waiting punctiliously with his silver tray to brush away the crumbs.

This was just what Gordon waited for. It had come to him as the only way. Courteously he drew aside, lifting the paper from the table and putting it in his lap, for just the instant while the butler did his work; but in that instant the paper with the red cross was slipped under the napkin, and the other paper took its place upon the table, back down so that its lack of a red cross could not be noted.

So far, so good, but how long could this be kept up? And the paper under the napkin—how was it to be got into his pocket? His hands were like ice now, and his brain seemed to be at boiling heat as he sat back and realized that the deed was done, and could not be undone. If any one should pick up that paper from the table and discover the lack of the red mark, it would be all up with him. He looked up for an instant to meet the gaze of the six men upon him. They had nothing better to do now than to look at him until the next course arrived. He realized that not one of them would have mercy upon him if they knew what he had done, not one unless it might be the tired, old–looking one, and he would not dare interfere.

Still Gordon was enabled to smile, and to say some pleasant nothings to his hostess when she passed him the salted almonds. His hand lay carelessly guarding the secret of the paper on the table, innocently, as though it just *happened* that he laid it on the paper.

Sitting thus with the real paper in his lap under his large damask napkin, the false paper under his hand on the table where he from time to time perused it, and his eye-glasses which made him look most distinguished still on his nose, he heard the distant telephone bell ring.

He remembered the words of his chief and sat rigid. From his position he could see the tall clock in the hall, and its gilded hands pointed to ten minutes before seven. It was about the time his chief had said he would be called on the telephone. What should he do with the two papers?

He had but an instant to think until the well-trained butler returned and announced that some one wished to speak with Mr. Burnham on the telephone. His resolve was taken. He would have to leave the substitute paper on the table. To carry it away with him might arouse suspicion, and, moreover, he could not easily manage both without being noticed. The real paper must be put safely away at all hazards, and he must take the chance that the absence of the red mark would remain unnoticed until his return.

Deliberately he laid a heavy silver spoon across one edge of the paper on the table, and an ice-cream fork across the other, as if to hold it in place until his return. Then, rising with apologies, he gathered his napkin, paper, and all in his hand, holding it against his coat most naturally, as if he had forgotten that he had it, and made his way into the front hall, where in an alcove was the telephone. As he passed the hat-rack he swept his coat and hat off with his free hand, and bore them with him, devoutly hoping that he was not being watched from the dining room. Could he possibly get from the telephone out the front door without being seen? Hastily he hid the cipher message in an inner pocket. The napkin he dropped on the little telephone table, and taking up the receiver he spoke: "Hello! Yes! Oh, good evening! You don't say so! How did that happen?" He made his voice purposely clear, that it might be heard in the dining-room if anyone was listening. Then glancing in that direction saw, to his horror, his host lean over and lift the cipher paper he had left on the table and hand it to the guest on his right.

The messenger at the other end had given his sentence agreed upon and he had replied according to the sentences laid down by the chief in his instructions; the other end had said good-bye and hung up, but Gordon's voice spoke, cool and clear in the little alcove, despite his excitement. "All right. Certainly, I can take time to write it down. Wait until I get my pencil. Now, I'm ready. Have you it there? I'll wait a minute until you get it." His heart beat wildly. The blood surged through his ears like rushing waters. Would they look for the little red mark? The soft clink of spoons and dishes and the murmur of conversation was still going on, but there was no doubt but that it was a matter of few seconds before his theft would be discovered. He must make an instant dash for liberty while he yet could. Cautiously, stealthily, like a shadow from the alcove, one eye on the dining-room, he stole to the door and turned the knob. Yet even as he did so he saw his recent host rise excitedly from his seat and fairly snatch the paper from the man who held it. His last glimpse of the room where he had but three minutes before been enjoying the hospitality of the house was a vision of the entire company starting up and pointing to himself even as he slid from sight. There was no longer need for silence. He had been discovered and must fight for his life. He shut the door quickly, his nerves so tense that it seemed as if something must break soon; opened and slammed the outer door, and was out in the great whirling city under the flare of electric lamps with only the chance of a second of time before his pursuers would be upon him.

He came down the steps with the air of one who could scarcely take time to touch his feet to the ground, but must fly.

3

ALMOST in front of the house stood a closed carriage with two fine horses, but the coachman was looking up anxiously toward the next building. The sound of the closing door drew the man's attention, and, catching Gordon's eye, he made as if to jump down and throw open the door of the carriage. Quick as a flash, Gordon saw he had been mistaken for the man the carriage awaited, and he determined to make use of the circumstance.

"Don't get down," he called to the man, taking chances. "It's very late already. I'll open the door. Drive for all you're worth." He jumped in and slammed the carriage door behind him, and in a second more the horses were flying down the street. A glance from the back window showed an excited group of his fellow-guests standing at the open door of the mansion he had just left pointing toward his carriage and wildly gesticulating. He surmised that his host was already at the telephone calling for his own private detective.

Gordon could scarcely believe his sense that he had accomplished his mission and flight so far, and yet he knew his situation was most precarious. Where he was going he neither knew nor cared. When he was sure he was far enough

28

from the house he would call to the driver and give him directions, but first he must make sure that the precious paper was safely stowed away, in case he should be caught and searched. They might be coming after him with motorcycles in a minute or two.

Carefully rolling the paper into a tiny compass, he slipped it into a hollow gold case which was among the things in the envelope the chief had given him. There was a fine chain attached to the case, and the whole looked innocently like a gold pencil. The chain he slipped about his neck, dropping the case down inside his collar. That done he breathed more freely. Only from his dead body should they take that away. Then he hastily put on the false eyebrows, mustache, and goatee which had been provided for his disguise, and pulling on a pair of light gloves he felt more fit to evade detection.

He was just beginning to think what he should say to the driver about taking him to the station, for it was important that he get out of the city at once, when, glancing out of the window to see what part of the city he was being taken through he became aware of an auto close beside the carriage keeping pace with it, and two men stretching their necks as if to look into the carriage window at him. He withdrew to the shadow instantly so that they could not see him, but the one quick glance he had made him sure that one of his pursuers was the short thick-set man with cruel jaw who had sat across from him at the dinner table a few minutes before. It this were so he had practically no chance at all of escape, for what was a carriage against a swift moving car and what was he against a whole city full of strangers and enemies? If he attempted to drop from the carriage on the other side and escape into the darkness he had but a chance of a thousand at not being seen, and he could not hope to hide and get away in this unknown part of the city. Yet he must take his chance somehow, for the carriage must sooner or later get somewhere and he be obliged to face his pursuers.

To make matters worse, just at the instant when he had

decided to jump at the next dark place and was measuring the distance with his eye, his hand even being outstretched to grasp the door handle, a blustering, boisterous motor-cycle burst into full bloom just where he intended to jump, and the man who rode it was in uniform. He dodged back into the darkness of the carriage again that he might not be seen, and the motor-cycle came so near that its rider turned a white face and looked in. He felt that his time had come, and his cause was lost. It had not yet occurred to him that the men who were pursuing him would hardly be likely to call in municipal aid in their search, lest their own duplicity would be discovered. He reasoned that he was dealing with desperate men who would stop at nothing to get back the original cipher paper, and stop his mouth. He was well aware that only death would be considered a sufficient silencer for him after what he had seen at Mr. Holman's dinner table, for the evidence he could give would involve the honor of every man who had sat there. He saw in a flash that the two henchmen whom he was sure were even now riding in the car on his right had been at the table for the purpose of silencing him if he showed any signs of giving trouble. The wonder was that any of them dared call in a stranger on a matter of such grave import which meant ruin to them all if they were found out, but probably they had reasoned that every man had his price and had intended to offer him a share of the booty. It was likely that the chief had caused it to be understood by them that he was the right kind of man for their purpose. Yet, of course, they had taken precautions, and now they had him well caught, an auto on one side, a motor-cycle on the other and no telling how many more behind! He had been a fool to get into this carriage. He might have known it would only trap him to his death. There seemed absolutely no chance for escape now—yet he must fight to the last. He put his hand on his revolver to make sure it was easy to get at, tried to think whether it would not be better to chew up and swallow that cipher message rather than to run the risk of its falling again into the hands of the enemy; decided that he must carry it intact to his chief if possible; and finally that he must make a dash for safety at once, when just then the carriage turned briskly into a wide driveway, and the attendant auto and motor-cycle dropped behind as if puzzled at the move. The carriage stopped short and a bright light from an open doorway was flung into his face. There seemed to be high stone walls on one side and the lighted doorway on the other hand evidently led into a great stone building. He could hear the puffing of the car and cycle just behind. A wild notion that the carriage had been placed in front of the house to trap him in case he tried to escape, and that he had been brought to prison, flitted through his mind.

His hand was on his revolver as the coachman jumped down to fling open the carriage door, for he intended to fight for his liberty to the last.

He glanced back through the carriage window, and the lights of the auto glared in his face. The short, thick-set man was getting out of the car, and the motor-cyclist had stood his machine up against the wall and was coming toward the carriage. Escape was going to be practically impossible. A wild thought of dashing out the opposite door of his carriage, boldly seizing the motor-cycle and making off on it passed through his mind, and then the door on his left was flung open and the carriage was immediately surrounded by six excited men in evening dress all talking at once. "Here you are at last!" they chorused.

"Where is the best man?" shouted some one from the doorway. "Hasn't he come either?" And as if in answer one of the men by the carriage door wheeled and called excitedly: "Yes, he's come! Tell him — tell Jeff — tell him he's come." Then turning once more to Gordon he seized him by the arm and cried: "Come on quickly! There isn't a minute to wait. The organist is fairly frantic. Everybody has been just as nervous as could be. We couldn't very well go on without you — you know. But don't let that worry you. It's all right now you've come.

Forget it, old man, and hustle." Dimly Gordon perceived above the sound of subdued hubbub that an organ was playing, and even as he listened it burst into the joyous notes of the wedding march. It dawned upon him that this was not a prison to which he had come but a church—not a courtroom but a wedding, and horror of horrors! They took him for the best man. His disguise had been his undoing. How was he to get out of this scrape? And with his pursuers just behind!

"Let me explain—" he began, and wondered what he could explain.

"There's no time for explanations now, man. I tell you the organ has begun the march. We're expected to be marching down that middle aisle this very minute and Jeff is waiting for us in the chapel. I sent the signal to the bride and another to the organist the minute we sighted you. Come on! Everybody knows your boat was late in coming in. You don't need to explain a thing till afterwards."

At the moment one of the ushers moved aside and the short, thick-set man stepped between, the light shining full upon his face, and Gordon knew him positively for the man who had sat opposite him at the table a few minutes before. He was peering eagerly into the carriage door and Gordon saw his only escape was into the church. With his heart pounding like a trip hammer he yielded himself to the six ushers, who swept the little pursuer aside as if he had been a fly and literally bore Gordon up the steps and into the church door.

A burst of music filled his senses, and dazzling lights, glimpses of flowers, palms and beautiful garments bewildered him. His one thought was for escape from his pursuers. Would they follow him into the church and drag him out in the presence of all these people, or would they be thrown off the track for a little while and give him opportunity yet to get away? He looked around wildly for a place of exit but he was in the hands of the insistent ushers. One of them chattered to him in a low, growling whisper, such as men use on solemn occasions:

"It must have been rough on you being anxious like this about getting here, but never mind now. It'll go all right. Come on. Here's our cue and there stands Jefferson over there. You and he go in with the minister, you know. The groom and the best man, you understand, they'll tell you when. Jeff has the ring all right, so you won't need to bother about that. There's absolutely nothing for you to do but stand where you're put and go out when the rest do. You needn't feel a bit nervous."

Was it possible that these crazy people didn't recognize their mistake even yet here in the bright light? Couldn't they see his mustache was stuck on and one eyebrow was crooked? Didn't they know their best man well enough to recognize his voice? Surely, surely, some one would discover the mistake soon — that man Jeff over there who was eyeing him so intently. He would be sure to know this was not his friend. Yet every minute that they continued to think so was a distinct gain for Gordon, puzzling his pursuers and giving himself time to think and plan and study his strange surroundings.

And now they were drawing him forward and a turn of his head gave him a vision of the stubbed head of the thickset man peering in at the chapel door and watching him eagerly. He must fool him if possible.

"But I don't know anything about the arrangements," faltered Gordon, reflecting that the best man might not be very well known to the ushers and perhaps he resembled him. It was not the first time he had been taken for another man — and with his present make-up and all, perhaps it was natural. Could he possibly hope to bluff it out for a few minutes until the ceremony was over and then escape? It would of course be the best way imaginable to throw that impudent little man in the doorway off his track. If the real best man would only stay away long enough it would not be a difficult part to play. The original man might turn up after he was gone and create a pleasant little mystery, but nobody would be injured thereby. All this passed through his mind while the usher kept up his sepulchral whisper:

"Why, there are just the usual arrangements, you know—nothing new. You and Jeff go in after the ushers have reached the back of the church and opened the door. Then you just stand there till Celia and her uncle come up the aisle. Then follows the ceremony—very brief. Celia had all that repeating after the minister cut out on account of not being able to rehearse. It's to be just the simplest service, not the usual lengthy affair. Don't worry, you'll be all right, old man. Hurry! They're calling you. Leave your hat right here. Now I must go. Keep cool. It'll soon be over."

The breathless usher hurried through the door and settled into a sort of exalted hobble to the time of the wonderful Lohengrin music. Gordon turned, thinking even yet to make a possible escape, but the eagle-eye of his pursuer was upon him and the man Jefferson was by his side:

"Here we are!" he said, eagerly grabbing Gordon's hat and coat and dumping them on a chair. "I'll look after everything. Just come along. It's time we went in. The doctor is motioning for us. Awfully glad to see you at last. Too bad you had to rush so. How many years is it since I saw you? Ten! You've changed some, but you're looking fine and dandy. No need to worry about anything. It'll soon be over and the knot tied."

Mechanically Gordon fell into place beside the man Jefferson, who was a pleasant-faced youth, well-groomed and handsome. Looking furtively at his finely-cut, happy features, Gordon wondered if he would feel as glad as this youth seemed to be, when he walked down the aisle to meet his bride. How, by the way, would he feel if were going to be married now, — going into the face of this great company of well-dressed people to meet Miss Julia Bentley and be joined to her for life? Instinctively his soul shrank within him at the thought.

But now the door was wide open, the organ pealing its best, and he suddenly became aware of many eyes, and of wondering how long his eyebrows would withstand the perspiration that was trickling softly down his forehead. His mustache — ridiculous appendage! why had he not removed it? — was it awry? Dared he put up his hand to see? His gloves! Would any one notice that they were not as strictly fresh as a best man's gloves should be? Then he took his first step to the music, and it was like being pulled from a delicious morning nap and plunged into a tub of icy water.

He walked with feet that suddenly weighed like lead, across a church that looked to be miles in width, in the face of swarms of curious eyes. He tried to reflect that these people were all strangers to him, that they were not looking at him, any way, but at the bridegroom by his side, and that it mattered very little what he did, so long as he kept still and braved it out, if only the real best man didn't turn up until he was well out of the church. Then he could vanish in the dark, and go by some back way to a car or a taxicab and so to the station. The thought of the paper inside the gold pencil-case filled him with a sort of elation. If only he could get out of this dreadful church, he would probably get away safely. Perhaps even the incident of the wedding might prove to be his protection, for they would never seek him in a crowded church at a fashionable wedding.

The man by his side managed him admirably, giving him a whispered hint, a shove, or a push now and then, and getting him into the proper position. It seemed as if the best man had to occupy the most trying spot in all the church, but as they put him there, of course it was right. He glanced furtively over the faces near the front, and they all looked quite satisfied, as if everything were going as it should, so he settled down to his fate, his white, strained face partly hidden by the abundant display of mustache and eyebrow. People whispered softly how handsome he looked, and some suggested that he was not so stout as when they had last seen him, ten years before. His stay in a foreign land must have done him good. One woman went so far as to tell her daughter that he was far more distinguished-looking than she had ever thought he could become, but it was wonderful what a stay in a foreign land would do to improve a person.

The music stole onward; and slowly, gracefully, like the opening of buds into flowers, the bridal party inched along up the middle aisle until at last the bride in all the mystery of her white veil arrived, and all the maidens in their flowers and many colored gauzes were suitably disposed about her.

The feeble old man on whose arm the bride had leaned as she came up the aisle dropped out of the procession, melting into one of the front seats, and Gordon found himself standing beside the bride. He felt sure there must be something wrong about it, and looked at his young guide with an attempt to change places with him, but the man named Jefferson held him in place with a warning eye. "You're all right. Just stay where you are," he whispered softly, and Gordon stayed, reflecting on the strange fashions of weddings, and wondering why he had never before taken notice of just how a wedding party came in and stood and got out again. If he was only out of this how glad he would be. It seemed one had to be a pretty all-around man to be a member of the Secret Service.

The organ had hushed its voice to a sort of exultant sobbing, filled with dreams of flowers and joys, and hints of sorrow; and the minister in a voice both impressive and musical began the ceremony. Gordon stood doggedly and wondered if that really was one eyebrow coming down over his eye, or only a drop of perspiration.

Another full second passed, and he decided that if he ever got out of this situation alive he would never, no, never, *no never,* get married himself.

During the next second that crawled by he became supremely conscious of the creature in white by his side. A desire possessed him to look at her and see if she were like

Julia Bentley. It was like a nightmare haunting his dreams that she *was* Julia Bentley somehow transported to New York and being married to him willy-nilly. He could not shake it off, and the other eyebrow began to feel shaky. He was sure it was sailing down over his eye. If he only dared press its adhesive lining a little tighter to his flesh!

Some time during the situation there came a prayer, interminable to his excited imagination, as all the other ceremonies.

Under cover of the hush and the supposedly bowed heads, Gordon turned desperately toward the bride. He must see her and drive this phantasm from his brain. He turned, half expecting to see Julia's tall, handsome form, though telling himself he was a fool, and wondering why he so dreaded the idea. Then his gaze was held fascinated.

She was a little creature, slender and young and very beautiful, with a beauty which a deathly pallor only enhanced. Her face was delicately cut, and set in a frame of fine dark hair, the whole made most exquisite by the mist of white tulle that breathed itself about her like real mist over a flower. But the lovely head drooped, the coral lips had a look of unutterable sadness, and the long lashes swept over white cheeks. He could not take his eyes from her now that he had looked. How lovely, and how fitting for the delightful youth by his side! Now that he thought of it she was like him, only smaller and more delicate, of course. A sudden fierce, ridiculous feeling of envy filled Gordon's heart. Why couldn't he have known and loved a girl like that? Why had Julia Bentley been forever in his pathway as the girl laid out for his choice?

He looked at her with such intensity that a couple of dear old sisters who listened to the prayer with their eyes wide open, whispered one to the other: "Just see him look at her! How he must love her! Wasn't it beautiful that he should come right from the steamer to the church and never see her till now, for the first time in ten long years. It's so romantic!"

"Yes," whispered the other; "and I believe it'll last. He looks at her that way. Only I do dislike that way of arranging the hair on his face. But then it's foreign I suppose. He'll probably get over it if they stay in this country."

A severe old lady in the seat in front turned a reprimanding chin toward them and they subsided. Still Gordon continued to gaze.

Then the bride became aware of his look, raised her eyes, and—they were full of tears!

They gave him one reproachful glance that shot through his soul like a sword, and her lashes drooped again. By some mysterious control over the law of gravity, the tears remained unshed, and the man's gaze was turned aside; but that look had done its mighty work.

All the experiences of the day rushed over him and seemed to culminate in that one look. It was as if the reproach of all things had come upon him. The hurt in the white dog's eyes had touched him, the perfect courage in the appeal of the child's eyes had called forth his deepest sympathy, but the tears of this exquisite woman wrung his heart. He saw now that the appeal of the dog and the child had been the opening wedge for the look of a woman which tore self from him and flung it at her feet for her to walk upon; and when the prayer was ended he found that he was trembling.

He looked vindictively at the innocent youth beside him, as the soft rustle of the audience and the little breath of relief from the bridal party betokened the next stage in the ceremony. What had this innocent-looking youth done to cause tears in those lovely eyes? Was she marrying him against her will? He was only a boy, any way. What right had he to suppose he could care for a delicate creature like that? He was making her cry already, and he seemed to be utterly unconscious of it. What could be the matter? Gordon felt a desire to kick him.

Then it occurred to him that inadvertently *he* might have been the cause of her tears; he, supposedly the best man, who had been late, and held up the wedding no knowing how long. Of course it wasn't really his fault; but by proxy it was, for he now was masquerading as that unlucky best man, and she was very likely reproaching him for what she supposed was his stupidity. He had heard that women cried sometimes from vexation, disappointment or excitement.

Yet in his heart of hearts he could not set those tears, that look, down to so trivial a cause. They had reached his very soul, and he felt there was something deeper there than mere vexation. There had been bitter reproach for a deep wrong done. The glance had told him that. All the manhood in him rose to defend her against whoever had hurt her. He longed to get one more look into her eyes to make quite sure; and then, if there was still appeal there, his soul must answer it.

For the moment his commission, his ridiculous situation, the real peril to his life and trust, were forgotten.

The man Jefferson had produced a ring and was nudging him. It appeared that the best man had some part to play with that ring. He dimly remembered somewhere hearing that the best man must hand the ring to the bridegroom at the proper moment, but it was absurd for them to go through the farce of doing that when the bridegroom already held the golden circlet in his fingers! Why did he not step up like a man and put it upon the outstretched hand; that little white hand just in front of him there, so timidly held out with its glove fingers tucked back, like a dove crept out from its covert unwillingly?

But that Jefferson-man still held out the ring stupidly to him, and evidently expected him to take it. Silly youth! There was nothing for it but to take it and hand it back, of course. He must do as he was told and hasten that awful ceremony to its interminable close. He took the ring and held it out, but the young man did not take it again. Instead he whispered, "Put it on her finger!"

Gordon frowned. Could he be hearing aright? Why didn't

the fellow put the ring on his own bride? If he were being married, he would knock any man down that dared to put his wife's wedding ring on for him. Could that be the silly custom now, to have the best man put the bride's ring on? How unutterably out of place! But he must not make a scene, of course.

The little timid hand, so slender and white, came a shade nearer as if to help, and the ring finger separated itself from the others.

He looked at the smooth circlet. It seemed too tiny for any woman's finger. Then, reverently, he slipped it on, with a strange, inexpressible longing to touch the little hand. While he was thinking himself all kinds of a fool, and was enjoying one of his intermittent visions of Julia Bentley's expressive countenance interpolated on the present scene, a strange thing happened.

There had been some low murmurs and motions which he had not noticed because he thought his part of this very uncomfortable affair was about concluded, when, lo and behold, the minister and the young man by his side both began fumbling for his hand, and among them they managed to bring it into position and place in its astonished grasp the little timid hand that he had just crowned with its ring.

As his fingers closed over the bride's hand, there was such reverence, such tenderness in his touch that the girl's eyes were raised once more to his face, this time with the conquered tears in retreat, but all the pain and appeal still there. He looked and involuntarily he pressed her hand the closer, as if to promise aforetime whatever she would ask. Then, with her hand in his, and with the realization that they two were detached as it were from the rest of the wedding party, standing in a little centre of their own, his senses came back to him, and he perceived as in a flash of understanding that it was *they* who were being married!

There had been some terrible, unexplainable mistake, and he was stupidly standing in another man's place, taking vows upon himself! The thing had passed from an adventure of little moment into the matter of a life-tragedy, two life-tragedies perhaps! What should he do?

With the question came the words, "I pronounce you husband and wife," and "let no man put asunder."

4

WHAT had he done? Was it some great unnamed, unheard-of crime he had unconsciously committed? Could any one understand or excuse such asinine stupidity? Could he ever hold up his head again, though he fled to the most distant part of the globe? Was there nothing that could save the situation? Now, before they left the church, could he not declare the truth, and set things right, undo the words that had been spoken in the presence of all these witnesses, and send out to find the real bridegroom? Surely neither law nor gospel could endorse a bond made in the ignorance of either participant. It would, of course, be a terrible thing for the bride, but better now than later. Besides, he was pledged by that hand-clasp to answer the appeal in her eyes and protect her. This, then, was what it had meant!

But his commission! What of that? "A matter of life and death!" Ah! but this was *more* than life or death!

While these rapid thoughts were flashing through his brain, the benediction was being pronounced, and with the last word the organ pealed forth its triumphant lay. The audience stirred excitedly, anticipating the final view of the wedding procession.

The bride turned to take her bouquet from the maid of honor, and the movement broke the spell under which Gordon had been held.

He turned to the young man by his side and spoke hurriedly in a low tone.

"An awful mistake has been made," he said, and the organ drowned everything but the word "mistake." "I don't know what to do," he went on. But young Jefferson hastened to reassure him joyously:

"Not a bit of it, old chap. Nobody noticed that hitch about the ring. It was only a second. Everything went off slick. You haven't anything more to do now but take my sister out. Look alive, there! She looks as if she might be going to faint! She hasn't been a bit well all day! Steady her, quick, can't you? She'll stick it out till she gets to the air, but hurry, for goodness' sake!"

Gordon turned in alarm. Already the frail white bride had a claim on him. His first duty was to get her out of this crowd. Perhaps, after all, she had discovered that he was not the right man, and that was the meaning of her tears and appeal. Yet she had held her own and allowed things to go through to the finish, and perhaps he had no right to reveal to the assembled multitudes what she evidently wanted kept quiet. He must wait till he could ask her. He must do as this other man said — this — this brother of hers — who was of course the best man. Oh fool, and blind! Why had he not understood at the beginning and got himself out of this fix before it was too late? And what should he do when he reached the door? How could he ever explain? His commission! He dared not breathe a word of that! What explanation could he possibly offer for his — his — yes — his *criminal* conduct? Why, no such thing was ever heard of in the history of mankind as that which had happened to him. From start to finish it was — it — was — He could not think of words to express what it was.

He was by this time meandering jerkily down the aisle,

attempting to keep time to the music and look the part that she evidently expected him to play, but his eyes were upon her face, which was whiter now and, if possible, lovelier, than before.

"Oh, just see how devoted he is," murmured the eldest of the two dear old sisters, and he caught the sense of her words as he passed, and wondered. Then, immediately before him, retreating backward down the aisle with terrible eyes of scorn upon him he seemed to feel the presence of Miss Julia Bentley leading onward toward the church door; but he would not take his eyes from that sweet, sad face of the white bride on his arm to look. He somehow knew that if he could hold out until he reached that door without looking up, her power over him would be exorcised forever.

Out into the vacant vestibule, under the tented canopy, alone together for the moment, he felt her gentle weight grow heavy on his arm, and knew her footsteps were lagging. Instinctively, lest others should gather around them, he almost lifted her and bore her down the carpeted steps, through the covered pathway, to the luxurious motor-car waiting with open door, and placed her on the cushions. Some one closed the car door and almost immediately they were in motion.

She settled back with a half sigh, as if she could not have borne one instant more of strain, then sitting opposite he adjusted the window to give her air. She seemed grateful but said nothing. Her eyes were closed wearily, and the whole droop of her figure showed utter exhaustion. It seemed a desecration to speak to her, yet he must have some kind of an understanding before they reached their destination.

"An explanation is due to you—" he began, without knowing just what he was going to say, but she put out her hand with a weary protest.

"Oh, please don't!" she pleaded. "I know—the boat was late! It doesn't matter in the least."

He sat back appalled! She did not herself know then that she had married the wrong man!

"But you don't understand," he protested.

"Never mind," she moaned. "I don't want to understand. Nothing can change things. Only, let me be quiet till we get to the house, or I never can go through with the rest of it."

Her words ended with almost a sob, and he sat silent for an instant, with a mingling of emotions, uppermost of which was a desire to take the little, white, shrinking girl into his arms and comfort her, "Nothing can change things!" That sounded as though she did know but thought it too late to undo the great mistake now that it had been made. He must let her know that he had not understood until the ceremony was over. While he sat helplessly looking at her in the dimness of the car where she looked so small and sad and misty huddled beside her great bouquet, she opened her eyes and looked at him. She seemed to understand that he was about to speak again. By the great arc light they were passing he saw there were tears in her eyes again, and her voice held a child-like pleading as she uttered one word:

"Don't!"

It hurt him like a knife, he knew not why. But he could not resist the appeal. Duty or no duty, he could not disobey her command.

"Very well." He said it quietly, almost tenderly, and sat back with folded arms. After all, what explanation could he give her that she would believe? He might not breathe a word of his commission or the message. What other reason could he give for his extraordinary appearance at her wedding and by her side?

The promise in his voice seemed to give her relief. She breathed a sigh of relief and closed her eyes. He must just keep still and have his eyes open for a chance to escape when the carriage reached its destination.

Thus silently they threaded through unknown streets,

strange thoughts in the heart of each. The bride was struggling with her heavy burden, and the man was trying to
think his way out of the maze of perplexity into which he
had unwittingly wandered. He tried to set his thoughts in
order and find out just what to do. First of all, of course came
his commission, but somehow every time the little white
bride opposite took first place in his mind. Could he serve
both? What *would* serve both, and what would serve *either*?
As for himself, he was free to confess that there was no room
left in the present situation for even a consideration of his
own interests.

Whatever there was of good in him must go now to set
matters right in which he had greatly blundered. He must
do the best he could for the girl who had so strangely crossed
his pathway, and get back to his commission. But when he
tried to realize the importance of his commission and set it
over against the interests of the girl-bride, his mind became
confused. What should he do? He could not think of slipping away and leaving her without further words, even if
an opportunity offered itself. Perhaps he was wrong. Doubtless his many friends might tell him so if they were consulted,
but he did not intend to consult them. He intended to see
this troubled soul to some place of safety, and look out for
his commission as best he could afterward. One thing he did
not fully realize, and that was that Miss Julia Bentley's vision troubled him no longer. He was free. There was only
one woman in the whole wide world that gave him any concern, and that was the little sorrowful creature who sat opposite to him, and to whom he had just been married.

Just been married! He! The thought brought with it a thrill
of wonder, and a something else that was not unpleasant.
What if he really had? Of course he had not. Of course such
a thing could not hold good. But what if he had? Just for
an instant he entertained the thought—would he be glad or
sorry? He did not know her of course, had heard her speak
but a few words, had looked into her face plainly but once,

and yet suppose she were his! His heart answered the question with a glad bound and astonished him, and all his former ideas of real love were swept from his mind in a breath. He knew that, stranger though she was, he could take her to his heart; cherish her, love her and bear with her, as he never could have done Julia Bentley. Then all at once he realized that he was allowing his thoughts to dwell upon a woman who by all that was holy belonged to another man, and that other man would doubtless soon be the one with whom he would have to deal. He would soon be face to face with a new phase of the situation and he must prepare himself to meet it. What was he going to do? Should he plan to escape from the opposite door of the automobile while the bride was being assisted from her seat? No, he could not, for he would be expected to get out first and help her out. Besides, there would be too many around, and he could not possibly get away. But, greater than any such reason, the thing that held him bound was the look in her eyes through the tears. He simply could not leave her until he knew that she no longer needed him. And yet there was his commission! Well, he must see her in the hands of those who would care for her at least. So much he had done even for the white dog, and then, too, surely she was worth as many minutes of his time as he had been compelled to give to the injured child of the streets. If he only could explain to her now!

The thought of his message, with its terrible significance, safe in his possession, sent shivers of anxiety through his frame! Suppose he should be caught, and it taken from him, all on account of this most impossible incident! What scorn, what contumely, would be his! How could he ever explain to his chief? Would anybody living believe that a man in his senses could be married to a stranger before a whole church full of people and not know he was being married until the deed was done — and then not do anything about it after it was done? That was what he was doing now this very minute. He ought to be explaining something somehow to that poor little creature in the shadow of the carriage. Perhaps in some way it might relieve her sorrow if he did, and yet when he looked at her and tried to speak his mouth was hopelessly closed. He might not tell her anything!!

He gradually sifted his immediate actions down to two necessities; to get his companion to a safe place where her friends could care for her, and to make his escape as soon and as swiftly as possible. It was awful to run and leave her without telling her anything about it; when she evidently believed him to be the man she had promised and intended to marry; but the real bridegroom would surely turn up soon somehow and make matters right. Anyhow, it was the least he could do to take himself out of her way and to get his trust to its owners at once.

The car halted suddenly before a brightly lighted mansion, whose tented entrance effectually shut out the gaze of alien eyes, and made the transit from car to domicile entirely private. There was no opportunity here to disappear. The sidewalk and road were black with curious onlookers. He stepped from the car first and helped the lady out. He bore her heavy bouquet because she looked literally too frail to carry it further herself.

In the doorway she was surrounded by a bevy of servants, foremost among whom her old nurse claimed the privilege of greeting her with tears and smiles and many "Miss-Celia-my-dears," and Gordon stood for the instant entranced, watching the sweet play of loving kindness in the face of the pale little bride. As soon as he could lay down those flowers inconspicuously he would be on the alert for a way of escape. It surely would be found through some back or side entrance of the house.

But even as the thought came to him the old nurse stepped back to let the other servants greet the bride with stiff bows and embarrassed words of blessing, and he felt a hand laid heavily on his arm.

He started as he turned, thinking instantly again of his

commission and expecting to see a policeman in uniform by his side, but it was only the old nurse, with tears of devotion still in her faded eyes.

"Mister George, ye hevn't forgot me, hev ye?" she asked, earnestly. "You usen't to like me verra well, I mind, but ye was awful for the teasin' an' I was always for my Miss Celie! But bygones is bygones now an' I wish ye well. Yer growed a man, an' I know ye must be worthy o' her, or she'd never hev consented to take ye. Yev got a gude wife an' no mistake, an' I know ye'll be the happiest man alive. Ye won't hold it against me, Mister George, that I used to tell yer uncle on your masterful tricks, will ye? You mind I was only carin' fer my baby girl, an' ye were but a boy."

She paused as if expecting an answer, and Gordon embarrassedly assured her that he would never think of holding so trifling a matter against her. He cast a look of reverent admiration and tenderness toward the beautiful girl who was smiling on her loyal subjects like a queen, roused from her sorrow to give joy to others; and even her old nurse was satisfied.

"Ah, ye luve her, Mister George, don't ye?" the nurse questioned. "I don't wonder. Everybody what lays eyes on her luves her. She's that dear—" here the tears got the better of the good woman for an instant and she forgot herself and pulled at the skirt of her new black dress thinking it was an apron, and wishing to wipe her eyes.

Then suddenly Gordon found his lips uttering strange words, without his own apparent consent, as if his heart had suddenly taken things in hand and determined to do as it pleased without consulting his judgment.

"Yes, I love her," he was saying, and to his amazement he found that the words were true.

This discovery made matters still more complicated.

"Then ye'll promise me something, Mister George, won't ye?" said the nurse eagerly, her tears having their own way down her rosy anxious face. "Ye'll promise me never to make her feel bad any more? She's cried a lot these last three months, an' nobody knows but me. She could hide it from them all but her old nurse that has loved her so long. But she's been that sorrowful, enough fer a whole lifetime. Promise that ye'll do all in yer power to make her happy always."

"I will do all in my power to make her happy," he said, solemnly, as if he were uttering a vow, and wondered how short-lived that power was to be.

5

THE wedding party had arrived in full force now. Carriages and automobiles were unloading; gay voices and laughter filled the house. The servants disappeared to their places, and the white bride, with only a motioning look toward Gordon, led the way to the place where they were to stand under an arch of roses, lilies and palms, in a room hung from the ceiling with drooping ferns and white carnations on invisible threads of silver wire, until it all seemed like a fairy dream.

Gordon had no choice but to follow, as his way was blocked by the incoming guests, and he foresaw that his exit would have to be made from some other door than the front if he were to escape yet awhile. As he stepped into the mystery of the flower-scented room where his lady led the way, he was conscious of a feeling of transition from the world of ordinary things into one of wonder, beauty and mysterious joy; but all the time he knew he was an imposter, who had no right in that silver-threaded bower.

Yet there he stood bowing, shaking hands, and smirking behind his false mustache, which threatened every minute to betray him.

People told him he was looking well, and congratulated him on his bride. Some said he was stouter than when he left the country, and some said he was thinner. They asked him questions about relatives and friends living and dead, and he ran constant risk of getting into hopeless difficulties. His only safety was in smiling, and saying very little; seeming not to hear some questions, and answering others with another question. It was not so hard after he got started, because there were so many people, and they kept coming close upon one another, so no one had much time to talk. Then supper with its formalities was got through with somehow, though to Gordon, with his already satisfied appetite and his hampering mustache, it seemed an endless ordeal.

"Jeff, " as they called him, was everywhere, attending to everything, and he slipped up to the unwilling bridegroom just as he was having to answer a very difficult question about the lateness of his vessel, and the kind of passage they had experienced in crossing. By this time Gordon had discovered that he was supposed to have been ten years abroad, and his steamer had been late in landing, but where he came from or what he had been doing over there were still to be found out; and it was extremely puzzling to be asked from what port he had sailed, and how he came to be there when he had been supposed to have been in St. Petersburg but the week before? His state of mind was anything but enviable. Beside all this, Gordon was just reflecting that the last he had seen of his hat and coat was in the church. What had become of them, and how could he go to the station without a hat? Then opportunely "Jeff" arrived.

"Your train leaves at ten three," he said in a low, business-like tone, as if he enjoyed the importance of having made all the arrangements. "I've secured the stateroom as you cabled me to do, and here are the tickets and checks. The trunks are down there all checked. Celia didn't want any nonsense about their being tied up with white ribbon. She hates all that. We've arranged for you to slip out by the fire-escape and down through the back yard of the next neighbor, where a motor, just a plain regular one from the station, will be waiting around the corner in the shadow. Celia knows where it is. None of the party will know you are gone until you are well under way. The car they think you will take is being elaborately adorned with white at the front door now, but you won't have any trouble about it. I've fixed everything up. Your coat and hat are out on the fire-escape, and as soon as Celia's ready I'll show you the way."

Gordon thanked him. There was nothing else to do, but his countenance grew blank. Was there, then, to be no escape? Must he actually take another man's bride with him in order to get away? And how was he to get away from her? Where was the real bridegroom and why did he not appear upon that scene? And yet what complications that might bring up. He began to look wildly about for a chance to flee at once, for how could he possibly run away with a bride on his hands? If only someone were going with them to the station he could slip away with a clear conscience, leaving her in good hands, but to leave her alone, ill and distressed was out of the question. He had rid himself of a lonely dog and a suffering child, though it gave him anguish to do the deed, but leave this lovely woman for whom he at least appeared to have become responsible, he could not, until he was sure she would come to no harm through him.

"Don't let anything hinder you! Don't let anything hinder you!"

It appeared that this refrain had not ceased for an instant since it began, but had chimed its changes through music, ceremony, prayer and reception without interruption. It acted like a goad upon his conscience now. He must do something that would set him free to go back to Washington. An inspiration came to him.

"Wouldn't you like to go to the station with us?" he asked the young man. "I am sure your sister would like to have you."

The boy's face lit up joyfully.

"Oh, wouldn't you mind? I'd like it awfully, and—if it's all the same to you, I wish Mother could go too. It's the first time Celia and she were ever separated, and I know she hates it fiercely to have to say good-by with the house full of folks this way. But she doesn't expect it of course, and really it isn't fair to you, when you haven't seen Celia alone yet, and it's your wedding trip—"

"There will be plenty of time for us," said the compulsory bridegroom graciously, and felt as if he had perjured himself. It was not in his nature to enjoy a serious masquerade of this kind.

"I shall be glad to have you both come," he added earnestly. "I really want you. Tell your mother."

The boy grasped his hand impulsively:

"I say," said he, "you're all right! I don't mind confessing that I've hated the very thought of you for a whole three months, ever since Celia told us she had promised to marry you. You see, I never really knew you when I was a little chap, but I didn't used to like you. I took an awful scunner to you for some reason. I suppose kids often take irrational dislikes like that. But ever since I've laid eyes on you to-night, I've liked you all the way through. I like your eyes. It isn't a bit as I thought I remembered you. I used to think your eyes had a sort of deceitful look. Awful to tell you, isn't it? But I felt as if I wanted to have it off my conscience, for I see now you're nothing of the kind. You've got the honestest eyes I ever saw on a man, and I'd stake my last cent that you wouldn't cheat a church mouse. You're true as steel, and I'm mighty glad you're my brother-in-law. I know you'll be good to Celia."

The slow color mounted under his disguise until it reached Gordon's burnished brown hair. His eyes *were* honest eyes. They had always been so—until to-day. Into what a world of deceit he had entered! How he would like to make a clean breast of it all to this nice, frank boy; but he must not! for there was his trust! For an instant he was on the point of trying to explain that he was not the true bridegroom, and getting young Jefferson to help him to set matters right, but an influx of newly arrived guests broke in upon their privacy, and he could only press the boy's hand and say in embarrassed tones:

"Thank you! I shall try to be worthy of your good opinion hereafter!"

It was over at last, and the bride slipped from his side to prepare for the journey. He looked hastily around, feeling that his very first opportunity had come for making an escape. If an open window had presented itself, he would have vaulted through, trusting to luck and his heels to get away, but there was no window, and every door was blocked by staring, admiring, smirking people. He bethought himself of the fire escape where waited his hat and coat, and wondered if he could find it.

With smiling apologies, he broke away from those around him, murmuring something about being needed, and worked his way firmly but steadily toward the stairs and thence to the back halls. Coming at last upon an open window, he slipped through, his heart beating wildly. He thought for a second that he was there ahead of the others; but a dark form loomed ahead and he perceived some one coming up from outside. Another second, and he saw it was his newly acquired brother-in-law.

"Say, this is great!" was his greeting. "How did you manage to find your way up alone? I was just coming down after you. I wanted to leave you there till the last minute so no one would suspect, but now you are here we can hustle off at once. I just took Mother and Celia down. It was pretty stiff for Mother to climb down, for she was a little bit afraid, but she was game all right, and she was so pleased to go. They're waiting for us down there in the court. Here, let me help you with your overcoat. Now I'll pull down this window, so no one will suspect us and follow. That's all right now, come on! You go ahead. Just hold on to the railing and go slow. I'll keep close to you. I know the way in my sleep. I've played fire here many a year, and could climb down in my sleep."

Gordon found himself wishing that this delightful brother-in-law were really his. There was evidently to be no opportunity of escape here. He meditated making a dash and getting away in the dark when they should reach the foot of the stairs; much as he hated to leave that way, he felt he must do so if there was any chance for him at all; but when they reached the ground he saw that was hopeless. The car that was to take them to the station was drawn up close to the spot, and the chauffeur stood beside it.

"Your mother says fer you to hurry, Mister Jefferson," he called in a sepulchral tone. "They're coming out around the block to watch. Get in as quick as you can."

The burly chauffeur stood below Gordon, helped him to alight on his feet from the fire-escape, and hustled him into the darkness of the conveyance.

They were very quiet until they had left in the dark court and were speeding away down the avenue. Then the bride's mother laid two gentle hands upon Gordon's, leaning across from her seat to do so, and said:

"My son, I shall never forget this of you, never! It was dear of you to give me this last few minutes with my darling!"

Gordon, deeply touched and much put to it for words, mumbled something about being very glad to have her, and Jefferson relieved the situation by pouring forth a volume of information and questions, fortunately not pausing long enough to have the latter answered. The bride sat with one hand clasped in her mother's, and said not a word. Gordon was haunted by the thought of tears in her eyes.

There was little opportunity for thinking, but Gordon made a hasty plan. He decided to get his party all out to the train and then remember his suitcase, which he had left checked in the station. Jefferson would probably insist upon going for it but he would insist more strenuously that the brother and sister would want to have this last minute together. Then he could get away in the crowd and disappear, coming later for his suit-case perhaps, or sending a porter from his own train for it. The only drawback to this arrangement was that it seemed a dishonorable way to leave these people who would in the nature of things be left in a most trying position by his disappearance, especially the sad little bride. But it could not be helped, and his staying would only complicate things still further, for he would have to explain who he was, and that was practically impossible on account of his commission. It would not do to run risks with himself until his mission was accomplished and his message delivered. After that he could confess and make whatever reparation a man in his strange position could render.

The plan worked very well. The brother of course eagerly urged that he be allowed to go back for the suit-case, but Gordon, with well-feigned thoughtfulness, said in a low tone:

"Your sister will want you for a minute all to herself."

A tender look came into the boy's eyes, and he turned back smiling to the stateroom where his mother and sister were having a wordless farewell. Gordon jumped from the train and sprinted down the platform, feeling meaner than he ever remembered to have felt in his whole life, and with a strange heaviness about his heart. He forgot for the moment that there was need for him to be on his guard against possible detectives sent by Mr. Holman. Even the importance of the message he carried seemed to weigh less, now that he was free. His feet had a strange unwillingness to hurry, and without a constant pressure of the will would have lagged in spite of him. His heart wanted to let suit-case and commission and everything else go to the winds and take him back to the state-room where he had left his sorrowful bride of an hour. She was not his, and he might not go, but he knew that he would never be the same hereafter. He would always be wondering where she was, wishing he could have saved her from whatever troubled her; wishing she were his bride, and not another's.

He passed back through the station gate, and a man in evening clothes eyed him sharply. He fancied he saw a resemblance to one of the men at the Holman dinner-table, but he dared not look again lest a glance should cost him recognition. He wondered blindly which way he should take, and if it would be safe to risk going at once to the checking window, or whether he ought to go in hiding until he was sure young Jefferson would no longer look for him. Then a hand touched his shoulder and a voice that was strangely welcome shouted:

"This way, George! The checking place is over to the right!"

He turned and there stood Jefferson, smiling and panting:

"You see, the little mother had something to say to Celia alone, so I saw I was *de trop,* and I thought I better come with you," he declared as soon as he could get his breath.

"Gee, but you can run!" added the panting youth. "What's the hurry? It's ten whole minutes before the train leaves. I couldn't waste all that time kicking my heels on the platform, when I might be enjoying my new brother-in-law's company. I say, are you really going to live permanently in Chicago? I do wish you'd decide to come back to New York. Mother'll miss Celia no end. I don't know how she's going to stand it."

Walking airily by Gordon's side, he talked, apparently not noticing the sudden start and look of mingled anxiety and relief that overspread his brother-in-law's countenance. Then another man walked by them and turning looked in their faces. Gordon was sure this was the thick-set man from Holman's. He was eyeing Gordon keenly. Suddenly all other questions stepped into the background, and the only immediate matter that concerned him was his message, to get it safely to its destination. With real relief he saw that this had been his greatest concern all the time, underneath all hindrances, and that there had not been at any moment any escape from the crowding circumstances other than that he had taken, step by step. If he had been beset by thieves and blackguards, and thrown into prison for a time he would not have felt shame at the delay, for those things he could not help. He saw with new illumination that there was no more shame to him from these trivial and peculiar circumstances with which he had been hemmed in since his start to New York than if he had been checked by any more tragic obstacles. His only real misgiving was about his marriage. Somehow it seemed his fault, and he felt there ought to be some way to confess his part at once—but how—without putting his message in jeopardy—for no one would believe unless they knew all.

But the time of danger was at hand, he plainly saw. The man whom he dared not look closely at had turned again and was walking parallel to them, glancing now and again keenly in their direction. He was watching Gordon furtively; not a motion escaped him.

There was a moment's delay at the checking counter while the attendant searched for the suitcase, and Gordon was convinced that the man had stopped a few steps away merely for the purpose of watching him.

He dared not look around or notice the man, but he was sure he followed them back to the train. He felt his presence as clearly as if he had been able to see through the back of his head.

But Gordon was cool and collected now. It was as if the experiences of the last two hours, with their embarrassing predicaments, had been wiped off the calendar, and he were back at the moment when he left the Holman house. He knew as well as if he had watched them follow him that they had discovered his—theft—treachery—whatever it ought to be called—and he was being searched for; and because of what was at stake those men would track him to death if they could. But he knew also that his disguise and his companion were for the moment puzzling this sleuth-hound.

This was probably not the only watcher about the station. There were detectives, too, perhaps, hired hastily, and all too ready to seize a suspect.

He marvelled that he could walk so deliberately, swinging his suit-case in his gloved hand at so momentous a time. He smiled and talked easily with the pleasant fellow who walked by his side, and answered his questions with very little idea of what he was saying; making promises which his heart would like to keep, but which he now saw no way of making good.

Thus they entered the train and came to the car where the bride and her mother waited. There were tears on the face of the girl, and she turned to the window to hide them. Gordon's eyes followed her wistfully, and down through the double glass, unnoticed by her absent gaze, he saw the face of the man who had followed them, sharply watching him.

Realizing that his hat was a partial disguise, he kept it on in spite of the presence of the ladies. The color rose in his cheeks that he had to seem so discourteous, but, to cover his embarrassment, he insisted that he be allowed to take the elder lady to the platform, as it really was almost time for the train to start, and so he went deliberately out to act the part of the bridegroom in the face of his recognized foe.

The mother and Gordon stood for a moment on the vestibule platform, while Jefferson bade his sister good-by and tried to soothe her distress at parting from her mother.

"He's all right, Celie, indeed he is," said the young fellow caressingly, laying his hand upon his sister's bowed head. "He's going to be awfully good to you; he cares a lot for you, and he's promised to do all sorts of nice things. He says he'll bring you back soon, and he would never stand in the way of your being with us a lot. He did indeed! What do you think of that? Isn't it quite different from what you thought he would say? He doesn't seem to think he's got to spend the rest of his days in Chicago either. He says there might something turn up that would make it possible for him to change all his plans. Isn't that great?"

Celia tried to look up and smile through her tears, while the man outside studied the situation a moment in perplexity and then strolled back to watch Gordon and the elder woman.

"You will be good to my little girl," he heard the woman's voice pleading. "She has always been guarded, and she will miss us all, even though she has you." The voice went through Gordon like a knife. To stand much more of this and not denounce himself for a blackguard would be impossible. Neither could he keep his hat on in the presence of this wonderful motherhood, a motherhood that appealed to him all the more that he had never known a mother of his own, and had always longed for one.

He put up his hand and lifted his hat slightly, guarding as much as possible his own face from the view of the man on the station platform, who was still walking deliberately, considerately, up and down, often passing near enough to hear what they were saying. In this reverent attitude, Gordon said, as though he were uttering a sacred vow:

"I will guard her as if she were—as if I were—as if I were—*you*"—then he paused a moment and added solemnly, tenderly—"Mother!"

He wondered if it were not desecration to utter such words when all the time he was utterly unable to perform them in the way in which the mother meant. "Impostor!" was the word which rang in his ears now. The clamor about being hindered had ceased, for he was doing his best, and not letting even a woman's happiness stand in the way of his duty.

Yet his heart had dictated the words he had spoken, while his mind and judgment were busy with his perilous position. He could not gainsay his heart, for he felt that in every way he could he would guard and care for the girl who was to be in his keeping at least for a few minutes until he could contrive some way to get her back to her friends without him.

The whistle of the train was sounding now, and the brakemen were shouting, "All aboard!"

He helped the frail little elderly woman down the steps, and she reached up her face to kiss him. He bent and took the caress, the first time that a woman's lips had touched his face since he was a little child.

"Mother, I will not let anything harm her," he whispered, and she said:

"My boy, I can trust you!"

Then he put her into the care of her strong young son, swung upon the train as the wheels began to move, and hurried back to the bride. On the platform, walking beside the train, he still saw the man. Going to the weeping girl, Gordon, stooped over her gently, touched her on the shoulder, and drew the window shade down. The last face he saw outside was the face of the baffled man, who was turning back, but what for? Was he going to report to others, and would there perhaps be another stop before they left the city, where officers or detectives might board the train? He ought to be ready to get off and run for his life if there was. There seemed no way but to fee the porter to look after his companion, and leave her, despicable as it seemed! Yet his soul of honor told him he could never do that, no matter what was at stake.

Then, without warning a new situation was thrust upon him. The bride, who had been standing with bowed head and with her handkerchief up to her eyes, just as her brother had left her, tottered and fell into his arms, limp and white. Instantly all his senses were called into action, and he forgot the man on the platform, forgot the possible next stop in the city, and the explanation he had been about to make to the girl; forgot even the importance of his mission, and the fact that the train he was on was headed toward Chicago, instead of Washington; forgot everything but the fact that the loveliest girl he had ever seen, with the saddest look a human face might wear, was lying apparently lifeless in his arms.

Outside the window the man had turned back and was now running excitedly along with the train trying to see into the window; and down the platform, not ten yards behind, came a frantic man with English-looking clothes, a heavy mustache and goatee, shaggy eyebrows, and a sensual face, striding angrily along as fast as his heavy body would carry him.

But Gordon saw none of them.

6

FIVE hours before, the man who was hurling himself furiously after the rapidly retreating train had driven calmly through the city, from the pier of the White Star Line to the apartment of a man whom he had met abroad, and who had offered him the use of it during his absence. The rooms were in the fourth story of a fine apartment house. The returning exile noted with satisfaction the irreproachable neighborhood, as he slowly descended from the carriage, paid his fee, and entered the door, to present his letter of introduction to the janitor in charge.

His first act was to open the steamer trunk which he had brought with him in the cab, and take therefrom his wedding garments. These he carefully arranged on folding hangers and hung in the closet, which was otherwise empty save for a few boxes piled on the high shelf.

Then he hastened to the telephone and communicated with his best man, Jefferson Hathaway; told him the boat was late arriving at the dock, but that he was here at last; gave him a few directions concerning errands he would like to have done, and agreed to be at the church a half-hour earlier than the time set for the ceremony, to be shown just what arrangements had been made. He was told his bride was feeling very tired and was resting, and agreed that it would be as well not to disturb her; they would have time enough to talk afterward; there really wasn't anything to say but what he had already written. And he would have about all he could do to get there on time as it was. He asked if Jefferson had called for the ring he had ordered and if the carriage would be sent for him in time and then without formalities closed the interview. He and Jefferson were not exactly fond of one another, though Jefferson was the beloved brother of his bride-to-be.

He hung up the receiver and rang for a brandy and soda to brace himself for the coming ordeal which was to bind him to a woman whom for years he had been trying to get in his power and whom he might have loved if she had not dared to scorn him for the evil that she knew was in him. At last he had found a way to subdue her and bring her with her ample fortune to his feet and he felt the exultation of the conqueror as he went about his preparations for the evening.

He made a smug and leisurely toilet, with a smile of satisfaction upon his flabby face. He was naturally a selfish person and had always known how to make other people attend to all bothersome details for him while he enjoyed himself. He was quite comfortable and self-complacent as he posed a moment before the mirror to smooth his mustache and note how well he was looking. Then he went to the closet for his coat.

It was most peculiar, the way it happened, but somehow, as he stepped into that closet to take down his coat, which hung at the back where the space was widest, the opening at the wrist of his shirt-sleeve caught for just an instant in the little knob of the closet latch. The gold button which held the cuff to the wristband slipped its hold, and the man was free almost at once, but the angry twitch he had made at the slight detention had given the door an impetus which set it silently moving on its hinges. (It was characteristic of George

Hayne that he was always impatient of the slightest detention.) He had scarcely put his hand upon his wedding coat
when a soft steel click, followed by utter darkness, warned
him that his impatience had entrapped him. He put out his
hand and pushed at the door, but the catch had settled into
place. It was a very strong, neat little catch, and it did its work
well. The man was a prisoner.

At first he was only annoyed, and gave the door an angry
kick or two, as if of course it would presently release him
meekly; but then he bethought him of his polished wedding
shoes, and desisted. He tried to find a knob and shake the
door, but the only knob was the tiny brass one on the outside of the catch, and you cannot shake a plain surface reared
up before you. Then he set his massive, flabby shoulder
against the door and pressed with all his might, till his bulky
linen shirt front creaked with dismay, and his wedding collar wilted limply. But the door stood like adamant. It was
massive, like the man, but it was not flabby. The wood of
which it was composed had spent its early life in the open
air, drinking only the wine of sunshine and sparkling air, wet
with the dews of heaven, and exercising against the north
blast. It was nothing for it to hold out against this pillow of
a man, who had been nurtured in the dissipation and folly
of a great city. The door held its own, and if doors do such
things, the face of it must have laughed to the silent room;
and who knows but the room winked back? It would be but
natural that a room should resent a new occupant in the absence of a beloved owner.

He was there, safe and fast, in the still dark, with plenty
of time for reflection. And there were things in his life that
called for his reflection. They had never had him at an advantage before.

In due course of time, having exhausted his breath and
strength in fruitless pushing, and his vocabulary in foolish
curses, he lifted up his voice and roared. No other word

would quite describe the sound that issued from his mighty throat. But the city roared placidly below him, and no one minded him in the least.

He sacrificed the shiny toes of the shoes and added resounding kicks on the door to the general hubbub. He changed the roar to a bellow like a mad bull, but still the silence that succeeded it was as deep and monotonous as ever. He tried going to the back of the closet and hurling himself against the door, but he only hurt his soft muscles with the effort. Finally he sat down on the floor of the closet.

Now the janitor's wife, who occupied an apartment somewhat overcrowded, had surreptitiously borrowed the use of this closet the week before, in order to hang therein her Sunday gown, whose front breadth was covered with grease-spots, thickly overlaid with French chalk. The French chalk had done its work and removed the grease-spots, and now lay thickly on the floor of the closet, but the imprisoned bridegroom did not know that, and he sat down quite naturally to rest from his unusual exertions, and to reflect on what could be done next.

The immediate present passed rapidly in review. He could not afford more than ten minutes to get out of this hole. He ought to be on the way to the church at once. There was no knowing what nonsense Celia might get into her head if he delayed. He had known her since her childhood, and she had always scorned him. The hold he had upon her now was like a rope of sand, but only he knew that. If he could but knock that old door down! If he only hadn't hung up his coat in the closet! If the man who built the house only hadn't put such a fool catch on the door! When he got out he would take time to chop it off! If only he had a little more room, and a little more air! It was stifling! Great beads of perspiration went rolling down his hot forehead, and his wet collar made a cool band about his neck. He wondered if he had another clean collar of that particular style with him. If he *only* could get out of this accursed place! Where were all the people? Why was everything so still? Would they never come and let him out?

He reflected that he had told the janitor he would occupy the room with his baggage for two or three weeks perhaps, but he expected to go away on a trip this very evening. The janitor would not think it strange if he did not appear. How would it be to stay here and die? Horrible thought!

He jumped up from the floor and began his howlings and gyrations once more, but soon desisted, and sat down to be entertained by a panorama of his past life which is always unpleasantly in evidence at such times. Fine and clear in the darkness of the closet stood out the nicely laid scheme of deviltry by which he had contrived to be at last within reach of a coveted fortune.

Occasionally would come the frantic thought that just through this little mishap of a foolish clothespress catch he might even yet lose it. The fraud and trickery by which he had an heiress in his power did not trouble him so much as the thought of losing her—at least of losing the fortune. He must have that fortune, for he was deep in debt, and—but then he would refuse to think, and get up to batter at his prison door again.

Four hours his prison walls enclosed him, with inky blackness all around save for a faint glimmer of light, which marked the well-fitted base of the door as the night outside drew on. He had lighted the gas when he began dressing, for the room had already been filled with shadows, and now, it began to seem as if that streak of flickering gas light was the only thing that saved him from losing his mind.

Somewhere from out of the dim shadows a face evolved itself and gazed at him, a haggard face with piercing hollow eyes and despair written upon it. It reproached him with a sin he thought long-forgotten. He shrank back in horror and the cold perspiration stood out upon his forehead, for the eyes were the eyes of the man whose name he had forged upon a note involving trust money fifteen years before; and the man, a quiet, kindly, unsuspecting creature had suffered the penalty in a prison cell until his death some five years ago.

Sometimes at night in the first years after his crime, that face had haunted him, appearing at odd intervals when he was plotting some particularly shady means of adding to his income, until he had resolved to turn over a new leaf, and actually gave up one or two schemes as being too unscrupulous to be indulged in, thus acquiring a comforting feeling of being virtuous. But it was long since the face had come. He had settled it in his mind that the forgery was merely a patch of wild oats which he had sown in his youth, something to be regretted but not too severely blamed for, and thus forgiving himself he had grown to feel that it was more the world's fault for not giving him what he wanted than his own for putting a harmless old man in prison. Of the shame that had killed the old man he knew nothing, nor could have understood. The actual punishment itself was all that appealed to him. He was ever one that had to be taught with the lash, and then only kept straight while it was in sight.

But the face was very near and vivid here in the thick darkness. It was like a cell, this closet, bare, cold, black. The eyes in the gloom seemed to pierce him with the thought: "This is what you made me suffer. It is your turn now. IT IS YOUR TURN NOW!" Nearer and nearer they came looking into his own, until they saw down into his very soul, his little sinful soul, and drew back appalled at the littleness and meanness of what they saw.

Then for the first time in his whole selfish life George Hayne knew any shame, for the eyes read forth to him all that they had seen, and how it looked to them; and beside the tale they told the eyes were clean of sin and almost glad in spite of suffering wrongfully.

Closer and thicker grew the air of the small closet; fiercer grew the rage and shame and horror of the man incarcerated.

Now, from out the shadows there looked other eyes, eyes that had never haunted him before, eyes of victims to whom he had never cast a half a thought. Eyes of men and women he had robbed by his artful, gentlemanly craft; eyes of innocent girls whose wrecked lives had contributed to his selfish scheme of living; even the great reproachful eyes of little children who had looked to him for pity and found none. Last, above them all were the eyes of the lovely girl he was to have married.

He had always loved Celia Hathaway more than he could have loved anyone or anything else besides himself, and it had eaten into his very being that he never could make her bow to him; not even by torture could he bring her to her knees. Stung by the years of her scorn he had stooped lower and lower in his methods of dealing with her until he had come at last to employ the tools of slow torture to her soul that he might bring low her pride and put her fortune and her scornful self within his power. The strength with which she had withheld him until the time of her surrender had turned his selfish love into a hate with contemplations of revenge.

But now her eyes glowed scornfully, wreathed round with bridal white, and seemed to taunt him with his foolish defeat at this last minute before the final triumph.

Undoubtedly the brandy he had taken had gone to his head. Was he going mad that he could not get away from all these terrible eyes?

He felt sure he was dying when at last the janitor came up to the fourth floor on his round of inspection, noticed the light flaring from the transom over the door occupied by the stranger who had said he was going to leave on a trip almost immediately, and went in to investigate. The eyes vanished at his step. The man in the closet lost no time in making his presence known, and the janitor, cautiously, and with great deliberation made careful investigation of the cause and reason for this disturbance and finally let him out, after having received promise of reward which never materialized.

The stranger flew to the telephone in frantic haste, called up the house of his affianced bride, shouting wildly at the operator for all undue delays, and when finally he succeeded in getting some one to the 'phone it was only to be told that neither Mrs. Hathaway nor her son were there. Were they at the church? "Oh, no," the servant answered, "they came back from the church long ago. There is a wedding in the house, and a great many people. They are making so much noise I can't hear. Speak louder, please!"

He shouted and raved at the servant, asking futile questions and demanding information, but the louder he raved the less the servant understood and finally he hung up the receiver and dashed about the room like an insane creature, tearing off his wilted collar, grabbing at another, jerking on his fine coat, searching vainly for his cuffs, snatching his hat and overcoat, and making off down the stairs; breathlessly, regardless of the demand of the janitor for the fee of freedom he had been promised.

Out in the street he rushed hither and thither blindly in search of some conveyance, found a taxicab at last, and, plunging in, ordered it to go at once to the Hathaway address.

Arrived there, he presented an enlivening spectacle to the guests, who were still making merry. His trousers were covered with French chalk, his collar had slipped from its confining button in front and curved gracefully about one fat cheek, his high hat was a crush indeed, having been rammed down to his head in his excitement. He talked so fast and so loud that they thought he was crazy and tried to put him out, but he shook his fist angrily in the face of the footman and demanded to know where Miss Hathaway was. When they told him she was married and gone, he turned livid with wrath and told them that that was impossible, as he was the bridegroom.

By this time the guests had gathered in curious groups in the hall and on the stairs, listening, and when he claimed to be the bridegroom they shouted with laughter, thinking this must be some practical joke or else that the man was insane. But one older gentleman, a friend of the family, stepped up to the excited visitor and said in a quieting voice:

"My friend, you have made a mistake! Miss Hathaway has this evening been married to Mr. George Hayne, just arrived from abroad, and they are at this moment on their way to take the train. You have come too late to see her, or else you have the wrong address, and are speaking of some other Miss Hathaway. That is very likely the explanation."

George looked around on the company with helpless rage, then rushed to his taxicab and gave the order for the station.

Arriving at the station, he saw it was within half a minute of departure of the Chicago train, and none knew better than he what time that train had been going to depart. Had he not given minute directions regarding the arrangements to his future brother-in-law? What did it all mean anyway? Had Celia managed somehow to carry out the wedding without him to hide her mortification at his non-appearance? Or had she run away? He was too excited to use his reason. He could merely urge his heavy bulk onward toward the fast fleeing train; and dashed up the platform, overcoat streaming from his arm, coat-tails flying, hat crushed down upon his head, his fat, bechalked legs rumbling heavily after him. He passed Jefferson and his mother; watching tearfully, lingeringly, the retreating mother did not notice and only said absently; "I think he'll be good to her, don't you, Jeff? He has nice eyes. I don't remember that his eyes used to seem so pleasant, and so — deferential." Then they turned to go back to their car, and the train moved faster and faster out of the station. It would presently rush away out into the night, leaving the two pursuers to face each other, baffled.

Both realized this at the same instant and the short, thickset man with sudden decision turned again and plunging along with the train caught at the rail and swung himself with dangerous precipitation to the last platform of the last car with a half-frightened triumph. Looking back he saw the other man with a frantic effort sprint forward, trying to do the same thing, and failing in the attempt, sprawl flat on the platform, to the intense amusement of a couple of trainmen standing near.

George Hayne, having thus come to a full stop in his head-long career, lay prostrate for a moment, stunned and shaken; then gathered himself up slowly and stood gazing after the departing train. After all, if he caught it what could he have done? It was incredible that Celia could have got herself married and gone on her wedding trip without him. If she had eloped with some one else and they were on that train what could he have done? Kill the bridegroom and force the bride to return with him and be married over again? Yes, but that might have been a trifle awkward after all, and he had enough awkward situations to his account already. Besides, it wasn't in the least likely that Celia was married yet. Those people at the house had been fooled somehow, and she had run away. Perhaps her mother and brother were gone with her. The same threats that had made her bend to him once should follow her wherever she had gone. She would marry him yet and pay for this folly a hundred fold. He lifted a shaking hand of execration toward the train which by this time was vanishing into the dark opening at the end of the station, where signal lights like red berries festooned themselves in an arch against the blackness, and the lights of the last car paled and vanished like a forgotten dream.

Then he turned and hobbled slowly back to the gates regardless of the merriment he was arousing in the genial trainmen; for he was spent and bruised, and his appearance was anything but dignified. No member of the wedding company had they seen him at this juncture would have recognized in him any resemblance to the handsome gentleman who had played his part in the wedding ceremony. No one would have thought it possible that he could be Celia Hathaway's bridegroom.

Slowly back to the gate he crept, haggard, dishevelled, crestfallen; his hair in its several isolate locks downfallen over his forehead, his collar wilted, his clothes smeared with chalk and dust, his overcoat dragging forlornly behind him. He was trying to decide what to do next, and realizing the torment of a perpetual thirst, when a hand was laid suddenly upon him and a voice that somehow had a familiar twang, said: "You will come with me, sir."

He looked up and there before him in the flesh were the eyes of the man who had haunted him for years, the eyes grown younger, and filled with more than reproach. They were piercing him with the keenness of retribution. They said, as plainly as those eyes in the closet had spoken but a brief hour before: "Your time is over. My time has come. You have sinned. You shall suffer. Come now and meet your reward."

He started back in horror. His hands trembled and his brain reeled. He wished for another cocktail to help him to meet this most extraordinary emergency. Surely, something had happened to his nerves that he was seeing these eyes in reality and hearing the voice, that old man's voice made young, bidding him come with him. It could not be, of course. He was unnerved with all he had been through. The man had mistaken him for some one — or perhaps it was not a man after all. He glanced quickly around to see if others saw him, and at once became aware that a crowd was collecting about them.

The man with the strange eyes and the familiar voice was dressed in plain clothes, but he seemed to have full assurance that he was a real live man and had a right to dictate. George Hayne could not shake away his grasp. There was a determination about it that struck terror to his soul, and he had a weak desire to scream and hide his eyes. Could he be coming down with delirium tremens? That brandy must have been unusually strong to have lasted so long in its effects. Then he made a weak effort to speak, but his voice sounded small and frightened. The eyes took his assurance from him.

"Who are you?" he asked, and meant to add, "What right have you to dictate to *me?*" but the words died away in his throat, for the plainclothes man had opened his coat and disclosed a badge that shone with a sinister light straight into his eyes.

"I am Norman Brand," answered the voice, "and I want you for what you did to my father. It is time you paid your debt. You were the cause of his humiliation and death. I have been watching you for years. I saw the notice of your wedding in the paper and was tracking you. It was for this I entered the service. Come with me."

With a cry of horror George Hayne wrenched away from his captor and turned to flee, but instantly three revolvers were levelled at him, and he found that two policemen in brass buttons were stationed behind him, and the crowd closed in about him. Wherever he turned it was to look into the barrel of a gun, and there was no escape in any direction.

They led him away to the patrol wagon, the erstwhile bridegroom, and in place of the immaculate linen he had searched so frantically for in his apartment they put upon his wrists cuffs of iron. They put him in a cell and left him with the eyes of the old man for company and the haunting likeness of his son's voice filling him with frenzy.

The unquenchable thirst came upon him and he begged for brandy and soda, but none came to slake his thirst, for he had crossed the great gulf and justice at last had him in her grasp.

7

MEANWHILE the man on the steps of the last car of the Chicago Limited was having his doubts about whether he ought to have boarded that train. He realized that the fat traveller who was hurling himself after the train had stirred in him a sudden impulse which had been only half formed before and he had obeyed it. Perhaps he was following a wrong scent and would lose the reward which he knew was his if he brought the thief of the code-writing, dead or alive, to his employer. He was half inclined to jump off again now before it was too late; but looking down he saw they were already speeding over a network of tracks, and trains were flying by in every direction. By the time they were out of this the speed would be too great for him to attempt a jump. It was even now risky, and he was heavy for athletics. He must do it at once if he did it at all.

He looked ahead tentatively to see if the track on which he must jump was clear, and the great eye of an engine stabbed him in the face, as it bore down upon him. The next instant it swept by, its hot breath fanning his cheek, and he drew back shuddering involuntarily. It was of no use. He could not jump here. Perhaps they would slow up or stop, and anyway, should he jump or stay on board?

He sat down on the upper step the better to get the situation in hand. Perhaps in a minute more the way would be clearer to jump off if he decided not to go on. Thus he vacillated. It was rather unlike him not to know his own mind.

It seemed as if there must be something here to follow, and yet, perhaps he was mistaken. He had been the first man of the company at the front door after Mr. Holman turned the paper over, and they all had noticed the absence of the red mark. It had been simultaneous with the clicking of the door-latch and he had covered the ground from his seat to the door sooner than anyone else. He could swear he had seen the man get into the cab that stood almost in front of the house. He had lost no time in getting into his own car which was detailed for such an emergency, and in signalling the officer on a motor-cycle who was also ready for a quick call. The carriage had barely turned the corner when they followed, there was no other of the kind in sight either way but that, and he had followed it closely. It must have been the right carriage. And yet, when the man got out at the church he was changed, much changed in appearance, so that he had looked twice into the empty carriage to make sure that the man for whom he searched was not still in there hiding. Then he had followed him into the church and seen him married; stood close at hand when he put his bride into a big car, and he had followed the car to the house where the reception was held; even mingling with the guests and watching until the bridal couple left for the train. He had stood in the alley in the shadow, the only one of the guests who had found how the bride was really going away, and again he had followed to the station.

He had walked close enough to the bridegroom in the station to be almost sure that mustache and those heavy eyebrows were false; and yet he could not make it out. How could it be possible that a man who was going to be married in a great church full of fashionable people would dare to flirt with chance as to accept an invitation to a dinner where he might not be able to get away for hours? What would have happened if he had not got there in time? Was it in the least possible that these two men could be identical? Everything but the likeness and the fact that he had followed the man so closely pointed out the impossibility.

The thick-set man was accustomed to trust his inner impressions thoroughly, and in this case his inner impression was that he must watch this peculiar bridegroom and be sure he was not the right man before he forever got away from him — and yet — and yet, he might be missing the right man by doing it. However, he had come so far, he risked a good deal already in following and in throwing himself on that fast moving train. He would stay a little longer and find out for sure. He would try and get a seat where he could watch him and in an hour he ought to be able to tell if he were really the man who had stolen the code-writing. If he could avoid the conductor for a time he would simply profess to have taken the wrong train by mistake, and maybe could get put off somewhere near home, in case he discovered that he was barking up the wrong tree. He would stick to the train for a little yet, inasmuch as there seemed no safe way of getting off at present.

Having decided so much, he gave one last glance toward the twinkling lights of the city hurrying past, and getting up sauntered into the train, keeping a weather eye out for the conductor. He meant to burn no bridges behind him. He was well provided with money for any kind of a tip and mileage books and passes. He knew where to send a telegram that would bring him instant assistance in case of need, and even now he knew the officer on the motor-cycle had reported to his employer that he had boarded this train. There was really no immediate need for him to worry. It was big game he was after and one must take some risks in a case of that sort. Thus he entered the sleeper to make good the impression of his inner senses.

Gordon had never held anything so precious, so sweet and beautiful and frail-looking, in his arms. He had a feeling that he ought to lay her down, yet there was a longing to draw her closer to himself and shield her from everything that could trouble her.

But she was not his—only a precious trust to be guarded and cared for as vigilantly as the message he carried hidden about his neck; she belonged to another, somewhere, and was a sacred trust until circumstances made it possible for him to return her to her rightful husband. Just what all this might mean to himself, to the woman in his arms, and to the man who she was to have married, Gordon had not as yet had time to think. It was as if he had been watching a moving picture and suddenly a lot of circumstances had fallen in a heap and become all jumbled up together, the result of his own rash but unsuspecting steps, the way whole families have in moving pictures of falling through a sky-scraper from floor to floor, carrying furniture and inhabitants with them as they descend.

He had not as yet been able to disentangle himself from the debris and find out what had been his fault and what he ought to do about it.

He laid her gently on the couch of the drawing-room and opened the little door of the private dressing-room. There would be cold water in there.

He knew very little about caring for sick people—he had always been well and strong himself—but cold water was what they used for people who had fainted, but was sure. He would not call in anyone to help, unless it was absolutely necessary. He pulled the door of the stateroom shut, and went after the water. As he passed the mirror, he started at the curious vision of himself. One false eyebrow had come loose and was hanging over his eye, and his goatee was crooked. Had it been so all the time? He snatched the eyebrow off, and then the other; but the mustache and goatee were more tightly affixed, and it was very painful to remove them. He glanced back, and the white limp look of the girl on the couch frightened him. What was he about, to stop over his appearance when she might be dying, and as for pain—he tore the false hair roughly from him, and stuffing it into his pocket, filled a glass with water and went back to the couch. His chin and upper lip smarted, but he did not notice it, nor know that the mark of the plaster was all about his face. He only knew that she lay there apparently lifeless before him, and he must bring the soul back into those dear eyes. It was strange, wonderful, how his feeling had grown for the girl whom he had never seen till three hours before.

He held the glass to her white lips and tried to make her drink, then poured water on his handkerchief and awkwardly bathed her forehead. Some hairpins slipped loose and a great wealth of golden-brown hair fell across his knees as he half knelt beside her. One little hand drooped over the side of the couch and touched his. He started! It seemed so soft and cold and lifeless.

He blamed himself that he had no remedies in his suitcase. Why had he never thought to carry something,—a simple restorative? Other people might need it though he did not. No man ought to travel without something for the saving of life in an emergency. He might have needed it himself even, in case of a railroad accident or something.

He slipped his arm tenderly under her head and tried to raise it so that she could drink, but the white lips did not move nor attempt to swallow.

Then a panic seized him. Suppose she was dying? Not until later, when he had quiet and opportunity for thought, did it occur to him what a terrible responsibility he had dared to take upon himself in letting her people leave her with him; what a fearful position he would have been in if she had really died. At the moment his whole thought was one of anguish at the idea of losing her; anxiety to save her precious life; and not for himself.

Forgetting his own need of quiet and obscurity, he laid her gently back upon the couch again, and rushed from the stateroom out into the aisle of the sleeper. The conductor was just making his rounds and he hurried to him with a white face.

"Is there a doctor on board, or have you any restoratives?" There is a lady—" He hesitated and the color rolled freshly into his anxious face. "That is—my wife." He spoke the word unwillingly, having at the instant of speaking realized that he must say this to protect her good name. It seemed like uttering a falsehood, or stealing another man's property; and yet, technically, it was true, and for her sake at least he must acknowledge it.

"My wife," he began again more connectedly, "is ill— unconscious."

The conductor looked at him sharply. He had sized them up as a wedding party when they came down the platform toward the train. The young man's blush confirmed his supposition.

"I'll see!" he said briefly. "Go back to her and I'll bring some one."

It was just as Gordon turned back that the thick-set man entered the car from the other end and met him face to face, but Gordon was too distraught at that moment to notice him, for his mind was at rest about his pursuer as soon as the train started.

Not so with the pursuer however. His keen little eyes took in the white, anxious face, the smear of sticking plaster about the mouth and eyebrows, and instantly knew his man. His instincts had not failed him after all.

He put out a pair of brawny fists to catch at him, but a lurch of the train and Gordon's swift stride out-purposed him, and by the time the little man had righted his footing Gordon was disappearing into the stateroom, and the conductor with another man was in the aisle behind him waiting to pass. He stepped back and watched. At least he had driven his prey to quarry and there was no possible escape now until the train stopped. He would watch that door as a cat watches a mouse, and perhaps be able to send a telegram for help before he made any move at all. It was as well that his impulse to take the man then and there had come to naught. What would the other passengers have thought of him? He must of course move cautiously. What a blunder he had almost made. It was not part of his purpose to make public his errand. The men who were behind him did not wish to be known, nor to have their business known.

With narrowing eyes he watched the door of the stateroom as the conductor and doctor came and went. He gathered from a few questions asked by one of the passengers that there was some one sick, probably the lady he had seen faint as the train started. It occurred to him that this might be his opportunity, and when the conductor came out of the drawing-room the second time he inquired if any assistance was needed, and implied that doctoring was his profession, though it would be a sorry patient that had only his attention. However, if he had one accomplishment it was bluffing, and he never stopped at any profession that suited his needs.

The conductor was annoyed at the interruptions that had already occurred and he answered him brusquely that they had all the help necessary and there wasn't anything the matter anyway.

There was nothing left for the man to do but wait.

He subsided with his eye on the stateroom door, and later secured a berth in plain sight of that door, but gave no order to have it made up until every other passenger in the car was gone to what rest a sleeping car provides. He kept his vigil well, but was rewarded with no sight of his prey that night, and at last with a sense of duty well done and the comfortable promise from the conductor that his deftly worded telegraphic message to Mr. Holman should be sent from a station they passed a little after midnight, he crept to his well-earned rest. He was not at home in a dress shirt and collar, being of the walks of life where a collar is mostly accounted superfluous, and he was glad to be relieved of it for a few hours. It had not yet occurred to him that his appearance in that evening suit would be a trifle out of place when morning came. It is doubtful if he had ever considered matters of dress. His profession was that of a human ferret of the lower order, and there were many things he did not know. It might have been the way he held his fork at dinner that had made Gordon decide that he was but a henchman of the others.

Having put his mind and his body at rest he proceeded to sleep, and the train thundered on its way into the night.

Gordon meanwhile had hurried back from his appeal to the conductor, and stood looking helplessly down at the delicate girl as she lay there so white and seemingly lifeless. Her pretty travelling gown set off the exquisite face finely; her glorious hair seemed to crown her. A handsome hat had fallen unheeded to the floor, and lay rolling back and forth in the aisle with the motion of the train. He picked it up reverently, as though it had been a part of her. His face in the few minutes had gone haggard.

The conductor hurried in presently, followed by a grave elderly man with a professional air. He touched a practised finger to the limp wrist, looked closely into the face, and then taking a little bottle from a case he carried called for a glass.

The liquid was poured between the closed lips, the white throat reluctantly swallowed it, the eyelids presently fluttered, a long breath that was scarcely more than a sigh hovered between the lips, and then the blue eyes opened.

She looked about, bewildered, looking longest at Gordon, then closed her eyes wearily, as if she wished they had not brought her back, and lay still.

The physician still knelt beside her, and Gordon, with time now to think, began to reflect on the possible consequences of his deeds. With anxious face, he stood watching, reflecting bitterly that he might not claim even a look of recognition from those sweet eyes, and wishing with all his heart that his marriage had been genuine. A passing memory of his morning ride to New York in company with Miss Bentley's conjured vision brought wonder to his eyes. It all seemed so long ago, and so strange that he ever could have entertained for a moment the thought of marrying Julia. She was a good girl of course, fine and handsome and all that, — but — and here his eyes sought the sweet sad face on the couch, and his heart suffered in a real agony for the trouble he saw; and for the trouble he must yet give her when he told her who he was, or rather who he was not; for he must tell her and that soon. It would not do to go on in her company — nor to Chicago! And yet, how was he possibly to leave her in this condition?

But no revelations were to be given that night.

The physician administered another draught, and ordered the porter to make up the berth immediately. Then with skillful hands and strong arms he laid the young girl in upon the pillows and made her comfortable, Gordon meanwhile standing awkwardly by with averted eyes and troubled mien. He would have like to help, but he did not know how.

"She'd better not be disturbed any more than is necessary to-night," said the doctor, as he pulled the pretty cloth travelling gown smoothly down about the girl's ankles and patted it with professional hands. "Don't let her yield to any nonsense about putting up her hair, or taking off that frock for fear she'll rumple it. She needs to lie perfectly quiet. It's a case of utter exhaustion, and I should say a long strain of some kind — anxiety, worry perhaps." He looked keenly at the sheepish bridegroom. "Has she had any trouble?"

Gordon lifted honest eyes.

"I'm afraid so," he answered contritely, as if it must have been his fault some way.

"Well, don't let her have any more," said the elder man briskly. "She's a very fragile bit of womanhood, young man, and you'll have to handle her carefully or she'll blow away.

Make her *happy,* young man! People can't have too much happiness in this world. It's the best thing, after all, to keep them well. Don't be afraid to give her plenty."

"Thank you!" said Gordon, fervently, wishing it were in his power to do what the physician ordered.

The kindly physician, the assiduous porter, and the brusque but good-hearted conductor went away at last, and Gordon was left with his precious charge, who to all appearances was sleeping quietly. The light was turned low and the curtains of the berth were a little apart. He could see the dim outline of drapery about her, and one shadowy hand lying limp at the edge of the couch, in weary relaxation.

Above her, in the upper berth, which he had told the porter not to make up, lay the great purple-black plumed hat, and a sheaf of lilies of the valley from her bouquet. It seemed all so strange for him to be there in their sacred presence.

He locked the door, so that no one should disturb the sleeper, and went slowly into the little private dressing-room. For a full minute after he reached it, he stood looking into the mirror before him, looking at his own weary, soiled face, and wondering if he, Cyril Gordon, heretofore honored and self-respecting, had really done in the last twelve hours all the things which he was crediting himself with having done! And the question was, how had it happened? Had he taken leave his senses, or had circumstances been too much for him? Had he lost the power of judging between right and wrong? Could he have helped any of the things that had come upon him? How could he have helped them? What ought he to have done? What ought he to do now? Was he a criminal beyond redemption? Had he spoiled the life of the sweet woman out there in her berth, or could he somehow make amends for what he had done? And was he as badly to blame for it all as he felt himself to be?

After a minute he rallied, to realize that his face was dirty. He washed the marks of the adhesive plaster away, and then, not satisfied with the result, he brought his shaving things from his suit-case and shaved. Somehow, he felt more like himself after his toilet was completed, and he slipped back into the darkened drawing-room and stretched himself wearily on the couch, which, according to his directions, was not made up, but merely furnished with pillows and a blanket.

The night settled into the noisy quiet of an express train, and each revolution of the wheels, as they whirled their way Chicagoward, resolved itself into the old refrain, "Don't let anything hinder you! Don't let anything hinder you!"

He certainly was not taking the most direct route from New York to Washington, though it might eventually prove that the longest way round was the shortest way home, on account of its comparative safety.

As he settled to the quiet of his couch, a number of things came more clearly to his vision. One was that they had safely passed the outskirts of New York without interference of any kind, and must by this time be speeding toward Albany, unless they were on a road that took them more directly West. He had not thought to look at the tickets for knowledge of his bearings, and the light was too dim for him to make out any monograms or letterings on inlaid wood panels or transoms, even if he had known enough about New York railroads to gain information from them. There was one thing certain: even if he had been mistaken about his supposed pursuers, by morning there would surely be some one searching for him. The duped Holman combination would stop at nothing when they discovered his theft of the paper, and he could not hope that so sharp-eyed a man as Mr. Holman had seemed to be would be long in discovering the absence of his private mark on the paper. Undoubtedly he knew it already. As for the frantic bridegroom, Gordon dreaded the thought of meeting him. It must be put off at any hazards until the message was safe with his chief, then, if he had to answer with his life for carrying off another man's bride, he could at least feel that he left no duty to his government undone. It was plain that his present situation was a dangerous one from two points of view, for the bridegroom would have no difficulty in finding out what train he and the lady had taken, and he was satisfied that an emissary of Holman had more than a suspicion of his identity. The obvious thing to do was to get off that train at the first opportunity and get across country to another line of railroad. But how was that to be done with a sick lady on his hands? Of course he could leave her to herself. She probably had taken journeys before, and would know how to get back. She would at least be able to telegraph to her friends to come for her. He could leave her money and a note explaining his involuntary villainy, and her indignation with him would probably be a sufficient stimulant to keep her from dying of chagrin at her plight. But as from the first every nerve and fibre in him rejected this suggestion. It would be cowardly, unmanly, horrible! Undoubtedly it might be the wise thing to do from many standpoints, but — *never!* He could no more leave her that way than he could run off to save his life and leave that message he carried. She was a trust as much as that. He had got into this, and he must get out somehow, but he would not desert the lady or neglect his duty.

Toward morning, when his fitful vigil became less lucid it occurred to him that he ought really to have deserted the bride while she was still unconscious, jumping off the train at the short stop they made soon after she fell into his arms. She would then have been cared for by some one, his absence discovered, and she would have been put off the train and her friends sent for at once. But it would have been dastardly to have deserted her that way not knowing even if she still lived, he on whom she had at least a claim of temporary protection.

It was all a terrible muddle, right and wrong juggled in such a mysterious and unusual way. He never remembered to have come to a spot before where it was difficult to know which of two things it was right to do. There had always before been such clearly defined divisions. He had supposed that people who professed not to know what was right were people who wished to be blinded on the subject because they wished to do wrong and think it right. But now he saw that he had judged such too harshly.

Perhaps his brain had been overstrained with the excitement and annoyances of the day, and he was not quite in a condition to judge what was right. He ought to snatch a few minutes' sleep, and then his mind would be clearer, for something must be done and that soon. It would not do to risk entering a large city where detectives and officers with full particulars might even now be on the watch for him. He was too familiar with the workings of retribution in this progressive age not to know his danger. But he really must get some sleep.

At last he yielded to the drowsiness that was stealing over him—just for a moment, he thought, and the wheels hummed on their monotonous song: "Don't let anything hinder! Don't let anything—! Don't let—! Don't! Hinder-r-r-r!"

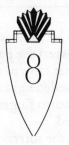

8

THE man slept, and the train rushed on. The night waned. The dawn grew purple in the east, and streaked itself with gold; then later got out a fillet of crimson and drew over its cloudy forehead. The breath of the lilies filled the little room with delicate fragrance, and mingled strange scenes in the dreams of the man and the woman so strangely united.

The sad little bride grew restless and stirred, but the man on the couch did not hear her. He was dreaming of a shooting affray, in which he carried a bride in a gold pencil and was shot for stealing a sandwich out of Mr. Holman's vest pocket.

The morning light grew clearer. The east had put on a vesture of gold above her purple robe, and its reflection shone softly in at the window, for the train was just at that moment rushing northward, though its general course was west.

The sleeper behind the thick green curtains stirred again and became conscious, as in many days past, of her heavy burden of sorrow. Always at first waking the realization of it sat upon her as though it would crush the life from her body. Lying still with bated breath, she fought back waking consciousness as she had learned to do in the last three months, yet knew it to be futile while she was doing it.

The sun shot up between the bars of crimson, like a topaz on a lady's gown that crowns the whole beautiful costume. The piercing, jewelled light lay across the white face, touched the lips with warm fingers, and the troubled soul knew all that had passed.

She lay quiet, letting the torrent sweep over her with its sickening realization. She was married! It was over—with the painful parting from dear ones. She was off away from them all. The new life she so dreaded had begun, and how was she to face it—the life with one whom she feared and did not respect? How could she ever have done it but for the love of her dear ones?

Gradually she came to remember the night before—the parting with her mother and her brother; the little things that brought the tears again to her eyes. Then all was blankness. She must have fainted. She did not often faint, but it must be—yes, she remembered opening her eyes and seeing men's faces about her, and George—could it have been George?— with a kinder look in his eyes than she had ever thought to see there. Then she must have fainted again—or had she? No, some one had lifted her into this berth, and she had drunk something and had gone to sleep. What had happened? Where was everybody? It was good to have been left alone. She grudgingly gave her unloved husband a fragment of gratitude for not having tried to talk to her. In the carriage on the way he had seemed determined to begin a long argument of some kind. She did not want to argue any more. She had written tomes upon the subject, and had said all she had to say. He was not deceived. He knew she did not love him, and would never have married him but for her mother's sake and for the sake of her beloved father's memory. What was the use of saying more? Let it rest. The deed was done, and they were married. Now let him have his way and make her suffer as he chose. If he would but let her suffer in silence and not inflict his bitter tongue upon her, she would try to bear it. And perhaps — oh, perhaps, she would not live long, and it would soon be all over.

As the daylight grew, the girl felt an inclination to find out whether her husband was near. Cautiously she lifted her head and, drawing back a corner of the curtain, peered out.

He lay quietly on the couch, one hand under his cheek against the pillow, the other across his breast, as if to guard something. He was in the still sleep of the over-wearied. He scarcely seemed to be breathing.

Celia dropped the curtain, and put her hand to her throat. It startled her to find him so near and so still. Softly, stealthily, she lay down again and closed her eyes. She must not waken him. She would have as long a time to herself as was possible, and try to think of her dear mother and her precious brother. Oh, if she were just going away from them alone, how well she could bear it! But to be going with one whom she had always almost hated —

Her brother's happy words about George suddenly came to her mind. Jefferson had thought him fine. Well, of course the dear boy knew nothing about it. He had not read all those letters — those awful letters. He did not know the threats — the terrible language that had been used. She shuddered as she thought of it. But in the same breath she was glad that her brother had been deceived. She would not have it otherwise. Her dear ones must never know what she had gone through to save them from disgrace and loss of fortune — disgrace, of course, being the first and greatest. She had feared that George would let them see through his veneer of manners, and leave them troubled, but he had made a better appearance than she had hoped. The years had made a greater change in him than she had expected. He really had not been so bad as her conjured image of him.

Then a sudden desire to look at him again seized her, to know once for all just how he really did seem. She would not want to notice him awake any more than she could help, nor dare, lest he presume upon her sudden interest, to act as if he had never offended; but if she should look at him now as he lay asleep she might study his face and see what she really had to expect.

She fought the desire to peer at him again, but finally it gained complete possession of her, and she drew back the curtain once more.

He was lying just as quietly as before. His heavy hair, a little disordered on the pillow, gave him a noble, interesting appearance. He did not seem at all a fellow of whom to be afraid. It was incredible that he could have written those letters.

She tried to trace in his features a likeness to the youth of ten years ago, whom she had known when she was but a little girl, who had tied her braids to her chair, and put raw oysters and caterpillars down her back, or stretched invisible cords to trip her feet in dark places; who made her visits to a beloved uncle—whom he also had the right to call uncle, though he was no cousin of hers—a long list of catastrophes resulting in tears; who had never failed to mortify her on all occasions possible, and once—But the memories were too horrible as they crowded one upon another! Let them be forgotten!

She watched the face before her keenly, critically, yet she could see no trace of any such character as she had imagined the boy George must have developed as a man; of which his letters had given her ample proof. This man's face was finely cut and sensitive. There was nothing coarse or selfish in its lines. The long, dark lashes lay above dark circles of weariness, and gave that look of boyishness that always touches the maternal chord in a woman's heart. George used to have a puffy, self-indulgent look under his eyes even when he was a boy. She had imagined from his last photograph that he would be much stouter, much more bombastic; but, then, in his sleep, perhaps those things fell from a man.

She tried to turn away indifferently, but something in his face held her. She studied it. If he had been any other man, any stranger, she would have said from looking at him critically that kindness and generosity, self-respect and respect for women, were written all over the face before her. There was fine, firm modelling about the lips and the clean-shaven chin; and about the forehead the look almost of a scholar; yet she thought she knew the man before her to be none of these things. How deceptive were looks! She would probably be envied rather than pitied by all who saw her. Well, perhaps that was better. She could the easier keep her trouble to herself. But stay, what was there about this man that seemed different? The smooth face? Yes. She had the dim impression that last night he wore a mustache. She must have been mistaken, of course. She had only looked at him when absolutely necessary, and her brain was in such a whirl; but still there seemed to be something different about him.

Her eyes wandered to the hand that lay across his breast. It was the fine white hand of the professional man, the kind of hand that somehow attracts the eye with a sense of cleanness and strength. There was nothing flabby about it. George as a boy used to have big, stumpy fingers and nails chewed down to the quick. She could remember how she used to hate to look at them when she was a little girl, and yet somehow could not keep her eyes away. She saw with relief that the nails on his hand were well shaped and well cared for.

He looked very handsome and attractive as he lay there. The sun shot one of its early daring bolts of light across his hair as the train turned in its course and lurched northward around a curve. It glinted there for a moment, like a miniature searchlight, travelling over the head, showing up every wave and curve. He had the kind of hair which makes a woman's hand instinctively long to touch it.

Celia wondered at the curious thoughts that crowded through her mind, knowing that all the while there was the consciousness that when this man should wake she would think of nothing but his hateful personality as she had known it through the years. And she was his wife! How strange! How terrible! How impossible to live with the thought through interminable weary years! Oh, that she might die at once before her strength failed and her mother found out her sorrow!

She lay back again on her pillows very still and tried to think, but somehow a pleasant image of him, her husband, lingered in her memory. Could it be possible that she would ever see anything pleasant in him? Ever endure the days of his companionship? Ever come to the point where she could overlook his outrageous conduct toward her, forgive him, and be even tolerant of him? Sharp memories crowded upon her, and the smarting years stung their way into her eyes, answering and echoing in her heart, "No, no, a thousand times, no!" She had paid his price and gained redemption for her own, but—forget what he had done? *Never!*

The long strain of weariness, and the monotony of the on-rushing train, lulled her into unconsciousness again, and the man on the couch slumbered on.

He came to himself suddenly, with all his senses on the alert, as the thumping noise and the motion of the train ceased, and a sudden silence of open country succeeded, broken now and again by distant oncoming and receding voices. He caught the fragment of a sentence from some train official: "It's a half-hour late, and maybe more. We'll just have to lie by, that's all. Here, you, Jim, take this flag and run up to the switch—" The voice trailed into the distance, ended by the metallic note of a hammer doing something mysterious to the under-pinning of the car.

Gordon sat up suddenly, his hand yet across his breast, where his first waking thought had been to feel if the little pencil-case were safe.

Glancing stealthily toward the curtains of the berth, and perceiving no motion, he concluded that the girl still slept.

Softly he slipped his feet into his shoes, gave one or two other touches to his toilet, and stood up, looking toward the curtains. He wanted to go out and see where they were stopping, but dared he go without knowing that she was all right?

Softly, reverently, he stooped and brought his face close to the opening in the curtains. Celia felt his eyes upon her. Her own were closed, and by a superhuman effort she controlled her breathing, slowly, gently, as if she were asleep.

He looked for a long moment, thrilled by the delicate beauty of her sleeping face, filled with an intoxicating joy to see that her lips were no longer white; then, turning reverently away, he unlocked the door and stepped forth.

The other occupants of the car were still wrapped in slumber. Loud snores of various kinds and qualities testified to that. A dim light at the further end contended luridly, and losingly, with the daylight now flooding the outside world and creeping mischievously into the transoms.

Gordon closed the door of the compartment noiselessly and went down the aisle to the end of the car.

A door was open, and he could hear voices outside. The conductor stood talking with two brakemen. He heard the words: "Three-quarters of an hour at least," and then the men walked off toward the engine.

Gordon looked across the country, and for the first time since he started on his journey let himself remember that it was springtime and May.

There had been a bitter wind the night before, with a hint of rain in the air. In fact, it had rained quite smartly during the ride to the hospital with that hurt child, but he had been so perturbed that he had taken little notice of the weather. But this was a radiant morning.

The sun was in one of its most charming moods, when it touches everything with a sort of unnatural glory after the long winter of darkness and cold. Every tree trunk in the distance seemed to stand out clearly, every little grass-blade was set with a glowing jewel, and the winding stream across a narrow valley fairly blazed with brightness. The very road with its deep, clean wheel-groves seemed like a well-taken photograph.

The air had an alluring softness mingled with its tang of winter that made one long to take a walk anywhere out into the world, just for the joy of being and doing. A meadowlark shot up from somewhere to a telegraph pole, let go a blithe note, and hurried on. It was glorious. The exhilaration filled Gordon's blood.

And here was the chance he craved to slip away from the train before it reached a place where he could be discovered. If he had but thought to bring his suit-case! He could slip back now without being noticed and get it! He could even go without it! But—he could not leave her that way—could he? Ought he? Perhaps he ought—But it would not do to leave his suit-case with her, for it contained letters addressed to his real name. An explanation would of course be demanded, and he could never satisfy a loving mother and brother for having left a helpless girl in such a situation— even if he could satisfy his own conscience, which he knew he never could. He simply could not leave her, and yet he *must* get away from that train as soon as possible. Perhaps this was the only opportunity he would have before reaching Buffalo, and it was very risky, indeed dangerous, to dare enter Buffalo. It was a foregone conclusion that there would be private detectives ready to meet the train in Buffalo with full descriptions and particulars and only too ready to make way with him if they could do so without being found out. He looked nervously back at the door of the car. Dared he attempt to waken her and say that they had made a mistake and must change cars? Was she well enough? And where could they go?

He looked off toward the landscape for answer to his question.

They were decidedly in the country. The train stood at the top of a high embankment of cinders, below which was a smooth country road running parallel to the railroad for some distance till it met another road at right angles to it, which stretched away between thrifty meadow-lands to a nestling village. The glorified stream he had first noticed far up the valley glinted narrower here in the morning light, with a suggestion of watercress and forget-me-nots in its fringes as it veered away under a bridge toward the village and hid itself in a tangle of willows and cat-tails.

How easy it would be to slide down that embankment, and walk out that road over the bridge to the village, where of course a conveyance of some sort could be hired to bear him to another railroad town and thence to — Pittsburgh, perhaps, where he could easily get a train to Washington. How easy if only he were not held by some invisible hands to care for the sweet sleeper inside the car! And yet, for her sake as well as his own, he must do something, and that right speedily.

He was standing thus in deep meditation, looking off at the little village which seemed so near and yet would be so far for her to walk, when he was pervaded with that strange sense of some one near. For an instant he resisted the desire to lift his eyes and prove to himself that no one was present in a doorway which a moment before he knew had been unoccupied. Then, frowning at his own nervousness, he turned.

She stood there in all the beauty of her fresh young girlhood, a delicate pallor on her cheeks, and a deep sadness in her great dark eyes, which were fixed upon him intently, in a sort of puzzled study. She was fully dressed, even to her hat and gloves. Every wave of her golden hair lay exquisitely in place under the purple hat, as though she might have taken an hour or two at her toilet; yet she had made it with excited haste, and with trembling fingers, determined to have it accomplished before the return of her dreaded liege lord.

She had sprung from her berth the instant he closed the door upon her, and fastened the little catch to bar him out. She had dashed cold water into her face, fastened her garments hurriedly, and tossed the glory of her hair into place with a few touches and what hairpins she could find on the floor. Then putting on her hat, coat, and gloves, she had followed him into the outer air. She had a feeling that she must have air to breathe or she would suffocate. A wild desire filled her to go alone into the great out-of-doors. Oh, if she but dared to run away from him! But that she might not do, for all his threats would then probably be made good by him upon her dear mother and brother. No, she must be patient and bear to the end all that was set down for her. But she would get out and breathe a little before he returned. He had very likely gone into the smoker. She remembered that the George of old had been an inveterate smoker of cigarettes. She would have time for a taste of the morning while he had his smoke. And if he returned and found her gone what mattered it? The inevitable beginning of conversations which she so dreaded would be put off for a time.

She never thought to come upon him standing thus alone, looking off at the beauty of the morning as if he enjoyed it. The sight of him held her still, watching, as his sleeping face had held her gaze earlier in the morning. How different he was from what she had expected! How the ten years had changed him! One could almost fancy it might have changed his spirit also — but for those letters — those terrible letters! The writer of those letters could not change, except for the worse!

And yet, he was handsome, intellectual looking, kindly in his bearing, appreciative of the beauty about him — she could not deny it. It was most astonishing. He had lost that baggy look under his eyes, and the weak, selfish, cruel pout of lip she remembered so keenly.

Then he turned, and a smile of delight and welcome lit up his face. In spite of herself, she could not keep an answering smile from glimmering faintly in her own.

"What! You up and out here?" he said, hastening closer to the step. "How are you feeling this morning? Better, I'm sure, or you would not be here so early."

"Oh, I had to get out to the air," she said. "I couldn't stand the car another minute. I wish we could walk the rest of the way."

"Do you?" he said, with a quick, surprised appreciation in his voice. "I was just wishing something like that myself. Do you see that beautiful straight road down there? I was longing to slide down this bank and walk over to that little village for breakfast. Then we could get an auto, perhaps, or a carriage, to take us on to another train. If you hadn't been so ill last night, I might have proposed it."

"Could we?" she asked, earnestly. "I should like it so much;" and there was eagerness in her voice. "What a lovely morning!" Her eyes were wistful, like the eyes of those who weep and wonder why they may not laugh, since sunshine is still yellow.

"Of course we could," he said, "if you were only able."

"Oh, I'm able enough. I should much rather do that than to go back into that stuffy car. But wouldn't they think it awfully queer of us to run away from the train this way?"

"They needn't know anything about it," he declared, like a boy about to play truant. "I'll slip back in the car and get our suit-cases. Is there anything of yours I might be in danger of leaving behind?"

"No, I put everything in my suit-case before I came out," she said, listlessly, as though she had already lost her desire to go.

"I'm afraid you are not able," he said, pausing solicitously as he scaled the steps.

She was surprised at his interest in her welfare.

"Why, of course I am," she said, insistently. "I have often taken longer walks than that looks to be, and I shall feel much better for being out. I really feel as if I couldn't stand it any longer in there."

"Good! Then, we'll try it!"

He hurried in for the baggage and left her standing on the cinder roadbed beside the train looking off at the opening morning.

## 9

IT was just at that instant that the thick-set man in his berth not ten feet away became broadly conscious of the unwonted stillness of the train and the cessation of motion that had lulled him to such sound repose. So does a tiny, sharp sound strike upon our senses and bring them into life again from sleep, making us aware of a state of things that has been going on for some time perhaps without our realization. The sound that roused him may have been the click of the stateroom latch as Gordon opened the door.

The shades were down in the man's berth and the curtains drawn close. The daylight had not as yet penetrated through their thickness. But once awake his senses were immediately on the alert. He yawned, stretched and suddenly arrested another yawn to analyze the utter stillness all about him. A sonorous snore suddenly emphasized the quiet of the car, and made him aware of all the occupants of all those curtained apartments. His mind went over a quick résumé of the nights before, and detailed him at once to duty.

Another soft clicking of the latch set him to listening and his bristly shocked head was stuck instantly out between the curtains into the aisle, eyes toward the stateroom door, just in time to see that a man was stealing quietly down the passageway out of the end door, carrying two suit-cases and an umbrella. It was his man. He was sure instantly, and his mind grew frantic with the thought. Almost he had outdone himself through foolish sleep.

He half sprang from his berth, then remembered that he was but partly dressed, and jerked back quickly to grab his clothes, stopping in the operation of putting them on to yank up his window shade with an impatient click and flatten his face against the window-pane!

Yes, there they were down on the ground outside the train, both of them; man, woman, baggage and all slipping away from him while he slept peacefully and let them go! The language of his mind at that point was hot with invectives.

Gordon had made his way back to the girl's side without meeting any porters or wakeful fellow-passengers. But a distant rumbling greeted his ears. The waited-for express was coming. If they were to get away, it must be done at once or their flight would be discovered, and perhaps even prevented. It certainly was better not to have it known where they got off. He had taken the precaution to close the stateroom door behind him and so it might be some time before their absence would be discovered. Perhaps there would be other stops before the train reached Buffalo, in which case their track would not easily be followed. He had no idea that the evil eye of his pursuer was even then upon him.

Celia was already on the ground, looking off toward the little village wistfully. Just how it was to make her lot any brighter to get out of the train and run away to a strange little village she did not quite explain to herself, but it seemed to be a relief to her pent-up feelings. She was half afraid that George might raise some new objection when he returned.

Gordon swung himself down on the cinder path, scanning the track either way. The conductor and brakemen were not in sight. Far in the distance a black speck was rushing down upon them. Gordon could hear the vibration of the rail of the second track, upon which he placed his foot as he helped Celia across. In a moment more the train would pass. It was important that they should be down the embankment, out of sight. Would the delicate girl not be afraid of the steep incline?

She hesitated for just an instant at the top, for it was very steep. Then, looking up at him, she saw that he expected her to go down with him. She gave a little frightened gasp, set her lips, and started.

He held her as well as he could with two suitcases and an umbrella clutched in his other hand, and finally, as the grade grew steeper, he let go the baggage altogether, and it slid briskly down by itself, while he devoted himself to steadying the girl's now inevitable and swift descent.

It certainly was not an ideal way of travelling, this new style of "gravity" road, but it landed them without delay, though much shaken and scratched, and divested of every vestige of dignity. It was impossible not to laugh, and Celia's voice rang out merrily, showing that she had not always wept and looked sorrowful.

"Are you much hurt?" asked Gordon anxiously, holding her hands and looking down at her tenderly.

Before she could reply, the express train roared above them, drowning their voices and laughter; and when it was past they saw their own train take up its interrupted way grumblingly, and rapidly move off. If the passengers on those two trains had not been deeply wrapped in slumber, they might have been surprised to see two fashionably attired young persons, with hats awry and clasped hands, laughing in a country road at five o'clock of a May morning. But only one was awake, and by the time the two in the road below remembered to look up and take notice, the trains were rapidly disappearing.

The girl had been deeply impressed with Gordon's solicitude for her. It was so out of keeping with his letters. He had never seemed to care whether she suffered or not. In all the arrangements, he had said what *he* wanted, indeed what he *would have,* with an implied threat in the framing of his sentence in case she dared demur. Never had there been the least expression of desire for her happiness. Therefore it was something of a surprise to find him so gentle and thoughtful of her. Perhaps, after all, he would not prove so terrible to live with as she had feared. And yet—how could anyone who wrote those letters have any alleviating qualities? It could not be. She must harden herself against him. Still, if he would be outwardly decent to her, it would make her lot easier, of course.

But her course of mental reasoning was broken in upon by his stout denunications of himself.

"I ought not to have allowed you to slide down there," he declared. "It was terrible, after what you went through last night. I didn't realize how steep and rough it was. Indeed I didn't. I don't see how you ever can forgive me."

"Why, I'm not hurt," she said gently, astonished at his solicitation. There was a strange lump in her throat brought by his kindness, which threatened tears. Just why should kindness from an unexpected quarter bring tears?

"I'm only a little shaken up," she went on as she saw a real anxiety in his brown eyes, "and I don't mind it in the least. I think it was rather fun, don't you?"

A faint glimmer of a smile wavered over the corners of her mouth, and Gordon experienced a sudden desire to take her in his arms and kiss her. It was a strange new feeling. He had never had any such thought about Julia Bentley.

"Why, I—why, yes I guess so, if you're sure you're not hurt."

"Not a bit," she said, and then, for some unexplained reason, they both began to laugh. After that they felt better.

"If your shoes are as full of these miserable cinders as mine are, they need emptying," declared Gordon, shaking first one well-shod foot and then the other, and looking ruefully at the little velvet boots of the lady.

"Suppose you sit down"—he looked about for a seat, but the dewy grass was the only resting place visible. He pitched upon the suit-cases and improvised a chair. "Now, sit down and let me take them off for you."

He knelt in the road at her feet as she obeyed, protesting that she could do it for herself. But he overruled her, and began clumsily to unbutton the tiny buttons, holding the timid little foot firmly, almost reverently, against his knee.

He drew the velvet shoe softly off, and, turning it upside down, shook out the intruding cinders, put a clumsy finger in to make sure they were all gone; then shyly, tenderly, passed his hand over the sole of the fine silk-stockinged foot that rested so lightly on his knee, to make sure no cinders clung to it. The sight and touch of that little foot stirred him deeply. He had never before been called upon to render service so intimate to any woman, and he did it now with half-averted gaze and the utmost respect in his manner. As he did it he tried to speak about the morning, the departing train, the annoying cinders, anything to make their unusual position seem natural and unstrained. He felt deeply embarrassed, the more so because of his own double part in this queer masquerade.

Celia sat watching him, strangely stirred. Her wonder over his kindness grew with each moment, and her prejudices almost dissolved. She could not understand it. There must be something more he wanted of her, for George Hayne had never been kind in the past unless he wanted something of her. She dreaded lest she should soon find it out. Yet he did not look like a man who was deceiving her. She drew a deep sigh. If only it were true, and he were good and kind, and had never written those awful letters! How good and dear it would be to be tenderly cared for this way! Her lips drooped at the corners, and her eyelids drooped in company with the sigh; then Gordon looked up in great distress.

"You are tired!" he declared, pausing in his attempt to fasten the little pearl buttons. "I have been cruel to let you get off the train!"

"Indeed I'm not," said the girl, brightening with sudden effort. At least, she would not spoil the kindness while it lasted. It was surely better than what she had feared.

"You never can button those shoes with your fingers," she laughed, as he redoubled his efforts to capture a tiny disc of pearl and set it into its small velvet socket. "Here! I have a button-hook in my hand-bag. Try this."

She produced a small silver instrument from a gold-link bag on her arm and handed it to him. He took it helplessly, trying first one end and then the other, and succeeding with neither.

"Here, let me show you," she laughed, pulling off one glove. Her white fingers grasped the silver button-hook, and flashed in and out of the velvet holes, knitting the little shoe to the foot in no time. He watched the process in humble wonder, and she would not have been a human girl not to have been flattered with his interest and admiration. For the minute she forgot who and what he was, and let her laugh ring out merrily; and so with shy audacity he assayed to take off the other shoe.

They really felt quite well acquainted and as if they were going on a day's picnic, when they finally gathered up their belongings and started down the road. Gordon summoned all his ready wit and intellect to brighten the walk for her, though he found himself again and again on the brink of referring to his Washington life, or some other personal matter that would have brought a wondering question to her lips. He had decided that he must not tell her who he was until he could put her in an independent position, where she could get away from him at once if she chose. He was bound to look after her until he could place her in good hands, or at least where she could look after herself, and it was better to carry it out leaving her to think what she pleased until he could tell her everything. If all went well, they might be able to catch a Pittsburgh train that night and be in Washington the next day. Then, his message delivered, he would tell her the whole story. Until then he must hold his peace.

They went gaily down the road, the girl's pale cheeks beginning to flush with the morning and the exercise. She was not naturally delicate, and her faint the night before had been the result of a series of heavy strains on a heart burdened with terrible fear. The morning and his kindness had made her forget for the time that she was supposed to be walking into a world of dread and sacrifice.

> *The year's at the spring,*
> *The day's at the morn*

quoted Gordon gaily,

> *Morning's at seven;*
> *The hill-side's dew-pearled —*

He waved an umbrella off to where a hill flashed back a thousand lights from its jewelled grass-blades thickly set.

> *The lark's on the wing;*
> *The snail's on the thorn*

went on Celia suddenly catching his spirit, and pointing to a lark that darted up into the blue with a trill of the morning in his throat.

Gordon turned appreciative eyes upon her. It was good to have her take up his favorite poet in that tone of voice — a tone that showed she too knew and loved Browning.

> *God's in his heaven,*
> *All's right with the world*

finished Gordon in a quieter voice, looking straight into her eyes. "That seems very true, to-day, doesn't it?"

The blue eyes wavered with a hint of shadow in them as they looked back into the brown ones.

"Almost—perhaps," she faltered wistfully.

The young man wished he dared go behind that "almost—perhaps" and find out what she meant, but concluded it were better to bring back the smile and help her to forget for a little while at least.

Down by the brook they paused to rest, under a weeping willow, whose green-tinged plumes were dabbling in the brook. Gordon arranged the suitcases for her to sit upon, then climbed down to the brookside and gathered a great bunch of forget-me-nots, blue as her eyes, and brought them to her.

She looked at them in wonder, to think they grew out here, wild, untended. She had never seen them before, except in pots in the florist's windows. She touched them delicately with the tips of her fingers, as if they were too ethereal for earth; then fastened them in the breast of her gown.

"They exactly match your eyes!" he exclaimed involuntarily, and then wished he had not spoken, for she flushed and paled under his glance, until he felt he had been unduly bold. He wondered why he had said that. He never had been in the habit of saying pretty things to girls, but this girl somehow called it from him. It was genuine. He sat a moment abashed, not knowing what to say next, as if he were a shy boy, and she did not help him, for her eyelashes drooped in a long becoming sweep over her cheeks, and she seemed for the moment not to be able to carry off the situation. He was not sure if she were displeased or not.

Her heart had thrilled strangely as he spoke, and she was vexed with herself that it should be so. A man who had bullied and threatened her for three terrible months and forced her to marry him had no right to a thrill of her heart nor a look from her eyes, be he ever so kind for the moment. He certainly was nice and pleasant when he chose to be; she must watch herself, for never, never, must she yield weakly to his smooth overtures. Well did she know him. He had some reason for all this pleasantness. It would surely be revealed soon.

She stiffened her lips and tried to look away from him to the purple-green hills; but the echo of his words came upon her again, and again her heart thrilled at them. What if — oh what if he were all right, and she might accept the admiration in his voice? And yet how could that be possible? The sweet color came into her cheeks again, and the tears flew quickly to her eyes, till they looked all sky and dew, and she dared not turn back to him.

The silence remained unbroken, until a lark in the willow copse behind them burst forth into a song and broke the spell that was upon them.

"Are you offended at what I said?" he asked earnestly. "I am sorry if you did not like it. The words said themselves without my stopping to think whether you might not like it. Will you forgive me?"

"Oh," she said, lifting her forget-me-not eyes to his, "I am not offended. There is nothing to forgive. It was — beautiful!"

Then his eyes spoke the compliment over again, and the thrill started anew in her heart, till her cheeks grew quite rosy, and she buried her face in the coolness of the tiny flowers to hide her confusion.

"It was very true," he said in a low, lover-like voice that sounded like a caress.

"Oughtn't we to hurry on to catch our train?" said Celia, suddenly springing to her feet. "I'm quite rested now." She felt if she stayed there another moment she would yield to the spell he had cast upon her.

With a dull thud of consciousness the man got himself to his feet and reminded himself that this was another man's promised wife to whom he had been letting his soul go out.

"Don't let anything hinder you! Don't let anything hinder you!" suddenly babbled out of the little brook, and he gathered up his suit-cases and started on.

"I am going to carry my suit-case," declared a very decided voice behind him, and a small hand seized hold of its handle.

"I beg your pardon, you are not!" declared Gordon in a much more determined voice.

"But they are too heavy for you—both of them—and the umbrella too," she protested. "Give me the umbrella then."

But he would not give her even the umbrella, rejoicing in his strength to shield her and bear her burdens. As she walked beside him, she remembered vividly a morning when George Hayne had made her carry two heavy baskets, that his hands might be free to shoot birds. Could this be the same George Hayne?

Altogether, it was a happy walk, and far shorter than either had expected it to be, though Gordon worried not a little about his frail companion before they came to the outskirts of the village, and kept begging her to sit down and rest again, but she would not. She was quite eager and excited about the strange village to which they were coming. Its outlying farm-houses were all so clean and white, with green blinds folded placidly over their front windows and only their back doors astir. The cows all looked peaceful, and the dogs all seemed friendly.

They walked up the village street, shaded in patches with flecks of sunshine through the young leaves. If anyone had told Celia Hathaway the night before that she would have walked and talked thus to-day with her bridegroom she would have laughed him to scorn. But now all unconsciously she had drifted into an attitude of friendliness with the man whom she had thought to hate all the rest of her life.

One long, straight, maple-lined street, running parallel to the stream, comprised the village. They walked to the centre of it, and still saw no signs of a restaurant. A post-office, a couple of stores and a bakery made up the business portion of the town, and upon enquiry it appeared that there was no public eating house, the one hotel of the place having been sold at auction the week before on account of the death of the owner. The early village loungers stared disinterestedly at the phenomenal appearance in their midst of a couple of city folks with their luggage and no apparent means of transit except their two delicately shod feet. It presented a problem too grave to be solved unassisted, and there were solemn shakings of the head over them. At last one who had discouragingly stated the village lack of a public inn asked casually:

"Hed a runaway?"

"Oh, no!" laughed Gordon pleasantly. "We didn't travel with horses."

"Hed a puncture, then," announced the village wise-acre, shifting from one foot to the other.

"Wal, you come the wrong direction to git help," said another languid listener. "Thur ain't no garridge here. The feller what uset to keep it skipped out with Sam Galt's wife a month ago. You'd ought to 'a' turned back to Ashville. They got a good blacksmith there can tinker ye up."

"Is that so?" said Gordon interestedly. "Well now that's too bad, but perhaps as it can't be helped we'll have to forget it. What's the next town on ahead and how far?"

"Sugar Grove's two mile further on, and Milton's five. They've got a garridge and a rest'rant to Milton, but that's only sence the railroad built a junction there."

"Has any one here a conveyance I could hire to take us to Milton?" questioned Gordon, looking anxiously about the indolent group.

"I wouldn't want to drive to Milton for less'n five dollars," declared a lazy youth after a suitable pause.

"Very well," said Gordon. "How soon can you be ready, and what sort of a rig have you? Will it be comfortable for the lady?"

The youth eyed the graceful woman in her dainty city dress scornfully. His own country lass was dressed far prettier to his mind; but the eyes of her, so blue, like the little weed-flowers at her breast, went to his head. His tongue was suddenly tied.

"It's all right! It's as good's you'll get!" volunteered a sullen-faced man half sitting on a sugar barrel. He was of a type who preferred to see fashionable ladies uncomfortable.

The youth departed for his "team" and after some enquiries Gordon found that he might be able to persuade the owner of the tiny white colonial cot across the street to prepare a "snack" for himself and his companion, so they went across the street and waited fifteen minutes in a dank little hair-cloth parlor adorned in funeral wreaths and knit tidies, for a delicious breakfast of poached eggs, coffee, home-made bread, butter like roses, and a comb of amber honey. To each the experience was a new one, and they enjoyed it together like two children, letting their eyes speak volumes of comments in the midst of the old lady's volubility. Unconsciously by their experiences they were being brought into sympathy with each other.

The "rig" when it arrived at the door driven by the blushing youth proved to be a high spring-wagon with two seats. In the front one the youth lounged without a thought of assisting his passengers. Gordon swung the baggage up, and then lifted the girl into the back seat, himself taking the place behind her, and planting a firm hand and arm behind the backless seat, that she might feel more secure.

That ride, with his arm behind her, was just one more link in the pretty chain of sympathy that was being welded about these two. Unconsciously more and more she began to droop, until when she grew very tired he seemed to know at once.

"Just lean against my arm," he said. "You must be very tired and it will help you bear the jolting." He spoke as if his arm were made of wood or iron, and was merely one of his belongings, like an umbrella or suit-case. He made it seem quite the natural thing for her to lean against him. If he had claimed it as her right and privilege as wife, she would have recoiled from him for recalling to her the hated relation, and would have sat straight as a bean-pole the rest of the way, but, as it was, she sank back a trifle deprecatingly, and realized that it was a great help. In her heart she thanked him for making it possible for her to rest without entirely compromising her attitude toward him. There was nothing about it that suggested anything loverlike; it seemed just a common courtesy.

Yet the strong arm almost trembled as he felt the precious weight against it, and he wished that the way were ten miles instead of five. Once, as Celia leaned forward to point to a particularly lovely bit of view that opened up as they wound around a curve in the road, they ran over a stone, and the wagon gave an unexpected jolt. Gordon reached his hand out to steady her, and she settled back to his arm with a sense of safety and being cared for that was very pleasant. Looking up shyly, she saw his eyes upon her, with that deep look of admiration and something more, and again that strange thrill of joy that had come when he gave her the forget-me-nots swept through her. She felt almost as if she were harboring a sinful thought when she remembered the letters he had written; but the joy of the day, and the sweetness of happiness for even a moment, when she had been for so long a time sad, was so pleasant that she let herself enjoy it and drift, refusing to think evil of him now, here, in this bright day. Thus like children on a picnic, they passed through Sugar Grove and came to the town of Milton, and there they bade their driver good-by, rewarding him with a crisp five-dollar bill. He drove home with a vision of smiles in forget-me-not eyes, and a marked inability to tell anything about his wonderful passengers who had filled the little village with awe and amazement, and had given no clue to anyone as to who or what they were.

10

BUT to go back to the pursuer, in his berth, baffled and frantic and raging. With hands that fumbled because of their very eagerness he sought to get into his garments, and find his shoes from the melée of blankets and other articles in the berth, all the time keeping one eye out of the window, for he must not let his prey get away from him now. He must watch and see what they were going to do. How fortunate that he had wakened in time for that. At least he would have a clue. Where was this? A station?

He stopped operations once more to gaze off at the landscape, a desolate country scene to his city hardened eyes. Not a house in sight, nor a station. The spires of the distant village seemed like a mirage to him. This couldn't be a station. What were those two doing down there anyway? Dared he risk calling the conductor and having him hold them? No, this affair must be kept absolutely quiet. Mr. Holman had said that if a breath of the matter came out it was worse than death for all concerned. He must just get off this train as fast as he could and follow them if they were getting away. It might be he could get the man in a lonely place—it would be easy enough to watch his chance and gag the lady—he had done such things before. He felt far more at home in such an affair than he had the night before at the Holman dinner table. What a pity one of the others had not come along. It would be mere child's play for two to handle those two who looked as if they would turn frightened at the first threat. However, he felt confident that he could manage the affair alone.

He panted with haste and succeeded in getting the wrong legs into his trousers and having to begin all over again, his efforts greatly hampered by the necessity for watching out the window.

Then came the distant rumble of an oncoming train, and an answering scream from his own engine. The two on the ground had crossed quickly over the second track and were looking down the steep embankment. Were they going down there? What fate that he was not ready to follow them at once! The train that was coming would pass — their own would start — and he could not get out. His opportunity was going from him and he could not find his shoes!

Well what of it? He would go without! What were shoes at a time like this? Surely he could get along barefoot, and beg a pair at some farmhouse, or buy a pair at a country store. He must get out at any cost, shoes or no shoes. Grasping his coat which contained his money and valuables he sprang from his berth straight into the arms of the porter who was hurrying back to his car after having been out to gossip with a brakeman over the delay.

"What's de mattah, sah?" asked the astonished porter, rallying quickly from the shock and assuming his habitual courtesy.

"My shoes!" roared the irate traveller. "What have you done with my shoes?"

"Quiet, sah, please sah, you'll wake de whole cyah," said the porter. "I put yoh shoes under de berth sah, righ whar I allus puts 'em aftah blackin' sah."

The porter stooped and extracted the shoes from beneath

the curtain and the traveller, whose experience in Pullmans was small, grabbed them furiously and made for the door, shoes in hand, for with a snort and a lurch and a preliminary jar the train had taken up its motion, and a loud rushing outside proclaimed that the other train was passing.

The porter, feeling that he had been treated with injustice, stood gazing reproachfully after the man for a full minute before he followed him to tell him that the wash-room was at the other end of the car and not down past the drawing-room as he evidently supposed.

He found his man standing in stocking feet on the cold iron platform, his head out of the opening left in the vestibuled train, for when the porter came in he had drawn shut the outer door and slammed down the movable platform, making it impossible for anyone to get out. There was only the little opening the size of a window above the grating guard, and the man clung to it as if he would jump over it if he only dared. He was looking back over the track and his face was not good to see.

He turned wildly upon the porter.

"I want you to stop this train and let me off," he shouted. "I've lost something valuable back there on the track. Stop the train quick, I tell you or I'll sue the railroad."

"What was it you lost?" asked the porter respectfully. He wasn't sure but the man was half asleep yet.

"It was a — my — why it was a very valuable paper. It means a fortune to me and several other people and I must go back and get it. Stop the train, I tell you, at once or I'll jump out."

"I can't stop de train sah, you'll hev to see de conductah sah, 'bout dat. But I specks there's mighty little prospec' o' gettin' dis train stopped foh it gits to its destinashun sah. We's one hour a'hind time now, sah, an' he's gotta make up foh we gets to Buff 'lo."

The excited passenger railed and stormed until several sleepers were awakened and stuck curious sleepy countenances out from the curtains of their berths, but the porter was obdurate, and would not take any measures to stop the train, nor even call the conductor until the passenger promised to return quietly to his berth.

The thick-set man was not used to obeying but he saw that he was only hindering himself and finally hurried back to his berth where he hastily parted the curtains, craning his neck to see back along the track and over the green valley growing smaller and smaller now in the distance. He could just make out two moving specks on the white winding ribbon of the road. He felt sure he knew the direction they were taking. If he only could get off that train he could easily catch them, for they would have no idea he was coming, and would take no precautions. If he had only wakened a few seconds sooner he would have been following them even now.

Fully ten minutes he argued with the conductor, showing a wide incongruity between his language and his gentlemanly attire, but the conductor would do nothing but promise to let him down at a water tower ten miles ahead where they had to slow up for water. He said sue or no sue he had his orders, and the thick-set man did not inspire him either to sympathy or confidence. The conductor had been many years on the road and generally knew when to stop his train and when to let it go on.

Sullenly the thick-set man accepted the conductor's decision and prepared to leave the train at the water tower, his eye out for the landmarks along the way as he completed his hasty toilet.

He was in no pleasant frame of mind, having missed a goodly amount of his accustomed stimulants the night before, and seeing little prospect of either stimulants or breakfast before him. He was not built for a ten-mile walk over the cinders and his flabby muscles already ached at the prospect. But then, of course he would not have to go far before he found an automobile or some kind of conveyance to help him on his way. He looked eagerly from the window for indications of garages or stables, but the river wound its silver way among the gray green willow fringes, and the new grass shone a placid emerald plan with nothing more human than a few cows grazing here and there. Not even a horse that might be borrowed without his owner's knowledge. It was a strange, forsaken spot, ten whole miles and no sign of any public livery! Off to the right and left he could see villages, but they were most of them too far away from the track to help him any. It began to look as if he must just foot it all the way. Now and then a small shanty or tiny dwelling whizzed by near at hand, but nothing that would relieve his situation.

It occurred to him to go into the dining car for breakfast, but even as he thought of it the conductor told him that the train would stop in two minutes and he must be ready to get off, for they did not stop long.

He certainly looked a harmless creature, that thick-set man as he stood alone upon the cinder elevation and surveyed the landscape o'er. Ten miles from his quarry, alone on a stretch of endless ties and rails with a gleaming river mocking him down in the valley, and a laughing sky jeering overhead. He started down the shining track his temper a wreck, his mind in chaos, his soul at war with the world. The worst of it all was that the whole fault was his own for going to sleep. He began to fear that he had lost his chance. Then he set his ugly jaw and strode ahead.

The morning sun poured down upon the thick-set man on his pilgrimage, and waxed hotter until noon. Trains whizzed mercilessly by and gave him no succor. Weary, faint, and fiercely thirsty he came at last to the spot where he was satisfied his quarry had escaped. He could see the marks of their rough descent in the steep cinder bank, and assaying the same himself came upon a shred of purple silk caught on a bramble at the foot.

Puffing and panting, bruised and foot-sore, he sat down at the very place where Celia had stopped to have her shoes fastened, and mopped his purple brow, but there was triumph in his ugly eye, and after a few moment's rest he trudged onward. That town over there ought to yield both conveyance and food as well as information concerning those he sought. He would catch them. They could never get away from him. He was on their track again, though hours behind. He would get them yet and no man should take his reward from him.

Almost spent he came at last to the village, and ate a surprisingly large dish of beef and vegetable stew at the quaint little house where Celia and Gordon had breakfasted, but the old lady who served it to them was shy about talking, and though admitting that a couple of people had been there that morning she was noncommittal about their appearance. They might have been young and good-looking and worn feathers in their hats, and they might not. She wasn't one for noticing people's appearance if they treated her civilly and paid their bills. Would he have another cup of coffee? He would, and also two more pieces of pie, but he got very little further information.

It was over at the corner store where he finally went in search of something stronger than coffee that he further pursued his investigations.

The loungers were still there. It was their only business in life and they were most diligent in it. They eyed the newcomer with relish and settled back on their various barrels and boxes to enjoy whatever entertainment the gods were about to provide to relieve their monotonous existence.

A house divided against itself cannot stand. This man's elegant garments assumed for the nonce did not fit the rest of his general appearance which had been accentuated by his long, hot, dusty tramp. The high evening hat was jammed on the back of his head and bore a decided dent where it had rolled down the cinder embankment, his collar was wilted and lifeless, his white laundered tie at half mast, his coat awry, and his fine patent leather shoes which pinched were covered with dust and had caused a limp like the hardest tramp upon the road. Moreover, again the speech of the man betrayed him, and the keen-minded old gossips who were watching him suspiciously sized him up at once the minute he opened his mouth.

"Saw anything of a couple of young folks walking down this way?" he enquired casually, pausing to light a cigar with which he was reinforcing himself for further travel.

One man allowed that there might have passed such people that day. He hardly seemed willing to commit himself, but another vouchsafed the information that "Joe here driv two parties of thet description to Milton this mornin'—jes' got back. Mebbe he could answer fer 'em."

Joe frowned. He did not like the looks of the thick-set man. He still remembered the forget-me-not eyes.

But the stranger made instant request to be driven to Milton, offering ten dollars for the same when he found that his driver was reluctant, and that Milton was a railroad centre. A few keen questions had made him sure that his man had gone to Milton.

Joe haggled, allowed his horse was tired, and he didn't care about the trip twice in one day, but finally agreed to take the man for fifteen dollars, and sauntered off to get a fresh horse. He had no mind to be in a hurry. He had his own opinion about letting those two "parties" get out of the way before the third put in an appearance, but he had no mind to lose fifteen dollars. It would help to buy the ring he coveted for his girl.

In due time Joe rode leisurely up and the impatient traveller climbed into the high spring wagon and was driven away from the apathetic gaze of the country loungers who unblinkingly took in the fact that Joe was headed toward Ashville, and evidently intended taking his fare to Milton by way of that village, a thirty-mile drive at least. The man would get the worth of his money in ride. A grim twinkle sat in their several eyes as the spring wagon turned the curve in the road and was lost to sight, and after due silence an old stager spoke:

"Do you reckon that there was their sho–fur?" he requested languidly.

"Naw!" replied a farmer's son vigorously. "He wouldn't try to showf all dolled up like that. He's the rich dad comin' after the runaways. Joe didn't intend he shell get 'em yet awhile. I reckon the ceremony'll be over 'fore he steps in to interfere." This lad went twice a month to Milton to the "movies" and was regarded as an authority on matters of romance. A pause showed that his theory had taken root in the minds of his auditors.

"Wal, I reckon Joe thinks the longest way round is the shortest way home," declared the old stager. "Joe never did like them cod–fish swells—but how do you 'count fer the style o' that gal? She wasn't like her dad one little bit."

"Oh, she's ben to collidge I 'spose," declared the youth. "They get all that off'n collidge."

"Serves the old man right fer sendin' his gal to a fool collidge when she ought to ben home learnin' to house-keep. I hope she gits off with her young man all right," said a grim old lounger, and a cackle of laughter went round the group, which presently broke up, for this had been a strenuous day and all felt their need of rest; besides they wanted to get home and tell the news before some neighbor got ahead of them.

All this time Celia and Gordon were touring Milton, serenely unconscious of danger near, or guardian angel of the name of Joe.

Investigation disclosed the fact that there was a train for Pittsburgh about three in the afternoon. Gordon sent a code telegram to his chief, assuring him of the safety of the message, and of his own intention to proceed to Washington as fast as steam could carry him. Then he took the girl to a restaurant, where they mounted two high stools, and partook with an unusually ravenous appetite of nearly everything on

the menu — corn soup, roast beef, baked trout, stewed toma-
toes, cole slaw, custard, apple, and mince pies, with a cup of
good country coffee and real cream — all for twenty-five
cents apiece.

It was a very merry meal. Celia felt somehow as if for the
time all memory of the past had been taken from her, and
she were free to think and act happily in the present, without any great problems to solve or decisions to make. Just
two young people off having a good time, they were, at least
until that afternoon train came.

After their dinner, they took a short walk to a tiny park
where two white ducks disported themselves on a seven-by-
nine pond, spanned by a rustic bridge where lovers had cut
their initials. Gordon took out his knife and idly cut C. H.
in the rough bark of the upper rail, while his companion sat
on the little board seat and watched him. She was pondering over the fact that he had cut her initials, and not his own.
It would have been like the George of old to cut his own and
never once think of hers. And he had put but one H. Probably he thought of her now as Celia Hayne, without the
Hathaway, or else he was so used to writing her name Celia
Hathaway, that he was not thinking at all.

Those letters! How they haunted her and clouded every
bright experience that she fain would have grasped and held
for a little hour.

They were silent now, while he worked and she thought.
He had finished the C. H., and was cutting another C, but
instead of making another H, he carefully carved out the letter G. What was that for? C. G.? Who was C. G.? Oh, how
stupid! George, of course. He had started a C by mistake.
But he did not add the expected H. Instead he snapped his
knife shut, laid his hand over the carving, and leaned over
the rail.

"Some time, perhaps, we'll come here again, and remember," he said, and then bethought him that he had no right
to hope for any such anniversary.

"Oh!" She looked up into his eyes, startled, troubled, the haunting of her fears in the shadows of the blue.

He looked down into them and read her trouble, read and understood, and looked back his great desire to comfort her.

His look carried further than he meant it should. For the third time that day a thrill of wonder and delight passed over her and left her fearful with a strange joy that she felt she should put from her.

It was only an instant, that look, but it brought the bright color to both faces, and made Gordon feel the immediate necessity of changing the subject.

"See those little fishes down there," he said pointing to the tiny lake below them.

Through a blur of tears, the girl looked down and saw the tiny, sharp-finned creatures darting here and there in a beam of sun like a small search-light set to show them off.

She moved her hand on the rail to lean further over, and her soft fingers touched his hand for a moment. She would not draw them away quickly, lest she hurt him; why, she did not know, but she could not — would not — hurt him. Not now! The two hands lay side by side for a full minute, and the touch to Gordon was as if a roseleaf had kissed his soul. He had never felt anything sweeter. He longed to gather the little hand into his clasp and feel its pulses trembling there as he had felt it in the church the night before, but she was not his. He might not touch her till she had her choice of what to do, and she would never choose him, never, when she knew how he had deceived her.

That one supreme moment they had of perfect consciousness, consciousness of the drawing of the soul to soul, of the sweetness of that hovering touch of hands, of the longing to know and understand each other.

Then a sharp whistle sounded, and a farmer's boy with a new rake and a sack of corn on his shoulder came sauntering briskly down the road to the bridge. Instantly they drew apart, and Celia felt that she had been on the verge of disloyalty to her true self.

They walked silently back to the station, each busy with his own thoughts, each conscious of that one moment when the other had come so near.

THERE were a lot of people at the station. They had been to a family gathering of some sort from their remarks, and they talked loudly and much, so that the two stood apart — for the seats were all occupied — and had no opportunity for conversation, save a quiet smiling comment now and then upon the chatter about them, or the odd remarks they heard.

There had come a constraint upon them, a withdrawing of each into his shell, each conscious of something that separated. Gordon struggled to prevent it, but he seemed helpless. Celia would smile in answer to his quiet remarks, but it was a smile of distance, such as she had worn early in the morning. She had quite found her former standing ground, with its fence of prejudice, and she was repairing the breaks through which she had gone over to the enemy during the day. She was bracing herself with dire reminders, and snatches from those terrible letters which were written in characters of fire in her heart. Never, never, could she care for a man who had done what this man had done. She had forgotten for a little while those terrible things he had said of her dear dead father. How could she have forgotten for an instant! How could she have let her hand lie close to the hand that had defiled itself by writing such things!

By the time they were seated in the train, she was freezing in her attitude, and poor Gordon sat miserably beside her and tried to think what he had done to offend her. It was not his fault that her hand had lain near his on the rail. She had put it there herself. Perhaps she expected him to put his over it, to show her that he cared as a bridegroom should care — as he did care, in reality, if he only had the right. And perhaps she was hurt that he had stood coolly and said or done nothing. But he could not help it.

Much to Gordon's relief, the train carried a parlor car, and it happened on this particular day to be almost deserted save for a deaf old man with a florid complexion and a gold-knobbed cane who slumbered audibly at the further end from the two chairs Gordon selected. He established his companion comfortably, disposed of the baggage, and sat down, but the girl paid no heed to him. With a sad, set face, she stared out of the window, her eyes seeming to see nothing. For two hours she sat so, he making remarks occasionally, to which she made little or no reply, until he lapsed into silence, looking at her with troubled eyes. Finally, just as they neared the outskirts of Pittsburgh, he leaned softly forward and touched her coat-sleeve, to attract her attention.

"Have I offended — hurt — you in any way?" he asked gently. She turned toward him, and her eyes were brimming full of tears.

"No," she said, and her lips were trembling. "No, you have been — most — kind — but — but I cannot forget *those letters!*" She ended with a sob and put up her handkerchief quickly to stifle it.

"Letters?" he asked helplessly. "What letters?"

"The letters you wrote me. All the letters of the last five months. I cannot forget them. I can *never* forget them! How could you *think* I could?"

He looked at her anxiously, not knowing what to say, and yet he must say something. The time had come when some kind of an understanding, some clearing up of facts, must take place. He must go cautiously, but he must find out what was the matter. He could not see her suffer so. There must be some way to let her know that so far as he was concerned she need suffer nothing further and that he would do all in his power to set her right with her world.

But letters! He had written no letters. His face lighted up with the swift certainty of one thing about which he had not dared to be sure. She still thought him the man she had intended to marry. She was not therefore troubled about that phase of the question. It was strange, almost unbelievable, but it was true that he personally was not responsible for the trouble in her eyes. What trouble she might feel when she knew all, he had yet to find out, but it was a great relief to be sure of so much. Still, something must be said.

"Letters!" he repeated again stupidly, and then added with perplexed tone: "Would you mind telling me just what it was in the letters that hurt you?"

She turned eyes of astonishment on him.

"How can you ask?" she said almost bitterly. "You surely must know how terrible they were to me! You could not be the man you have seemed to be to-day if you did not know what you were doing to me in making all those terrible threats. You must know how cruel they were."

"I am afraid I don't understand," he said earnestly, the trouble still most apparent in his eyes, "Would you mind being a little more explicit? Would you mind telling me exactly what you think I wrote you that sounded like a threat?"

He asked the question half hesitatingly, because he was not quite sure whether he was justified in thus obtaining private information under false pretenses, and yet he felt that he must know just what troubled her or he could never help her, and he was sure that if she knew he was an utter stranger, even a kindly one, those gentle lips would never open to inform him upon her torturer. As it was she could tell him her trouble with a perfectly clear conscience, thinking she was telling it to the man who knew all about it. But his hesitation about prying into an utter stranger's private affairs, even with a good motive, gave him an air of troubled dignity, and real anxiety to know his fault that puzzled the girl more than all that had gone before.

"I cannot understand how you can ask such a question, since it has been the constant subject of discussion in all our letters!" she replied, sitting up with asperity and drying her tears. She was on the verge of growing angry with him for his petty, wilful misunderstanding of words whose meaning she felt he must know well.

"I do ask it," he said quietly, "and, believe me, I have a good motive in doing so."

She looked at him in surprise. It was impossible to be angry with those kindly eyes, even though he did persist in a wilful stupidity.

"Well, then, since you wish it stated once more I will tell you," she declared, the tears welling again into her eyes. "You first demanded that I marry you—demanded—without any pretense whatever of caring for me—with a hidden threat in your demand that if I did not, you would bring some dire calamity upon me by means that were already in your power. You took me for the same foolish little girl whom you had delighted to tease for years before you went abroad to live. And when I refused you, you told me that you could not only take away from my mother all the property which she had inherited from her brother, by means of a will made just before my uncle's death, and unknown except to his lawyer and you; but that you could and would blacken my dear dead father's name and honor, and show that every cent that belonged to Mother and Jefferson and myself was stolen property. When I challenged you to prove any such thing against my honored father, you went still further and threatened to bring out a terrible story and prove it with witnesses who would swear to anything you said. You knew my father's white life, you as much as owned your charges were false, and yet you dared to send me a letter from a vile creature who pretended that she was his first wife, and who said she could prove that he had spent much of his time in her company. You knew the whole thing was a falsehood, but you dared to threaten to make this known throughout the newspapers if I did not marry you. You realized that I knew that, even though few people and no friends would believe such a thing of my father, such a report in the papers — false though it was — would crush my mother to death. You knew that I would give my life to save her, and so you had me in your power, as you have me now. You have always wanted me in your power, just because you love to torture, and now you have me. But you cannot make me forget what you have done. I have given my life but I cannot give any more. If it is not sufficient you will have to do your worst."

She dropped her face into the little wet handkerchief, and Gordon sat with white, drawn countenance and clenched hands. He was fairly trembling with indignation toward the villain who had thus dared impose upon this delicate flower of womanhood. He longed to search the world over for the false bridegroom; and, finding, give him his just dues.

And what should he do or say? Dared he tell her at once who he was and trust to her kind heart to forgive his terrible blunder and keep his secret till the message was safely delivered? Dared he? Had he any right? No, the secret was not his to divulge either for his own benefit or for any other's. He must keep that to himself. But he must help her in some way.

At last he began to speak, scarcely knowing what he was about to say:

"It is terrible, *terrible,* what you have told me. To have written such things to one like you — in fact, to any one on earth — seems to me unforgivable. It is the most inhuman cruelty I have ever heard of. You are fully justified in hating and despising the man who wrote such words to you."

"Then, why did you write them?" she burst forth. "And how can you sit there calmly and talk that way about it, as if you had nothing to do with the matter?"

"Because I never wrote those letters," he said, looking her steadily, earnestly, in the eyes.

"You never wrote them!" she exclaimed excitedly. "You dare to deny it?"

"I dare to deny it." His voice was quiet, earnest, convincing.

She looked at him, dazed, bewildered, indignant, sorrowful. "But you cannot deny it," she said, her fragile frame trembling with excitement. "I have the letters all in my suit-case. You cannot deny your own handwriting. I have the last awful one — the one in which you threatened Father's good name — here in my hand-bag. I dared not put it with the rest, and I had no opportunity to destroy it before leaving home. I felt as if I must always keep it with me, lest otherwise its awful secret would somehow get out. There it is. Read it and see your own name signed to the words you say you did not write!"

While she talked, her trembling fingers had taken a folded, crumpled letter from her little handbag, and this she reached over and laid upon the arm of his chair.

"Read it," she said. "Read it and see that you cannot deny it."

"I should rather not read it," he said. "I do not need to read it to deny that I ever wrote such things to you."

"But I insist that you read it," said the girl.

"If you insist I will read it," he said, taking the letter reluctantly and opening it.

She sat watching him furtively through the tears while he read, saw the angry flush steal into his cheeks as the villainy of a fellow man was revealed to him through the brief, coarse, cruel epistle, and she mistook the flush for one of shame.

Then his true brown eyes looked up and met her tearful gaze steadily, a fine anger burning in them.

"And you think I wrote that?" he said, a something in his voice she could not understand.

"What else could I think? It bears your signature," she answered coldly.

"The letter is vile," he said, "and the man who wrote is a blackguard, and deserves the utmost that the law allows for such offenses. With your permission, I shall make it my business to see that he gets it."

"What do you mean?" she said, wide-eyed. "How could you punish yourself? You cannot still deny that you wrote the letter."

"I still deny that I wrote it, or ever saw it until you handed it to me just now."

The girl looked at him, nonplussed, more than half convinced, in spite of reason.

"But isn't that your handwriting?"

"It is not. Look!"

He took out his fountain pen, and holding the letter on the arm of her chair, he wrote rapidly in his natural hand her own name and address beneath the address on the envelope, then held it up to her.

"Do they look alike?"

The two writings were as utterly unlike as possible, the letter being addressed in an almost unreadable scrawl, and the fresh writing standing fine and clear, in a script that spoke of character and business ability. Even a child could see at a glance that the two were not written by the same hand — and yet of course, it might have been practised for the purpose of deception. This thought flashed through the minds of both even as he held it out for her to look.

She looked from the envelope to his eyes and back to the letter, startled, not knowing what to think.

But before either of them had time for another word the conductor, the porter, and several people from the car behind came hurriedly through, and they realized that while they talked the train had come to a halt, amid the blazing electric lights of a great city station.

"Why," said Gordon startled, "we must have reached Pittsburgh. Is this Pittsburgh?" he called out to the vanishing porter.

"Yas sah!" yelled the porter, putting his head around the curve of the passageway. "You bettah hurry sah, foh dis train goes on to Cincinnati pretty quick. We's late gittin' in you see."

Neither of them had noticed a man in rough clothes with slouch hat and hands in his pockets who had boarded the train a few miles back and walked through the car several times eyeing them keenly. He stuck his head in at the door now furtively and drew back quickly again out of sight.

Gordon hurriedly gathered up the baggage, and they went out of the car, the porter rushing back as they reached the door, to assist them and get a last tip. There was no opportunity to say anything more, as they mingled with the crowd, until the porter landed their baggage in the great station and hurried back to his train. The man with the slouch hat followed and stood unobtrusively behind them.

Gordon looked down at the white, drawn face of the girl, and his heart was touched with compassion for her trouble. He must make her some satisfactory explanation at once that would set her heart at rest, but he could not do it here, for every seat about them was filled with noisy chattering folk. He stooped and whispered low and tenderly:

"Don't worry, little girl! Just try to trust me, and I will explain it all."

"Can you explain it?" she asked anxiously, as if catching at a rope thrown out to save her life.

"Perfectly," he said, "if you will be patient and trust me. But we cannot talk here. Just wait in this seat until I see if I can get the stateroom on the sleeper."

He left her with his courteous bow, and she sat watching

his tall, fine figure as he threaded his way among the crowds to the Pullman window, her heart filled with mingling emotions. In spite of her reason, a tiny bit of hope for the future was springing up in her heart and without her own will she found herself inclined to trust him. At least it was all she could do at present.

12

BACK at Milton an hour before, when the shades of dusk were falling and a slender moon hung timidly on the edge of the horizon, a horse drawing a spring wagon ambled deliberately into town and came to a reluctant halt beside the railroad station, having made a wide detour through the larger part of the country on the way to that metropolis.

The sun had been hot, the road much of it rough, and the jolts over stones and bumps had not added to the comfort of the thick-set man, already bruised and weary from his travels. Joe's conversation had not ceased. He had given his guest a wide range of topics, discoursing learnedly on the buckwheat crop and the blight that might be expected to assail the cherry trees. He pointed out certain portions of land infested with rattlesnakes, and told blood-curdling stories of experiences with stray bears and wild cats in a maple grove through which they passed till the passenger looked furtively behind him and urged the driver to hurry a little faster.

Joe, seeing his gullibility, only made his stories of country life the bigger, for the thick-set man, though bold as a lion in his own city haunts, was a coward in the unknown world of the country.

When the traveller looking at his watch urged Joe to make haste and asked how many miles further Milton was, Joe managed it that the horse should stumble on a particularly stony bit of road. Then getting down gravely from the wagon he examined the horse's feet each in turn, shaking his head sadly over the left fore foot.

"Jes' 'z I 'sposed," he meditated dreamily. "Stone bruise! Lame horse! Don't believe I ought to go on. Sorry, but it'll be ruination of the horse. You ain't in a hurry I hope."

The passenger in great excitement promised to double the fare if the young man would get another horse and hurry him forward, and after great professions of doubt Joe gave in and said he would try the horse, but it wouldn't do to work him hard. They would have to let him take his time. He couldn't on any account leave the horse behind anywhere and get a fresh one because it belonged to his best friend and he promised to bring it back safe and sound. They would just take their time and go slow and see if the horse could stand it. He wouldn't think of trying it if it weren't for the extra money which he needed.

So the impatient traveller was dragged fuming along weary hour after weary hour through the monotonous glory of a spring afternoon of which he saw nothing but the dust of the road as he tried to count the endless miles. Every mile or two Joe would descend from the wagon seat and fuss around with the horse's leg, the horse nothing loth at such unprecedented attention dozing cozily by the roadside during the process. And so was the traveller brought to his destination ten minutes after the last train that stopped at Milton that night had passed the station.

The telegraph office was not closed however, and without waiting to haggle, the passenger paid his thirty dollars for the longest journey he ever took, and disappeared into the station, while Joe, whipping up his petted animal, and whistling cherrily:

"Where did you get that girl—"

went rattling down the short cut from Milton home at a surprising pace for a lame horse. He was eating his supper at home in a little more than an hour, and the horse seemed to have miraculously recovered from his stone bruise. Joe was wondering how his girl would look in a hat with purple plumes, and thinking of his thirty dollars with a chuckle.

It was surprising how much that thick-set man, weary and desperate though he was, could accomplish, when once he reached the telegraph station and sent his messages flying on their way. In less than three minutes after his arrival he had extracted from the station agent the fact that two people, man and woman, answering the description he gave, had bought tickets for Pittsburgh and taken the afternoon train for that city. The agent had noticed them on account of their looking as if they came from the city. He especially noticed the purple plumes, the like of which he had never seen before. He had taken every minute he could get off from selling tickets and sending telegrams to watch the lady through his little cobwebby window. They didn't wear hats like that in Milton.

In ten minutes one message was on its way to a crony in Pittsburgh with whom the thick-set man kept in constant touch for just such occasions as the present, stirring him to strenuous action; another message had winged its mysterious way to Mr. Holman, giving him the main facts in the case; while a third message caught another crony thirty miles north of Pittsburgh and ordered him to board the evening express at his own station, hunt up the parties described, and shadow them to their destination, if possible getting in touch with the Pittsburgh crony when he reached the city.

The pursuer then ate a ham sandwich with liberal washings of liquid fire while he awaited replies to some of his messages; and as soon as he was satisfied that he had set justice in motion he hired an automobile and hied him across country to catch a midnight express to Pittsburgh. He had given orders that his man and accompanying lady should be held in Pittsburgh until his arrival, and he had no doubt but that the orders would be carried out, so sure was he that he was on the right track, and that his cronies would be able and willing to follow his orders.

There was some kind of an excursion on at Pittsburgh, and the place was crowded. The train-men kept calling off specials, and crowds hurried out of the waiting room, only to be replaced by other crowds, all eager, pushing, talking, laughing. They were mostly men, but a good many women and some children seemed to be of the number; and the noise and excitement worried her after her own exciting afternoon. Celia longed to lay her down and sleep, but the seat was narrow, and hard, and people were pressing on every side. That disagreeable man in the slouch hat would stand too near. He was most repulsive looking, though he did not seem to be aware of her presence.

Gordon had a long wait before he finally secured the coveted state-room and started back to her, when suddenly a face that he knew loomed up in the crowd and startled him. It was the face of a private detective who was well known about Washington, but whose headquarters were in New York.

Until that instant, it had not occurred to him to fear watchers so far south and west as Pittsburgh. It was not possible that the other bridegroom would think to track him here, and, as for the Holman contingent, they would not be likely to make a public disturbance about his disappearance, lest they be found to have some connection with the first theft of government property. They could have watchers only through private means, and they must have been wily indeed if they had anticipated his move through Pittsburgh to Washington. Still, it was the natural move for him to make in order to get home as quickly as possible and yet escape them. And this man in the crowd was the very one whom they would have been likely to pick out for their work. He was as slippery in his dealings as they must be, and no doubt was in league with them. He knew the man and his ways thoroughly, and had no mind to fall into his hands.

Whether he had been seen by the detective yet or not, he could not tell, but he suspected he had, by the way the man stood around and avoided recognizing him. There was not an instant to be lost. The fine state-room must go untenanted. He must make a dash for liberty. Liberty! Ah, East Liberty! What queer things these brains of ours are! He knew Pittsburgh just a little. He remembered having caught a train at East Liberty Station once when he had not time to come down to the station to take it. Perhaps he might get the same train at East Liberty. It was nearly two hours before it left.

Swooping down upon the baggage, he murmured in the girl's ear:

"Can you hurry a little? We must catch a car right away."

She followed him closely through the crowd, he stooping as if to look down at his suit-case, so that his height might not attract the attention of the man whose recognition he feared, and in a moment more they were out in the lighted blackness of the streets. One glance backward showed his supposed enemy stretching his neck above the crowd, as if searching for some one, as he walked hurriedly toward the very doorway they had just passed. Behind them shadowed the man in the slouch hat, and with a curious motion of his hand signalled another like himself, the Pittsburgh crony, who skulked in the darkness outside. Instantly this man gave another signal and out of the gloom of the street a carriage drew up at the curb before the door, the cabman looking eagerly for patronage.

Gordon put both suit-cases in one hand and taking Celia's arm as gently as he could in his haste hurried her toward the carriage. It was the very refuge he sought. He placed her inside and gave the order for East Liberty Station, drawing a long breath of relief at being safely out of the station. He did not see the shabby one who mounted the box beside the driver and gave his directions in guttural whispers, nor the man with the slouch hat who watched from the doorway and followed them to a familiar haunt on the nearest car. He only felt how good it was to be by themselves once more where they could talk together without interruption.

But conversation was not easy under the circumstances. The noise of wagons, trains and cars was so great at the station that they could think of nothing but the din, and when they had threaded their way out of the tangle and started rattling over the pavement the driver went at such a furious pace that they could still only converse by shouting and that not at all satisfactorily. It seemed a strange thing that any cabman should drive at such a rapid rate within the city limits, but as Gordon was anxious to get away from the station and the keen-eyed detective as fast as possible he thought nothing of it at first. After a shouted word or two they ceased to try to talk, and Gordon, half shyly, reached out a reassuring hand and laid it on the girl's shrinking one that lay in her lap. He had not meant to keep it there but a second, just to make her understand that all was well, and he would soon be able to explain things, but as she did not seem to resent it nor draw her own away, he yielded to the temptation and kept the small gloved hand in his.

The carriage rattled on, bumpety-bump, over rough places, around corners, tilting now and then sideways, and Celia, half frightened, was forced to cling to her protector to keep from being thrown on the floor of the cab.

"Oh, are we running away?" she breathed awesomely into his ear.

"I think not, — dear," he answered back, the last word inaudible. "The driver thinks we are in a hurry but he has no need to go at this furious pace. I will tell him."

He leaned forward and tapped on the glass, but the driver paid no attention whatever save perhaps to drive faster.

Could it be that he had lost control of his horse and could not stop, or hadn't he heard? Gordon tried again, and accompanied the knocking this time with a shout, but all to no purpose. The cab rattled steadily on. Gordon discovered now that there were two men on the box instead of one and a sudden premonition sent a thrill of alarm through him. What if after all the presence of that detective had been a warning, and he unheeding had walked into a trap? What a fool he had been to get into a carriage where he was at the mercy of the driver. He ought to have stayed in open places where kidnapping would be impossible. Now that he had thought of it he felt convinced that this was just what the enemy would try to do, — kidnap him. The more fruitless he found his efforts to make the driver hear him the more he felt convinced that something was wrong. He tried to open the door next him and found it stuck. He put all his strength forth to turn the catch but it held fast. Then a cold sweat stood out upon him and horror filled his mind. His commission with its large significance to the country was in imminent jeopardy. His own life was in all probability hanging in the balance, but most of all he felt the awful peril of the sweet girl by his side. What terrible experiences might be hers within the next hour if his brain and right arm could not protect her. Instinctively his hand went to the pocket where he had kept his revolver ready since ever he had left Washington. Danger should not find him utterly unprepared.

He realized, too, that it was entirely possible, that his alarms were unfounded; that the driver was really taking them to the East Liberty Station; that the door merely stuck, and he was needlessly anxious. He must keep a steady head and not let his companion see that he was nervous. The first thing was to find out if possible where they really were, but that was a difficult task. The street over which they rattled was utterly dark with the gloom of a smoky city added to the night. There were no street lights except at wide intervals, and the buildings appeared to be blank walls of darkness, probably great warehouses. The way was narrow, and entirely unknown. Gordon could not tell if he had ever been there before. He was sure from his knowledge of the stations that they had gone much farther than to East Liberty, and the darkness and loneliness of the region through which they were passing filled him again with a vague alarm. It occurred to him that he might be able to get the window sash down and speak to the driver, and he struggled with the one on his own side for awhile, with little result, for it seemed to have been plugged up with wads of paper all around. This fact renewed his anxiety. It began to look as if there was intention in sealing up that carriage. He leaned over and felt around the sash of the opposite door and found the paper wads there also. There certainly was intention. Not to alarm Celia he straightened back and went to work again at his own window sash cautiously pulling out the paper until at last he could let down the glass.

A rush of dank air rewarded his efforts, and the girl drew a breath of relief. Gordon never knew how near she had been to fainting at that moment. She was sitting perfectly quiet in her corner watching him, her fears kept to herself, though her heart was beating wildly. She was convinced that the horse was running away.

Gordon leaned his head out of the window, but immediately he caught the gleam of a revolver in a hand that hung at the side of the driver's box, pointed downward straight toward his face as if with intention to be ready in case of need. The owner of the hand was not looking toward him, but was talking in muffled tones to the driver. They evidently had not heard the window let down, but were ready for the first sign of an attempt on the part of their victims to escape.

Quietly Gordon drew in his head speculating rapidly on the possibility of wrenching that revolver out of its owner's hand. He could do it from where he sat, but would it be wise? They were probably locked in a trap, and the driver was very likely armed also. What chance would he have to save Celia if he brought on a desperate fight at this point? If he were alone he might knock that revolver out of the man's hand and spring from the window, taking his chance of getting away, but now he had Celia to think of and the case was different. Not for a universe of governments could he leave a woman in such desperate straits. She must be considered first even ahead of the message. This was life and death.

He wondered at his own coolness as he sat back in the carriage and quietly lifted the glass frame back into place. Then he laid a steady hand on Celia's again and stooping close whispered into her ear:

"I am afraid there's something wrong with our driver. Can you be a little brave, — dear?" He did not know he had used the last word this time, but it thrilled into the girl's heart with a sudden accession of trust.

"Oh, yes," she breathed close to his face. "You don't think he has been drinking, do you?"

"Well, perhaps," said Gordon relieved at the explanation. "But keep calm. I think we can get out of this all right. Suppose you change seats with me and let me try if that door will open easily. We might want to get out in a hurry in case he slows up somewhere pretty soon."

Celia quietly and swiftly slipped into Gordon's seat and he applied himself with all his strength and ingenuity gently manipulating the latch and pressing his shoulder against the door, until at last to his joy it gave way reluctantly and he found that it would swing open. He had worked carefully, else the sudden giving of the latch would have thrown him out of the carriage and given instant alarm to his driver. He was so thoroughly convinced by this time that he was being kidnapped, perhaps to be murdered, that every sense was on alert. It was his characteristic to be exceedingly cool during a crisis. It was the quality that the keen-eyed chief had valued most in him, and the final reason why he had been selected for this difficult task in place of an older and more experienced man who at times lost his head.

The door to the outside world being open, Gordon cautiously took a survey of the enemy from that side. There was no gleaming weapon here. The man set grimly enough, laying on the whip and muttering curses to his bony horse who galloped recklessly on as if partaking of the desperate desires of his master. In the distance Gordon would hear the rumbling of an on-coming train. The street was still dark and scarcely a vehicle or person to be seen. There seemed no help at hand, and no opportunity to get out, for they were still rushing at a tremendous pace. An attempt to jump now would very likely result in broken limbs, which would only leave them in a worse plight than they were. He slipped back to his own seat and put Celia next to the free door again. She must be where she could get out first if the opportunity presented itself. Also, he must manage to throw out the suitcases if possible on account of the letters and valuables they contained.

Instinctively his hand sought Celia's in the darkness again, and hers nestled into it in a frightened way as if his strength gave her comfort.

Then, before they could speak or realize, there came the rushing sound of a train almost upon them and the cab came to a halt with a jerk, the driver pulling the horse far back on his haunches to stop him. The shock almost threw Celia to the floor, but Gordon's arm about her steadied her, and instantly he was on the alert.

13

GLANCING through the window he saw that they were
in front of a railroad track upon which a long freight train
was rushing madly along at a giddy pace for a mere freight.
The driver had evidently hoped to pass this point before the
train got there, but had failed. The train had an exultant sound
as if it knew and had outwitted the driver.

On one side of the street were high buildings and on the
other a great lumber yard, between which and their carriage
there stood a team of horses hitched to a covered wagon,
from the back of which some boards protruded, and this was
on the side next to Celia where the door would open! Gordon's heart leaped up with hope and wonder over the miracle of their opportunity. The best thing about their situation
was that their driver had stopped just a little back of the covered wagon, so that their door would open to the street
directly behind the covered wagon. It made it possible for
the carriage door to swing wide and for them to slip across
behind the wagon without getting too near to the driver.
Nothing could have been better arranged for their escape and
the clatter of the empty freight cars drowned all sounds.

Without delay Gordon softly unlatched the door and
swung it open whispering to Celia:

"Go! Quick! Over there by the fence in the shadow. Don't look around nor speak! Quick! I'll come!"

Trembling in every limb yet with brave starry eyes Celia slipped like a wraith from the carriage, stole behind the boards and melted into the shadow of the great fence of the lumber yard, and her purple plumes were depths of shadow against the smoky planks. Gordon, grasping the suit-cases moved instantly after her, deftly and silently closing the carriage door and dropping into the shadows behind the big wagon, scarcely able to believe as yet that they had really escaped.

Ten feet back along the sidewalk was a gateway, the posts being tall and thick. The gate itself was closed but it hung a few inches inside the line of the fence, and into this depression the two stepped softly and stood, flattening themselves back against the gate as closely as possible, scarcely daring to breathe, while the long freight clattered and rambled its way by like a lot of jolly washerwomen running and laughing in a line and spatting their tired noisy feet as they went; then the vehicles impatiently took up their onward course. Gordon saw the driver look down at the window below him and glance back hastily over his shoulder, and the man on the other side of the box, looked down on his side. The glitter of something in his hand shone for an instant in the glare of the signal light over the track. Then the horse lurched forward and the cab began its crazy gait over the track and up the cobbled street. They had started onward without getting down to look in the carriage and see if all were safe with their prisoners, and they had not even looked back to see if they had escaped. They evidently trusted in the means they had used to lock the carriage doors, and had heard no sounds of their escaping. It was incredible, but it was true. Gordon drew a long breath of relief and relaxed from his strained position. The next thing was to get out of that neighborhood as swiftly as possible before those men had time to discover that their birds had flown. They would of course know at once where their departure had taken place and come back swiftly to search for them, with perhaps more men to help; and a second time escape would be impossible.

Gordon snatched up the suit-cases with one hand, and with the other drew Celia's arm within his.

"Now, we must hurry with all our might," he said softly. "Are you all right?"

"Yes." Her breath was coming in a sob, but her eyes were shining bravely.

"Poor child!" his voice was very tender. "Were you much frightened?"

"A little," she answered more bravely now.

"I shall have hard work to forgive myself for all this," he said tenderly. "But we mustn't talk. We have to get out of this quickly or they may come back after us. Lean on me and walk as fast as you can."

Celia bent her efforts to take long springing strides, and together they fairly skimmed the pavements, turning first this corner, then that, in the general direction from which Gordon thought they had come, until at last, three blocks away they caught the welcome whirr of a trolley, and breathless, flew onward, just catching a car. They cared not where it went so that they were safe in a bright light with other people. No diamonds on any gentleman's neckscarf ever shone to Celia's eyes with so friendly a welcome as the dull brass buttons on that trolley conductor's coat as he rang up their fares and answered Gordon's questions about how to get to East Liberty Station; and their pleasant homely gleam almost were her undoing, for now that they were safe at last the tears would come to her eyes.

Gordon watched her lovingly, tenderly, glad that she did not know how terrible had been her danger. His heart was still beating wildly with the thought of their marvellous escape, and his own present responsibility. He must run no further risks. They would keep to crowded trolleys, and trust to hiding in the open. The main thing was to get out of the city on the first train they could manage to board.

When they reached East Liberty Station a long train was just coming in, all sleepers, and they could hear the echo of a stentorian voice:

"Special for Harrisburg, Baltimore and Washington! All aboard!" and up at the further end of the platform Gordon saw the lank form of the detective whom he had tried to avoid an hour before at the other station.

Without taking time for thought he hurried Celia forward and they sprang breathlessly aboard. Not until they were fairly in the cars and the wheels moving under them did it occur to him that his companion had had nothing to eat since about twelve o'clock. She must be famished, and in a fair way to be ill again. What a fool he was not to have thought! They could have stopped in some obscure restaurant along the way as well as not, and taken a later train, and yet it was safer to get away at once. Without doubt there were watchers at East Liberty, too, and he was lucky to have got on the train without a challenge. He was sure that detective's face lighted strangely as he looked his way. Perhaps there was a buffet attached to the train. At least, he would investigate. If there wasn't, they must get off at the next stop — there must be another stop surely somewhere near the city — he could not remember, but there surely must be.

They had to wait some time to get the attention of the conductor. He was having much trouble with some disgruntled passengers who each claimed to have the same berth. Gordon finally got his ear, and showing his stateroom tickets enquired if they could be used on this train.

"No," growled the worried conductor. "You're on the wrong train. This is a special, and every berth in the train is taken now but one upper."

"Then, we'll have to get off at the next stop, I suppose, and take the other train," said Gordon dismally.

"There isn't any other stop till somewhere in the middle of the night. I tell you this is a special, and we're scheduled to go straight through. East Liberty's the last stop."

"Then what shall we do?"asked Gordon inanely.

"I'm sure I don't know," snapped the conductor. "I've enough to do without mending other people's mistakes. Stay aboard, I suppose, unless you want to jump off and commit suicide."

"But I have a lady with me who isn't at all well," said Gordon, with dignity.

"So much the worse for the lady," replied the conductor inhumanly. "There's one upper berth, I told you."

"An upper berth wouldn't do for her," said Gordon decidedly. "She isn't well, I tell you."

"Suit yourself!" snapped the harassed official. "I reckon it's better than nothing. You may not have it long. I'm likely to be asked for it the next half minute."

"Is that so? And is there absolutely nothing else?"

"Young man, I can't waste words on you. I haven't time. Take it or let it alone. It's all one to me. There's some standing room left in the day-coach, perhaps."

"I'll take it," said Gordon meekly, wishing he could go back and undo the last half-hour. How in the world was he to go and tell Celia that he could provide her nothing better than an upper berth?

She was sitting with her back to him, her face resting wearily on her hand against the window. Two men with largely checked suits, big seal rings, and diamond scarf-pins sat in the opposite seat. He knew it was most unpleasant for her. A nondescript woman with a very large hat and thick powder on her face shared Celia's seat. He reflected that "specials" did not always bear a select company.

"Is there nothing you can do?" he pleaded with the conductor, as he took the bit of pasteboard entitling him to the last vacant berth. "Don't you suppose you could get some man to change and give her a lower berth? It'll be very hard for her. She isn't used to upper berths."

His eyes rested wistfully on the bowed head. Celia had

taken off her plumed hat, and the fitful light of the car played with the gold of her hair. The conductor's grim eye softened as he looked.

"That the lady? I'll see what I can do," he said briefly, and stumped off to the next car. The miracle of her presence worked its change upon him.

Gordon went over to Celia and told her in a low tone that he hoped to have arrangements made for her soon, so that she could be comfortable. She must be fearfully tired with the excitement and fright and hurry. He added that he had made a great blunder in getting on this train, and now there was no chance to get off for several hours, perhaps, and probably no supper to be had.

"Oh, it doesn't matter in the least," said Celia wearily. "I'm not at all hungry." She almost smiled when she said it. He knew that what she wanted was to have her mind relieved about the letters. But she readily saw that there was no opportunity now.

She even seemed sorry at his troubled look, and tried to smile again through the settled sadness in her eyes. He could see she was very weary, and he felt like a great brute in care of a child, and mentally berated himself for his own thoughtlessness.

Gordon started off to search for something to eat for her, and was more successful than he had dared hope. The newsboy had two chicken sandwiches left, and these, with the addition of a fine orange, a box of chocolates, and a glass of ice-water, he presently brought to her, and was rewarded by a smile this time, almost as warm and intimate as those she had given him during their beautiful day.

But he could not sit beside her, for the places were all taken, and he could not stand in the aisle and talk, for the porter was constantly running back and forth making up the berths. There seemed to be a congested state of things in the whole train, every seat being full and men standing in the aisles. He noticed now that they all wore badges of some fraternal order. It was doubtless a delegation to some great convention, upon which they had intruded. They were a good-natured, noisy, happy crowd, but not anywhere among them was to be found a quiet spot where he and Celia could go on with their suddenly interrupted conversation. Presently the conductor came to him and said he had found a gentleman who would give the lady his lower berth and take her upper one. It was already made up, and the lady might take possession at once.

Gordon made the exchange of tickets, and immediately escorted Celia to it. He found her most glad to go for she was now unutterably weary, and was longing to get away from the light and noise about her.

He led the way with the suit-cases, hoping that in the other car there would be some spot where they could talk for a few minutes. But he was disappointed. It was even fuller than in the first car. He arranged everything for her comfort as far as possible, disposed of her hat and fixed her suit-case so that she could open it, but even while he was doing it there were people crowding by, and no private conversation could be had. He stepped back when all was arranged and held the curtain aside that she might sit on the edge of her berth. Then stooping over he whispered:

"Try to trust me until morning. I'll explain it all to you then, so that you will understand how I have had nothing to do with those letters. Forget it, and try to rest. Will you?"

His tone was wistful. He had never wanted to do anything so much in all his life as to stoop and kiss those sweet lips, and the lovely eyes that looked up at him out of the dusky shadows of the berth, filled with fear and longing. They looked more than ever like the blue tired flowers that drooped from her gown wearily. But he held himself with a firm hand. She was not his to kiss. When she knew how he had deceived her, she would probably never give him the right to kiss her.

"I will try," she murmured in answer to his question, and

then added: "But where will you be? Is your berth near by?"

"Not far away—that is, I had to take a place in another car, they are so crowded."

"Oh!" she said a little anxiously. "Are you sure you have a good comfortable place?"

"Oh, yes, I shall be all right," he answered joyously. It was so wonderful to have her care whether he was comfortable or not.

The porter was making up the opposite berth, and there was no room to stand longer, so he bade her good night, she putting out her hand for a farewell. For an instant he held it close, with gentle pressure, as if to reassure her, then he went away to the day-coach, and settled down into a hard corner at the very back of the car, drawing his travelling cap over his eyes, and letting his heart beat out wild joy over that little touch of her dear hand. Wave after wave of sweetness went over him, thrilling his very soul with a joy he had never known before.

And this was love! And what kind of a wretch was he, presuming to love like this a woman who was the promised bride of another man! Ah, but such a man! A villain! A brute, who had used his power over her to make her suffer tortures! Had a man like that a right to claim her? His whole being answered "no."

Then the memory of the look in her eyes, the turn of her head, the soft touch of her fingers as they lay for that instant in his, the inflection of her voice, would send that wave of sweetness over his senses, his heart would thrill anew, and he would forget the wretch who stood between him and this lovely girl whom he knew now he loved as he had never dreamed a man could love.

Gradually his mind steadied itself under the sweet intoxication, and he began to wonder just what he should say to her in the morning. It was a good thing he had not had further opportunity to talk with her that night, for he could not have told her everything; and now if all went well they would be in Washington in the morning, and he might make some excuse till after he had delivered his message. Then he would be free to tell the whole story, and lay his case before her for decision. His heart throbbed with ecstasy as he thought of the possibility of her forgiving him, and yet it seemed most unlikely. Sometimes he would let his wild longings fancy for just an instant what joy it would be if she could be induced to let the marriage stand. But he told himself at the same time that that could never be. It was very likely that there was someone else in New York to whom her heart would turn if she were free from the scoundrel who had threatened her into a compulsory marriage. He would promise to help her, protect her, defend her from the man who was evidently using blackmail to get her into his power for some purpose; most likely for the sake of having control of her property. At least it would be some comfort to be able to help her out of her trouble. And yet, would she ever trust a man who had even unwittingly allowed her to be bound by the sacred tie of marriage to an utter stranger?

And thus, amid hope and fear, the night whirled itself away. Forward in the sleeper the girl lay wide awake for a long time. In the middle of the night a thought suddenly evolved itself out of the blackness of her curtained couch. She sat upright alertly and stared into the darkness, as if it were a thing that she could catch and handle and examine. The thought was born out of a dreamy vision of the crisp brown waves, almost curls if they had not been short and thick, that covered the head of the man who had lain sleeping outside her curtains in the early morning. It came to her with sudden force that not so had been the hair of the boy George Hayne, who used to trouble her girlish days. His was thin and black and oily, collecting naturally into little isolated strings with the least warmth, and giving him the appearance of a kitten who had been out in the rain. One lock, how well she remembered that lock! — one lock on the very crown of his head had always refused to lie down, no matter how much persuasion was brought to bear upon it. It had been the one point on which the self-satisfied George had been pregnable, his hair, that scalp lock that would always arise stiffly, oilily, from the top of his head. The hair she had looked at admiringly that morning in the dawning crimson of the rising sun had not been that way. It had curved clingingly to the shape of the fine head as if it loved to go that way. It was beautiful and fine and burnished with a sense of life and vigor in its every wave. Could hair change in ten years? Could it grow brown where it had been black? Could it become glossy instead of dull and oily? Could it take on the signs of natural wave where it had been as straight as a die? Could it grow like fur where it had been so thin?

The girl could not solve the problem, but the thought was most startling and brought with it many suggestive possibilities that were most disturbing. Yet gradually out of the darkness she drew a sort of comfort in her dawning enlightenment. Two things she had to go on in her strange premises: he had said he did not write the letters, and his hair was not the same. Who then was he? Her husband now undoubtedly, but who? And if deeds and hair change so materially, why not spirits? At least he was not the same as she had feared and dreaded. There was so much comfort.

And at last she lay down and slept.

14

THEY were late coming into Washington, for the Special had been sidetracked in the night for several express trains, and the noisy crowd who had kept one another awake till after midnight made up by sleeping far into the morning.

Three times did Gordon make the journey three cars front to see if his companion of yesterday were awake and needed anything, but each time found the curtains drawn and still, and each time he went slowly back again to his seat in the crowded daycoach.

It was not until the white dome of the capitol, and the tall needle of the monument, were painted soft and vision-like against the sky, reminding one of the pictures of the heavenly city in the story of Pilgrim's Progress, and faintly suggesting a new and visionary world, that he sought her again, and found her fully ready, standing in the aisle while the porter put up the berth out of the way. Beneath the great brim of her purple hat, where the soft fronds of her plumes trembled with the motion of the train, she lifted sweet eyes to him, as if she were both glad and frightened to see him. And then that ecstasy shot through him again, as he realized suddenly what it would be to have her for his life-companion, to feel her looks of gladness were all for him, and have the right to take all fright away from her.

They could only smile at each other for good-morning, for everybody was standing up and being brushed, and pushing here and there for suit-cases and lost umbrellas; and everybody talked loudly, and laughed a great deal, and told how late the train was. Then at last they were there, and could get out and walk silently side by side in the noisy procession through the station to the sidewalk.

What little things sometimes change a lifetime and make for our safety or our destruction! That very morning three keen watchers were set to guard that station at Washington to hunt out the government spy who had stolen back the stolen message, and take him, message and all, dead or alive, back to New York; for the man who could testify against the Holman Combination was not to be let live if there was such a thing as getting him out of the way. But they never thought to watch the Special which was supposed to carry only delegates to the great convention. He could not possibly be on that! They knew he was coming from Pittsburgh, for they had been so advised by telegram the evening before by one of their company who had seen him buying a sleeper ticket for Washington, but they felt safe about that Special, for they had made inquiries and been told no one but delegates could possibly come on it. They had done their work thoroughly, and were on hand with every possible plan perfected for bagging their game, but they took the time when the Pittsburgh Special was expected to arrive for eating a hearty breakfast in the restaurant across the street from the station. Two of them emerged from the restaurant doorway in plenty of time to meet the next Pittsburgh tain, just as Gordon, having placed the lady in a closed carriage, was getting in himself.

If the carriage had stood in any other spot along the pavement in front of the station, they never would have seen him, but, as it was, they had a full view of him; and because they were Washington men, and experts in their line, they recognized him at once, and knew their plans had failed, and that only by extreme measures could they hope to prevent the delivery of the message which would mean downfall and disaster to them and their schemes.

As Gordon slammed shut the door of the carriage, he caught a vision of his two enemies pointing excitedly toward him, and he knew that the blood-hounds were on the scent.

His heart beat wildly. His anxiety was divided between the message and the lady. What should he do? Drive at once to the home of his chief and deliver the message, or leave the girl at his rooms, 'phone for a faster conveyance and trust to getting to his chief ahead of his pursuers?

"Don't let anything hinder you! Don't let anything hinder you! Make it a matter of life and death!" rang the little ditty in his ears, and now it seemed as if he must go straight ahead with the message. And yet—"a matter of life and death!" He could not, must not, might not, take the lady with him into danger. If he must be in danger of death he did not want to die having exposed an innocent stranger to the same.

Then there was another point to be thought of.

He had already told the driver to take him to his apartments, and to drive as rapidly as possible. It would not do to stop him now and change the directions, for a pistol-shot could easily reach him yet; and, coming from a crowd, who would be suspected? His enemies were standing on the threshold of a place where there were many of their kind to protect them, and none of his friends knew of his coming. It would be a race for life from now on to the finish.

Celia was looking out with interest at the streets, recognizing landmarks with wonder, and did not notice Gordon's white, set face and burning eyes as he strained his vision to note how fast the horse was going. Oh, if the driver would only turn off at the next corner into the side street they could not watch the carriage so far, but it was not likely, for this was the most direct road, and yet—yes, he had turned! Joy! The street here was so crowded that he had sought the narrower, less crowded way that he might go the faster.

It seemed an age to him before they stopped at his apartments. To Celia, it had been but a short ride, in which familiar scenes had brought her pleasure, for she recognized that she was not in strange Chicago, but in Washington, a city often visited. Somehow she felt it was an omen of a better future than she had feared.

"Oh, why didn't you tell me?" she smiled to Gordon. "It is Washington, dear old Washington."

Somehow he controlled the tumult in his heart and smiled back, saying in a voice quite natural:

"I am so glad you like it."

She seemed to understand that they could not talk until they reached a quiet place somewhere, and she did not trouble him with questions. Instead—she looked from the window, or watched him furtively, comparing him with her memory of George Hayne, and wondering in her own thoughts. She was glad to have them to herself for just this little bit, for now that the morning had come she was almost afraid of revelation, what it might bring forth. And so it came about that they took the swift ride in more or less silence, and neither thought it strange.

As the carriage stopped, he spoke with low, hurried voice, tense with excitement, but her own nerves were on a strain also, and she did not notice.

"We get out here."

He had the fare ready for the driver, and, stepping out, hurried Celia into the shelter of the hallway. It happened that an elevator had just come down, so it was but a second more before they were up safe in the hall before his own apartment.

Taking a latch-key from his pocket, he applied it to the door, flung it open, and ushered Celia to a large leather chair in the middle of the room. Then, stepping quickly to the side of the room, he touched a bell, and from it went to the telephone, with an "Excuse me, please, this is necessary," to the girl, who sat astonished, wondering at the homelikeness of the room and at the "at-homeness" of the man. She had expected to be taken to a hotel. This seemed to be a private apartment with which he was perfectly acquainted. Perhaps it belonged to some friend. But how, after an absence of years, could he remember just where to go, which door and which elevator to take, and how to fit the key with so accustomed a hand? Then her attention was arrested by his voice:

"Give me 254 L please," he said. . . . "Is this 254 L? . . . Is Mr. Osborne in? . . . You say he has *not* gone to the office yet? . . . May I speak with him? . . . Is this Mr. Osborne? . . . I did not expect you to know my voice. . . . Yes, sir; just arrived, and all safe so far. Shall I bring it to the house or the office? . . . The house? . . . All right, sir. Immediately. . . . By the way, I am sure Hale and Burke are on my track. They saw me at the station. . . . To your house? . . . You will wait until I come? . . . All right, sir. Yes, immediately. . . . Sure, I'll take precaution. . . . Good-by."

With the closing words came a tap at the door.

"Come, Henry," he answered, as the astonished girl turned toward the door. "Henry, you will go down, please, to the restaurant, and bring up a menu card. This lady will select what she would like to have, and you will serve breakfast for her in this room as soon as possible. I shall be out for perhaps an hour, and, meantime, you will obey any orders she may give you."

He did not introduce her as his wife, but she did not notice the omission. She had suddenly become aware of a strange, distraught haste in his manner, and when he said he was going out alarm seized her, she could not tell why.

The man bowed deferentially to his master, looked his admiration and devotion to the lady, waited long enough to say:

"I'se mighty glad to see you safe back, sah —" and disappeared to obey orders.

Celia turned toward Gordon for an explanation, but he was already at the telephone again:

"46! . . . Is this the Garage? . . . This is The Harris Apartments. . . . Can you send Thomas with a closed car to the rear door immediately? . . . Yes. . . . No, I want Thomas, and a car that can speed. . . . Yes, the rear door, *rear,* and at once. . . . What? . . . What's that? . . . But I *must.* . . . It's *official* business. . . . Well, I thought so. Hurry them up. Good-by."

He turned and saw her troubled gaze following him with growing fear in her eyes.

"What is the matter?" she asked anxiously. "Has something happened?"

Just one moment he paused, and, coming toward her, laid his hands on hers tenderly.

"Nothing the matter at all," he said soothingly. "At least nothing that need worry you. It is just a matter of pressing business. I'm sorry to have to go from you for a little while, but it's necessary. I cannot explain to you until I return. You will trust me? You will not worry?"

"I will try!"

Her lips were quivering, and her eyes were filled with tears. Again he felt that intense longing to lay his lips upon hers and comfort her, but he put it from him.

"There is nothing to feel sad about," he said, smiling gently. "It is nothing tragic only there is need for haste, for if I wait, I may fail yet—It is something that means a great deal to me. When I come back I will explain all."

"Go!" she said, putting out her hands in a gesture of resignation, as if she would hurry him from her. And though she was burning to know what it all meant there was that about him that compelled her to trust him and to wait.

Then his control almost went from him. He nearly took those hands in his and kissed them, but he did not. Instead, he went with swift steps to his bedroom door, threw open a chiffonier drawer, and took therefrom something small and sinister. She could see the gleam of its polished metal, and she sensed a strange little menace in the click as he did something to it. He came out with his hand in his pocket, as if he had just hidden something there.

She was not familiar with firearms. Her mother had been afraid of them and her brother had never flourished any around the house, yet she knew by instinct that some weapon of defence was in Gordon's possession; and a nameless horror rose in her heart and shone from her blue eyes, but she would not speak a word to let him know it. If he had not been in such haste, he would have seen. Her horror would have been still greater if she had known that he already carried one loaded revolver and was taking a second in case of an emergency.

"Don't worry," he called as he hurried out the door. "Henry will get anything you need, and I shall soon be back."

The door closed and he was gone. She heard his quick step down the hall, heard the elevator door slide and slam again, and then she knew he was gone down. Outside an automobile sounded and she seemed to hear again his words at the phone, "The rear door." Why had he gone to the rear door? Was he in hiding? Was he flying from someone? What, oh what, did it mean?

Without stopping to reason it out, she flew across the room and opened the door of the bedroom he had just left, then through it passed swiftly to a bathroom beyond. Yes, there was a window. Would it be the one? Could she see him? And what good would it do her if she could?

She crowded close to the window. There was a heavy sash with stained glass, but she selected a clear bit of yellow and put her eye close. Yes, there was a closed automobile just below her, and it had started away from the building. He had gone, then. Where?

Her mind was a blank for a few minutes. She went slowly, mechanically back to the other room without noticing anything about her, sat down in the chair, putting her hands to her temples, and tried to think. Back to the moment in the church where he had appeared at her side and the service had begun. Something had told her then that he was different, and yet there had been those letters, and how could it possibly be that he had not written them? He was gone on some dangerous business. Of that she felt sure. There had been some caution given him by the man to whom he first 'phoned. He had promised to take precaution—that meant the little, wicked, gleaming thing in his pocket. Perhaps some harm would come to him, and she would never know. And then she stared at the opposite wall with wonder-filled eyes. Well, and suppose it did? Why did she care? Was he not the man whose power over her but two short days ago would have made her welcome death as her deliverer? Why was all changed now? Just because he had smiled upon her and been kind? Had given her a few wild flowers and said her eyes were like them? Had hair that waved instead of being straight and thin? And where was all her loyalty to her dear dead father's memory? How could she mind that danger should come to one who had threatened to tell terrible lies that should blacken him in the thoughts of people who had loved him? Had she forgotten the letters? Was she willing to forgive all just because he had declared that he did not write them? How foolish! He said he could prove that he did not, but of course that was all nonsense. He must have written them. And yet there was the wave in his hair, and the kindness in his eyes. And he had looked—oh, he had looked terrible things when he had read that letter; as if he would like to wreak vengeance on the man who had written it. Could a man masquerade that way?

And then a new solution to the problem came to her. Suppose this—whoever he was—this man who had married her, had gone out to find and punish George Hayne? Suppose— But then she covered her eyes with her hands and shuddered. Yet why should she care? But she did. Suppose he should be killed, himself! Who was he if not George Hayne and how did he come to take his place? Was it just another of George's terrible tricks upon her?

A quick vision came of their bringing him back to her. He would lie, perhaps, on that great crimson leather couch over there, just as he had lain in the dawning of the morning in the state-room of the train, with his hands hanging limp, and one perhaps across his breast, as if he were guarding something, and his bright waves of brown hair lying heavy about his forehead—only, his forehead would be white, so white and cold, with a little blue mark in his temple perhaps.

The footsteps of the man Henry brought her back to the present again. She smiled at him pleasantly as he entered, and answered his questions about what she would have for breakfast; but it was he who selected the menu, not she, and after he had gone she could not have told what she had ordered. She could not get away from the vision on the couch. She closed her eyes and pressed her cold fingers against her eyeballs to drive it away, but still her bridegroom seemed to lie there before her.

The colored man came back presently with a loaded tray, and set it down on a little table which he wheeled before her, as though he had done it many times before. She thanked him, and said there was nothing else she needed, so he went away.

She toyed with the cup of delicious coffee which he had poured for her, and the few swallows she took gave her new heart. She broke a bit from a hot roll, and ate a little of the delicious steak, but still her mind was at work at the problem, and her heart was full of nameless anxiety.

He had gone away without any breakfast himself, and he had had no supper the night before, she was sure. He probably had given to her everything he could get on the train. She was haunted with regret because she had not shared with him. She got up and walked about the room, trying to shake off the horror that was upon her, and the dread of what the morning might bring forth. Ordinarily she would have thought of sending a message to her mother and brother, but her mind was so troubled now that it never occurred to her.

The walls of the room were tinted a soft greenish gray, and above the picture moulding they blended into a woodsy landscape with a hint of water, greensward, and blue sky through interlacing branches. It reminded her of the little village they had seen as they started from the train in the early morning light. What a beautiful day they had spent together and how it had changed her whole attitude of heart toward the man she had married!

Two or three fine pictures were hung in good lights. She studied them, and knew that the one who had selected and hung them was a judge of true art; but they did not hold her attention long, for as yet, she had not connected the room with the man for whom she waited.

A handsome mahogany desk stood open in a broad space by the window. She was attracted by a little painted miniature of a woman. She took it up and studied the face. It was fine and sweet, with brown hair dressed low, and eyes that reminded her of the man who had just gone from her. Was this, then, the home of some relative with whom he had come to stop for a day or two, and, if so, where was the relative? The dress in the miniature was of a quarter of a century past, yet the face was young and sweet, as young, perhaps, as herself. She wondered who it was. She put the miniature back in place with caressing hand. She felt that she would like to know this woman with the tender eyes. She wished her here now, that she might tell her all her anxiety.

Her eye wandered to the pile of letters, some of them official-looking ones, one or two in square, perfumed envelopes, with high, angular writing. They were all addressed to Mr. Cyril Gordon. That was strange! Who was Mr. Cyril Gordon? What had they—what had she—to do with him? Was he a friend whom George—whom they—were visiting for a few days? It was all bewildering.

Then the telephone rang.

Her heart beat wildly and she looked toward it as if it had been a human voice speaking and she had no power to answer. What should she do now? Should she answer? Or should she wait for the man to come? Could the man hear the telephone bell or was she perhaps expected to answer? And yet if Mr. Cyril Gordon—well, somebody ought to answer. The 'phone rang insistently once more, and still a third time. What if *he* should be calling her? Perhaps he was in distress. This thought sent her flying to the 'phone. She took down the receiver and called:

"Hello!" and her voice sounded far away to herself.

"Is this Mr. Gordon's apartment?"

"Yes," she answered, for her eyes were resting on the pile of letters close at hand.

"Is Mr. Gordon there?"

"No he is not," she answered, growing more confident now and almost wishing she had not presumed to answer a stranger's 'phone.

"Why, I just 'phoned to the office and they told me he had returned," said a voice that had an imperious note in it. "Are you sure he isn't there?"

"Quite sure," she replied.

"Who is this, please?"

"I beg your pardon," said Celia trying to make time and knowing not how to reply. She was not any longer Miss Hathaway. Who was she? Mrs. Hayne? She shrank from the name. It was filled with horror for her. "Who is this, I said," snapped the other voice now. "Is this the chambermaid? Because if it is I'd like you to look around and inquire and be quite sure that Mr. Gordon isn't there. I wish to speak with him about something very important."

Celia smiled.

"No, this is not the chambermaid," she said sweetly, "and I am quite sure Mr. Gordon is not here."

"How long before he will be there?"

"I don't know really, for I have just come myself."

"Who is this to whom I am talking?"

"Why—just a friend," she answered, wondering if that were the best thing to say.

"Oh!" there was a long and contemplative pause at the other end.

"Well, could you give Mr. Gordon a message when he comes in?"

"Why certainly, I think so. Who is this?'"

"Miss Bentley. Julia Bentley. He'll know," replied the imperious one eagerly now. "And tell him please that he is expected here to dinner to-night. We need him to complete the number, and he simply mustn't fail me. I'll excuse him for going off in such a rush if he comes early and tells me all about it. Now you won't forget, will you? You got the name, Bentley, did you? B, E, N, T, L, E, Y, you know. And you'll tell him the minute he comes in?"

"Yes."

"Thank you! What did you say your name was?"

But Celia had hung up. Somehow the message annoyed her, she could not tell why. She wished she had not answered the 'phone. Whoever Mr. Cyril Gordon was what should she do if he should suddenly appear? And as for this imperious lady and her message she hoped she would never have to deliver it. On second thought why not write it and leave it on his desk with the pile of letters? She would do it. It would serve to pass away a few of these dreadful minutes that lagged so distressfully.

She sat down and wrote: "Miss Bentley wishes Mr. Gordon to dine with her this evening. She will pardon his running away the other day if he will come early." She laid it beside the high angular writing on the square perfumed letters and went back to the leather chair too restless to rest yet too weary to stand up.

She went presently to the back windows to look out and then to the side ones. Across the housetops she could catch a glimpse of domes and buildings. There was the Congressional Library, which usually delighted her with its exquisite tones of gold and brown and white. But she had no eyes for it now. Beyond were more buildings, all set in the lovely foliage which was much farther developed than it had been in New York State. From another window she could get a glimpse of the Potomac shining in the morning sun.

She wandered to the front windows and looked out. There were people passing and repassing. It was a busy street, but she could not make out whether it was one she knew or not. There were two men walking back and forth on the opposite side. They did not go further than the corner of the street either way. They looked across at the windows sometimes and pointed up, when they met, and once one of them took something out of his pocket and flashed it under his coat at his side, as if to have it ready for use. It reminded her of the thing her husband had held in his hand in the bedroom and she shuddered. She watched them, fascinated, not able to draw herself away from the window.

Now and then she would go to the rear window, to see if there was any sign of the automobile returning, and then hurry back to the front, to see if the men were still there. Once she returned to the chair, and, lying back, shut her eyes, and let the memory of yesterday sweep over her in all its sweet details, up to the time when they had got into the way train and she had seemed to feel her disloyalty to her father. But now her heart was all on the other side, and she began to feel that there had been some dreadful mistake, somewhere, and he was surely all right. He could not, could not have written those terrible letters. Then again the details of their wild carriage ride in Pittsburgh and miraculous escape haunted her. There was something strange and unexplained about that which she must understand.

15

MEANTIME, Gordon was speeding away to another part of the city by the fastest time an experienced chauffeur dare to make. About the time they turned the first corner into the avenue, two burly policemen sauntered casually into the pretty square in front of the house where lived the chief of the Secret Service. There was nothing about their demeanor to show that they had been detailed there by special urgency, and three men who hurried to the little park just across the street from the house could not possibly know that their leisurely and careless stroll was the result of a hurried telephone message from the chief to police headquarters immediately after his message from Gordon.

The policemen strolled by the house, greeted each other, and walked on around the square across the little park. They eyed the three men sitting idly on a bench, and passed leisurely on. They disappeared around a corner, and to the three men were out of the way. The latter did not know the hidden places where the officers took up their watch, and when an automobile appeared, and the three stealthily got up from their park bench and distributed themselves among the shrubbery near the walk, they knew not that their every movement was observed with keen attention. But they did wonder how it happened that those two policemen seemed to spring out of the ground suddenly, just as the auto came to a halt in front of the chief's house.

Gordon sprang out and up the steps with a bound, the door opening before him as if he were expected. The two grim and apparently indifferent policemen stood outside like two stone images on guard, while up the street with the rhythmic sound rode two mounted police, also coming to a halt before the house as if for a purpose. The three men in the bushes hid their instruments of death, and would have slunk away had there been a chance; but, turning to make a hasty flight, they were met by three more policemen. There was the crack of a revolver as one of the three desperadoes tried a last reckless dash for freedom — and failed. The wretch went to justice with his right arm hanging limp by his side.

Inside the house Gordon was delivering up his message, and as he laid it before his chief, and stood silent while the elder man read and pondered its tremendous import, it occurred to him for the first time that his chief would require some report of his journey, and the hindrances that had made him a whole day late in getting back to Washington. His heart stood still with sudden panic. What was he to do? How could he tell it all? What right had he to tell of his marriage to an unknown woman? A marriage that perhaps was not a marriage. He could not know what the outcome would be until he had told the girl everything. As far as he himself was concerned he knew that the great joy of his life had come to him in her. And he must think of her and protect her good name in every way. If there should be such a thing as that she should consent to remain with him and be his wife he must never let a soul know but what the marriage had been planned long ago. It would not be fair to her. It would make life intolerable for them both either together or apart. And while he might be and doubtless was perfectly safe in confiding in his chief, and asking him to keep silence about the matter, still he felt that even that would be a breach of faith with Celia. He must close his lips upon the story until he could talk with her and know her wishes. He drew a sigh of weariness. It was a long, hard way he had come, and it was not over. The worst ordeal would be his confession to the bride who was not his wife.

The chief looked up.

"Could you make this out, Gordon?" he asked, noting keenly the young man's weary eyes, the strained, tense look about his mouth.

"Oh, yes sir; I saw it at once. I was almost afraid my eyes might betray the secret before I got away with it."

"Then you know that you have saved the country, and what you have been worth to the Service."

The young man flushed with pleasure.

"Thank you, sir," he said, looking down. "I understood it was important, and I am glad I was able to accomplish the errand without failing."

"Have you reason to suppose you were followed, except for what you saw at the station in this city?"

"Yes, sir; I am sure there were detectives after me as I was leaving New York. They were suspicious of me. I saw one of the men who had been at the dinner with me watching me. The disguise—and—some circumstances—threw him off. He wasn't sure. Then, there was a man—you know him, Balder—at Pittsburgh?—"

"Pittsburgh!"

"Yes, you wonder how I got to Pittsburgh. You see, I was shadowed almost from the first I suspect, for when I reached the station in New York I was sure I recognized this man who had sat opposite me a few minutes before. I suppose my disguise, which you so thoughtfully provided, bothered him, for though he followed me about at a little distance he didn't speak to me. I had to get on the first train that circumstances permitted, and perhaps the fact that it was a Chicago train made him think he was mistaken in me. Anyhow I saw no more of him after the train left the station. Rather unexpectedly I found I could get the drawing room compartment, and went into immediate retirement, leaving the train at daylight where it was delayed on a side track, and walked across country till I found a conveyance that took me to Pittsburgh train. It didn't seem feasible to get away from the Chicago train any sooner as the train made no further stops, and it was rather late at night by the time I boarded it. I thought I would run less risk by making a detour. I never dreamed they would have watchers out for me at Pittsburgh, and I can't think yet how they managed to get on my track, but almost the first minute I landed I spied Balder stretching his neck over the crowds. I bolted from the station at once and finding a carriage drawn up before the door just ready for me I got in and ordered them to drive me to East Liberty Station.

"I am afraid I shall always be suspicious of handy closed carriages after this experience. I certainly have reason to be. The door was no sooner closed on me than the driver began to race like mad through the streets. I didn't think much of it at first until he had been going some time, fully long enough to have reached East Liberty, and the horse was still rushing like a locomotive. Then I saw that we were in a lonely district of the city that seemed unfamiliar. That alarmed me and I tapped on the window and called to the driver. He paid no attention. Then I found the doors were fastened shut, and the windows plugged so they wouldn't open.

"I discovered that an armed man rode beside the driver. I managed to get one of the doors open after a good deal of work, and escaped when we stopped for a freight train to pass; but I'm satisfied that I was being kidnapped and if I hadn't got away just when I did you would never have heard of me again or the message either. I finally managed to reach East Liberty Station and jumped on the first train that came in, but I caught a glimpse of Balder stretching his neck over the crowd. He must have seen me and had Hale and Burke on the watch when I got here. They just missed me by a half second. They went over to the restaurant—didn't expect me on a special, but I escaped them, and I'm mighty glad to get that little paper into your possession and out of mine. It's rather a long story to tell the whole, but I think you have the main facts."

There was a suspicious glitter in the keen eyes of the kind old chief as he put out his hand and grasped Gordon's in a hearty shake; but all he said was:

"And you are all worn out—I'll guarantee you didn't sleep much last night."

"Well, no," said Gordon; "I had to sit up in a day-coach and share the seat with another man. Besides, I was somewhat excited."

"Of course, of course!" puffed the old chief, coughing vigorously, and showing by his gruff attitude that he was deeply affected. "Well, young man, this won't be forgotten by the Department. Now you go home and take a good sleep. Take the whole day off if you wish, and then come down tomorrow morning and tell me all about it. Isn't there anything more I need to know at once that justice may be done?"

"I believe not," said Gordon, with a sigh of relief. "There's a list of the men who were at dinner with me. I wrote them down from memory last night when I couldn't sleep. I also wrote a few scraps of conversation, which will show you just how deep the plot had gone. If I had not read the message and known its import, I should not have understood what they were talking about."

"H-m! Yes. If there had been more time before you started I might have told you all about it. Still it seemed desirable that you should appear as much at your ease as possible. I thought this would be best accomplished by your knowing nothing of the import of the writing when you first met the people."

"I suppose it was as well that I did not know any more than I did. You are a great chief, sir! I was deeply impressed anew with that fact as I saw how wonderfully you had planned for every possible emergency. It was simply great, sir."

"Pooh! Pooh! Get you home and to bed," said the old chief quite brusquely.

He touched a bell and a man appeared.

"Jessup, is the coast clear?" he asked.

"Yessah," declared the man. "Dey have jest hed a couple o' shots in de pahk, an' now dey tuk de villains off to der p'lice station. De officers is out der waitin' to 'scort de gemman."

"Get home with you, Gordon, and don't come to the office till ten in the morning. Then come straight to my private room."

Gordon thanked him, and left the room preceded by the gray-haired servant. He was surprised to find the policemen outside, and wondered still more that they seemed to be going one in front and the other behind him as he rode along. He was greatly relieved that he had not been called upon to give the whole story. His heart was filled with anxiety now to get back to the girl, and tell her everything, and yet he dreaded it more than anything he had ever had to face in all his life. He sat back on cushions, and, covering his face with his hands, tried to think how he should begin, but he could see nothing but her sweet eyes filled with tears, think of nothing but the way she had looked and smiled during the beautiful morning they had spent together in the little town of Milton. Beautiful little Milton. Should he ever see it again?

Celia at her window grew more and more nervous as an hour and then another half hour slipped slowly away, and still he did not come. Then two mounted policemen rode rapidly down the street following an automobile, in which sat the man for whom she waited.

She had no eyes now for the men who had been lurking across the way, and when she thought to look for them again she saw them running in the opposite direction as fast as they could go, making wild gestures for a car to stop for them.

She stood by the window and saw Gordon get out of the car, and disappear into the building below, saw the car wheel and curve away and the mounted police take up their stand on either corner; heard the clang of the elevator as it started up, and the clash of its door as it stopped at that floor; heard steps coming on toward the door, and the key in the latch. Then she turned and looked at him, her two hands clasped before her, and her two eyes yearning, glad and fearful all at once.

"Oh, I have been so frightened about you! I am so glad you have come!" she said, and caught her voice in a sob as she took one little step toward him.

He threw his hat upon the floor, wherever it might land, and went to meet her, a great light glowing in his tired eyes, his arms outstretched to hers.

"And did you care?" he asked in a voice of almost awe. "Dear, did you *care* what became of *me?*"

"Oh yes, I *cared!* I could not help it." There was a real sob in her voice now, though her eyes were shining.

His arms went around her hungrily, as if he would draw her to him in spite of everything; yet he kept them so encircling, without touching her, like a benediction that would enwrap the very soul of his beloved. Looking down into her face he breathed softly:

"Oh, my dear, it seems as if I must hold you close and kiss you!"

She looked up with bated breath, and thought she understood. Then, with a lovely gesture of surrender, she whispered, "I can trust you." Her lashes were drooping now over her eyes.

"Not until you know all," he said, and put her gently from him into the great arm-chair, with a look of reverence and self-abnegation she felt she never would forget.

"Then, tell me quickly," she said, a swift fear making her weak from head to foot. She laid her hand across her heart, as if to help steady its beating.

He wheeled forward the leather couch opposite her chair, and sat down, her head drooping, his eyes down. He dreaded to begin.

She waited for the revelation, her eyes upon his bowed head.

Finally he lifted his eyes and saw her look, and a tender light came into his face.

"It is a strange story," he said. "I don't know what you will think of me after it is told, but I want you to know that, blundering, stupid, even criminal, though you may think me, I would sooner die this minute than cause you one more breath of suffering."

Her eyes lit up with a wonderful light, and the ready tears sprang into them, tears that sparkled through the sunshine of a great joy that illumined her whole face.

"Please go on," she said softly, and added very gently, "I believe you."

But even with those words in his ears the beginning was not easy. Gordon drew a deep breath and launched forth.

"I am not the man you think," he said, and looked at her to see how she would take it. "My name is not George Hayne. My name is Cyril Gordon."

As one might launch an arrow at a beloved victim and long that it may not strike the mark, so he sent his truth home to her understanding, and waited in breathless silence, hoping against hope that this might not turn her against him.

"Oh!" she breathed softly, as if some puzzle were solving itself. "Oh! — "this time not altogether in surprise, nor as if the fact were displeasing. She looked at him expectantly for further revelation, and he plunged into his story headlong.

"I'm a member of the Secret Service, — headquarters here in Washington, — and day before yesterday I was sent to New

York on an important errand. A message of great import written in a private code had been stolen from one of our men. I was sent to get it before they could decipher it. The message involved matters of such tremendous significance that I was ordered to go under an assumed name, and on no account to let anyone know of my mission. My orders were to get the message, and let nothing hinder me in bringing it with all haste to Washington. I went with the full understanding that I might even be called upon to risk my life."

He looked up. The girl sat wide-eyed, with hands clasped together at her throat.

He hurried on, not to cause her any needless anxiety.

"I won't weary you with details. There were a good many annoying hindrances on the way, which served to make me nervous, but I carried out the program laid down by my chief, and succeeded in getting possession of the message and making my escape from the house of the man who had stolen it. As I closed the door behind me, knowing that it could be but a matter of a few seconds at longest before six furious men would be on my track, who would stop at nothing to get back what I had taken from them, I saw a carriage standing almost before the house. The driver took me for the man he awaited, and I lost no time in taking advantage of his mistake. I jumped in, telling him to drive as fast as he could. I intended to give him further directions, but he had evidently had them from another quarter, and I thought I could call to him as soon as we were out of the dangerous neighborhood. To add to my situation I soon became sure that an automobile and a motor-cycle were following me. I recognized one of the men in the car as the man who sat opposite to me at the table a few minutes before. My coachman drove like mad, while I hurried to secure the message so that if I were caught it would not be found, and to put on a slight disguise—some eyebrows and things the chief had given me. Before I knew where I was, the carriage had stopped before a building. At first I thought it was a prison — and the car and motor-cycle came to a halt just behind me. I felt that I was pretty well trapped."

The girl gave a low moan, and Gordon, not daring to look up, hurried on with his story.

"There isn't much more to tell that you do not already know. I soon discovered the building was a church, not a prison. What happened afterward was the result of my extreme perturbance of mind, I suppose. I cannot account for my stupidity and subsequent cowardice in any other way. Neither was it possible for me to explain matters satisfactorily at any time during the whole mix-up, on account of the trust which I carried, and which I could on no account reveal even in confidence, or put in jeopardy in the slightest degree. Naturally at first my commission and how to get safely through it all was the only thing of importance to me. If you keep this in mind perhaps you will be able to judge me less harshly. My only thought when the carriage came to a halt was how to escape from those two pursuers, and that more or less pervaded my mind during what followed so that ordinary matters which at another time would have been at once clear to me, meant nothing at all. You see, the instant that carriage came to a standstill someone threw open the door, and I heard a voice call 'Where is the best man?' Then another voice said, 'Here he is!' I took it that they thought I was best man, but would soon discover that I wasn't when I came into the light. There wasn't any chance to slip away, or I should have done so, and vanished in the dark, but everybody surrounded me, and seemed to think I was all right. The two men who had followed were close behind eyeing me keenly. I'm satisfied that they were to blame for that wild ride we took in Pittsburgh! I soon saw by the remarks that the man I was supposed to be had been away from this country for ten years, and of course then they would not be very critical. I tried twice to explain that there was a mistake, but both times they misunderstood me and thought I was saying I couldn't go in the procession because

I hadn't practised. I don't just know how I came to be in such a dreadful mess. It would seem as if it ought to have been a very easy thing to say I had got into the wrong carriage and they must excuse me, that I wasn't their man, but, you see, they gave me no time to think nor to speak. They just turned me over from one man to another and took everything for granted, and I, finding that I would have to break loose and flee before their eyes if I wished to escape, reflected that there would be no harm in marching down the aisle as best man in a delayed wedding, if that was all there was to do. I could disappear as soon as the ceremony was over, and no one would be the wiser. The real best man would probably turn up and then they might wonder as they pleased for I would be far away and perhaps this was as good a place as any in which to hide for half an hour until my pursuers were baffled and well on their way seeking elsewhere for me. I can see now that I made a grave mistake in allowing even so much deception, but I did not see any harm in it then, and they all seemed in great distress for the ceremony to go forward. Bear in mind also that I was at that time entirely taken up with the importance of hiding my message until I could take it safely to my chief. Nothing else seemed to matter much. If the real best man was late to the wedding and they were willing to use me in his place what harm could come from it? He certainly deserved it for being late and if he came in during the ceremony he would think some one else had been put in his place. They introduced me to your brother—Jefferson. I thought he was the bridegroom, and I thought so until they laid your hand in mine!"

"Oh!" she moaned, and the little hand went to help its mate cover her face.

"I knew it!" he said bitterly. "I knew you would feel just that way as soon as you knew. I don't blame you. I deserve it! I was a fool, a villain, a dumb brute—whatever you have a mind to call me! You can't begin to understand how I have suffered for you since this happened, and how I have blamed myself."

He got up suddenly and strode over to the window, frowning down into the sunlit street, and wondering how it was that everybody seemed to be going on in exactly the same hurry as ever, when for him life had suddenly come to a standstill.

16

THE room was very still. The girl did not even sob. He turned after a moment and went back to that bowed golden head there in the deep crimson chair.

"Look here," he said, "I know you can't ever forgive me. I don't expect it! I don't deserve it! But please don't feel so awfully about it. I'll explain it all to every one. I'll make it all right for you. I'll take every bit of blame on myself, and get plenty of witnesses to prove all about it—"

The girl looked up with sorrow and surprise in her wet eyes.

"Why, I do not blame you," she said, mournfully. "I cannot see how you were to blame. It was no one's fault. It was just an unusual happening—a strange set of circumstances. I could not blame you. There is nothing to forgive, and if there were I would gladly forgive it!"

"Then what on earth makes you look so white and feel so distressed?" he asked in a distracted voice, as a man will sometimes look and talk to the woman he loves when she becomes a tearful problem of despair to his obtuse eyes.

"Oh, don't you know?"

---

"No, I don't," he said. "You're surely not mourning for that brute of a man to whom you had promised to sacrifice your life?"

She shook her head, and buried her face in her hands again. He could see that the tears were dropping between her fingers, and they seemed to fall red hot upon his heart.

"Then what is it?" His tone was almost sharp in its demand, but she only cried the harder. Her slender shoulders were shaking with her grief now.

He put his hand down softly and touched her bowed head.

"Won't you tell me, Dear?" he breathed, and, stooping, knelt beside her.

The sobs ceased, and she was quite still for a moment, while his hand still lay on her hair with that gentle, pleading touch.

"It is — because you married me — in — that way — without knowing — Oh, can't you see how terrible — "

Oh, the folly and blindness of love! Gordon got up from his knees as if she had stung him.

"You need not feel bad about that any more," he said in a hurt tone. "Did I not tell you I would set you free at once? Surely no one in his senses could call you bound after such circumstances."

She was very still for an instant, as if he had struck her, and then she raised her golden head, and a pair of sweet eyes suddenly grown haughty.

"You mean that *I* will set *you* free!" she said coldly. "I could not think of letting you be bound by a misunderstanding when you were under great stress of mind. You were in no wise to blame. *I* will set *you* free."

"As you please," he retorted bitterly, turning toward the window again. "It all amounts to the same thing. There is nothing for you to feel bad about."

"Yes, there is," she answered, with a quick rush of feeling that broke through her assumed haughtiness. "I shall always feel that I have broken in upon your life. You have had a most trying experience with me, and you never can quite forget it. Things won't be the same—"

She paused and the quiet tears chased each other eloquently down her face.

"No," said Gordon still bitterly; "things will never be the same for me. I shall always see you sitting there in my chair. I shall always be missing you from it! But I am glad—glad. I would never have known what I missed if it had not been for this." He spoke almost savagely.

He did not look around, but she was staring at him in astonishment, her blue eyes suddenly alight.

"What do you mean?" she asked softly.

He wheeled around upon her. "I mean that I shall never forget you; that I do not want to forget you. I should rather have had these two days of your sweet company, than all my lifetime in any other companionship."

"Oh!" she breathed. "Then, why—why did you say what you did about being free?"

"I didn't say anything about being free that I remember. It was you that said that."

"I said I would set you free. I could not, of course, hold you to a bond you did not want—"

"But I did not say I did not want it. I said I would not hold you if *you* did not want to stay."

"Do you mean that if you had known me a little—that is, just as much as you know me now—and had come in there and found out your mistake before it was too late, that you would have *wanted* to go on with it?"

She waited for his answer breathlessly.

"If you had known me just as much as you do now, and had looked up and seen that it was I and not George Hayne you were marrying, would *you* have wanted to go on and be married?"

Her cheeks grew rosy and her eyes confused.

"I asked you first," she said, with just a flicker of a smile.

He caught the shimmer of light in her eyes, and came toward her eagerly, his own face all aglow now with a dawning understanding.

"Darling," he said, "I can go farther than you have asked. From the first minute my eyes rested upon your face under that mist of white veil I wished with all my heart that I might have known you before any other man had found and won you. When you turned and looked at me with that deep sorrow in your eyes, you pledged me with every fibre of my being to fight for you. I was yours from that instant. And when your little hand was laid in mine, my heart went out in longing to have it stay in mine forever. I know now, as I did not understand then, that the real reason for my not doing something to make known my identity at that instant was not because I was afraid of any of the things that might happen, or any scene I might make, but because my heart was fighting for the right to keep what had been given me out of the unknown. You are my wife, by every law of heaven and earth, if your heart will but say yes. I love you, as I never knew a man could love, and yet if you do not want to stay with me I will set you free; but it is true that I should never be the same, for I am married to you in my heart, and always shall be. Darling, look up and answer my question now."

He stood before her with outstretched arms, and for answer she rose and came to him slowly, with downcast eyes.

"I do not want to be set free," she said.

Then gently, tenderly, he folded his arms about her, as if she were too precious to handle roughly, and laid his lips upon hers.

It was the shrill, insistent clang of the telephone bell that broke in upon their bliss. For a moment Gordon let it ring, but its merciless clatter was not to be denied; so, drawing Celia close within his arm, he made her come with him to the 'phone.

To his annoyance, the haughty voice of Miss Bentley answered him from the little black distance of the 'phone.

His arm was about Celia, and she felt his whole body stiffen with formality.

"Oh, Miss Bentley! Good morning! Your message? Why no! Ah! Well, I have but just come in—"

A pause during which Celia, panic-stricken, handed him the paper on which she had written Julia's message.

"Ah! Oh, yes, I have the message. Yes, it is very kind of you—" he murmured stiffly, "but you will have to excuse me. No, really. It is utterly impossible! I have another engagement—" his arm stole closer around Celia's waist and caught her hand, holding it with a meaningful pressure. He smiled, with a grimace toward the telephone which gladdened her heart. "Pardon me, I didn't hear that," he went on. . . . "Oh, give up my engagement and come? . . . Not possibly!" His voice rang with a glad, decided force, and he held still closer the soft fingers in his hand. . . . "Well, I'm sorry you feel that way about it. I certainly am not trying to be disagreeable. No, I could not come to-morrow night either. . . . I cannot make any plan for the next few days. . . . I may have to leave town again. . . . It is quite possible I may have to return to New York. Yes, business has been very pressing. I hope you will excuse me. I am sorry to disappoint you. No, of course I didn't do it on purpose. I shall have some pleasant news to tell you when I see you again—or—" with a glance of deep love at Celia, "perhaps I shall find means to let you know of it before I see you."

The color came and went in Celia's cheeks. She understood what he meant and nestled closer to him.

"No, no, I could not tell it over the 'phone. No, it will keep. Good things will always keep if they are well cared for you know. No, really I can't. And I'm very sorry to disappoint you to-night, but it can't be helped. . . . Good-by."

He hung up the receiver with a sigh of relief.

"Who is Miss Bentley?" asked Celia, with natural interest. She was pleased that he had not addressed her as "Julia."

"Why, she is—a friend—I suppose you would call her. She

has been taking possession of my time lately rather more than I really enjoyed. Still, she is a nice girl. You'll like her, I think; but I hope you'll never get too intimate. I shouldn't like to have her continually around. She—" he paused and finished, laughing—"she makes me tired."

"I was afraid, from her tone when she 'phoned you, that she was a very dear friend—that she might be some one you cared for. There was a sort of proprietorship in her tone."

"Yes, that's the very word, proprietorship," he laughed. "I couldn't care for her. I never did. I tried to consider her in that light one day, because I'd been told repeatedly that I ought to settle down, but the thought of having her with me always was—well—intolerable. The fact is, you reign supreme in a heart that has never loved another girl. I didn't know there was such a thing as love like this. I knew I lacked something, but I didn't know what it was. This is greater than all the gifts of life, this gift of your love. And that it should come to me in this beautiful, unsought way seems too good to be true!"

He drew her to him once more and looked down into her lovely face, as if he could not drink enough of its sweetness.

"And to think you are willing to be my wife! My wife!" and he folded her close again.

A discreet tap on the door announced the arrival of the man Henry, and Gordon roused to the necessity of ordering lunch.

"Come in a minute, Henry," he said. "This is my wife. I hope you will henceforth take her wishes as your special charge, and do for her as you have done so faithfully for me."

The man's eyes shone with pleasure as he bowed low before the gentle lady.

"I is very glad to heah it, sah, and I offers you my congratchumlations, sah, and de lady, too. She can't find no bettah man in the whole United States dan Mars' Gordon. I's mighty glad you done got ma'ied, sah, an' I hopes you bof have a mighty fine life."

The luncheon was served in Henry's best style, and his dark face shone as he stepped noiselessly about, putting silver and china and glass in place, and casting admiring glances at the lady, who stood holding the little miniature in her hand and asking questions with a gentle voice:

"Your mother, you say? How dear she is! And she died so long ago! You never knew her? Oh, how strange and sweet and pitiful to have a beautiful girl-mother like that!"

She put out her hand to his in the shelter of the deep window, and they thought Henry did not see the look and touch that passed between them; but he discreetly averted his eyes and smiled benignly at the salt-cellars and the celery he was arranging. Then he hurried out to a florist's next door and returned with a dozen white roses, which he arranged in a queer little crystal pitcher, one of the few articles belonging to his mother that Gordon possessed. It had never been used before, except to stand on the mantel.

It was after they had finished their delightful luncheon, and Henry had cleared the table and left the room, that Gordon remarked:

"I wonder what has become of George Hayne? Do you suppose he means to try to make trouble?"

Celia's hands fluttered to her throat with a little gesture of fear.

"Oh!" she said. "I had forgotten him! How terrible! He will do *something,* of course. He will do *everything.* He will probably carry out all his threats. How could I have forgotten! Perhaps Mamma is now in great distress. What can we do? What can *I* do?"

"Don't be frightened," he soothed her. "He cannot do anything very dreadful, and if he tries we'll soon silence him. What he has written in those letters is blackmail. He is simply a big coward, who will run and hide as soon as he is exposed. He thought you did not understand law, and so took advantage of you. I'm sure I can silence him."

"Oh, do you think so? But Mamma! Poor Mamma! It will

kill her! And George will stop at nothing when he is crossed. I have known him too long. It will be *terrible* if he carries out his threat." Tears were in her eyes, agony was in her face.

"We must telephone your mother at once and set her heart at rest. Then we can find out just what ought to be done," said Gordon soothingly. "It was unforgivably thoughtless in me not to have done it before."

Celia's face was radiant at the thought of speaking to her mother.

"Oh, how beautiful! Why didn't I think of that before? What perfectly dear things telephones are!"

With one accord, they went to the telephone table.

"Shall you call them up, or shall I?" he asked.

"You call, and then I will speak to Mamma," she said, her eyes shining with her joy in him. "I want them to hear your voice again. They can't help knowing you are all right when they hear your voice."

For that, he gave her a glance very much worth having.

"Just how do you account for the fact that you didn't think I was all right yesterday afternoon? I have a very realizing sense that you didn't. I used my voice to the best of my ability, but it did no good then."

"Well, you see, that was different! There were those letters to be accounted for. Mamma and Jeff don't know anything about the letters."

"And what are you going to tell them now?"

She drew her brows down a minute and thought.

"You'd better find out how much they already know," he suggested. "If this George Hayne hasn't turned up yet, perhaps you can wait until you can write, or we might be able to go up to-morrow and explain it ourselves."

"Oh, could we? How lovely!"

"I think we could," said Gordon. "I'm sure I can make it possible. Of course, you know a wedding journey isn't exactly in the program of the Secret Service, but I might be able to work them for one. I surely can in a few days if this Holman business doesn't hold me up. I may be needed for a witness. I'll have to talk with the chief first."

"Oh, how perfectly beautiful! Then you call them up, and just say something pleasant—anything, you know, and then say I'll speak to Mamma."

She gave him the number, and in a few minutes a voice from New York said, "Hello!"

"Hello!" called Gordon. "Is this Mr. Jefferson Hathaway? . . . Well, this is your new brother-in-law. How are you all? . . . Your mother recovered from all the excitement and weariness? . . . That's good. . . . What's that? . . . You've been trying to 'phone us in Chicago? . . . But we're not in Chicago. We changed our minds and came to Washington instead. . . . Yes, we're in Washington—The Harris Apartments. We have been very selfish not to have communicated with you sooner. At least I have. Celia hasn't had any choice in the matter. I've kept her so busy. Yes, she's very well, and seems to look happy. She wants to speak for herself. I'll try to arrange to bring her up to-morrow for a little visit. I want to see you too. We've a lot of things to explain to you. . . . Here is Celia. She wants to speak to you."

Celia, her eyes shining, her lips quivering with suppressed excitement, took the receiver.

"Oh, Jeff dear, it's good to hear your voice," she said. "Is everything all right? Yes, I've been having a perfectly beautiful time, and I've something fine to tell you. All those nice things you said to me just before you got off the train are true. Yes, he's just as nice as you said, and a great deal nicer besides. Oh, yes, I'm very happy, and I want to speak to Mamma please. Jeff, is she all right? Is she *perfectly* well, and not fretting a bit? You know you promised to tell me. What's that? She thought I looked sad? Well, I did but that's all gone now. Everything is perfectly beautiful. Tell mother to come to the 'phone please—I want to make her understand."

"I'm going to tell her, dear," she whispered, looking up at

Gordon. "I'm afraid George will get there before we do and make her worry."

For answer he stooped and kissed her, his arm encircling her and drawing her close. "Whatever you think best, dearest," he whispered back.

"Is that you, Mamma?" With a happy smile she turned back to the 'phone. "Dear Mamma! Yes, I'm all safe and happy, and I'm sorry you have worried. We won't let you do it again. But listen; I've something to tell you, a surprise—Mamma, I did not marry George Hayne at all. No, I say I *did not* marry George Hayne at all. George Hayne is a wicked man. I can't tell you about it over the 'phone but that was why I looked sad. Yes, I was *married* all right, but not to George. He's oh, so different, Mother you can't think. He's right here beside me now, and Mother, he is just as dear—you'd be very happy about him if you could see him. What did you say? Didn't I mean to marry George? Why Mother, I never wanted to. I was awfully unhappy about it, and I knew I made you feel so too, though I tried not to. But I'll explain all about it. . . . No, there's nothing whatever for you to worry about. Everything is right now and life looks more beautiful to me than it ever did before. What's his name? Oh;" she looked up at Gordon with a funny little expression of dismay. She had forgotten and he whispered it in her ear.

"Cyril—"

"It's Cyril, Mother! Isn't that a pretty name! Which name? Oh, the first name of course. That last name?"

"Gordon—" he supplied in her ear again.

"Cyril Gordon, Mother," she said, giggling in spite of herself at her strange predicament. . . . "Yes, Mother. I am very, very happy. I couldn't be happier unless I had you and Jeff, too, and"—she paused, hesitating at the unaccustomed name,—"and Cyril says we're coming to visit you tomorrow. We'll come up and see you and explain everything. And you're not to worry about George Hayne if he comes.

Just let Jeff put him off by telling him you have sent for me, or something of the sort, and don't pay any attention to what he says. What? You say he did come? How strange — and he hasn't been back? I'm so thankful. He is dreadful. Oh, Mother, you don't know what I've escaped! And Cyril is good and dear. What? You want to speak to him? All right. He's right here. Good-by, Mother, dear, till to-morrow. And you'll promise not to worry about anything? All right. Here is — Cyril."

Gordon took the receiver.

"Mother, I'm taking good care of her, just as I promised, and I'm going to bring her for a flying visit up to see you to-morrow. Yes, I'll take good care of her. She is very dear to me. The best thing that ever came into my life."

Then a mother's blessing came thrilling over the wires, and touched the handsome, manly face with tenderness.

"Thank you," he said. "I shall try always to make you glad you said those words."

They returned to looking in each other's eyes, after the receiver was hung up, as if they had been parted a long time. It seemed somehow as if their joy must be greater than any other married couple, because they had all their courting yet to do. It was beautiful to think of what was before them.

There was so much on both sides to be told; and to be told over again because only half had been told; and there were so many hopes and experiences to be exchanged; so many opinions to compare, and to rejoice over because they were alike on many essentials. Then there were the rooms to be gone through, and Gordon's pictures and favorite books to look at and talk about, and plans for the future to be touched upon — just barely touched upon.

The apartment would do until they could look about and get a house, Gordon said, his heart swelling with the proud thought that at last he would have a real home, like his other married friends, with a real princess to preside over it.

Then Celia had to tell all about the horror of the last three months, with the unpleasant shadows of the preceding years back of it. She told this in the dusk of the evening, before Henry had come in to light up, and before they had realized that it was almost dinner-time. She told it with her face hidden on her husband's shoulder, and his arms close about her, to give her comfort at each revelation of the story. They tried also to plan what to do about George Hayne; and then there was the whole story of Gordon's journey and commission from the time the old chief had called him into the office until he came to stand beside her at the church altar and they were married. It was told in careful detail with all the comical, exasperating and pitiful incidents of white dog and little newsboy; but the strangest part about it all was that Gordon never said one word about Julia Bentley and her imaginary presence with him that first day, and he never even knew that he had left out an important detail.

Celia laughed over the white dog and declared they must bring him home to live with them; and she cried over the story of the brave little newsboy and was eager to visit him in New York, promising herself all sorts of pleasure in taking him gifts and permanently bettering his condition; and it was in this way that Gordon incidentally learned that his wife had a fortune in her own right, a fact that for a time gave him great uneasiness of mind until she had soothed him and laughed at him for an hour or more; for Gordon was an independent creature and had ideas about supporting his wife by his own toil. Besides, it seemed an unfair advantage to have taken a wife and a fortune as it were unaware.

But Celia's fortune had not spoiled her, and she soon made him see that it had always been a mere incident in her scheme of living; a comfortable and pleasant incident to be sure, but still an incident to be kept always in the background, and never for a moment to be a cause for self-congratulation or pride.

Gordon found himself dreading the explanation that would have to come when he reached New York and faced

his wife's mother and brother. Celia had accepted his explanations, because, somehow by the beautiful ways of the
spirit, her soul had found and believed in his soul before the
truth was made known to her, but would her mother and
brother be able also to believe? And he fell to planning with
Celia just how he should tell the story; and this led to his
bringing out a number of letters and papers that would be
worth while showing as credentials, and every step of the
way, as Celia got glimpse after glimpse into his past, her face
shone with joy and her heart leaped with the assurance that
her lot had been cast in goodly places, for she perceived not
only that this man was honored and respected in high places,
but that his early life had been peculiarly pure and true.

The strange loneliness that had surrounded his young
manhood seemed suddenly to have broken ahead of him,
and to have opened out into the glory of the companionship of one peculiarly fitted to fill the need of his life. Thus
they looked into one another's eyes reading their life-joy, and
entered into the beautiful miracle of acquaintanceship.

17

THE next morning quite early the 'phone called Gordon to the office. The chief's secretary said the matter was urgent.

He hurried away leaving Celia somewhat anxious lest their plans for going to New York that day could not be carried out, but she made up her mind not to fret even if the trip had to be put off a little, and solaced herself with a short visit with her mother over the telephone.

Gordon entered his chief's office a trifle anxiously, for he felt that in justice to his wife he ought to take her right back to New York and get matters there adjusted; but he feared that there would be business to hold him at home until the Holman matter was settled.

The chief greeted him affably and bade him sit down.

"I am sorry to have called you up so early," he said, "but we need you. The fact is, they've arrested Holman and five other men, and you are in immediate demand to identify them. Would it be asking too much of an already over-worked man to send you back to New York to-day?"

Gordon almost sprang from his seat in pleasure.

"It just exactly fits in with my plans, or, rather, my wishes," he said, smiling. "There are several matters of my own that

I would like to attend to in New York and for which of course I did not have time."

He paused and looked at his chief, half hesitating, marvelling that the way had so miraculously opened for him to keep silence a little longer on the subject of his marriage. Perhaps the chief need never be told that the marriage ceremony took place on the day of the Holman dinner.

"That is good," said the chief, smiling. "You certainly have earned the right to attend to your own affairs. Then we need not feel so bad at having to send you back. Can you go on the afternoon train? Good! Then let us hear your account of your trip briefly, to see if there are any points we didn't notice yesterday. But first just step here a moment. I have something to show you."

He flung open the door to the next office.

"You knew that Ferry had left the Department on account of his ill-health? I have taken the liberty of having your things moved in here. This will hereafter be your headquarters, and you will be next to me in the Department."

Gordon turned in amazement and gazed at the kindly old face. Promotion he had hoped for, but such promotion, right over the heads of his elders and superiors, he had never dreamed of receiving. He could have taken the chief in his arms.

"Pooh! Pooh!" said the chief. "You deserve it, you deserve it!" when Godon tried to blunder out some words of appreciation. Then, as if to cap the climax, he added:

"And, by the way, you know some one has got to run across the water to look after that Stanhope matter. That will fall to you, I'm afraid. Sorry to keep you trotting around the globe, but perhaps you'll like to make a little vacation of it. The Department'll give you some time if you want it. Oh, don't thank me! It's simply the reward of doing your duty, to have more duties given you, and higher ones. You have done well, young man. I have here all the papers in the Stanhope case, and full directions written out, and then if you can plan for it you needn't return, unless it suits your pleasure. You understand the matter as fully as I do already. And now for business. Let's hurry through. There are one or two little matters we must talk over and I know you will want to hurry back and get ready for your journey." And so after all the account of Gordon's extraordinary escape and eventful journey home became by reason of its hasty repetition a most prosaic story composed of the bare facts and not all of those.

At parting the chief pressed Gordon's hand with heartiness and ushered him out into the hall, with the same brusque manner he used to close all business interviews, and Gordon found himself hurrying through the familiar halls in a daze of happiness, the secret of his unexpected marriage still his own—and hers.

Celia was watching at the window when his key clicked in the lock and he let himself into the apartment his face alight with the joy of meeting her again after the brief absence. She turned in a quiver of pleasure at his coming.

"Well, get ready," he said joyfully. "We are ordered off to New York on the afternoon train, with a wedding trip to Europe into the bargain; and I'm promoted to the next place to the chief. What do you think of that for a morning's surprise?"

He tossed up his hat like a boy, came over to where she stood, and stooping laid reverent lips upon her brow and eyes.

"Oh, beautiful! Lovely!" cried Celia, ecstatically. "Come sit down on the couch and tell me all about it. We can work faster afterward if we get it off our minds. Was your chief much shocked that you were married without his permission or knowledge?"

"Why, that was the best of all. I didn't have to tell him I was married. And he is not to know until just as I sail. He need never know how it all happened. It isn't his business and it would be hard to explain. No one need ever know except your mother and brother unless you wish them to, dear."

"Oh, I am so glad and relieved," said Celia, delightedly. "I've been worrying about that a little, —what people would think of us, —for of course we couldn't possibly explain it all out as it is to us. They would always be watching us to see if we really cared for each other; and suspecting that we didn't, and it would be horrid. I think it is our own precious secret, and nobody but Mamma and Jeff have a right to know, don't you?"

"I certainly do, and I was casting about in my mind as I went into the office how I could manage not to tell the chief, when what did he do but spring a proposition on me to go at once to New York and identify those men. He apologized tremendously for having to send me right back again, but said it was necessary. I told him it just suited me for I had affairs of my own that I had not had time to attend to when I was there, and would be glad to go back and see to them. That let me out on the wedding question for it would be only necessary to tell him I was married when I got back. He would never ask when."

"But the announcements," said Celia catching her breath laughingly, "I never thought of that. We'll just have to have some kind of announcements or my friends will not understand about my new name; and we'll have to send him one, won't we?"

"Why, I don't know. Couldn't we get along without announcements? You can explain to your intimate friends, and the others won't ever remember the name after a few months—we'll not be likely to meet many of them right away. I'll write to my chief and tell him informally leaving out the date entirely. He won't miss it. If we have announcements at all we needn't send him one. He wouldn't be likely ever to see one any other way, or to notice the date. I think we can manage that matter. We'll talk it over with your—" he hesitated and then smiling tenderly added, "we'll talk it over with *Mother*. How good it sounds to say that. I never knew my mother, you know."

Celia nestled her hands in his and murmured, "Oh, I am so happy, — so happy! But I don't understand how you got a wedding trip without telling your chief about our marriage."

"Easy as anything. He asked me if I would mind running across the water to attend to a matter for the Service and said I might have extra time while there for a vacation. He never suspects that vacation is to be used as a wedding trip. I'll write him, or 'phone him the night we leave New York. I may have to stay in the city two or three days to get this Holman matter settled, and then we can be off. In the meantime you can spend the time reconciling your mother to her new son. Do you think we'll have a very hard time explaining matters to her?"

"Not a bit," said Celia, gaily. "She never did like George. It was the only thing we ever disagreed about, my marrying him. She suspected all the time I wasn't happy and couldn't understand why I insisted on marrying him when I hadn't seen him for ten years. She begged me to wait until he had been back in the country for a year or two, but he would not hear to such a thing and threatened to carry out his worst at once."

Gordon's heart suddenly contracted with righteous wrath over the cowardliness of the man who sought to gain his own ends by intimidating a woman — and this woman, so dear, so beautiful, so lovely in her nature. It seemed the man's heart must indeed be black to have done what he did. He mentally resolved to search him out and bring him to justice as soon as he reached New York. It puzzled him to understand how easily he seemed to have abandoned his purposes. Perhaps after all he was more of a coward than they thought, and had not dared to remain in the country when he found that Celia had braved his wrath and married another man. He would find out about him and set the girl's heart at rest just as soon as possible, that any embarrassment at some future time might be avoided. Gordon stooped and

kissed his wife again, a caress that seemed to promise all reparation for the past.

But it suddenly occurred to the two that trains did not wait
for lovers' long loitering, and with one accord they went to
work. Celia of course had very little preparation to make.
Her trunk was probably in Chicago and would need to be
wired for. Gordon attended to that the first thing, looking
up the number of the check and ordering it back to New
York by telegraph. Turning from the telephone he rang for
the man and asked Celia to give the order for lunch while
he got together some things that he must take with him. A
stay of several weeks would necessitate a little more baggage
than he had taken to New York.

He went into the bedroom and began pulling out things
to pack but when Celia turned from giving her directions
she found him standing in the bedroom doorway with an
old-fashioned velvet jewel case in his hand which he had just
taken from the little safe in his room. His face wore a wonderful tender light as if he had just discovered something
precious.

"Dear," he said. "I wonder if you will care for these. They
were mother's. Perhaps this ring will do until I can buy you
a new one. See if it will fit you. It was my mother's."

He held out a ring containing a diamond of singular purity and brilliance in quaint old-fashioned setting.

Celia put out her hand with its wedding ring, the ring that
he had put upon her finger at the altar, and he slipped the
other jewelled one above it. It fitted perfectly.

"It is a beauty," breathed Celia, holding out her hand to
admire it, "and I would far rather have it than a new one. Your
dear little mother!"

"There's not much else here but a little string of pearls and
a pin or two. I have always kept them near me. Somehow
they seemed like a link between me and mother. I was keeping them for — " he hesitated and then giving her a rare smile
he finished:

"I was keeping them for you."

Her answering look was eloquent, and needed no words, which was well, for Henry appeared at that moment to serve luncheon and remind his master that his train left in a little over two hours. There was no further time for sentiment.

And yet, these two, it seemed, could not be practical that day. They idled over their luncheon and dawdled over their packing, stopping to look at this and that picture or bit of bric-a-brac that Gordon had picked up in some of his travels; and Henry finally had to take things in his own hands, pack them off and send their baggage after them. Henry was a capable man and rejoiced to see the devotion of his master and his new mistress, but he had a practical head and knew where his part came in.

18

THE journey back to New York seemed all too brief for the two whose lives had just been blended so unexpectedly, and every mile was filled with a new and sweet discovery of delight in one another; and then, when they reached the city they rushed in on Mrs. Hathaway and the eager young Jeff like two children who had so much to tell they did not know where to begin.

Mrs. Hathaway settled the matter by insisting on their going to dinner immediately and leaving all explanations until afterward; and with the servants present of course there was little that could be said about the matter that each one had most at heart. But there was a spirit of deep happiness in the atmosphere and one couldn't possibly entertain any fears under the influence of the radiant smiles that passed between mother and daughter, husband and wife, brother and sister.

As soon as the meal was concluded the mother led them up to her private sitting room, and closing the door she stood facing them all as half breathless with the excitement of the moment they stood in a row before her:

"My three dear children!" she murmured. Gordon's eyes

lit with joy and his heart thrilled with the wonder of it all. Then the mother stepped up to him and placing her hand on his arm led him over to the couch and made him sit beside her, while the brother and sister sat down together close by.

"Now, Cyril, my new son," said she, deliberately, her eyes resting approvingly upon his face, "you may tell me your story. I see my girl has lost both head and heart to you and I doubt if she could tell it connectedly."

And while Celia and Jeff were laughing at this, Gordon set about his task of winning a mother, and incidentally an eager-eyed young brother who was more than half committed to his cause already.

Celia watched proudly as her handsome husband took out his credentials, and began his explanation.

"First, I must tell you who I am, and these papers will do it better than I could. Will you look at them, please?"

He handed her a few letters and papers.

"These papers on the top show the rank and position that my father and my grandfather held with the government and in the army. This is a letter from the president to my father congratulating him on his approaching marriage with my mother. That paper contains my mother's family tree, and the letters with it will give an idea of the honor in which my mother's family was held in Washington and in Virginia, her old home. I know these matters are not of much moment, and say nothing whatever about what I am myself, but they are things you would have been likely to know about my family if you had known me all my life; and at least they will tell you that my family was respectable."

Mrs. Hathaway was examining the papers, and suddenly looked up exclaiming: "My dear! My father knew your grandfather. I think I saw him once when he came to our home in New York. It was years ago and I was a young girl, but I remember he was a fine looking man with keen dark eyes and a heavy head of iron gray hair."

She looked at Gordon keenly.

"I wonder if your eyes are not like his. It was long ago of course."

"They used to say I looked like him. I do not remember him. He died when I was very young."

The mother looked up with a pleased smile.

"Now tell me about yourself," she said and laid a gentle hand on his.

Gordon looked down, an embarrassed flush spreading over his face.

"There's nothing great to tell," he said. "I've always tried to live a straight true life, and I've never been in love with any girl before —" he flashed a wonderful, blinding smile upon Celia.

"I was left alone in the world when quite young and have lived around in boarding-schools and college. I'm a graduate of Harvard and I've travelled a little. There was some money left from my father's estate, not much. I'm not rich. I'm a Secret Service man, and I love my work. I get a good salary and was this morning promoted to the position next in rank to my chief, so that now I shall have still more money. I shall be able to make your daughter comfortable and give her some of the luxuries, if not all, to which she has been accustomed."

"My dear boy, that part is not what I am anxious about —" interrupted the mother.

"I know," said Gordon, "But it is a detail you have a right to be told. I understand that you care far more what I am than how much money I can make, and I promise you I am going to try to be all that you would want your daughter's husband to be. Perhaps the best thing I can say for myself is that I love her better than my life, and I mean to make her happiness the dearest thing in life to me."

The mother's look of deep understanding answered him more eloquently than words could have done, and after a moment she spoke again.

"But I do not understand how you could have known one another and I never have heard of you. Celia is not good at keeping things from her mother, though the last three months she has had a sadness that I could not fathom, and was forced to lay to her natural dread of leaving home. She seemed so insistent upon having this marriage just as George planned it—and I was so afraid she would regret not waiting. How could you have known one another all this time and she never talked to me about it, and why did George Hayne have any part whatever in it if you two loved one another? Just how long have you known each other any way? Did it begin when you visited in Washington last spring, Celia?"

With dancing eyes Celia shook her head.

"No, Mamma. If I had met him then I'm sure George Hayne would never had had anything to do with the matter, for Cyril would have known how to help me out of my difficulty."

"I shall have to tell you the whole story from my standpoint, and from the beginning," said Gordon, dreading now that the crisis was upon him, what the outcome would be. "I have wanted you to know who and what I was before you know the story, that you might judge me as kindly as possible, and know that however I may have been to blame in the matter it was through no intention of mine. My story may sound rather impossible. I know it will seem improbable, but it is nevertheless true, everything that I have to tell. May I hope to be believed?"

"I think you may," answered the mother searching his face anxiously. "Those eyes of yours are not lying eyes."

"Thank you," he said simply, and then gathering all his courage he plunged into his story.

Mrs. Hathaway was watching him with searching interest. Jeff had drawn his chair up close and could scarcely restrain his excitement, and when Gordon told of his commission he burst forth explosively:

"Gee! But that was a great stunt! I'd have liked to have been along with you! You must be simply great to be trusted with a thing like that!"

But his mother gently reproved him:

"Hush, my son, let us hear the story."

Celia sat quietly watching her husband with pride, two bright spots of color of her cheeks, and her hands clasping each other tightly. She was hearing many details now that were new to her. Once more, when Gordon mentioned the dinner at Holman's Jeff interrupted with:

"Holman! Holman! Not J. P.? Why of course — we know him! Celia was one of his daughter's bridesmaids last spring! The old lynx! I always thought he was crooked! People hint a lot of things about him—"

"Jeff, dear, let us hear the story," again insisted his mother, and the story continued.

Gordon had been looking down as he talked. He dreaded to see their faces as the truth should dawn upon them, but when he had told all he lifted honest eyes to the white-faced mother and pleaded with her:

"Indeed, indeed, I hope you will believe me, that not until they laid your daughter's hand in mine did I know that I was supposed to be the bridegroom. I thought all the time her brother was the bridegroom. If I had not been so distraught, and trying so hard to think how to escape, I suppose I would have noticed that I was standing next to her, and that everything was peculiar about the whole matter, but I didn't. And then when I suddenly knew that she and I were being married, what should I have done? Do you think I ought to have stopped the ceremony then and there and made a scene before all those people? What was the right thing to do? Suppose my commission had been entirely out of the question, and I had had no duty toward the government to keep entirely quiet about myself, do you think I ought to have made a scene? Would you have wanted me to for your daughter's sake? Tell me please," he insisted, gently.

And while she hesitated he added:

"I did some pretty hard thinking during that first quarter of a second that I realized what was happening, and I tell you honestly I didn't know what was the right thing to do. It seemed awful for her sake to make a scene, and to tell you the truth I worshipped her from the moment my eyes rested upon her. There was something sad and appealing as she looked at me that seemed to pledge my very life to save her from trouble. Tell me, do you think I ought to have stopped the ceremony then at the first moment of my realization that I was being married?"

The mother's face had softened as she watched him and listened to his tender words about Celia and now she answered gently:

"I am not sure — perhaps not! It was a very grave question to face. I don't know that I can blame you for doing nothing. It would have been terrible for her and us and everybody and have made it all so public. Oh, I think you did right not to do anything publicly — perhaps — and yet — it is terrible to me to think you have been forced to marry my daughter in that way."

"Please do not say forced, —" said Gordon laying both hands earnestly upon hers and looking into her eyes, "I tell you one thing that held me back from doing anything was that I so earnestly desired that what I was passing through might be real and lasting. I have never seen one like her before. I know that if the mistake had been righted and she had passed out of my life I should never have felt the same again. I am glad, glad with all my heart that she is mine, and — Mother! — I think she is glad too!"

The mother turned toward her daughter, and Celia with starry eyes came and knelt before them, and laid her hands in the hands of her husband, saying with ringing voice:

"Yes, dear little Mother, I am gladder than I ever was before in my life."

And kneeling thus, with her husband's arm about her, her

face against his shoulder, and both her hands clasped in his, she told her mother about the tortures that George Hayne had put her through, until the mother turned white with horror at what her beloved and cherished child had been enduring, and the brother got up and stormed across the floor, vowing vengeance on the luckless head of poor George Hayne.

Then after the mother had given her blessing to the two and Jeff had added an original one of his own, there was the whole story of the eventful wedding trip to tell, which they both told by solos and choruses until the hour grew alarmingly late and the mother suddenly sent them all off to bed.

The next few days were both busy and happy ones for the two. They went to the hospital and gladdened the life of the little newsboy with fruit and toys and many promises; and they brought home a happy white dog from his boarding place whom Jeff adopted as his own. Gordon had a trying hour or two at court with his one-time host, the scoundrel who had stolen the cipher message; and the thick-set man glared at him from a cell window as he passed along the corridor of the prison whither he had gone in search of George Hayne.

Gordon, in his search for the lost bridegroom, whom for many reasons he desired to find as soon as possible, had asked the help of one of the men at work on the Holman case, in searching for a certain George Hayne who needed very much to be brought to justice.

"Oh, you won't have to search for him," declared the man with a smile. "He's safely landed in prison three days ago. He was caught as neatly as rolling off a log by the son of the man whose name he forged several years ago. It was trust money of a big corporation and the man died in his place in a prison cell, but the son means to see the real culprit punished."

And so Gordon, in the capacity of Celia's lawyer, went to the prison to talk with George Hayne, and that miserable man found no excuse for his sins when the searching talk was over. Gordon did not let the man know who he was, and merely made it understood that Celia was married, and that if he attempted to make her any further trouble the whole thing would be exposed and he would have to answer a grave charge of blackmail.

The days passed rapidly, and at last the New York matter for which Gordon's presence was needed was finished, and he was free to sail away with his bride. On the morning of their departure Gordon's voice rang out over the miles of telephone wires to his old chief in Washington: "I am married and am just starting on my wedding trip. Don't you want to congratulate me?" And the old chief's gruff voice sounded back:

"Good work, old man! Congratulations for you both. She may or may not be the best girl in all the world; I haven't had a chance to see yet; but she's a lucky girl, for she's got *the best man I know.* Tell her that for me! Bless you both! I'm glad she's going with you. It won't be so lonesome."

Gordon gave her the message that afternoon as they sailed straight into the sunshine of a new and beautiful life together.

"Dear," he said, as he arranged her steamer rug more comfortably about her, "has it occurred to you that you are probably the only bride who ever married the best man at her wedding?"

Celia smiled appreciatively and after a minute replied mischievously:

"I suppose every bride *thinks* her husband is the best man."

## About the Author

Grace Livingston Hill is well known as one of the most pro-
lific writers of romantic fiction. Her personal life was fraught
with joys and sorrows not unlike those experienced by many
of her fictional heroines.

Born in Wellsville, New York, Grace nearly died during
the first hours of life. But her loving parents and friends
turned to God in prayer. She survived miraculously, thus her
thankful father named her Grace.

Grace was always close to her father, a Presbyterian minister, and her mother, a published writer. It was from them that
she learned the art of storytelling. When Grace was twelve, a
close aunt surprised her with a hardbound, illustrated copy of
one of Grace's stories. This was the beginning of Grace's
journey into being a published author.

In 1892 Grace married Fred Hill, a young minister, and
they soon had two lovely young daughters. Then came 1901,
a difficult year for Grace—the year when, within months of
each other, both her father and husband died. Suddenly Grace
had to find a new place to live (her home was owned by the
church where her husband had been pastor). It was a struggle
for Grace to raise her young daughters alone, but through

everything she kept writing. In 1902 she produced *The Angel of His Presence, The Story of a Whim,* and *An Unwilling Guest.* In 1903 her two books *According to the Pattern* and *Because of Stephen* were published.

It wasn't long before Grace was a well-known author, but she wanted to go beyond just entertaining her readers. She soon included the message of God's salvation through Jesus Christ in each of her books. For Grace, the most important thing she did was not write books but share the message of salvation, a message she felt God wanted her to share through the abilities he had given her.

In all, Grace Livingston Hill wrote more than one hundred books, all of which have sold thousands of copies and have touched the lives of readers around the world with their message of "enduring love" and the true way to lasting happiness: a relationship with God through his Son, Jesus Christ.

In an interview shortly before her death, Grace's devotion to her Lord still shone clear. She commented that whatever she had accomplished had been God's doing. She was only his servant, one who had tried to follow his teaching in all her thoughts and writing.

# *Grace*
# LIVINGSTON HILL
### AMERICA'S BEST-LOVED STORYTELLER

## *LADYBIRD*

**LIVING BOOKS®**
Tyndale House Publishers, Inc.
Wheaton, Illinois

This Tyndale House book
by Grace Livingston Hill
contains the complete text
of the original hardcover edition.
NOT ONE WORD
HAS BEEN OMITTED

FRALEY MacPherson stood in the open door of the cabin, looking out across the mountains. The peace of the morning was shining on them and the world looked clean and new made after the storm of the night before. She gave a little wistful sigh, her heart swelling with longing, and joy in the beauty, and a wish that life were all like that beauty spread out so wondrously before her.

For a moment she reveled in the Spring tints of the foliage, the tender buds of the trees like dots of coral over their tops, the pale green of the little new leaves, the deep darkness of the stalwart pines, that seemed like great plumy backgrounds for the more delicate tracery of the other trees that were getting their new season's foliage. Her glance swept every familiar point in the landscape, from the dim purple mountains in the distance, as far as eye could reach, with the high light of snow on the peaks, to the nearer ones, gaunt with rocks or furred with the tender green of the trees; then down to the foothills, and the valley below.

There was one place, off to the right, where her eyes never lingered. It was the way to the settlement, miles beyond, the trail that led past a sheer precipice, where her father had fallen to his death five months before. She always had to suppress a little shudder as she glanced past the ominous yawning cavern, that crept, it seemed to her sensitive gaze, nearer and nearer to the trail each month. It was the one spot in all the glorious panorama that spoiled the picture if she let herself see it, not only because of that terrible memory, but also because it was the way the men of the household came and went to and from the far off world.

Peace, and contentment came into Fraley's life only when the men of the household were gone somewhere into the world. Peace and contentment fled when they returned, terror and dismay remained.

The girl was good to look upon as she stood in the doorway, the sunshine on her golden hair that curled into a thousand ripples and caught the gleams of light till she looked like a piece of the morning herself.

Her eyes were bits of the sky, and the soft flush that came and went in her cheeks was like a wild mountain flower. She looked like a young flower herself as she stood there in her little faded shapeless frock, one bare foot poised on the toe behind the other bare heel— pretty feet, never cramped by shoes that were too tight for her, seldom covered by any shoe at all.

Her arms were round and smooth and white, one raised and resting against the door frame. The whole graceful little wild sweet figure, drenched with the morning and gazing into life, a fit subject for some great artist's brush.

Something of all this came into the weary mind of the dying woman who lay on the cot across the room and watched her, and a weak tear trickled down her pallid cheek.

Fraley's eyes were resting on a soft cloud now, that

nested in the hollow of a mountain just below its peak. She had eyes that could see heavenly things in clouds, and she loved to watch them as they trailed a glorious panorama among the peaks and decked themselves in the colors of the morning; or the blaze of white noon; or the vivid glory of the sunset. This cloud she was watching now had wreathed itself about until she saw in it a lovely mother, holding a little child in her arms. She smiled dreamily as the cloud mother smiled down at the little leaping babe in her arms, that, even as she watched, sank back into sleep, and became a soft billow of white upon the mountain. How the mother looked down and loved it, the little billow of cloud baby in her arms!

"Fraley!"

The voice was very weak, but the girl, anxious, startled, her smile fading quickly into alarm, turned with a start back to the sordid room and life with its steadily advancing sorrow that had been drawing nearer every hour now for tortuous days.

"Fraley."

The girl was at her mother's side in an instant, kneeling beside the crude cot.

"Yes, Mother?" There was pain in her voice, and a forced cheer. "You want some fresh water?"

"No, dear! Sit down close—I must tell you something—"

"Oh, don't talk, Mother!" protested the girl anxiously, "It always makes you cough so."

"I must!—Fraley—the time—is—going fast—now—It's almost run out."

"Oh, don't, Mother! You were better last night. You haven't coughed so much this morning. I asked that strange man last night to get word to a doctor. He promised. Maybe he will come before night!"

"No, Fraley, child! It's too late! No doctor can cure

me. Listen child—Don't let's waste words—Every minute is precious—I must tell you something—I ought to have told you before—Come close—I can't speak—so—loud."

The girl stayed her tears, and leaned close to the beloved lips, a wild fear growing in her eyes. Persistently she had tried to hide from herself the fact that this beloved mother, her only beloved in all the world, was going from her; tried not to think what her lot would be when she was gone.

Persistently now she put the thought from her and tried bravely to listen.

"Fraley—when I'm gone—you—can't stay here."

Fraley nodded, as if that had long been a settled fact between them.

"I hoped—I hoped—I always hoped I'd get strength to go with you and get away—somehow—only I never—did. I never found a way—nor money enough for us both—even for one—"

"Don't, Mother!" moaned the girl with a little quick catch in her breath—"don't *apologize*. As if I didn't know what you've been through. Just tell me what you want me to know, and don't bother with the rest. I *understand.*"

The feeble hand pressed the girl's strong one, and the pale lips tried to smile.

"Dear child!" she murmured, then struggled through a spell of coughing, lay panting a moment, and struggled on.

"There isn't enough—yet—not even for you—" she panted.

"I don't need money," scorned the young voice. "I can take care of myself."

"Oh, my dear!" sighed the woman, and then girded herself to go on.

"There's only fifteen dollars. It's in—three little gold fives. Never mind how I got it. I sold the heifer they thought went astray—to that stranger that rode up here two months ago. I had to bear a beating—but it gave me the last five. The first I brought out here to the wilderness with me and the second I got from the man who came here the day your father was killed. I—sold my wedding ring to him—but that was all he would give—"

"Oh, Mother! You oughtn't to talk," pleaded the girl, as the mother struggled with another fit of coughing.

"I must, dear! Don't hinder now—the time is so short!"

"Then tell it quick, Mother, and let's be over with it," cried the girl, lifting the sick woman's head tenderly and helping her to sip a little water from a tin cup that stood on a bench by the cot.

"It's here"—she pressed her hand over her heart, "sewed in the cloth—You must rip it out. Put it in the little clean bag I made for it, and tie it around your waist. If Brand Carter should lay his hands on it once you'd never see it again! Twice—he's tried to see if I had anything—once when he thought I was asleep. He suspected, I think. Take it now, Fraley, and fix it out of sight around your waist. Here, take the knife and rip the stitches—quick— You can't always tell if one of the men might come back! Go look down the mountain before you begin. Hurry!"

In a panic the girl sprang to the door, and gazed in the direction of the trail, but the morning simmered on in beauty, and not a human came in sight. A wild bird soared, smote the morning with his song—smote her young heart with sorrow. Oh, why did that bird have to sing now?

She sprang back and deftly cut the stitches. Through blinding tears she sewed the coins into the bit of girdle her mother had crudely made from a cotton salt bag—most of their clothing was made from bags, flour and salt and sometimes cotton sugar bags—and solemnly girded herself with it as her mother bade her.

"Now, Fraley," said the mother, when this was done to her satisfaction, "You're to guard that night and day. It won't be long till I'm gone. And you're not to think you must spend any of it on—me—on burying—or 1-like that—"

A sob from Fraley stopped her, and she laid a wasted hand upon the bright rough head that was buried in the flimsy bed cover.

"I know—little girl—Mother's little girl! That's hard—but—that's a *command!* Understand, Fraley? It's Mother's last wish!"

The girl choked out an assent.

"And you're not to stay for *anything* like that. It wouldn't be *safe!* Oh, I ought—to have got you out of here long ago! Only I—didn't see the way clear—I couldn't let you go—without me—You—were so young—!"

"I know, Mother dear, I know!" sobbed the girl, trying to smile bravely through her tears. "I wouldn't have gone—you know—not without you!"

"Well, I should have gone—we should have gone together long ago and found a nice place in the wilderness, if there wasn't any other way, a place where they would never think to look, where we could die together. That would have been better than this—than leaving you *here* all alone. You—all—alone!"

"Mother, don't blame yourself! Please! I can't bear it!"

A wild rabbit scurried across the silence in front of the cabin and a hawk in the sky circled great shadows that moved over the spot of sunshine on the cabin floor. Fraley with ears attuned to the slightest sound in her wide silent world, sprang up and darted to the door to survey the wilderness, then came back reassured.

"It's no one," she said, laying her firm young hand on the cold brow, "Now, Mother, can't you rest a little? You've talked too much."

"No, No!" protested the sick woman, "The time is going! I must finish! Fraley, go look behind the loose board under your bed. There's a bag there! Bring it! I want to show you! Quick!"

Fraley came back with a bundle of gray woolen cloth which she examined wonderingly.

"I made it from your father's old coat," explained the mother eagerly. "It's some worn, and there's a hole or two I had to darn, but it will be better than nothing."

"But what is it for, Mother?" asked the girl puzzled.

"It's a travelling bag for you when you start. It's all packed. See! I washed and mended your other things, and made a little best dress for you out of my old black satin one that had been put away in the hole under the floor since before you were born. It may not be in fashion now—but it's the best I could do. I cut it out when you were asleep, and sewed it while you gathered wood for the fire."

"Oh, Mother! And you so sick."

"I loved to do it, dear—I'd always thought—how some day—maybe I'd get where I could buy you—pretty things—maybe some day a white—wedding—dress! But now—!"

"Oh, Mother!" burst forth the girl with uncontrollable tears, "I shan't ever need a wedding dress! I don't *want* a wedding dress! I hate men! I hate the sight of them all. My father never made you happy! All the men around here only curse and get drunk and swear. I shall never get married—!"

"I'm sorry, dear child, you should never have known

all—this—sin, this terror—Oh, I dreamed I'd get you out of this—into a clean world some day! But I've failed—! There *are* good men—!"

Fraley set her lips, but said nothing. She doubted that there were good men.

"Fraley, we must hurry! My strength—is—going—fast."

"Don't talk Mother! Please."

"But I must! Look in the bag, child. I've put the old Book there! It's almost worn out, but I've sewed it in a cloth cover. Fraley—you'll stick to the old Book?"

"Yes, Mother, I promise. I'll never let anybody take it from me!"

"But if it should be lost—or stolen—Fraley, you've much of it in your heart. You'll never forsake it, Fraley?"

"Never, Mother. I promise!" said the girl solemnly.

"Well, then I'm satisfied!" sighed the mother, closing her eyes. "Now, child, hide the bag again! Everything is there I could give you. Even your father's picture and mine when we were married, and a few papers I've kept. Put them away, and come back—I want to tell you—what I've never told you before!"

Fraley obeyed trembling at what revelation might be coming.

"Come closer, child, I'm—short—of breath—again—And—I—must tell—I should have told—before—!"

Fraley nestled close, and held her mother's cold hand in hers.

"Child, I did a wrong and foolish thing—when I was a girl! I had a good home—I've never talked—much about it! I couldn't bear to! My heart was breaking for it—all the—time!"

Fraley held her mother's hand closer in sympathy.

"Child, I ran away from that home and got married.

I've never seen—nor heard—from any of—my own—since—"

There was a great sob like a gasp at the end of the words!

"Oh, Mother!" gasped the girl in wonder and sorrow, "Oh, Mother—if you'd only told me—I might have helped you more!"

"Fraley—darling—you have been everything! You have been wonderful! You have—been—my world—my life—! Oh, if I could take you with me where I am going—now! But—you'll *come?* You'll be *sure* and—come?"

"Yes, I'll come! That will be *everything*—for me, Mother!"

"But I—must—hurry on."

"Mother—did you have—" the girl hesitated, almost shyly, "Did you have a Mother like you? You told me once my grandmother was dead. Was she dead—when—you went?"

"Yes, child. She had been gone a year. You—think I would not have gone—if she—had been there? Well—perhaps—I do not know. I was young—and headstrong. Even before she went she warned me against Angus MacPherson. But I did not heed! Perhaps she worried herself into the grave about me. While she lived—I did not go with him—*much!* But—she knew where my heart—was turning! I was mad with impatience to be out—like other girls!"

Fraley listened as to a fairy story. *Her mother*, young and wild like that!

"Angus was young and handsome. He had dark curls, and a cleft in his chin—and he was very much—in love—with me—then—! No, child, you mustn't look like—*that!* You mustn't think—hard of *him!* He was—all right—always—till he took to drink—!"

"He didn't have to drink, Mother!" said the fierce young voice. "He must have known what drink was."

"Well—child—it came little by little! You don't understand. He never meant—to be like that—not when he started—He—was always wild and independent. He didn't care what folks thought—of him—but—he wasn't bad! Not bad! And when he came and told me he was in a hole—someone had framed him up to a life in the penitentiary—to cover a gang's doings—and that there wasn't any thing for him—but to—disappear—forever—I believed him! I believe him—yet, Fraley! He didn't do the robbing, nor he didn't forge the check—there's all the papers in the bag there to prove it! But he wouldn't go back—on one fellow—who had been—innocent! If he got free, and told the truth—the other boy—would have to bear it—and he had a sick old mother. He was like that, Fraley—your father was—he wouldn't go back on some one who had been—his friend!"

"But he went back *on you!*" said the fierce young voice again. "He brought you out away from everybody that loved you—and then—he treated you—!" the girl's voice broke in a sob of indignation.

"Not then, child—" pleaded the mother's voice. "He was tender and loving, but he put it up to me! It was either go with him then—or—never see him—again! Fraley—I—loved him—!"

"Don't mind me, Mother!" said the girl struggling for control of her feelings. She could remember the cruel blows he had given the frail mother. She could remember so many things!

"It was the drink that did it," pleaded the mother, reading the thoughts of the sensitive girl and struggling for breath as a paroxysm of coughing seized her.

The old dog trotted in from his wanderings after the

cow, snuffed around the cot lovingly and lay down with a soft thud of his paws on the bare floor. Fraley put the tin cup of water to her mother's lips again, and after a time she rallied:

"I—must—hurry!" she gasped as she lay back on the pillow. "I can't stand many more—like—that!"

"I wish you wouldn't," begged the girl, "What difference will it make? I love you—anyway—and I don't care anything about all the rest. It's you—you, I want. I can't bear to see you suffer!"

"No, child," the feeble hand lifted just the slightest in protest, "let—me—finish!"

Fraley's answer was a soft hand on the thin gray hair around her mother's temples.

"Go on, Mother dear!" she breathed softly.

"My father was a stern man, especially since my mother's death—" the sick woman whispered the story with the greatest difficulty. "He had said—if I—married—Angus—I need never—come back!"

The old dog heaved a deep sigh as if he, too, were listening.

The sick woman paused for breath, then went on, her words very low.

"That night I slipped out—of the house—when he—was asleep! We were married in a little out of the way church—I pasted the marriage certificate and license—into the Bible—you'll find—it—" she paused as if her task were almost done, then hurried on.

"When—we got out here—we found—this was a place of—outlaws."

"Outlaws!" said Fraley, startled—"What does that mean?"

"It means—that every man for miles around—has committed some crime—and is afraid—to go back—where he—came from."

Fraley turned her startled eyes toward the open door and her faraway mountains.

"Was—my—father—?" she faltered at last.

"No! No! I told you he was innocent—"

"Why didn't he get away then?"

"He couldn't—child—even if he had had money—which he hadn't—not a cent! The men here wouldn't let him go. They would have shot us all first! Your father—knew too much! There were—too many—notorious criminals on this mountain. There—wouldn't have been—a chance for the three of us— You see—we didn't find it all out—not till after you came. You were five months old—the day—your father—told me!"

A chill hand seemed to be clutching the girl's throat as she stared unseeingly at the spot of sunshine on the floor beside the old brown dog.

"We tried—to think of some way—but your father—knew too much. He'd been out with the other men—rustling cattle—He'd have been implicated with them in their crime—of course. At first he didn't understand—at first he thought it was cattle that belonged to them. He was green, you know, and didn't understand! The man who brought him out here had made great promises. He had expected to go back rich—some day. I had thought how proud I would be to show my father I had been right about Angus. I thought he would—be a—successful man, and we would go home—rich!"

The old dog stirred and snapped at a bug that crept in the doorway and the sick woman looked around with a start.

"It's all right, Mother, no one is coming," said the girl with a furtive look out the door.

The mother struggled on with her story.

"When your father—found out, when he saw he too had been stealing, and there was no hope—to get away—it seemed he just gave up—and let go. He said we had to live—and there was no other—way. He had always been wild—you know—and it seemed as though—he kind of got used to things—and fitted right in with the others after a while. When I cried and blamed him—then he took to drinking hard—and after—that—he didn't care, though sometimes he was—very fond—of you. But when he got liquor, then he didn't care!"

"Drinking didn't make it any better!" said the fierce young voice.

"No—It didn't," went on the dreary voice—"No—and then he brought the men—here! I couldn't help it—I tried. But I saw they had some kind—of a hold—on him! He was *afraid*—!"

The dog made a quick dash out the door after a rabbit that had shot by, and the woman stopped and looked up sharply.

"Listen!" she said, gripping the firm young hand in an icy clasp, "I must say the rest quick!" She was half lifted from her pillow with her frightened eyes turned toward the door, "I might go—or they might come—any minute now. Listen! I had a brother. He went to New York. He was Robert Fraley. You—must go—to him! It's all written down in the cover of the Bible—under the cloth I sewed over it. You—must find him! He—loved—me. Angus—had people too—but they were—ashamed of him! They were rich—but it's all written down. You must get out of here at once. Promise me! I—can't—die—till—you promise!"

"I promise!"

"Promise—you—won't wait—not even—for any—burying!"

"But, Mother—!"

"No 'but' Fraley! They'll bury me deep all right, don't

worry! They'll want me out of their sight—and mind! Many's the time—I've told them—before your father went—what I thought of them! I told them—about the wrath of God!—Oh—I know—they've had me in their power—since—I was—sick! I—had to shut up! But—when I'm gone—they'll take it out on you! Fraley, my girl—they can't hurt—my dead body. No matter what happens—God will know—how to find it—again—at the resurrection. But they can do—terrible things—to you, my baby! You're safer—dead—than here alive, if it comes—to that! Now promise me! Promise!"

Fraley choked back the racking sobs that came to her throat, and promised. The woman sank back and closed her eyes. It seemed she hardly breathed. The girl thought she was asleep and kept quite still, but after a time the stillness frightened her, and she lifted her trembling hand and touched the cold cheek. Her mother opened her eyes.

"I've been—praying!" she murmured, "I've—put you—in *His* care!"

There was a flicker of a smile on the tired lips, and the cold hand made a feeble attempt at a pressure on the warm vivid one it held.

After that she seemed to sleep again.

The girl, worn with sorrow and apprehension, sank in her cramped position on the floor into a troubled sleep herself, and the old dog, padding softly back from the hunt with delicate tread slunk silently down near her, closing sad eyes, and sighing.

Tired out, the girl slept on, past the noon hour, into the afternoon, never knowing when the cold hand grew moist with death damp, never seeing the shadow that crept over the loved face, the faint breaths, slow, and farther between, as the dying soul slipped nearer to the brink.

The dog, hungry, patient, sighed and sighed again, closed his eyes and waited, understanding perhaps what was passing in the old cabin, his dog heart aching with those he loved.

The shadows were changing on the mountain tops, and the long rays of the setting sun were flinging across the cabin floor, laying warm fingers on the old brown dog, bright fingers on the gold of the girl's hair, and a glory of another world on the face of the passing soul. Suddenly the dying eyes opened and with a gasp the woman clutched at the young relaxed hand that lay in hers.

"Fraley—! Child—! The old Bible!" The words were almost inarticulate except to loving ears, but the girl started awake and put her warm young arm about her mother.

"Yes, Mother! I'll keep it! I'll always keep it! I'll not forget! I'll never let anyone take it from me!"

Her words seemed to pierce the dying ears, and a smile trembled feebly on the white lips. For a long moment she lay in Fraley's young arms, as if content, like a nestling child. Then, with superhuman strength the dying woman lifted herself, and a light broke into her face, a light that made her look young and glad and well again, as her child could never remember her having looked:

"He's *come* for me!" she cried joyously as if it were an honor she had not expected, and then, her eyes still looking up as if hearing a communication—"He's going to keep *you* safe! Good-by! Till—you come!"

With the smile still on her lips she was gone! The girl, stunned, dazed with her sorrow, yet understanding that the great mystery of passing was over, laid her back on the flabby pillow and gazed on the face so changed, so rested in spite of its frailty, its wornness; that face already taking on itself the look of a closed and uninhabited dwelling. She watched the glory fade into stillness of death, wrote it down, as it were, in her secret heart, to recall all through her life, and then, as sometimes when she had watched the sunset dropping behind the mountain and all the world grow dark, she knew it was over, and she sank down on her knees beside all that remained that was dear to her in the great world, and broke into heart-broken sobs.

The dog came and whined about her, nosing her face and licking her hands, but she did not feel him. Her heart seemed crushed within her. All that had passed between herself and her mother during that long, terrible, beautiful parting, had faded for the time, and she was throbbing with one fearful thought. She was gone, gone, gone beyond recall! For the moment there was no future, nothing to do but to lie, broken, and cry out her terrible pain. It seemed as though the pent-up torrent of her sorrow, now that it had fallen upon her, had obliterated everything else.

Then, suddenly, a low, menacing growl beside her startled her back to the present. She lifted her face and turned quick, frightened eyes toward the neglected watch she had been keeping, and her heart stood still. There in the door, silhouetted dark against the blood-red light of the setting sun, stood Brand Carter, her mother's enemy—and hers!

IT was incredible that a girl could have grown to Fraley's years in this wilderness, this mountain fastness of wickedness, so fine and sweet and unsoiled as this girl was. Nobody but God would ever know at what expense to herself the mother had been able to guard her all her years, especially the last few months since her father died.

Like the matchless beauty of the little white flower that grows in the darkness of a coal pit and, protected by some miraculous quality with which its petals are endowed that will not retain the soil, lifts its starry whiteness amid the smut, so the child had grown into loveliness, unstained.

And now the frail hand that had shut her from the gaze of unholy eyes more times than she would ever know, the strong soul that in a weak body had protected her from dangers unspeakable, was gone; cold, silent, still, it could no more protect her. The time that her mother had warned her against had come, and caught her unaware! She had been merely weeping!

She sprang to her feet in a terror she had never felt before. There had been times in the past when she had been deathly frightened, but never like this. Her very heart stood still, and would not beat. Her breath hurt her in her lungs, her eyes seemed bursting as she gazed, her mind would not function. He had come. It was too late! It was useless to flee!

Then with sudden realization she glanced toward the silent form on the cot beside her, with an instinct to protect her who could no longer protect herself. But the majesty in that dead face brought the realization that the dead need no protection. She caught her breath in one quick gasp and tried to think.

But even that glance had been enough to break the spell that rested on the room. The man's eyes went to the dead face too, and with an oath he made a move to come forward.

The old dog gave a low growl and sprang with fangs exposed, but a cruel boot caught him midway, and sent him sprawling outside the door, where for a second, he lay stunned by the well-aimed blow.

"Ugh! Croaked at last!" said the man, coming close to the cot, peering down at the dead face, lifting a waxen eyelid roughly, and glaring into the dead eye, "Well, she took long enough about it!"

Then he turned to the trembling girl, who, with enraged eyes, watched him.

"Now, young 'un, *you* git out and milk the cow and git us a good supper. The men are coming, and we're hungry. See? Now, *git!*"

He seized her in a rough grip and flung her through the door, almost into the arms of another man who had just sprung from his horse and was coming toward the cabin. He was a young man with an evil face and lustful eyes. Pierce, they called him, Pierce Boyden, lately come to the wilderness. Fraley hated him, and feared him.

"Here, you—Pierce, come in here! We gotta get rid of this old woman! Give us a hand!"

Then, turning to the other three men who drove up he gave his orders.

"Pete, you stand there with your gun and watch that girl while she milks that cow and gits us some grub. Whist, you and Babe get your shovels and be quick about it."

Fraley darted around the house to where the cow stood waiting to be milked. Every word that was spoken stung its terrible meaning into her frightened soul. Scarcely knowing what she did she went at the task, a task from which her mother had saved her as long as she could. The angry voice of Brand rang out from the house where he was going about, roughly shoving a chair across the floor, flinging the old tin cup against the wall in his anger. She shuddered as she thought of what the men were doing. Her precious mother!

The tears that had been flowing seemed to sting backward in her eyes. Her cheeks scorched dry, her heart came choking to her throat. Her hands were numb and could scarcely hold the pail in place. The milk was going everywhere.

The voice of Brand, drunker than usual, sailed out into the twilight from the open doorway:

"You, Pete! Stay there till I come back. If she starts to run shoot her in the feet, then she can't go fur!"

He laughed a terrible haw, haw, and then she could hear the awful procession going down the mountain!

She knew what they were doing. She could hear the ring of a shovel against a rock. It seemed that every clod they turned fell across her quivering heart.

Pete, with his gun, stood guard at the corner of the house. Pete, the silent one with the terrible leering eyes of hate. Pete who never smiled—not even when he was drunk. And now he was drunk! Oh, why had she lost her senses? Why had she not gone before they came, as her mother had meant her to do?

The old dog hobbled to her and began to lick the tears from her face, and she felt comforted, and less afraid. She whispered to him to lie down and he obeyed her, sneaking into a shadow behind the cow.

Pete stalked nearer and gruffly bade her make haste. She managed to finish her milking, though her hands still felt more dead than live, and stumbled into the house. The old dog slunk after her, and hid in the bushes near the door. The shadows were growing long and deep on the grass, and on the mountains across the dark valley, where they had taken—No!—it was not her mother! Merely the worn-out dress with which she was done! Hadn't Mother tried to make her understand that?

She tried to take a deep breath and hold her shoulders up as she marched about the room, tried not to see the empty space where the cot had stood. Tried not to think, tried just to get the supper, and get the men to eating. There were hungry now, and they would not bother her till they were fed, if she fed them quickly.

She started the coffee boiling, and put some salt meat on to cook. She fried a great skillet of potatoes, and mixed up the crude corn bread. The familiar duties seemed to take her hours, and all the while her heart was listening in terror for the sound of returning feet. Pete had come into the house and was sitting in the corner with his gun aimed toward her. She shuddered when she looked at him, not so much because of the gun as because of the cunning look in his eyes, and once—as she glanced up because she could not keep her eyes away from his shadowy corner—he laughed, a horrid cackle, almost demoniacal. Pete, who never even smiled! It was as if he had her in his power. As if he were gloating over it. She would rather Brand had left almost any of the men than Pete. There was something about him that did not seem quite human.

Feverishly she worked, her head throbbing with her haste, setting out the old table with the tin plates, the cracked cups. She could hear the men's voices. They were coming back up the mountain now. They were singing one of those terrible songs about hanging somebody by the roadside, the one that had always made her mother turn pale.

Fraley sprang to the stove and broke eggs into the hot fat beside the meat. She would give them such a supper as would make them forget her for the moment.

The corn bread was ready, smoking hot on the table as the men came noisily in. Brand watched her as he towered above the rest, his evil eyes gloating, she thought, with the same look that had been in Pete's eyes. She brought the coffee pot and set the frying pan with its sizzling meat and eggs in the middle of the table, and the men, with drunken satisfaction, sat down and drew up their chairs. They were joking among themselves about their task just completed, in words that froze her heart with sorrow and horror. But she was glad to have their attention for the moment taken from herself.

They were all busy with the first mouthfuls now—like hungry wolves, too busy to spring.

She turned stealthily and her foot touched something. It was the old tin cup that Brand had kicked away in his anger. With quick instinct she stooped and picked it up. She might need it. Some bits of dry bread that were on the shelf as she passed she swept into it, and hiding the cup in the scant gathers of her cotton dress, she made a stealthy movement toward the door of the room that had been her refuge from the terrors of the world ever since she could remember.

The men did not notice her. They were eating.

Silently, as unobtrusively as she could move, she glided to the door and slipped within. They had not seemed to notice she was gone. She pushed the bolt quickly. It was a large bolt, and her mother had kept it well oiled so that it would move quickly and silently if need be. There was a bar, too, that slipped across the bottom of the door. That too, her mother had cunningly, crudely, arranged. Probably it would not endure long in a united attack, but it was a brief hindrance at least. If she only dared draw the old trunk across the door! But that would make a noise.

Stealthily she moved in the dark little room that was scarcely larger than a closet. With fingers weak with fear she lifted the loose board beneath the cot and pulled out the woolen bag. Suppressing the quick sob at thought of her mother, she opened the flap of the bag and stowed away the tin cup and bread, then, standing on tip toe, she lifted the bag to the little high window over the bed and pushed it softly over the sill. As it fell she listened breathlessly. What if the men should hear it drop, or Larcha the old dog should begin to bark, and the men should go out to look around!

Softly she took down the old coat that had hung on a peg in the wall ever since her father died, and put it on. The men were talking loudly now. Two of them seemed to be fighting over something that a third had said. It would perhaps come to blows. It often did. She welcomed the noise. It would cover her going. But as she stepped upon her little bed her heart suddenly froze in her breast! What was this terrible thing they were saying? It was about herself they were fighting. They were saying unspeakably awful things. For an instant she seemed paralyzed and could not move. Then fear set her free, and she was stung into action. It was not an easy matter to climb from the creaky little cot to the high narrow window sill above without making a particle of noise, and she was trembling in every nerve.

The window was barely large enough to let her slenderness through, and it required skill to swing outside, cling to the window sill and then drop with catlike softness to the ground, but it was not the first time she had accomplished it. There had been other times of stress in the little cabin when her mother had sent her away in a hurry to a refuge she had, out in the open, and that experience helped her now. But there was no time to pause and be cautious, for at any moment the men might discover her absence and call for her. Then they would rush outside to hunt her down, and death itself would be better than life!

With the awful words of the men ringing in her ears she dropped from the window, praying that she might not make a false landing. Her head seemed dizzy and there was a beating in her throat. For an instant her body felt too heavy to rise up, and she lay quite still where she had dropped, holding her breath and listening.

The old dog came softly whining and licking her face as if he understood she was in trouble and new panic seized her. She hushed him into quiet, picked up her bag and slung it over her shoulder by its strap, then, her hand upon the dog's head, she moved like a small shadow across the ground, her bare feet making no sound, her heart beating so wildly that it seemed as if it could be heard a mile away.

It was not toward the trail she directed her steps, and she did not look back to the awful pass where the precipice was, nor down the valley where they had carried her precious mother's form. Into the wilderness where there was no trail, into the darkness she went.

Like a voice there silently stole into her heart a phrase

from the words she had learned for her mother, sitting morning after morning in the cabin door in the sunshine, learning her lesson out of the old Book, the only book she had, or huddled in a blanket when the weather was cold and the fire was low, learning, learning, always learning beautiful words to repeat to her mother. It was the only school she had ever known and she loved to study, and to repeat the words she had learned; pleased to be able to say them perfectly, often asking what they meant, but only half comprehending what her mother tried to tell her. Now suddenly it seemed that these words had taken on new, wide meaning.

"He knoweth—the way—that I take. He knoweth the way—He knoweth—"

As she stole along cautiously, her accustomed feet finding the pathway in the dark, her heart fearful, her eyes looking back in dread, the words began to come like an accompaniment to her silent going, and their meaning beat itself into her soul.

Suddenly, back through the clear stillness of the starlit night came a sharp cracking sound, a snap and a sound of rending wood, then a kind of roar of evil bursting from the door of the cabin. Casting a frightened look back she could see the light from the cabin door which was flung wide now, could hear the men's voices calling her angrily, shouting imprecations, swearing a tumult of angry menace. It put new terror into her going, new tremblings into her limbs. She hastened her uncertain steps blindly on toward an old tree that had been her refuge before in times of alarm, her arms outstretched to feel for obstructions in her path as she fled down the side of the mountain.

She could hear the clatter of hoofs now, ringing out on the crisp night air, as the horses crossed the slab of rock that cropped out a little way from the house. Yes, some of them at least, were coming this way. She had hoped they would search the trail first, but it seemed they were taking no chances. They would be upon her very soon and her limbs were trembling until she felt they would crumple under her! Her feet were so uncertain as they stepped! Her heart was beating so that it seemed as if it would choke her. Weakly she snatched at a young sapling and swung herself up to a cleft place in a great rock she knew so well. If she could only make it now, and reach the foot of the old tree!

Breathlessly on she climbed, not pausing now to look back, and at last she reached it.

As she swung herself up in the branches she remembered the old dog who had followed her. Where was he? Had he gone back? Much as she loved him, and wanted his company on her journey, she realized now that she should have shut him in the cow shed where he could not have followed her. Now, if he lingered at the foot of the rock, he would give away her hiding place to the enemy!

For an instant she paused, but the ring of horses' hoofs on the rock-strewn path she had just left warned her that she had no time to spare. They were hot-foot on her track. Possibly it was Pete, and it might be he had searched out her haunt. Pete had a way of appearing at the shack of late when everybody thought he had gone afar. Pete might have seen her going or coming to her tree.

The thought sent the blood hurrying through her veins with feverish rapidity. Her hands almost refused to hold on to the branches, so frightened was she. She tried to think. If this tree was no longer a refuge, where could she go? It was too late to go back, to hope to get down this sheer rock on the other side and make the valley before she would be heard, even though the dark did hide her. It would be folly. She would be dashed to pieces in the dark, for the way down the precipitous incline was dangerous even in the daytime when one could pick and choose a cranny for a footing, step by step. It was a long and slow and fearsome descent. To make it in the dark, and in haste, would be impossible. To go back to where she had begun to descend to this rock would be to meet the enemy face to face. There was nothing for it but to climb to the topmost limbs and wait. Yet, if it was Pete, and he should find her, he would not hesitate to cut down the tree! She would be at his mercy!

In terror she climbed to heights she had never ventured before, till she clung at the very top of the great tree, enveloped in its resinous plumes. Even in the light of day it would have been hardly discoverable that the tree was inhabited, so thick were the branches. It had been Fraley's playhouse in her childhood and her refuge in many a time of fear. But she had always guarded her goings so that she thought no one but her mother knew of her whereabouts. Now, however, in this, her most trying crisis, she began to wonder whether, perhaps, some of the men might not recently have spied upon her.

Clinging to the old pine, her arms about its rough trunk, her feet curled into the crotch of the slender branch upon which her weight rested, the woolen bag her mother had made dragging heavily from her shoulder, she waited, her heart beating wildly.

If it had been daytime she could have almost looked into the eyes of her pursuer, though his horse's feet traveled ground far above where the tree stood, for the tree top was almost on a level with him. But she could see nothing now but the black night ahead of her and a high line of dim starry sky far above the mountain. But she knew by the sound that her pursuers were almost opposite her, and that a moment more would tell her whether they had discovered her trail, for now if they guessed where she was they would turn abruptly down the mountain toward her. And, Oh, what had become of Larcha, the old dog? If he only would have sense enough not to whine!

Suddenly a sound broke on her startled ear, like the hurtling of some heavy object through small branches and dry sticks, a rush, a menacing growl, followed by curses, and the sound of a plunging horse, rearing and stumbling on the slippery hillside.

Instantly her forest-trained ears understood. It was almost as if she could see what was being enacted before her in the dark. Old Larcha, the dog, had tried to help. He had cunningly stolen above the trail where the enemy was coming, and at the right instant had plunged down upon the horse and his rider, had dared to attack in defense of the girl he loved, had been intelligent enough to try to mislead her pursuer into making chase higher up the mountain, and so covering her hiding place.

Instantly she knew, now, even if she had not heard the rough curses, that it was Pete who rode that horse. Larcha had always shown deep dislike to him, and fear in his presence. It had been a joke among the men to send Larcha to Pete and hear him growl. And Pete had been cruel to the dog, kicking him brutally whenever opportunity offered, throwing stones at him without provocation, pointing the gun at him. The dog would always hide when he came around. Fraley had often noticed how the hair would rise on the brown back, and how the dog would lift his upper lip and show his teeth whenever the man came in sight. He would always disappear, hiding for hours together, till his enemy had left the place. Larcha had cause of his own, now, to fight her pursuer. Yet Fraley knew he would have done this even without the personal cause. Since she was a little child Larcha had been her one playmate, and comrade whenever she strayed away from her mother. Larcha was all the friend she had left in the world. And now that friend was offering up himself for her. For Fraley had little doubt what Pete would do to the dog. The answer to her fear came sharp and quick in a shot that rang out over the mountain, followed by the dull thud of a body falling on the ground and rolling a few paces.

Then into the night came the sound of curses, and of other horses riding, and cries.

A sharp little light shot out from the rider of the horse, and twinkled over the ground till it focused on a dark, huddled object at the foot of a tree. Pete had recently come from a surreptitious visit to the outside world, and had brought back with him a number of these strange little flashlights. Yes, there was no question but that her pursuer was Pete, and that, if he wanted to, he would shoot her as readily as he had shot Larcha. At least he would shoot to disable, perhaps not to kill.

The other horses were coming on, Brand's big roan stumbling with his lame foot, and two others. They would surround her now. Oh, if she could only be sure they would kill her. The awful words she had heard the men speak a few moments before still rang, menacing, in her ears.

One of the horses caught his foot in a root, and stumbling, began to slide down a steep place. His rider was evidently thrown forward. There was a sound of struggling and more curses as the horse righted himself and the drunken rider remounted.

A consultation in low tones followed. Fraley could catch a word now and then. Pete was laughing that awful cackle of triumph, telling of Larcha's attack and finish. She held her breath and clung to the tree with arms that were numb with tensity, expecting momently that the wicked little flashlight would play upon her face and reveal her to her enemies.

Then she heard Brand cry out:

"Which way did the dog come? Up there? We'll soon have her then. She can't make time up hill. All set?"

The four horses wheeled and went up the mountain, directly away from where she clung in mid air.

Larcha's ruse had worked. He had not died in vain.

# 3

FRALEY'S head reeled as she clung to the tree and listened to the receding hoof beats. She could feel the old tree sway under her; she had climbed so near to the top that her anchorage seemed very uncertain. She had a feeling that she was high above the world, held somehow in the hollow of God's hand, and she laid her white face against the rough old trunk and closed her eyes. It seemed as if she scarcely dared to breathe yet, lest the men return, much less could she think of descending from her stronghold.

The searchers climbed higher and higher, till they were silhouetted for a moment against the distant bit of starry sky, and then disappeared down the other side of the mountain. They had gone to search for her among their own kind, thinking she had taken refuge with some one. Their voices which at first had been loud and clear, floating back in angry snatches, were suddenly shut off as they dropped from view. She drew a deep breath of relief.

But—they would come back! When they failed to find her there they would come this way again and search! It was not safe to go down now. There was no other spot for hiding that she knew of within miles, and she dared not venture into the unknown while they were yet hot on her trail. Besides, she knew that her progress must be slow indeed for she must go cautiously. Well had she learned that there were many other men hiding within these strange mountain fastnesses, who would be no safer companions than the ones from whom she would escape. Indeed, the way before her seemed as beset as the way behind.

How good it would have been if the shot that had stilled old Larcha's barking, had reached her own heart, and sent her out of a world that was only full of sorrow and terror.

As the immediate fear of the men died away, and strength began to return to the girl's tired limbs, and steadiness to her heart, she began to think about the dog. Had he died at once, or was he lying there in pain and wondering why she did not come to him? Her last defender, the only one in the world left who loved her, and he was stilled—probably forever! There had not been a whimper from him since that shot and the dull thud that followed. And she had thought that he would go with her on her long strange journey! Now she must go alone!

It seemed hours that she clung there to her frail support high in the old pine. The night shut down more darkly. The stars flicked little pricks in the strip of sky above the mountain more distinctly, and a thread of a moon came up and hung like a silver toy in the east, far off to the right. She shrank even from the bit of light it gave, lest her enemy might return. She dared not try to run away yet.

She tried to make a plan for her going, but somehow everything seemed all mixed up. She could not be sure which way the men would return. Also, there were cabins, deep hidden among the spurs of the foothills, where dangerous characters abode. These she must avoid, although she had not even a very definite idea where they were located. There were paths which her mother had always warned her against in a general way, and yet, they lay, some of them, between her and the great east which she must seek. Arriving each time from her round of problems she would just close her eyes and pray: "Oh God, you show me the way please! You go with me!"

It was hours later that she was startled into alertness again.

Voices had suddenly risen on the night air, detached, drunken voices, booming up along the horizon as if they had just emerged from another world.

She shifted her hands on the resinous tree, and found them stiff and painful with their long clinging. She changed her position, and shrank closer to the tree. The men were coming back!

Terror seized her once more with its iron grip. She peered fearfully up at the strip of sky. She could see a slow procession of four, silhouetted against the brightness, riding crazily, but they were not coming toward her. They were going along the ridge of the mountain toward the cabin, drooping and swaying on their horses. They had been somewhere with their kind and were debauched with drink. How well she knew their attitude! How familiar were the noisy curses that floated back to her!

"Well—l-l-let 'er—go!" stuttered Brand as he righted himself after a turn in the saddle to look back. "S-s-she—c-c-an't git fur before m-morning! We'll round 'er up with Shorty's hounds! Good sport. What say, boys?"

A chorus of drunken laughter followed, and the voices

drowned themselves back of the cow shed, then disappeared behind the slammed door of the cabin. How often she had wakened in the night and heard them! Only now she was alone, and in their power!

She waited while the night grew wide and still. No more sounds came from the cabin. Then she began to ease herself slowly down to the lower branches, listening at every move. Her hearing, trained in the open, was attuned to the noises of the night. She was not afraid of the creatures that lived in the forest, that hid, and stirred, and stole abroad in the dark for prey. She felt herself akin to them as she stood at last with her feet again upon the ground and listened. She could tread the forest aisles as silently as they. She could go like a shadow of the night. She could make herself a part of the black background, and shrink into it at the first approach of alarm.

Stealthily, for she was aware that the men might have left some one of their number in hiding to watch the surrounding country, she crept from the shelter of the great rock on which the old pine grew, and, turning, gave one glance back and up at it. If she succeeded in escaping she would probably never see it again. She could not conceive of herself ever coming willingly back to that place, so she looked her farewell with eyes that were blurred with grateful tears. That tree had been her true friend.

Adjusting the bag that seemed almost to have worn a groove in her slender shoulder she went softly, swiftly forward until she reached the higher ground where the horses had stood.

There lay the old dog right across her path. She stumbled and almost fell over him, his body still warm. Dear old Larcha! He had died for her! Or had he? Perhaps he was not dead after all? She must not stay for even such a defender, but might she not carry him with her, a little way at least? If she left him here he would be a prey for wild beasts. She could not bear to think of old Larcha, suffering perhaps, deserted. A little farther on was the river. She could see the gleam of it in the faint light of the little new moon. Perhaps down there she could minister to the old dog, and he might get up and go with her after all.

With sudden hope she stooped and picked him up and started toward the stream. But it was a heavy tug, and more than once her heart failed her, for she began to realize that he was dead. The inert way the body lay in her weary young arms told her so.

At last, near the water's edge, she laid him down and looked at him. There was no hope. She had known that even before she stooped, for the chill of his body had been growing upon her. She knew too that she could not carry him farther. She must save her own strength.

Sadly picking him up once more she waded out into the water and dropped him in.

"Dear Larcha!" she whispered softly as the water closed over the faithful head, "I'll never forget you!"

Then she turned and waded down the pebbly bed of the stream.

The water was cold and sent a chill over her as she tried not to envy old Larcha. How simple it would all have been if only she might have died too!

When the water grew too cold for her to stand it any longer she stepped out upon the bank and ran to get warm, but soon took to the stream again, knowing that if the threat of following her with the hounds should be made good, it would be harder for the dogs to trace her scent.

Later in the night, when the little silver boat of a moon hung low and seemed to ripple at her from the water like a tiny lamp, she found a fallen tree lying across the stream in a shallow place. Its top branches were touching the bank she was on, and its roots had been torn from the opposite bank and were standing high in the air like a wall. It might be dangerous, but she decided to cross on that tree.

Tucking her scant skirts about her she waded out as far as she dared, for the current was stronger here, and then clutched for the topmost branches.

The water was cold and black, but looking behind she seemed already very far from shore, so taking firm hold of the branches she pulled herself along, slipping and almost falling, until she could clamber into the tree top and so work her way along the trunk until she came to the rampart of roots towering above her in the dark, like an impassable wall. Had she been a fool to try to get across, she wondered?

She sat down on the tree trunk to get her breath and examine the precious woolen bag that she had taken the precaution to strap high on her shoulders before entering the stream. It was not very wet. Only the least little bit on the lower edge. Her precious Bible and the things her mother had put in it would be safe! That was something to be thankful for, at least.

She sat down to rest for a moment on the trunk of the tree before she would explore what was back of that wall of gnarled roots and mud and moss. The dim bank of the other side of the stream seemed not far away. Could she climb over the roots and get to the land or would the water be too deep for wading?

Across the stream lay the darkness from which she had come. There was no gleam of light anywhere. The cabin on the mountain where her drunken enemies slept was in darkness. She could not even locate it. She seemed to have been traveling for years and to have come miles and miles, but her knowledge of the wilderness and the vast open country told her that the cabin was probably not far away. In the daylight she would be able to see it easily. She had never been so far as this before. Her mother had always limited her going. But the old mountains were over there, the mountains she knew so well. Her journey would be a matter of years, perhaps, before she got to a place that would really seem safe. With a feeling of hopelessness she turned and faced the task before her. Some hiding place must be found before daylight, where she could rest in safety till another night gave her cover to go on.

She found the roots above her hard to climb. They had been worn smooth and slippery by many waters, before they were uprooted. But at last, after several failures, she found a place where she could work herself around, clinging carefully from root to root, till she had gained the black shadow behind them. The bag on her back hindered her, and took her strength, the roots were uncertain and gave way in the most unexpected manner, switching her face, and sometimes proving stubborn where they should have yielded. When she gained the spot where she could look across the blackness that separated her from the shore, the bank seemed steep and abrupt, and the water black as night. If it had not been for the little stars reflected in its darkness she could not have told whether it was water or mere black space. Gradually her eyes grew accustomed to the blackness that reigned behind those roots, and she saw that the other end almost touched the shore with one big root, heavier than the rest. A little star was twinkling right beneath it and plainly showed a big flat stone where one could step.

Softly, cautiously, she put an investigating foot down and tested the water under her. If she could only swing herself by these wiry old roots, over toward that stone, she could get up to the bank she was sure.

The first root she tried snapped, and left her with only a single hold, her foot went down several inches into soft spongy mud, but she clutched for another root and caught it, and was finally able to get a footing farther on. At last she stood on the stepping stone and caught at the bending branches of another tree that arched over the water.

It was a hard, dangerous climb, even then, for her feet were wet and the bank was slippery and steep. Moreover her pack had become painfully heavy, and its straps cut deep into her weary shoulders. When she scrambled at last to the top she had only strength left to draw her feet after her, and sink down where she lay to get her breath. Now that she was safe across the water it did not seem to matter. There might be dangers twice as great as those she had escaped but her tired eyelids dropped over her eyes, and she lay there panting and disheartened, wondering how she was to go on. Suddenly the memory that her mother was gone surged deep into her soul, and everything was for the moment forgotten in the overwhelming realization. Nothing mattered but to weep her young soul out.

It seemed the more bitter to her that she had not been able to attend her beloved to her final resting place. She longed inexpressibly to go back and make sure that all was safe and right, but that was impossible. There would be no escape if she did, for that would be the spot where the men would look for her first. She shuddered at the thought of being found there, at the possibility of the terrible things they would say. The harsh unfeeling words of Brand when he had discovered that her mother was dead had seemed to her more cruel than all the rest. Her soul writhed at the memory. Out of all proportion to her other injuries this seemed to loom as the one unforgivable thing.

Silent sobs racked her weary young frame as she lay there under the low spreading tree. She dared not cry aloud, but there was some relief in letting the tears come.

A little stir high up over her head made her suddenly start and sit up, looking around her in the darkness. Was someone watching her? Had perhaps the men traced her to this refuge too?

But though she listened she heard only a little scratching of tiny forest feet, some bird or chipmunk perhaps in the branches, and the soft sighing of winds stirring a twig against a limb. It was very dark here, for the foliage grew thick and heavy, and the night seemed to have settled closer. Peering hard she could discern nothing but tree trunks, and concluded she must be in the woods. This would be a good place to sleep, but she dared not sleep. The night would be all too short for putting distance between herself and her enemies, without stopping for sleep. She would stretch out for just a few minutes to relax her tired limbs, and then she must grope on. It would not do to be getting out in the open at daylight. She must get somewhere under cover by dawn lest the men be out after her early. They would want their breakfast, and would be impatient at not finding her back. No, she had no time to waste resting. So in a very short time she gathered herself up, re-slung her pack on her back, and started groping on through the woods.

The trees fringed the river bank thickly here, and she dared not stay near the edge where it was lighter, because the bank was steep, and she was in danger of slipping down into the water. She must penetrate the woods, and get to the other side if possible before daybreak.

Looking up occasionally where the trees were not quite so close together she could see the distant stars, but they seemed very far away. If she only had a match or a candle! Yet she would not have dared light it if she had, she reasoned, lest someone see her and hinder her going. No, the dark was a friend, for God was in the dark, and He would show her the way.

Resting her soul in this thought she groped on from tree to tree, sometimes stumbling over a root, often coming in sharp contact with brush that scratched her face, clung to her garments, and left thorns in her hands.

It seemed that she had already been hours in that forest when she suddenly came to a break in the darkness, a soft lightening of the blackness that seemed almost bright in contrast.

Cautiously she went forward, for now she sensed some soft sound ahead of her, something more than the night wind. Nearer and nearer she drew to the sound and streak of light, till suddenly she was on the edge of the woods, and the sound was as of a giant breathing. She stood quite still, steadying herself by a tree, her own breath withheld, and listened.

Yes, decidedly, that was breathing!

Had some human being camped just ahead of where she stood? Perhaps there was more than one person. Perhaps she had come on some of her enemies resting in their search till daylight.

With her hand on her heart she stood trying to still its wild thumping and to get strength to go on, forward or back, she could not tell which. At last she began to steal cautiously around the tree, and made her way slowly along the edge of the wood, keeping near to the clearing because it was easier going and not so pitchy black!

As a misty dawn began to break she saw that the open space was like a wide valley with dark mountains beyond again reaching up to the vault of dim stars. If she could only get across that valley perhaps she would be out of the region of danger. That would be wonderful! And yet, there might be people camped here who would see her as the lights grew stronger, and she might not be able to get to hiding before the morning really came. But there was danger anywhere, and she must take a risk. Also, she was burning with thirst and there ought to be water in a valley. Of course she was faint with hunger, too, but she must not think of stopping to eat. If she could only get far enough away so that word of her would not travel back, then she could take her own time. But now she must press on.

Ahead of her under the shadow of a tree that stood out a little way from the rest, she saw a dark outline, seemingly an out-cropping of rock. She would go and sit down upon it for a moment and rest. Her limbs were so tired they trembled under her. And now she noticed other dark shapes scattered over the open space. Yes of course they were rocks. She must get away from the idea that they were people camped here. What a foolish idea! People would not scatter around like this to camp.

Then she heard the soft breathing again. Could that be a man wrapped in his blanket, sleeping under the stars?

To her right came more breathing, and a movement, as if some one stirred in his sleep. Startled, she turned her eyes back toward the woods which were not far behind her, and imagined she saw something moving there, and heard more breathing. It certainly sounded like human beings.

In utter panic she turned, she knew not which way, and started to run, but she caught her foot in the long grass and fell headlong. Her hands went wildly out to save herself, and came in startling contact with warm, soft, living fur!

4

SHE was too frightened and stunned to think, and things began happening right away.

To begin with, the rock that was covered with fur gave a snort, and a quick investigating nose came cold and wet to her face. There came a leap and a bellow, rending of the earth close to her, a blinding shower of dirt and grass in her face, a sound of prancing and a great body hurled about.

Suddenly all around her other dark shapes came alive and reared and roared and bellowed, and she knew what she had done. This was a herd of wild cattle and she had trespassed into their territory. In a moment more, if it were daylight, she would be torn and trampled to a horrible death. They were preparing to stampede. She knew enough of cattle raising to understand their habits. She was as good as dead now if they could see her.

But the darkness hung like a curtain between them and her.

The creature she had fallen against had backed off, and was snuffing about uncertainly, with angry roars, sleep and mist in its eyes, making it very plain that once it got a sight of this unknown enemy in the dark, there would be a quick ending.

Fraley held her breath and lay quite still for an instant and the big steer, turned and backed off again, facing away from her. Could she make an escape? Would her limbs obey her? If she could only get to a tree! Now she must move, while its back was turned. Those other dark shapes were forming in a mass. She could hear an ominous bewildered roar. If they should stampede! If they should turn this way—!

With a quick catlike stealth she lifted her body an inch or two from the earth, and began to creep on hands and feet, inch by inch, away from the dark creature. Its own bellowing drowned the soft sound of her movement at first, and then as she grew bolder and moved faster something clinked in the bag that hung across her shoulders, as it swung down and hit the ground in her turning. Whatever it was, the creature about-faced and gave another roar. Trembling so that she seemed almost paralyzed, Fraley sprang to her feet and fled blindly, in the dark.

The race was on. The enemy sounded the battle cry, and a stamping of hoofs told her that she was pursued. A thousand giants, breathing hard, came behind her, a living angry fiery tornado. Was she going to the woods, or out into the open? There was so much dirt in her eyes she could not make out. Was she going to fall again? Would she never—reach—*anywhere?*

It was at this instant that her outstretched hand touched the trunk of a small sapling, and, straining her eyes ahead, she saw that the darkness of the woods was just before her. But how was she to find a tree to climb in the dark? Could she escape from those angry, flying creatures if they ventured in among the trees?

The roar behind her now was deafening, and they

were coming full toward her. Could they see her? Did they have eyes that could see in the dark like a cat?

An instant more and she swung herself under the low branches of another tree, and gained a footing inside the darkness! Sharply she turned to her right, and dashed in and out among the trees, slid behind a tall old oak, out of breath, her heart feeling as if it would burst with fright and exertion.

She peered around her tree, and saw that the cattle had paused, baffled at the barrier of trees for the moment. But she dared not trust to that. They were still making angry sounds, a mob cry. Perhaps they were consulting how they might find her and vent their anger for their rude awakening. She had heard awful tales about those who had got the ill will of a herd of cattle!

Putting out a groping hand her fingers touched the plumy branch of a pine! Her soul thrilled! Another pine! There would be branches she could climb!

It was not a great king of a tree like the one that had been her refuge before, but it was taller than the cattle that were after her. For now she could hear the crash of a branch, the crumpling of bushes under the heavy tread as first one creature and then another ventured blindly within the thicket. Without more hesitation she clung to the trunk, and drew herself up with new strength born of her necessity.

The tree swayed as she put her foot at last upon the lower branches, and the stir of swinging branches drew on the enemy. She clutched the resinous trunk tenaciously as her foot slipped, and almost fell back to earth again, but struggling desperately she at last got a footing, and crept up. The whole tree swayed with her weight, and trembled. But she was above those awful horns at last, unless the creatures tore the tree down. Could they do that? The one that had followed her was snorting and pawing just below. His horns were tangled in a branch, tossing the piney plumes.

Then a curious thing happened.

While she waited breathlessly, swaying in the tree top, a call sounded out below in the meadow, the cry of the angry leader of the beasts. In quick reply the whole herd turned and stampeded in the other direction, those struggling, tangled in the edge of the wood, crashing behind. The limbs cracked and snapped as they passed. Young saplings bent and were trampled under foot. Old dead branches that reached low enough for the flying horns were broken off like pipe stems, and the whole dark bellowing pack hurled themselves away toward the valley.

Fraley hung there in wonder and listened to their going. Then she closed her eyes and put her tired face against the gummy pine trunk and cried softly.

When the sound of the flying herd grew faint in the distance she opened her eyes and looked to the edge of the forest.

Little faint streaks of pink had taken the place of the starry strip above the mountains, though it was still very dark in the woods, but she could see that out in the open it was gray with dawning.

Softly, cautiously, listening at every move, she slid down at last to the ground. She was stiff and sore and moved painfully. Also she was faint with hunger, but this was no place to stop and eat. This must be the beginning of the cattle lands. She must get away from here before daylight. There would be men coming when morning broke and that would be worse perhaps than those awful cattle. She had heard all about this region. There were not only wild stretches of rich pasture land filled with cattle—many of them stolen cattle—but they were guarded by men, outlaws, such as those from whom she had fled. She must be on her guard every instant, or she would only be rushing into new dangers.

It was growing lighter now, even in the woods, and she was able to steer her course.

But now she began to be painfully aware of her burden, for the straps had become twisted and were cutting into her flesh. Also the old coat dragged heavily upon her and her hands and feet were torn and bleeding with the branches and bark. She had a stone bruise on one foot, and a deep cut where she had slipped on a sharp stone in the river. All these aches began now to cry out for relief. She began to wonder how many thousand miles she had yet to go. Could she ever make it? Here she had only been out one awful night and she felt ready to lie down and die. Oh, if she only could!

Bravely she drew a deep breath and struggled on, but there were tears running down her white cheeks, though perhaps she was not even aware that she was crying.

The dawn was creeping up fast now. Overhead there was a rosy glow.

Presently she heard a soft tinkle of water over stones, and came upon a little brook rippling along through the forest. Ah, here was refreshment!

She remembered the old tin cup, and unslung her bag to search for it.

She would have breakfast here beside this brook, and then perhaps she would be rested enough to go on.

But when she came to open the bag the tears started afresh, for it brought back so clearly her last talk with her dear mother.

Tenderly she unfastened the strings that held the bag shut, and looked within. The scanty folded bits of coarse clothing made from salt bags and the like, smote her with fresh sorrow. The little pockets along the sides of the bag, made with her mother's neat stitches, even though the thread was coarse with which they had been set! How dear every stitch would always be! And mother had made it for her!

It was light enough now to see everything, but she went through her investigation with great care so that nothing should slip out and be lost in the woods.

One pocket held needles, thread, a few buttons, the old scissors with one broken point, the other point stuck into a cork for safety, a pencil, some folded bits of cloth for patches, a pincushion with a few pins. Another held a broken comb, and a tiny broken mirror that had been one of the wonders of her childhood. That pocket was her little vanity case. Another held a small piece of soap and a wash rag neatly hemmed. There was a larger pocket that held some little bags, one filled with corn meal, perhaps a pint in all, another a small piece of salt pork wrapped in paper, and a piece of cheese. There was a handful of shelled corn in another. Then tucked in between the bags, and wrapped carefully in cloth were two little glass bottles with screw tops of metal. She knew her mother treasured them as relics of her own childhood that she had brought them with her into her far western home. One of them contained sugar and the other was half full of salt. This was her little pocket of supplies, and, save for the bits of corn bread she had brought, they were all that stood between her and starvation. And she knew that these had been saved at infinite risk and sacrifice to the dear mother who had packed the bag, for Brand, who brought home all supplies, kept a keen watch upon everything.

Fraley did not discover all these things at first. She was too weary and faint to look carefully, too overwrought with sorrow to identify everything. Also the light was not even yet strong enough to tell sugar from salt there in the woods. But she knew that her mother's tender hand had been on everything, and her love had put them all in. Later she discovered that another pocket contained a small piece of candle, and a few matches in a tiny box wrapped up in a bit of woolen cloth.

But it was the sight of the old Bible sewed into its neat cotton cover that broke her down, so that for a few minutes she sat there and sobbed softly to herself.

At last she roused herself. The tinkle of the water was so inviting. She took out the old tin cup and dipped herself a drink of water. Oh, how good it tasted. She drank deeply, and then leaned down to the brook and washed her face and hands, using the bit of soap, and setting up the broken mirror against a tree while she combed out her pretty hair and tried to make it tidy.

She felt a little better then, and ate a part of the corn bread she had brought. She must not eat it all, for it might be a long time before she could get more when this was gone, although there was the meal and the matches. When she got far enough away where it would be safe she might make a little corn cake and bake it on a hot stone over a fire of twigs. But not now. She must hoard every crumb of the corn bread.

She drank some more water, and then lay down and shut her eyes. It felt so good to stretch out flat and relax. She must not go to sleep, but she would rest a little while, five minutes, perhaps.

When she opened her eyes again she did not know where she was.

Two slender fingers of warm sunshine were touching her cheek, and shining on her golden hair, and a bird was singing over her head. She looked up to the trees, and down to the brook, and at the knapsack lying open beside her, and then she remembered.

As long as she lived she would never forget that moment when she awoke and realized that she had been asleep—perhaps a long time—and had been cared for and was safe. The words that came to her lips with a kind of sweet amazement were:

"I will both lay me down in peace and sleep, for thou Lord only makest me to dwell in safety." God had made good that promise to her in her terror and loneliness! There was almost triumph in her face as she looked over the things in her traveling bag, and found them all there.

Presently, realizing that the warm color of the two rays of sunshine that had penetrated the trees above showed that it was late in the day, perhaps even past midday, she gathered herself together to go on. She dashed more cold water from the brook in her face, and felt refreshed and able to travel. She drank again of the brook and was glad of the sweet water. She dipped her feet in for a last wash before she started, and then she began to strap up her bag. But in stuffing the things back again she found two hard objects which she had not noticed earlier in the morning in the dim light. They were wrapped carefully in the clean garments her mother had made and tied about with bits of string. Curious, she unknotted the string and found, first an empty bottle with a good tight cork. It seemed to be perfectly clean, and a bit of paper had been pasted around it which said "FOR WATER" printed with pencil.

Again quick tears came to her eyes at the thoughtfulness that had provided for all her little needs as well as it was possible. Now, she would be able to carry a little water with her for a time of need for it was not likely that brooks of clear water like this one would be frequent along the way.

She filled the bottle from the clear deep spot where the water bubbled up in a little pool, corked it firmly and set it upright in one of the pockets so there would be little danger of its upsetting. Then she investigated the other bundle, and almost cried out with pleasure when she found that it contained the old field glass which had been her father's and which, from her earliest memory, it had been the delight of her life to look through. She had not seen it since her father's death, and supposed, of course, some of the other men had appropriated it, as they had almost everything else that had belonged to him, in spite of all her mother could do. But it seemed she had been able to save this, hidden away perhaps under the old board beneath the bed which had been their only treasure chest.

Eagerly she unwrapped it and adjusted it, turning it toward the distance in each direction, delighted when she sighted a tiny bird in the branches, a squirrel sitting under a distant tree eating a nut it had just unearthed from last winter's store. Now she would be able to sight the distance, and see if an enemy was at hand! And her mother had known that. Oh, what a wonderful mother! It was almost as if her guiding hand were still there, to find all these things ready. A hungering came over her to unwrap the old Bible and see what had been written in it, but she knew that she must not take the time to do it now. Her first business was to get out of this region as fast as her two feet could carry her. Something over two thousand miles she had to go in all.

How far had she come already? As much as ten? She could not tell. No journey in her past compared with this one. But the thought of it was appalling, as the figures loomed before her, ten into two thousand—even supposing she had already made ten! She knew that ten was nothing to the men on horseback. She knew they thought little of a journey of a hundred and fifty miles. They could easily come after her and catch her although she had been doing her best for days, if they chose to think it worth while. The country was so wide and open, and her knowledge of it so very limited. Oh, it was a terrible chance she was taking to expect to get away from seven determined men with seven good horses and unlimited friends to whom they might appeal for help all along the way. Yet she must go on and do her best.

She buckled the old strap of the field glass across one shoulder, fastened up her bag carefully, and sprang to her feet. She must get on. The slant of the sunbeams was decidedly low, it might even be late afternoon. She must get some idea of where she was before night fell again. She must not risk another attack of wild cattle.

She decided to follow the brook a little way, and before long came out to the edge of the larger stream again, but, she judged, much farther down toward the East than she had been when she entered it, for she could see no trace of the fallen tree on which she had crossed. There was probably a curve in the stream that hid it, and the woods grew close, the trees leaning far over the water in some places.

The sun was already far down to the western horizon. She must have slept even longer than she had thought. She gave one quick searching glance about and finding no one near she held up her field glass and searched the valley.

There were some cattle grazing quietly across the stream. She could even see the mark of their branding on one or two near by, but she was safe here. They were too far away to notice her. She searched the valley behind her, the way she must have come last night, as far as she could see, but only cattle here and there dotted the peaceful scene. There were no horses nor riders. She turned her glass up toward the heights across the valley, and searched them step by step, back as far as her eye could reach. Was that her old pine that had given her refuge the night before? It stood out like a dark spike against the sky, with rock below, and other trees around, but it was so tiny, and so far away in the shimmer of the afternoon sunshine, that she could not even be sure it was the same tree. Behind it and above it, she could not see. If it were her tree the cabin would probably be out of sight from the point where she stood. But, if it were her tree, how far had she come? Could one see ten miles even with a glass? She did not know. She did know that a great mountain might be many miles away and still be visible, soft and purple against the sky, but one could not see detail on a great mountain, one could not tell one tree from another at a great distance.

She searched the way again, on the ridge along the mountain up which the men had ridden after they had shot Larcha, but there was no sign of horse or rider, and with a breath of relief she turned and hurried along the edge of the stream.

It was rough going here, and took more time than she ought to spare, because, for every rod she progressed, she must travel three or four sometimes in getting around trees and climbing steep banks, but it was very peaceful and lovely here and gave her comfort and a sense of safety.

As she hurried along she occasionally raised her glass and searched the horizon again in either direction, and at last saw, through an opening in the woods, that the forest was past, and she was approaching a place where the trees were thick only along the stream.

That would mean that there were broad pasture lands perhaps, and she must be wary. It would also mean that she would be out in open where her moving form could be seen unless she stuck close to the fringe of trees along the stream. She remembered how often her mother had spoken about being able to see her coming a long way off because the sun shone on her gold hair as if it were bright metal. She must do something about that before she went out into the sunshine. Would there be something in her bag she could tie over her head? Then she remembered an old gray rag in the pocket of the old coat she wore. It was the remnant of a silk handkerchief her father had owned in his better days, but long since worn beyond recognition as such. The edges were frayed and frowsy, and there was more than one hole in it, but it was large enough to tie around her head.

Gravely she took it out and adjusted it, spreading it over her whole head and covering the bright curls till not a thread of them showed, tying the ends in the back of her neck firmly. Then she buttoned the old coat to her throat, slung the bag around under her arm like a fishing basket, and marched on. If anyone sighted her perhaps they would think she was a boy out fishing. If she had only thought to hunt out her father's old hat, but she was not sure that it had not been taken by the other men. Nothing had been safe after he was gone.

She hurried along as fast as she could, for she began to feel again the weight of her bag, and her feet and limbs ached with the continuous going.

She had been used to running free in the open all her life, but a long continuous plodding journey she had not known. For sixteen years she had lived in the cabin, her only excitement the wandering to the limits her mother had set for her, her only pleasure climbing trees and looking off at a world she did not know, and might not explore. Well and strong she was indeed, and able to stand much hardships, for she had never known even comfort in her life, but this long strain of going over rough uncertain ground, her loss of sleep and lack of food, added to the sorrow she was bearing, were beginning to tell on even her splendid young constitution. She longed to drop down again and sleep, but she knew she must not. This was her best time for going. She must get to a good sleeping place before night.

So she plodded on, keeping as near as possible, when she emerged from the woods, to the fringe of trees along the river bank.

But finally the fringe of trees grew thin, and then stopped entirely, and the river broadened into a sheet of silver. And now the land on either side was flat for long distances, with mountains far away on either hand, and she could see far and wide, even without the glasses. The sun was distinctly behind her and her own shadow went flat and small and black before her, so she knew she was travelling in the right direction.

She trudged along several miles in this wide open space, growing more and more secure as she went on. There seemed to be no cattle on either side as far as she could see, just wide, lonely landscape, and she was glad. But she was beginning to feel as if she could not drag her feet very much farther, and kept looking ahead for a spot where she could rest securely.

The landscape, however, offered no refuge at this point, and the horizon stretched ahead bright and golden in the low afternoon sun. It seemed to her as she looked through her glass with a faint despair at her heart, that she could see almost to New York, and there was nothing between. Would she ever be able to make it?

At last she sank down in the grass and opened her bag. She must have something to eat. There was a sudden weakness upon her. So she took out her stores and ate another portion of corn bread, and a few small bites of the salt meat. To her starved appetite it tasted like the most savory meal. Then she drank a cup of water, corked the bottle carefully, tied up her kit and stood up.

The river was off at her left now, a rod or two away, for the ground where she was seemed to be an easier path for her feet than close by the river bank. The sun had turned the river into a broad band of gold, and the west was bright with its horizontal rays, blending sky and earth at the horizon into a golden haze as if an eternal city were just beyond that point. With her glass Fraley swept the land back of her and to either side and came at last to the view straight ahead, catching her breath at the beauty of the day that was departing, the exquisite tintings of the foliage, and sky and clouds, rejoicing that there was not even a sign of cattle anywhere about, save a few scattered ones miles away behind her.

Then, suddenly, as she looked, fear crept into her body like a great hand that gripped her as in a vise, for, out from the golden distance, along the ridge that led from as far as she could see, back along the line of the opposite mountain, and on toward the cabin she had left, there moved a little black dot!

At first she thought it must be a speck on the glass, and she carefully breathed upon it and polished it with her sleeve, but no, when she looked again the dot, growing rapidly larger, was moving on toward her. As she watched it, scarcely daring to breath, it gradually became three moving dots, one lighter than the rest, and still coming on over that ridge of the opposite mountain.

She tried to tell herself that she was nervous, excited, seeing things—that this was some sort of mirage. Her mother had told her of mirages on the desert—but this was not the desert.

Larger and larger the dots grew, nearer and nearer they came, racing along the ridge. They were so near now that through the glass she could distinctly see that they were horses, bearing riders. A conviction grew upon her that it was some of the men from the cabin out on a search party after her, and her knees grew so weak they shook. She dropped to the earth suddenly as if she had been shot as this fear grew to a certainty, and, keeping a sharp lookout, with lowered head, she crept on hands and knees toward a clump of bushes down by the river bank. Oh, if she had stayed over there instead of daring to take the more open ground! Perhaps they had already sighted her. Yet, unless they were carrying a field glass, they might not have seen her. Brand had a field glass she knew. But was it Brand or some of the others? Or was it only some passing cowboys who knew nothing at all about her?

When she reached the screen of the bushes she crept close, and thus in ambush trained her glass once more on the riders.

They were almost opposite her range now, and she could see them plainly, although they must be a long distance away. The air was clear and still, and she could hear them shout to one another, though she could not hear what they said, and once she thought she heard a curse flung into the golden evening. But as they came opposite she saw distinctly that two horses were dark, and one was white, and the white one was lame in his left hind foot.

Like little silhouettes they moved across the opposite ridge of mountain. Now she was sure, though she could not see the men's faces, that the one on the forward dark horse was Pete, the other dark one would be Shorty— they always went together; and the white horse was Pierce Boyden's, the man she hated and dreaded most of all except Brand Carter.

As she watched them through the screen of the bushes, they suddenly drew rein, and stood together, pointing off in her direction, as if consulting about their route. Then they turned their course and came down from the ridge of the mountain, winding like tiny puppets into the dark pathways of the mountain side. There was a patch of trees that hindered the sunlight and hid them now from view, and Fraley lay in her covert trembling. Oh, had they seen her through a glass, and were they coming to trap her here as she hid?

Perhaps Brand had called out Shorty's vicious hounds, and they were even now coming upon her from the other direction. Perhaps that pointing on the mountain ridge had been signalling to the others. They might all be upon her in a few minutes, and what could she do? There was positively no place to which she could flee in the wide open landscape, and there was no possibility that these sparse bushes would cover her if a search party came near. Oh, if there were only a hole in the ground!

Then it came to her that she might cover herself with grass. Perhaps they would not get here before the sun was much lower, and they might not notice, though the hounds would surely search her out if they were along. But it seemed the only thing she could do, so she fell to pulling the grass about and piling it into a great heap beside her.

She crouched as close to the bushes as she could get, burrowing her body into the loose soil, till the old coat was almost on a level with the surrounding ground, and the precious bag containing her treasures was beneath her. Then she set to work as well as she could to cover herself with the grass she had pulled, satisfied at last that she would not be noticeable unless some one came quite near. She put her face down on her arms, and lay still under her camouflage, and, before long there came a sound of voices, and of hoof beats ringing across the water.

Fraley in her flimsy refuge, cringed, and held her breath!

5

FRALEY'S worst fears were realized as the enemy drew near. It was indeed, as she had guessed, the three men, Pete and Shorty and Pierce, and, as she had thought, they had come that way in answer to a signal from Brand who had found the body of the dead dog lying in the clear water of the river.

The three men came riding down from the mountain, and halted a little way from the water just across from the clump of bushes that hid the trembling girl, and there they waited till Brand came riding up on the other side. He forded the river not two rods above the little grass mound which covered Fraley's old coat, and she held her breath and tried to keep from trembling, as she listened to the splash of his horse's feet when he stepped out into the water.

She could hear all they said. They were not drunk now, and their curses were so much the more cold blooded and deliberate, as each man told with a coarse laugh what he would do to the culprit when he found her. Fraley shut her eyes and wondered if hell were like this, and wondered again, as she had done many times of late, why God made men.

It appeared that there were other search parties out for her now. Shorty had been warned, and was to pass the word along. Not a man within the outlaw's territory but would rise to the occasion and keep a keen lookout along his border. She heard them name the places, and gathered much helpful information from their discussion, the only trouble with it being that there did not seem to be any direction she could turn in which she might find egress into the world beyond. They had shut up the gates of their world, and guarded all their defenses. How could she hope to escape?

She had no words with which to pray, but she lay there calling in her heart to God, and presently, seemingly without reason, the men all turned their horses and galloped away across the valley. Cautiously she peered through the thicket to watch them, marveling that they were gone, not daring to come out of her covert lest there be someone still in ambush lurking behind her.

She lay there until the damp ground chilled her to the bone, and a sick dizziness descended upon her. She wondered how long it took people to die of starvation. She was not near that yet, for there were still stores within her bag, but she felt a strange apathy about eating anything. If she could only lie there and sleep herself away out of this life!

But Fraley had been too well taught to let herself give up so easily, and soon the stillness all about her began to give her renewed assurance. Now was the time for her to find another hiding place The sun had gone lower in the west. It was almost down to the horizon.

Cautiously she peered out. It was all very still.

She rolled herself softly over and looked about. She took out the glass and searched in every direction. Far away to the northeast she could see those small specks climbing the mountain again. Dared she rise and get across the wide stretch of open space now? If they looked back with field glasses could they sight her?

She decided to keep low, and move slowly. No one could notice a flat thing on the ground. So she crawled until her muscles were too tired to go that way any longer, then she rose half way and ran a few steps, dropping to her knees and lying flat down again, till she made another survey, and so she slowly progressed across a space that seemed interminable. She kept going and going and never getting any nearer to anything.

And now the ground began to rise. She was sorry for that, for it would make her more visible from afar, but a careful survey of the horizon showed her three enemies just going over the ridge of the opposite mountain and the other riding far off to the northeast. She would be safe from them for a little while at least, and perhaps could get over beyond the hill somehow. Perhaps it was safer south than north, although she had an inner conviction that it was in that direction she would find the great herds of cattle. She rose and ran again, till she was ready to drop.

There was a tree on the little hill. Its foliage was scant, and would give little shelter from an enemy's eye, but it might give her an outlook beyond, and help her to know where to go, or where not to go which was much more important.

As she climbed the hill she began to hope again. If she could only get beyond the bounds where these men had no holdings—out beyond where they dared to go! She knew there were such bounds for her mother had often told her so, and warned her to keep close around the cabin where she belonged, for until she was beyond these bounds there was no safety. And now she began to understand why her mother had not dared to try to get away. It was hard enough for one to hide. Two could not have done it even so long. Neither could her frail little mother have endured the long journey on foot, and the exposure.

The sun had slipped its last gold-bound crimson edge behind the mountain as Fraley reached the tree, and she stood up with more assurance now. There was no brilliant sunlight to pick out her little figure as it stood upright upon the hill.

The tree was not quite at the top of the hill, but from its highest branch she felt she could see over, so she unstrapped her burden and laid it on the ground, while she took a tired hold of the tree, and began to go up, hand over hand, knees gripping the trunk hard, feet clinging like well-trained hands. Oh, she knew how to climb. It had been her one sport as she ranged her own mountain, keeping in sight of mother's signal, an old cloth she hung out on the line behind the cabin whenever she wanted Fraley to return.

So now, she went easily up into the branches, and clung there, searching with her glasses first the place whence she had come, then the opposite mountain, lying dark against a bright sky. It all lay peaceful and serene. She could now see bunches of cattle grazing here and there, or going down to patches of water to drink. Then she turned her eyes to the south.

The ground sloped down here to another valley which stretched out and narrowed farther on into a deep pass or cut between more mountains she did not remember having seen before. They were hidden from the cabin on her own mountain by the range that shut in this side of the valley she had just crossed.

There were no cattle in this pass, though she could see them farther back in the new valley, and as she studied every bit of ground within sight she could see, just below her, half hidden among a group of trees, a little log cabin. That startled her, for she feared it might belong to some of the gang of outlaws against which she had been warned. Her impulse was to slide down the tree at once and fly again, but a certain intuition warned her not to be in a hurry. So she clung quietly to her tree and studied the little log house in the waning light. Its single window on this side reflected the faint glow of the flame in the sunset sky, but there was no light of candle within, and the rude chimney gave forth no smoke, although this was the hour for preparing an evening meal if the occupant were at home. The place looked lonely and deserted, and she half decided that no one lived there till she noticed, a few rods beyond it, half way up the crest of the hillside, a cow tethered to a long rope. Then she decided that the householder was gone from home, and might return at any time now. For no one who valued his cow would remain away without milking it. It would certainly be wise to get beyond this house before the owner came back.

Having thus decided, she gave one sweep of the landscape with her glass to make sure all was right, then slid down the tree, took up her bag and hurried froward, keeping just below the crest of the hill where she could study the house, ready to fly back over on the other side if she saw signs of human approach.

When she had got past the back of the cabin and nearer to where the cow was tethered, the creature broke out bawling, and Fraley, accustomed to the ways of a cow, noticed that her bag was full. The poor thing needed milking, and no one was at home.

With sudden pity for the cow, she paused and looked around sharply. The landscape was very still, and deep shadows were beginning to gather in every hollow and crevice. It was twilight down there by the log cabin. If she only had a pail she could relieve the poor cow, and perhaps get some milk for herself. That would help greatly. Yes, down there on a bench by the door of the cabin was a pail turned upside down. Dared she steal down there and get it? Perhaps she was a fool to think of it, but she could not bear to see the poor cow suffering.

She hesitated and the cow started bawling again, as if she knew what the girl was thinking, and Fraley took a sudden resolve. This was something she must do.

Softly, cautiously, she stole down and secured the pail, swiftly flew back again up the hillside and behind the cow. With quick furtive glances about she knelt and began to milk, and soon the pail was foaming with the sweet warm liquid. The fragrance of it made the famished girl faint with her need of it. And when she had finished and the cow was comfortable again, she took out her tin cup and drank deeply. She had a right to that much surely, after having performed this service for the cow.

When she had drank all that she could she took out her little water bottle and carefully filled that full, setting the cork tight again. Then she carried the pail carefully down the hill and put it on the bench. There was nothing near with which to cover it, but at least she had done what she could. Then, having tiptoed away from the house, she fled up the hill and away, on feet that were suddenly frenzied at the thought of what she had done. Perhaps the owner of that cow was a friend of Brand's and would presently meet her and punish her for having drank his milk, and meddled with his cow.

Yet she was going now on the strength of that milk, with fleeter step than she had traveled all day long. New strength seemed to have come into her veins with that sweet warm draught.

There were woods beyond, and if she could gain them before she met any returning householder, perhaps she would be safe for another night. She had her eyes upon that narrow pass, out between the mountains. If she could gain that, and get beyond, perhaps she would be out in the world where safety lay.

It was growing dusky now, and the way was dim and indefinite. Rough stones cropped up and almost tripped her, little hollows appeared in unsuspected places and almost threw her. Yet her feet seemed to have been given wings for the moment; she fled over all difficulties, and, breathless at last, gained the shadow of the scattered woods.

The rose color and the flame, the golden and the green were fading now from the western sky, and the little pink clouds catching reflected glory in the east were scurrying away to the dark. There seemed to be no creature stirring, and the ground where she was travelling had grown rough and pebbly. The grass was scant, which gave her relief, for she knew there would be no cattle about, and she did not want to repeat the wild terror of the night before.

She kept along the edge of the woods again, with her face ever toward the mountain pass in the distance. She would go as long as she could see, then find a place to drop down and rest till the moon came up, and get on a little farther. So she kept on at an incredible pace—for one who had traveled as far and been through as many strenuous experiences as she had—until suddenly she came to a little nook that seemed made for rest, two trees with their roots locked together in a kind of natural couch.

The woods were behind her as she dropped down upon it, and the ground below her sloped away to a sort of gravelly bed, perhaps the bed of an old stream. Across a wide stretch of this she could see the looming darkness of the mountain beyond, that continued on to the pass which was almost invisible now that it was quite dark.

There were more of the friendly stars above than there had been the night before. She looked up and was glad they were there.

She gathered the old coat about her, drew closer the knot of the old handkerchief that covered her bright curls, placed her bag on the roots, curled her feet under her coat, lay down with her head pillowed on the old Bible, and soon fell asleep.

Back across two mountains and a valley her enemies drank and plotted to ensnare her, while behind her, and around her, were creatures of the dark, but none of them came near her, as she slept guarded by an angelic band or perhaps, even by the loved mother whose body was lying in a rude grave in the other valley. Who knows?

The moon rose, and grew bright. It sailed on high for hours, looked down on the little soul hid among the branches, and stole away on its course to the west. The stars twinkled dimly, and the night waned.

Up through the mountain pass on horses came two riders through the night. Their voices were low but distinct in the clear air. Their horses were weary, as though they had come a long way that day, and they rode slowly and talked deliberately. The horses' feet clinked on the rocky road as they went. The sound pierced the night and seemed to stir the little shadows as they came.

Something reached the young sleeper as they drew nearer, and she woke sharply in alarm, but did not stir. Her senses seemed to be startled into breathlessness. Were these her enemies come again to find her? And dared she try to escape again through those dark un-known woods? She felt too stupid with sleep to dare to climb a tree, and the travelers were too near now for her to move without giving them warning of her presence. No, she must just lie still, with her face hidden, and hope they would pass by without noticing her.

The voices came on, low, angry, troubled, disheartened. They did not sound like drunken voices; and with relief she noticed now that they were not any voices that she knew.

"It was that Pierce Boyden done it!" said the voice of one of the riders resentfully. "I seen him. But you can't do nothin' about it. He's too slick with his gun. You gotta let him get by with it."

"She was there, then? You're sure she was there?" the other voice questioned anxiously.

"Oh, yes, she was there. I seen her all right. I trailed her down—" Fraley's heart stood still with horror. These must be some of Brand's gang, and they had been trailing her! But what had Pierce Boyden to do with it? Had he some fiendish plan to trap her, and make her pay for her escape?

Then the older voice spoke again, gravely as if perplexed:

"But I thought that woman was dead. I thought they told you they saw her buried."

"Oh, you mean the old 'un," said the other man. "Yep, she's dead alrighty. No mistake! But the young 'un is at the old stand, an' she's ninety times as peppy as her ma! She's a looker, too, got bleached hair an' has the boys right on her string. She keeps 'em all a guessing, too."

"And you think Boyden did it for her sake?" questioned the elder.

"Positive! He's jealous as a cat. I stood right beside him an' I saw him look at her an' then I saw him draw a bead—!"

The riders suddenly rounded a curve behind the trees and their voices were drowned in a breeze that sprang up and tossed the branches about.

Fraley sat up and strained her ears, but could only catch detached words now and then that meant nothing, and there she sat for some time trying to make out what the men had meant. Draw a bead. Then they were not talking about her after all, perhaps. It must be some other girl. Who were these men? They did not sound as if they were friends of Pierce Boyden. The older voice sounded sad and different from the men hereabout. Perhaps it was the owner of the log cabin where she had milked the cow.

But she could take no chances. She must get away from here as soon as it was light enough to see a step before her. It would not do to go yet however. The men might be returning soon, or others of their party might straggle on behind. She must wait until she could see ahead of her or she would run into more difficulties.

She let her head drop back again on her hard pillow and closed her eyes. She did not intend to go to sleep again, just to rest until she felt it was safe to go on; but the weariness of her young flesh asserted itself, and she was soon soundly sleeping again, so sound that she did not hear a stealthy foot on the trail ten feet from her couch, nor hear the sniff of an inquisitive nose, as the creature paused and tried to analyze the new scent. Then across the valley a dark shadow stole into deeper shadows, and all was still again.

Day was just dawning when she was awakened again, this time by a leaf softly fluttering down on her face. Looking up startled she saw two bright eyes above her, as a saucy chipmunk frisked away on a slender limb and chattered noisily.

She sat up and looked about her cautiously. The

woods were very dim behind her yet, and still, save for a stray bird note now and then as some old chorister gave his warning cry preparatory to the early matins. Gray and dim also was the valley stretching out to the grim mountain beyond. But down at the end of the valley toward which she was facing, the mountain pass was lit with the rising sun, just the first pale streaks in the sky, rosy and golden, framed by the sentinel mountains on either hand—a wondrous picture to gaze at. Fraley caught her breath at the beauty of it.

But this was no time to gaze at beautiful pictures. She must be on her way before the enemy was on her track. If she could make the mountain pass before anyone came by, she felt she would have some chance. But it was a long way off, and she could not tell but perhaps it might be an all day's walk. Distances were deceptive. She had learned that yesterday.

Reaching in her bag she took out the little bottle of milk and drank its contents. She might need it more later, but by then it might have soured, and she must not run the risk of losing it.

She started on her way in the mist before the dawning, walking toward the rising sun. She found herself stiff and sore from lying on her humpy bed, and from the exertions of the day before, but the milk had heartened her, and she stepped forth briskly, trying to keep a straight course to the mountain pass.

The going was easier than the day before, for the trail was clearly defined as if it were in frequent use, and she got on faster than she had hoped. Before the sun was up above the mountain she was fairly beneath the grim straight shadow of this great stone gateway into the next valley—into a new world for her, she hoped. Nearer and nearer she drew to its foot, and passed between the rocky walls, looking up, straight up to heaven with a new awe upon her. She had never been right at the foot of a great sheer mountain like this before, and it almost oppressed her with its grandeur. It somehow surprised her to note that there was foliage draped upon its rugged breast, trailing vines putting out new leaves of tender green, gray moss and lichens covering the bare rocks in other places, here and there a small windflower growing, unafraid, from a crack in the stone, and blossoming a childish pink or blue, blowing in the wind as happily as if it had opened its eyes in a safe sweet meadow instead of on this bare cliff. And up toward the summit one or two temerarious pines had set courageous fingers in a crevice, and were growing out above the pass like truants, daring others to swing high and wide and free.

As she entered the gloom of the pass itself she paused and took a brief survey of the country she was leaving behind her. It lay green and still in the early light, and the few cattle she could distinguish were, most of them, lying down as if they had not wakened yet. There was no sign of human kind, no horses even in sight, and with relief she turned and hurried forward, wishing to get beyond this place before anyone could meet her or come behind her.

The trail was rougher here, and stony. It hurt her feet sometimes so that she had to stop and rub them, but she had no time to think of discomfort. It seemed so long to the end of the pass. The mountains were as thick through as they were high. It was like a great tunnel without a top through which she was passing. If she were caught in here there would be no place to hide. Perhaps she should not have attempted it in this growing daylight! She dared not linger.

The sun was three hours' high when she reached the end, her breath coming in quick painful gasps, for she had almost run the last mile, so great had been her panic.

The sound of a stone rolling down the mountain, the dripping of water from the crevices of rock startled her like shouts in the open. She kept a furtive watch behind and before for other travelers, and when she found she had really reached the end of the gloomy pass without molestation she could hardly believe her senses.

It was bright morning now, out in the world to which she had come. The valley was filled with grass, and dotted here and there with trees. This latter fact gave her new hope, for at least a tree was a place of refuge from cattle, if not from men. Cattle and men were her two enemies. There were some cattle in this new valley, but they were off to the left, and seemed to be quietly grazing. Perhaps she could pass beyond them without attracting their attention. The way was wide and comparatively smooth, and though she was worn with the excitement of the past hours, still she could walk fairly fast, and made good progress. Every step onward meant one nearer to freedom for her, and though the bag on her shoulders dragged heavily sometimes, she went forward with good heart, determined to get across one more wide open stretch before she need fear meeting other travelers abroad.

In the wide distance there glittered water, like a sheet of silver, but it seemed as far away as fairyland or heaven. To it her eager footsteps were now directed. It was as if she were in a wide sort of cup, with mountains all around, and mountains in the distance just beyond the glittering water. She felt safe and protected. And yet it was through this same valley that the two men who passed her last night must have come. She must not be too trustful.

Thus reasoning, she kept a constant scanning of the distance in every direction, and arrived about high noon at a small foothill where there were groups of young trees, and a spring of water that trickled down into a tiny stream and disappeared in the valley again. She was thirsty now, for she had eaten some of the salt pork, and the last of her corn bread as she walked along, and for the last half hour had been parched for a drink. She dipped her cup in the spring and enjoyed the clear cold water, dashing some in her face, smoothing her hair back with her wet hands and tying the kerchief over her head again. But she could not stop for more than this tidying. She felt that she must utilize every moment of this bright peace and quiet to get on into safety. This long-continued absence of anything to make her afraid was almost too good to be true, and she must not rest secure.

She hurried up the hill, after cooling her hot feet in the water for a moment, and when she almost reached the top she flung herself full length upon the ground and began to creep up. She would not make herself a target for any eyes that might be searching the landscape. So she crept up till she could peer over, and then slid slowly back, her heart beating fast. The valley below her was full of cattle, and riding among them were three horsemen, seemingly rounding them up. Far away, at the upper end of the range, she could see two more horsemen riding toward the others. Her one quick glance was enough to tell her that Pierce Boyden was one of the men among the cattle, and that he was riding his white horse. The back of another looked like Pete but she could not be sure, and she waited no longer to identify the others, for a great panic had seized her. She rolled down that hill, and darted out into the golden day across the open like a frenzied creature. She ran and ran until she was breathless, and still she kept on, staggering through high grass, crushing through brush and brambles, wading a little stream that came in her way regardless of its depth, and the fact that it was wetting her brief skirt, and soaking up the edges of the old coat she wore. She seemed to have always been running, and still she ran on, panting for breath, her eyes blinded now, unable to see whither she was going, until suddenly she stumbled and fell across a tree trunk that had been hidden by tall grass. She lay there trying to get her breath and wishing she need never have to rise again, afraid to open her congested eyes lest the sun would blind her, too weary to even think.

6

IN a few minutes it began to dawn upon her senses that she was no longer out in the sunlight but was lying in the cool shade somewhere, and all about her everything was very still. Cautiously she opened her eyes and saw she was lying in the shade of a mountain that loomed above her, and off beyond it she could see the water flashing, a silver sheet in the sun.

She sat up and looked around, half dazed by her fall, her head feeling queer and dizzy. She got out her field glass and put it up to her bewildered eyes, but presently she identified the low green hill in the distance as the one she had crept up a while before. She had then come safely across the wide spaces, and was close to the water, incredible as it seemed. She had thought that water a whole day's journey away when she sighted it from the little hill.

Glad and thankful she rose and tried to walk. Her whole body was stiff and sore, and her feet were swollen and bruised with the stones, for she had not tried to save them in her flight. But she felt she must keep on around that mountain till she was out of sight of the valley she was leaving.

It was just as she reached the turn where a moment more would open up a new vista to her troubled gaze, that she turned back once more to look and saw the big drove of cattle pouring from a narrow pass between the little hill and the opposite mountain, and among them were five riders!

Horrified, she flattened herself against the rock that loomed above her, and peered through the branches of a tree that grew out from the side of the mountain, watching, fascinated, dumb with hopelessness. They were a long way off, but it would not take them long to catch up with her, and where could she flee? Unless the rocks and the mountains opened up and took her in, or fell on her to hide her she was lost; for the moving procession seemed to be coming straight her way.

She hugged the rock, her fingers reaching out along its surface, like a child who clings for protection, and a strange thing happened. Her hands found a wide crevice in the rock, a sort of fissure, and looking, she saw it was an opening where the rock had split away, making a fissure some seven or eight inches wide, with part of the split rock fallen out making a screen in front. It was wet inside as if a small stream or spring had worked a way behind the rock, and the opening was small. But could she slip inside? If she could she would be practically hidden.

Shifting her bundle, she flattened herself as much as she could and squeezed between the rocks. A sharp jagged edge bruised her shoulder, and her foot slipped on the mossy stones as she went through so that she struck her face, but she accomplished it, and slid behind the fallen pieces of mountain.

Safely hidden, she found that she could peep through

the crevice and watch the oncoming group. There was a great bunch of cattle, and the men were riding hard to keep them in check. They seemed to be coming directly toward her, and were probably going round this mountain straight to the lake, toward which, five minutes before, she herself had been happily hurrying, thinking to find safety. The men on horseback were so close now that she could see the ugly set of Pierce Boyden's jaw, the cruel blue eyes, the sensuous lips, as he dug his spurs deep into his horse's flanks and rounded up a tricky steer. And now she could see the long scar on his cheek that glowed an angry red. In a moment more he would be where he could see straight into her hiding place!

She shrank back and fell to trembling, not daring to look any longer, slipped down to her knees on the cold wet stones, with her face against the wet rock, her eyes closed, and prayed.

The cattle herd swept on, with trampling of hoofs, and shouting of the men, but she began to realize that they were not going on toward the water, but were rounding the mountain back of her. Perhaps the cattle had tried to stampede for the water, and that was why they came so far out of their straight course; but at any rate they were going on, and in a very short time they were out of sight and sound.

It was a long time before the girl dared creep from her hiding place, and then so fearfully, so tremblingly that she found it hard work to squeeze through the tiny opening. Fearfully she gazed about her, studying the farthest corner with her glass. Her enemies were gone again and she safe once more!

With her hand touching the great rock, she crept on around her mountain, knowing that her strength was spent. She must find a place in which to rest.

Perhaps a mile further on, around the other side of the

mountain, she came upon another great rock split away from the mountain, leaving a hollow place behind it like a cave. Here was shelter surely, and before her lay the great sheet of silver water, almost round, and clear as crystal.

The shore line seemed deserted. There was no sign of shack or habitation of any sort in sight. If there were humans living about, it must be beyond the thick foliage which clustered at the upper end, and that would be too far to see a small lone figure creeping in behind a rock. She needed food, but she was too tired to eat the salt meat, or the dry meal which was all that she had left, so she crept to the edge of the lake, filled her cup, drank plenty of water, then stole back to her cave, arranged her hard pillow and lay down. There might be processions of enemies going by, but she was out of sight; the mountain behind which she hid might be full of wild animals, but the thought did not occur to her. Utterly spent, she lay down and slept, and knew not when the second sun went down upon her pilgrimage, nor when the stars came out or the young moon like a silver boat was reflected in her lake, upside down. It might even have been that some night creatures crept about her feet and sniffed at their strange companion, but she slept on.

It was early morning when she woke again, startled and wondering where she was. A sparkling new day lay before her, with the lake in white ruffled wavelets, lapping softly on the pebbly shore.

She stole from her hiding place and looked around, but there was no one in sight. She would have liked to take a swim in the clear water, as she and her mother had often done on days when the men were away and the trail to the river free from intrusion, but she dared not, so near the enemies' territory. Those cattle were probably being driven somewhere to be sold, and it might be that while Pierce and Pete and the others were away, she would be more free to escape from this region entirely. She must not delay. So, adjusting her bag to her shoulders comfortably, she went down to the water's edge, filled her water bottle, tucking it safely into the bag, and then stooped for a refreshing dash of water in her face and on her arms. She took a long drink, too, lapping the water Gideon fashion, and felt better. Now she would hurry on at once.

But before she could rise, the sense of another presence near by brought a great fear. Turning her head she saw not five feet away from her, standing beside his black horse, her old enemy Pete. He leered at her with a wicked grin of triumph, knowing that he now had her in his power.

For an instant she was too frightened to think or move, and the strength seemed to be ebbing out through her feet leaving her helpless there before him, as he stood gloating over her. Oh, if the water would but rise and receive her out of his sight! She had a wild thought of flinging herself into it, though she knew Pete carried a wicked weapon, and would shoot with unerring aim, only to wound and capture her at last. Pete was a great swimmer too. She could not escape that way.

Then in her terror she seized upon the only weapon at hand, the pebbles and sand at her feet. With a quick motion, so deadly quick and subtle that Pete was taken off his guard, she flung the two handfuls of sand and tiny pebbles straight into those two evil eyes, and springing past him as he cringed with sudden maddening pain she flung herself toward the fiery black horse. Would he let her mount? He was known as an ugly brute, and had always seemed to her to possess a demon spirit like his owner. But he was her only hope now to get away.

Perhaps the horse too was taken unaware by the

daring of this slip of a girl, a little white, frightened, flying creature who hurled herself upon his back and dug her bare heels into his sides.

The bridle had been flung over the saddle, but she had no time to grasp it, for when the beast felt this new rider upon his back, he began to rear and plunge and she could only throw her arms about his neck and cling with a desperation born of her terrible plight.

Failing to dislodge her at the third plunge, the horse whirled with a peculiar motion all his own that would almost have flung off a leech, and started to run. The running was almost like a bolt of lightning, or a ball shot from a cannon, and had not Fraley been trained by her father to ride a wild western pony fearlessly when she was a little child, she would have stood no chance whatever in this race with death. But she had early learned to hold on, and now as the horse fairly flew through the world with a wild unbridled freedom that was breath taking and horrifying, she clung as she had never clung before, each second seeming a year of horror. The bag across her shoulders banged its weight against her, and each instant seemed about to be torn away from her by the motion—would she ever be able to find it again if it dropped off?—Her hair blew wildly over her eyes and whipped her face unmercifully. She expected momently to be flung to earth, and her heart was beating so wildly that it seemed to her it was about to burst. Was that a shot she heard? She could not be sure, but she felt rather than saw that they had skirted the lake and already left it behind.

Then just when it seemed that her strained muscles could not hold on another second the horse stopped stock-still so suddenly and unexpectedly that the aching muscles, set rigidly for the motion of swiftly shooting forward, suddenly lost their grip; and when the horse as suddenly rose upon his hind legs and shook himself with a spiral motion, Fraley went limp and slid to earth in a crumpled little heap, everything gone black around her.

When she came to herself and looked around the horse was gone, and a deadly inertia was upon her. She felt too languid even to raise her head or her hand, and somehow did not seem to care whether she was in danger or not! She wondered if perhaps she was dying.

Gradually her memory returned, and with it the sense of danger. She began to bestir herself slowly and at last rose to a sitting posture and took account of stock.

Her first anxiety came when she discovered that the bag was not about her shoulders. But on further examination she found that it was lying only a few feet away, one strap torn and some of the contents scattered about.

With trembling limbs she crept over to it and began gathering up her things, the slow tears rolling down her cheeks.

When she came to the field glass she remembered Pete. Perhaps he was already almost upon her. She put the glasses to her eyes, and searched the distance fearfully, but there was no sign of living creatures as far as the eye could reach, not even a glimmer of a lake. The horse must have brought her a long way, but he would probably return to his master. It would not take Pete long to give the warning to his mates, and they would surround her. For by this time Pete was probably recovered from the sand she had thrown in his eyes, and he would be angrier than ever. No torture would be too great for her punishment.

In new panic she looked around and discovered a forest not far away. Could she get to it? Fear winged her feet and gave her new strength, and she started in haste for the only shelter offered.

And then it took nearly an hour to get to the edge of

the woods. By this time she was faint with hunger and worn with anxiety, and could hardly drag one foot after the other. She sank down at last in the heart of the forest, too spent to do anything for a time but lie with closed eyes and just be thankful she was sheltered.

She was not hungry now. The anxiety and fatigue and the shock of the fall had taken her appetite away, but she was sick and dizzy for lack of food and knew she should eat something.

She dared not make a fire to bake her meal into cakes, and she dared not eat salt pork alone lest she be tormented with thirst. She had taken the precaution to wash and fill her water bottle when she first went down by the lake, but that would not last long, and there was no telling how far she might have to go before she found water again.

But she must eat or she could not go on, so she took out the little bag of meal and forced herself to chew some of the dry meal slowly, washing it down with sparing sips of water, till at last she felt a little better.

And now her uncharted course led her through the forest, one of the tall primeval kind, with dim sweet light filtering from far above, and distant birds flying from branch to branch and singing strange sweet songs. Little squirrels raced and chattered from bough to bough, and the air was delicious with balsam breath. The paths were smooth here, soft and resinous with pine needles, and little pretty cones she longed to stop and pick up. It was a place she would have loved to linger in, and once she sat down at the foot of a great tree, looked up the length of its mighty trunk, and drew a deep breath of relief. It was like finding sanctuary from trouble to walk these forest aisles and she dreaded to leave it.

It was late in the afternoon when she finally stepped fearfully out from the woods, wondering if after all she had not better remain there for another night. The sun could not be more than two hours from setting now, and the world looked strange and different as she paused and tried to get her bearings. There were still some mountains in the distance, but they did not look quite like the mountains she knew. They were far away, and purple with a misty light upon them, and the land ahead of her looked flatter, and had been fenced in places, though there were still wide stretches of land without fences, with just a sort of hard flat trail over them. This must be what men in the world called a road.

Strange that just going through a forest, even a wide forest like the one she had traversed, should make things different. Here there seemed to be no friendly hidings, few trees together that could be climbed in time of need. She hardly knew how to adjust herself to this new outlook.

She stepped timidly down from the wooded bank, and started along the cleared smooth way. It was even easier going than in the forest, and she made good time. But what, she wondered, should she do if enemies on horseback came along that way and met her? Here were no convenient holes in which to burrow, no kindly mountain to offer shelter, only the open country wide and frightening and different. It seemed so far to anywhere, yet there was a way marked out, and on the beaten path she took her unknown course.

It might have been an hour she walked along, her feet growing sore with the dust between her toes, and longing for rest again, when a strange foreign noise began to grow upon her consciousness. It came from behind her, and she stopped in a nameless dread, as she saw an old horse jogging along the road at a steady pace, drawing a shackly vehicle of the type known as a buckboard. It was the rattle of the wobbling wheels, more than the thud

thud of the old horse's feet on the dirt road, that had made the queer noise, but the sight of the oncoming equipage frightened the little pilgrim more than anything that had come her way yet.

There was nothing to do but stand aside till the thing had passed, or take to the open and run, and she had sense enough to see that this course would lay her open to suspicion far more than to sit by the wayside and rest. So she sat down a little off the beaten track, and looked toward the sunset, as if she had come out for that purpose, even as she might have done at home by the old cabin in the mountains.

She could not yet see the driver of the equipage very clearly, but she knew that none of her immediate enemies drove such things as that, they all went horseback. Of course it might be some of their gang who had been sent to trace her, but if it was she would have to face it out somehow. She selected deliberately a spot of ground that was a bit higher than the road, and throwing her bag down, flung herself beside it, resting one elbow on the firm square of the old Bible, her hand slipped through the strap, if there came a need for sudden flight.

On came the buckboard, and presently she could see the driver quite plainly. It was a woman, dressed in an old dark cotton frock, with a man's felt hat on the back of her head. A few straggling gray locks of hair hung down around her ears, and her skin was darkly tanned like old tired leather. She sat slouched forward on the rickety seat, occasionally looking over her shoulder to a box of things that were lashed to the back of the rig. When she got opposite to Fraley she drew rein and stopped, gazing at her pleasantly, and not at all curiously.

"Howdy!" she said with a kindly leather smile, "want a lift?"

Fraley half rose, a frightened look in her eyes, ready for almost anything, but glad that it was a woman.

"Want a—*what?*" she asked doubtfully.

"Goin' my way?" explained the woman questioningly. "Want a lift? It's late fer walkin'. Hop in!"

"Oh!" said the girl, beginning to comprehend. "Thank you—I—How much will it be to ride a little way?"

"Not a cent!" responded the woman heartily. "We don't charge fer lifts out our way. I'm gettin' back to the ranch before dark ef I kin make it. Left the children alone with the dogs. Gettin' oneasy about 'em, so hop in quick! I ain't got time to waste!"

Fraley was coming down the bank swiftly now. The invitation sounded too good to be true, for her weary feet would hardly carry her down the slope, and the bag dragged heavily on her shoulder as if it were weighted with iron.

"You—are—very kind!" she said shyly, as she climbed up beside the woman. It was only after the old horse had started on his jog trot again that she bethought her this might possibly be a person sent by her enemies to lure her back to them. So she rested the heavy bag in her lap, and sat tongue-tied, choking over the thought.

"How fur be you going?" asked the woman turning kindly, uncurious eyes upon her.

"A good many miles," stated Fraley noncommittally. "I'm sure I'm much obliged for the ride," she added, as her mother had taught her was proper.

"Well, you mustn't let me carry you outta your way," said her hostess. "My ranch turns off to the right about fifteen miles beyond here."

"Oh, that's all right," said Fraley, relieved that it did not turn to the left. Somehow her instinct taught her that the Southern route was best, at least until she was farther east.

"Come fur?" asked the woman, still eyeing her admiringly.

"Yes, a good ways," said Fraley laconically.

"Well, where are you goin'? I don't wantta take you outta yer way."

"Why, down this road," said the girl, "I—you see, I'm just travelling."

"Ummm!" observed the woman in a tone that implied her answer was inadequate.

"I'm on my way to New York!" she added desperately, feeling that she must make some explanation. The woman reminded her a little of her mother.

"Umm! Yer young to be goin' that fur alone!" observed the woman affably. "What's yer ma think o' yer goin'? I hope ye ain't running away. Ef ye are I ken tell ya it don't pay! I done it, and look at me!"

"Oh," said Fraley, her tired eyes suddenly filling with tears, "my mother is dead! She told me to go. Yes, I'm running away, but not from anybody that has a right—"

"There, there, honey child, don't you cry! I hadta ast. You see I'm a mother, an' you is too little and sweet eyed to be trampin' around these here diggin's alone so near night. There's them that might do ya harm."

"But I have to go. I have—people—in the east."

"Well, thank goodness fur that!" said the woman warmly, "an' I'll take ye home with me to-night, and you can have a good supper and a nice sleep before you start on. You look all beat out. And in the morning my Car'line'll harness up an' give ya a lift over ta the railroad. It ain't so fur, an' she's used ta drivin' alone. She can take Billy along fer comp'ny on the way back."

"Oh, thank you," said Fraley again, still frightened at the way her affairs were being managed for her. She didn't want to go to a strange ranch. There would be men there, and there might be friends of Brand's or Pierce's. Then she would not be safe ever, for they would come and hunt her wherever she went if they once got track of her. They would claim she was theirs.

"My old man died three years back and left me with five children," went on her would-be hostess. "I thought we'd come to the end, but I stuck it out, and now Jimmie is fifteen, and he can do a man's work. I useta have a hired man, but he got drunk and I got tired of it, so now we just look after things ourselves."

"Oh," said Fraley suddenly relieved there were no men to face at the ranch.

"That's one reason I'm hurryin' home. Jimmie's plantin' t'day, an' he'll be tired, and Car'line's got a cut on her hand an' can't milk. I got two cows, and they'll be bawlin' fit ta kill. I don't let the young children milk; they're too fresh. Last time Billy tried he knocked a whole pail of milk over on himself."

"Oh, I can milk," said Fraley eagerly. "If you'll let me milk to pay for staying, I'd be glad to come to your house to-night."

"You got such little hands I wouldn't think you could bring the milk down," remarked the woman eyeing Fraley's little brown hands that lay relaxed in her lap.

"But I can," said the girl earnestly.

"All right. You can try. I've got an awful lot to do to red up. I'm expecting a man t'morra from over beyont the mountain. His name's Carter, Brand Carter. Mebbe you've heard of him. He's coming to look over some steers I've got for sale!"

7

FRALEY'S face grew white as milk, and her heart seemed almost to cease to beat. The sustaining power seemed to ebb away from her arms and shoulders, and her whole body slumped. With the relaxing of her position the bag on her lap began to slide, and in a second more would have gone out onto the road. But she rallied and caught it, and covered her confusion well with the effort.

"Say, you don't need ta hold that heavy bundle!" exclaimed the woman, alert at once to be kindly. "Here! Lemme put it back in my box. There's plenty a room there, and it can't get out! You're all beat out, an' you're white as a sheet!"

"Oh, thank you—but I'm all right!" urged Fraley, gripping her precious bag close once more. "I'd rather hold it. There are some very special things in it. They might fall out. It doesn't fasten very close together."

"But ain't it heavy? My land! I don't see how you ever managed carrying all that, hiking it! I think it's better to travel light. What you got in there? Can't you ship 'em on by freight?"

"Oh, no!" said Fraley aghast, "I wouldn't want to trust it that way! It's my Bible, that's the only heavy thing, and I couldn't be without it. Besides, I wouldn't be sure just where to send it till I got there."

"Why, ain't you got your folks' address?"

"Yes, I have the old address, but they might have moved," said Fraley evasively.

"Hmmm! Well, you could leave it to my house till you got fixed and let me know where to send it. Me, I wouldn't bother about just a Bible. You can buy 'em cheap anywhere."

"Oh, no!" said the girl horrified, "not like this one. This was my mother's Bible. She taught me to read out of it. It has things written down in the cover—things that she wrote for me! I promised her I'd never let it away from me!"

"Oh, well, that's diffrunt, of course, ef your maw wrote things down fer you to remember. I thought ef 'twas jest a common Bible why you cud git one most ennywheres. I don't see what use they is ennyhow! Except ta sit round on the parlor table like a nornament and hev ta dust all the time. Me, I didn't even bring mine with me when I cum out here. I hed too much else ta think about. I never missed it. I was too busy ta dust books. Besides, I never had no parlor table. Say, why don't you stay ta our house awhile? You cud be comp'ny fer my Car'line. Mebbe she wouldn't be so crazy to git out an' see the world ef she hed a girl her own age to talk to. She's got men comin' to see her, a'ready, an' she ain't much older'n you. There's one comes ridin' over the crest of the mountain every oncet an' a while. She's allus fussin' up when he comes. His name's Pierce somethin'. I didn't rightly git the last name, an' I won't ast Car'line, it would give her too much satisfaction. But I don't like his eye. It ain't nice. I donno why, but it ain't.

Say, whyn't you stay over a week er so an' be comp'ny fer Car'line? It might kinda make her more contented like."

"Oh, I couldn't!" said Fraley in a small disturbed voice. "I'm sorry, but I just couldn't. I really ought to go on to-night. You see I'm in a great hurry. I'll just ride as far as you go, and by that time I'll be rested and can go on. I really must get on to-night."

There was actual panic in her voice. Brand and Pierce! Then she was not out of their region after all! Perhaps she was getting into an even worse place. Perhaps Brand or Pierce would come to-night and find her in this woman's house!

"Naw, you can't go on ta-night!" said the woman eyeing her curiously, "I ain't lettin' no kid like you go gallivantin' out in the dark. There's wolves beyond the ranch in the forest. They come out sometimes. My Jimmy seen 'em. You ain't got no gun, hev ye? Well, you jest better wait till daylight. It'll be plumb dark now afore we git to my shack, an' time fer you ta rest. My Car'line, she'll git ya off at daybreak, ef that'll suit ya, but I ain't lettin' no child wander off ta get lost in the desert this time o' night. Ef you'd get inta the desert alone, an' lose yer way yer bones might bleach white afore anyone found 'em. You trust me."

Fraley's face could turn no whiter, but she said nothing more. Perhaps there would be a chance to steal away in the night.

The sky ahead was showing pearly tints with blue and green and fire pink like an opal. When she turned to looked behind her the sun was a burning ball just touching the rim of the horizon, and poised above a dark mountain. But she was relieved to see that so far there was no traveler in the long beaten strip of white road that rose and fell and rose again mile after mile as far as she could see, till the forest through which she had come intercepted.

The woman began to talk of her home, and the children, telling bits of family life, till Fraley grew interested. Her heart leaped at the thought of knowing another girl. Only once or twice had she seen girls of her own age, once when a party of tourists lost their way and stopped at the cabin to inquire. There had been two pretty girls in that company, dressed in lovely garments the like of which she had never seen before; and once she had seen some girls in the town when her father took her with him to buy her shoes. The ride had taken all day, and she had been very tired. He never took her again. He said it was too much trouble. It would be nice to know a girl—and to see some children. There had been no children near the cabin since her baby brother died of croup, and she was a tiny thing then herself.

It was quite dark when at last they came in sight of a speck of light in the distance. She could see nothing in the blackness but that light like a red berry, and she began to be afraid again.

"That's my place!" announced the woman cheerfully. "Now, we'll have some grub. I'm gettin' hongry. What about you? There! Hear the dogs howl! They know it's me jest as well zif they cud see me. We keep five dogs about the place an' there couldn't no stranger come within a half a mile 'thout we'd know it. You like dogs? Ever have one?"

"I had a dog—But—it is dead!" said Fraley in a low voice, and the woman could see the tears were not far away.

"Well, they will die, too. That's so! But they're right useful whilst they live. I reckon Car'line's got hot bread fer supper. You like hot bread? Car'line kin make it good. She knows how to housekeep real well, an' she c'n work the farm too, only I won't let her. I say that's man's work. Though goodness knows I've done enough of it myself, too. But that's diffrunt! Car'line ain't gonta!"

They were nearing the ranch house now, a long low building made of logs. The door was flung open wide, and a stream of light shot out into the night. A sudden shyness descended upon Fraley. She wondered what to say to these strange people. She had had no dealings with her own kind, and she remembered keenly the mirthful glances of the two daintily dressed girls in the lost party on the mountain. They had made fun of her bare feet, she knew as well as though she had heard the words they were whispering. What would this Caroline think of her?

Then the dogs broke about them with barks of joy, and leaped at the woman, as she halted the old horse in front of the door.

Fraley stood, in a moment more, inside the open door, holding her precious bag in her arms, looking like a frightened rabbit.

She did not know that she made a picture as she stood there in her bare feet, and the old coat and kerchief, with the light of a big log fire flickering on the golden curls that strayed from under the binding silk. The other children stood off, suddenly shy, and watched her, and she eyed them, and then stared at the great beautiful fire in bewilderment. She had never been in a room like this, nor seen a fire in an open fireplace.

Off at one side was a table set with dishes, neatly, and chairs drawn up. There was a foaming pitcher of milk and another of molasses, and there was a pile of corn cakes keeping warm on a tin on the hearth. There was a smell of appetizing meat cooking sending up exquisite steam from a kettle slung over the fireplace.

The baby of the house ran and jumped into her mother's arms, and the others stood around evidently happy that she had come home. It seemed like heaven to Fraley.

Car'line stood by the side of the fire and stared at the girl her mother had brought home. Said "Howdy" perfunctorily when her mother told her to, and went on looking at her curiously. The other children stood around and watched her.

There was a certain dignity about Fraley, even as she stood there in bare feet clasping her bundle, that made the others feel shy. But suddenly one of the dogs sprang through the door, went wagging from one member of the family to the other, wagged up to the stranger, sniffing about her skirts, and laying his muzzle against her hand. Fraley stooped down, and began to pat him, snuggling her arm around him. Here was someone she understood, and who understood her.

"Oh, he is a dear dog!" she said looking up, and he wagged his tail and whined in pleasure at her attention.

There was something in the tone of her voice, or the way she said it, that made the children stare again. This was a person of another kind. There was something fine in the quality of her speech that they recognized as beyond theirs, which Car'line, perhaps resented a little.

"He's fell fer you all right," said the mother as she removed the old felt hat she wore and hung it on a peg between the logs.

"I ken see he thinks you're jest right. Swing that kettle round, Car'line, you'll have that stew burned before we get a chance to get it et up. Whar's Jimmy?"

The boy appeared at the door, awkward in the presence of the stranger, but melted into a grin as he saw how the dog had made friends with her.

"She's a girl I picked up on the road," introduced his mother informally. "She's goin' to stay with us t'night. She's all right."

"I bet she is," vouched Jimmy. "Buck wouldn't take up with 'er ef she wasn't. Say, girl, you gotta dog t'home, ain't ya? He smells it on ya I guess."

"I did have," said Fraley sadly, drooping her head to hide the tears that stung her eyes, "He—got—shot,— two days—ago!"

"Aw shucks! Ain't that a dirty shame!" said Jimmy sympathetically.

Fraley liked Jimmy from that time, and the rest of the children gathered around her with clumsy affection, feeling that her love for dogs had made her kin to them.

They gathered around the table while Car'line took up the stew in big tin plates. Fraley had a nicked thick white one because she was company.

She took off her head kerchief and washed her hands at the tin basin on the bench as the rest did. Then she sat down as a guest at a table with strangers for the first time in her life.

And here, as before, they noticed a difference in her. She did not reach out and grab for things. She did not make a noise with her lips as she ate, nor swoop up gravy with her spoon; she did not fill her mouth too full, nor talk when she was chewing. She seemed to eat without doing so. She put things into her mouth with quiet little unobtrusive movements, as if eating were quite a secondary thing, yet she seemed to enjoy what they gave her and accepted the second helping when it was offered.

The children watched her fascinated, the candle light playing on her gold hair, and on her delicate features. She seemed like a creature from another world to them. Yet she was telling their mother that she had lived all her life in these parts, and the garments she wore were no better than their own.

It appeared that the cows had been milked by Car'line and Jim, so the guest had no opportunity to prove her abilities in that line, but she promised to be up bright and early next morning to do it before she left.

It was after the supper was cleared away and Fraley had helped with the washing up, that they gathered around the fire, and Fraley felt a sudden loneliness in the midst of this friendly family. She and her mother had been like this together, even though there had been but two of them, and now there was no one! If only this were thousands of miles away from the home cabin gladly would she have accepted the earnest invitation of her hostess to stay on indefinitely and visit. But the thought of the men who were expected on the morrow to buy steers filled her with terror.

"Say, why'n't you git out yer Bible an' read to us all?" asked the mother presently, reaching forward to stir up the fire with a long stick that lay on the hearth. "I'd like to see what it sounds like after all these years; an' it wouldn't do these children any harm to hear it oncet, too."

Fraley shrank from bringing out the dear relic, sewed so carefully into its cotton covers by the hand of the beloved; but she could not refuse when they had been so kind to her. She must do something to repay them for her supper and night's lodging. So she went to the corner where she had laid by her gray woolen bag and took out the Bible for the first time since her mother had committed it to her care. She was a little troubled as she did so because of the papers which her mother had told her were inside the book, but when she unwrapped the outer sheathing of cotton, she found that the cover was fitted tightly over the old worn boards of the original, and that the papers were securely placed within this outer jacket of cloth with a fold of the cloth turned inside over their edges. Then she need not explain everything to these strangers, and have them fingering over her precious papers and asking her all sorts of questions when she had scarcely seen the papers herself.

With quiet reserve she took the chair that her hostess had placed for her beside the table, where two candles pierced the gloom of the room outside the ring of firelight.

"Where shall I read?" she asked lifting her serious big eyes to look about the group.

"Any place!" said Car'line peering over her shoulder curiously, "Is it a story?"

"Yes, it's full of stories."

"Read what you like," said the mother.

So Fraley turned to a favorite chapter to repeat it.

The candle light flickered on the worn page, the edge almost in tatters, where the little Fraley had fingered it long ago when she learned it; and the sweet earnest face of the girl was bent over the book for a moment and then lifted, with her gaze across to the firelight, as she spoke the wonderful words.

The family watched her spellbound.

"Say, you ain't lookin' on that there book, how can you know what it says?" interrupted Jim finally, too puzzled to wait till she was done. "Are you all makin' that up?"

Fraley smiled.

"Oh, no. I know it all by heart. I forgot I was not looking on. I learned it when I was a very little girl."

"You learned that whole book?" asked Car'line incredulously.

"Oh, no, but a great many parts. I used to learn a chapter a week, and sometimes more. I know a lot of the gospels, and the epistles, and a great many psalms. You see this was the only book we had. I never went to school, so Mother made me learn out of here.

"Car'line went a whole two terms when we was back

in Oregon," boasted her mother, "but she can't read good like that."

"Oh, I can't be bothered!" said Car'line with a toss of her head, "I allus hev too much to do. And ennyhow, where's the good of readin'? I'd never hev ennythin' to read."

"I'm gonta send fer us one o' them Bibles, an' you better git practiced up, Car'line, fer I meanta hev it read now an' then."

"Gwan!" said Jim, "I wanta hear what it's like. Mebbe I'll read it."

So Fraley went on with her chapter, being many times interrupted in the course of her recitation.

The room was very still. Even the little ones listened with round wondering eyes, and the mother, nodding now and then as her memory brought back her vague former knowledge of the story that was being told, although it had never reached her soul before as a thing that had aught to do with her personally.

As the story of the death on the cross changed into the glory of resurrection, the faces round the fire grew vivid with excitement, and Fraley, led on by their interest told of Christ's appearance to the different disciples, and to the women.

As she paused, the great log that had been burning in the fireplace fell in two and sent up a shower of sparks, and the mother, more deeply stirred by the story than she cared to have her children see, rose and fixed the fire again, but Jimmy leaned forward eagerly:

"An' wot happened then? Gwan!"

So Fraley told of the ascension, taking the words from the first chapter of Acts.

"Oh Gosh! Then He's gone!" said the boy flinging himself back in dismay. "Wot was the use of risin' from the dead then? He might just as well be dead as up in the sky."

"Oh, no," said Fraley earnestly, "Because He's coming again. Listen!" and she began to recite again:

"'This same Jesus which is taken up from you into heaven, shall so come in like manner as ye have seen Him go into heaven.' And you know in that first chapter I read, He said, 'If I go away I'll come again.'"

"Well, did He?" The boy's brows were drawn in a frown of earnestness.

"Not yet. But He's coming sure, sometime. There are lots of places in the Bible where it tells about it. He might come to-night, or to-morrow. It says it will be when no one knows—not even the angels know. But it's going to be wonderful!"

"Gosh! Then you can't tell us the rest of it t'night!" he said in a disappointed tone. "I don't see why He had ta go away 'tall ef He was comin' back."

"Why," said Fraley puckering her brows in her effort to explain, "because He had something to do for us up there before He came back."

"What 'e hav ta do?"

"He had to take our sins up there and tell God He'd taken them all on Him when He died."

"Gosh! What for?"

"Because we were all sinners."

"Well, what did God care about that?"

"He cared because He loved everybody. He made them to be His children, and do right, and be His family, and everybody went and did what He told them not to do, and He felt bad. He had said everybody that sinned had to die, and He had to keep His word or He'd be a liar, so He sent His Son to die and make a way for everybody that wanted to come back and be forgiven."

The boy who had lived all his young life on the edge

of an outlaw's country opened his eyes in wonder at this, and silence filled the room for a long moment, while each listener thought over this new version of what life and sin and death meant.

Then suddenly the mother turned toward the stranger and saw that her face looked worn and her eyelids were drooping.

"Say," she said eagerly. "Whyn't you stay? You'all could stay awhile, ennyhow, and git good en rested, an' read this Book to us a spell!"

"Oh, I couldn't!" said Fraley starting up in alarm. "I ought not to have stopped over night—really!"

"Well, you all gotta go to bed now. It's way after bed time."

"Aw, maw!" protested Jim. "It's jes' this one night an' we wanna hear more."

"Yes, jes' this one night for you all, but this child's gotta go a journey in the early mawnin' and Car'line an' Billy gotta take her down to the railroad. Hustle down quick now, an' no more words."

Fraley slept with Car'line in a loft overhead that they reached by a ladder at the far end of the room, and presently the house was still, the fire banked, the door barred, and no chance to steal away as she had half contemplated doing. Jimmy was sleeping on the cot in the big room down stairs, just at the foot of the ladder. The little window up here was too small to crawl through even if she dared drop so far, and the mother with her brood slept at the other end of the loft. so Fraley, with her hand out on the bag that carried her old Bible, fell asleep. To-morrow, perhaps early in the morning, Brand was coming to buy steers, and maybe Pierce Boyden with him. But she was safe to-night.

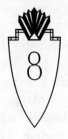

## 8

THE household was astir early, for the roosters began to crow at daylight, and all the other creatures seemed to think it was time to wake up. Fraley made a hurried toilet and got down even before Car'line, who was prinking a bit for the ride to town.

She milked both cows in spite of their protests, for they somehow felt that she was above such work. But she insisted sweetly, and carried her point, and then they all sat down to breakfast, Jimmy in open admiration now for a girl who could both read books and milk cows.

"Gosh, ef you'd stay," he urged with his mouth full of corn cake, "we'd have a great time! Wouldn't we, Maw?"

"I reckun we would!" said the mother with a sigh of regret. "But p'raps she'll come back sometime when she gits done visitin' her kinfolks."

Fraley smiled. She was in a frenzy to be gone, but she could not hurry Car'line, who was enjoying her breakfast, and had just reached over and helped herself to another piece of fried meat.

"We don't have meat fer breakfast every day," vouchsafed Billy with his mouth full. "It's jes' cause o' you. I wisht you'd stay."

It was just as they were leaving that Fraley ventured her request in the mother's ear, as she said good-by.

"Please don't say anything about my being here to any of those men that come from around the mountain," she whispered. "There's someone I'm afraid of that might follow me, and I don't want anyone to find out where I'm gone."

"All right, child, I won't," promised the woman with a kindly pat. "You're a good girl, an' ef anybody worries you, you jus' come right back to us. We'll see that no harm don't come to ya. I'll see that Jimmy don't say nothin' too. Don't ya worry! Good luck to ya, an' don't cher fergit the Bible!"

"No, I won't," promised Fraley, "I've put the address safe in the Bible, so I can't lose it."

Then she went out and climbed up into the buckboard beside Car'line, her precious bag across her lap, and they started, Billy riding on behind atop of the wooden box that held the groceries yesterday, his legs hanging down and swinging.

Away they drove over the winding brown ribbon of a road, over humps and hollows, till suddenly and surprisingly the log cabin was lost to view, and the country stretched wide before them, taking on a new aspect with the mountains far away and very dim.

Fraley kept glancing behind her every little while to see if there was anyone coming. She made the excuse of talking to Billy, but the morning was new and no one else in the wide world seemed abroad at this hour.

They were coming into country where the land was often fenced in little detached portions, and small bunches of cattle were kept meekly within bounds. Car'line discoursed wisely of the different ranches that could be seen as they went along, talked of the people who owned them, and of cattle raising, as if it were a kind of sport. But mostly her talk was of the young men about, and of their interest in herself. She found Fraley not very responsive on such topics, but a good listener, and she grew more confidential and related how a man named Pierce Boyden came to see her sometimes, and how he had kissed her the last time he came.

"Oh, Car'line!" exclaimed Fraley startled out of her reticence, "I wouldn't let him!"

"Why not?" asked Car'line sharply.

"Because——" said Fraley earnestly, and then stopped, realizing what it might mean if she let this girl know she knew the man and hated him. "Because—why—men are—Why, Car'line, do you know anything about this man? He may be—a *bad* man, Car'line! Does your mother know he kissed you?"

"Well, I guess not!" said Car'line proudly. "He wouldn't do it before her! He's a gentleman, he is! He has great big black eyes, and black hair all sort of curly, and when he smiles he looks just like a king! You oughtta see him! He's the best looker I ever saw!"

"But he might be—a—cattle thief or—something! He might kiss—other girls!" Then mindful of the midnight conversation she had heard concerning Pierce, and feeling she ought to give a warning she added:

"I know a man—like that—hair and eyes and all—and he—he—kissed a girl down in a town beyond where we lived. She wasn't a nice girl. Men talked about her—at night—that is they said awful things about him—too! I wish you wouldn't do it, Car'line. Your mother has been good to me, an' I wish you wouldn't do it. You tell her what I said about that man, and you ask her if she thinks you ought to, won't you?" she pleaded earnestly.

"Like fun I will!" snapped Car'line angrily, "an' don't

you go to writing no highflown letters to her about it neither ur I'll tell her you did it because you are jealous of me, see?"

"Oh, Car'line!" said Fraley in distress. "You wouldn't!"

"Sure I would!" said Car'line gaily. "Just you try me!"

"But it wouldn't be true!" said Fraley quietly, as if that robbed the threat of its sting.

"I'm not so sure it ain't," said Car'line impishly, eyeing her companion with a furtive look, "I'll bet you know him!"

But Fraley's answer after a long wait surprised her.

"Yes, I know him."

"You do?" The other girl was startled. "Mebbe he's kissed you, too."

"Never!" said Fraley and her face was grim with indignation. "I would rather be—*dead* than have him touch me!"

Car'line laughed.

"Gosh!" she said. "Well, you would. You're one of them saints! I didn't know they had 'em round her s'near ta Rogues Valley. Well, I ain't. I'm jes' flesh an' blood an' b'lieve me, I know a handsome man when I see him."

From then on Car'line had the conversation all to herself and she rattled on proudly about the devotion of the different young men she had met till Fraley turned her thoughts away in self-defense.

The country round would have been interesting to her if she had not been in a frenzy of fear. Now she had given herself away to this girl who had no sense of loyalty to a confidence, and here she was almost as badly off as if she had just started from her home mountain. If Pierce found out she had been here he would get the word to Brand at once, and Brand would call the gang and ride after her. There was no use in trying to doubt that. Brand thought she was his property. The last few sentences she had heard him and his drunken companions speak on the terrible night of her escape left no doubt whatever what her fate would be if she were caught. She could not even claim the protection of this good woman with whom she had passed the night. Brand and his crew were stronger than a mere woman. He would ride and take her, that would be all of it, and after that she were better dead!

What could she do about it? Would any appeal reach this girl as it seemed to have her mother?

The town, as they called it, turned out to be five houses widely scattered, a general store, and a station. Car'line drew up at the station with a flourish of her broken whip, and a smile and a gay word for the two men who stood on the platform which was returned in none too courteous a manner.

"Well, here you be," said Car'line. "You got a hour an some minutes to wait I reckon, but I'll hev to be gettin' back. Pierce Boyden said he might be comin' down today an' I don't wantta miss him."

But here Billy rose:

"Aw, Car'line! Maw said you wasta wait till her train come. I wanna wait an' see the train come in. I ain't seen it only twicet in my life. I wanna wait!"

"You shet up!" said the elder sister in an ugly tone. "You shet up er I'll tell maw you're a cry baby!"

But Fraley was already getting out of the conveyance. Car'line's decision had brought intense relief to her. She did not mean to wait around any station and give Pierce or Brand a chance to waylay her, and if Car'line went now it would make her way much easier.

"No, don't wait," she said eagerly, "I don't need

anyone. It was kind of you to bring me, and I hope I'll be able sometime to repay you."

She wanted to ask Car'line please to say nothing about her being there, but when she looked again at the girl's angry eyes and arrogant chin she decided to leave things as they were. Perhaps Car'line would keep still on her own account, but if she did not she certainly would not do so for the asking. She was evidently angry at what Fraley had told her of the young man. Well, let it go at that. There were difficulties everywhere and this was just one more.

"Good-by, Billy," said Fraley wistfully, "and thank your mother for the pleasant time. When I come back I'll bring you something nice. Good-by, Car'line, and thank you for the ride."

Car'line lingered a minute to flirt with the two men on the platform, obviously showing off to the younger girl, and then, with a careless wave of her hand toward Fraley she drove away and was soon a mere speck in the distance.

Fraley, giving a quick furtive glance around, moved away from the vicinity of the two men. She looked up and down the shining track that gleamed sharply in the morning sun, and ran away in a bright ribbon as far as her eyes could see in either direction. She marveled that this was a thing to bind the distance. Her mother had talked about the railroad. She had come west—on the railroad—years ago. Fraley knew about the sleeping cars and diners, and the common cars. She of course could only afford a common car when she came to taking the railroad, but she was not ready yet. She would trust nothing but her two feet for the present. This getting mixed up with other people only seemed to make more and more trouble. But how was she going to get away with those two men watching her?

She studied the surroundings and read the sign over the store door. A store! She would buy something more to eat, some cheese, or crackers or something that would be easily carried. It would be interesting to go into a store, and she would have an excuse to get away from the station without attracting their attention.

So she hurried across the space between, and up the wooden steps of the store.

She had taken the precaution to tie one of her precious gold pieces from her belt, into the corner of her crude handkerchief, and knot it round her wrist under her sleeve, for she had expected to have to pay something if she had to take the train, so now with confidence she entered the store and looked around.

It was as interesting to her wilderness eyes as a great city emporium would have been to a villager, and she longed to stay and examine the wares, of which there were a great variety, all the way from plow and shoes to crackers and cheese and dress goods. The bright tin pans were fascinating, also a nest of yellow bowls, and there was a piece of cotton cloth covered with little pink flowers. But she had no time for such things now. She looked about and saw some dried prunes. Sometimes her father had brought home prunes with the groceries. Those were things that could be eaten raw, also there were apples. She bought two apples, after carefully asking the price, a quarter of a pound of prunes, ten cents' worth of cheese, for hers was all gone, three eggs, and a box of stale crackers that had been in the store indefinitely. The eggs she meant to use in mixing up her corn meal when she found a safe place to make a fire by the wayside. They would be hard to carry, but would make the corn meal go a great way.

She put the things in her coat pocket, placing the eggs carefully on the opposite side from the one on which she carried her bag, and while she waited for the store-keeper to make change she asked a few questions. The store-keeper told her about the trains, gave her an old time-table, and was quite voluble in explaining the dif-ference between local and express trains. He informed her that the next train east would be there in exactly one hour and fifteen minutes "if she wa'n't late, which she usually was." He invited her to be seated and offered her a Kansas City newspaper a week old to read. He said his wife came from "back east in Kansas," but she thanked him and declined. She said she would go out in the sunshine awhile and walk around, and so she slipped away.

The two men were just getting into a cart driven by a third man when she emerged from the door, and she waited by the door to examine a pair of shoes that hung just outside, tied together by its strings. She admired the smooth stiff surface, and decided that some day she would buy a pair, but she must not spare the money now. She did not even ask the price, but the shoes kept her back in the shadow till the men had driven away, and then she ventured forth.

She walked back to the station, glanced around, and seeing nobody watching her, and nothing in sight either way, she began slowly to walk the rail that was next to the platform, balancing herself with her arms out, as if to amuse herself. When she had walked a few steps she turned and walked back, and the store-keeper nodded across to her and called:

"When ye git tired come over an' set" and she called back a smiling "Thank you," and kept on walking the rail.

The man went in presently, and she turned and walked the other way. This time she did not walk back, but kept on down the track toward the east. The man had said there was no train till the eastern local came by an hour from now. She need not be afraid, so she walked on and on till the little gray station and the little gray store were mere specks in the bright distance. And if the store-keeper came to look out at her again and missed her he did not trouble himself long about a stray stranger. She was going to take the train and she would likely look after herself.

But Fraley, when she came to a road that turned at right angles to the railroad, sprang from the track and started out across country, glad to get her feet off the hot steel, and on to the cool ground again.

The road she took led across a hill, and when she had climbed the gentle slope she looked around, took her bearings again, and after studying the long bright ribbon of tracks, decided to keep them in view as much as possible, for at least they were a clue to the world she sought and eventually they would lead her on the right way.

She sat there resting, sheltered by a group of trees. Feeling in her pocket she found that the eggs were still unbroken, and decided to eat one of the apples, for it seemed a long time since breakfast and she might not find such a good place to rest in again for several hours. The country here was broad and flat, and much of the forest had been removed.

As she enjoyed her apple, she suddenly heard a rumbling in the distance, and starting to her feet, she looked wildly around her in every direction, until finally she discovered a dark speck back on the railroad track coming along like a wild steer, or a whole herd of wild steers. In amazement she dropped down in the grass again and watched it, breathless, her eyes shining with wonder. This must be the train she was supposed to have taken!

How did people stay in their seats on a thing that went as fast as that?

Her mother had told her about the railroad trains, but she had never imagined it would be like that.

She watched it as it came on, and in another moment it was before her. Like a flash it passed, and was gone, a darting, disappearing speck in the distance! How strange! How wonderful!

She sat there visualizing the sight again, the great black puffing monster ahead. That would be the engine. Cars and cars hitched together, with little windows in most of them, windows close together, and the outline of heads of people inside at each window. At the last car there had been a black man wearing a white kind of cap that looked like paper, and a white coat and apron. He would be the cook for the dining car, or one of the waiters. Her mother had described it all. But somehow she had never thought it would be like this, rushing so fast! She was glad she had not taken that train, it would have frightened her. She resolved to wait as long as possible before she took to the railroad.

When Fraley started on again she had a sense of being comparatively safe for the time at least. If Car'line had told her plans to either of her enemies, at least they had not been able to find her at the train, even if they could have reached there in time. And perhaps if they thought she had taken the train, they would stop their search for her in that region. She did not realize that she had already gone beyond the bounds that outlaws had set for themselves, and that they would come no further out in the open seeking her. If they carried on their search they would have to conduct it through others, and it might be that those others would be in the most unexpected places, even far from where she started.

She did remember later that the store-keeper might

have seen her walking the track, and perhaps told some-one, and so her old uneasiness returned to keep her on the alert.

With very little rest she kept on her pilgrim way during most of the day, but at sunset, well spent, she discovered a little nook where two small hills came together, leaving a tiny point of land jutting between them at their base. There were trees above, leaning over and quite sheltering the retreat, and a small brook, that had been wandering around all the afternoon in the general direction that the railroad took, ambled not far away. It was an ideal spot to make a fire, hardly visible from any direction. Fraley gathered sticks, and finding three large stones, put the flat one across the other two, making a very good fireplace. She soon had a brisk little fire of twigs and sticks, and the top stone heating nicely.

She examined her eggs in the right-hand pocket and found only one cracked, and that she broke into her tin cup. She had no spoon or fork, but she stirred it with her finger, and began mixing in the corn meal, with a pinch of salt, and a little water from her fresh filled water bottle. As soon as the stone was hot enough to sizzle at a drop of water she dropped her little hoe cake on the stone and it began to bake, sending forth such a savory odor that she was almost afraid it would attract some wild thing of the forest, or perhaps some wilder humans, but the cake went on baking, and the soft blue smoke from the tiny fire rose straight up between the sheltering pines on the banks above, and nothing came to molest or make her afraid.

She was just eating the last crumb of the hoe cake when there came that low terrifying rumble that beto-kened a train. Three times that afternoon, since the first train in the morning, had the silence of the open been broken by that sound, and now that she was becoming more accustomed to it, it seemed even friendly.

So she sat quite still by her little fire, and watched a freight train slamming by, down beyond the mist of the meadowland. The smoke from the engine sent up a fiery glow in the twilight, and the end of the long, long train carried a little red berry-like light, that waved and winked and twinkled jauntily, as the train flung on into the prairie vastness.

When the train was entirely out of sight, Fraley put out every vestige of fire, even trampling the dirt into the spot where it had been, and pushed the stones under the bank where no curious passer would notice them. She then ascended the bank to find a night's lodging. She would not be afraid if she could find the right kind of a tree. True a tree was not always as restful as the ground, but it was safer, and could be ascended in a hurry.

She found one to her purpose just up the bank, a big pine—for she always took a pine if there was one about, she loved its sweet odor and its plumy tassels—and swinging up into it a few branches high settled herself and her bag quite comfortably for a rest. Even supposing she should turn in her sleep, there would be little danger of falling far, for the branches were wide and low and closely interlaced. She could almost rest back upon their springy resinous arms. She was high enough from the ground so that no animal would be likely to disturb her, and near enough to good climbing branches to easily get herself out of harm's way in case anything came to trouble her.

A drawing-room train from California swept along the railroad track near enough to be interesting, and Fraley, lying among her branches, watched. She could see bright windows and people sitting cosily together, doing something at little tables. Some of them seemed to be eating. She watched in wonder till the train swept out of sight, and then she thought of the pleasant home where she had spent the last night. Hungrily she wished for such a home. If only Mother were back, and they two could have a home of their own, where joy and safety and love abode!

She remembered each little incident of the evening before; the faces with the flickering firelight on them, the wonder in their eyes when she read the Word of God. She had not realized before that some people did not know the Bible—except perhaps such men as Brand who had deliberately chosen to go away from God. And sometimes even he spoke in his anger words that showed he must have heard some of the Bible.

From the branches she could see the stars coming out one by one, and the moon beginning to climb the heavens, and she repeated softly to herself: "When I consider Thy heavens, the work of Thy fingers, the moon and the stars which Thou hast ordained, what is man that Thou art mindful of him—"

On through the psalm her mind went, as if she were talking to the invisible One. But she was not quite finished before her eyelids drooped and she was asleep, rocked in the arms of the great pine.

The Atlantic and Pacific Express woke her in the early dawning, rattling through the land in two sections, its sleepers still dark-windowed where the travelers lay asleep. Rubbing the sleep from her eyes to watch its trail against the dawning, she found thanksgiving in her heart that the night was past and she was still safe.

Slipping down from her piney bough, a little stiff from her cramped position, she pattered softly down to the stream, to a spot where she had noticed low growing trees, and a sheltered pool. Here shut in by the foliage and the dark she could safely bathe.

Ten minutes later she returned to her shelter of the night before, assembled her fireplace and some wood, and baked another little cake out of the last of her meal. She might not find another opportunity to do this conveniently, and the meal would be wasted.

She had put on fresh undergarments, and washed out the brief ones she had been wearing since she left the cabin, and now she hung the wet things around the fire to dry while the cake was baking. With her bit of comb, and the broken mirror she combed her hair out and spread it to dry over her shoulders, and then she ate her cake, saving a small piece to eat on her way. There was one more egg in her pocket, still unbroken, and that she could eat raw for lunch if there were no chance to cook it.

By the time she had put out her fire and broken camp, the flimsy garments hanging on the low limb over the fire were dry. She wrapped them up, stuffed them into the bag and started on into a new day, almost sorry to leave the pleasant retreat that had housed her so comfortably.

The morning proved long and uneventful. The way was rough in some places, unless she wanted to climb the hills and get farther away from the railroad, but she felt that it was the only guide she had to her unknown port, so she trudged on, through boggy land, or rough stubble grass, and about noon she came in sight of a small village.

9

IT was only a small straggling village, a settlement it would have been called in the east, but it looked like a swarming hive of population to the girl whose eyes were trained by mountain loneliness. She stood uncertain afar and studied it through her glass.

The railroad wandered before her, cutting a clean steel gash across the country shining in the midday sun. She studied the buildings in detail, and finally came to the one closest to the tracks. That would likely be a station. Then her heart stood still. There were two riders just arriving, and one rode a white horse!

That was enough for Fraley. She put down her glass and dashed into the bushes, making a wide detour around that village, and resolving to keep as far as possible from human habitation for the next several days. Would she never be free from her enemies?

The detour carried her far out of her course, and for three hours she lost track of her railroad entirely, and began to think she would never find it again, but it rediscovered itself to her toward evening near a brown lake set about with reeds and reflecting dark pines in its depths.

She had steadily avoided human habitation so far, but as night drew on again she felt a strange dread of the loneliness. The lake looked large and dark, and the world seemed interminable. A dislike of passing that sheet of dark water possessed her, and she was aching in every muscle with fatigue. She was hungry too. She had eaten the raw egg early in the day, the apple at noon with the last bit of corn cake, and later in the afternoon had eaten some of the dried prunes with a few of the stale crackers and a little cheese. Her store of eatables was growing very low, and how could she go on unless she ate. Even though she had dipped deep into her supply she was not satisfied, but felt empty and faint as she dragged on her weary way.

As it neared the lake the railroad plunged into a dark forest and was lost again, and Fraley, half running, found herself sobbing as she tried to keep on higher ground because it was wet down near the tracks, but at last in desperation went splashing across the marshy land straight over to where the railroad grade rose up high and dry.

She had been watching the trains ever since she had left the station where Car'line had conducted her. She knew that there would be no train either way now for some time, for the usual afternoon expresses had passed. Should she venture to walk the track a little way? She could keep a sharp lookout, and roll down the grade quickly if she heard a train coming. There was a double track, and she had noticed two freights passing yesterday. She could walk toward the one that would be coming west.

She stood, hesitating, at the foot of the steep grade, and then started upward. It was difficult climbing, especially with that heavy bag to carry, but she struggled up, and at last reached the top of the grade and stood, palpitating, on a tie. She looked back and saw nothing but track and landscape as far as her eye could reach. She looked forward and saw the dark lake at the foot of gloomy mountains on one hand, and marsh land on the other, the track plunging into the depths of the forest just beyond the lake. But there was light beyond. She could see that the wooded place was not of great extent. Should she try it?

The memory of those two riders she had seen at that village gave her impulse and she decided to press on.

It was hard, nervous work walking the ties, and her feet were sore from the climb through the cinders, her head dizzy with watching her steps and both distances at the same time. It seemed the longest walk she had ever taken, but at last she got beyond the woods and came out into a wide stretch of country that was brilliant with sunshine.

"Oh," she said aloud, "oh, I'm so glad!" and found there were tears running down her face. It had been a terrible strain, walking that track through the dark wood, with water on either side down below the grading, and the dread of a special train, perhaps, rushing at her unawares.

She slid down the grade as soon as she got beyond the marshy land, and was glad, indeed, to get on firm, dry ground once more.

The place about here looked more inviting than where she had been all day. There was a house a long way off and, apparently, roads going here and there. There was even a stretch of land that seemed to have been made ready for planting. A plow stood in a furrow as if it had just been left for a while. Also there were pleasant, friendly trees along the way, and a smooth road presently presented itself to be walked on. She was almost too tired to keep on much longer, but she must until she found a safe place to sleep.

She was watching the way to choose smooth spots for her feet were very sore, when suddenly she looked up and saw a rider coming toward her on a black horse, and her heart stood still with fear.

There was not time to study him through her glass and see if he was one of her enemies. It might be that he had not yet noticed her. She turned and fled like a streak of light but, to her horror, as she ran she heard the man calling. She did not stay to hear whether he was calling her or someone else. She fled for her life back on the road, back to the last tree she had passed. She flung herself upon its trunk as she had often done before, and shinned up into the thick branches, where she was completely hidden from view. The branches were so luxurious that she could not even look out herself without parting them, and she did not dare do that. Silently she waited, seated on a high bough, frightened eyes staring down, ears strained to listen to the horse's hoof beats on the hard earth.

Yes, he was coming on. Had he seen her? Was it Brand, or Pete? Was she caught at last? It was of no use to cry out, for that house was too far away, even if there might be friendly people in it. Her only chance was to keep silent and hope he had not seen her. Perhaps he lived in that house and had been calling to someone on the porch. Perhaps he had not seen her at all, or if he had he might have missed where she went and would ride straight by.

But no, the horse had stopped. There was a sound of someone springing to the ground, and then she heard steps. He was coming toward the tree.

"Oh, I say, you up there? What are you? A bird or a

girl? What do you seem to think you are doing up there anyway?"

The voice was crisp and hearty, and the eyes that looked up were full of merry twinkles. Fraley leaned forward and stared down and answered in a frightened little voice:

"I'm—just resting—a little!"

"Oh, I see!" said the young man jovially. "Well, would you mind if I interrupted you a minute to inquire the way? I'm a stranger around here, and I guess I've made a wrong turn. I want to get to the log schoolhouse, wherever that is. Can you tell me? You see I'm lost."

Fraley looked down at his nice, lean, tanned face, noticed the wave in his brown hair, and the merry twinkle in his eyes, and lost some of her fear.

"But—you see—I'm lost too!" she said gravely.

"The dickens! You are?" said the young man, and bent over, laughing, "Say now, that's a great joke, isn't it? Well, perhaps I can help you then. Where were you going?"

"I—don't—quite know," she vouchsafed in a small voice. "I'm travelling."

"Oh, I see!" said the young man sobering down and giving her a quick, surprised glance.

"Well," he said at last, "I see you're a lady, and, I should judge, a lady in distress, and I hope I'm a gentleman. You needn't be afraid of me, if that's what's the matter. I'm perfectly respectable. Suppose you come down and let's talk this thing over. Where were you really heading for?"

Fraley sat very still for a minute, and then answered slowly, "Why—I—suppose New York, in the end. But it seems to be a long ways off."

"You bet your life it is!" said the young man bitterly. "I'd like right well to be there myself if I hadn't been chump enough to promise to stay out here and hold down another fellow's job while he goes to the hospital. But I'm here, and I guess I'll have to stick it out. How about it, will you come down and help me decide which way we ought to go, or do I have to come up there?"

Fraley looked wildly about and at once uncurled her feet from under her dress, where they had been tucked out of sight.

"Let me help you," said the young man, reaching up a friendly hand.

"Thank you," said Fraley solemnly, "I can get down alone," and she proceeded to swing herself off the high bough and drop with a graceful little spring to the ground as if she had really been the bird he had suggested.

"Well, that was some jump!" declared the young man, surveying her as she stood silently before him, watching him with wise, half-frightened eyes.

The kerchief had caught in the branches, and was hanging on her back, and her golden hair was flowing in waves about her shoulders. Even in the old overcoat she was lovely; barefoot and tired and ragged, she made a picture there in the wilderness.

"Now, what are we going to do about it?" asked the young man after he had surveyed her. "What good jokes do you know?"

"Jokes?" she said looking puzzled. "I'm not sure what you mean. But there's a railroad over there, just behind those bushes, down there. It goes east that way, because that's where the sun rises."

"The dickens it does? I take it you've watched it rise too. Well that's something, only the sun isn't rising now."

"No, it's almost sunset time," said the girl gravely, "were you going east or west?"

"Well, now, that's what I don't know. You see, I started from a ranch where this friend of mine is supposed to board, and I'm due at that log schoolhouse at seven o'clock. I've got to get there or bust because I told this fellow I would. He's counting on me! It isn't my kind of a job, but I'll have to do the best I can with it, and I've got to get there. By the way, how can I serve you? You said you were going to New York. Do you want to get to a station? I should suppose there would be one somewhere along a railroad eventually, although you can't, most always, sometimes, tell in a new country like this. I could perchance take you to a station if we could find one lying around loose."

"No, thank you. I thought I would walk a little farther first," said Fraley shyly, "it costs a lot of money, I guess, to ride on the cars, and I haven't very much."

"Oh!" said the young man, "so it's money is it? That's my bugbear too. Not for myself you understand. I happen to have been born with plenty and I can help you out in that way if you'll let me."

"Oh, no," said Fraley shrinking away, "I'll be all right. But I'm sorry I can't help you. I've been travelling all day and I haven't seen any log schoolhouse—that is nothing that looked like that—"

"I see," said the young man. "Well, what about some supper? I'm getting perfectly hollah! Suppose we just sit down here under this tree and have a bite and talk it over. Perhaps that will help."

"I'm sorry," said Fraley again, "but I have nothing but some crackers and a few prunes. You are welcome to half of those if you like. They are not very nice."

"Oh, but I've got a real lunch," said the young man. "The lady at the ranch put it up for me. There's enough for a regiment, and I do hate like the dickens to eat alone. Won't you share it with me? Then we can decide what's best to be done."

Fraley looked troubled. It was not quite her idea of etiquette nor safety, this picking up a strange young man in the wilderness and going out to dinner with him under a casual tree, but he waited for no acquiescence. He stepped over to his horse and began to unstrap a box from the back of the saddle.

"Gaze on that!" said the young man opening the box and disclosing neat packages wrapped in wax paper, and glimpses of golden oranges.

"Oh," said Fraley looking with amazement at the arrangement, "that is wonderful!"

"Now, let's sit down here and eat. I'm simply ravenous. We had lunch at eleven o'clock, and I expected to reach this place an hour ago and have time to get all primed up for the evening. Here, let me fix that knapsack of yours so you'll be comfortable!" He sprang forward and lifted the bag from her tired shoulders and placed it down by the tree trunk.

"Now, tree-lady, drop down there and rest against that. There's nothing breakable in it I'm sure, the way you lighted down from that tree."

She obeyed him because she did not know just what else to do, and because she was too tired to stand up longer.

He dropped down on the grass in front of her and opened the box again, handing her out one of the little wax paper parcels.

"How's that? Open it and see what it turns out to be. If I can judge by the lunch we had it'll be something pretty delectable. They think because I'm taking the job of their preacher that I must be fed on nectar and ambrosia."

"Is this nectar and ambrosia?" asked Fraley seriously looking down at the package she held, still unopened.

The young man laughed.

"Something like that," he said. "Try it."

"Oh, but I mustn't," said Fraley handing it back to him. "You will need every crumb you can get if you're really lost. It's such a long way to anywhere out here. I know for I've tried it."

"The dickens you have!" said the young man. "Well, now, that's too bad because I never eat alone, and if you won't I won't, you see, and we'll just starve together!"

Fraley looked at him in astonishment and then she laughed, a rich sweet childish gurgle of fun.

"I'll eat some," she agreed, and opened her little package.

She found delicate slices of fine white bread with slices of chicken breast laid in between. And when she put it in her mouth she thought it was the best thing she had ever tasted.

There were other little packages with other sandwiches, some with fragrant slices of pink ham between them. There were hard boiled eggs rolled in paper. There were olives and pickles, and chocolate cake, and cookies, and white grapes and oranges, a feast for a king! There was coffee amazingly hot in a thermos bottle! And in the wilderness!

Fraley ate silently at first, until the faint sick feeling was gone, and then she looked up with a smile:

"This is just like Elijah under the juniper tree, isn't it?"

The young man stared at her.

"Beg pardon, who did you say?"

"Elijah! Don't you know? The first time he was in the wilderness the ravens fed him, and then the time he was so discouraged under the juniper tree an angel came and baked him a little cake—"

"Am I to understand that I am an angel or a raven?" asked the young man. "Consider, I beg you, for it will make a great difference to me whether you think I'm a raven or an angel."

Fraley looked up and laughed.

"But I mean it seriously," said the young man helping himself to his third ham sandwich, "It may make a great difference to me all my life whether you consider me a raven or an angel. And who is this person Elijah that you seem so intimate with?"

Her face grew sober again.

"Oh, don't you *know* Elijah?"

"Sorry but I never had the pleasure of meeting him," said this strange merry gentleman as he handed her a bunch of luscious grapes. "I'm a graduate of one of the best colleges of the land, too, and I suppose I ought to have heard of him at least, but I simply can't recall his identity."

Fraley looked troubled.

"It's a long story," she said, "I'd have to begin at the beginning to tell it all, but you can read it."

"I detest waiting for a thing when I want to know it at once. Just give me some clue, I may know the gentleman after all."

"Why, he was a prophet, you know," began Fraley looking at him hopefully.

"A weather prophet?" asked the young man catching the word lightly.

"Yes," said Fraley with a clearing of her expression. "That's the one. I was sure you knew him. He told Ahab you know, that there wasn't going to be any dew nor rain and it made him so angry that he told the prophet to get out of the country, and he went where there was a brook and the ravens brought him bread and flesh in the morning, and bread and flesh in the evening and he drank of the brook."

"Oh, I see," said the young man, "but that's the raven, where does the angel come in? I don't seem to recall the rest of the story. Where did the ravens get the sandwiches do you think?"

"Why, they weren't sandwiches," said the girl earnestly. "I don't think people fixed them like this then, it doesn't say anything about it, but God sent the ravens you know. He told Elijah He was going to do it, and He sent the angel to him too you know."

"No, I don't know," said the young man. "Where do you get all this? I don't recall ever having heard it. Tell me the rest. It sounds interesting. We have ten minutes before we have to start. I'm sure that will give us plenty of time to hunt out that schoolhouse, for it ought to be within a mile of us somewhere. I know just where I got off the track."

Fraley looked at the sun.

"It's getting late," she said uneasily. "I ought to start right away myself. I've got to get somewhere for the night."

"That's all right," said the young man easily. "I'll take you wherever you want to go. That horse is good for two riders as well as one. You can come on with me till I get this job done I'm in for, and then I'll carry you wherever you say. Why not come on back to the ranch with me till morning? My landlady will be delighted to take you in, I'm sure. I'll just tell her I picked you up on the road, and you need a night's lodging."

Fraley's eyes were filled with alarm.

"Oh, I couldn't really!" she said, getting to her feet. "I must be getting along fast. It is time I was gone now. The sun is going down, see, and I must find—I must get—somewhere—before it is quite dark."

"Where is it you have to get?" asked the young man springing up also.

"I—why—I—have to find the place. I don't know just where—and so I must hurry."

"Do you mean you are going to some house where friends live?" he asked eying her keenly.

The alarm was growing in her eyes and, when she did not answer immediately, he went on.

"Because there isn't any house anywhere near here except that one up there, I can tell you that, I've been riding around quite a bit, and I've got a pretty good idea of the lay of the land. Where is it you think you are going? You know it isn't safe for a nice little ladybird like you to be cutting around lonely places all alone like this. You don't *live* around here, do you? You don't *live* up in that old empty house up there, do you? Because I happen to know it's perfectly empty, for I applied my eye to one of the windows a few minutes ago, meaning to ask the shortest way to my schoolhouse. There isn't a stick of furniture in the place."

"No, I don't live there—" she said, "but I can find a place—I always do—!"

"Do you mean to say you've been hiking it like this for long?"

"Oh, not very long," evaded Fraley, intensely worried now and anxious only to get away.

He looked at her steadily, and there was something strong and clean in his eyes that allayed her fears. Then he spoke.

"Well, I may as well tell you the truth, I'd been watching you for half an hour from that upper road up there. Several times I saw you drop down as if you were all in, and you dragged along as if you couldn't go much farther. Being somewhat lost myself a little farther didn't matter, so I thought I'd come down and offer you a lift.

But when I saw you run and disappear into a tree I just didn't know what to make of it, and so I thought I'd come and see anyway. Now, Ladybird, you needn't tell me any more than you want me to know, but I certainly don't intend to leave you in this God-forsaken spot alone at this time of night, unless you tell me you have a protector lurking somewhere in the neighborhood that will see that no harm comes to you. The people I'm staying with told me there were some tough characters not far from here, and it isn't safe for a girl to be here alone."

"I know," said Fraley gently, "but this isn't a God-forsaken place, it isn't really. God has taken care of me in a wonderful way—if you knew."

"Well, that may be so," said the young man, "but I guess He's sent me to do the job this time, and I intend to do it. You can take me for a raven or an angel whichever you like, but I'm going to stick by till I see you in a safe place. You look too much like a stray angel yourself to be lying around loose on the desert. Now, shall we go?"

"But—where are you going?" asked Fraley wide eyed again, and troubled.

"Why, we are going to find that schoolhouse. I'm going straight back to the crossroads and take the other road. If it isn't this one then it has to be the other one. I was more than half sure it was when I took this one, but I wanted to see where this led. I've never been out to this part of the country before. Come, lady, let's mount. You ride in the saddle and I'll sit behind. The horse looks long enough to hold half a dozen."

"Oh, I can easily walk beside you," said the girl shyly.

"Walk, nothing! What do you think I am, Ladybird, a sheik of the desert? No, you get on. We'll manage fine. I went to a military school once for a year and the horses was the best thing I did there. Now, are we all set? Well, how about continuing that serial story? I want to hear about those angelic sandwiches. What was it, bread and meat in the morning?"

"Oh, the angel baked a little cake. It was another time you know, under the juniper tree, after the big testing on Mount Carmel!"

"The testing? What was that?"

Fraley began to tell the story, and as she told it the young man marvelled at her simple, pure language. How was it that a girl in these wilds, dressed as she was, could yet speak English as if she had been well educated? She must have been away to school somewhere. And yet, there was a lack of sophistication that made that seem impossible.

But there was something about that simply-told story that was gripping. He stopped his wondering about the speaker and listened to the tale.

Where did she get the language in which she spoke? For Fraley as usual was using the words of the Book, the matchless words that cannot be improved. Occasionally she condensed in a few words of her own, but for the most part she clung pretty closely to the text.

The sunset lay upon the world as she reached the ending of her story.

"I say, where did you get that tale?" asked the young man as the sweet earnest voice ceased speaking. "It's rare, and I never heard it before."

"Why," said Fraley, "it's just in the Bible. How could you miss it?"

"Well," said the young man studying her curiously, "you see I've been rather busy with a lot of other things, and well—I stopped before I got to that, I guess. But I can see now my education has been badly neglected. That's a great tale. And you say it's in the Bible? Do you know about what page? Perhaps you could help me find it. It might be just the thing I need to-night."

"To-night?" said Fraley, puzzled. "Why, yes, of course I can find it. It's in the first book of Kings, about the middle somewhere. But you don't find things in the Bible by pages. You find them by books and chapters, you know."

"Oh yes, of course, that was what I meant of course. I wonder if they will have a Bible at the schoolhouse. One would think they ought to, but you can't always tell. You see I haven't brought one with me. I came away in a hurry."

"Why, I have my Bible with me," said Fraley, half reluctant to have a stranger handle it. "You can read out of mine."

"The dickens, you have?" said the young man, astonishment in his voice. "Well, now that's rare. You see I have to hold a service to-night in that schoolhouse and I was just figuring what to do about it. It isn't really my job, but as I told you I couldn't refuse to help a fellow out when he was in such straits, and he swore he wouldn't go to the hospital unless I'd promise faithfully to get someone here in time for this service to-night, and failing in finding any of the people he suggested I had to come myself."

"Are you a minister?" There was a ring of interest in the girl's voice that almost amounted to awe as she asked the question. "Then you *are* an angel! God's ministers are called angels several times in the Bible."

The young man gave her a startled look, and then suddenly, he discovered that he was passing the cross-roads, and drew the rein sharply to the left, starting down a better worn trail than the one they had been traveling.

"This is the way, I'm positive," said he, taking a card out of his pocket and consulting a diagram traced on it with pencil. "Yes, this is where I should have turned before. But in that case I shouldn't have seen you and that would have been bad, wouldn't it? I couldn't have been even a raven then. The schoolhouse ought to be about two miles from here, and then we'll have plenty of time to look up that story in your Bible. Now, what was that question you asked?"

10

"YOU are a minister!" declared Fraley joyously. "To think that I should have found you out here in the wilderness. You see I never saw one before and so I did not know you. I thought a minister would look older."

"They do come young, sometimes," affirmed the young man, eyeing her curiously. "But where have you lived, angel lady, that you never saw one before. I fear you're kidding me."

"What is kidding?" she turned her large serious eyes on him, and he found it rather difficult to explain.

"I mean you are joking with me, birdlady. You surely could not have lived your years to this time without having seen many a preacher?"

"No, I haven't really," she said earnestly. "I lived on a mountain and we never saw anybody except men who came now and then. They—were not the kind—of men, ministers would come to see!"

"You don't say!" said the young man thoughtfully, and watched the pure outline of the girl's profile as she sat before him, her head slightly turned towards him, the warm tints of the setting sun bringing out the delicacy of the features, the soft modeling of the sun-browned flesh.

"I am so glad I know you are a minister. Now I do not need to be afraid of you any more. My mother has told me what wonderful men ministers are!"

Ah! There had been that kind of a mother! That explained some things.

"But you see, I'm not!" said the young man after a thoughtful pause. "I'm all kinds of sorry to disappoint you, but you see I'm only a raven after all."

"Why—but—you said you were going to hold a service?" she questioned with a look as if she had leaned upon something that looked strong and found it failed her.

"That's what I'm undertaking to do. I don't know how well I'll make out, but I'm making the best kind of a stab at it that I know how. You see it was this way. This fellow that was coming out here is a minister all right I guess. I don't really know much about him. He was a poor gink that had studied himself pretty near into the grave and hadn't any strength left. He got up from a sick bed to go to his train so he would get here in plenty of time to get settled and begin on this service to-night. He's a stranger to me. I only saw him about half an hour before I had to leave. You see he was taken awfully sick in the street, and was almost knocked down. In fact he fell as he was crossing the street toward the station, and we picked him up unconscious. I happened to be driving my car that way and was the first one to pick him up, and of course I landed him at the hospital and thought that would be the end of it, but on the way there the poor boob came to, and insisted that I take him to the train instead of the hospital, and he wouldn't take no for an answer till I promised I'd see somebody took his place out here. Of course there was nothing to do but promise, but when I got him to the hospital and the doctor got on the job he found there had to be an operation, and the poor guy was so upset that I just stuck around a few minutes. He seemed to cling to me like a drowning passenger to a lifeboat, and boy! I couldn't shake him. He said he had three friends, any one of which could take this job and I promised to see that one of them went by the next train, and stuck on the job till he got there. So he went happy to the operating room and I went to hunt my man and get him shipped out here."

Fraley's vivid little face was turned to listen and he paused to wonder again at the delicacy and refinement of it. It was like finding a rare exotic in a wilderness.

"Well?" she said breathlessly.

"Well, would you believe it, I couldn't get one of these guys to come. The first one had got married and gone on his wedding trip, the second one was off in Maine being headmaster of a boys' camp, an all summer job; and the third had gone down to Jersey to take charge of a church. There I was, and by the time I got the last man chased to his hiding place it was just about time to leave. There wasn't a soul I knew would come out here even for a week till I got time to hunt somebody else. I called up several men I knew that do this sort of thing but they were all busy for the summer. I tried to sleep over it but I couldn't get asleep so I got up and took the midnight train. I couldn't get away from that guy's face when he made me promise to come, and here I am. I had to keep my promise, didn't I?"

"Of course," said Fraley. "But—how are you going to do it? Doesn't a man—have to know how? And doesn't he have to be set apart, or—or—blest or something the way they did with the Levites before they could minister before the Lord? You—might make some—mistake!"

"Blest if I know. I'm doing my best, aren't I? Angels could do no more," the glib tongue replied.

The girl looked serious and troubled.

"I—should think you'd—be—afraid. You know God sent down fire from heaven on Nadab and Abihu for doing something like that."

"The dickens He did? What did they do?"

"They offered strange fire. I don't know just what that means, but it was something they hadn't been told to do. Something they were not supposed to do."

"How did you know all that?" he asked wonderingly.

"Why, it's all in the Bible," she said simply as if that settled it.

"Say," said he wonderingly. "You know a lot, don't you? I wish I knew some of those things. I never realized there were things like that in a Bible!"

"Why it's easy. You could begin now. You learn a few verses every day," she said, as if that were the most natural thing in the world.

"You don't say!" he responded studying her earnest young face and wondering how a soul like this had come to be on the bad old earth.

But now, with a little turn of the road around the side of a hill, they came suddenly upon the log schoolhouse.

It was still light and the young man alighted and turned to help the girl, but found she had sprung to the ground before he could get to her.

She sat down on the step and began to open her bag at once while he tethered his horse, and when he came back to her she handed out the Bible in its cotton binding.

He took it curiously and marked the worn condition of its pages. Truly this old book had seen hard usage. He gazed at it reverently. The Book of God. Some inkling of what the Book had been meant to be to the human heart was revealed to him as he looked at the worn pages and then at the face of the lovely girl who had been fed upon it.

"Well, now, where is that man Elijah?" he asked gravely. "I've been thinking, don't you think it would be all right if I just read that story to the folks? That ought to be something anybody could do, to read a story."

She pointed out the place where it began and ended, and he sat down on the step of the schoolhouse and began to read in the dying light. And when the light failed he took out a pocket flash he was carrying and turned it on the page.

Fraley dropped down in the grass and leaned against a tree watching him as he read, and wondering what her mother would think if she knew she was here alone with a strange young man.

The young man was still reading when the first member of the congregation arrived. He swung himself from his saddle, a long lank man with a discouraged droop to his shoulders, and a kindly look in his eyes. And behind him on two mules rode his bright-eyed wife and her two boys.

The man said "Howdy" and unlocked the schoolhouse door. Presently light streamed forth from the door, from a swinging kerosene lamp and from four candles in different parts of the dim interior of the building.

The young missionary with his finger between the leaves of the old Bible rose and went inside, and Fraley stole into a shadowed corner, slipping into a seat and looking about her in wonder.

So this was a schoolhouse! All these desks for the scholars, two to a desk. And that smooth dark surface running around the front and sides of the room must be a blackboard. She had heard her mother describe it all.

People began to drop into the schoolhouse now by ones and twos. The tall thin first comer rang an old cracked bell, and the echo of its reverberations seemed to come back in relays from the mountains round about. Fraley sat in her corner and listened with awe. No visitor in a great cathedral could have felt more thrill than she as she listened for the first time to the call to worship as it rang out in that primitive countryside.

Most of the people who came looked old and tired, although there were a few with little children. Perhaps it was the shadows of the weird candlelight, and the high smokey kerosene beacon overhead that made them all look so scared and sad.

Three women came in together, and a little, little boy. Two more and a man. A little girl and her father. Then some more men, three of them. You could hear the thud of their horses' feet as they arrived, or the rattling of old sun-warped wheels on the hard earth. They seemed to steal almost furtively in, and slide into their seats. Finally the place was half full. Fraley counted them as they came, until thirty-nine had arrived. She had never seen so many people together in her life. But as each man came, she shrank back farther into the shadow, and scanned him anxiously. She was always looking for Brand, or Pete, or Pierce. Yet none of them would be likely to come to a prayer meeting unless they came for some evil purpose. And, as each new man entered, she quickly glanced from him to the young man sitting by the table in front. He was her friend, he would protect her, she felt sure, in case anyone should come after her.

So, at last, she settled back into comparative comfort to enjoy what was going on. It was all wonderful to her.

There was a thing up near the table that looked like a brown box, and presently a woman that looked younger than the rest came up and opened its lid and sat down before it. There seemed to be a lot of little white and black stripes inside, and Fraley wondered what it could be. There was a pile of books on the top of one of the front desks and the old man who rang the bell took them and distributed them. Fraley accepted hers wonderingly, and puzzled over the queer lines with dots on them that went between the reading.

The young missionary was whispering now with the woman who sat before the box, and looking through one of the books, and presently he announced that they would sing number ninety-three. Everybody opened the books and fluttered the leaves through and Fraley opened hers and found there were numbers on each page. She had no trouble in finding the right one. Then a strange sound broke the stillness. The woman at the box was moving her fingers up and down the black and white stripes and making the sounds, and it was a tune—a tune Fraley's mother used to sing to her sometimes, when they were very happy together, all alone:

> *"Rock of Ages, cleft for me,*
> *Let me hide myself in Thee."*

Why, that was like the place in the rock she had hidden behind! She had not thought of it then, for her mother had not sung the song for a long time.

And this must be a hymn book she was holding. The box was some kind of musical instrument, perhaps a piano, or an organ. Her mother used to play the piano. She had told her about that, and Fraley had always had a longing to play one sometime.

She joined her flute-like voice to the tide of dragging song that was sweeping round the little log schoolhouse, and lo, the hymn rose and soared as if a million songbirds had suddenly joined the company. Tired old voices, rose to the key, and felt thrilled with the music, because this sweet, new voice had broken into their worship. The young man at the desk heard, and looked up in pleased surprise, presently adding a fine baritone, and the little schoolhouse rang with the old, old song. Flickering candles, smoking lamp, breath of the pines drifting in, weird shadows in dusty corners, sad, tired, sinsick souls, one sorrowful lonely child of God, and one astonished flabbergasted man of the world, trying to do something he did not in the least understand!

When they had sung three songs the young man stood up. He looked around on the people, and the light from the candle that stood on the table before him flickered over his face and made him look like a nice, shy, little boy standing there facing into the shadowy schoolroom.

"Friends," he said looking about on them with his engaging smile, "I'm not the minister you expected here to-night. He's very sick in the hospital, back east, having an operation for appendicitis. I'm just the man that picked him up on the street and carried him to the hospital, and I promised him I'd see that somebody came out here to take his place. He wouldn't go under the operation till I'd promised. He said he had given his word that he would be here without fail. I tried to get somebody else to come that knew how, but I couldn't, so here I am. But it's a new job for me, and you'll have to excuse me if I don't do it very well. Perhaps you'll all help me."

Then he opened Fraley's cotton-covered Bible and began to read at the beginning of the story of Elijah.

The room was very still as he finished with the touch of the angel's hand on Elijah's shoulder, bidding him rise and eat and go forward.

The young man closed the Bible and looked at his

strange audience half bewildered for a moment, then he said, as if it came right out of his heart:

"My friends, I guess there is something in this story that will do us all good, to-night. I know it has made me think a lot. Suppose we each one think about it. Now I wonder if anybody else has anything to say?"

Back in the corner by the door the tall thin man arose and began to pray, and then another and another of the old men who looked like gnarled sticks but had kindly eyes, followed him, and a very old man leaning on a stick testified that he had served the Lord seventy years and found joy in doing it, and then a little tired looking woman asked for a hymn, and so the meeting unrolled itself till the young leader sat in amazement and watched.

The climax came when one man prayed "for our young brother who has brought us the word of God to-night" and Fraley thought she saw her missionary man brush away a tear as he rose when that prayer was over.

"Well, friends, I guess God heard all those prayers," he said. "I sure feel I've got something out of it."

They lingered after the closing hymn to shake hands with the new leader, and with the little stranger back by the door, and their kindly welcome seemed lovely to the girl.

She looked back wistfully at the long, low, shadowy room as she stepped out. It would always be a sweet memory to her, the hour spent there in the candleglow.

Out in the starlight the sky seemed to stoop lower, as if God were very near.

The tall man padlocked the schoolhouse door, and one by one the worshippers mounted their horses, or climbed into their shackly conveyances, and disappeared into the darkness, and Fraley was left standing on the steps while the young man went for the horse.

When they were mounted again and on their way he said gravely.

"Well, you had the right dope, little girl. I guess that service got by, didn't it?"

"It was wonderful!" said Fraley, starry eyed.

"Oh, I don't think that," he answered seriously, "but I can see there is a lot more in it than I ever thought there was. Jove! Think of that old man, poor and lame and almost blind, saying he's happy! But now, little sister," he said, bringing his attention back to Fraley, "we've got to make some plans for you."

"Oh," said Fraley, suddenly brought back to earth, "you mustn't take any more trouble with me. I've been thinking about that. If you'll let me down at your ranch house and just tell me the way the road goes I'll keep right on to-night. I feel real rested now and I mustn't waste any more time."

"Look here, little tree-lady!" said the young man, pulling the horse up short and leaning around where he could look at her. "I thought we settled that thing long ago. You are not going to be left to wander the darkness alone! Understand that? I was made a man so I could protect woman and I'm going to do it! And from all they told me at the ranch to-day I know this region around here is no fit place for you, even in the daytime, let alone night. So that's that! Do you understand?"

"But—" said Fraley, a worried pucker between her brows.

"No buts, please. I've got a plan. Listen to me. First, tell me a thing or two. Why are you traveling alone like this? You know you haven't explained yourself at all. Beyond the fact that you're a sort of a lady-tramp, bound ultimately for New York, I know nothing at all about you. Don't you think I have a right to an explanation? Can't you trust me?"

"WHAT do you want to know?" asked Fraley almost sadly, suddenly reminded of her sorrowful past.

"Where did you come from, where are your people, and where are you going?" asked the young man. "You may trust me absolutely. If there is something you want kept secret I'll be as mum as an oyster, if you know what that is."

"I've never had one," said Fraley smiling, "but my mother had."

"Well, an oyster never tells anything," said the young man solemnly, and Fraley suddenly laughed.

"I'm not afraid of you," she said, "but it's not a happy story. I lived in a cabin on a mountain, and I've hardly ever been away from there. A little while ago my father was killed, and the men that were with my father raising cattle were not good men. My mother was sick, and before she died she told me to get away as quick as I could. She had a brother in New York, and I am going to find him."

"But why did you start out to walk? Do you know how far it is to New York?"

"I know it seems very far," she said with a sigh, "but if I keep on I'll get there some day I guess."

"You poor little ladybird," said the young man with his voice full of tenderness. "But tell me, why did you not take the train? If you didn't have money, surely some of your friends would have loaned you some—"

"We hadn't any friends," said Fraley gravely.

"No friends? Well—but—why, surely your father's friends—the men you spoke of—even if you didn't like them they aren't inhuman are they?"

"I think perhaps they are," said the girl seriously. "They wouldn't have let me go if they had known. They wanted me to stay and cook for them. They—" the girl's voice shook and her slender shoulders quivered at the memory, "they came home drunk—and I heard them talking— They were *terrible!* I was afraid, and I got out of the window and ran away. I meant to get gone before they came back, but I couldn't bear to leave my mother lying there all alone, dead. She told me to go without waiting, but they came—sooner than I thought—"

"You poor kiddie!" said the young man, his own voice full of feeling. He felt a great longing to comfort her somehow, yet he laid no finger upon her. She was a little, white soul—like an angel.

"You poor, brave little kid! Didn't they find out you had gone?"

"Yes, pretty soon they broke down the door and got in and found me gone. I could hear them break it as I ran. They came after me, and they shot Larcha—!"

"Who is Larcha?"

"My dear dog. He was going with me, and he rushed at them to keep them from finding me. He threw them off the trail—"

"But where were you?"

"Up in my big pine tree—"

"Up a tree! Oh, so that wasn't the first time you shinned up a tree when you were frightened. Do you always go up a tree when you see a man coming?"

"There was nowhere else to go."

"You poor dear little kid!"

Little by little he drew from her the whole tale of her journey thus far.

"I don't wonder you were afraid of me!" he said when she had finished the tale. "You are a wonderful brave little kid. And now, it seems to me you have done this bravery act to a finish and it's high time someone took care of you. How would you like to stay at the ranch house where I board for a little while till you can write to these friends of yours to come after you?"

"Oh, no!" said Fraley. "I must get away. You don't know what those men are. They would find out. They may know even now about where I am, and they would find a way to get a hold of me."

"Let them come on," said the young man gaily, "I'd just like to wring their necks for them."

"Oh, no!" said Fraley with fright in her voice. "No, you must never go near them. Never! They would kill you as soon as they would kill a dog. They don't care for anything. They would get behind you in the dark, and nobody would ever know where you were. My father—"

"You think they killed your father?" he asked looking at her keenly.

"I'm not sure," she said, "I think my mother thought so! Oh, promise me you won't ever have anything to do with them. Please, please let me get down now and go away somewhere in the dark! They must not ever know that you were kind to me, or your life won't be safe."

"Now look here, Ladybird, calm yourself. If you are so determined to go away I'll see you safe to somewhere in the morning, and I'll make good and sure that it is safe too, but to-night you ride with me to the ranch, and sleep in a real bed. You needn't worry about me. I can kid the eyeteeth out of any man that ever walked the earth or shot a gun if I try. In fact I've shot guns too, over in France, and I know how. I'm not afraid, and I won't run any risks. You needn't worry about that."

"You promise that?"

"I sure do. And now listen, I've been thinking. I have a whole perfectly good return trip ticket to New York. I bought it thinking I was going right back. I meant to telegraph and get somebody else to take this job out here before another service came due. But after to-night I've a notion to stick it out, at least till somebody else turns up that can do it better than I. So there's my ticket going to waste. It's only good for five days, and if you begin to use it to-morrow morning it will take you on the train to New York. How about it? Will that help any?"

"Oh, that would be wonderful!" said Fraley hesitating. "But would you let me pay you for it sometime when I have earned some money?"

"Why if that's necessary to your peace of mind, sister, perhaps I would, but it isn't in the least necessary. You see the ticket is no good to me if I stay here awhile, and you might as well use it."

By the time he had reached the ranch house he had convinced her that the ticket really needed to be used, and she was doing him service to ride on it, and she drew a long breath of relief.

"All right, Ladybird, that's settled. And now, I want you to do something for me. When you get to New York, just as soon as it is at all convenient for you, I want you to go to a bookstore and buy me a Bible. I'll give you some money to pay for it, and I want a very nice Bible, with a soft leather cover, the kind a minister ought to have. Will you remember? You see I haven't any friends back home just now that I care to have pick me out a Bible, they wouldn't understand. It needs somebody who loves it to pick it out, I imagine. Can you do that?"

"Oh, I shall be glad to do it," said Fraley, her eyes shining at the prospect. "That will be two Bibles I shall have to buy."

"Two Bibles? How is that?"

And then she told him of the woman who had befriended her on the drive and kept her overnight, and of the evening when she had read her Bible to them. The young man listened.

"So you too have been called to be a minister by the wayside," he said thoughtfully. "Well, I want you to let me pay for that Bible too. I would like a share in that if you'll let me. I'll give you the money in the morning, and I want you to use whatever is left over for something that you want for yourself, something to remember me by. Will you?"

Fraley solemnly promised, and soon after that they came within sight of the ranch house, its windows glowing red with friendly light.

Fraley shrank back as the door was opened. Somehow she dreaded this new contact.

The room was more formal than the one at the other log house, and the hostess a different kind of woman entirely. She was gracious and lovely, an entirely new type to the girl. Her hair was waved, and she wore dainty pretty garments. She had a lovely smile, and was graciousness itself when the young man introduced her as a young sister who had been at meeting and was on her way to the railroad station.

"I have promised to see her safely to her train," he said, quite as if that were one of the duties of a missionary preacher, "and I told her I thought you would be good enough to put her up for the night so that she might catch the morning train, as she has come a long distance, Mrs. Hartwick."

The lady swept Fraley a lovely smile, just taking her for granted as one of the natives, and that was all.

"Oh, surely, Mr. Seagrave. We've plenty of room, and are quite used to having people stop on their way. We always keep open house. I'm glad you brought her. Molly," motioning to a colored woman, "show this girl to the end bedroom. See if she would like something to eat before she retires. Good night, my dear. I hope you will rest well."

Another smile and Fraley found herself dismissed.

She could not understand why she felt so humiliated as she walked across the lovely room full of easy chairs, deep soft rugs, wonderful pictures and bright lamps. The lady had been pleasant. She had said nice things. But she had shoved her out. She had made her feel like a stranger and an interloper.

She followed the colored woman out through a little hall, but as she went through the door she looked back and caught one look from the young man who had brought her, and something in his eyes gave her comfort, it was a light and interest, and a dazzling smile, and she knew she was not alone.

The lady was watching her with amused eyes. It was good that Fraley could not hear what she said as the door closed behind her.

"It is well that girl is not staying around here, she is much too good looking to be riding around with our young minister!" she said, and laughed a little warning laugh that had a snarl at the end of it.

Seagrave turned inquiring eyes on his hostess.

"Good looking?" he said, "and what has that to do

with it?" The lady laughed, but the young man began to talk of something else and did not return to the topic. It was the next morning that the hostess got in her final sting for Fraley.

They were sitting at the breakfast table, which was abundantly laden with good things, but the girl was too overawed to eat more than a bite or two. She felt uncomfortable and only longed to get away. The woman and her husband were kind, and passed her everything, but otherwise ignored her, and again she felt that she was where she was not wanted, and her sensitive nature was crushed by the burden of it.

"Mr. Seagrave," said the hostess, "We've made other plans for you this morning. We're going to take you off on a riding party to another ranch about fifty miles away, and we're starting right after breakfast. We've arranged to send this little charge of yours down to her train with Molly and Jim, and they will reach there in plenty of time to put her in the car and see to everything for her."

A quick fright came into Fraley's eyes, and suddenly she spoke, surprising them all at her gentle accent and refined tone:

"Thank you," she said politely, "You need not trouble to do that. I am quite used to walking, and would much rather go by myself. I don't want to be a burden on anybody. You have been very kind to take me in overnight, and I thank you, but that is all I shall need, and if you will excuse me I would like to start at once."

She rose from the table with a grace and ease made possible by her eagerness for flight, and they all looked up amazed at her poise. The lady was almost embarrassed.

"Oh, no, my dear. You misunderstood me. It is no trouble whatever to send you down to the train. We always arrange to do that for our guests. You see the man usually drives over every day or two anyway on errands, and it will be no trouble whatever. We were glad to have you with us."

But the young man interrupted her, rising with his watch in his hand.

"I beg your pardon, Mrs. Hartwick. I'm sorry to spoil your plans but I've given my word to personally see this little sister on the train and I must do it. Another time I'll be glad to ride with you if I may. And now, I wonder if you can spare another horse for my friend to ride. Or, perhaps we can manage as we did last night."

"Oh, you can have the horses of course," laughed the lady to hide her chagrin, "but it seems to me you might be a little easier on your conscience. Jim and Molly would do it just as well as you."

"That may be so, but I'm going," said the young man pleasantly.

"Well, then, John, we'd better go too, and go on from the station. It will only make the ride a little farther," said the lady determinedly.

Fraley's heart sank. She felt like darting out the door and flying anywhere to get away, but Seagrave caught her eye with reassurance.

"Sorry," he said, "I'll have to spoil your plans again. I've got a lot of business to attend to down at the station. I've got to send telegrams and wait for answers, and I simply couldn't make it to-day. I'll have to hang around and wait for Long Distance connection with the hospital too. I want to ask how our friend Dudley is getting on, and if he is in shape at all, I need to find out several things before I can go on here."

"Oh, you could wait to write," pleaded the lady.

But Seagrave was firm.

"I've got to get things straightened out," he declared, and then, in the nicest and easiest way possible he made his apologies and got Fraley out of that house and onto a horse, and together they started away in the sunshine, leaving the lady looking most discontented.

"I don't think she liked you to go," said Fraley, solemnly, after they had ridden in silence about a mile.

"That doesn't spoil the sunshine a particle for me," said Seagrave, smiling. "If I were thinking of staying out here indefinitely I might even change my boardinghouse, but I guess, as it is, we shall manage to rub along and be good friends. I really didn't come out here for the purpose of amusing that woman, even if she does know how to put up a good lunch. Say, little sister, just hand me over that bag and let me carry it. It looks like a heavy load for you."

"Oh, no," said Fraley, "I like it. My mother made it for me."

"In that case I suppose it isn't heavy, but you needn't be selfish about it," and he reached over and lifted the strap from her shoulder, putting it over his own.

"You are very kind," she said, "I feel sorry to take you all this way just for me. I really can do very well alone."

"Well, I've expressed my views on that subject several times before so we won't need to say any more," he said jovially. "But listen now, there are a lot of things I need to know, and some things I must tell you before we get interrupted again. No telling but those persistent people may tag us after all, and give us no chance to talk. In the first place, you haven't told me your name."

"It's Fraley MacPherson."

"Fraley MacPherson," he repeated, taking out a pencil and writing it down. "That's an extraordinary name. I like it."

"And now, where are you going? Have you got the address with you?"

"My mother said she had put it inside the cover of the

Bible. I have not looked at it yet. There hasn't been any time, and I didn't need to know till I got somewhere near, but it is in New York somewhere."

"Well, we'll stop when we get over that hill out yonder, and let you look it up. I've got to know where you are going. I want to find you when I come back."

"Oh," smiled Fraley, "that will be nice. Then I won't be so lonesome."

"Well, now, do you know what to do when you get to New York?"

"Why, just get off the train, don't I?"

"Well, yes, but you know New York is a large place, and you want to be careful. You just go up into the station, you'll see how everybody else does, and when you get upstairs where the waiting room is you go and ask for the Traveler's Aid woman. She'll be around there somewhere. You can ask any of the red-capped porters, or officials and they will show you where she is. Then you tell her where you are going and she will tell you just how to take a taxi and get there."

"What is a taxi?" asked Fraley wonderingly.

"Why it's a public conveyance that you can hire to take you anywhere in the city. But you better get the woman agent to show you where to get it or you'll be lost in two seconds."

Fraley looked frightened.

"Oh, you'll get on all right," he reassured her, "but you better just let the agent manage things for you. It's her business to help travelers that don't know the city, and show them where to stay all night when they haven't any friends. You are sure you'll be all right when you get to your family?"

"Oh, yes," said Fraley, "my mother said her brother was very nice. He was always very fond of her."

The young man looked down at the sweet eyes lifted

to his, and felt grave misgivings at sending this young innocent out alone into the world. She read the thought in his eyes.

"You needn't worry about me, really," she laughed. "I'm perfectly all safe, and you know God is in New York too. The Bible says He is."

"I believe it," he said seriously; "I didn't know it before. Say, are there any more stories as good as Elijah in that Bible of yours?"

"Oh, many, many!" she said eagerly. "There's the blind man."

"Well, you hurry and send that Bible back to me. I've got to get up something to read on Sunday, you know."

"Oh, yes, take the blind man. I love that story! It's the ninth chapter of John."

"Very well, that's the one I shall read next Sunday!"

They had come to the other side of the hill now, and under a group of trees they stopped while Fraley took out her Bible and found the address she wanted.

"What's this MacPherson one?" he asked looking over her shoulder.

"That's my father's people," she said with reserve. "I might look them up too—I'll see when I get there."

"I know some MacPhersons," he said thoughtfully, marking the initials, "but they're not likely the same people. This address is away downtown in old New York."

That meant nothing at all to Fraley. She carefully put back the bits of paper on which her mother had written the addresses, and put away the Bible in her bag. The young man noticed with wonder the tenderness with which she handled it, almost as if the bag and its contents were holy things.

"It seems as if I oughtn't to let you go this journey all

alone," said Seagrave looking troubled; "you seem so little and unprotected."

She smiled up into his face.

"You are the first person except my mother that I ever felt was all right," she said innocently.

He smiled down at her with a worshipful look in his eyes.

"You are the first girl I ever met that seemed just as God meant her to be," he said gravely, and then knew that if he sat there looking down into her eyes any longer he might be tempted to say more.

"Now," he said looking at his watch, "we'll have to be getting on. I can't have you missing that train. But I want to give you this envelope first. I've written out a lot of directions for you there about the train and what you are to do, about new York and how to get about easily. You probably won't need them when you find your friends, but I wanted to provide against your being in a muddle. It's a big town, you know, and you can't trust everybody. Remember that! Trust God all you want to but don't trust men—nor many women either."

She took the envelope and looked at it interestedly.

"And here, in this purse I've put the money for the Bible, and the ticket, and a little extra change. You'll need it for tipping the porter."

"Tipping? What's that? And what's the porter?"

"Why, the man who looks after you on the train. You'd better get reservations right away. I'll try to get near a porter or the Pullman conductor myself and arrange that for you, but in case I don't, you ask for the Pullman conductor and get a reservation yourself. You'll have no trouble. I've written down what you'll likely have to pay for it. But you can give the porter a little something for waiting on you, and then you'll need to go into the diner for your meals."

"Oh!" said Fraley round-eyed. She wasn't sure she would dare. She wasn't sure that she was going this journey on the cars. If any chance at all presented itself for her to get away so that he wouldn't know it, she might slip off into the desert or somewhere and pursue her weary way, even yet. Now that she was getting near to the station she began to be more and more frightened at the idea of traveling on the cars with a lot of strangers.

They had lingered longer than they realized, and at the last had to hurry their horses to reach the station in time.

She found herself trembling as the great iron monster drew nearer to them, and Seagrave, kind and thoughtful for her, slipped his hand within her arm.

"You mustn't forget me, little ladybird," he said wistfully. "I'm coming to hunt you up when I get back. You know you are my friend. You'll remember that, won't you?"

"Oh, I won't forget you ever," said Fraley earnestly, "and I'm so glad I have one friend. I'm very grateful to you for what you have done for me, and I'll keep remembering your beautiful meeting."

"It wasn't mine, little sister, it was yours," he said, and then as the train drew to a halt he suddenly stooped and kissed her gravely, reverently, on her forehead.

"Good-by, little sister. You've done a lot for me, I think. Here, get on here, in this car. Yes, that's right, go in that door. The porter will look after you. Here, Porter!"

She stood an instant trembling, looking after him as he spoke to the colored man with the white coat, and then the train began to move, the porter swung on, and

Seagrave walked alongside, tipping his hat to her, and waving his hand. She watched him through sudden blinding tears, and tried to smile, watched him till the train whirled out of his sight, and then she turned to go inside.

12

IT seemed a strange unfriendly place that she had entered, somewhat like the entrance to a cave, solid walls,
and a passage only wide enough for one to walk. The
motion of the train, too, frightened her. She could climb
trees, and walk out on a slender limb, she could wade
rivers, she could brave the dangers of the night and the
menace of wild cattle, but the motion of that train simply
paralyzed her. It seemed that the earth beneath her was
rocking and about to fall.

She put out both hands and steadied herself, and so,
after a minute, began slowly to go onward again, inching
along, and sliding her hands on the wall.

The porter with whom Seagrave had talked had vanished into the car behind her, and there seemed no one
left in the wide world again. Why had she trusted herself
to this strange way of traveling? Would she not see
anybody at all all the way, and to where did this queer
narrow room lead?

She came at length to the main part of the car, and saw
high backed seats with green cushions, and people sitting
in them, some facing each other. Some men were

playing ards in one section, and their intent looks as they threw down their cards on the little table between them reminded her of Brand and Pierce when they were playing that way. She shrank back, and turned to her right to return to the door again. It was hot in this place, and she felt as if she could not breathe. But suddenly a little doorway hung with a dark green curtain presented itself. The curtain was shoved back, and there was a small room, with long green seats. By the window sat a lady who looked up curiously at her.

Fraley gave her a shy questioning smile, and the lady smiled back pleasantly enough. She was a curiously dressed lady, with trim, close-fitting, very short tresses, and a little tight dark hat. She was slim as a girl, though you could see by her face that she wasn't young. She wore a necklace made of beads that looked like drops of dew when the sun rises, and she had more colored stones in rings on her hands.

"Is this a place where I could sit?" she asked, shyly stepping within the door.

"Why, I guess so," said the lady with a swift startled glance at the slender bare feet. "You have probably got in the wrong car, but you can stay there till the conductor comes and he will tell you where to go."

Fraley sat down thankfully on the edge of the long seat.

"I have a ticket," she said as if presenting her credentials, "and some money," she added earnestly. "I can pay for my seat."

"Well, I'm sure the conductor will fix you up all right," said the lady kindly, wondering at the pure speech and refined accent of this barefoot child, and fascinated by her loveliness.

Fraley's eyes wandered to the window, startled.

"How fast we go!" she exclaimed. "I've never been on a train before!"

"You haven't?" exclaimed the lady. "That's strange. Where are you going?"

"I'm going to New York," said the girl, still watching the landscape. "Why, see! It's only the near-by things that are going fast. The ones that are far off, the mountains hardly seem to move at all. There! There they go! The mountains are going now. They're just shadows of themselves. Oh, I didn't think we could get away from the mountains so fast!"

The lady smiled and watched her amusedly. Presently she spoke again.

"Haven't you some shoes and stockings in that bag?" she asked practically. "I think you'd better put them on if you have. You know it isn't the custom to ride in the train barefoot. The conductor might not like it."

Fraley's eyes came to the lady's face now with quick alarm, and a flood of lovely color went over her face.

"Oh!" she said, and glanced down at her small white feet.

"They—are—perfectly clean. I washed them just before I started and we rode all the way."

"Yes, I see that," said the lady trying to make her voice sound less amused and more kindly, "but it just isn't the custom, you know. You might feel awkward, and I'm sure the conductor would feel he ought to speak to you about it. That's why I mentioned it."

Fraley's eyes went to the lady's exquisite little feet clad in sheerest gun metal silk stockings, and patent leather slippers with sparkling buckles. Then she tucked her own feet back as far as they would go curling one around the other unobtrusively.

"I didn't know," she said sadly, "or I wouldn't have come this way. I'd better get off the next time the train stops. Perhaps the conductor won't get around before that to see me. I can walk of course, only it will take longer."

"Walk!" said the lady laughing. "Why you would be an old woman before you got there."

"Well," said Fraley, "I suppose it wouldn't matter then."

"How absurd!" said the startled lady laughing. "Why don't you put on your shoes and stockings?"

"But I haven't any," said the girl, and there were almost tears in her eyes. "I had a pair once, but the stockings wore out, and then the shoes got too little and hurt me. They were red shoes and they had little tassels at the top. It was a long time ago."

The lady stared. Where had this amazing child lived without shoes and grown into lovely womanhood? Did she belong to some strange sect who didn't believe in footgear, or what?

"But why haven't you had shoes and stockings?" asked the lady curiously.

The color waved over the sweet face again. She lifted shamed eyes.

"Because we hadn't money to buy them. And anyhow they weren't necessary, like things to eat."

"Oh," said the lady with a little gasp as if she were in pain. As if anybody could be so poor as that!

She stared at the girl a moment and then she suddenly arose and sharply shut the little door between the drawing-room and the outer car.

"We've got to do something about this before the conductor comes," she said kindly. "I've got plenty of stockings here in my bag, and you go into the little dressing room here and put on a pair. I think maybe I have a pair of shoes that will fit you, too, nice low-heeled sports ones; we'll see. It simply won't do for the conductor to see you that way. He'll never let you stay in his car looking like that."

The lady swung open another little door and switched on a mysterious flood of light, and lo, there was a tiny washroom with towels and a looking-glass and sweet scented soap. Fraley's mother had told her about such an arrangement but she never expected to see one.

"Now," said the lady in a business-like tone, "we've got to work fast. You go in there and take off that coat, and that thing off your head, and I'll bring you some stockings. Have you any garters? No, of course you wouldn't have."

The lady vanished and Fraley stared at herself in the mirror critically, dimly realizing for the first time what part clothes play in the scheme of living.

The lady reappeared bearing biscuit-colored silk stockings and a pair of low-cut tan golf shoes with rubber soles.

"I should think you might get these on," she said as she put the shoes on the floor. "Now, let's see how the stockings fit. Your foot must be about the size of mine."

Fraley was not expert at putting on stockings, and the lady had to take a hand, and turn the toe inside, helping to sheathe the wild little foot in silk for the first time in its life.

"My! Aren't they pretty!" said Fraley surveying them in wonder after her two feet were arranged in the stockings.

Then she bent to the task of getting on the shoes, and found, to the lady's satisfaction, that they went on easily. They were even a little large, which was well for a first shoeing.

Fraley stood up and looked down at her feet. She took a trial step, and looked up.

"You couldn't walk up a mountain in these," she said with a comical helpless little pucker in her brow.

"Well, I think I'd make a better showing in those than without them," laughed the lady. "However, I'm glad they fit."

"How much—are these?" Fraley asked shyly, hesitating between the words, and not quite sure whether this was the correct thing to say or not.

"How much?" asked the amazed lady. "Why nothing, child. You're welcome to them. They're just old ones. I seldom wear golf shoes a second year, the style changes so often."

"The what changes?"

"The style. The way they're cut—the fashion, you know."

"Oh," said Fraley, "that's like 'The fashion of this world passeth away,' isn't it? I never knew that meant shoes too."

"You odd child! What extremely unique remarks you make! Really I can't quite classify you. But listen, is that your best dress?"

"No," said the girl looking down at herself doubtfully. "Don't you think this is clean enough? I washed it out in the brook not long ago. But I've got another one. It was made out of one my mother had when she was married. I am going to be very careful of it because it's the last thing she made for me before she died and I want to keep it always, but if you say I ought to put it on now, I will. I want to look right. Mother would have wanted me to look all right."

"Let me see your other dress!" ordered the lady.

Fraley went down to the bottom of her bag, under the Bible and the tin cup and the little packages, and fished out the old black satin frock, which was made something after the pattern of a flour bag.

The lady shook it out and surveyed it critically.

"It's rather mussed," she said dubiously, searching around for a good excuse, because she could see the girl's pride in her best dress, "and I think perhaps on the whole you'd better put it way if you want it for a keepsake. Traveling is rather hard on clothes, you know. Just let me see if I haven't something you could wear. You're about my size and I have several dresses I am tired of. I would just give them to my maid when I got home anyway. If you don't mind we'll put one on you and freshen you up."

"You're very kind," said Fraley with quaint courtesy, "But I don't think my mother would think it was right for me to take so much. Besides, your maid will be disappointed."

"Your mother would want you to look right," said the lady firmly, "and since she is not here why you'll have to let me decide that in her place. As for my maid she is just rolling in things I've given her, and won't know whether she gets one more or not. Wait, I think I have a little blue frock that will be the very thing."

The lady opened her suitcase again and produced an armful of bright silky things.

"These things go with it," she stated briefly as she handed out some flimsy little silk underwear of pale pink trimmed with frills of fine lace and set with a rosebud here and there. The lady was having the best time she had had since her childhood's last doll, dressing up this lovely child just to please herself and see how she would look in the right clothes.

Fraley looked at the pink things puzzled.

"What are these?" she said.

"They're undergarments that go with that dress to make it set right."

"But I have some nice clean underthings on," said Fraley proudly. "My mother made them."

"Well, take them off and put them away in your bag with your dress, and put these on. The dress won't hang right without the things that were made for it," said the lady as if that settled the matter.

Fraley accepted them because that seemed the thing to do.

"This one goes on first," said the lady, pointing to a much befrilled article, "and then this, and this."

The lady went out and Fraley took off her own things and slowly put on the strange slippery ones, and looked down at herself in wonder.

"I suppose," she said as the lady came back with a shimmery dark blue dress over her arm, "I suppose the fashion of my underthings is passed away, isn't it? And mother didn't know because we've been out there on the mountain so long."

"I guess that's it," said the lady with a mental note of the child's discernment. "Now, slip this over your head, and put your arms in here—"

The dark blue dress settled down over the girl's slimness and gave her distinction at once as all such little creations of a great foreign designer usually do. Fraley stared down at herself in delight, fingering the bright buckle with which the dress was fastened.

"Now, we've got to do something with that hair," said the lady speculatively. "Suppose you sit down on that stool and let me try something. You want to look like other girls of your age before we go out to the diner, you know. Your mother would want that. She wouldn't want you to look queer."

"Did I look queer?" asked Fraley studying this new self in the mirror over the wash-bowl.

"Well, just a little different, you know," said the lady with a smile. "Now, do you mind if I arrange your hair?"

"Oh, no," said the girl with a sigh of pleasure, "I wouldn't know how, I'm sure. You're very kind." Then after a minute, she added, "My hair is clean. I washed it in the brook night before last."

"You washed it in the brook!" exclaimed the lady in horror. "How on earth did you manage that? Were you in swimming?"

"Yes—" said Fraley hesitating a little to make sure this was quite true, "at least, I couldn't swim much, it wasn't deep enough."

"Well, it's lovely," said the lady in admiration. "Now, let's try a new way."

Fraley watched in the glass while the older woman combed her soft gold hair, parting it from forehead to the nape of the neck, and gathering each mass of golden curls into a softly coiled wheel over her ears.

"There!" she said standing off to survey the finished effect. "I think that's a good style for you. Now, wait till I get the hat that goes with that dress."

She came back with a little blue hat of soft straw with a bright pin gleaming at one side. She had also brought a string of curiously carved beads, and a little wrist watch which she said Fraley would need.

The girl stood up and looked down at herself, and then looked in the glass and turned back to the lady.

"It's like being clothed with Christ's righteousness, isn't it?" she said turning luminous eyes to her benefactor. "I wouldn't know myself at all."

"Mercy, child, what uncanny things you do say!" said the startled lady. "I think you look very well myself. You'd get by anywhere now."

"Yes," said Fraley shining-faced, "I think it will be a

good deal like this when I get up to heaven and see myself all dressed in the white linen!"

The lady looked at her aghast and said quickly:

"I don't know in the least what you mean, but don't try to tell me now, for it's time for the conductor to be coming around. What have you done with your ticket? You said you had a ticket, didn't you?"

"Yes," said the girl, "it's here in this envelope," and she drew it forth from the bag where she had slipped it when she came in to put on her stockings.

"Oh, well, you'll have to have a hand bag," said the lady and went out again to her suitcase, returning with a small strap bag of dark blue leather trimmed in silver.

"This will do. Now, put your ticket in there, and your money. They don't carry things around uncovered that way. And, what about that gray bag you have your things in? You want to keep all those things, do you? You wouldn't want to throw them away?"

"Oh, no indeed!" said the girl, a frightened look coming into her eyes. "My mother made the bag for me. It's been so convenient."

"Well, I was just thinking. They're not using that pattern of bag quite so much this season. Suppose I let you have this one of mine. I can easily put what things I have left in it, into my suitcase. We sent so many things home by parcel post that there really wasn't enough left to fill all the bags, but I didn't just care to throw it away."

So the old gray woolen bag found sanctuary in the extremely correct patent-leather overnight bag that the lady emptied for the purpose. Fraley went out in her new attire and sat down opposite the little door which was now opened for the coming of the official, and wondered at herself.

Then she began to wonder what her mother would have said to all this lovely array, and what her enemies would think if they could see her now. She had a passing wish that Caroline might have seen these clothes, and the lady who kept looking at her feet when she tried to keep the young missionary from going to the station with her.

And then her breath came a little faster, and her cheek flushed softly pink, at thought of that same young man, and the words he had said and the farewell he had given her. She could feel the touch of his lips upon her brow even yet, and she told herself it was like a blessing.

The lady was watching her with satisfaction. Not in years had she been so interested in anything as in transforming this lovely creature from a wild thing to a maid of the world. And yet, she would perhaps never be just like other girls. There was a freshness and a freedom about her that she would not want to have spoiled. A little training and she would be a wonder! An idea had come to her, and she was turning it over. As she was musing and watching Fraley, the conductor arrived.

The lady leaned forward with her own ticket, and told Fraley to get out hers. The conductor eyed her sharply.

"This young lady is traveling with me," she said handing over the two tickets. "She got on at the last stop. Can you arrange to put her here with me?"

"Tell the Pullman conductor," growled the official who snipped a hole or two in Fraley's ticket and handed it back.

Fraley took the ticket and studied it in wonder, reading its inscription as if it were something really interesting.

Suddenly she looked up at the lady who was still watching her.

"You have been wonderful to me," she said with a smile. "I can never thank you enough."

The lady spoke almost crossly:

"I've done nothing but what I pleased. Don't bother to thank me. I haven't enjoyed anything so much in a long time. Come, let's go and get some luncheon!"

13

FRALEY was very much intrigued with the diner. It seemed to her like a playhouse with all those little tables. With the pleasure of a child she sat down in the chair opposite to the lady.

The menu card interested her, too, and she studied it with fascination, but she knew very few of the names that were on its list.

"Would you like me to order?" the lady asked, watching her perplexity.

"Please," said Fraley. "Get me something that doesn't cost much. Just some bread and milk perhaps if that is cheap, or don't they have a cow on a train?"

The lady laughed.

"No cow, but plenty of milk! Don't you want tea or coffee?"

"No," said the girl decidedly, "Mother thought it wasn't good for me."

When the order was brought the girl opened her eyes in astonishment.

"Won't this cost a lot?" she asked with a troubled look.

"You're not to bother about the cost," smiled the lady. "You are my guest on this trip. You'll have use enough for your money when you get to New York."

"But that isn't right!"

"Yes, it's right if I want to. Now, eat your soup."

With a healthy young appetite she did as she was bid, and surprised her patroness with the easy way in which she handled her spoon and knife and fork, and the beautiful way she ate. Where did she learn it all? There was a mystery about this.

Nothing that went on escaped the bright eyes. After the lady paid the bill she laid some money beside the plate.

"What is that for?" the girl asked.

"A tip for the waiter."

"I thought so," said Fraley with satisfaction. "A friend told me about that. I ought to tip the porter too, he said."

"You needn't bother; I've done that. Who is this friend? Have you know him a long time?"

"His name is Seagrave. He is a good man. He had a service last night in a schoolhouse. I was there. I've only know him yesterday and to-day, but he was very kind. He brought me to the station and told me some of the things I would need to know."

"Is he young or old?"

"Why—he's young—with nice eyes, and a smile."

"H'm!" said the lady, "some theological student out earning his next winter's tuition, I suppose. What did he tell you?"

"Oh, how to get off the train, and up into the Pennsylvania station," recited the careful student. "He told me to go to the Traveler's Aid to find out about taking a taxi, and where to look for my friends, and where to find a place to board in case they were not at home."

"So you have friends?"

It almost sounded as if the lady were not glad.

"Yes. My mother's brother lives in New York. And my father's people live there too," she added the last as an afterthought.

"It's time you told me your name. I am Mrs. Wentworth, but you may call me Violet if you like. A great many of my friends call me that."

"Oh, what a lovely name. It's like your eyes. I'd like to pick you some of the flowers. They grow all over my mountain where I came from."

The lady smiled. This was the kind of thing she liked.

"But my name is just Fraley MacPherson," said the girl. "My mother was Alison Fraley and I have her last name, because she didn't want to forget it."

"That's strange," said the lady; "I know an Alison Fraley. She lives on Riverside Drive very near my home. But of course it can't be a relative of yours. I know some MacPhersons too, but they are very rich people. Where are your people living?"

Fraley told the address as she remembered it from having read it to Seagrave that morning.

"Yes, that's way downtown. Strange it happens to be the same initials. The one I know is Robert Fraley, too. He is a multimillionaire."

"What is that?" asked Fraley mildly interested.

"A man who is very rich indeed, richer than almost anybody else except just a few others like himself."

"That wouldn't be right, would it?" asked the girl with a worried frown. "A man ought not to keep more than his share, ought he?"

"Tell that to the millionaires and see what they'd say," laughed the lady. "I think you're rare. Tell me, how did you get your education if you've lived away off on the mountain? Was there a school anywhere near you?"

"Oh, we had a Book," said Fraley and opened her eyes wide in a way she had when she was astonished. "My mother used to hear me say my lessons every morning. I always learned a chapter a week at least, and then we had numbers, different kinds of them, and other things."

"All out of the same book?" asked the lady more amused than ever.

"Yes."

"What was the book?"

"The Bible."

"The Bible! How could you possibly study numbers out of that?"

"Oh, easily. At first I just had the numbers of the chapters and the verses. I counted them, and added them, and subtracted them and divided them. And then I began to hunt out the numbers of things in the stories. There were seventy of the children of Israel that went down into Egypt, you know, counting Joseph and his family. And there were six hundred and three thousand, five hundred and fifty of them when they came back four hundred years later."

The woman of the world stared as if she thought the girl had gone crazy.

"There was an old rock up a little way from our back door," Fraley went on eagerly, her eyes shining with joy at the remembrance. "I used to do my sums on that with a piece of limestone that made nice white marks on it. When I got the answers mother would come out and look at them to see if they were right."

"What did you do when the rock was full?" asked the lady interested.

"Oh, I washed it off, or sometimes the rain would

wash it off for me. I used to play games with the stories in the Old Testament sometimes. I would gather pebbles of different sizes for the people. There was a smooth white stone I always called David and a big rough red one with mica in it that was Goliath, and I used to set the armies out on the cabin floor, and then bring Goliath down to challenge them and little David would come and say he would fight the giant. I had a stone for the king too."

"Your mother must have been a very original woman!" said the lady listening interestedly. "I would like to have known her. The perfect idea of educating a child out of one book and doing all that!"

"Oh, but the book was the Bible, you know," explained the young student. "I used to have English work too. I used to have to write the stories off in other words, so mother could see if I understood. That was fun, putting it in another way but telling the same story."

The lady's eyes narrowed.

"You speak singularly pure English," she said. "I wonder—" but she did not finish her sentence. She was studying the girl's eager face and wondering what it would be like to have a young thing like this around her all the time.

"And what are you going to do first when you get to New York?" the lady asked at length.

"Why, first—the very first thing I'm going to hunt up a store where they sell Bibles. I have to buy two and send them back to people who are waiting for them."

"Bibles?" said the lady startled again. "Why should people be waiting for Bibles? I should think you would find a place to stay, first of all, and then hunt up your people."

"No, I must get the Bibles first," said Fraley firmly. "I promised. You see they are really needed."

"Whom are they for?"

"One is for a woman I stayed overnight with. She hadn't ever read it, and I recited some for her, and she wanted some more so much that I told her I would be sure to send her one. She wouldn't let me pay for my supper and my night's lodging, and you see I must let her know right away that I have not forgotten."

"Sort of a bread and butter Bible, then!" laughed the lady.

"A what?" asked Fraley. Sometimes this lady almost acted as if she were making a joke out of things.

"I mean you are sending it out of courtesy," she explained, her eyes sobering pleasantly.

"Not altogether," said Fraley. "There's a little boy there. He wants to read it."

"And why should you care whether he reads it or not? It seems abnormal for a child like you to be talking about reading the Bible. You are young and ought to be interested in all the gay things that are going on. You'll just love everything when you get to New York. You need to dance and flirt and have a good time generally. You've been too solemn and not had the right kind of a childhood. You are morbid. But New York will soon take it out of you, I'm afraid."

"If I thought that," said Fraley earnestly, "I'd get right off this train and go back. I would rather live out my life on a mountain than forget my Bible. It's the dearest thing in life to me, and I promised my mother I would never let go of it."

The lady shrugged her shoulders, and spoke soothingly:

"Oh, well, child, don't take me too seriously. Tell me who the other Bible is for?"

"It's for my friend, Mr. Seagrave. He had to go out there to preach without any Bible because he was called to go in a hurry in place of someone who was sick, and he gave me some money and asked me to send him back a Bible as soon as I possibly could. He needs it for Sunday. I am going to mark some of the stories in it that he is to read in his service. They are stories we talked about and he asked me to mark them for him."

"It seems to me he got rather intimate in one day," remarked the lady.

"Oh, no," said Fraley. "He was just friendly. He was what my mother used to tell me a gentleman was like. I never saw one before."

"H'm! What did you say his name was?"

"Seagrave," said Fraley, and suddenly felt a reserve coming over her speech. Was there the least bit of a sneer for her friend in this lady's eyes, and on her red lips?

"There are Seagraves in New York of course," said the lady thoughtfully, but Fraley kept her own counsel, and let her eyes wander happily out on the brightness of the landscape.

"Are your mother's people poor?" asked the lady suddenly.

The girl brought her gaze back to the lady thoughtfully.

"Why, I'm not sure," she said, "perhaps they are. I never thought. But what difference would that make?"

"You'd not want to be dependent on them if they were," suggested the lady, "perhaps they wouldn't be able to support you."

"Oh, I wouldn't want anybody to support me," said the girl happily. "I can get some work to do. I must take care of myself of course."

"But what could you do?"

"I could milk," was the eager answer. "I've done that a great deal, and I do it nicely."

The lady laughed amusedly.

"We don't keep cows in New York. The city is too crowded. So you'll have to give up the idea of being a dairymaid."

"You don't keep cows?" she asked perplexed. "How do you get along without milk?"

"Oh, we have milk. It comes on milk trains, in cans and bottles, packed in ice."

"Real milk? Where does it come from?"

"Farms and dairies."

"Then perhaps I'd have to go out to a farm or dairy and get work," sighed the child disappointedly, "but I'd rather be near people who belonged to my mother."

"Oh, they wouldn't take a girl to do that work. It is all done by men, or machines, nowadays."

"Machines? How could a machine milk a cow?"

"I'm sure I don't know. I never saw one, but I've heard that all the milking in large dairies is done by some kind of an electric contrivance that is made a good deal like a human hand. But what else can you do?"

"I can wash," she said brightly, "and cook a little. I can learn to do almost anything, I guess."

Looking at her the woman thought perhaps it might be possible.

"How would you like to come and work for me?" she asked.

"Oh, could I? That would be beautiful!" said the child enthusiastically. "What would you let me do for you? I could learn to do fine cooking like what we had to eat to-day perhaps."

"But I already have a cook, and a waitress, and a maid and several other servants. I don't need another. How would you like to be my social secretary? A sort of companion, you know."

"That's not work," said Fraley disappointed; "that's

play. I couldn't earn money honestly for doing a thing like that."

"Oh, yes, you could," said the lady, "and it's not play by any means. You would have to keep track of my engagements, and see that I didn't forget any of them. You would look after sending my laces to be mended and my jewels to be repaired or cleaned, or restrung, you know—and you would have to learn to answer my notes and send out invitations—all those things. Can you write?"

"Oh, yes," said the girl eagerly.

"Write something for me. Write me a letter. Here, take this and see what you can do."

The lady opened a gold-mounted handbag and took out a small notebook and a gold fountain pen and handed them to her.

Fraley examined the pen, and handed it back.

"I'd better get my own pencil. I'm not used to that yet, but I'll practice with it later if you want me to."

She opened the newly acquired bag, dug out her own little stub of a pencil and went to work. In a few minutes she handed over the paper. It was written in a neat plain hand and the spelling was perfect.

> *Dear Mrs. Wentworth:*
> *I am glad I met you, and I love you. I hope God will bless you for helping me.*
>
> > *With affection,*
> > *Fraley MacPherson.*

Mrs. Wentworth looked up surprised.

"Who taught you the form of a letter?"

"My mother used to make me write one to her every morning for a while, till she thought I understood. Sometimes she let me sign the end like the epistles in the

Bible. 'The grace of our Lord Jesus Christ be with your spirit.' I like that, but I didn't know whether that would do for the kind of letters you want or not so I didn't put it in."

"It would not," said the lady a bit sharply. "You showed good sense. Well, then, shall we call it a bargain? I'll hire you at a salary of two hundred a month. That will give you enough to buy some clothes right away. You'll need a good many for you will go out with me a lot. Do you think you will like it?"

"I'm sure I'll like to be with you and do whatever you want done if I can do it right," said Fraley. "I think you are lovely."

"Well, you may not think so after you've been with me a while. And if you get tired of the job of course I shall not hold you. I don't want you to feel under any obligation. I'm having my fun out of this, and I don't feel you owe me anything. But there's one thing I would suggest. Don't drag the Bible in everywhere. People don't all care for it as much as you do, and you'll turn everybody against you. You wouldn't want to do that, would you?"

"Why no, of course not."

The lady gave her a queer look, almost as if she were going to laugh and then she turned away and looked out of the window a long time. After which she turned back and said earnestly, "Fraley, you're a dear little girl. Don't let anything I've said worry you. I'm really rather a cranky old thing."

"Don't say that, please, Mrs. Wentworth."

"I told you you might call me Violet."

"I know. But it doesn't seem quite respectful. Mother taught me to be respectful."

"Well, I don't want respect. That makes me feel old

and I'm getting old fast enough without it. I'd rather you'd call me Violet."

"I'll try—Mrs.—Violet," she smiled timidly.

"That's right," said the lady. "Now, can you play bridge?"

"Bridge?" said Fraley. "What is that?"

"It's a game of cards."

Fraley's face darkened.

"No, I cannot play cards."

"I will teach you then."

"No, Mrs.—I mean Violet, please. I would rather not learn. My mother hated cards. The men played them when they were drunk. She thought it was what made my father lose—everything. I wouldn't feel right playing them."

"That's absurd, of course. However, I shan't press the matter now. You'll learn soon enough when you get into another world that those are all things of the past. You are leaving them behind and there will be new standards which you will have to accept if you want to be a success in New York. I am going to teach you how to be a success, little Fraley."

Fraley smiled but she did not look wholly convinced. She examined the tips of the smart little shoes she was wearing which had already become irksome; she smoothed down the satin of her chic little frock, and let the afternoon sunshine twinkle on the tiny platinum watch she was wearing, but somehow she felt a great depression. The new life began to look complicated. She looked wistfully out of the window, and thought of the Raven, her new friend, and that reverent kiss he had laid upon her brow at parting. She wished she could go to her own dear mother and talk it all over and find out what was right.

She drew a deep sigh. It was very stuffy in the train and her eyelids were heavy with sleep!

"You're tired, child," said the lady sympathetically. "Take off your hat and shoes and lie down there. We can draw the curtain or close the door and no one will disturb you. I want to read awhile."

So Fraley took off the new hat and hung it respectfully on the long brass hook over her head, took off the fine shoes and stood them in a corner by her couch, and nestled down on the pillow that the porter brought. She was soon sound asleep. One silk clad arm was under her head, and the long dark lashes lay on the lovely rounded cheek. A little late beam of sunshine laid bright touches on the coil of soft hair over her ear, and brought out exquisite tintings in the warm flesh. What a picture she made as she lay there sleeping like a baby, the little girl pilgrim, all alone! Something deeper than she understood stirred in the woman who watched her, over the book she was not reading. What if she should make this girl something more than social secretary! She would make a great sensation in her world, if she were launched in the way that she knew well how to launch a girl. Perhaps she would do it. She would go slow. She would find out first what kind of people she belonged to, whether they were likely to turn up later and spoil all her plans. Perhaps it would be well to investigate them before the girl had opportunity, and if they were undesirable, keep her from going to them at all. It would not be hard to do so, she judged, for the child was most tractable.

So the afternoon waned, and the sun went down behind the long express train hurrying east, and the sky on either side was spread with lovely colors left over from the main display.

Fraley woke up in time to see it, and to wonder for a

moment where she was, in such a noisy rush. She laughed when the lady smiled at her.

"I thought I was hiding behind a great rock in the hot sun," she said, sitting up and rubbing her eyes. "I guess I must have gone to sleep. Why, it is getting night, isn't it?"

"It surely is," said the lady closing her book. "Go smooth your hair and let us go to dinner. I like to eat while the sky is in good form. It makes it seem like a banquet."

Fraley got up and made ready, and they wended their way once more to the diner.

"I don't really need to eat so often," said the girl. "It costs a lot and I'm not used to meals very often."

"That is silly," said the lady. "People have to eat, and besides it is all there is to do here."

"Oh, I think there is a great deal to do," said Fraley happily. "There is so much to see. Such wide pictures out of the window, it is almost like climbing a tree and looking high over the world."

"Can you climb a tree?" asked the lady studying her and realizing her loveliness again. How well she looked in that dark blue. It brought out all the tints of her perfect skin.

"Oh yes," laughed the girl, "I always could do that. Can't you?"

"Well, no," said the lady, "not that I ever remember. I'm afraid I wouldn't look like much up a tree. There are no trees to climb in New York, you know," she reminded.

"Perhaps you do not need them," said the girl gravely, thinking how often a tree had been her only refuge.

"Need them? Oh, for shade? Well, no, we have our cool houses you know, and in summer we always go away anyway."

"I mean to climb to get out of danger," explained Fraley.

"Danger? What kind of danger?"

"Oh, bad men, and wild animals, and angry cattle," she answered coolly.

"Mercy!" said the lady. "Have you ever encountered such things?"

"Oh, yes."

"And taken refuge in a tree?"

"Yes, I don't know where I would have gone if there hadn't been a tree. I think God planted them just where He saw I would need them."

The lady smiled superciliously.

"Do you think He bothers about us to that extent?"

"Oh, yes," said the girl, opening her eyes wide in her earnestness. "I know He does. He took care of me every step of the way here."

"Well, what kind of ice cream do you want? I suppose the vanilla with fudge sauce would be the best, unless you prefer fresh strawberries."

"Oh, yes, strawberries! I've picked them on the mountain. How my mother loved them!"

"How you loved your mother!" sighed the lady enviously. "I wish I might have been your mother, but I'm afraid you wouldn't have been half so lovely as you are."

"Oh," said Fraley thoughtfully, gazing out at the violet and gold of the dying sunset. "It makes a difference where we are born, doesn't it?"

"It certainly does, princess in disguise."

"If I couldn't have been the child of my own dear mother, I think the next best thing would have been to have been yours," she said at last prettily, with a shy smile.

14

THE wonder of the night was having the berths made up in the cosy little drawing-room, and lying on the long couch at the side, with the lady over in the other berth in the soft noisy dark. The wheels beat a monotonous rhythm underneath her, and the night came close as they hurried along safe and protected through the dark land. The engine needed no guide. It had a set track to go on and it made no mistakes.

And Fraley thought how just as plainly her own little track was perhaps marked out where God who was her engineer could see it, and guide her.

Then as she heard the steady breathing of her room-mate and privacy settled down around her, she began to go over her meeting with the young man in the wilderness, and all the way they had come in their friendship in those few short hours. That kiss he had given her at parting sat upon her brow like a holy thing. She had a friend, and something told her he would always be her friend. Would he like her better in these new clothes she had put on? Had he liked her less for her bare feet, and faded clothing? It did not seem that he had noticed them. Out there in the wilderness perhaps it sort of fitted in with everything, and she was glad that he liked her first in her own plain simple things that she had always worn. Afterward, if she ever met him again she would like to have him know that she knew how to look as the world expected her to look, but she would always remember that he had not despised her in her old garments, and bare feet.

Then she remembered with a thrill of anticipation, that she had a letter in her new pocketbook from him that she had not read. She would get it out and read it in the morning while the lady was in the little dressing-room getting dressed. She shrank from reading it before her; she would ask so many questions. Instinctively she felt that this new Violet woman would not understand her friendship with this man in the desert.

She went back in her thoughts to the dim smoky schoolhouse with its candle light and quavering prayers; the sweet songs they had sung; and the voice of the young man as he read the familiar words from the Book. How close she felt to him as she thought of it, for he had enjoyed her Book, and had wanted one for himself. He had a sympathy and understanding for it that she felt the lady did not have.

When she woke in the morning the lady was still asleep.

Softly Fraley tiptoed up and got her letter, stealing into the little dressing-room to read it.

In a little delicate embroidered gown and kimono of silk that the lady had provided for her, she stood by the light and read, breathless with the pleasure of having a real friend who would write to her like that.

*My dear Ladybird: [he wrote]*
*I am sitting up to write this because I am afraid I may*

*not have a chance to say these things in the morning
without someone by to bother, and I do not want you to
go into the wilderness of New York without some knowledge of what you are up against.*

There followed some minute directions about ways and
means, and what was wise and unwise to do in a great
city when a young girl was all alone. Warnings that young
Seagrave's friends would have been surprised he knew
how to give.

She read them all through carefully, and then there
came another bit of himself at the end:

*And now, I don't just know how to tell you, Ladybird,
what you have done for me. I was pretty much of a good
for nothing when you found me on the desert yesterday,
or when I found you in a tree. I don't mean I've ever been
very sinful, you know, just careless, and always living for
a good time. But you've somehow given me a new
viewpoint, and I want to thank you for it. I mean to stick
to the job. I'll just tell some of the stories, and put the folks
to studying the Book. When you send me my Bible I'll
get to work on it myself, and perhaps now and then, you'll
remember to put up a prayer for the poor raven who was
sent to feed you when you were hungry. I shall always be
glad I met you, Angel lady, and please don't forget when
you get settled to give me your address, for it may be your
people are not at home and you'll have to find a boarding
place. Don't forget that on any account, for I want to write
you about my services and how you helped me through
them, if you'll let me.*

*Your new friend,
A Raven.*

And down in the lower corner of the sheet was written

*George Rivington Seagrave,*

with two addresses, one in the west, the other in New York.

But Fraley could hear that the lady was stirring in her berth now, and she folded the precious letter and tucked it safely away. She dressed quickly and came out looking fresh as a new-blown rose.

"Did I do my hair all right?" she asked, starry-eyed from her letter.

"You certainly did," said the lady admiringly, lifting a haggard face with the make-up sadly in need of repair. "You look like a new-born babe, my child. How do you manage it? I don't know but what you've improved on my coiffure. You certainly got the knack quickly. Well, I'll be ready shortly. I suppose you are hungry."

"Don't hurry," said Fraley happily, "I'll sit here and look out of the window. Isn't the world wonderful! And I want to read my Bible a few minutes too, I always do every morning."

Marveling, the elder woman took her way to the dressing-room, almost envying this child her relish for simple sights, and wondering whether after all she would ever be able to give sophistication to this strange young creature who seemed to be almost from another world.

"You certainly look a picture!" she said a little while later coming out in all her delicate war paint. "Put up your old Book now and let's go get some breakfast. They always have waffles on these trains. Do you like waffles?"

"I never saw one," said Fraley with the air of a joyous explorer.

Breakfast was a success. The morning was sparkling,

and the scenery wonderful through which they were passing. The people who sat at the little tables in the dining car were a never-failing source of interest to the girl whose circle of acquaintance had been so exceedingly restricted.

At one or two places during the day when the train stopped for some minutes, they got out and walked around, and Fraley managed her new shoes very well, although she confided to her new friend that it was much, much easier to walk without them.

"We'll have some that really fit you when we get to New York," said the new mentor, and noted with satisfaction how the girl beside her attracted all eyes, and how she went through this open admiration without a particle of self-consciousness. In fact she did not even seem to be aware of it. Perhaps that was because public opinion had as yet no part in her life, and pride of self had not entered into her soul.

Violet Wentworth felt that she had found a treasure in this lovely unspoiled girl, and she meant to use her as a new attraction to adorn her charming home. There was nothing like a new girl, with character and distinction, to bring a throng. She was proud of her sons, and of her reputation as a hostess. She was beginning to think that perhaps she would drop the social secretary idea and introduce Fraley as a young friend who was visiting her for a year. She would see how it worked out. Of course she would have to keep up the form of secretaryship for the time, until the girl got some of that Puritanism rubbed off, for she could see she would not be easily persuaded to accept her living for nothing indefinitely, not even in friendship—and of course it would be hard to make the unsophisticated child understand the real reason why she wanted her. And if she did understand, half the value would be gone from her fine simplicity. As soon as she got to know her own loveliness, it would vanish in pride and selfishness. Violet Wentworth had seen this happen many a time before with the different protégés she impulsively picked up here and there, but she somehow had a warmer feeling for this pretty child, and wanted to keep her as she was.

Secretly studying the child all the time as she conversed with her, Violet Wentworth was deciding just what coaching she needed to make her most quickly ready to move among the people of her own circle. Late in the afternoon she handed over a magazine she had been reading.

"There is a good little story; read it, Fraley. You ought to read a great many magazine stories, and novels. They will be excellent for teaching you the ways of the world. I don't know any way you can get atmosphere as quickly as by reading society stories. Unless perhaps the movies, and the theatre. Of course they are a wonderful help. Little habits and customs that no one would think to tell you about, you would acquire by watching, without realizing you were learning something new. It would simply come to you the way a baby learns the habits of her household into which she had been born."

Fraley took up the magazine and went dutifully to reading the story set for her. But as she read her face grew grave; and graver still as it progressed, and the color came brightly in her cheeks.

Violet Wentworth, watching her could not quite understand her reaction. But she did not seem to be enjoying what she had considered a little romance quite amusing and out of the ordinary. The child's eyes were flashing, and her lips were parted as if she were about to protest at something. When she had finished she handed over the magazine.

"Are people in the world all like that?" she flashed at the astonished lady.

"What do you mean, like that?" asked the lady, "Didn't you like the story? I thought it exceedingly well written."

"Oh," said the girl, "you mean the way it is told. Yes, I suppose it is well told. But why did they want to write such a horrible thing? It isn't like the dreadful stories in the Bible. They were all told to warn people or to teach some great truth that the people needed to know. But this story teaches a thing that isn't so."

"What can you mean, you funny little girl!" exclaimed Violet Wentworth, taking up the magazine and glancing down its columns to refresh her memory of the story which had already gone from her mind.

"Why, it makes that secretary girl fall in love with a man who already has a wife, and marry him, and *be happy* with him! Mother said that was a sin! The Bible says so too!"

"Oh, my dear!" laughed the lady. "What a little old-fashioned thing you are, to be sure. You'll have to get over talking about sin! There is no such thing nowadays, and people don't look at it that way. It is quite the fashion now to divorce and marry again, and nobody thinks anything of it. Perhaps half of the people you will meet will have been divorced once or twice. You mustn't think of it in the horrified way. The world is changing all the time, you know, and we are getting away from the antiquated ideas, and see that we have to do what fits the times. It certainly is better to be divorced if you are unhappy, and to marry someone you will be happy with. It makes the world a better place to live in for everybody to be happy, you know."

Fraley pondered this sophistry for a while and then she said with a troubled look:

"But God doesn't feel that way about it. The Bible says divorce is wrong. And besides, everybody wasn't meant to be happy. God said his children would have to bear hard things sometimes."

Violet smiled wisely.

"My dear, the world has progressed, and we must keep up with the times. You know the Bible is a very old-fashioned book. Come, let's forget it, and watch the sunset. I think it is going to be better than last night. Look at the lovely orchid next to the green."

Fraley turned her eyes toward the window, but there was a disturbed look in her face that her companion did not like. She must deal wisely with this prejudiced child if she wished to conquer in the end. It would not do to antagonize her. Therefore she put out her hand and patted the young hand that lay in the blue satin lap.

"You mustn't think that I object to your beloved Bible, little Fraley," she said. "It's all right, and it's very lovely for you to be so devoted to it, and all that. It really makes you quite unique and charming, only of course you have been shut in a good deal from the world, and you have got a narrow viewpoint. There's no harm in it, at all. It's really attractive for a young girl in this age of the world to believe in something uplifting like that. Only you have got some things a little out of proportion. But that will right itself. When you get to going to dances and house parties, and week ends, and theatre parties and the like, and when you have read some of the current literature, and gone to the movies a little you will find all this falling into line, and taking its place as it ought to do. But you must remember you don't know the world, and it is the world you live in, not heaven, now, and you've got to be like the world or you won't have a good time, and the world won't like you."

Fraley's face was still troubled, and she did not answer.

Violet saw that the girl was in no state of mind to accept her sophistries so she soothed her.

"I've been thinking," she said pleasantly, as if the other subject were finished, "that we ought to plan just what we will do when we get to New York. There are always so many things to think about just before one gets off a train. You said you wanted to send those two books before you do anything else. Suppose we attend to that the very first thing. You can have the addresses all written out for sending them, and it won't take much time to select what you want. We'll drive to the store straight from the station and get that off your mind. Then you can enjoy New York."

She had struck the right note at last. Fraley smiled and new light came into her eyes. She sat watching the changing colors of the sunset, and when the darkness came down, and the lights were turned on in the car her face was bright again.

15

THERE was one thing in which Violet Wentworth utterly failed to interest her new protégée. It was a matter that she had never found to fail before and she was utterly at a loss to understand. Fraley MacPherson had no interest at all in the subject that has been all-absorbing to the most of womankind since Eve wore her first fig leaf, the question of wherewithal shall we be clothed.

Pleased she was with her new garments, often touching the cloth of her little frock gently as if she admired it, careful lest the least dust should fall upon it, guarding her hat from crushing with an instinct of one who had always worn good garments; yet when she was asked what else she would like to have in her wardrobe she smiled dreamily and said:

"Why I think I have enough, now, thank you."

Violet Wentworth was nonplused.

"Wait till we get in the shops," she said easily, "you'll see. You'll be charmed with everything."

"But I wouldn't need anything else but this," said Fraley genuinely surprised. "I've been very careful with this. It won't be hurt a bit by the traveling. I can save it

186

for best and wear my other own old ones for work. This will do for dressing up."

"Well, that, little Fraley, is another thing you will have to wait till you get to New York to understand. Life is very different where I live. We don't go to bed at dark, and we have different clothes for all the places we go. Evening clothes, and sports clothes, and afternoon clothes, and street things, and party things. Oh, there is no end to the clothes one can use."

"Isn't it a lot of trouble?"

"Why, no. It's very interesting. Don't you like pretty things?"

"Oh, yes. I have always loved pretty things. The mountains in a mist, the sun rising across the valley, little green eggs in a robin's nest, the lichens on a great rock, an old tree against the sky when the sun has fallen the night before—and—my mother's face! My mother was lovely!"

"She must have been," said Violet Wentworth almost wistfully, watching the vivid little face before her.

The child was such a contrast to the feverish, artificial life she led, that it made her more than ever dissatisfied with everything; yet here was she at that very moment planning how she might force Fraley into the very same mould with all her little earth. Life was a strange contradiction, and a glimmer of the truth flashed at her now and then through the face and words of this unspoiled child.

The days on the train seemed like weeks to the girl. She began to grow weary of the confinement, but now they were coming to settlements, nearer and nearer together, and these were sources of great interest, seeing so many houses together, the paved streets, the many automobiles parked about the stations, the people coming and going in crowds, till it seemed to her that all the people of the earth must have congregated at one city.

Once there was a real procession passing the station just at the time the train stopped there, in fact they had come down with brass bands and all their nobility to see off some distinguished guest who was boarding the very train on which she was riding, and Fraley exclaimed at the throng.

"Oh, see, that must be something like the way the children of Israel looked when they started out of Egypt. There are women and children too, only of course there are no cattle nor sheep!"

The lady smiled indulgently, and Fraley quick to catch the lack of sympathy in her face, flushed softly and closed her lips. She was learning fast not to speak of her Book where it could not be appreciated. Would it always be like that in the new life to which she was going?

But each new town was a new pleasure. She longed to get out of the warm train and walk all over the streets till she knew the place as she would know a friend. What pleasure it would be to travel everywhere and get to know the world as she knew each individual mountain back where she had come from!

Chicago amazed her with its miles of buildings huddled close, and at her first sight of the lake she seemed almost frightened.

"Look!" she cried in an awestruck whisper. "Is that a—a—cloud—or—what?"

And when she learned it was called a lake, "But it is so big!" she said. "And it melts into the sky in such a strange way. I thought it must be an ocean."

The lady assured her that the ocean was much larger, and she sat with her face pressed against the window, watching till it was out of sight.

After they left Chicago the world was a continual

revelation to the girl from the mountains. So many, many houses, and people in them all. So many towns and cities, and always more on ahead! The wide stretching fields all plowed and harrowed and ready for the sowing, the miles of fences, the great barns and store houses. The groups of cattle and sheep grazing, the comfortable-looking homes, white with green blinds nestled among tall elms, or the great old stone farmhouses that had been there for years and looked to the young stranger as if carved out of her own mountain. She asked more questions than her benefactor could possibly answer, and the woman wondered that a girl could care so much for so many things that seemed to her utterly uninteresting. Why, some of those questions had never occurred to her, though she had traveled through this region all her life. She could not tell why certain types of fences seemed to be used to fence in cattle, and why some fields had only stone walls. She did not even know whether there was a reason or it was only a happening. She had never noticed that it was so. And it bored her to be asked.

But it continued to interest her to watch this girl, this new type of humanity, as she sat and planned how soon she could turn her into her own kind. Another pretty face on a useless creature of the world. That was what she wanted to make out of this lovely child of God.

And now, at last, New York!

Fraley was so excited she could hardly keep her seat. She wanted to stand up and press her face against the window, and watch each new station. She watched the porter curiously as he went from seat to seat brushing off the dust from passengers, polishing shoes and collecting baggage.

She almost protested when he came and took the handsome bag that now contained all the possessions she had brought from home.

"Perhaps I ought to take my Bible out," she whispered to the lady. "I mustn't lose that you know."

"He won't lose it," laughed the lady. "See, he has all my luggage, too. When we get out there we shall find our bags waiting for us. You will see."

She was much disappointed that they entered the station through an underground passage. She had thought New York would burst upon her like a vision of the heavenly city, shining and great in the noonday sun, and here they were rushed through darkness, with a ringing in her ears, and a strange bursting feeling in her head, and presently arrived in a great walled-in space lined with something that resembled stone, framed above with great stairs and galleries.

She stepped out carefully to the platform that was on a level close to the floor of the car, and stood looking up.

"Go on, Fraley, don't stop to look around now," whispered the lady. "You are holding up other people."

Fraley started with quick color in her cheeks and followed Mrs. Wentworth.

They got into a small cage a few steps from where they had stepped out, and the door shut and the whole little bunch of people with them began to rise into the air. It was a very terrible sensation not at all like being in the top of a tree, and Fraley's face expressed distress, but a glance at her companion showed that amused look that she had learned to dread, and she dropped her frightened gaze and tried to act as if she had been accustomed to ascend mountains in an elevator.

Violet Wentworth knew just what to do. They walked across a great open plain, with many people going in different directions, yet all having plenty of room. A great voice coming forth from above their heads somewhere announced a train to Washington, and another back to the Pacific Coast. She felt that she was standing in the center of the ways of the world. Here she was in New York! Yet she felt more of a pilgrim than ever. It was all so strange and cold and far away.

They walked across the wide space and through an archway and a great yellow chariot drew up before them as if by magic. It had no horse, and it looked magnificent to the unaccustomed eyes of the girl from the wilderness. The lady gave an order, and they both got inside. Then the red-capped man put some of their bags in with them and piled the rest in the front with the driver, and they rode away.

"Can this—be—a—a—taxi?" Fraley asked in awe. "It looks like—" But here she remembered and closed her lips.

"Yes, it's a taxi," said her mentor. "What do you think it looks like?"

"I was just thinking it looked something like what I thought a chariot might be."

"Oh!" said the lady, amused again. "I never saw one, but this is a mighty shabby old taxi. We'll have our own car by this evening, I hope. I telegraphed on to have it put in shape for immediate use, but as I wasn't sure then which train I would take I couldn't let them know when to meet me."

"Have you a family?" asked Fraley eagerly, half shrinking from the thought of sharing her new friend with others. "Have you any little children? Was that what made you so kind to me, because you are a mother yourself?"

"On, no," said the lady laughing. "Nothing like that, thank goodness. I've nobody to bother about but myself."

"But you have a husband?" said the girl fearfully. Men were such an uncertain quantity in this world.

"No!" said the lady quite crossly, "I haven't!"

"Oh, did he die?" she asked with sympathy in her voice. A dead man could do her no harm.

The lady was silent a moment staring out of the window, and then she answered sharply:

"No, he didn't! I might as well tell you for if I don't someone else will. I divorced him last fall. I've nobody but myself."

"Oh!" said Fraley in a little stricken voice and sat back silently thinking over the things she had said about people who were divorced; thinking of all the kind things the lady had done; of the pretty clothes she was wearing at her expense; trying to think of something that would be both suitable and true to say. But no words came to her lips. She could only sit back quietly and slide her small hand into the slim elegantly gloved one with a warm human pressure.

But the embarrassing silence was soon broken by their arrival at a book store, and Fraley's delight was great. Books! Books! Books! More than she had ever dreamed were in the world! Beautiful red and blue and gold and brown books. Books on shelves and on long tables that went down the room on either side.

Fraley's eyes sparkled with joy as she made her careful selections: a beautiful, expensive limp covered Scofield Bible with India paper and clear type for Seagrave, because the salesman recommended it as being most popular with ministers on account of its wonderful notes; and a large-print red-covered one with colored pictures for Jimmy.

They left careful directions for the mailing of the books, and Fraley proudly paid for them, and turned away with a shining in her eyes that was wholly unexplainable to the woman of the world.

"Now," said the lady, "are you ready to come home

with me, or do you think you've got to racket around first and locate your family?"

"Oh, no," said the girl seriously, "I'll look them up another time. I want to get started first and feel that I have a place to call home somewhere. I don't want to have them think they've got to do anything for me. They might not like it, you know."

"I see," said Violet Wentworth, with a shrewd look in her eyes and a satisfied set of her lips. Then there would not be any immediate interference of a family in her plans, until she had tried some things out and knew what she wanted to do. She got into the taxi and gave her order, feeling that everything was working out nicely.

Riverside Drive meant nothing at all to the little girl from the mountains, but when she saw the river, wide and shining in the afternoon sun, with the many strange boats plying back and forth upon its surface or clustered along its banks, she exclaimed with joy.

"Oh, this is going to be a wonderful place!" she said. "I'm going to love it. Now I can look off and see far away. It is almost as good as my mountains, this wonderful river. I felt so—shut in—before I saw this!"

She went up the steps of the Wentworth mansion with more wonder upon her, but turned before she entered the door and looked again upon the river, and at the palisades across.

"I shall come out here often and just enjoy this," she said as she turned to follow her friend into the house.

But inside the great hall she stopped and looked about her bewildered. The ceilings were so high, and the rooms so large, that she had a sense of desiring to reach out and hold on to something, lest she would fall.

There were thick rugs under her feet, and beautiful vistas opening out from wide doorways, with great mirrors in which she saw her small self reflected in several different views, and thought it someone else. There was one room in the distance where the walls were lined with books behind glass doors, and off in the other direction she could see a table set with dishes, and candles burning over a crystal bowl of flowers.

There were people there, also, a man who opened the door, and somehow reminded her of the porter on the Pullman. In the background was a woman, wearing a black dress and a white apron and cap or curious little white bonnet on her head; a young man, a boy almost, with brass buttons on his short jacket, lighting a fire in a room opposite the door. It was all bewildering.

She presently sensed without being told that these people were servants. She watched them and wondered how she should greet them, but found they did not expect anything but her shy smile.

The boy carried the bags up a beautiful staircase, and Fraley mounted it with interest. She had never seen a stair so high, and cushioned with velvet so that no sound came from a footfall.

There seemed to be unlimited rooms on the second floor, and Fraley was given one that opened across the hall from her hostess, a great beautiful room with windows looking out on the river, and a steamer hurrying down the river made a wondrous sight. She walked straight over to the window and watched it till it was out of sight before she even took off her hat.

"It is going to be wonderful here," she said turning as Violet Wentworth entered the door and stood watching her. "I am afraid I shall not do enough work with all this to look at."

"Well, forget it now," said the lady pleasantly. "I want to show you your room. I'm putting you here right across from me so that I can have you close at hand when I need you."

She did not explain that this room she was giving the girl was one which she had usually kept for honored guests, and that she was putting the child here because she wanted her near her, because she was growing fond of her, and because she longed to give her the best she had and see what reaction it would bring.

Fraley turned and looked at the beautiful room, stately in proportion, decorated and furnished by one of the greatest decorators in New York City, and at a fabulous sum. The effect was charming. To Fraley it seemed too spacious for her small self, too formal and beautiful for common use, too wonderful for the girl who had slept in a little seven by nine bedroom off the corner of the cabin on the mountain. But her heart swelled with appreciation of it all.

When the door to the white tiled bathroom was open, disclosing its shining spotlessness, with all its perfect appointments for comfort, she stopped and dared not enter. It was so white it dazzled her. White floor, white walls, silver-trimmed fixtures, and a lovely rose silk curtain to the bath!

"You do not mean that this is all for me, alone?" she said turning to the lady, and there were tears upon her lashes. "Oh, if my mother could know I have all this, she would be so glad. Oh, if she could only have had it I would be willing to go back to the cabin and stay alone. She had it so hard!"

"Well, she is probably glad you are here," said the lady, stirred almost to tears herself by the wistfulness of the young voice, "so just be as happy as you can. Now, will you unpack your own things, or do you want the maid to do it for you?"

"Oh, I will do it," said Fraley. "I want to do everything, myself."

"You can put your things in these drawers, and here

is one you can lock if you have any special treasures that you don't want the maid to touch when she comes in to wait on you."

"Oh, please, I don't want to be waited on," said the girl pleadingly, "I wouldn't know how to act."

"As you please. You'll get acquainted with all the ways pretty soon and then you won't feel so. Jeanne is very good, and knows how to put the last touches on a costume delightfully. She can teach you a great many things you ought to know. I shall tell her you have always lived your life quietly, and she will understand and not bother you. She is quick-witted. You will like her."

Fraley unpacked her shining bag, and took out the old gray woolen bag her mother had made for her. She locked her door and with the bag in her arms went and knelt by the smooth white bed and laid her face on the bag, beginning to cry.

"Oh, mother, mother, mother," she sobbed softly, "if only you were back again, I'd rather be on the mountain with you. Oh, I would!"

But presently she dried her tears and looked around trying to grow accustomed to her surroundings, and realize that this room was to be her home spot now, this beautiful room! If she could have seen a vision of this to which she was coming while she lay behind that riven rock, for instance, or while she was fleeing from the wild steers, or from the men who were her enemies, how astonished she would have been. So this was what God had been leading her to, all this time.

Slowly she unpacked the bag, taking out the old Bible, and looked around for a suitable place to put it, where she could easily use it every day.

Beside her bed was a little night table, with a silken-shaded lamp, a Dresden shepherdess under a pink umbrella. She laid the old Bible with its cotton covers down upon this table under the shade of the pink umbrella.

She put her mother's bag with the crude little cotton garments in the safe drawer and locked it. She realized by this time how odd they were beside the things that other people wore. She was not too proud to wear them still, but she knew that the lady would not like her to appear odd, and neither would her mother wish it; and moreover she did not want the critical eye of strangers on the precious garments that her dear mother had made with her last dying strength. So she locked them away tenderly.

Then she made herself sweet and neat and went softly out into the hall.

As the door across the hall was shut, and there were no sounds except far away downstairs, she went back to her room and sat down by the window to watch the river.

It was like having a new picture in place of her mountains, that great still river down there with the busy boats, so many of them, and off at the left, very far away in an evening mist of gold a place that looked like a very forest of boats, ships with tall masts.

She watched the pearly mists that began to rise as the evening came on, watched the sunset tints, and thought how even now they were out there in her western sky, back at the home mountain, and back at the ranch house where the missionary friend would be at this time of night perhaps.

She wondered if he had forgotten her by this time? It seemed a long, long two days since she bade him goodby. Was he sticking by his job?

Then suddenly she became aware of someone standing in the open door, and looking up there she saw the stiff young person in her black dress and white apron and bonnet.

"Dinner is served. Madam says will you come down to the dining room?"

Fraley arose, fear born of formality upon her and followed the maid.

16

IT was an awesome room to which she was led, with high paneled walls in cream color, and rich heavy draperies over the white curtains at the windows.

The dishes were fragile and glittering, some of them like frostwork. There was a great deal of silver, and rich damask napkins with great embroidered initials. It was not at all like the neighborly little tables in the dining car. Fraley suddenly felt very small and awkward. It seemed a long walk from the door over to the table where Mrs. Wentworth stood, like some stranger in a wonderful sleeveless low-cut gown of deep rich velvet in dark red tones. There were ropes of little pearls about her neck and hanging low on the front of her gown. Fraley felt as if she did not know her till she looked up and smiled, but even the smile was rather absent-minded.

She was reading a letter, and seemed annoyed at something.

The tall gentleman in strange black clothes was standing at the door, and the maid who had brought her word about dinner being ready was at the other end of the room.

"When did this come, Saxon?"

"This morning, ma'am," said the gentleman, bowing obsequiously.

"And did you tell them when I would arrive?"

"I told the messenger that you were expected to arrive this afternoon."

"And nothing has come since? No telephone message even?"

"Nothing ma'am, except a box of flowers. I had it put in the ice box, madam."

"Have them brought in," said the lady curtly, and swept to her seat at the head of the table. The man pulled her chair out for her, and pushed it in when she was seated and then came and did the same for Fraley. The girl wished he would not. It only made it harder, but she tried to do just what Mrs. Wentworth had done, and to act as though it were nothing new.

There was nothing to eat on the table but little long-stemmed glasses of delicious fruit, and the lady began to eat it at once, tasting daintily, not seeming to care much about it. But to the girl it tasted like a wonderful heavenly nectar.

The butler brought the flowers in, wonderful roses and strange weird fluted things that her hostess said were orchids, tinted a queer green with brown markings. The roses looked like a sunset. Fraley had never seen roses before, not roses like those. Her mother had cultivated a sickly little bush from a root she had got somewhere before Fraley was born, and it produced little tight, red, purply pink button roses without any fragrance. But these looked as if they must have fallen from heaven, and the fragrance was like all sweet winds and perfumes melted together and flung upon the air.

The lady called for a crystal bowl and directed the maid in arranging the flowers in water. She seemed far more interested in them than in the delicious soup that was presently put before them. Fraley wondered if the flowers came from the lady's husband, but she did not dare ask. Perhaps he was feeling bad about their divorce, and wanted to make it right again. She watched the lady's lovely head as it was bent over the flowers, her white fingers, flashing with precious stones, giving a touch to the flowers skillfully, making them lie in the water as if they grew there, and lift their lovely heads like little people. Fraley was very much in love with the lady. She hoped with all her heart that she would make it up with her husband. The lady seemed absorbed and was not talking, so Fraley kept still and watched her.

"Rather nice ones, aren't they? One of my admirers sent them," and she laughed.

Somehow Fraley felt disappointed, but she tried to answer with a shy smile.

"I'd—like to—send you—some as nice—some day!" she said wistfully.

"Well, you can," said the lady as the butler took her only half-finished soup. "But if I were you, I wouldn't bother. You'll have plenty of uses for your money, and I get a lot of flowers. Sometimes I'm perfectly fed up on them."

The girl had a feeling that she was only half thinking of her. Presently the telephone rang, and the butler brought a message. It meant nothing to the girl, something about someone coming to call at nine o'clock, but after that, the lady was more cheerful, and the dinner went briskly.

There was half a little bird for the next course, and the mountain girl, who had lived on corn bread and bacon nearly all her life, with eggs and milk when it could be spared, felt wicked and wasteful, with so much all for her own. There were delicious vegetables and queer little entrées and a salad even more unusual than the things she had on the train, and the meal finished off with a delicate frozen pudding.

Black coffee was served in tiny cups and when Fraley declined it, the lady said to the butler, "See that there is milk for Miss MacPherson in the morning. She prefers milk."

"Now," said the lady as they rose from the table, "I am expecting callers. I wonder what you would like to do? As soon as we do some shopping for you I shall want you to come in sometimes and meet my friends, but to-night you can amuse yourself as you like. There's the library. Perhaps you'll find some books you'll enjoy, unless you think it's wicked to read any book but the Bible. And there are folios of engravings, and some signed etchings, and water colors in the drawer of the big table. There's the radio, too, and the victrola. I'll show you how to turn them off and on, and you can do what you like. I suppose perhaps you're tired anyway, after the journey. I surely am, but I shall be busy this evening."

"Oh, I'm not tired," said Fraley happily. "I'll love just to look around. And of course I shall enjoy looking at the books. This is such a wonderful house! I should think you would be the happiest woman in the world. You have just everything you want, don't you? Everything there is."

A strange look passed over the woman's face.

"No, I'm afraid not, little girl," said the woman sadly; "there are several things I would have liked that never came my way."

"But you never were hungry, or cold—or afraid—!" mused the girl.

"Yes—I've often—been afraid!" said the woman more as if she were talking to herself than the girl.

"We don't need to be afraid," said Fraley softly, with

her eyes full of a far-off longing, as if she were reminding herself of deliverance in the past. "God will always take care of us—if we trust Him. He sent—you—to me!"

Violet Wentworth suddenly walked over to the girl, with a quite new and tender look in her face, and putting her arms about her, kissed her. Then she walked away quickly into the other room, as if to hide her emotion.

Fraley went into the library and browsed around among the books. They were all of course utterly unknown to her. She had not even heard their names. Things beyond what she had seen herself she knew of only through her mother's telling. A bit of newspaper wrapped around something from the distant store, once a year perhaps, had been as near to a newspaper as she had ever come; and that was only a scrap now and then, treasured and puzzled over, but seldom complete enough to demand any real interest. Save for the old Bible which her mother had probably carried away with her more as a matter of superstition and sentiment, than for any real love of it at the time, no other book had come her way.

That Bible had become a liberal education to the isolated child, for from its pages alone her mother had contrived to give the little Fraley a rare knowledge of English and composition, an intelligent if not extensive idea of mathematics, a curious fragment of oriental geography, a vague glimpse into geology, botany, zoölogy and astronomy to say nothing of a thorough knowledge of theology.

So Fraley stood before those walls of books delighted, reading their titles, and wondering over them. They were not all of them such as a mother of such a girl would have selected for her daughter's perusal, but Fraley did not know that, and went over their titles selecting such as invited her interest.

Violet Wentworth's taste in literature was extremely modern. All the lurid, liberal, daring novels of the day were set in flaring rows across her shelves without discretion. For convention's sake she had of course, other rows, on the higher shelves—all the classics—and it was to these, after a dip into about twenty titles on the lower shelves, that the girl found herself drawn.

"They are more like the Bible," she explained later to Violet when she pointed out that those books on the lower shelves were the newer ones and therefore more important for her to read, as everybody would be talking about them and she must be ready to take her part in the conversation.

"But I don't like the people in those books," objected Fraley. "Now this one," she went on, taking up a volume of George Eliot, "has real people in it. They are living in earnest. But those other books down on the lower shelves, why, the people in them *like* to be bad! They just seem to be trying to hunt out new ways to do wrong! They are like the people before the flood!"

"They are up-to-date," said Violet with a firm line to her lips, "and they are what you ought to read to be well informed on your times. They will do a lot for you. They will show you how to move in the circle of my acquaintances, and do your work right. I want you to read them."

Fraley looked appalled.

"I'll try," she said slowly, "but—it doesn't—seem quite—right. Some of them—just make me *sick!*"

Her mentor laughed.

"You'll get over that, my dear. It's the way of the world, and if you live in New York you've got to grow up. You can't be a wild bird all your life. It's a part of your education."

"Of course I'll try to do what you want me to do,"

said Fraley looking worried, "but it seems like being among a lot of wicked, dirty-minded people."

"Well, you've got to get used to the world, or how can you ever live in it?" asked the elder woman with a firm set to her lips.

Fraley was silent for a full minute with her eyes wide and serious, then she said slowly, almost as if she thought the other woman would not understand:

"The Bible says you must keep your garments unspotted from the world!"

Violet Wentworth went upstairs from that discussion feeling that she had just put over another slaughter of the innocents.

Fraley continued to browse among the books, delighting in the top shelves, and dutifully skimming a few of the books on the lower ones.

But on this first evening she did little more than browse.

A little later when she was on her way upstairs with several books she had selected to read, she caught a glimpse of the caller as he entered.

She did not like his face. For an instant she almost thought it was Pierce Boyden come for her, so like he seemed to the other. Even the swift, furtive glance he cast about seemed like the way Pierce had always entered the cabin. She shrank back into the shadows of the landing startled, and so became an unintentional witness to the intimate greeting he gave to Violet who came forward at once from the big room on the right of the hall without waiting for the butler to announce the visitor.

The sight was most disturbing, the girl could not quite tell why. It was none of her business of course what this lady of hers did, or what relation she bore to this unpleasant caller, but she did long to feel that she was beyond reproach in every way.

So she went up to her lovely room with an oppression upon her which she could not shake off.

The room was in a soft light from a rose-shaded lamp by the bedside, and the covers were turned back for her convenience. A rose-colored satin quilt lay like a bright cloud across the foot of the bed, and on a chair lay rosy garments for the night, and a delightful negligee of rose and white chiffon with frills and tiny rosebuds of ribbon. Think of having things like this to wear when she was all by herself in her room! Nobody else to share its beauty! A sense of reluctance was upon her that she should have luxury when her mother had gone without everything lovely most of her life, and was lying now in that hasty unmarked grave in the distant valley. If only her mother could have shared all this!

She turned her back on the beautiful room, and went to the window to gaze out on the dark river.

There were lights below on the drive, cars hurrying by, lights off to the left where she knew the crowded city lay, lights across in the little park between the drive and the river, lights everywhere along the shore, and out on the river, on the boats. There were even lights twinkling across on the opposite shore, and high above on the palisades, where dim outlines of tower and roof marked noble mansions among the trees.

And up in the wide sky there were lights, her dear stars, come to New York with her. She would not be able to locate them all perhaps, but she found the Little Dipper at once, and it made her feel at home. God's sky, how wide and dear it was!

She stood within the shadow of the draperies that shrouded the windows and tried to shake off the oppression that was upon her about her dear lady, and she found tears upon her cheeks. Oh, mother! If only you were here! Oh God, show me how to walk!

There was a slight stirring and she turned to see the white-capped maid standing in the doorway.

"I am Jeanne, madam's maid. Madam told me to ask if there was anything I could do for mademoiselle."

"Oh, no thank you, Jeanne," said Fraley turning and smiling at the maid. "I have put all my things away."

"I could draw your bath," said the woman, "any time when mademoiselle is ready, and perhaps mademoiselle would like me to brush her hair. Mademoiselle has pretty hair."

"You are very kind, Jeanne, but I've never been waited upon. I've always done everything for myself, and I wouldn't know how to be taken care of. Only my mother ever did anything for me."

"One's mother is always best," said the maid unbending from her formal tone. "Is mademoiselle's mother far away?"

"She is in heaven!"

"Oh, that's too bad, mademoiselle!" apologized the maid sympathetically. "I beg your pardon, mademoiselle, I didn't know. But you're going to stop here in this house, now, and there'll be plenty of gay times to help you to forget."

"Oh, I don't want to forget, Jeanne; I love to think about my dear mother, but sometimes I feel just as if I had to cry."

"You poor little dear!" said the maid, now thoroughly won over. "Now, you just get a nice book and sit here and read, or get into bed if you like. I'll fix the pillows for you. That's what madam generally does. She most generally reads herself to sleep."

"I shall not need to read myself to sleep to-night,"

laughed the girl. "I'm sleepy already. That bed looks wonderful!"

"Well, then, I'll just draw the water for your bath," said the maid. "I know madam would be better pleased if I helped you and I'll get you some of madam's nice bath salts. They have such a pleasant odor, mademoiselle will like it I know."

"Call me Fraley, won't you, please?" said the girl. "It sounds more friendly."

"Very well, Miss Fraley," said the maid in a pleased tone. "Now, you undress and I'll have the water ready for you at once," and the persistent maid marched into the bathroom and prepared the bath.

Jeanne put the lovely rosy folds of the kimono about her shoulders and then departed, but when Fraley came out from her bath she was there at the door again.

"I just thought I'd come back and fix your hair for the night," she said. "It'll be a pleasure for me to handle such hair as yours. I used to work in a beauty parlor before I took a place as lady's maid, and they gave me all the fine ladies to do their hair. But now since everybody's bobbed there is little of that to be done any more. I was always sorry madam bobbed her hair. Of course she looks more distinguished this way, but she had such lovely hair, Miss Fraley, it was such a pity to do away with it. And she's so chic herself she could have got away with hair on her very well. You never bobbed yours, did you, Miss Fraley?"

"Do you mean cut it? No, mother liked it to grow. And then, I was living out west on a mountain, where I never saw other girls. I had only mother to please. But I wouldn't like my hair cut. God gave it to me and I'd like to keep it."

"That's what I always say, Miss Fraley, I say keep as near to nature as you can. Of course a bit of paint and powder now and then for pale people, but you, now, you don't need any. Your skin is like a baby's. You've got an odd name, Miss Fraley, is it a family name?"

"Yes, my mother's name was Alison Fraley."

"Why, that's odd now. There's an Alison Fraley lives on the drive. Is she related to you?"

"Oh, no, I don't suppose so. Mrs. Wentworth spoke of her on the train, but I've never heard of her. It is odd, isn't it, my mother's name?"

"She might be some kin, you can't tell. You'll have to ask her when you get to know her. She comes here a lot. Her mother is one of Mrs. Wentworth's crowd, and they entertain a great deal. You'll probably see a good deal of her. But she's not like you, one could see that at a glance. Of course she's handsome in her way, and very stylish, goes to all the extremes, and like that. But she hasn't got a good skin like yours, and her ways are very proud like. She'd not be conversing with a maid, kind like you are, Miss Fraley. She thinks she's above everybody. She'd be more like to throw her shoe at me if I spoke of anything but my work."

"Oh!" said Fraley distressed, "I am afraid I shan't like her."

"Oh, she'll not be like that to you, not if you are Mrs. Wentworth's friend. She dotes on Mrs. Wentworth. She went to Europe with her three months last summer. She's tall and dark, and a bit too bold looking to my thinking, but she's very popular. I can see you're going to be quite popular, too, Miss Fraley. You've got a way with you that makes people like you. Now Miss Alison, she is popular more because people are afraid she'll turn them down than because they like her."

"I'm sorry she's that way," said Fraley looking troubled. "I don't like to think anybody that has my mother's name is disagreeable. My mother was so dear!"

"I'll bet she was, Miss Fraley, or you wouldn't be what you are. I'll tell you frankly, there's not many girls to-day is as unspoiled and friendly as you are and that's a fact. Now, Miss Fraley, if you'll just step into bed I'll fix the pillows for you, and the light, and then you can read as long as you like. Can I get your book for you?"

"Oh, this is my book," said Fraley gathering the old cotton-covered Bible from the little bedside stand. "It was my mother's and I love it."

"It's not many young ladies nowadays reads the Bible," commented the maid, hovering about and patting the pillows, "I've never read it myself, but I've heard it has some very good things in it."

"Oh, it has, Jeanne! Sit down and let me read to you."

Fraley turned the pages and began to recite one of her favorite chapters.

The maid stood at the foot of the bed and listened curiously.

"That's beautiful, Miss Fraley," she said enthusiastically when the chapter was finished, "I never knew it was like that. If I had an education I might read it too, but somehow, when you read it, it sounds nice. I'd like to hear it again sometime, Miss Fraley, if you ever have time."

"Oh, I'll read to you every night, Jeanne, if you can come up here!" said Fraley eagerly. "I'd love to."

"I certainly appreciate that, Miss Fraley. I'll never forget your offer, but I know the madam when she gets herself going, will have your evenings all full. You'll be going out with her a lot."

"Oh, I don't think so, not much," said the girl, lying back on her pillow. "You know I'm here to work for her, don't you? I'm not here just visiting."

"I know she's taken you up, Miss Fraley, and that means you're just like a guest in the house, or a member of the family, and I've seen enough of this house to know she'll keep you going. But I'll be glad to hear you read, Miss Fraley, whenever you have the time. And now, would you like a glass of milk or something before you sleep?"

"No indeed," laughed Fraley, "I've already had more to eat to-day than I needed. Good-night, Jeanne, and don't forget to come to-morrow night."

"Thank you, Miss Fraley, for being so good to me. It's been a long time since I've seen a young lady I've been so drawn to as you, and I'll do anything I can for you, bless your little heart."

The maid withdrew and closed the door, and Fraley lay back on her pillows and watched the lights across from her windows and soon fell asleep.

17

THE maid brought a tray to Fraley's room next morning, and found her fully dressed sitting by the window absorbed in watching the boats on the river and the automobiles in the street.

"Here's your breakfast, Miss Fraley," explained Jeanne setting down a dainty tray on the little stand, and drawing up a chair. "You could have had it earlier if I had known you were up, but I was afraid to disturb you."

"Oh, you don't need to bring me anything, Jeanne. Couldn't I go down? I've been waiting for Mrs. Wentworth to open her door. I did go downstairs once, but there was nobody about and I concluded she had sat up late and had overslept."

"She always sits up late in New York, Miss Fraley, but she never rises before ten anyway. She takes her breakfast in bed, and she doesn't have it till she rings for it. I haven't heard a sound from her yet this morning, but I thought I'd venture to see if you were awake, as you went to bed pretty early last night."

"Oh," said Fraley, somewhat dismayed at a state of things like this. On the mountain she had usually arisen at dawn or a little after, and gone to bed with the birds. "Well, then after this I'll come down and get my breakfast. That'll be less trouble for you, won't it? And I don't need a thing but a glass of milk and a little bread or something. Don't let anybody bother getting a breakfast for me."

"It's no bother, Miss Fraley. The breakfast is always cooked anyway, for the servants, and it's less trouble for me to bring a tray up than for you to have the table set in the dining room just for you."

So Fraley ate her delicious breakfast hungrily, and presently Jeanne returned with a message.

"Madam says you're to go shopping with her this morning and she'll be ready in half an hour."

Fraley had put on the little cotton frock of her mother's make when she first got up, but when she stood before the pier glass and surveyed herself, she realized that it looked queer, here in this grand new home. She did not understand it because it had always seemed nice and appropriate enough, a whole, clean frock without any ugly patches; but now, since she had travelled in a Pullman, and watched the people in the diner, and more than all since she had been with this lovely lady, she did not like her own looks in this mountainmade frock of faded cotton. So she had changed into the borrowed one again. Now she was glad she had done so for her dear Violet would not have liked her to go shopping in her old dress, of course.

So she put on hat and coat and gloves and sat down by the window to count her money. How much did dresses cost? She seemed to have a lot of money left from those Bibles, but one could never tell in this new world to which she had come. There might be only enough for a pair of shoes. The dear lady had said she must have shoes.

But before her problem was solved there came the summons to start, and Fraley went down to find her lady arrayed in a smart street suit, with her face so startlingly fresh and lovely that she almost exclaimed over it.

But she seemed a distant lady, this variable new friend this morning. She was all business-like, giving orders for the day before she left, and somehow the girl did not like to speak intimately.

The car was at the door, a wonderful shining limousine, glittering and luxurious, with deep soft upholstery.

"Isn't this wonderful!" she said before she could stop herself as she sat down on the deep cushions and looked out of the clear glass at her side. "Why, it's like a little house!" The lady smiled:

"Do you like the car? It's a new one. It seems comfortable, doesn't it? Now, let's begin to talk about what you need. We want to get your wardrobe all in order before people find out that I'm home and begin to come, and I have so many engagements that I can't attend to anything else."

"I was thinking about it this morning," said Fraley, "I put on one of my old dresses and it looked kind of queer after I'd worn yours, so I guess perhaps I'd better buy a new dress to save this one if you think I've got money enough. The Bibles didn't cost as much as I expected, and I haven't spent any of the money my mother gave me, except for crackers and prunes and apples and cheese. How much do everyday dresses cost?"

"Oh, you needn't bother about that, child, I'll attend to all that. You'll need a lot of things besides an everyday dress if you're going to stay with me, and I'll just have them charged and then we'll take it out of your first month's salary. How is that?"

"Why, that is very kind—but—suppose something

happened to me and I couldn't do the work right, or I got sick and died. Then I wouldn't have paid for them."

"Well, I'd still have the dresses and things, wouldn't I?" smiled the lady. "And anyhow that's my affair. I say you've got to have the things if you stay with me, so I'll take the chance of your doing what I want you to do in payment."

"All right," said Fraley with a pleased sigh, "only I want to be honest. You see I don't know anything about what clothes cost, so I can't judge, but it seems to me my work won't be worth very much at first, anyway, though I mean to try very hard."

"You don't know how much of an asset you are, little Fraley," smiled Violet Wentworth, looking into the clear eyes, and noticing the sweet sincerity and purity that was an open vision to all who looked that way.

Fraley wondered what an asset was but she did not ask. She kept her eyes busy out of the window, for now they had come to the shopping district and the traffic was jammed.

"Why, it's just the way God takes us through hard things, isn't it?" she exclaimed suddenly, and then caught herself and flushed. She had not meant to think out loud that way any more, since she knew the lady was amused by it.

"I mean," she explained when she saw the look of question in her companion's eyes, "I mean the car, and the man who drives it. We don't have to worry about getting across that street, or be afraid we'll be run over, because the car carries us straight through, and the man who drives it is doing all the worrying."

"You certainly ought to have been a theologian," said the lady crossly. "Your mind is always running on things like that. But you mustn't call Burton 'the man who drives,' you must say, 'Chauffeur.' You'll have to remember that because it will mark you as utterly green if you don't. Burton! Stop here! Yes, the shoes! There's a place where you can park around on the side street. It's too crowded here for you to wait. We'll come around to the usual place."

The quiet elegance of the shoe shop overawed the child of the wilderness. She followed where she was led, and sat down as she was bidden. Violet Wentworth did all the rest.

"Shoes!" she ordered curtly, "for this young lady! She's not been used to high heels. Yes, sports shoes and street shoes, and don't make the heels too high even on the evening slippers! Make it an easy grade from the low flat school-shoe type, you know. Her foot has never been cramped."

Fraley sat and wondered and said very little.

Shoes and shoes they tried on her, now and again asking her if they were comfortable.

Bewildered, the girl had no idea how many or if any shoes had been bought until Mrs. Wentworth said:

"I think she had better wear this pair and send the old ones home with the order. You would like to wear the dark blue ones, wouldn't you, Fraley? They go so well with your dress. They are perfectly comfortable, aren't they? Yes, you may send the rest up, Mr. Kennard. We are going to a fitting and these are a nice height of heel for that, don't you think?"

Fraley did not even have to assent, for they hadn't noticed her at all, and so she found herself standing in new dark blue kid pumps, and wondering if those were really her feet, so trim and pretty and like other people's feet.

The next store they entered was a lingerie shop, and for half an hour Violet tossed over piles of silk trifles that passed for underwear, little French importations, with exquisite hand work expended upon them. Now and then she appealed to Fraley to know which one she liked best of two, and the girl supposed she was purchasing all these things for herself. It was not until they reached home that she discovered there were dozens of things being bought for her, but by that time she was a day wiser.

They next drove to an exclusive shop and the chauffeur was told to return in an hour and a half.

The place was quiet and elegant, and Fraley who was already worn with the noise and confusion of the city sank into a chair gladly to wait. She was thinking how nice it would be to get back to the house and read some of those beautiful books, curled up in a big chair with the river outside of her window and the stillness of the house surrounding her. The shop did not look very interesting.

Violet introduced her to a large imposing woman called Madam who gave her a chair and called her "my dear," and then stood off, studying her. The shop seemed a stupid place and Fraley was not deeply interested in it. She wondered why they were there till Violet said in a low tone:

"This is the gown shop. We are going to see some models." Madam went away back across the gray-velveted aisle with mirrors on each side, and presently she returned and talked with her customer about the weather and where she had been during the winter.

Then there was a little stir down the gray-velvet aisle and a girl no larger than Fraley, with a startlingly red mouth and hard black eyes, came sauntering toward them in a daring red and black outfit.

The mountain girl watched her come, and turned away. She did not like the bold black eyes and the red mouth.

"It's hardly her type," said Violet scanning the model carefully. "Very clever cut, of course, but I scarcely think I'd care for it."

"Well, perhaps," said Madam, "but it's a useful little frock for in between you know."

Another young thing had entered the gray aisle and was lingering for a signal to come on. Madam gave it, and there arrived a girl in green. She had deep red hair and brown eyes, and Fraley liked her better, but she too had that terrible red mouth that looked like a wound.

"That's not bad," said Violet. "I'm not sure but it would do. Of course she's a different coloring, but green and gold are lovely. You might have that laid aside and we'll let her try it on."

The procession seemed endless and amounted to little or nothing so far as a fashion show was concerned, to the girl from the mountain. She continued to look at the faces of the models, and to regret their red, red mouths. How did all these girls of New York get such red lips? She had noticed it just the least bit in her beloved Violet's lips, too, this morning. It must be something in the climate or the water. Perhaps her own would grow that way after a time, but she did not like it.

When a number of street dresses had been selected for further consideration, and several afternoon costumes added to their number, the various models returned, garbed now in evening wear, the first in an evening cloak of gold cloth trimmed with ermine, which when removed revealed an elaborate affair of turquoise malines cut in myriads of points, and standing out like blue spray about the frail ankles of the slim thing that wore it, but scarcely draping the upper part of her anatomy at all. It was held in place by a garland of silver roses over one shoulder.

"That! Now, that would go with her eyes," said Violet, interested. "Don't you like that, Fraley dear?"

Fraley responded instantly to the "dear," and turned her smile toward the matter in hand.

"It's a pretty color," she said, "but there isn't any top to it. It looks as if those roses were going to break and let it all down."

The models looked at one another and grinned contemptuously. The Madam said: "Oh, my dear!" and laughed affectedly, then turning to Violet Wentworth she said, "She's witty, isn't she? A clever remark!"

Fraley could see that her Violet was vexed with her, and she felt mortified, though she did not know exactly what she had done.

"Do you wear a coat over it?" she asked in a low voice, but Violet did not answer.

"I think," she said crossly, "that it's getting late and we will not bother with evening dresses this morning. We'll just let her try on the green frock, and possibly that little brown model."

Then Madam rose suavely to the occasion. A customer like this was not to be lost if anything could keep her.

"I think," said she, "if you will just have patience for one more, I would like to try something. There is a little model,—it has just occurred to me, and pardon me, but perhaps the young lady is right. The ingénue. That is the type. I have a lovely thing here in white velvet I would just like you to see—!"

There was not a model in that establishment that had the make up for wearing that white velvet, but Madame chose her most demure maiden, and bade her wash off the rouge, and hurry. By all means hurry.

In the end Violet bought the white velvet, of course.

Fraley, robed in it, looked like a saint from some old

castle retreat. Its draperies fell from the shoulders and came around to tie in front in long sash-like ends, clasped with a knot of yellow gold.

"There is jewelry to go with this," and Madam slung a rope of gold about the girl's neck, clasped bracelets on her arms, and brought forth earrings.

Fraley shrank back when she saw what Madam was intending to do to her, and put her hands to her ears.

"Please no," she said, and looked pleadingly toward her lady.

"She is right," said Violet, "they do not belong to the type. A saint wouldn't wear long dangling things in her ears. And you may keep the chain and armlets too. I think pearls would be better. These are too noisy. She needs something quieter. The clasp is good perhaps. I'll take the dress."

Fraley looked at herself in the mirrors dubiously. She was not sure of herself. But it was better than some. The draperies covered her arms partially at least, and the neck was modest in its cut, so she said nothing.

A blue taffeta was next forthcoming, with tiny sweetheart rosebuds on long wisps of silver cord hanging from a rosette of rosebuds at the little round waist, a full long skirt of bound scallops drawn into the round waist gave it a childish charm. Fraley could see that her lady liked it, so when asked if she liked it she said:

"All but the arms. I'd like some sleeves!"

The Madam laughed.

"It's an evening dress you know, Fraley," said Violet, "everybody wears them that way. You mustn't be a silly!"

"Wait!" said Madam seeing another sale in the offing. "I've an idea. Clotilde, go bring that lace bertha, the very thing. It's on that new model that just came in."

Clotilde brought the lace, fine as a cobweb, and the Madam flung it over Fraley's head, and adjusted it.

"The very thing!" she cried. "She's a clever girl. She knows what she needs to bring out her best style."

The lace hung in soft cobwebby folds from the round neck, deep as the waist line in the back, a little shorter in front, but covering the sweet round arms to the elbow. Violet was vexed with her charge but she could not but admit that the little mountain girl dressed thus looked very sweet and modest, and that the lace brought out the charm by which she had been attracted at the first.

So they bought the blue taffeta.

"But I can't work in any of those," said Fraley when at last they left the place.

"No, of course not, you silly! Did you think we were buying working clothes? We'll get some plain tailored things, and some sports clothes for that. We're going to lunch now, but after lunch we'll go to some of the big department stores and look around. There are several more of these little exclusive shops, too, where you can pick up really original clothes quite reasonably if you know how to look for them. I want to look around and send some more things home for you to try on. There's nothing like trying a garment in the environment in which it is to be worn to find out its defects and its good points. Of course if I find something better than these I can return them. But I'm sure the white velvet is good, and the blue taffeta is darling! We must keep that in any event."

Fraley got back into the car feeling far more worn than from a day of her pilgrimage. Such a lot of work just to get something to put on! There seemed to be a great many pretty things in the shop windows they passed. Why wouldn't any of them do? But she said nothing more. She saw that Violet was happy in this thing that she was doing.

After a frugal but costly lunch of salads and ices they went on their way again hunting more clothes.

"I don't see when I can possibly use all these," said Fraley wearily when at last they were in the car on their way back home, "I can't ever wear out so many."

"You don't wear them out, child," said Violet complacently, "you give them away when you are tired of them—or sell them. Many people sell them, but it's a lot of bother, and you have to give a maid things anyway or she gets dissatisfied."

Safe in her quiet room that night, with Violet entertaining callers downstairs, Fraley pondered on the strange ways of this new world into which she had come.

## 18

THE days that followed were full of shopping, and while she gradually grew more intelligent in the matter of choosing garments suitable for the occasions in which she was supposed to wear them, and acquired a certain simplicity in taste that was surprising, considering the contrast in her present circumstances from those that had surrounded her in her childhood, still Fraley was more or less bored with it all. She wanted to be doing so many other things in this wonderful city.

There was the river with its endless procession of boats going back and forth. She wanted to ride on all those boats. She wanted to climb the palisades and find out how far she could see from the top. She wanted to tramp the length of the river and then cross over and tramp back. Sometimes she wanted to get out and away from all the strange, cramping, hindering clutter of sights and sounds into her own native wilderness and beauty.

Then there were the great buildings that she gradually learned were of historic interest. She knew very little of world history or even of the history of her own country, and when she once discovered books of history she read

with eager appetite. The local landmarks and great buildings that commemorated some discovery or victory or
happening took on new interest, and seemed to stand out
from their neighbors on the street almost as if they had
been painted a different noble color.

But gradually the two great closets connected with
her lovely room began to be filled with charming
clothes, for morning and afternoon and evening, for hot,
for cold, and for medium weather, and she began to hope
that the days of toil in the shops were almost over.

To say she had not enjoyed it would be wrong, because
she loved beauty, but to get it entirely out of its relation
to other things in life wearied her. After the first few days,
when she entered a shop, her quick eyes would rove
about and search out one or two distinguished garments
or articles from all the other commonplace ones, and
Violet soon learned that she could trust her selection
almost every time. Simplicity of line and color were her
keynote, and she went unerringly to the few things in
each shop that bore those distinctions.

So the first month passed, the month of April, and
Fraley felt that she had worked hard for her first month's
salary, even though she had done little else for her lady
but select the clothes she felt were so necessary for the
job. Not until she was earning some real money did she
intend to write the letter she had promised to her
friend—the raven of the wilderness as he had called
himself. She wanted to have something real to tell him
about how she was getting on. So far she had done
nothing but get ready to live. As soon as the shopping
tours were over she meant to begin to look around and
get acquainted with New York.

But lo! when the shopping was completed, Violet
began to talk of going away for the summer. Mountains,

or seashore, or a water trip. She couldn't decide which to take.

"Why, you have just got home," said Fraley in dismay. "It is so lovely here. We can take our books and go out there in the park and sit on a bench and read when the hot weather comes."

Violet smiled at her simplicity.

"Nobody stays in the city in the summer, unless they are absolutely tied," she told her.

"But why?"

"It is very hot here! All the best houses are closed, and people go away to get rested from the winter and enjoy themselves."

It was of no use to talk. Going was the order of the day, so Fraley submitted, marveling over the change in her circumstances since she had started from the old cabin through her bedroom window, with only her father's coat and neckerchief for outfit, and the old gray bag containing the Bible for baggage.

Bags and suitcases and hatboxes! There seemed no end to the number that had to be packed. All those pretty dresses shut away in wardrobe trunks! She had no faith that she would ever have use for more than one or two.

And so began a round of gaiety in strange hotels, utterly foreign to the child whose life had hitherto been so quiet and isolated.

There were many people whom Violet Wentworth knew at these hotels where they stopped for a week, sometimes two or three weeks, before moving on elsewhere. The days passed in a round of sea bathing, automobile riding, teas, bazaars, and the like. Fraley learned to play tennis and golf, and, being the free little athlete that she was, it did not take her long to become fairly proficient in both. Her arms were strong and sinewy, her eye was true, her brain was keen, and she was as lithe as a young sapling. Presently she began to be in demand to play these games because she could play well and she really enjoyed it hugely.

Violet insisted on teaching her to dance, but she balked at the first dance she attended.

"It would be lovely if I could do it alone," she said, "but I don't like strange men, or any men, getting so familiar. My mother taught me—"

"There!" said Violet, "it's time you learned that your mother was so far out of the world for so long that she was no guide for what you should do now. You have a right to choose your own life."

Fraley was silent a moment, then she said:

"Then I do choose. And I choose not to dance. I do not want any man to put his arm around me the way they do. I watched you dancing last night and I didn't like the way your partner touched you and looked at you. You are too dear and lovely. You—! He—! He reminded me of a bad man I knew out on the mountains!"

"Stop!" said Violet flushing angrily. "You are getting impudent. You should dance of course. But I don't want to hurry you into things you don't understand. You must get over labeling everything either good or bad. That's ridiculous! You just watch, this summer, and by fall you'll feel differently about it. Come, let's go and dress for dinner."

So the days went by, and the evenings. Fraley in blue taffeta with sweetheart roses, or in white velvet with gold clasps and pearls, or in some other richly simple costume would hover on the outer edge of the things her patroness enjoyed and watch sorrowfully. But sometimes she would wander off by herself for a while and watch the sea in the darkness.

The work she was supposed to be doing for Mrs.

Wentworth seemed so indefinite and desultory that it often troubled her. It seemed to her that she was not giving enough service for all she was receiving. Of course there were always a few letters to be answered every day, and she had learned to answer them in a manner apparently quite satisfactory to her employer; at least she never found fault with her, beyond correcting a few trifling mistakes. She seemed entirely content with this slight service, and a few small errands occasionally. Her main desire seemed to be to have Fraley on call at any hour of the day or night. A less humble girl would have found out before many weeks had passed that Violet Wentworth wanted her to show her off, that she looked upon her as a sort of possession wherewith to wield her social scepter. But Fraley was never thinking of herself. It never entered her head that she was wanted for anything except the work that she could do, and she was most grateful always.

But one night she decided the time had come to write to her friend of the desert, the "Raven," as she still called him.

In her rosy tulle she sat down to the pleasant task, and she made a lovely picture indeed, with a smile on her lips and her eyes starry with memory.

It was a charming letter she wrote, frank and true, opening her heart concerning her many perplexities in the new life which she could not tell to anyone else. The writing of it gave her great content. But, she forgot to put in her New York address and they were leaving for the mountains the next day. She had not even thought to write on hotel paper to give a clue to her whereabouts. This letter did not seem to her like other letters. It was almost like sending out a little prayer. She scarcely ex-pected an answer.

The fall was coming on and the mountains were

touched with crimson and gold, the woodbine on the rocks like flaming embroidery.

The hotel was swarming with people. Many of Mrs. Wentworth's friends were there.

There was one tall gentleman at the next table in the dining room who troubled her greatly because he was constantly reminding her of someone, yet she could not think who it was. He had a great head of wavy white hair, and keen, blue, rather unhappy eyes. His mouth was drawn down at the corners as if he wanted everybody to get out of his way and Fraley always got out of it if she possibly could.

He had a wife who never came down to breakfast, but neither did a lot of the other women there. This woman was wrinkled and painted and wore her hair marcelled so smoothly that it looked as if the waves were painted on a piece of white satin and fitted smoothly over her head. They had a grandson about fourteen who was always at odds with his grandfather and grandmother, particularly his grandfather.

One day Fraley found this boy out at the golf links, with no one to play with and she scraped an acquaintance with him and played nine holes. They got along very well together, and walked back to the hotel quite chummily. Just as they reached the steps the boy told her his name was James MacPherson, and he was being sent off to school the next day, and he didn't want to go.

"Why, isn't that funny!" said Fraley, "So is my name MacPherson. Perhaps we are distant relatives somewhere back, who knows?"

"No such luck," said the boy, "Gee, I wish I had a relative like you. You're all right!"

She played tennis with him that afternoon, and they went down to the game room in the evening and played pingpong in the hotel in the evening. He was a nice boy.

She felt sorry for him. He said his father and mother were in Europe for a year, and his sister was in California, and he hated boarding school. He said he'd like to stay at home, but "Gramp had a grouch on and couldn't see it." Fraley got up the next morning early and played nine more holes of golf with him before he had to go, and then felt forlorn and lonely as she saw him grinning good-by to her as he drove off in the hotel bus down the mountain to the station.

After that she used to watch the grandfather and grandmother every day just because they belonged to the boy. She was sorry for them, they looked so discontented.

Looking at them and knowing they bore the same name, made her think of her own father's father, and wonder if he was living.

She resolved to hunt him up as soon as she got back to New York, and not delay any longer. No matter who he was or in what circumstances, she ought to look him up. Whether she revealed her identity or not would depend on conditions, but she must find him and know what sort of person he was. Her mother evidently had wished that.

That very evening when they both came up to go to bed Violet called her into her room and talked with her awhile. She asked her more about her own home, and who her father and mother had been, and Fraley, naturally reticent, and anxious to keep the secrets of her family, told very little. Her mother and father had married against the wishes of their parents and gone west and lost sight of their respective families. That was all. She acknowledged that she knew nothing of her relatives' financial standing, though she supposed they would be comfortably off. Her mother had always spoken of having a good home, and she had spoken as if the

MacPhersons were rather proud people. That was all she knew.

Violet Wentworth narrowed her eyes as she watched Fraley under their lashes.

"Fraley," she said, "if you should find out that any of these relatives are well off and want you, would you wish to leave me and go to them?"

"I would not want to leave you," said Fraley with a wistful look, "but I could not tell what I ought to do until I knew all about it. Their being well off would not make any difference. I would go to them sooner if they were poor for they might need me to help them some way."

"You're a dear child," said Violet Wentworth with a sudden unusual gust of emotion, and kissed her for the second time.

"Now, run off to bed, or you'll lose your complexion and be just as bad as I am."

It was a great day for Fraley when they got back to New York. She settled all her beautiful fineries in the two great closets, fineries that she had grown accustomed to, now, and took for granted as she did her golden hair, and the slimness of her ankles. That slimness was the envy of all the women in the hotel, though Fraley didn't even know it.

Two days after they got home, she happened to over-hear Violet answering a call on the telephone.

"Oh, is that you, Alison? I thought you weren't coming back till next week. I'm so glad you are here. Listen, Alison, I've got a young girl staying with me this winter—brought her back from my western trip. She's a girl I'm very fond of indeed and I want to show her a good time. I'm depending on you to take her to the country club and introduce her to all our young friends, and I wish you'd run over and take tea with us this afternoon informally. I want you two to know each other at once. She's charming. I'm sure you will like her."

Fraley stood still by the window in her own room and heard the receiver click as it was hung up. So, that was the way that Violet was introducing her. A friend from the west who was staying there! Not a social secretary at all! There was something disturbing in the knowledge, though Fraley could not just tell why. It did not seem wholly honest to her truth-loving soul.

And so Alison Fraley was coming to see her!

She shrank from meeting this other girl who bore her mother's dear name. Perhaps it was what Jeanne had said that had prejudiced her, and that was not right of course. So she tried to put such thoughts out of her mind, and sitting down she wrote to Seagrave the letter she had promised to write as soon as she was back in New York.

It was only a few sentences, but even that contact of the mind with the fine, true spirit who had been so wonderful to her on her journey, seemed to give her new courage. She wrote:

> *Dear Raven:*
>
> *We are at home at last and I am glad. I am sending you the address as I promised. I hope you will write me about the services in the log schoolhouse. I have never forgotten about that meeting.*
>
> *Your friend,*
>
> *Fraley MacPherson.*

With the letter in her hand she was starting out to mail it as Violet came out of her room.

"Where are you going, child? Not away I hope. I have a friend coming in to have tea with us in a few minutes, and I want you to meet her. She's the natural friend for you at this stage of the game and will do you a lot of good. Is that one of my letters?" and Violet took the letter out of Fraley's unresisting hand.

There it was, George Rivington Seagrave! There simply couldn't be two of that name, not with Rivington in it!

"What are you doing writing to Rivie Seagrave?" Violet asked in wide astonishment, searching Fraley's face suspiciously. "Wherever in the world did you meet him?"

"Out on the prairie somewhere, under a tree. I told you about it on the train. He's the man I sent the Bible to."

"Yes, you said his name was Seagrave, I remember, but you didn't say it was Rivington. How could that possibly be? I couldn't think of any man less likely to want a Bible than Rivington Seagrave, yet you said, didn't you, that he was preaching or something like that. It certainly must have been a practical joke of some kind. Of course, it can't be Riv. He would no more know how to preach than I would."

"He said he didn't know how," said Fraley gravely. "He was doing it for some poor fellow that was taken to the hospital just before train time. The other man was afraid he would lose his job if somebody didn't hold it down for him."

"Well, that sounds more like him. He's always been kind hearted, but dear me! Riv Seagrave. That's rich!"

Something in Fraley's heart rose in defense.

"He had a wonderful meeting," she said, "I went to it. He read the Bible, and he sang like the heavenly choirs."

"Yes, I'll admit he can sing like an angel, but Riv Seagrave reading the Bible! That's too good a joke!"

Fraley froze.

"He did not make a joke out of it," she said quietly, and in her voice was a gentle rebuke.

"Well, that may be so," said Violet, "but he certainly must have met with a change of heart, then."

"I think he has," Fraley said quietly.

"Well, I advise you to lay off that young man, Fraley," said Violet good naturedly as she handed back the letter. "You see he's almost as good as engaged to Alison Fraley, and I want you two to be friends. I wouldn't mention him to her if I were you."

Fraley went quietly on down the stairs, out the door and down to the corner where she mailed her letter, but she no longer smiled.

She dropped her letter in the post office box at the corner and turned to go back to the house, when suddenly it came to her that she ought not to have mailed that letter. Her raven was engaged to another girl, and she had no right to be writing him letters, even such simple friendly letters as this. There was no longer need for her to write him, because he had a Bible and that would give him all the light he needed for his work. She had been crazy to think she needed to write him any more. He had probably forgotten all about her anyway by this time.

Of course, she had promised to let him know where she was, but—well the letter was gone now, unless she stayed out there and asked the postman to give it back to her, which he wouldn't likely do.

Well, never mind, it could do no harm, and if he ever came back to New York or if he wrote her a nice little note thanking her for anything, she would let him understand that she knew it was all in friendliness. She would simply drop the thought of him out of her heart. But oh, how was she going to do it? Her one friend! And that kiss! What was she going to do with the memory of that kiss? She could not bury it as if it were dead. She could not extract it as if it were a thorn. It was there on her brow forever, and it was hers, rightfully or no, it was hers and did not belong to another.

Then she remembered that he had called her an angel. That was it! That made it all right on his part to have kissed her. He had not looked upon her as a young girl, not as he would have thought of the girl to whom he was engaged, but as a dear little girl, a sort of angel. Angels were holy beings and he had simply given her a high tribute with that kiss as if she were someone set above himself. He was a raven and she was an angel, and there was nothing meant by that kiss but a kind of homage.

So she reasoned it over and over, trying to make the situation assume a different aspect in her mind.

She walked up and down the block several times trying to get adjusted so that that kiss would not be a thorn in her heart. Trying to tell herself that she had never taken it to have any special meaning other than tenderness for a lost child.

When she went back to the house there was a sad little smile on her face, and she held her head up proudly.

Back in her room she tried to face the immediate present.

"She is coming!" she told herself, "the girl he loves! I must go down and meet her pretty soon. I must not think of that kiss as anything that ever belonged to me."

Then Jeanne tapped at the door.

"Miss Fraley, Madam would like you to come down. Tea is served in the library and Miss Alison Fraley is there."

Fraley smoothed her hair, dashed cold water in her face, dabbed it with a soft towel, and went downstairs with a look of peace upon her brow.

19

ALISON Fraley was lounging in a corner of a couch, her long slim legs crossed and stretched out to their fullest extent. She was smoking a cigarette.

Fraley had of course not been away all summer in fashionable hotels and restaurants without knowing that women nowadays smoked, but she had a strange aversion to it which, so far, Violet Wentworth had been unable to break down, though Violet herself had never yet smoked in the presence of the mountain girl.

Fraley came into the room, with an air of sweet aloofness. Her fine patrician chin was lifted just the least bit but not haughtily, her lips made a firm little line of courage and in her eyes was a look that puzzled the two women who awaited her.

Fraley had a lack of self-consciousness in the presence of strangers that constantly astonished her benefactress. Violet called it poise, though one usually thinks of poise as a thing that is acquired, not inherited. If this girl had acquired her poise she had got it from her mountain distances, and her close touch with holy things. The world troubled her, but it did not embarrass her.

She came forward quite easily and acknowledged the introduction, but there was a reservation in her attitude, a lack of response—save by a distant little smile—when Violet said she hoped these two girls would be friends. It was as if she held her friendship in abeyance until she should find out whether the other girl were such as she could take into the innermost citadel of her heart.

The other girl showed her lack of poise by her rudeness. She did not rise from her slouching attitude, nor show any courtesy of tone as she spoke, and she puffed a stream of smoke into the air even before she nodded.

"Well, it seems we're booked to have a crush on each other," she flung out almost insolently, "I can't imagine either of us picking out the other for a pal, but Vi seems to think we should, so I suppose we shall. How about Thursday morning? We'll go to the country club and have some golf. Vi says you play."

"Thank you," said Fraley simply and tried to smile.

She was studying this other girl, with her long slim legs slung out before her, the cigarette drooping from her listless fingers, with her sullen discontented eyes. She was wondering how a girl like this came to be a friend of the breezy, healthy, vivid man of the wilderness. She saw him now in memory as he stood in the dim shadows of the old log schoolhouse reading from her mother's cotton-covered Bible, the candle light flickering on his earnest face and putting glints into the crispness of the wave of hair over his forehead. She heard his voice again, reading the Bible, groping his way to the truth as if he meant it, and she could not think of this girl as having been present, or entering into the spirit of the gathering.

Violet was busying herself with the tea things, making sharp, clinking little sounds with the spoons as she laid them down in the egg-shell saucers. Fraley could see that she was watching her furtively, and presently she spoke, but it was to the other girl she directed her conversation.

"What do you hear from Riv?" she asked casually. But suddenly Fraley understood why she had asked the question. Riv was the strange name she had called Mr. Seagrave. That was what she must call him now, *Mr.* Seagrave. Even "raven" that he had asked her to use would be too intimate, now that she knew he was to marry someone else. Of course she had never expected him to marry *her.* She had not thought anything at all about it except that he was her friend, and as long as he had a perfect right to be that nothing more had occurred to her. But now that she knew he belonged to another, she felt that she had no right to a special friendship like that with him. There was an inborn fineness in her soul which her mother had, perhaps almost unconsciously, fostered.

It occurred to Fraley suddenly as she tried not to start at Violet's question, that perhaps Mr. Seagrave had written to this other girl all about finding her in the desert in a tree, and a wave of color swept up softly into her cheeks as she turned her grave eyes to hear the answer to Violet's question.

"Riv? Oh, I'm off him for life," said the slow insolent voice, as the slim arm went lazily out to accept the cup of tea her hostess was passing her. "He's off on a trip somewhere. I haven't heard a word from him all summer. He got one of his stubborn fits, insisted he had to go somewhere else when Gwen had a house party at the shore and particularly wanted him, and he hasn't turned up since. But he'll come soon now I suppose. He's always on deck when things begin. He'll be back in time for the tournaments. He never misses those. I suppose he thinks he's been giving me a much needed lesson, staying away all summer without a word, but I've been having the time of my life with Dicky Whitehead. You know he's just got a divorce and he's like a bird let loose."

Something fiery glowed in Fraley's eyes, but she busied her gaze with the little cakes on her plate, and gave the two women who were watching her no satisfaction. She wondered if Violet had said anything to her guest about the letter before she came down, but she maintained a discreet silence, and got over the hard place.

Alison Fraley presently turned to her and began to talk golf and tennis, putting Fraley through a catechism to see if she knew anything at all. Finding her quite intelligent, she decided she would make it a point to be at the golf links on Thursday.

The conversation touched on books. Alison wanted to borrow a new book that Violet had just bought.

"That is, when you both have read it of course," she added with unusual politeness.

"Oh, you can have it now," said Violet ringing for the maid, "I finished it last night, read till half past two. Fraley would not care for it."

"Fraley?" said the other girl with a sudden startled survey of the mountain girl, and a sharp look toward her hostess, "Is that your name?"

Fraley nodded.

"Where on earth did you get that name? It's mine, you know."

"Yes," said Fraley, "I know. Mine is a family name." She felt oddly averse to telling this girl that the whole name she bore had belonged to her mother.

"It would be odd, wouldn't it, if you and I should turn out to be relatives," said the other girl, again with that startled look in her bold eyes, and another swift survey of Fraley, from correct shoe tip to beautifully arranged coiffure. Well, if it should be that way of course she was nothing to be ashamed of. But, how odd!

"Did you get us here just to spring this on us, Vi?" asked Alison.

"Well, why not?" answered Violet enigmatically, but did not seem disposed to talk further about it. "When did you say your people are returning?" she asked, as if weary of the other subject.

"Dad is crossing this week, but mother is waiting to come till Aunt Greta is ready. It may be a fortnight yet. Aunt Greta is afraid of the September storms, and made such a fuss mother had to give in."

Violet's eyes narrowed.

"Bring your father over some evening when he gets back. We'll have a little bridge. But you'll have to get somebody else to make a fourth. Fraley won't learn. Perhaps Rivington will be back by that time."

"Perhaps—" said the girl yawning indifferently, "or I'll bring Dicky. He is simply great at bridge you know. But why don't you play?" she asked turning suddenly to Fraley.

"It bores her," said Violet sharply answering for the girl.

Alison took out a little gold case and handed it over to the other girl.

"Have a smoke with me," she said watching her narrowly.

Fraley drew back. She felt as if she were being put through a series of tests.

"Thank you, no," she said summoning a withdrawing smile.

But the other girl still held out the gold case.

"Oh, cut it," she said, "this is as good a time as any to begin if you don't like it. You'll soon get over that. You know you'll never get anywhere if you don't smoke or play bridge."

Fraley turned wide, amused eyes upon her.

"That depends on where you want to get," she said.

"What's the matter, does your mother object?" asked Alison with scorn in her voice, "you know that doesn't cut any ice in the world to-day."

"My mother," said Fraley with a slight lift of her lovely head, "is in heaven," and there was a look of sudden tears suppressed in the shining eyes with which she looked straight at the other girl.

It may be that Alison was embarrassed, but if she was it took the form of rudeness again:

"That must be comfortable," she said with a half sneer. "It must leave you pretty free! But of course," she added as she saw a dangerous look in the stranger's eyes, "if you don't feel that way it's rather rotten."

"I don't feel that way," said Fraley briefly, struggling to hide the desire to rush from the room and cry.

"She doesn't care for me, Vi," said Alison amusedly, turning to the older woman, "I haven't got on at all, and here I have been doing my best to be amusing."

"You're all right," said the lady, pouring another cup of tea for herself, "you don't understand each other yet. You have to find the keynote first before you can play harmoniously you know. Fraley's a dear if you just know how to take her, and when to let her have her own way."

Fraley twinkled into an appreciative smile. If Violet was pleased, and cared enough to defend her, what did it matter what this other girl said or thought?

But though the atmosphere was not quite so electrically charged after that, and the talk went on for perhaps a half hour more before the visitor took her languid leave, Fraley said very little. She could not get away from her own thoughts enough to think of something to say in this strange new environment. Hitherto this kind of thing had only revolved in a wide circle about the place where she was, but now she had been pushed intimately into it and she felt like a fish out of water.

When Alison left, Violet went to lie down for a little while and Fraley put on her hat and went out. She wanted to be in the great out-of-doors, and get the cobwebs swept out of her brain, and the tired feeling out of her heart. Nothing else could do it but the open, even though it was but a city street.

She longed for the great wide spaces of the west, for her mountain and its distant vision, for the sense of being near to God's sky. Even the river and the palisades seemed too small and near to-day.

The wind was blowing wildly as it sometimes does on Riverside Drive, and when she came to the corner where she usually turned off to go across to the little park where she loved to sit and watch the boats, she had to stop and bend forward to keep her footing. The wind swept down the side street, and almost took her with it across the street. As she lifted her head to go forward again something dark and soft swept by her face and out into the street.

In an instant she saw that it was a man's soft hat, and that it was bound across the street and down toward the river as fast as wind could carry it.

Ignoring the oncoming cars, she darted across the street after it, threading her way between traffic, almost putting her hand upon the hat only to have the wind snatch it once more and hurl it a little farther down the bank. Nimbly she darted after it again, though it evaded her several times, till in a sudden lull she pounced upon it and held it tight.

When she rose and turned around to see where it belonged she saw a tall hatless figure standing above her on the pavement, his white hair blowing wildly in the wind, his glasses dancing at the end of a long black ribbon, and his long arm and gloved hand that held a correct walking stick, waving dignifiedly at her. There was something strangely familiar about the man, but she did not stop to identify it then. She hurried up the steep bank, all out of breath from her chase, her cheeks rosy with the exercise, and her eyes bright at her success in getting the hat. She was smiling like a child when she handed it to him, and then she saw that he had put his hand in his pocket and was bringing out some money. Her laugh rang out happily as she ignored his outstretched hand.

"I just loved getting it," she said gaily, and at her cultured voice he perceived his mistake and stared.

"I beg your pardon," he said hurrying the money back into his pocket and putting on his glasses. "I thought—" and then he perceived that he did not want to tell her what he thought. "You are very kind I'm sure," he blustered. "Not many young girls to-day would want to take the trouble to run after a passing hat. Why—why— haven't I seen you somewhere, my child? Your face looks familiar. Perhaps I ought to have known you at first, but my eyes are not so good as they were. You live somewhere along here? Perhaps I have seen you passing."

"You are Mr. MacPherson," laughed Fraley, "you saw me up at the mountain house. I used to play tennis and golf with your grandson."

"Oh, you don't say so! That must be it then. I'm sure I am deeply grateful to you. You are a nice girl. I wish there were more like you—"

Fraley laughingly protested that it was nothing and hurried away down the path to the river, leaving the old man looking after her, half perplexed lest he ought to have given her something after all. She looked such a child in the little trim knit suit she had donned before going out for her walk, and she ran so lightly down the steep incline as if she had wings on her feet. He stood for sometime looking after her, and then turned sighing away, wondering what it was in the past that stirred his memory when he looked at her. Something sweet and painful that was gone.

That night at dinner Fraley's face was bright and peaceful. She had walked off her depression, and there was peace in her eyes and soul; she could smile.

Violet watched her in admiration, for she had seen the struggle the girl had gone through while the visitor put her through her paces, and she knew she had been deeply stirred. There was something in this sweet young soul that others surely did not have, to be able to come out of it sunny and strong and wholesome.

"Well, how did you like your cousin?" asked Violet at length when the main course had been served and the butler had withdrawn for a few minutes and left them alone.

Fraley looked up with startled eyes. Their deep blue seemed almost to change to black as she looked. She went white about her lips.

"My cousin!" she exclaimed, "oh, what do you mean? Do you know something about my people that I do not know?"

"Well, I haven't quite proved it yet," admitted Violet, "but I'm rather reasonably sure."

"Did she—? Have you asked her? Did she know that I—?"

"No, she knows nothing about it yet," said Violet crossly. She was vexed that this child of the wilds was not apparently pleased at her prospect of a high connection. "You heard all she knows. I've merely put the idea to working in her mind. She's clever and she'll probably work it out after a while, and question you. You didn't think I would give you away to her without letting you know first, did you?"

"No," said the girl slowly, "I hoped you wouldn't. I trusted—that you wouldn't. Please don't say anything more to her—if you can help it."

"Well, I can help it of course if I think it is wise. But why on earth don't you want her to know? It puts you on a level with her. It gives you social standing, don't you see?"

"No," said Fraley, "I'm not sure I want that. I am not sure I want her ever to know. If I had been I would have hunted up my people right away. You see, I am—myself, and she is—herself—"

"Obviously," said Violet dryly.

Fraley smiled wanly.

"I know that sounds silly," she admitted, "but you don't understand."

"I understand perfectly," said the woman. "You don't care a little bit about social position, or wealth or anything in this world. But that is silly, and you've got to get over it. You have a right to take your own place in the world."

"I'm not sure that I have any place in the world," said the girl thoughtfully. "If I have it is not dependent on other people. God puts people up or down, where He wants them. But that isn't what I'm thinking about at all."

"No, of course not!" interrupted Violet a trifle bitterly.

"Please," said Fraley, "you don't understand. My mother went away and married my father, and I'm not sure how they feel toward her, if they even remember her at all. I don't want anybody to think that my mother's child has come back to be a burden on any-body!"

"Fiddlesticks and nonsense!" said Violet crossly. "There is no talk of that. You are here, looking after yourself, aren't you? You are not asking to be a burden on anybody. You are supporting yourself."

"You mean, you are supporting me," said Fraley, look-ing at the woman with honest eyes. "I don't know why you do it this way. I know I'm doing nothing in payment for a home like this."

"You're doing more than you know," was the crabbed response. "Now, let's talk about something else. Have you got that list addressed that I gave you? I want those invitations to go out to-morrow afternoon without fail or I shall have to change the date. It is not correct to send invitations any later."

"They are all ready. I stamped them just after lunch," said Fraley happily.

"And yet you say that you don't do anything for me!" snapped the woman. "I never had my invitations done so quickly and so entirely without mistakes before, not even when I had a trained secretary!"

The girl smiled her shy pleasure.

After the dessert had been brought in and they were alone once more the girl looked up.

"I would like you to tell me please what makes you think that girl may be my cousin."

Violet eyed her for a moment speculatively and then answered:

"Because I went and hunted up the addresses you gave me when we first got here, and found that the people had moved. I had them traced by a detective, and found that the Mr. Robert Fraley who used to live downtown at the address your mother gave you was the father of Alison Fraley who lives on the drive."

"But isn't he a very rich man?" asked the girl after a moment's thoughtful wonder.

"Yes. He's counted one of the very rich men of the city now."

"But he used to be poor. That is, he was just a clerk somewhere."

"Well, he didn't stay a clerk," said Violet. "Sometimes they don't. He probably learned to play the market. Most people up here do."

"What's that?"

"Oh, investing their money well, even if it isn't but a little, and selling when it is at a good price and then doing it over again."

"Is—that—quite—right? Doesn't somebody have to lose?"

"I'm sure I don't know!" snapped Violet, "that hasn't anything to do with the case. I suppose it depends on how you do it. Your idea I suppose is to find out if your uncle is honest. But you really have nothing to do with that. You can't make everybody over to suit your ideas, not even if they are relatives. However, for your comfort, I can tell you that Robert Fraley is quite the correct thing in every way so far as I know. I have never heard a breath of suspicion against his morals or the way he got his fortune. He's one of those "honest Scotchmen" who are clever enough to turn a penny, and keep in with religion too. He's very prominent in one of the big Fifth Avenue churches."

"Oh," said Fraley, and watched the varying changes of her informer's face as she said these half sarcastic things about the newly discovered uncle.

Violet was going out that evening, and disappeared into her room almost immediately after the evening meal. There was no further chance to question her that night. Fraley went up to her room with much to think

about. She sat down in the window where she could see
the lights on the river, with her Bible in her lap. There
was a reading lamp close by that she would turn on
presently when she had thought her way through. But
now she loved to sit with her hand on the dear old Bible,
while she thought. It was more as if her mother were
talking it all over with her! Oh, if she could but hear her
voice, and could lay her head in her lap as she used to do
and tell all that was in her heart, and see what the mother
thought about it!

Fraley had long ago purchased with the money left
over from Seagrave's Bible a Scofield Bible, such as she
had bought for the young missionary, for after much
deliberation she had decided that she would rather have
that for a keepsake of him than anything else. She wanted
to see what she had sent him, and she enjoyed the
thought that perhaps she was reading the same things
that he was reading, because she had the same kind of a
copy. So she was devouring the Book again as if it were
a new book, looking up all the marginal references, and
reading all the enlightening footnotes, and getting daily
new light on the Word. It was all very precious. But
to-night, she had unlocked her treasure drawer and taken
out the old cotton-covered Book because she felt that
she needed the comfort of her mother's presence and
guidance, and because, too, she felt that perhaps her
reading of the other copy with the thought of the young
man in mind, had been a thing she ought not to have
done, at least, in the light of her present knowledge that
he was as good as engaged to her cousin. She must get
out of that habit.

So she sat there in the dusk of the city in her darkened
room, and thought.

It seemed to her as if everything had been turned
upside down again in her life. Her friend was gone, and

she had in his place an unwanted cousin and an unknown uncle—and there would be an aunt too, of
course, who was a still more unknown quantity. Silently,
in the darkness, the tears began to slip down her cheeks.
She longed inexpressibly to run away and get back to her
mountain. If only those men could be taken away from
there and she might have the place in quietness and
peace, she thought it would be a wonderful refuge. She
believed at that moment that she would be content to
stay there alone for the rest of her days, if she need not
fear those enemies of hers. But it seemed there were
enemies of one kind or another in the world whichever
way one turned.

Presently, as her fingers slipped between the worn
precious leaves, she felt two that seemed to stick together,
and idly her fingers sought to free the soft jagged edges
from each other. But they would not come apart. She
began to realize that there seemed to be a soft layer of
paper or something between them.

Curious, she snapped on the light, and began to
examine them.

She had not read much in this book since she purchased her new one. In fact she had only used it that first
night or two in reading to Jeanne, because she had
bought the new one the second or third day she was out
shopping. She had put this one away for safekeeping, not
only lest its leaves should become more worn, but also to
protect it from the amused and curious glances of anyone
who might enter her room, for she had been quick to see
that they thought it very queer in its cotton covering. To
have it viewed by unsympathetic eyes was like laying bare
her heart.

She found that the two pages that were stuck together
were in between the Old and New Testaments. Perhaps
that was why she had not noticed them when she read

to Jeanne, because she had not had to open between them.

And now she saw that "For Fraley, dear" was scrawled in pencil in her mother's hand as if she had written it in her last hours when she was too sick and weak to write her best.

Eagerly, carefully, the girl sought a paper knife that was a part of the outfitting of the beautiful desk that adorned her room. The pages were pasted together most carefully so that the torn edges fitted each other, and it hurt her to separate them, because they kept tearing in little jagged fringes. But when she finally got them apart she found a letter within written by her mother on an old piece of paper bag. It was folded small, and addressed to her.

As if she had heard a voice from another world, she laid her hand on her heart and looked at it, smiling through the sudden tears that came. A letter from her dear mother! And that it should come just now when she was particularly sorrowful and in great doubt! Perhaps God had sent it to help her to know what to do.

20

*Mother's dear little girl:* [the letter began]

*Some day you will find this letter between two pages in the old Bible, and it will be like me speaking to you again.*

*It's terribly hard for me to leave you all alone, but I feel that God is going to take care of you and when you read this you will I hope be far away from here with good people somewhere who will help you find a way to earn your living.*

*But there will be times when things all look black, for life is like that. And perhaps this letter will help you then, and you will remember that your mother thought ahead and wished she could bear all the hard things for you. But I suppose you have to have your hard testings like everybody else, to get you ready for the life everlasting. Remember you don't have to do it all alone. If you ever get where you don't know what to do go to God, and tell Him just as you used to tell me everything.*

*I can't write any more. My strength is almost gone, and this is all the paper there is, but you know I love you and I'll be waiting for you when you come home.*

*If, where I am going, they let mothers like me be guardian angels, I'll ask to be allowed to guard you, precious child, till we meet in heaven.*
> Your loving mother,
> Alison Fraley MacPherson.

For a long time Fraley sat reading this letter over and over until she had each line by heart. It seemed so wonderful to hear her mother's words spoken out of the grave, and to have the letter come just now when her soul was tried. It seemed to make all the things that had troubled her sink into insignificance before the fact that she was in this world being tested, and that if anything that she desired was not the Father's will she must not want it, that was all. It might seem to her that she could not live without it, but that would not be so, for the Lord knew best, and He was able to bring her through a thing of the Spirit as well as He had brought her through the perils of her pilgrimage.

She went to bed that night with her mother's letter under her cheek, and a more peaceful look upon her brow than she had worn for several days.

Violet Wentworth did not arise early, and it was understood that the mornings were Fraley's to do with as she pleased, unless there were letters to be written.

Fraley had planned to go downtown this morning, so she started out early, intending to walk until she was tired and then take the bus.

As she came out to the pavement she saw old Mr. MacPherson coming down the street with his stately tread, looking keenly at her, evidently recognizing her. The smile that lit his crabbed old face gave her a new view of what the man might have been.

Fraley smiled up at him, and would have let him pass, but he halted and spoke to her.

"Good morning, little maid," he said with a somewhat courtly manner. "Are you feeling any the worse for your sprint after my hat yesterday?"

"Oh no," laughed Fraley, "I was glad to have a good run. There isn't often so good an excuse for running in the city you know, and I'm supposed to be grown up."

"Are you, indeed!" smiled the old man watching her sparkling beauty with admiration. "And is this where you live?"

He glanced up sharply at the house.

Fraley said it was.

"And are you going out to walk? May I walk with you a little way? We are neighbors, we ought to be acquainted."

Fraley said she was and would be glad of his company, and they fell into step along the pavement.

"I suppose I ought to know you," said the old man smiling down at her scrutinizingly. "But I'm not very good at remembering names and faces. Your face however is not hard to remember. Whose house is that where you came out, anyway? I declare I'm not quite sure."

"Mrs. Wentworth lives there," said Fraley.

"Oh!" said the old man, and *"Oh!"* in quite a revealing tone. It was most evident that he did not approve of Mrs. Wentworth. "And—you are—her—*daughter?"* he asked and Fraley fancied his tone was now less cordial.

"No," said the girl, "I'm just staying there for a little while. I'm helping her. She calls it social secretary work."

"I see," said her companion more cordially. "Well, that's good. You are a good little girl I'm sure. Always keep yourself sweet and unspoiled the way you are now. I'm glad you don't paint your lips. It's ghastly the way the girls do that. You couldn't smile the way you do if your lips were painted. You make me think of something sweet I lost once."

"Oh," said Fraley shyly, "I'm sorry! I wouldn't want to trouble you."

"You don't trouble me," he said gruffly, "I like to watch you."

They walked a long distance toward downtown till the old man said he would have to go back, that he was getting beyond his beat. So Fraley took the bus and went on down, wondering at the strange friendship she had picked up with this old man who bore the same name that she did. There seemed to be a wistfulness about him as if he were hungering for something he could not find.

Fraley's errand that morning was to look up the addresses her mother had put in the old Bible. She felt that she wanted to know for a certainty about her mother's people before she went with Alison. She wanted to be sure that Violet's information was correct.

She had no trouble in locating the address of Robert Fraley, and, as Violet had experienced before her, she was sent to an old crippled shoemaker across the street to gain information about the former occupants of the house.

"Yes, I been here thirty years," he informed her eyeing her curiously. "Yes, I knowed Robert Fraley all right; a right nice sort of feller he useta be afore he made his pile. Always had a pleasant word. I've mended many a shoe fer him in his younger days afore he got up in the world. He had a pretty little wife, an' she useta wheel her kid up an' down this street. I made the kid a pair o' shoes outa pretty red leather oncet. Her name was Allie—little Allie—fer a sister o' hisn who married a poor stick an' went out west—"

Fraley sank down on the wooden chair offered her and listened and questioned till she had no more doubt left in her mind but that Alison Fraley was her own cousin.

"They don't talk any more," went on the garrulous old man, "they *ride,* they do, an' not in no trolley car neither. They has their limousines now, more'n one, and they resides on Riverside Drive when they ain't abroad, which they are just now. I seen it in the paper the other day. 'Mr. Robert Fraley and wife after a winter in Yorrup is sailin' fer home, an' booked to arrive in N'York about the twenty-fif'.' That's the way they write it. But I ain't seen him fer a matter of ten year now. He don't never come down this way any more. He's got too high hat fer this street—at least his wife an' kid have. He was a nice man, I will say that fer him. An' ef he were to meet me now, allowin' he knowed me after all these years, I wouldn't put it past him to speak as pleasant as ever he done. But her, now, she's another kind. And I've heard say the kid is more high steppin' than them all."

When Fraley left the dusty old shoe shop and went her way back to Riverside Drive, her heart was very heavy. She seemed to have come suddenly very close to her dear mother again, and to feel with her, the great isolation from her family. Mother had felt that her brother Robert was the salt of the earth, and would care for his niece. But Mother never knew of this rise in circumstance. Mother had not spoken much about her brother's wife, and now Fraley felt as if she knew the reason why. The sister-in-law was of another kind. This crooked old cobbler had keen little discerning eyes. Fraley felt she understood the whole situation. She was sure beyond the shadow of a doubt that Alison Fraley was her own cousin, and she felt also very sure that she did not care to claim relationship, at least not until she knew her better. But she had completely forgotten to look up the MacPherson side of the house at all.

"What is the matter with you?" asked Violet crossly at breakfast the next morning, watching the lovely, troubled face jealously. "I've asked you a question twice and you don't seem to even hear me."

"Oh, I beg your pardon," said Fraley getting pink, "I'm sorry. I was just thinking."

"Thinking about what?" asked Violet suspiciously. "Because if it's about that young man you wrote to, you better cut it out. You're much too young to be thinking about young men. You need to wait another year or two anyway."

Fraley's face was flaming now.

"I was not thinking about any young man," she said, tremulously, "I don't think you should talk to me that way. There is nothing wrong about that young man. He was just kind to me when he met me when I was lost, and couldn't find my way to anywhere. I had promised him that I would let him know when I found a place to stay."

Violet still eyed her suspiciously.

"Why should he want to know where you were? Was there anything between you? You know a young man like that doesn't mean any good to a girl he picks up on the desert."

Fraley rose, her face growing white with anger, and her eyes darkening with feeling.

"You shall not say things like that about Mr. Seagrave!" she said. "He was wonderful to me. He took care of me as if he had been my own brother. He wanted me to write so he could be sure I was safe. He was just kind."

"Oh, well, you needn't cry about it!" said Violet contemptuously, "I was just warning you. You've got a lot to learn and you may as well find it out first as last.

Well, if you weren't thinking about him who were you thinking about?"

"I was thinking about Joseph."

"Joseph who?" with new alarm in her voice.

"Joseph in the Bible," said Fraley desperately. "I was reading about him this morning how he was sold into Egypt. You don't like me to talk about the Bible or I would have told you at once."

"The Bible again," said Violet in great annoyance. "I certainly am Bibled to death. I can't teach you the things you need to know when your head is full of this Bible stuff. You know enough about that. It's time you got some worldly wisdom. Now, run along and don't bother me any more, and for pity's sake don't look so glum! I didn't ask you here to look like a tombstone!"

Sadly Fraley went up to her room to dress for the golf game with her stranger cousin. Life certainly did not look very rosy just now to her. She could not anticipate the coming ordeal with anything but dread.

As she was going out to the car where Alison Fraley awaited her the postman arrived and the butler stood in the hall with his hands full of letters.

"Here's one for you, Miss Fraley," he said as he sorted them over. "Will you have it now or shall I put it up in your room?"

"Oh, I'll take it now," said Fraley, curious to know who could possibly have written to her. But a glance at the letter flooded her face with color. She had seen that handwriting but once but she never would forget it, and it did not need the inscription in the left hand corner, "Return to G. R. Seagrave" to tell her that her friend of the wilderness had not forgotten her.

Tremulously she hid the letter in her pocket and ran down the steps to the car.

All the morning she had a guilty feeling with that

letter crackling whenever she turned, and she could not get away from the longing to run away somewhere and see what it contained. She tried her best to concentrate on what she was doing and play a good game, but her thoughts were far away.

Alison gossiped a great deal about the different people on the golf links. Also she told Fraley much about Violet Wentworth's past which she would rather not have known, and which filled her with a new dismay. Was Violet really like that? And was all this mess the reason why Mr. MacPherson had lost his cordiality when he found out where she was living—when he thought she was a relative of Violet's?

"Now," said Alison, "we're going into the club house and have a cocktail. Vi said I was to teach you to like them, and I give you fair warning there's no use trying to get out of it. Then we're going to have a smoke. It's time you learned."

Fraley walked thoughtfully toward the club house, her mouth set in a firm little line. When they reached the porch she paused.

"Come on," said Alison pointing to a group, "the gang's all here and Vi said I was to introduce you to them. This is Teddy and Rose Frelingheysen, May Ellen Montgomery, Martha Minter, Jill Rossiter, Jack Schuyler, Sam Van Rensalaer, and Dick Willoughby."

For the "gang" had thronged over to where they stood as if by preconcerted arrangement, and there was no opportunity to escape.

"And here come the drinks!" cried the one they called Dick, as if that were the end and aim of all mornings.

"I'll wait in the car, Alison, if you'll excuse me," said Fraley with sudden determination.

"Not on your life you won't!" cried Alison laughing, "I've given my word to initiate you before I go home.

Put her in a chair, boys, and let her see we mean business."

Laughingly they laid hands upon her, those maidens and elegant youths, dressed in the latest importation of fashion, children of fortune who had no need to do anything in the world but play. They literally carried her to a veranda chair with a great whorl of a back that looked like the top of a king's throne, and placed her in it. And then the youth called Jack laughingly held a glass to her lips.

Now it is well known that though you may lead a horse to water you cannot make him drink, and Fraley, though her arms were pinioned to the straw arms of the great chair, and though there were so many of her tormentors that she could not hope to get free if she tried, resolutely held her lips closed.

At last the youth who held the glass stood back and said, "Why won't you taste it? Just taste it!"

Fraley looked him in the eyes.

"If I had no reason for not drinking it I certainly would not drink it now. I will not be *made* to eat or drink or do anything. I would not drink it if you tried to kill me for it."

There was something in her quiet tone that brought them to their senses, and they looked at one another. There were times perhaps when this group, after they had been drinking all night at a dance, would have kept up the buffoonery even under the gravest circumstances, but it was morning yet, and none of these young people had been drinking that day. They perceived that they were carrying a joke a little too far, and even Violet Wentworth might not uphold them in the torture they were putting upon this fair stranger.

"I'll tell you what we'll do," drawled Alison now, standing in front of her cousin. "If you'll tell us why you won't drink nor smoke nor play bridge, we'll let you off, but it's got to be a real honest to goodness reason, and I'm to be the judge, or else we're going to stay right here till you drink it."

"Yes, I'll tell you the reason," said Fraley, "though I don't like the way you are trying to force me to it. I don't play cards, nor smoke nor drink because I've seen criminals doing all those three things in the mountain cabin where I was born, till they were beside themselves. I've seen them lose every cent they had, and turn and curse my little sweet mother, and throw things at her, and then take my father who tried to make them pay what they owed him and drag him out and push him off the cliff and kill him!"

Fraley's lips were trembling with feeling and her eyes were flashing blue fire. And as they watched her the group gradually let go of her hands, and stepped back almost respectfully, shocked and amazed, but recognizing the girl's courage. Fraley looked at them steadily, and then turned her eyes on Alison, saw a curl of a sneer on her lips, and was stung into words again.

"And you," she said, "you who have always had everything you needed all your life, who never knew what it was to be hungry or cold or afraid, who have always been sheltered and cared for, are willing to do the same things that those vile men do. And not only that but you are trying to make me do them. Alison Fraley, my mother was your father's only sister, and she gave her life to protect me and keep me clean. Do you suppose I would let you undo what she gave her lifetime to do, even if you killed me in the attempt?"

Fraley stood up, free. They were all watching her in amazement now, and drinks were forgotten. They were looking at Alison in startled question. There was a quality, too, in their looks, of admiration, as Fraley stood forth, and faced them all, a little lovely angry thing with enraged righteousness in her eyes.

"I will go back by myself now," she said to Alison. "You need not come with me!" and she turned and walked off the piazza and down the winding drive of the country club.

"Imposter!"

The word followed her like a hissing serpent.

"So that's her game!" said the voice of Alison angrily, purposely loud so that she might hear it. "She is going to blackmail the family. She is expecting to get some money out of my father to finance herself. But she'll find my father is not so easily taken in. My father *had no* sister!"

But Fraley walked steadily on out the gate of the country club and down the road out of sight.

GEORGE Rivington Seagrave was taking a horseback ride by himself. He had wearied of the attention of his hostess and had pleaded a promised call on members of his parish to shake her for the day. And now he had ridden out along the way where he had found the little pilgrim in a tree on his first day in the west.

It did not take him long to find the place, and identify the tree.

"The little squirrel!" he said to himself as he stood looking up into the branches, "she must be some climber! Now to think of her going up into that tree as if she were a bird."

He threw the horse's rein over the saddle and sat down at the foot of the tree, going over that experience which was now several months away, for he lingered, week after week holding down the job for the poor fellow who was slowly recovering but was not yet able to take up his work. The pitiful letters scrawled from the hospital cot were the first thing that held him in the wilds, but later he grew to be interested in the queer gnarled people who inhabited these forlorn log cabins so far from most human habitation, and who were willing to take such long toilsome journeys just to hear him read the word of God once or twice a week. It was a continual miracle to him to see them come straggling into the schoolhouse faithfully on Sunday morning, and one evening a week.

Sitting under the tree Seagrave took out the Bible that Fraley had bought for him and after much fumbling around and referring to the paper he carried in his pocket, found the place which the girl had showed him sitting under that same tree. For a while he sat and read, chapter after chapter, thinking of the quaint comments the child had made as she told him the story, seeing again her sweet pure face, looking down at him from the tree when he first accosted her; smiling back to him from the saddle as they rode together; gleaming out at him from the shadows of the old schoolhouse as he told over the story himself. Oh, she was a sweet child, and how had she taken hold upon him even in that one short day! It was strange. He had never seen a human being who so stirred him. He was beginning to think now that it was something more than human, it was God, speaking through the lovely lips of the girl.

He wondered again as he had wondered many times since she left him, what had been the circumstances of her own life that had so perfected her sweet young womanhood even out in the wilds, with only one book for contact with the great world. That, too, must have been a miracle. But he would like to know. He would like to find the place where she was born, and see some of the people with whom she had associated. She had said they lived alone on a mountain, but of course that could not have been literally so. There must have been a settlement somewhere near by. They must have had some contacts with life. How interesting to search them out. What if he should do it some day? Of course he had no idea how far she had come from her home before he met her. She had not given him any data to go by, and it might be a wild goose chase, but on the other hand she had been walking with a rather heavy burden for such slender shoulders, and she could not have come far. He had the day on his hands, why not ride around and see if he could get any clue of her. She was far enough away now so that no harm could come to her by it, and anyhow he could be careful of whom he asked questions.

So he mounted his horse again and rode fast up the road where he had first seen Fraley that day in early spring.

He loved the soft tints of the distant mountains, and the lovely shadings of the woods. So he skirted the forest through which Fraley had come, that last long day of her pilgrimage, and eventually reached the far side of her lake near which she had camped on her last night out.

A fresh, spirited horse can quickly cover ground that a girl's weary feet had taken hours to walk, and Seagrave found himself, though he did not know it, going over almost the same ground that Fraley had trod on her way out.

He kept for the most part down in the valleys, for he had little knowledge of scaling mountains. He was amazed to find that he could ride so far without coming to human habitation. The house where Fraley had milked the cow was the only one he saw, for he had kept his course several miles south of the log house where she stayed all night with the woman.

And now, the sun began to warn him that he would better turn back, and looking at his watch he was startled to find that it was so late. He would scarcely be able to reach the ranch in time for supper unless he hurried.

But when he tried to find his way back he was

bewildered. The horse insisted on going one way when he felt sure he ought to go the other. He took his own turn and found himself winding up a trail above a steep precipice. He felt sure he had been in no such high path all day, but it seemed to be a well beaten track, and he argued that it might be a shorter cut to where he wanted to go. In fact there was likely to be human habitation at the end of this trail somewhere, and he might inquire the way, or perhaps even stay overnight if the house were reasonably clean, and go back the next day.

So, hurrying his horse onward he came to a turn in the trail, where up a little higher he could see the outlines of a cabin. Ah! He had been right in coming. Now, if it were not vacated he would be able to get direction.

The trail wound along narrowly, dizzily close to the precipice, and because he did not care to risk his horsemanship in such a straitened path he took to the woods just above the trail and circled about behind the cabin, and beyond, studying it from afar. There was no smoke coming from the chimney, but he thought he heard the cackling of hens a little distance from the house. Holding his horse in check he came slowly round the back intending to approach from the front, when all at once before him there arose a big rock, high and smooth, and on it he saw writing in a clear round hand. He paused surprised. Perhaps here was a sign to guide strangers on their way. "The angel of the Lord encampeth round about them that fear Him, and delivereth them," he read, and underneath it was signed "Fraley MacPherson."

Ah! He was on the right track. His little girl had been here. That was her name, Fraley MacPherson. Could it be possible that she used to live in that cabin?

He gazed off at the mountains in the distance, and

something of the greatness of the view impressed him. Here was beauty. Perhaps this was part of the explanation of her loveliness. This and the Book from which she had learned day after day.

So he picked his way among the rocks, and came around in front of the cabin, dismounted, and knocked. If there was anybody still living here perhaps they could tell him who the girl was and what about her people. He would be careful of course and not mention her, for she had seemed to be afraid of someone. But he could find out a great deal just by judicious questioning.

So he tapped at the cabin door.

There was a sound like hollow surprise through the place, and then a harsh movement, like a heavy bench being shoved back. Heavy boots too, dragging across the floor. A fumbling with the lock, and then the door was open a crack, and a gleaming sinister metal eye looked out, its cold menace almost in the face of the young man. Behind the gun there was a hand, gnarled and hairy, and behind the hand there appeared a face, dirty, unkempt, wild-eyed and full of hate.

"I beg your pardon," said Seagrave stepping back a pace, "I'm not an enemy; I merely stopped to inquire the way. I seem to be lost."

But the shining gun did not withdraw a hair's breadth.

"Lost! I guess ya air! In more ways 'n you know. Don't you stir now. I'm goin' to shoot around ya, just to give the rest of the gang a call!"

And the words were scarcely spoken when a bullet whistled by Seagrave's ear, almost grazing it.

The door was opened a little wider, showing more of the ugly, unshaven face, and bleared eyes. The breath of whisky came strongly out like an evil wind and struck his nostrils. It was combined with the smell of unwashed flesh and unlaundered garments.

"Now, stand still!" ordered the voice. "A fella never comes up here without intendin' and he never goes out when he gets here. Stand still!"

Seagrave measured the distance from himself to his horse which had reared and backed at the sound of the explosion. He guessed at his chance if he tried to bolt, and decided not to risk it.

"Oh, I say," he began putting on his best manner, "what's your grouch, pardner? I had no intention of getting in bad with you. I'm just a stranger from the east out riding. I lost my way, that was all. If you'll tell me which way to go I'll get out and never trouble you again. I'm just the guy that's holding down the preacher's job over at the log schoolhouse till the right man gets here."

"Oh, that's who you are, is it? I been layin' fer you. So you're the man that's stole my girl away from me."

"Your girl?" asked Seagrave guilelessly. "Who is your girl, and how could I steal her? I haven't got any girl."

"You haven't got any girl, haven't ye? You didn't take her over ta the railroad an' put her on the train didn't ya? I learnt all about it. I got watchers everywheres, I know what you was doin'. I heard how you an' she rid to the meetin', and then went off to where you was stayin' an' next mornin' you took 'er to tha train. I just ben waitin' till I got good'n ready to come over an' lay ya out, but now you've saved me the trouble, an' we'll fight it out right here an' now!"

Brand threw the cabin door open wide revealing the dreary room where Fraley had lived her young life, and where her poor mother had died without comfort.

"We got 'nother grudge agin ye, too. One of our men's got a girl, name o' Car'line. She's no good to him any more 'count o' you. You got 'er goin' on that there meetin' stuff, an' readin' the Bible, an' she's just natur'ly ruined fer his purposes. See? So I'm comin' out there an' shoot ya up. I'd like ta wait till the boys get here ta he'p enjoy it, but I ain't s' sure they wouldn't take the job from me ef I did, so I'll just leave 'em look on the corpse after the work's done. Air ya ready? When I shoot I shoot to kill!"

Seagrave had not spent nine months at the front in France for nothing.

"Well," he responded airily, "if I had known it was to be an affair of this sort of course I would have brought my gun along, but since I came in peace—just a min- ute—!"

Suddenly Brand's gun flew up in the air, and Brand took a blow on his jaw bone that banished from his drunken mind all knowledge of what was happening, and left him lying unconscious across the threshold of the cabin door.

Seagrave waited only to pick up the gun and unstrap the cartridge belt from Brand's waist and then he swung to his horse and was off.

Not down the trail where the narrow precipice lay, but out into the open, past Fraley's big pine, past rock and river and valley on and on as fast as his horse's flying feet could go.

He had sense enough to know that if there were a gang anywhere near, the sound of those shots would summon them and they knew better how to follow him than he knew how to run from them, therefore he must not lose a moment. He knew now that he must be within those mysterious limits that were known as Bad Man's Land, and he knew that his life depended on getting out of those limits before darkness dropped down.

This time he did not try to guide the horse. He let him take his own way, and the beast seemed to understand and picked his way with marvellous sense.

Half an hour they must have been on their way, before Seagrave heard shots behind him, very far away it is true, but still it meant serious business.

The sun was very low almost dropping behind the distant mountains when he reached a spot that he seemed to recognize, and a little later he came around the mountain and out to the lake that he had passed earlier in the day. But soon after that he heard more shots not far away now, and he thought that after all he was lost. He tried to turn the horse into the woods where he would be out of sight, but the animal knew where he was going and he fairly flew, mile after mile, over the soft earth, his hoofs making no sound, as the dusk grew deeper and the stars came out. And all at once Seagrave saw ahead of him the tree where he had found Fraley, and knew where he was. Then hope began to rise. He might be able to make it after all! There was only ominous silence behind, but once he thought he heard a bullet whistle through the air not far away.

Then, for the first time, Seagrave really prayed.

"Oh God! If you bring me out of this I'm going to serve you the rest of my days."

He said it aloud to the night as he flew by, and he set his lips. There was some glory perhaps in dying in France for the good of the whole world, but only ignominy in being shot in his tracks for a foolish blunder, because he was a tenderfoot. He wanted to come through this unharmed. But more than anything, he wanted to live to find little Fraley and guard her the rest of her life from all dangers. He had never realized before what womanhood could go through till he saw that drunken brute, and the inside of that cheerless cabin.

It was not long after that however, that he reached the familiar road which he rode every day, and he knew that he was safe.

As he realized this he looked up, with a reverent gaze. "I guess it's a promise!" he said aloud to the stars.

And then, there came back to his memory the verse that he had found written on the rock with the girl's name signed to it, and the miracle of his escape seemed to him a direct fulfillment of its promise.

It was like Seagrave that he said nothing of this incident when he arrived at the ranch house. He merely told his hostess that he had been detained longer than he expected at a place where he had called, and couldn't get back sooner. When they asked him where he was, he said he had neglected to ask the name, and he sat down at the piano and whistled a love song, playing the accompaniment while his hostess was setting out food for him.

He ate his supper, but when he went to his room and took off his clothes, he looked hard at a spot of blood on his sleeve, then washed it carefully and bound up a nasty little wound in his arm that had been teasing and stinging him all the way home. "The angel of the Lord—the angel of the Lord—" What was the rest of the verse? He knew it must be in the Bible, and he meant to find it before he slept.

He sat down by his flaming candle, and opened the book, turning to the concordance in the back and finding the word angel. He was a bright young man and it hadn't taken him long, in this land whose main attractions were horseback riding and the unwanted attentions of one's flirtatious hostess, to find out and use the means provided for his knowledge of this hitherto unknown book. Before long he had the verse and was reading the whole psalm, hearing the little girl's voice in it all. For had he not seen her lovely name signed to the words, written high on the rock?

That night before he slept, after the candle was extinguished, he knelt beside his bed, and approached God for the first time in his life on his own behalf. He had made that promise out in the open, more as a promise to himself than a prayer. But this was a prayer. He had come before the Almighty God whom he had ignored all his life, to acknowledge that he was wrong, and to put himself into the attitude of humility before his Maker. He had many things yet to learn about sin in himself and the way of salvation, but he had taken the first step to put himself right with God.

Two days later the mail down at the station contained a crude letter for Seagrave, addressed to the preacher at the schoolhouse.

"Yu got off this tim but it ant fur long. Ile plug yo wen yo ant lukin, so wach out. Ya kant cum in bad Mans land an git awa withit. Ile blo yurbloomin branse out onles you quit this preachin, Brand."

Seagrave read this with much difficulty and then, while still in the post office, wrote an answer.

"Thanks for the warning, but you see, I'm working for God and I can't quit till He says so. If I'm worth anything to Him He'll take care of me."

Brand's answer was unprintable, but Seagrave wired east for a couple of good revolvers and some ammunition and always went armed thereafter.

The news that came from the young man in the hospital was not encouraging. There had been complications. He was promised that if he would keep quiet and not try to work for six more weeks he might be able to take up his work. Seagrave, with a wistful glance toward the east wrote him that he would stand by until he was able to come.

By this time the merry, breezy young preacher had created quite a sensation in the wide neighborhood. People rode for fifty and a hundred miles on horseback to attend one of his services. Word went out that he didn't exhort, he told stories out of the Bible, and more than one poor man came bringing a tattered dollar bill and asking if the preacher could send east for a Bible for him, that his gal or his boy "wanted to read them there stories out of it fer theirsel's."

Seagrave sent a large order east to a bookstore, and in due time Bibles enough for the whole circuit arrived and were given out to the eager applicants.

"If I never can do any good here myself," mused Seagrave as he rode home after that service, thinking of the happy faces of those who had received the Bibles, "I can at least get people to read the greatest book in the world." For by this time Seagrave had reached that conclusion about the Bible.

Then Seagrave set to work in earnest to study the Bible for himself.

He made a regular business of it, beginning at the beginning, and looking up every reference in the margin. The enlightening footnotes became a joy to him, as day by day he came to know the plan of salvation from the beginning of the universe, and the way the whole Bible fitted together like a wonderful picture puzzle.

"Not a contradiction anywhere from start to finish," he said to himself after a morning of hard study. "There seems to be a reason for every chapter and verse, for every book in the whole combination, each is a part of the other. I never saw anything like it. Just that fact ought to be enough to convince anybody of its divine origin. No man or men could have possibly done that." And he had always heard that the Bible was just full of contradictions.

Day after day he grew more interested, shutting himself in his room every morning for a couple of hours, or else going off to some quiet place out of doors where he could read.

"Yes, he's a great student," admitted the lady of the ranch to the few friends with whom she had thought it worth while in this wide land to make contacts. It was most disappointing to her that she was unable to draw him into all her interests, and make of him a gay companion. Surely if George Rivington Seagrave's friends in New York could have looked in on him at this time, they would have been amazed at his new attitude toward life. He had been known as being one of the gayest, merriest, idlest, most playful fellows in the world. With all the money he needed, and friends on every hand, he had rollicked through life thus far, with seemingly not a serious thought in the world. He had always been eager for all sorts of amusement. Now he withdrew early from the great living room where were often pleasant things going on, and went to his room to read awhile before he slept.

He was taking the Bible as a man reads an exciting novel, and he could not bear to break off the thread of the story for long. Some power had gotten hold of him that he did not understand.

Then one day he came on the doctrine of the new birth. And he came, spirit led with Nicodemus, by night to His Lord, and heard the mysterious word that a man must be born again before he can enter the kingdom of God. He searched out diligently all the references and cross-references on this subject, and in one of these he came upon the fact that one must die to self and sin and the things of this world if he would share Christ's risen life. He understood that if he accepted Christ and His death on the cross as a propitiation for his sins—he had reached the point some days back where he knew he was a sinner—he should die with Him as far as his old self was concerned. He spent hours on the sixth chapter of Romans. He read and reread the verses:

> *For he that is dead is freed from sin. Now if we be dead with Christ, we believe that we shall also live with Him. For in that He died, He died unto sin once, but in that He liveth, He liveth unto God. Likewise reckon ye also yourselves to be dead indeed unto sin, but alive unto God through Jesus Christ our Lord. Let not sin therefore reign in your mortal body, that ye should obey it in the lusts thereof. Neither yield ye your members as instruments of unrighteousness unto sin: but yield yourselves unto God, as those that are alive from the dead, and your members as instruments of righteousness unto God.*

Those last sentences got him.

He took them out in the desert and spent the day alone, trying to face God, and decide the great question for himself. One verse from his Bible study kept going over in his mind. "As many as received Him to them gave He power to become the sons of God, even to them that believe on His name." The question was, was he willing to receive Him? He had already an intellectual belief, but was it an active belief, one that went all the way, and received Christ into His life without reservation? For he knew that if he did it at all he would want to go the whole way.

All day he threshed it out in the wilderness, sitting sometimes under the very tree where he had met the little pilgrim with her guide book, and had first been introduced to the Bible.

That night he went home late, under the stars, with a new light in his eyes and a new peace on his face. He knew that he had been accepted, that he was born again, that he was a new creature in Jesus Christ, and he was happier than he ever remembered to have been in his life.

Stealing quietly into the house because everybody was in bed, he went to his room, lighted his candle, and there on his table lay Fraley's letter, telling him where she was living.

A thrill passed through him as he opened it and saw an address at the top of the page. Now he could write and tell her what a wonderful thing had come to pass that night in his soul. He was now a child of God, and she would be glad, for she was a child of God also. Of all the wide circle of his acquaintances she was the only one to whom he felt he could tell his new joy, who would understand it and be glad with him.

Before he slept he wrote the little girl a letter, and the next morning he rode to the station to mail it himself. He could not trust it to the ranch hands who were driving down; he wanted to put it in the letter box himself and be sure it went safely.

Turning away from the letter box he looked up to see a tall shadow standing in the open door, a young man with a scarred face, that might have been handsome once perhaps, but was marred not only by the scar, but by a leer of evil in the eyes.

As was his custom in this friendly country, he bowed and smiled. He was by nature friendly with all men, anyway, and he had found that in his capacity of preacher out here, it was universally expected of him to speak to everybody.

But this dark, evil young face did not break into a courteous smile as most did. Instead the man stood frowning at him, with an ugly leer in his eyes, and as he passed, there broke from him a taunting laugh.

Seagrave turned, with astonished eyes and looked the man straight in the face, and he saw a murderous challenge in the other's eyes. Well, this must be one of those men from Bad Man's Land. He looked it. Seagrave hesitated, and almost went back to speak to him, then thought better of it, and with firm set lips, walked on to where his horse stood and mounted it. But he turned and looked steadily once more at the man who was still standing in the doorway watching him with that sneer on his lips and the challenge in his eyes.

That night was the night for the evening worship in the old schoolhouse. Seagrave rode off as usual with his mind intent on what he was going to say. For the first time in his ministrations to these people he meant to preach a sermon himself. Hitherto he had been content to read them the Bible, occasionally throwing in a word or phrase of his own to make the meaning simpler—that is when he was sure he understood it himself. Now he was going to tell those people about the new birth, and how he had been born again. He was going out to witness what the Lord had done for him, and his heart was full of joy.

It was a wonderful meeting in the old log schoolhouse. The very presence of the Lord Jesus seemed to be there, and the sorrowful lonely members who came their long journeys to get this little time of worship, were stirred to tears and prayers of longing and surrender, and one, Car'line, sitting back by the door in the shadow, having stayed the day and night with a friend so she could be present, lingered to talk with the young preacher, and ask if there was a way for one who had sinned greatly to be born again.

The old man and woman with whom she had come lingered outside in an old spring wagon, waiting for her. Seagrave and she stood beneath the smoky oil lamp, straight in view of the open door, and talked. Seagrave had then his first opportunity to really point the way of life to a seeking soul, and right there under the flare of that light they knelt together, while with unaccustomed lips he asked the Lord to accept this girl, and to forgive her.

Out in the darkness, behind the wooded roadside, a shadow lurked, still and grim, but the old man and woman in the spring wagon did not see it move, and crouch, and look, nor did the old man who lingered to put out the smoky lamp and lock the door.

The girl came out and got into the wagon and the old man drove away. Seagrave came out with a cheery goodnight to the old man as he lingered till he had locked the door, and then both mounted their horses and drove away in opposite directions.

The moon came up and made a silvery light along the way, and Seagrave was filled with joy. He felt like singing. He began to hum the tune of one of the hymns they had sung in the meeting, his clear baritone ringing far on the still stretches of the open.

Then, suddenly there came a stinging pain in his side, another an instant later through his right arm. He felt himself sliding from his horse, and the light of the moon going out.

A dark shadow stole away from a group of trees back on the road he had come, and slid along through the woods till it mounted a horse, and disappeared into the night.

But Seagrave lay where he had fallen, with the moonlight shining silver over his white face, and his horse whinnying beside him.

22

FRALEY had walked a great part of the way back to the city, her mind in such turmoil of anger and humiliation, and penitence that she could not reason. It was several hours later when she arrived at the house and walked straight up to Violet, who happened to be downstairs reading in the library.

"I've done a terrible thing," she said her face white and her eyes dark with emotion. "You won't like it at all. I lost my temper, and I've been rude to a lot of your friends at the country club. I made what you'll call a scene right before everybody! I'm very sorry if I have mortified you, but I couldn't do what they tried to make me. I wouldn't, not if they killed me!" she finished, her lips stern and set.

"What in the world do you mean, been rude? Made a scene at the country club? Why did you have to do that? For pity's sake stop being excited and explain!" said Violet coldly, at once on the defensive. Here was probably some more of the child's outrageous puritanism and it had got to be nipped in the bud. It couldn't go on any longer.

Fraley leaned back against the doorway and closed her tired eyes for an instant, drawing a deep breath, and then she gathered strength and began.

"They were trying to force me to drink liquor!" she said with a fierce little intake of breath.

"Who were?" asked Violet, her voice like an icicle.

"Alison and her friends. She said you had told her she must teach me before I came home." There was a question in Fraley's voice, almost a pleading, but Violet would not let herself respond to it. She looked steadily, coldly at the girl, and after an instant a weary little shadow passed over the sweet face, and Fraley went on.

"They caught me, all those young men, and put me in a big chair and held me! They had no right to touch me!"

She was still struggling between her sense of being wronged, and her penitence for having lost her temper.

"They said they would not let me up and they held the glass to my lips and tried to pry my lips open, and force me to take it!"

Still there was no relenting in the cold eyes of the woman who listened. The white lids fluttered down and up again bravely.

"I wouldn't. It was a long time, and I wouldn't! They hurt me holding my arms so hard, I suppose that was one thing that made me so angry. They hurt my neck, and they hurt my lips. But I shouldn't have been so angry. And then, when they said they would let me go if I would tell them why I would not play bridge, nor smoke nor drink, it seemed as though I just had to. So I told them."

"What did you tell them?" Violet's tone was tense now.

"I told them about the cabin on the mountain where I was born, and the men who used to play cards with my father and smoke and drink and curse my mother, and throw things at her; and how they got drunk and pushed my father off the cliff and killed him!" Fraley paused for a desperate breath. "Alison Fraley had been sneering at me, and I looked right at her and told her that my dear mother who had to stand all that was her father' sister, and that she had no right to try to make me do what my mother had spent her life in teaching me not to do."

"You told Alison that you were related to her!"

"Yes!" Fraley lifted brave steady eyes.

"Well," said Violet at last after a brief interval of thought in which conflicting emotions played over her face, "you certainly have made a pretty mess of things. I might have known that a young savage like you couldn't be trusted to go off alone among civilized people. Now, there has got to be an understanding between you and me and we might as well have it over with. It's been coming to you for some time. You've got to learn that if you stay here you must conform to my habits and customs. For instance, next week I'm giving that dinner and I want you to be present. That's one of the things I got you for, to help entertain my guests. That's why I bought you all those imported frocks and things. But you can't come to a dinner and act like a puritan. You've got to do your part and be a lady of the world. This matter of cocktails is most important. A lady knows how to drink in a ladylike way, and there is no reason whatever why a cocktail in a drawing room, or a glass of champagne at a dinner table among respectable men and women of society should remind you of a lot of boors in the wilderness who are too low down and sottish to be spoken of as human beings. Now, young lady, you may take your choice. You either make up your mind to drink what is set before you, and behave yourself, or you go out of my house! Do you understand that?"

Violet had grown very angry as she talked. She was incensed that this frail little girl with no background whatever should dare to stand against her. It offended her pride. She wanted Fraley to adore her and think her word was law. It was Fraley's admiration that had won her in the first place to take this child of the wilds and try to make her over. She wanted somebody who was lovely to glorify Violet Wentworth and help to make her name great, and she was filled with fury that she was not paramount in the girl's thoughts. She was jealous of her fine allegiance to God and her Bible, and the things her mother had taught her.

Fraley stood very still and looked at her, her eyes growing large and dark with sorrow, her face growing whiter. It seemed as if she could not believe that her friend, who had done so much for her, had spoken those awful words.

Violet saw how the child was stirred and pressed her advantage.

"I mean every word that I have said!" she said sternly. "You've got a whole week to decide. You can go upstairs now and think it over."

Fraley suddenly dropped her white lids like curtains drawn quickly, and two large tears rolled down her cheeks and splashed on the floor by her little dusty shoes.

There was silence in the room for a full minute while the girl struggled to gain her self-control. Then she lifted her eyes again, bright with sorrow, and spoke bravely:

"All right!" she said, with her lips quivering, "but there's something I must tell you first. You ought to know."

"Go on," said the cold voice.

"It's about that man, that Mr. Easton that comes here to see you. I've found out he's a bad man. I saw him at the country club in an alcove this morning kissing that

Lilla Hobart. He had her in his arms and was looking down into her face the way I saw him look at you the first night I came. I thought you ought to know."

"Get out!" shouted Violet in a fury, her face red and her eyes terribly angry. "You are meddling with things that are none of your business! Get out of my sight!"

Meekly, with her whole slender form drooping in sorrow, her head bent, Fraley turned and went out of the room. She walked slowly up the stairs and into her room, and locked the door. Then she dropped upon her knees and her body shook with a tempest of tears, while she tried to pray. Somehow, this seemed to her worse than anything that had come to her since her mother's death.

But she had no time for weeping, and her prayer was short, just a cry for help and guidance. Then she arose with determination in her face, and began to undress. There was no doubt in her mind what she had to do.

As she drew off the pretty sports dress that she had worn at the country club the letter that she had tucked in the pocket fell to the floor. She stooped and with a startled look picked it up. She had forgotten it. But the sight of it brought her no joy. It was only a reminder of another pleasant thing in her life lost.

She went to the bureau and put the letter safely inside her hand bag, the one that Violet had given her on the train. She had kept it carefully, and used it when she went out in the morning by herself. Somehow it had seemed to belong to her more than the elegant trifles that Violet had bought for her to go with the new costumes to be used in her capacity as social secretary.

Fraley put on the dress and hat that had been given her on the train, and selected the shoes and stockings that were bought to go with it that first day of shopping. Then she sat down at the desk and wrote two notes.

*My dear lady: [the first began]*

*I am going away at once as you have said I must, and I cannot stand it to say good-by to you, because I have loved you so much and you have been so good to me. But I want to tell you just once more how grateful I am to you for all you have done, and for the things you have wanted to do for me. I am sorry I cannot please you by doing the things you wanted me to, but they are things I cannot do. They are things that would not be right for me to do. I think you will understand some day. I am going to pray God to make you understand why I could not do it. I am going to pray to Him to help you to love Him and His Bible, and then you will be very happy.*

*I am wearing away the first things you gave me, because it might shame you if I went out of your house in the things I wore from the mountain, but they were things you said you were going to give away anyway, and some day I hope I will earn money enough to pay you for the beautiful shoes and other things.*

*I ask your pardon for anything I may have done to trouble you, and I shall never forget how good you were to me,*

*Lovingly,*
*Fraley MacPherson*

The other note was to Jeanne, and read as follows:

*Dear Jeanne:*

*I am so sorry but I find I have to go away quite suddenly and unexpectedly. I shall miss the Bible readings with you, and I hope you will keep on reading by yourself. I shall always pray for you. Sometime, perhaps, I can see you again, and I shall not forget you.*

*In haste, and very lovingly,*
*Fraley MacPherson*

When she had addressed these notes she laid them on the desk where she was sure they would be noticed. Then she went to the treasure drawer and unlocked it, taking out the old woolen bag her mother had made, and the little garments made of salt bags, and all the things she had brought with her from the mountain. She packed them carefully, putting the old Bible in first, and tucking the other things around it. She hesitated with her own little Scofield Bible as she was about to put it in, and then with a sigh laid it out on her bureau. She had bought it with her own money, and had loved it and marked some of the verses in it that she loved the best, but now it occurred to her that she was leaving this house without a Bible. If she left it here perhaps Violet would sometimes open it and read, or Jeanne would come in when nobody was about. She would not dare give the Bible to Violet, but if she left it there as if she had forgotten it God might let it do its work somehow. Of course she had the old Bible, and it wouldn't matter so much now how it looked, there would be no one but herself to mind the cotton covers. By and by when she was earning something she would dare to spend the money for another one, and until then she could do with the old one.

So she left her new Bible on the bureau.

She found a large piece of wrapping paper in the hall closet and wrapped up her bag carefully. Then with a sorrowful look about the room that would be hers no more she turned and went slowly, softly, down the stairs, and let herself out of the door. There was no one about, and though she looked back for a last good-by to the spot that had grown so dear, she saw nobody at the windows.

Then she knew that till this last minute she had somehow hoped that Violet would relent and call her back, and tell her she did not mean that awful sentence of exile she had pronounced upon her.

With tears blinding her eyes she stumbled on down the street, block after block, narrowly escaping being run over as she heedlessly crossed the side streets.

At last, when she had gone a long distance from the house, and knew that she was beyond the sight of any one who knew her, she went across to the strip of park and sat down on a bench. She had often sat here before, when she was taking walks by herself, and watched the river in its varying moods, but now it only looked sad to her, for she was leaving this neighborhood forever and would not feel like going back to it again.

Then she remembered her letter, and a sharp pang came at the thought that this friend, too, must be renounced because he belonged to someone else. Nevertheless, she must read that letter.

She opened it with fingers that trembled with the excitement of actually hearing from him again, but at the first words a beautiful light broke over her face.

> *Dear Ladybird: [it read]*
>
> *At last you have sent me your address and I can write to you. I have been very anxious about you all these months of silence for many reasons, but now I am glad to get your letter. And glad it came just this night too, for I have something to tell you that I think will make you glad.*
>
> *I have this night given my old self over to your Jesus Christ, and I feel that I am born again. You probably know more than I do about that wonderful miracle, so I do not need to tell you, but I want you to know that it is because of you that I have found out that I was a sinner and needed to be born again. I can't think of words great enough to thank you for what you have done little*

*Ladybird, and now I am no more just a raven, nor an angel either, thank God, for I can sign myself a child of God, and I guess that is better than being an angel. Anyhow it looks good to me.*

*I've been a bit worried about you though, since you told me you had been picked up by Violet Wentworth. I know her well, but she isn't your kind, little girl, she's a woman of the world, and a hard-boiled one I'm afraid, and although I'm deeply grateful to her for having helped you over a hard place, I don't want you to stay too long with her. She might somehow make you forget the wonderful things God has taught you out of His book. She doesn't know anything about such things, and I don't want you spoiled, Ladybird.*

*My sick man is about well now. He's coming out of the hospital next week, and then very soon he'll come on and take his work, and I'll come home. There are a great many things I mean to do when I get there, for my whole life is changed now, and I'm a new man in Christ Jesus, but the first thing I am going to do is to see that you are safe and happy.*

*So write to me, little friend, for we are going to be friends always you know, and tell me all about yourself, and soon I'll be home and come at once to see you.*

*Your friend who is more grateful to you than you can ever understand, for leading him to Jesus,*

*Sincerely,*

*George R. Seagrave.*

With heart almost bursting with joy and renunciation, Fraley read this letter twice and three times before she folded it and put it away. Then she gathered up her bundle and started out into a new world, and a new life again. As before she was leaving all behind but her Bible, but God was with her, and she could trust Him to bring her where He wanted her. That ought to be enough.

About that time, Violet, who had gone to her room after Fraley left her, and had failed to be able to get to sleep as usual because she was strangely disturbed, came down the stairs to the library to get her book. She could not get away from the thought of the great distressed eyes, the pitiful white face, and the glint of the two tears that had rolled down and splashed on the floor. She wanted to absorb herself in her book again to drive the vision from her. This was going to be excellent discipline for Fraley and she must not be soft-hearted and relent just because of two tears.

She had just settled herself in her favorite chair again when the bell rang and Alison walked in, unannounced, her face dark and angry.

"I thought I'd find you here!" she said as she flung herself into another chair, and took out her cigarette case. "Such a day as I've had! I just thought I'd run in and tell you how well I succeeded in carrying out your orders. Where is that little viper? Is she anywhere around? I'd like to tell you before her what she said to me."

Violet looked up, her eyes fully as cold as they had been when talking with Fraley.

"You certainly don't seem to have exercised much common sense or taste in doing it," she remarked coolly. "You ought to have known you couldn't get anywhere by force with a girl of as strong character as that one."

"Strong character!" sneered Alison, "I'll say so! The way she slung words around. Wait till I tell you what she did!"

"She has told me," said Violet, again strangely drawn to defend her protégée.

"She *told* you!" exclaimed Alison incredulously. "I'll bet she told you a good story for herself!"

"She always tells the truth," said Violet, almost against her will.

"Well, she didn't this time. Wait till I tell you what she said about her mother and my father."

"But that happens to be true too."

"Vi! What can you mean?"

"I mean just what I said. I've known it for a long time, but I didn't mean to tell it till you two got to be friends, and you knew what a really rare character she has."

"Rare temper, I'd say! But Vi, it can't be true? Daddy never had a sister."

"Yes, he did. I have proof. There's an old man living downtown now, unless he has died in the last three months, who remembers her. Her name was Alison Fraley and you must be named after her. He told me that he remembered the look on your grandfather Fraley's face the day he discovered that his only daughter had run away with the good-for-nothing son of James MacPherson. He never smiled after that, he said, and died not many months later. That was when your people lived down in that row of little houses just off—"

"Oh, for Pete's sake don't bring all that up, Vi. Of course I knew Dad used to be poor, but there's no advantage in raking out old things like that. He isn't poor now. And so the little snake has got the MacPhersons mixed up with it too, has she? Well, but I don't see how she has put it over on you. I thought you were keen and knew a fraud when you saw one. Coming around here with her soft pretty ways and her big eyes and pretending to be good, and all the while a suit for blackmail up her sleeve. She's probably under the direction of some bold western lover who has sent her on here to play the game and get a lot of money out of two respectable old families, for them to go to housekeeping on. I didn't think you'd be fooled by a little sly thing like that."

"I tell you I have the proof, Alison," said Violet coldly. "I went and got all her papers that her mother gave her before she died. I copied them one day when she was out of the house for the morning, and then I went to the addresses given and looked up everything. I even got an expert detective on the job and had him hunt out a lot of old records and things, till I knew all the two families had done since away back. And Fraley herself doesn't even know yet that she belongs to the MacPhersons."

"But I've seen her out walking with old Mr. Mac-Pherson, several times, in the mornings."

"Oh, she met him at the mountain house this summer. He was a guest there and she played tennis with the kid grandson. But she hasn't an idea he is any connection of hers."

"Don't you fool yourself!" said Alison. "She's working a deep game, that girl is. I'd like to put her in jail. She's the most contemptible little piece I've ever seen. Just you wait till dad gets home. He'll fix her! He wouldn't stand for anybody treating me the way she did at the club house to-day. I shouldn't be at all surprised, from what she says, but that she has drunk worse than cocktails many a time. Has she ever told you what kind of men came to the house where she lived on that mountain? It sounds to me like the worst kind of a roadhouse, and she pretends to be so terribly good! Just you question her and you'll find out a few things that will open your eyes, Vi Wentworth!"

"Very well," said Violet putting her hand out to the bell and summoning the maid. "We'll send for her and ask her a few questions. Incidentally, I'll tell her about her Grandfather MacPherson and you may watch her face and see whether you'll be satisfied that she doesn't know a thing."

"By all means send for her," said the girl contemptuously. Alison arose and began pacing up and down the room as Jeanne appeared at the door.

"Tell Miss MacPherson I want her to come down to the library at once!" ordered Violet.

Jeanne disappeared, and a silence ensued. It seemed almost a hostile silence. Violet could not quite understand her own feelings.

The door bell sounded faintly in the distance and they could hear the butler going to open the door, and letting someone in. Presently he appeared at the door.

"Mr. MacPherson to see Mrs. Wentworth," he announced. "Shall I say you are engaged?"

Violet looked up astonished.

"I told you so," said Alison pausing in her restless walk, "he's found her out too, very likely. Now you'll see I was right."

Violet's face hardened. She accepted the challenge.

"Show Mr. MacPherson in here," she said, with a glitter of daring in her eyes. "We might as well have the whole show at once and be over with it," she added with a hard little laugh, "though, of course, I hadn't planned it just in this way."

"I should hope not!" muttered Alison.

They could hear Mr. MacPherson's slow step, and the tap of his cane as he followed the butler with stately tread down the hall.

He appeared at the door and looked from one lady to the other, a trifle annoyed perhaps to find someone else present besides the person he sought.

He paused in the doorway. They noticed that he held a small package in his hand.

"Good afternoon, Mrs. Wentworth. We ought to

know one another, I suppose," he said in a rather haughty way, "neighbors of course—"

"Won't you have a chair, Mr. MacPherson?" said Violet rising and greeting him pleasantly.

"Oh, no," he said. "You have a guest. I'll not trouble you. I just wanted to ask a favor of you. It won't take a moment. I have a little trifle here—a small gift—that is—You have a young girl here, a very sweet little unspoiled thing, working for you? Social secretary I think she said she was. She was very kind one day to run after my hat and capture it when it blew away in a high wind. She ran almost down to the river after it, and she would accept nothing for her services. That is—I saw of course after I had suggested it that she was a very superior little girl, and I shouldn't maybe have offered it. But I would like to do something in recognition of her kindness. Not only because she was so pleasant and quick about it, but because she reminds me strangely of some one I loved long ago. I have met her by accident a couple of times since and walked a few blocks with her till our ways parted, but I have never got quite to the place where it seemed possible to offer it to her. She seems to have so much—what should I call it—not exactly self-respect, nor dignity. Perhaps you might call it refinement. I was afraid she might not like my offering it, and so I thought I would come to you, that perhaps you would know how to give it to her without hurting her feelings. It's just a little wrist watch. I thought it might be useful in her work. She seems a charming child. And another thing, you know I don't know her name, but you surely know who I mean. There can't be two like her working for you."

Violet was standing with her hand on the back of a chair listening, mingled emotions passing over her face like the shadow of clouds on a windy day. There was a kind of triumph in the glance she swept toward Alison.

"You mean Fraley MacPherson, I suppose," she said when the old gentleman came to a pause in his lengthy, embarrassed speech.

"What! Is that her name? MacPherson? Why—why— I wonder how—Perhaps that might explain my strange feeling that there was a likeness—I've even spoken to my wife about it. Perhaps she might be a distant connection somehow. Do you know where her people came from?"

Over Violet Wentworth's face there swept a look of sudden resolve.

"I know a little about her people, Mr. MacPherson, but she can tell you more. I have just sent for her. She will be down in a moment and will tell you what she knows. But there is one thing I can tell you before she comes, Mr. MacPherson. Fraley is your grandchild. You had a son Robert, didn't you, who married a Miss Fraley—Alison Fraley? Well, Fraley is his daughter. Won't you sit down? She will be here in a moment I think."

The old man stood stock still and looked for a moment as if he were going to fall. Then suddenly a light broke over his face.

"My grandchild? You say she is my grandchild? You say she is my lost Robert's daughter? That sounds too good to be true!" and the old man stumbled into the chair that was offered him, and took out his immaculate handkerchief, mopping his brow which was wet with cold sweat.

Jeanne appeared at the door just then. Her eyes were red with weeping which she made no effort to conceal.

"Mrs. Wentworth, Miss Fraley has gone!" she said with a woebegone look.

"Gone," said Violet sharply. "Where has she gone? How do you know?"

"She left these notes," said Jeanne, her lip beginning to tremble, "and Madam, she doesn't say where she is gone, but it seems as though she did not mean to come back."

Jeanne handed over the two notes, and Violet with sudden premonition tore open her own, her face growing white and stern as she read.

"Well, I hope you are satisfied, Alison," she said lifting her eyes to the sullen girl who stood watching her curiously. "She's gone and she hasn't left a clue behind her." There was a ring of almost triumph in her voice. "It is like her," she added in a curiously gentle voice.

"What?" asked the old man looking up, "what do you say? She is gone? You have not let my granddaughter go off without knowing her destination have you? You expect her to return, don't you?"

"I don't know," said Violet with sudden trouble in her voice, "she can't have been gone an hour. Surely we ought to be able to find her. You see, we had a little trouble. It was only a trifle of course, but I think—she must have misunderstood me. She is very sensitive—she thought she had done something that would hurt me very much, and that I would not forgive. But it was not her fault—" She darted a vindictive look at Alison. "I foolishly told her she must do something I wanted or she could leave, and she has taken me literally. I should have known—she is so gentle—and so easily hurt—" There was almost a sob in her voice now. Then with quick anxiety in her face she called:

"Jeanne, go to the phone and call my lawyer, quick. He will tell us what to do. Surely she can be found. And Jeanne, tell Saxon to go out and search the neighborhood. Tell him not to wait to change to his street things, she may be right near here somewhere. She wouldn't know where to go!"

"I have lost her, just when I had found her?" said the old man, passing a trembling hand over his cold forehead. They noticed that the little box that held the watch was shaking in his hold.

"Jeanne, as soon as you have got the lawyer you run out yourself. She likes you and maybe you can find her," Violet called distractedly.

"I will go out myself and look for her," said the old gentleman rising tremulously and starting toward the door. "I—I—don't know who this young lady is, but perhaps she will go with me. You are—perhaps—her friend?"

"This is Alison Fraley, her cousin, Mr. MacPherson," said Violet pausing in her mad rush of issuing commands. "Certainly she will go out and help to hunt her cousin. The whole world will soon know it if she doesn't," and Violet gave Alison a look that made her open her eyes in astonishment.

That was the beginning of the long search, that lasted all the fall, and into the early winter, and still no trace had been found of Fraley.

Old Mr. MacPherson aged visibly, Violet Wentworth canceled all her social engagements and gave herself to the search. She even sent a telegram out to George Rivington Seagrave at the strange, brief address in the west that she remembered to have read on Fraley's letter, asking if he knew Fraley's present address, but a reply came back the next day. "Seagrave too ill to read your telegram." And signed with a name she had never heard.

The best skilled service of the great city was employed, at first quietly, and by and by using every means, even the radio, to find the lost girl. But none of them came anywhere near little Fraley, hid away safely in the hollow of His hand, till His time had come to reveal her hiding place.

Even Alison had become depressed with the terrible mystery that hung over her unknown cousin. Her father and mother had returned, and of course had been called upon to help in the search. Her father's keen anxiety when he heard of the unknown niece at once convinced Alison that she had been wrong, and she dared not let her father know what part she had played in this tragedy. Even her mother who had never known the beloved sister Alison Fraley, was warm in her sympathy and earnest in her efforts to find that sister's child. Alison's friends at the Club House also, grew interested in the girl who had so bravely and so completely defied them, and made Alison's life miserable by constant questions, until she began to stay away from her usual haunts, and became sullen and morose. The young people who had tormented Fraley that memorable day of her disappearance were fast making her into a heroine.

And then the terrible thought came creeping with sinister shadow of fear into the hearts of those who cared, that perhaps the child had been killed somewhere in the awful city. The records of the morgue were sought, but nothing anywhere gave up the secret of Fraley's disappearance.

And at last Violet Wentworth, from loss of sleep, and lack of food, for she neither ate nor slept much, and perhaps from other anxieties which only her own soul knew, fell ill with a fever.

23

IT was characteristic of Fraley that she was not deeply concerned for her own homeless condition. A bird of the wilderness, she felt that there might be a lodging tree almost anywhere, and crumbs would somehow come to her lot. She was asking no more of life.

The beautiful glimpse she had had of luxuries that others were enjoying had not spoiled her. She went on her winged way trusting in a higher power for the things needful, and she shed things worldly as if they were a foreign substance.

She had walked a good many miles before it gradually came to her consciousness that she was not getting anywhere, and she did not know where she was going.

The streets about her looked strange and foreign. Little children in scanty attire scuttled in groups here and there, and dishevelled parents hung forlornly about unattractive doors, watching her with hostile eyes. Now and then an old person hurried furtively by with a haunted look like one who had come a long way, and there were men lounging about who stared at her and reminded her of Brand and his kind. This was not the

New York she had known since she had been with Violet Wentworth. She must have wandered into some strange quarter. Many of these people were foreigners for they spoke unknown languages.

She was hungry, too, and suddenly felt that she could scarcely drag herself another step. It was growing dark and she felt afraid. She turned about and tried to retrace her steps but when she reached a corner she could not tell which way she had come, and the surroundings seemed only to grow worse.

At last she ventured up to a group of women who had been eyeing her critically and asked if they could direct her to a nice quiet place where she could get something to eat.

They looked at her dress, they looked at her shoes, and hat, all bearing an unmistakable air of refinement and money, and they laughed a mirthless meaningful laugh.

"Right acrost the street an' up them stairs!" pointed one, with a toothless upper gum and a gray bushy bob "That's where you b'long my pretty! You'll get all that's comin' to you up there!" and she laughed again. The sound of her mockery sent a shudder through Fraley; but just to get away from it if for nothing else she crossed the street and stood hesitating in the entrance, while they watched her like an evil menace.

The stairs were narrow and dirty, but a light shone up at the top and there was music. It was not the kind of music Violet made on the grand piano at Riverside Drive, but, from the unfriendly street, there was a certain jazzy cheer in it and she went up.

It was a strange scene that met her gaze. Lights and color, and crudity. Girls in flimsy bright dresses were dancing with men in the middle of the room and a mingling of cheap perfume and unwashed flesh met her nostrils. But there were little tables about the walls of the big room, and she was famished. She slipped into a chair by a table that was comparatively sheltered and gave a shy order. "Could you bring me a bowl of soup and some crackers, please?"

He laughed.

"We don't serve soup, lady. You picked the wrong dump. We just serves drinks and ices and sandriges and that like."

The waiter's intimate tone and searching look he gave her brought the quick color to Fraley's cheeks, but she said hastily:

"Oh, then please bring me a cup of coffee and a sandwich."

The waiter lingered, a dirty tray balanced above his shoulder.

"Want I should interjuce ya to some nice man?"

"Oh, no! Thank you!" said Fraley in a weak frightened voice. "I'm in—rather of a hurry!"

"I see!" said the waiter still watching her as he made slow progress to a door at the back of the room.

She noticed that he stopped at a table where four men sat drinking something in tall foamy glasses and spoke to them, and that they all turned and looked her way.

Fraley grew more frightened every instant. She turned her eyes away, as if she didn't see them, but when she looked up again one of the men was coming toward her, and he had eyes like Pierce Boyden's. Strange how many eyes like that there seemed to be in the world!

More frightened than ever now she rose to her feet, but he was beside her.

"Hello, Baby darlin'!" he addressed her. "I ben waitin' fer you all my life. Let's you and me have a dance while we're waitin' fer the drinks!" He slid his arm boldly about her waist and tried to draw her into the middle of the room.

Fraley drew back and braced herself against the wall, her face very white. She could smell the liquor on his breath.

"Oh, no!" she said. "Please don't! I don't dance! I must have made a mistake. I thought this was a restaurant—I must go!"

She was edging away as he talked. Long experience with drunken men had led her to use strategy rather than to make outcry.

"Go anywhere you shay, Baby darlin'," said the man with a silly grin.

Fraley looked about for help, but saw only the waiter back by the door, grinning, and the other three men rising and apparently coming forward eagerly to join in the discussion. Fraley, in her terror, measured the brief distance to the stairs. She must get there before the other men arrived. She gave a frantic pull and tried to get away from her captor, but he had her pretty well pinioned between the table and the wall, and she was sure now there was to be no help from anyone in that awful room. Even the band men were laughing and calling out in time to their music. Was there nothing she could do?

Then she noticed the glass half full of water standing on the sloppy table beside her, and instinct once more served her. She seized it with her free hand and flung its contents full in the face of the man who was trying to hold her. Then snatching up her little bundle she fled down the steep stairs out into the street.

Mocking laughter and angry cries followed her, and somewhere above her she thought she heard a shot. They were coming after her! She could hear loud stamping feet on the bare boards! She flew down the street past detaining hands and mocking voices, straight into the arms of a great policeman, who took hold of her firmly, and said in a gruff voice:

"Well, what are you trying to put over, kid?"

He had a hard face, scarred and unkindly, but he was knocking the crowd away with his club, as if they had been so many dogs trying to devour her.

"Oh, please!" said Fraley in a small little voice full of sobs and terror, "won't you show me the way to the Pennsylvania station? I—think—I—ammm—a little lost—!"

The man eyed her suspiciously.

"Well, if you ain't now you soon will be, if you stay long down here," he said roughly. "If you was huntin' for the Pennsylvania station what was you doin' up in a joint like that?" he asked looking her severely in the eyes. "That's the toughest joint in New York City, barrin' none—"

"Oh!" said Fraley, aghast, "those ladies across the street said it was a restaurant—"

"Ladies?" the policeman repeated lifting his eyes to the group of slatternly women pressing near, gloatingly. "Ladies! Ha-ha! Say, you better come along 'ith me, kid!"

"Oh, thank you!" breathed Fraley with relief. "If you'll just show me where I can get a bus, or a taxi. Would it be very expensive to take a taxi to the station?"

The policeman looked at her curiously. This was a new specimen. There was something in the quality of her voice that showed him that she did not belong in this quarter.

"Say, Miss," he said, "what are you anyway? Where'd you fall from?"

Fraley tried to explain.

"I'm from the west. I haven't been in the city long and I must have got turned around. If I can only get to the Pennsylvania station I shall know my way all right."

He took her by the arm and cleared a way through the

crowd, conducting her several blocks and questioning her. But by the time they reached a bus line he had somehow satisfied himself that this was no young criminal, merely a babe-in-the-woods who had strayed. Fraley never knew how very near she came to being taken to the station-house that night and locked up. Then she would have had to call for assistance from Violet Wentworth, and incidentally would have saved a great deal of trouble to those who loved her. Though it is doubtful if even under such trying circumstances her proud spirit would have been willing to trouble the woman who had sent her from her home. Fraley had strange vital ideas of self-respect and honor, and would never flinch even in the face of absolute disaster.

So the policeman of the tenderloin, who bore the title of "hard-boiled," put her carefully into a bus going stationward, and Fraley was once more saved from peril.

She spent that first night in the Pennsylvania station.

She wandered through its palatial vistas back and forth until she began to understand its various passages and windings, and finally discovered a ladies' waiting room where were rocking-chairs and a couch.

The couch was occupied by a tired-looking woman with a baby in her arms, but there was a vacant rocking-chair and Fraley sank into it gratefully. She was not at all sure she would be allowed to stay here long, but at least she would rest until someone told her to move on.

By this time the gnawing hunger had ceased to trouble her. She was only utterly weary. She let her head rest back and closed her eyes, too tired even to think of her recent horrible experiences.

The next thing she knew, someone touched her on the shoulder and she opened her eyes and started up. It seemed a long time since she had sat down, and she knew by the feeling of her eyes that she must have been asleep.

She looked around, half bewildered. Perhaps they were going to arrest her for having dared to go to sleep here.

But it was only the woman who had been lying on the couch. She was smiling at her.

"I just thought maybe you'd like to take the couch," she said in a kindly tone. "You look awfully tired, and I'm leaving in a few minutes. I take the midnight train, and if you get on here before I leave nobody else will get ahead of you."

"Oh," said Fraley relieved. "That's very kind of you. Would I be allowed to lie there the rest of the night?"

"Sure, I think you would, unless somebody was to come in real sick. Anyhow you can stay till someone puts you off."

So Fraley curled herself gratefully on the hard leather couch, watched her benefactor trudge off with her sleeping baby, and then dropped promptly off to sleep herself, too dazed to worry over her present situation, too drugged with trouble and weariness to even remember much about it.

She had two good hours of sleep on the couch before the caretaker roused her to give the couch to a woman more in need. But afterwards, dozing in another rocker, she began to come to her senses again.

Then it came to her that life in a great city with no friends was not going to be much better than life in a desert hiding from enemies. There seemed to be enemies on every hand everywhere.

As morning dawned grayly, and the time drew nearer when she would have to leave this brief haven and go out to find a new place in the world, she bethought herself of the advice her friend of the desert had given her. The Travelers' Aid! She would go to the Travelers' Aid and ask advice!

She dozed in her chair till morning was fully come and

the rush of the workaday world began to breeze through the waiting room. Then she tidied herself, picked up her little package and went to the restaurant.

A cup of coffee and some toast seemed to be about the cheapest thing she could get to eat, and after it was swallowed she felt courage rising within her.

During her morning meditations, it had occurred to her that there was still an unknown grandfather who might be applied to perhaps, for advice. But her proud young spirit shrank from going to her relatives a pauper. Not for worlds would she reveal her present condition to the family who had turned against her father for marrying her precious, saintly mother, even if she could find them. She had set her feet to walk a thorny path, and did not falter.

The Travelers' Aid asked several questions; where she had come from and where she was going. Fraley was not fond of giving information about herself, but she managed to evade the main issue, very cleverly.

"I'm from the west and my parents are dead," she stated quietly. This in answer to a query, why she had come to the city. "Yes, I had work but the lady wanted me to do some things that I did not think were right and I had to leave her. No, I would not feel like asking for a reference. I would rather find something for myself. Yes, I have some relatives in the city but—they are not in a position—that is I do not wish to ask help from them. I have a very little money, and I want to get a decent room where I will not be afraid, and something to do. I was told you could direct me."

There was a grave sweet dignity about the child that stopped further questions, and the Travelers' Aid with secret admiration began to look over her list of rooms.

"There are rooms of course as low as twenty-five cents a night, but they are not very nice. They are clean, but they are small and dark, and up several flights of stairs."

"Oh, that's all right," said Fraley with relief. "I can climb stairs. I'll take one, if you please."

"They are not in a very pleasant neighborhood, and there is very little furniture, only a cot and a table, perhaps a chair," said the woman eyeing the rich material of Fraley's imported frock, trim slippers and chic hat.

"Do you mean there would be bad men in the neighborhood?" asked Fraley, a frightened look coming in her eyes.

"Oh, no!" said the woman kindly. "We only recommend rooms in a respectable neighborhood of course. I mean the houses are not very attractive and the rooms are quite bare."

"I don't mind that!" said Fraley with a relieved sigh. "Now, do you know how I should go about getting a job? I'm willing to do anything."

"But you know you can't get a really good job without a reference, my dear."

The fright came back to the girl's eyes.

"Not *any*thing?" she asked pathetically.

"Well, not anything that pays very well. There are a few places, of course, that are not so very particular. I'll give you a list and you can try."

Armed with the list and promising to come back if she got into difficulties, Fraley went on her way, full of good advice and directions.

The first three places on the list were filled, but the fourth turned out to be still vacant. Fraley shrank from the eyes of the proprietor, who looked her over as if she were a piece of merchandise, and finally hired her at an exceedingly small wage, so small that she knew that she must take the very cheapest room that was to be had in the city, and then scrimp at every turn. Even then she must eke out her needs with the few dollars left from her store brought from the west.

Her duties began that afternoon. She was to pull bastings from coarse finished garments that a dozen other women in the grimy room were making, on a dozen noisy sewing machines.

The room she finally took after a long search, was on the fourth floor overlooking chimney roofs and chimney pots through its tiny grimy window. It contained a gaunt cot scantily furnished, and absolutely nothing else. There were lavatory privileges on the floor below, all very dismal and utterly repelling. But the sad, sharp-faced, sick-looking proprietress looked decent at least and Fraley took the room because it was cheap.

In a cheap little shop not far away she purchased a dark cotton dress for a dollar, paid ten cents at a grocery for an empty orange box, purchased a box of crackers, some cheese and a bottle of milk, and set up housekeeping. The orange box she set on end for a combined table and pantry, put her Bible on the top, and her supplies on the shelf below. Then she changed into the cotton dress, ate a hasty lunch and hurried off to her work.

The atmosphere of the first workroom was almost unbearable, both morally, and physically. The air was bad, reeking of the unwashed, the language which her fellow workwomen used was worse, and their hostile manner reminded her of the women who had sent her into the dance hall the night before. Moreover, the proprietor was half drunk most of the time, and so cross that one could never please him, though Fraley tried with all her might. Her fingers were cut with the threads, and sore from contact with the rough goods, and her spirit was sore with the alien atmosphere about her.

When, at the end of a week, the proprietor refused to pay her but half the scanty wage promised her because he said that was all she was worth to him while she had been learning her job, she turned aghast and walked out of the shop.

Her next employment was in a small forlorn shop where derelict furniture found harbor and changed hands occasionally. The wages were a few cents more than in the tailor shop, but the proprietor required her to lie about the furniture, producing all sorts of fairy tales concerning articles on display, stories about former owners of renown, and finally dismissing her without pay because she had refused to lie about a chair with a broken leg when a customer asked if it hadn't been mended.

She grew thin and sorrowful as one experience of this sort after another met her. Her rounded cheeks lost their curves and rose tints, her eyes wore no more glints of happiness. Yet it never once entered her mind to go back to Violet Wentworth and give in to her conditions.

At last Fraley got a position as a waitress in a restaurant. It was not a high-class restaurant. In fact Fraley did not know how very low-class it was. A girl who roomed in the same house with her had told her of it. Her predecessor had died the night before of pneumonia, and the restaurant needed someone at once. The wages were better than any she had had so far, and though the hours were long and the duties heavy she started in happily.

Just one small pleasure she permitted herself. She did answer Jimmie MacPherson's letter, and his breezy reply gave her much comfort.

But a new trouble arose on the horizon when the proprietor began to grow fond of her, and insisted on making love to her.

She avoided him as much as possible at first, and went on her sweet impersonal way, keeping to herself, doing her hard work well and quickly, moving among her sordid surroundings like a young queen, and breaking her heart at night when she crept to her cot, too weary to even grieve long over the situation. Like her mother before her, she seemed to be caught on the wheel of circumstance, and to be condemned to go on because there was no way of getting off.

But a crisis arose late in November when Max, the dark-browed Russian proprietor, asked her to go to a movie with him that night.

It was during the six o'clock supper rush that it occurred. The headwaiter told her to go up to the desk, that Max wanted to see her.

With fear and trembling she obeyed, thinking perhaps she was to be dismissed, for she had broken some dishes that morning when the cook ran against her full tray. Also, she knew that he had been cross at her ever since she had refused to go to a dance with him the week before. But she had tried to be smiling and pleasant about it, and not anger him. She had told him that time that she did not feel well, and wanted to get straight home to bed. Now, she watched him anxiously as she threaded her way among the tables toward the desk. It was not that she dreaded leaving, for the work was terrible and the hours almost unbearable, but even such work was better than none at all, and the cold weather was at hand. She needed a warm coat. She had nothing but a thin sweater for a wrap, that she had bought at a second hand store for fifty cents, and carefully washed and mended.

So, when Max spoke in his most winning tones and asked her how she was feeling that night, she gave him a relieved smile. She did not see a dark fellow with lowering eyes across the room at a table in her own territory, who watched her narrowly with an evil gaze.

"Well, how about a picture tanight?" smiled Max wetting his voluptuous red lips, and watching the pretty color drain out of the smooth cheeks. "You and me has gotta get tagether, Birdie. I let you off tonight at seven, see? You can get dolled up and I meet you here at ten ta eight. See?"

Fraley's face was white now and her eyes troubled and earnest.

"Oh, Mr. Kirschmann, I couldn't. I really couldn't. I have some work I have to do this evening, and I really can't do my work here well if I stay up late nights—"

But she could see that her excuses were not getting her anywhere, and she drew back in dismayed protest.

"I ain't takin' no excuses. See?" went on Max, and reaching out his great grimy paw he caught both her hands and held them like a vise. "What I say goes. If you've gotta date with some other guy, break it. See? You're goin' out with me tanight an' that's straight. We're mebbe takin' dinner in a cabaret afterwards too, so put on yer best rags an' do me proud."

"But—" said Fraley wide-eyed and struggling to get free, aware of the hostile glances of her fellow laborers.

"Ain't no buts," said Max gruffly. "You gotta date 'ith me tanight. Ef you're to high hat ta go with Max you c'n leave the job *tanight!* See? But ef you do the right thing by me I'll see you sit pretty, my cherry! Now, run back ta yer table. There's a bird ben waitin' there five minutes an' he looks mad enough ta shoot. Run!"

Fraley ran, a great fear growing in her soul. Trouble was looming ahead of her. She could see that plainly. She must either go with this wild Russian fellow or she must give up her job. There was no use trying to get out of it. She could see that he was quite determined. She had seen enough men of this type to know and fear.

She was so concerned with her own thoughts that she scarcely noticed where she was going, and arriving at her table handed a grubby-looking menu card to her customer without noticing him.

But when he spoke:

"Get me a beef stew and make it snappy!" her eyes came about to look into his with horror, and he looked up and met her gaze with a dark insolence that searched her to the soul. It was Pierce Boyden himself sitting before her at the table!

For an instant it seemed to Fraley that she hung suspended between life and death. This surely was the end! He had searched her out forlorn and helpless! There was no one in the world to whom she could turn for protection unless she chose to appeal to her employer and accept his repulsive attentions. Perhaps he might be strong enough to outwit even Pierce Boyden, though she doubted it.

All this flew through her consciousness while she stood for that instant wondering if she were about to fall, and then to her surprise she turned and walked away from the table with the menu card in her hand, back to the kitchen. She was perfectly conscious, every step she took, that Pierce Boyden's eyes were upon her as she walked, and yet she was able to go steadily as if nothing unusual had happened. She felt that some power beyond herself was enabling her to do this, for in herself she had only awful weakness.

Back in the kitchen out of sight for the moment she seized the arm of a waitress just returning with a tray laden with soiled dishes.

"Anna! Take my customer! I don't feel well! He wants a beef stew in a hurry. You may have my tip."

She did not wait for the other girl to answer. She did not even wait to get her old grey sweater. She slipped out the back door into the dark alley, and was gone into the night. How many minutes would it be before Pierce would be after her? Perhaps even now he was on her track. Perhaps Max, too, had been watching her!

Her feet seemed to be made of lead, her arms weighed heavily at her sides, and although she did not seem to be making much progress, she was panting wildly. She longed for the wilds of the desert, and a friendly place to hide. She was afraid of every nook and corner of this alley, afraid of the streets she had to pass through, afraid of the whole awful city.

Though it seemed like ages, she did finally arrive at her stopping place, climb step by step up to the fourth floor, and was locked at last into her room. Then she fell upon her knees beside the bed, panting, breathless, her heart breathing an inarticulate prayer for help.

In a moment or two when the wild beating of her heart was somewhat quieted she sprang into action.

Quickly tearing off her work dress she put on her one good frock, threw her few possessions together into the old faithful gray bag her mother had made, put on her hat and hurried out of the room and down the stairs. She must get out of this place before any one came after her! She felt certain that Max would come even if Pierce was not able to find her at once. Some of the girls in the restaurant knew where she roomed, and Max would lose no time in finding her. She must get away at once and she must get away from this part of the world forever. She would go north or south or somewhere that Pierce Boyden could never find her! Perhaps she would even be able to find something to do on a ship and get away from the country altogether!

And how fortunate it was that she did not have to stop and talk with her landlady! She had paid her week's rent in advance three days ago, so that poor creature would not be out anything by her sudden flight.

This was her thought as she rounded the stair railing on the third floor and started down the dark narrow stairs to the second; and then suddenly she came face to face with a tall form, and would have fallen if strong arms had not caught her.

It was very dark in that upper hall, for the screaming uncertain gas jet had gone out, and as she struggled with her unknown adversary she felt herself falling. When she lost her footing her senses seemed to swim and swing in the balance, and she wondered if this might be what they called fainting, and then she felt herself lifted firmly and carried down to the floor below.

He had found her then, her enemy! Pierce or Max. It did not seem to matter; they were all one to her tired heart and brain. It was no use to struggle. This was the end!

24

FROM the start Violet's illness was desperate, and the physician and nurses and friends looked gravely at one another. And then she began in her delirium to call for Fraley. Night and day she tossed, and asked everyone who came in the room if they had found her yet.

They tried to pacify her with lies, but she paid no heed to them, only kept looking toward the door, and calling out to her to come. And the cry grew into a strange sentence.

"Come here! I'm going to die. I've got to see you about my sins! I don't know what to do!"

Over and over she would call it, till in desperation they sent for a minister of the fashionable church she had attended occasionally.

He tried to soothe her, to tell her she had no sins worth speaking of, to tell her it was all right, and he prayed a worthy and happy prayer to pave the way straight to heaven for her worried feet. But she only stared at him bewildered, and tossed her head and moaned: "It's Fraley I want. I've got to see her about my sins. She's the only one that knows what to do. She has a Bible."

So Jeanne came one day, with fear and trembling, and Fraley's Bible she had found on the bureau, and began to read in a low voice verses that Fraley had marked for her, verses about sins.

"As far as the east is from the west so far hath He removed our transgressions from us." "He hath put thy sins behind His back." "He hath drowned them in the depths of the sea." "For God so loved the world that He gave His only begotten son that whosoever believeth in Him should not perish, but have everlasting life." "For God sent not His son into the world to condemn the world, but that the world through Him might be saved."

And then that other chapter, the fourteenth of John, the first that Fraley had read to Jeanne: "Let not your heart be troubled, ye believe in God, believe also in me—"

The weary head turned, and the sunken fevered eyes looked at Jeanne, and she seemed to listen. On and on Jeanne read, her voice low and soothing, the tears continually blinding her.

At last a weak voice that sounded almost natural said:

"But that's not for me, Fraley knows. Oh, if Fraley would come and tell me about my sins!"

Said the doctor, who had come in during the reading and was watching the patient with practiced finger on the fluttering pulse:

"Where is this Fraley person that she talks about continually? Isn't there some way to get in touch with her? She might live if she came. Such things turn the tide sometimes."

They told this to old Grandfather MacPherson when he came to inquire, and he went sadly back to his wife, and reported it.

Jimmy was home from school for Thanksgiving vacation, and was in the next room listening.

"Fraley?" he said strolling to the door, "Fraley? Do you mean Fraley MacPherson? The girl I played golf with last summer? Why I know where she is. I had a letter from her last week. I've got her address, I'm going to see her tomorrow and take her one of my school pennants. She said she would like it to put in her room. She's been writing to me all fall."

Grandfather MacPherson started up and was wanting to go right off without his hat, till his wife protested. But Jimmy said:

"Aw, Gee. Lemme have the car, Grampa, I'll bring her back in no time. Naw, you needn'ta go along. Well, have it your own way, but she's gonta sit in front with me."

That was the wildest drive that the old man ever took in the midst of the traffic of a great city, and more than one officer of the law held up a worthy hand, and cried out, but Jimmy stopped not on the order of his going. Yet if his grandfather had to pay a fine next day, Jimmy never knew it. The old gentleman had his hat in his hand. He had not thought to put it on even when it was given him, and his wavy silver hair tossed wildly in the breeze as they sailed down Fifth Avenue at a speed no one in his senses dared to go.

And so it was Jimmy who went in after her, who mounted the stairs himself because the apathetic landlady said she didn't know whether the lodger was in or not and she was too tired to go and see. It was Jimmy who caught her on the wing and kept her from falling down stairs, who carried her down to the front door.

"Oh, gee! I'm glad I found ya!" he said setting her down at last, bewildered, overjoyed to find her enemy a friend. "Just suppose you'd gone out! You *were* going out, weren't ya? Say, they wantya bad down at yer house. That Mrs. Wentworth is awful sick and she keeps calling fer ya, and the doc says she's gotta have ya! And my grandad has been carrying on something fierce. If they'd just asked me before, I coulda told 'em!"

She ran before them all when she reached the house, past the overjoyed butler who opened the door, past frightened Alison who sat in the hall at her father's command to await a possible message to him, past the doctor who stood gravely at Violet's door, and the nurse who was putting away the medicine she had just administered.

Softly she knelt beside the bed and took the hot hand that picked at the coverlet.

"I've come," she whispered softly, "Violet, did you want me?"

The moaning stopped, the restless head turned to look, and the fevered eyes lit with sanity.

"Oh, you've come, Fraley, you've come! And now, you'll forgive me, won't you? I'm sorry, Fraley, little girl, I'm sorry! And what shall I do about my sins?"

"I've nothing to forgive, dear lady," said Fraley with her soft lips against the pale fingers, "I love you and I've come back. And don't worry about the rest. Jesus loves you, and died to save you."

"But I've sinned!" moaned the woman, "it's just as you knew. I've sinned!"

"Yes, Jesus knew all that. That's what He died for," said the girl with wonderful tenderness.

"Are you sure?"

"Perfectly sure."

"How do you know?"

"He told me so in His book."

"And will you stay right here and not go away any more?"

"Yes, I'll stay right here—"

Softly the white lids dropped over the bright restless eyes, more quietly the breath began to come, while Fraley knelt and held the frail hand, and the watchers stood outside the door and waited.

Perhaps an hour passed, and the doctor tiptoed in, touched the white wrist again, and nodded, looking at his watch.

Out in the hall later, when they had motioned Fraley away to get some rest the doctor told her:

"Little sister, you have saved her life. I think she'll pull through now, if you stay around. But you came just in time. Another hour and it would have been too late."

There were others waiting for Fraley down in the hall, waiting all the time that she knelt by the sick bed, until the night nurse took charge, promising to call her if she were needed. Old Mr. MacPherson waited with white face, and eager eyes, to clasp the child of his long-lost son, waited to take her home to her grandmother, where she was eagerly anticipated. Jimmy waited grim and important, feeling that he ought to have come before. All this fuss about something he could have straightened out in a minute. Now, perhaps his grandfather would see it would be best for him to stay around home instead of going back to that old stuffy school the next semester.

Alison waited to make a sullen apology to the girl she knew she must accept.

Jeanne waited to welcome her beloved Miss Fraley back and tell her she had never forgotten to read the blessed book.

But while they all waited, Alison, and Jimmy and MacPherson in the hall near the foot of the stairs, Jeanne just behind the reception room portiere where she could not be seen, the butler back farther in the hall, the door bell rang. Its muffled peal stirred on their strained senses like the boom of a cannon.

Fraley had just started down the stairs as the butler reached the door to open it, and paused looking down to see who it was. All the others started up eagerly, even Alison, relieved that the long wait was over. Saxon opened the door. A young man with a white face and one arm in a sling entered.

"I want to see Mrs. Wentworth right away, Saxon, please," rang out a voice that Fraley never would forget, a voice that thrilled through her heart and made her forget everything except that she was hearing it again.

"I'm sorry, Mr. George," said Saxon in a low apology,—for Saxon used to work for the Seagraves in the years that were past. "Mrs. Wentworth has been very ill indeed, sir. She is very low to-night."

The young man's face was full of sympathy.

"Oh!" he said, "I'm sorry, I didn't know."

His glance went around the group in the hall without perceiving who they were, and lifted to the stairs. Then his whole face lit with a wonderful joy.

"Ladybird!" he cried and sprang up the stairs to meet her. "My Little Ladybird! Thank God!"

## About the Author

Grace Livingston Hill is well known as one of the most prolific writers of romantic fiction. Her personal life was fraught with joys and sorrows not unlike those experienced by many of her fictional heroines.

Born in Wellsville, New York, Grace nearly died during the first hours of life. But her loving parents and friends turned to God in prayer. She survived miraculously, thus her thankful father named her Grace.

Grace was always close to her father, a Presbyterian minister, and her mother, a published writer. It was from them that she learned the art of storytelling. When Grace was twelve, a close aunt surprised her with a hardbound, illustrated copy of one of Grace's stories. This was the beginning of Grace's journey into being a published author.

In 1892 Grace married Fred Hill, a young minister, and they soon had two lovely young daughters. Then came 1901, a difficult year for Grace—the year when, within months of each other, both her father and husband died. Suddenly Grace had to find a new place to live (her home was owned by the church where her husband had been pastor). It was a struggle for Grace to raise her young daughters alone, but through everything she kept writing. In 1902 she produced *The Angel of His Presence, The Story of a Whim,* and *An Unwilling Guest.* In 1903 her two books *According to the Pattern* and *Because of Stephen* were published.

It wasn't long before Grace was a well-known author, but she wanted to go beyond just entertaining her readers. She soon included the message of God's salvation through Jesus Christ in each of her books. For Grace, the most important thing she did was not write books but share the message of salvation, a message she felt God wanted her to share through the abilities he had given her.

In all, Grace Livingston Hill wrote more than one hundred books, all of which have sold thousands of copies and have touched the lives of readers around the world with their message of "enduring love" and the true way to lasting happiness: a relationship with God through his Son, Jesus Christ.

In an interview shortly before her death, Grace's devotion to her Lord still shone clear. She commented that whatever she had accomplished had been God's doing. She was only his servant, one who had tried to follow his teaching in all her thoughts and writing.